ALSO BY ALICE ADAMS

Careless Love

Families and Survivors

Listening to Billie

Beautiful Girl (stories)

Rich Rewards

To See You Again (stories)

Superior Women

Return Trips (stories)

Second Chances

After You've Gone (stories)

Mexico: Some Travels and Travellers There

Caroline's Daughters

Almost Perfect

A Southern Exposure

Medicine Men

The Last Lovely City (stories)

After the War

The Stories of Alice Adams

The Stories of

Alice Adams

Alfred A. Knopf   New York   2002

THIS IS A BORZOI BOOK
PUBLISHED BY ALFRED A. KNOPF

Copyright © 2002 by The Estate of Alice Adams Linenthal
All rights reserved under International and Pan-American Copyright
Conventions. Published in the United States by Alfred A. Knopf,
a division of Random House, Inc., New York, and simultaneously
in Canada by Random House of Canada Limited, Toronto.
Distributed by Random House, Inc., New York.

www.aaknopf.com

Knopf, Borzoi Books, and the colophon are registered
trademarks of Random House, Inc.

Library of Congress Cataloging-in-Publication Data
Adams, Alice, 1926–1999
[Short stories]
The stories of Alice Adams.—1st ed.
p.   cm.
ISBN 0-375-41285-9 (alk. paper)
1. United States—Social life and customs—20th century—Fiction.   I. Title.
PS3551.D324 A6 2002
813'.54—dc21   2002070940

Manufactured in the United States of America
First Edition

Contents

Contents

The Stories of Alice Adams

Verlie I Say Unto You

Every morning of all the years of the thirties, at around seven, Verlie Jones begins her long and laborious walk to the Todds' house, two miles uphill. She works for the Todds—their maid. Her own house, where she lives with her four children, is a slatted floorless cabin, in a grove of enormous sheltering oaks. It is just down a gravelly road from the bending highway, and that steep small road is the first thing she has to climb, starting out early in the morning. Arrived at the highway she stops and sighs, and looks around and then starts out. Walking steadily but not in any hurry, beside the winding white concrete.

First there are fields of broomstraw on either side of the road, stretching back to the woods, thick, clustered dark pines and cedars, trees whose lower limbs are cluttered with underbrush. Then the land gradually rises until on one side there is a steep red clay bank, going up to the woods; on the other side a wide cornfield, rich furrows dotted over in spring with tiny wild flowers, all colors—in the winter dry and rutted, sometimes frosted over, frost as shiny as splintered glass.

Then the creek. Before she comes to the small concrete bridge, she can see the heavier growth at the edge of the fields, green, edging the water. On the creek's steep banks, below the bridge, are huge peeling poplars, ghostly, old. She stands there looking down at the water (the bridge is halfway to the Todds'). The water is thick and swollen, rushing, full of twigs and leaf trash and swirling logs in the spring. Trickling and almost dried out when summer is over, in the early fall.

Past the bridge is the filling station, where they sell loaves of bread and cookies and soap, along with the gas and things for cars. Always there are men sitting around at the station, white men in overalls, dusty and dried out. Sometimes they nod to Verlie. "Morning, Verlie. Going to be any hot day?"

Occasionally, maybe a couple of times a year, a chain gang will be along there, working on the road. The colored men chained together, in their dirty, wide-striped uniforms, working with their picks. And the thin, mean guard (a white man) with his rifle, watching them. Looking quickly, briefly at Verlie as she passes. She looks everywhere but there, as her heart falls down to her stomach and turns upside down. All kinds of fears grab at her, all together: she is afraid of the guard and of those men (their heavy eyes) and also a chain gang is one of the places where her deserting husband, Horace, might well be, and she never wants to see Horace again. Not anywhere.

After the filling station some houses start. Small box houses, sitting up high on brick stilts. On the other side of the highway red clay roads lead back into the hills, to the woods. To the fields of country with no roads at all, where sometimes Mr. Todd goes to hunt rabbits, and where at other times, in summer, the children, Avery and Devlin Todd, take lunches and stay all day.

From a certain bend in the highway Verlie can see the Todds' house, but she rarely bothers to look anymore. She sighs and shifts her weight before starting up the steep, white, graveled road, and then the road to the right that swings around to the back of the house, to the back door that leads into the kitchen.

There on the back porch she has her own small bathroom that Mr. Todd put in for her. There is a mirror and some nails to hang her things on, and a flush toilet, ordered from Montgomery Ward, that still works. No washbasin, but she can wash her hands in the kitchen sink.

She hangs up her cardigan sweater in her bathroom and takes an apron off a nail. She goes into the kitchen to start everyone's breakfast.

They all eat separate. First Avery, who likes oatmeal and then soft-boiled eggs; then Mr. Todd (oatmeal and scrambled eggs and bacon and coffee); Devlin (toast and peanut butter and jam); and Mrs. Todd (tea and toast).

Verlie sighs, and puts the water on.

Verlie has always been with the Todds; that is how they put it to their friends. "Verlie has always been with us." Of course, that is not true. Actually she came to them about ten years before, when Avery was a baby. What they meant was that they did not know much about her life before them, and also (a more important meaning) they cannot imagine their life without her. They say, "We couldn't get along without Verlie," but it is unlikely that any of them (except possibly Jessica, with her mournful, exacerbated and extreme intelligence) realizes the full truth of the remark. And, laughingly, one of them will add, "No one else could put up with us." Another truth, or perhaps only a partial truth: in those days, there and then, most maids put up with a lot, and possibly Verlie suffers no more than most.

She does get more money than most maids, thirteen dollars a week (most get along on ten or eleven). And she gets to go home before dinner, around six (she first leaves the meal all fixed for them), since they—since Mr. Todd likes to have a lot of drinks and then eat late.

Every third Sunday she gets off to go to church.

None of them is stupid enough to say that she is like a member of the family.

Tom Todd, that handsome, guiltily faithless husband, troubled professor (the 10 percent salary cuts of the Depression; his history of abandoned projects—the book on Shelley, the innumerable articles)—Tom was the one who asked Verlie about her name.

"You know, it's like in the Bible. Verlie I say unto you."

Tom felt that he successfully concealed his amusement at that, and later it makes a marvelous story, especially in academic circles, in those days when funny-maid stories are standard social fare. In fact people (white people) are somewhat competitive as to who has heard or known the most comical colored person, comical meaning outrageously childishly ignorant. Tom's story always goes over well.

In her summer sneakers, shorts and little shirt, Avery comes into the dining room, a small, dark-haired girl carrying a big book. Since she has learned to read (her mother taught her, when she was no bigger than a minute) she reads all the time, curled up in big chairs in the living room or in her own room, in the bed. At the breakfast table.

"Good morning, Verlie."

"Morning. How you?"

"Fine, thank you. Going to be hot today?"

"Well, I reckon so."

Avery drinks her orange juice, and then Verlie takes out the glass and brings in her bowl of hot oatmeal. Avery reads the thick book while she eats. Verlie takes out the oatmeal bowl and brings in the soft-boiled eggs and a glass of milk.

"You drink your milk, now, hear?"

Verlie is about four times the size of Avery and more times than that her age. (But Verlie can't read.)

Verlie is an exceptionally handsome woman, big and tall and strong, with big bright eyes and smooth yellow skin over high cheekbones. A wide curving mouth, and strong white teeth.

Once there was a bad time between Avery and Verlie: Avery was playing with some children down the road, and it got to be suppertime. Jessica sent Verlie down to get Avery, who didn't want to come home. "Blah blah blah blah!" she yelled at Verlie—who, unaccountably, turned and walked away.

The next person Avery saw was furious Jessica, arms akimbo. "How are you, how *could* you? Verlie, who's loved you all your life? How could you be so cruel, calling her black?"

"I didn't—I said blah. I never said black. Where is she?"

"Gone home. Very hurt."

Jessica remained stiff and unforgiving (she had problems of her own); but the next morning Avery ran down into the kitchen at the first sound of Verlie. "Verlie, I said blah blah—I didn't say black."

And Verlie smiled, and it was all over. For good.

Tom Todd comes into the dining room, carrying the newspaper. "Good morning, Avery. Morning, Verlie. Well, it doesn't look like a day for getting out our umbrellas, does it now?"

That is the way he talks.

"Avery, please put your book away. Who knows, we might have an absolutely fascinating conversation."

She gives him a small sad smile and closes her book. "Pass the cream?"

"With the greatest of pleasure."

"Thanks."

But despite the intense and often painful complications of his character, Tom's relationship with Verlie is perhaps the simplest in that family. Within their rigidly defined roles they are even fond of each other. Verlie thinks he talks funny, but not much more so than most men—white men. He runs around with women (she knows that from his handkerchiefs, the lipstick stains that he couldn't have bothered to hide from her) but not as much as Horace did. He bosses his wife and children but he doesn't hit them. He acts as Verlie expects a man to act, and perhaps a little better.

And from Tom's point of view Verlie behaves like a Negro maid. She is somewhat lazy; she does as little cleaning as she can. She laughs at his jokes. She sometimes sneaks drinks from his liquor closet. He does not, of course, think of Verlie as a woman—a woman in the sense of sexual possibility; in fact he once sincerely (astoundingly) remarked that he could not imagine a sexual impulse toward a colored person.

Devlin comes in next. A small and frightened boy, afraid of Verlie. Once as he stood up in his bath she touched his tiny penis and laughed and said, "This here's going to grow to something nice and big." He was terrified: what would he do with something big, down there?

He mutters good morning to his father and sister and to Verlie.

Then Jessica. Mrs. Todd. "Good morning, everyone. Morning, Verlie. My, doesn't it look like a lovely spring day?"

She sighs, as no one answers.

The end of breakfast. Verlie clears the table, washes up, as those four people separate.

There is a Negro man who also (sometimes) works for the Todds, named Clifton. Yard work: raking leaves in the fall, building a fence around the garbage cans, and then a dog kennel, then a playhouse for the children.

When Verlie saw Clifton the first time he came into the yard (a man who had walked a long way, looking for work), what she thought was: Lord, I never saw no man so beautiful. Her second thought was: He sick.

Clifton is bronze-colored. Reddish. Shining. Not brown like most colored (or yellow, as Verlie is). His eyes are big and brown, but dragged downward with his inside sickness. And his sadness: he is a lonesome man, almost out of luck.

"Whatever do you suppose they talk about?" Tom Todd says to Jessica, who has come into his study to help him with the index of his book, an hour or so after breakfast. They can hear the slow, quiet sounds of Verlie's voice, with Clifton's, from the kitchen.

"Us, maybe?" Jessica makes this light, attempting a joke, but she really wonders if in fact she and Tom are their subject. Her own communication with Verlie is so mystifyingly nonverbal that she sometimes suspects Verlie of secret (and accurate) appraisals, as though Verlie knows her in ways that no one else does, herself included. At other times she thinks that Verlie is just plain stubborn.

From the window come spring breaths of blossom and grasses and leaves. Of spring earth. Aging plump Jessica deeply sighs.

Tom says, "I very much doubt that, my dear. Incredibly fascinating though we be."

In near total despair Jessica says, "Sometimes I think I just don't have the feeling for an index."

The telephone rings. Tom and Jessica look at each other, and then Verlie's face comes to the study door. "It's for you, Mr. Todd. A long distance."

Clifton has had a bad life; it almost seems cursed. The same sickness one spring down in Mississippi carried off his wife and three poor little children, and after that everything got even worse: every job that he got came apart like a bunch of sticks in his hands. Folks all said that they had no money to pay. He even made deliveries for a bootlegger, knocking on back doors at night, but the man got arrested and sent to jail before Clifton got any money.

He likes working for the Todds, and at the few other jobs around town that Mrs. Todd finds for him. But he doesn't feel good. Sometimes he thinks he has some kind of sickness.

He looks anxiously at Verlie as he says this last, as though he, like Jessica, believes that she can see inside him.

"You nervous," Verlie says. "You be all right, come summertime." But she can't look at him as she says this.

They are standing in the small apple orchard where Verlie's clotheslines are. She has been hanging out the sheets. They billow, shuddering in the lively restive air of early spring.

Clifton suddenly takes hold of her face, and turns it around to his. He presses his mouth and his body to hers, standing there. Something deep inside Verlie heats up and makes her almost melt.

"Verlie!"

It is Avery, suddenly coming up on them, so that they cumbersomely step apart.

"Verlie, my father wants you." Avery runs away almost before she has stopped speaking.

Clifton asks, "You reckon we ought to tell her not to tell?"

"No, she's not going to tell."

Verlie is right, but it is a scene that Avery thinks about. Of course, she has seen other grown-ups kissing: her father and Irene McGinnis or someone after a party. But Verlie and Clifton looked different; for one thing they were more absorbed. It took them a long time to hear her voice.

Tom is desperately questioning Jessica. "How in God's name will I tell her?" he asks.

Verlie's husband, Horace, is dead. He died in a Memphis hospital, after a knife fight, having first told a doctor the name of the people and the town where his wife worked.

"I could tell her," Jessica forces herself to say, and for a few minutes they look at each other, with this suggestion lying between them. But they both know, with some dark and intimate Southern knowledge, that Tom will have to be the one to tell her. And alone: it would not even "do" for Jessica to stay on in the room, although neither of them could have explained these certainties.

. . .

Having been clearly (and kindly) told by Tom what has happened in Memphis, Verlie then asks, "You sure? You sure it's Horace, not any other man?"

Why couldn't he have let Jessica tell her, or at least have let her stay in the room? Tom is uncomfortable; it wildly occurs to him to offer Verlie a drink (to offer Verlie a drink?). He mumbles, "Yes, I'm afraid there's no doubt at all." He adds, in his more reasonable, professorial voice, "You see, another man wouldn't have said Verlie Jones, who works for the Todd family, in Hilton."

Incredibly, a smile breaks out on Verlie's face. ("For a minute I actually thought she was going to *laugh*," Tom later says to Jessica.)

Verlie says, "I reckon that's right. Couldn't be no other man." And then she says, "Lunch about ready now," and she goes back into the kitchen.

Jessica has been hovering in the dining room, pushing at the arrangement of violets and cowslips in a silver bowl. She follows Verlie into the kitchen; she says, "Verlie, I'm terribly sorry. Verlie, wouldn't you like to go on home? Take the afternoon off. I could drive you . . ."

"No'm. No, thank you. I'd liefer get on with the ironing."

And so, with a stiff and unreadable face, opaque dark-brown eyes, Verlie serves their lunch.

What could they know, what could any of them know about a man like Horace? Had any of them seen her scars? Knife scars and beating scars, and worse things he had done without leaving any scars. All the times he forced her, when he was so hurting and quick, and she was sick or just plain exhausted. The girls she always knew he had. The mean tricks he played on little kids, his kids. The dollars of hers that he stole to get drunk on.

She had always thought Horace was too mean to die, and as she cleans up the lunch dishes and starts to sprinkle the dry sheets for ironing, she still wonders: *Is* Horace dead?

She tries to imagine an open casket, full of Horace, dead. His finicky little moustache and his long, strong fingers folded together on his chest. But the casket floats off into the recesses of her mind and what she sees is Horace, alive and terrifying.

A familiar dry smell tells her that she has scorched a sheet, and tears begin to roll slowly down her face.

"When I went into the kitchen to see how she was, she was standing there with tears rolling down her face," Jessica reports to Tom—and then is appalled at what she hears as satisfaction in her own voice.

"I find that hardly surprising," Tom says, with a questioning raise of his eyebrows.

Aware that she has lost his attention, Jessica goes on. (Where *is* he—with whom?) "I just meant, it seems awful to feel a sort of relief when she cries. As though I thought that's what she ought to do. Maybe she didn't really care for Horace. He hasn't been around for years, after all." (As usual she is making things worse: it is apparent that Tom can barely listen.)

She says, "I think I'll take the index cards back to my desk," and she manages not to cry.

Picking up the sheets to take upstairs to the linen closet, Verlie decides that she won't tell Clifton about Horace; dimly she thinks that if she tells anyone, especially Clifton, it won't be true: Horace, alive, will be waiting for her at her house, as almost every night she is afraid that he will be.

Sitting at her desk, unseeingly Jessica looks out across the deep valley, where the creek winds down toward the sea, to the further hills that are bright green with spring. Despair slowly fills her blood so that it seems heavy in her veins, and thick, and there is a heavy pressure in her head.

And she dreams for a moment, as she has sometimes before, of a friend to whom she could say, "I can't stand anything about my life. My husband either is untrue to me or would like to be—constantly. It comes to the same thing, didn't St. Paul say that? My daughter's eyes are beginning to go cold against me, and my son is terrified of everyone. Of me." But there is no one to whom she could say a word of this; she is known among her friends for dignity and restraint. (Only sometimes her mind explodes, and she breaks out screaming—at Tom, at one of her children, once at Verlie—leaving them all sick and shocked, especially herself sick and shocked, and further apart than ever.)

Now Verlie comes through the room with an armful of fresh, folded sheets, and for an instant, looking at her, Jessica has the thought that Verlie could be that friend, that listener. That Verlie could understand.

She dismisses the impulse almost as quickly as it came.

Lately she has spent a lot of time remembering college, those distant happy years, among friends. Her successes of that time. The two years when she directed the Greek play, on May Day weekend (really better than being in the May Court). Her senior year, elected president of the secret honor society. (And the springs of wisteria, heavily flowering, scented, lavender and white, the heavy vines everywhere.)

From those college days she still has two friends, to whom she writes, and visits at rarer intervals. Elizabeth, who is visibly happily married to handsome and successful Jackson Stuart (although he is, to Jessica, a shocking racial bigot). And Mary John James, who teaches Latin in a girls' school, in Richmond—who has never married. Neither of them could be her imagined friend (any more than Verlie could).

Not wanting to see Jessica's sad eyes again (the sorrow in that woman's face, the mourning!), Verlie puts the sheets in the linen closet and goes down the back stairs. She is halfway down, walking slow, when she feels a sudden coolness in her blood, as though from a breeze. She stops, she listens to nothing and then she is flooded with the certain knowledge that Horace is dead, is at that very moment laid away in Memphis (wherever Memphis is). Standing there alone, by the halfway window that looks out to the giant rhododendron, she begins to smile, peacefully and slowly—an interior, pervasive smile.

Then she goes on down the stairs, through the dining room and into the kitchen.

Clifton is there.

Her smile changes; her face becomes brighter and more animated, although she doesn't say anything—not quite trusting herself not to say everything, as she has promised herself.

"You looking perky," Clifton says, by way of a question. He is standing at the sink with a drink of water.

Her smile broadens, and she lies. "Thinking about the social at the church. Just studying if or not I ought to go."

"You do right to go," he says. And then, "You be surprise, you find me there?"

(They have never arranged any meeting before, much less in another place, at night; they have always pretended that they were in the same place in the yard or orchard by accident.)

She laughs. "You never find the way."

He grins at her, his face brighter than any face that she has ever seen. "I be there," he says to her.

A long, hot summer, extending into fall. A hot October, and then there is sudden cold. Splinters of frost on the red clay erosions in the fields. Ice in the shallow edges of the creek.

For Verlie it has been the happiest summer of her life, but no one of the Todds has remarked on this, nor been consciously aware of unusual feelings, near at hand. They all have preoccupations of their own.

Clifton has been working for the Macombers, friends and neighbors of the Todds, and it is Irene Macomber who telephones to tell Jessica the sad news that he had a kind of seizure (a hemorrhage) and that when they finally got him to the Negro hospital (twelve miles away) it was too late, and he died.

Depressing news, on that dark November day. Jessica supposes that the first thing is to tell Verlie. (After all, she and Clifton were friends, and Verlie might know of relatives.)

She is not prepared for Verlie's reaction.

A wail—"Aieeeee"—that goes on and on, from Verlie's wide mouth, and her wide, wild eyes. "Aieee—"

Then it stops abruptly, as Verlie claps her hands over her mouth, and bends over and blindly reaches for a chair, her rocker. She pulls herself toward the chair, she falls into it, she bends over double and begins to cough, deep and wrackingly.

Poor shocked Jessica has no notion what to do. To go over to Verlie and embrace her, to press her own sorrowing face to Verlie's face? To creep shyly and sadly from the room?

This last is what she does—is all, perhaps, that she is able to do.

.   .   .

"You know," says Tom Todd (seriously) to Irene McGinnis, in one of their rare lapses from the steady demands of unconsummated love, "I believe those two people had a real affection for each other."

Verlie is sick for a week and more after that, with what is called "misery in the chest." (No one mentions her heart.)

Thinking to amuse her children (she is clearly at a loss without Verlie, and she knows this), Jessica takes them for a long walk, on the hard, narrow, white roads that lead up into the hills, the heavy, thick, dark woods of fall, smelling of leaves and earth and woodsmoke. But a melancholy mood settles over them all; it is cold and the children are tired, and Jessica finds that she is thinking of Verlie and Clifton. (Is it possible that they were lovers? She uncomfortably shrugs off this possibility.)

Dark comes early, and there is a raw, red sunset at the black edge of the horizon, as finally they reach home.

Verlie comes back the next day, to everyone's relief. But there is a grayish tinge to the color of her skin that does not go away.

But on that rare spring day months earlier (the day Horace is dead and laid away in Memphis) Verlie walks the miles home with an exceptional lightness of heart, smiling to herself at all the colors of the bright new flowers, and at the smells of spring, the promises.

Winter Rain

Whenever in the final unendurable weeks of winter, I am stricken, as now, to the bone with cold—it is raining, the furnace has somehow failed—I remember that winter of 1947–1948 in Paris, when I was colder than ever in my life, when it always rained, when everything broke down. That was the winter of strikes: GRÈVE GÉNÉRALE, in large strange headlines. And everyone struck: Métro, garbage, water, electricity, mail—all these daily necessities were at one time or another with difficulty forgone. Also, that was the first winter of American students—boys on the G.I. bill and girls with money from home, Bennington meeting Princeton in the Montana Bar. There were cellar clubs to which French friends guided one mysteriously: on the Rue Dauphine the Tabu, with a band; the Mephisto, just off the Boulevard Saint-Germain; and further out on Rue Blomet the wicked Bal Nègre, where one danced all night to West Indian music, danced with everyone and drank Pernod. It was a crowded, wild, excited year.

I think of friends of that time—I have kept up with none of them, certainly not with Bruno, nor Laura, nor Joe, not even with Mme. Frenaye. And it gloomily occurs to me that they may all be dead, Bruno in some violent Italian way, Laura and Joe in Hollywood, and Mme. Frenaye of sheer old age, on the Rue de Courcelles, *"tout près,"* as she used to say, *"du Parc Monceau."* Though we parted less than friends, it is she of whom I think most often.

Madame and I really parted, as from the first I should have known we would, over money. And, more than I regret the loss of our connection, I regret the sordidness of its demise. But I should have known; the process was gradual but clear. As was the fact that I, and not she, would lose face in any conflict.

Winter Rain

. . .

To begin with, she extracted from me an enormous amount of money for permission to live at the cold end of the long drafty hall in her flat. Of course I didn't have to take the room, or to accept the arrangement at all, but from the first I was seduced. I had heard, from friends, that a Mme. Frenaye might be willing to take a nice American girl student into her charming home. I inquired further, and was invited to tea. It was raining dreadfully, even in September, and I wore, all wet and shivering, a yellow summer coat and summer dress since, probably owing to a strike somewhere, my trunk of winter clothes had not arrived. The street seemed impossibly gray, chilled and forbidding, but the central room of the flat into which I was ushered by Madame was warm and graceful. There were exquisite white Louis XVI chairs, a marvelous muted blue Persian rug, a mantel lined with marble above a fireplace in which a small fire blazed prettily.

Mme. Frenaye was a great goddess of a woman. She must have been sixty, or even seventy—I was never sure—but she was very tall and she held herself high; she was Junoesque indeed. She still mourned her husband, dead five years, and wore only black, but her effect was vivid. Her hair was bright gold and she wore it in a thick crowning braid across the waves that rose from her brow. Her eyes were very blue, capable of a great spectacle of innocence or charming guile, and she wore mascara heavily on her long lashes. She had dimples and perfect white teeth.

We took tea from a beautiful table before the fire, and we talked about Antibes, where I had spent the summer. Mme. Frenaye poured a little rum from a pretty porcelain jug into the tea, and said, "I would not have thought of going to the Riviera in the summer. So crowded then. But of course you are so young, you have not been to France before."

She seemed prepared to forgive, and I did not want to protest that I had had a very good time.

She went on, "But a winter in Paris, there you have chosen wisely, this time you will not regret your choice. Theatre, opera, it is all here for you, the best in the world. And of course the Sorbonne, since you have chosen to study." She was vastly amused to learn that the name of my course at the Sorbonne was *Cours de la civilisation française.* "But you will spend the rest of your life—" she said, and I agreed.

We talked, and drank our tea, and ate small delicious cakes, until it occurred to me that I had perhaps stayed too long and so rose to leave. I think I had really forgotten that I had come about a room, or perhaps such a crass consideration seemed inappropriate in Louis XVI surroundings. Instead, on the way out I admired a painting. Mme. Frenaye said, "Ah, yes, and it has a gross value." I translate literally to give the precise effect of her words on me. My French was not good, and I thought I had misheard her, or not known an idiom. I would not be warned.

Then, at the door, while helping me with my still damp yellow coat, she said that she had heard that I needed a pleasant place to live, that she would be willing to let me live there, that she would serve me breakfast and dinner, and she named an outrageous number of francs. Even translated into dollars it was high. I was so stunned by her whole method that I accepted on the spot, and it was agreed that I would bring my things on the following Monday. That I did not even ask to see the room is evidence of my stupor; I must have thought it would be exactly like the salon.

And sometimes now I wonder whether she had any idea that I would accept; or made up that ridiculous figure simply to let me off. And I wonder too if I did not want to prove that I could do better than yellow coats and summer dresses in a cold September rain; behind me there were sound American dollars, and, as my father would have said, more where they came from. So, from our combined dubious motives, we were joined, to live and eat and talk together throughout those difficult historic months from September until February, until our private war became visible and manifest, and I left.

The room was actually not as bad as it might have been, taken on such dazzled faith. It was not large, nor warm, nor did it contain a desk or a bookcase; however, the bed was regally gilded and huge and soft, and I slept under comforting layers of down, between pink linen sheets. Madame sighed, her beautiful eyes misted as she showed the bed to me and I felt badly about so depriving her until I realized that her own small bed-sitting room had been astutely chosen as the warmest room in the house. And the grand bed would not fit into it.

. . .

When I said such things to Laura and Joe, later to Bruno, as we hunched over beers in the steamy Café de Flore or the Deux Magots, they reasonably exclaimed, "But why on earth do you stay there?" (Laura and Joe were Marxists, and I was acceptable to them partly because my arrangement with Mme. Frenaye left me with virtually no money at all.) In any case I did not think that they would feel the charm of Mme. Frenaye, and so I would say to them, "But the food is fantastic, and see how my French is improving."

Both of these things were quite true. I have never since tasted anything to compare with her *poisson normand,* that beautifully flaking fat white fish baked with tiny mushrooms, tiny shrimps and mussels in white wine. I have the most vivid sensual memories of her crisp green salads. I would arrive cold and usually wet from my long Métro trek, and hurriedly unwrap myself from my coat just in time to enter that small warm room where she had placed the white-clothed table. The room was full of marvelous delicate smells of hot food, and Madame in passage from the kitchen would greet me. *"Bon soir, Patience. Mais vous avez froid. Asseyez-vous, je viens tout de suite. Oh, mais j'ai oublié l'essentiel—"* and she was off to fetch the decanter of wine.

And my French did improve. She knew no English, and we talked animatedly throughout those months of dinners. She was endlessly curious about America, though she pretended to disbelieve half of what I told her. "But, Patience, surely you exaggerate," she would chide, in a tone of amused tolerance. Sometimes, fresh from Joe's lectures, I became heavily sociological. She listened intently, nodded appropriately. Only when I hit on American anti-Semitism did I strike some chord in her— she found it absolutely incomprehensible. She adored American Jews. Her husband had been a cotton merchant, and in his business the only Americans he met were Jewish or from Texas. And the Texans, according to Madame, were appalling: they ordered the most expensive champagne or cognac and then got drunk on it. The Jewish families whom she met were quite another story. *"Tellement cultivées, tellement sensibles."* Her most admired American friends, the Berkowitzes (*"Ah, les Berkowitz"*), went to museums daily, to the theatre and the opera; the Texans never. She felt that *"les Berkowitz"* too squandered their money but in less visible and offensive ways. One of her most loved stories was of going shopping for a brassière, a *soutien-gorge,* with Marion Berkowitz. *"C'était tout, tout petit,"* she would say, with her thumb and forefinger gesturing a pinch of nothing, *"et ça coûtait tellement cher!"* This contradiction never ceased to amaze and delight her.

The truth was that I liked Mme. Frenaye. I admired her beauty and her charm; and her scorn, her assumption of superiority to the world, comforted me since I felt that she counted me on her side. Moreover, I simply could not imagine a scene in which I told her that I was going to leave. I think that if I had not met Bruno, near Christmas, during one long night in the Bal Nègre, where I had reluctantly gone with Laura and Joe, I would have lived on the Rue de Courcelles until June, when I took that huge and final boat for New York.

My memory of Bruno is also involved with the cold: I see the two of us clinging together in a garish white-lit Métro entrance, because it was too cold outside, and our partings were endless and all unendurable. We walked together. I remember my ungloved hand pressing against his, together jammed deeply into his shabby tweed pocket, as we walked past steamed bright windows in the iron cold, stopping to kiss.

Even Bruno seems legendary to me now; both our romantic intensity and the facts of his life sound mythic. His father was an Italian anti-Fascist who had left Italy in the twenties. Bruno was born in Toulouse, and spent his fifteenth birthday in a Vichy concentration camp, his sixteenth in a similar camp in Italy. He had fought with the Maquis, and with guerrilla fighters in the Italian Alps. He had no scars nor any limp to show for all of this; he was tall and sturdy, smooth-skinned, clear-eyed as any innocent American boy—in fact he was often taken for a G.I., which amused him and privately annoyed me. He studied law in Paris, and lived with relatives out in the 14th arrondissement. Thus in the cold we had no place to go, and between partings we dreamed of a furnished room, warm and light, anywhere in Paris. I can no longer remember the substance of our quarrels, nor of our talk, but both went on forever, punctuating each other, and all the time our eyes held together, our hands touched.

Out of some misguided sense of duty I spent Christmas Day that year with Madame rather than with Bruno. And it was a bad day. Madame was far from being at her best. She sniffed deprecatingly at my gift of a tiny bottle of perfume from Worth, telling me she had once calculated the contents of all the bottles on her dressing table and it came to more than two liters. "You can imagine," she said, "how much that would be worth." She had given me a pair of felt slippers from Trois Quartiers, and they were not very pretty.

We rallied somewhat at dinner. There was an incredible roast chicken, an unheard-of luxury in Paris that year. But then, with the token glass of brandy, Mme. Frenaye grew sad again, and spoke of the death of her husband. "Over and over he said to me, 'Ah, how good you are,'" and her great eyes misted. I was wildly impatient to go; I had promised to meet Bruno at the Flore at nine. I wanted to hear of no other love, no death.

That night we fought because I lived so far away. Bruno found incomprehensible my refusal to move. "On purpose you isolate yourself in your gray prison," he said. (Once he had accompanied me home, had seen from the outside the fortress of apartments on the Rue de Courcelles.) He said, his clear blue eyes near mine, "How much more time we would have if you even lived near the Sorbonne—I think you don't want to be with me—you would rather stay safely beside your little fire." I protested this violently, but in a sense it was perfectly true. I was afraid of him; life with Madame, though difficult, seemed safer than the exposure of a room alone.

But at the same time that I resisted Bruno I found my fortress more and more impossible. I was extremely tense; the most petty annoyances grew large. I once calculated that with all the small sums of money which Madame had borrowed from time to time to tip porters, buy stamps, I could have bought Bruno a gaudy present.

And there was the matter of my CARE packages. My anxious mother sent them punctually each month, thus assuring herself that I would never starve. I had written and asked her not to. Their arrival embarrassed me; I was sure the porter who carried them upstairs knew what they were, and thought of his own hungry family. I wanted badly to give them to him, but some misplaced shyness held me back. Madame adored all that American food. She appropriated each package and opened it on the marble-topped kitchen table. She exclaimed over, and later used, the boxes of cake mix, and she devised a marvelous method of stuffing baked potatoes with the liver pâté that came in large cans. The pancake mix she especially loved. *"Ah, les crêpes américaines,"* she would cry out lovingly, expressing her whole indulgent fondness for the young rich crazy country of dollars and handsome brave G.I.s, of fantastic machines that did everything, of her cherished Berkowitzes and of me.

But in my new mood of sullen resentment I protested her appropriation. How dare she charge me ruinous rates for food and lodging and then accept such a bulk of food from my mother? In silence and secrecy my list of grievances against her mounted; that they were petty and degrading of course made them more unbearable. Also that I lacked the courage to say anything.

It was perfectly appropriate to that year that my dilemma was finally resolved by a strike. And by Bruno.

All during January, Bruno snarled and complained at my living arrangements. I remember an afternoon in the upstairs part of the Flore, where it was always warm and with luck one could stay for hours, seated on the plaid-covered banquettes, without having to order anything. We had, I remember, not enough money between us for hot chocolate— which we both felt could have saved the afternoon. Unkindly, Bruno reminded me that if I lived in the Quarter, in a cheap room, I could now be making hot chocolate and serving it in privacy. There was always a sort of European practicality about him—even in love, I thought—and in the phrase betrayed how American was my own romanticism. He gave a sense of the pressure of time, of destiny, as though along his way he could not be troubled with incidents of geography and money. By the end of the afternoon we had agreed never to meet again, and I wept conspicuously all the long Métro ride from Odéon to Place Péreire.

The next week was unendurable. There was a violent cold black rain. The heat failed again in Madame's long flat, the fires spluttered and would not burn. Wholly miserable, I mourned my forever lost love.

Then came the mail strike. No letters at all, from anywhere. The papers described mountains of paper piled fantastically on post-office floors. I was completely dependent on letters from home for money, and now I could not pay Madame on the day when my fee came due. At dinner I tried to mention it casually to her. Much in the spirit of the times, I said, "After all, this strike can't go on forever."

But Madame's spirit was not at all with the times. "Strike or not, I have to shop for groceries," she said with uncharacteristic terseness. I was totally upset; life, I felt, was too much for me; I had no resources. And even Madame, stronger and wiser and infinitely more charming, fell down. Apropos of nothing she told me again the story of Marion Berkowitz and the buying of the *soutien-gorge,* but the mention of high prices made us both nervous and we failed to be amused.

That night, hunched frozen between the pink linen sheets, I decided that if I did not see Bruno again I would die.

At breakfast my final long-delayed scene with Mme. Frenaye took place, over cups of powdered American coffee from my latest CARE package. I found that I had to say everything all at once. "I have to move," I said. "It's very nice here but I simply can't afford it any longer. And really, you know, no one pays so much for a pension, I mean even in America this would be considered high. And also this is too far from my classes at the Sorbonne—you remember during the Métro strike I couldn't even get there."

Madame listened to this somewhat with the air of a teacher of speech. And indeed it was a tribute to the French I had learned with her that I was able to get it out. She seemed, on the whole, to approve both my eloquence and my logic, for at the end she said, *"Certainement,"* in a final tone.

I needed her to argue with me, and I added defiantly, "I want to live in the Latin Quarter."

"Oui, le Quartier Latin." But she was not thinking about my proposed life on the Left Bank; her tone was completely neutral. And hearing it I realized suddenly that as far as she was concerned I had already gone. Also, and this was doubly infuriating, I realized that she had undoubtedly known for some time that I would go. Probably from that first wet day when we took our tea by her pretty fire she had known that I would not last the year. Any concession on her part—if she had said she could wait for the rent—might have made me weaken. But she was far too realistic and too economical for any emotional waste.

．　．　．

And so I packed that afternoon in a fury of frustration. I felt that I had been taken, conned out of my moment of righteous defiance by some ageless European trick of charm. As I hunted for shoe bags, I thought furiously that she had completely turned the tables. I was the one who had ended by being mercenary, petty.

She came to the door later, and asked perfunctorily if there was anything that she could do to help, and I wanted to shout "No!" at her, but I did not; I only muttered negatively. She said, "Well, in that case I will say *au revoir, Patience, et bonne chance.*"

We shook hands at the door to my erstwhile bedroom, and I said that I would call her when I was settled, and she said, "But please do," and smiled with her beautiful wise blue eyes and was gone. I had no true parting scene.

The room that I found late that afternoon was on the Rue de Seine. My high narrow windows overlooked the entrance to the Club Mephisto; I could see a fish market where the fat silver bellies were piled high, and a fruit stand bright with winter tomatoes and bunches of dark rose chrysanthemums. At the corner hardware store I bought a saucepan and a small tripod burner with some cans of Sterno, and felt myself prepared for warm domestic peace with Bruno.

But though reunited we were never peaceful. In spite of my room, of which he approved, our passionate partings continued. I can hear now the angry sound of his boots on the narrow steep stairs as he left stormily after an impossible argument. And I remember lying half awake dreaming that he would come back.

One afternoon, during a rift with Bruno that was more prolonged than usual, on an impulse I called Mme. Frenaye and asked her to have tea with me at the Ritz. She would be delighted, she said, and I remember that I wore my first New Look dress, which was gray silk with a terribly long skirt. The occasion was a great success. I was struck by how glad I was to see her. It seemed to me then that I had missed her, and that my life alone had been more difficult. Certainly that afternoon Madame was at her best. She complained pleasantly that the service was not what it had been before the war, nor the pastry, and after our tea we gossiped happily about the other women in the room.

Madame did not ask me about my present living arrangements. Since I had come prepared to boast, this was slightly irritating, but at the same time I was relieved. Nor did she, as I had rather expected, say that she missed me. She was quite impersonally charming, and we parted with an exchange of pleasantries, but with no talk of a further meeting.

The rain and cold continued into April. I remember bitterly deciding that the lyric burst one expected of spring in Paris would never come, that it was a myth.

Joe and Laura had left, apologizing, for Hollywood in March. I went to lectures at the Sorbonne and in the lengthening intervals when I did not see Bruno I wandered alone about the city, hunched against the rain, wrapped in American tweed.

Then, around the first of May, the weather changed, the chestnut and plane trees along the boulevards feathered into delicate green and the sky behind the square stone tower of Saint-Germain-des-Prés was pink and soft in the long light evenings.

For at least a month Bruno and I got along happily. It was the tender penultimate stage of a love affair, before it became clear that I really wanted him to come to America and marry me, and that he had to live in Italy and did not want to get married, clear to us both that I was hopelessly domestic and bourgeois. He said, finally, that I would not be a suitable companion for an Italian statesman, and of course he was perfectly right.

But before this finality, in some spirit of bravado, I called Mme. Frenaye and asked her to come to tea in my room—and asked Bruno to come too. I am not at all sure what I expected of either of them; perhaps I felt the dramatic necessity of a meeting between the two people who had that year been, variously, most important to me.

Or perhaps this was my last defiance of Madame. If that were so I failed utterly, foiled again by her aplomb. Of course Bruno helped; he appeared uncharacteristically in a white shirt and tie, his brown hair brushed smooth; he could not have looked less like an Italian radical with a violent past. Mme. Frenaye first took him to be a nice American boy; her whole demeanor spoke a total acceptance and approval of him. She thought it very wise of him to study law in Paris, and she raised her lovely innocent blue eyes in attractive horror when he told her how many hours he had to study each day. "But then you are so young and strong," she said, with a tender and admiring smile. Of course he liked her—who could not?

She even approved of my room, though she sat rather stiffly and gingerly on the single straight wooden chair. She looked across the street to the piles of fish and remarked that she had noticed lower prices here than in her own *quartier,* but this was her only suggestion that I had come down in the world. And I thought then, but did not speak, of her beautiful *poisson normand.* She only said, "Such a nice clean room, Patience, and it must be so convenient for you."

I made tea, boiling the water over Sterno which Madame thought terribly ingenious, and we ate the pastries which I had bought. Bruno and Madame talked about the beauties of Italy, of Florence in early spring, Venice in October. And painting. I could imagine her saying of him, *"Tellement cultivé, ce jeune Italien, tellement sensible."*

After that day everything deteriorated. The weather turned cold and it rained fiercely as though to remind us all of the difficult past winter. When, finally, I booked passage on a boat which was to leave the third of June, I felt that my exit was being forced, the city and the time would have no more of me. I had accepted the impossibility of Bruno—we still saw each other but I wept and it always ended badly. I did not see Madame again. I did call her, meaning to say good-bye, but there was no answer.

Sometimes it occurs to me to write to Madame, to send her pictures of my husband, my house and my children, as though to convince her that I have grown up, that I am no longer that odd girl who came to her in the wet summer coat, or who tried to charm her with tea made over Sterno in an unlikely room. Or I try to imagine her here, perhaps as the great-aunt whom, on shopping trips into town, I occasionally visit. But this is impossible: my aunt, an American Gothic puritan with a band of black grosgrain ribbon about her throat, my aunt laughing over the purchase of a tiny *soutien-gorge,* bringing in wine, *l'essentiel*? This won't do. And I am forced to leave Madame, and Bruno of whom I never think, as and where they are, in that year of my own history.

Ripped Off

The gentle, leafy day made Deborah high; she came home from her morning job light in her head and heart. When she saw that the small drawer from her desk had been pulled out and taken over to the bed and left there, its contents spilled out over the tousled blue sheets, she first thought, Wow, Philip, what are you trying to tell me? Philip lived with her in the Russian Hill flat, and what was—or had been—in the drawer were notes from him, notes or bits of paper that for one reason or another he had put his name on or drawn some small picture on. A couple of the messages said "Gone for walk. Later." But on one, a torn-off match cover, he had written "I love you," and passed it to her across a table in a restaurant. There was even a canceled check made out to and endorsed by him, from a couple of months ago when Deborah had lent him some money.

Her second reaction was one of surprise; Philip was not nosy or jealous. Once she had known a boy, Juan, from Panama, who was both—violently so. She had had to burn her old letters and diaries so that he would not find them. In fact, he had finally left her because (he said) she was so friendly with other men. (She did not see herself as especially friendly to anyone.) It was not like Philip to search through her desk. She thought he must have been looking for a stamp or something. Still, why bring the drawer over to the bed? What was he trying to tell her?

Deborah was a tall, rather oddly shaped girl. Her breasts were large but her body was otherwise skimpy, and with her long thin legs she had somewhat the look of a bird that might topple over but never quite did. Big front teeth made her appear shy, which she was. Her wide dark-brown eyes could show a great deal of pain or love. She wore her brown hair long and straight, but for her Kelly Girl job—taken for two reasons:

to give herself freedom of movement (she only took morning work), and to embarrass her mother, who expected her to have some kind of career—she dressed in short non-mini skirts and straight shirts. She tended to look for clothes that would hide her—hide her identity as well as her breasts. Her mother and some of the neighbors in that expensive San Francisco block—she and Philip lived in a building owned by Deborah's stepfather, who charged a ritualistic fifty a month for a high, wide studio room with an overwhelming view of the Bay and the ocean— described her as a hippie. Deborah felt that that was not quite right, although she could not have said what she was. She read a lot, and thought. Now she was mainly thinking about what to make for dinner for Philip, in case he came home for dinner.

As she picked up the bits of paper (nothing missing) and replaced the drawer and made the bed—bending awkwardly, tugging at the recalcitrant sheets—her discovery seemed less funny all the time. It was painful for Philip to know she was so sentimental. She blushed and pressed her fingers over her mouth. Nobody but a thirteen-year-old or a middle-aged woman (her mother, with all her dead father's Navy things, and pressed dead gardenias in a book of poems by Dorothy Parker) would keep stuff around like that. What would Philip think? Nothing between them was at all explicitly stated or defined. He had moved into the room shortly after they had met (at the Renaissance Fair, in Marin County—beautiful!) without much comment or any real plan, and he could presumably leave the same way. No one said anything about how long. Deborah sometimes thought he was there simply because of the coincidence in time between meeting her and the disbanding of his Mendocino commune and the start of a new term at the Art Institute. He was a little younger than she was—twenty-one to her twenty-three. His presence was kindly and peaceful, but he talked little, and it was not possible to tell what was in his mind. Sometimes he sang a line or two, like "It ain't me, babe, it ain't me you're looking for, babe." (Did he mean her?) Or, "Lay, lady, lay, lay across my big brass bed." (Had he met a new girl?)

As she straightened up from her own bed (the headboard of linen, not brass) she noticed what was incredible that she had not seen before: Philip had taken his zebra-skin rug. Loss hit her hard—so hard that she sat down on the bed and stared at the dusty space where the skins had been. He's used that silly drawer as an excuse to go, she thought. Of course. That was why he emptied it onto the bed. He was telling her that she was a terrible, possessive woman, hoarding souvenirs (like her mother), trying to hang on to him. The rug was the first thing he had brought over, by way of moving in, and despite their ambivalence about it (they disapproved of hunting, and too, the skins had a suggestion of decorator chic), it had picked up the look of the room, enhancing Deborah's wicker and white linen and black leather chairs—leavings from her mother's tasteful (the taste of five years back) country house.

Deborah was given to moments of total panic such as this, when the world seemed to lurch beneath her like the fun-house floor at Playland-at-the-Beach, when she gasped for air and found it hard to breathe. A psychiatrist had explained this tidily to her as a syndrome: she feared abandonment. Her father had gone off to war and been killed ("At three, you would have viewed this as a desertion—a deliberate one"), and it seemed (to the psychiatrist) that she tried to repeat that situation. She readily felt abandoned, and picked people who would abandon her, like Panamanian Juan. But no, she thought, she was at least able to make an effort to think things through in a reasonable way. She controlled her breathing (with Yoga breaths) and remembered that Philip had been talking about having the rug repaired. There was a rip in it that could get larger, or could trip one of them. It made sense—Philip finally took the rug off to be sewn. He had mentioned some people on Union Street who did things with hides and who had the right machines for skins.

Having decided so rationally on what had happened, Deborah felt better, but not very much better. Some cobweb of fear or anxiety clung to her mind, and she could not brush it off. She knew that she would not feel entirely well and reassured until she spoke to Philip. She concentrated on his phone call, which always came early in the afternoon, though by no stated arrangement. They would say whatever had happened in the day so far, and make some plan for the evening. Or Philip would say that he would see her later—meaning ten or eleven that night.

Naturally, since she was eager for Philip to call, several other people did instead, and each time her heart jumped as she answered, "Hello?"

Her mother said, "Darling, how are you? I was wondering if you and Philip are possibly free to come to dinner tomorrow? A couple of my professors from State are coming—you know, the ones who were out on strike—and I thought you might have fun with them."

Meaning: her mother thought the professors, who must have been quite young, would have a better time (and think better of her) if they met her hippie daughter with her long-haired, bearded boyfriend.

"Sure. I'll check with Philip," Deborah said, and then listened to her mother's continuing voice, which was grateful and full of love.

Once, when she was stoned, Deborah had said to Philip, "My mother's love comes at me like jelly. I have to be careful and stay back from it, you know? All that total approval I get poured over me. She doesn't even know who I am."

Philip's mother, in Cincinnati ("She pronounces it with a broad 'a'—can you imagine? Cincin*nah*ti." He, too, was a person displaced from the upper middle class), did not approve of him at all—his beard or his long hair, his Goodwill or Army-surplus clothes. Dropping out of Princeton to come to an art school in San Francisco. She had not been told about the commune in Mendocino; nor, presumably, about Deborah. "I don't mind her," he said. "She's sort of abrasive, bracing, like good sandpaper. She does her own thing, and it's very clear where we're both at."

Philip talked that hip way somewhat ironically, hiding behind it. "I think I'm what those idiot behavioral scientists call a post-hippie," he once said. "Sounds sort of like a wooden Indian, doesn't it?" But he had indeed put various things behind him, including drugs, except for an occasional cigarette. For him, Deborah had thrown out all her posters, and with him she had moved from Hesse and Tolkien to Mann and Dostoevski. "Let's face it, babe, they've got more to say. I mean, they've really got it all together."

After her mother's call, two friends called (about nothing), and finally there was the call from Philip.

She said, "Wow, Philip, what are you trying to tell me?" as she had planned to, but she felt no conviction.

"What?"

"The desk drawer on the bed."

"What drawer?"

"Did you take the zebra rug to be sewn?"

"No. Deb, are you trying to tell me that we've been ripped off, as they say?"

Crazily enough, this was a possibility she had not considered, but now she thought, Of course, it happens all the time.

"Debby," he was saying, "would you please look around and see what else is gone?"

As best she could, she did look around; she found her shoe box full of jewelry—the ugly inherited diamonds that she never wore—intact under her sweaters, and the stereo safely in its corner. The books, the records. His pictures. She came back to the phone and told him that.

"But aside from the stereo what else could they have taken?" she asked. "We don't have TV and appliances, stuff like that. Who wants our books?" She felt herself babbling, then said, "I'm really sorry about your rug."

"Oh, well. Maybe I wasn't supposed to have it."

"Shall I call the cops?"

"I guess. I'll be home for dinner, O.K.?"

Relief made Deborah efficient. Philip had not moved out, and he was coming home for dinner. She began to put together a rather elaborate lamb stew. (She always bought meat on the chance that he would come home, even though sometimes after several days of his absences she would have to throw it out.) She shaved fresh ginger into the lamb, and then she called the police.

The two officers who arrived perhaps twenty minutes later were something of a surprise. They were young—about her age. (Who of her generation would want to be a cop, she wondered.) One of them was blond and looked a little like a short-haired, clean-shaven Philip. They were quite sympathetic and soft-spoken; they gave sensible advice. "Use the double lock when you go out," the blond one said. "This one could be picked in a minute. And fix the bolt on the kitchen door."

"Do it soon," said the other. "They could be back for more."

"It's sort of funny they didn't take the stereo, too," Deborah said, conversationally.

"Hippies love those fur rugs," they told her, unaware that they were not talking to a nice girl from the right side of Russian Hill, and that for her they had just become the enemy.

"More likely junkies than hippies, don't you think?" she coldly said.

For Deborah, the preparation and serving of food were acts of love. She liked to serve Philip; she brought in plates and placed them gently before him, like presents, although her offhand manner denied this.

"It's that Indian stuff," she said of the stew. Then, so that he would not be forced to comment on her cooking, she said, "It's funny, their moving that drawer from my desk."

"Probably thought you kept valuables there—bonds and bank notes and stuff." He was eating as though he were starved, which was how he always ate; he barely paused to look up and speak.

She felt herself inwardly crying, "I do! You are infinitely valuable to me. Anything connected with you is valuable—please stay with me!" She managed not to say any of this; instead she blinked. He had been known to read her eyes.

"This stew is really nice," he told her. "And the wine—cool! Like wow!"

They both laughed a little, their eyes briefly meeting.

She asked, "How's school? How's the graphics class?"

"Pretty good."

Philip was thin, with knobby bones at his wrists, protuberant neck bones and tense tendons. He had dark-blue, thoughtful eyes. His fine hair flew about when he moved. He looked frail, as though a strong wind (or a new idea) could carry him off bodily. "I tend to get into head trips" is how he half ironically put it, not saying what kind of trips they were. He seemed to be mainly concerned with his work—drawing, etching, watercolors. Other things (people, weather, days) passed by his cool, untroubled but observant gaze—as someday, Deborah felt, she, too, might pass by.

At the moment, however, she was experiencing a total, warm contentment. There was Philip, eating and liking the stew she had made, and they had been robbed—ripped off—and nothing of value was gone.

"What was in the drawer?" he asked.

"Oh, nothing. Just some stuff I keep around."

Again their quick glances met, and they smiled; then both ducked away from prolonged contact. Deborah had to look aside because she had suddenly thought how marvelous it would be if they could have a child, a straw-blond baby that she would nurse (she had heard that breast-feeding made big breasts smaller) and Philip would always love. The intensity of this wish made her dizzy. For concealment, she asked, "You really won't miss those skins?"

"Really not. You know I always hated them as much as I liked them. Good luck to whoever took them is how I feel."

. . .

After dinner Deborah cleared and cleaned the kitchen, while Philip read in the living room. Early on in their life together, he had helped or at least offered to, but gradually they both realized that cleaning up was something Deborah did not mind doing. She liked that simple interval of being alone, with nothing demanded of her that she could not accomplish. Her mother said of her that she was a throwback—"my quaint hippie daughter." Deborah supposed that there was something to that. She liked to polish the wineglasses and to shine the chrome and porcelain on the stove and sink. She did all that tonight, and then went into the living room, where Philip was, and sat near him with a book of her own. With evening, the fog had begun to roll in. Outside, the distant foghorns announced a cold, moist black night. Wind shuddered against the windows, beyond which nothing was visible. The surrounding dark and cold made an island of their room—to Deborah, an enchanted island. She thought, We could live like this forever; this peace is better than any high. She thought, Do I want to get married, is that what I mean that I want? And then, No, I only mean to stay like this, with no change. But someday a baby.

They read for several hours. Absorbed in his book (*Doctor Faustus,* for the second time), Philip fought off sleep until he and then Deborah went into fits of yawns, and they gave up and went to bed.

While they were undressing, Deborah opened the drawer where she kept her scarves.

It was gone—her largest, most beautiful, pale striped silk scarf, all lavenders and mauves and pinks, the only present from her mother that she had ever liked. Wearing any dress at all, she could wrap herself in that scarf and be instantly elegant. Soon after she and Philip had met, she wore it to a party at the Institute, and he thought it was a wonderful scarf. The enormity of its absence had surely summoned her and made her for no reason open that drawer.

She felt hurt enough to cry, which, with a conscious effort, she did not do. Her second decision was not to tell Philip. This was less rational, and even as she slipped into bed beside him she was not sure why. Obviously, someday he would ask why she never wore it anymore. But at the moment she only knew that she felt diminished, as though without that scarf Philip would love her less, as though their best times together were over.

Philip turned on his side; having kissed her good night, he quickly fell asleep. She lay there in the dark, listening to the erratic mourning noise of the foghorns. She was thinking that even if she had a child he would grow up and go away. Finally, she couldn't stand it; all her thoughts were unbearable, and she turned and pressed her body against the length of Philip's slender warm back, holding him tightly with her arms, as though she could keep him there.

The Swastika on Our Door

Normally, Karen Washington took a warmly nostalgic interest in stories about and especially pictures of her husband's former girls. They had all been pretty, some beautiful. And they reminded her that her very successful and preoccupied lawyer husband had once been a lively bachelor, vigorously engaged in the pursuit of women. But the large glossy picture of Roger and his brother Richard, who was now dead, and a girl, that she found on the top shelf of her husband's shirt closet disturbed her considerably. Why had Roger put it there? She was not jealous; she did not suspect that he perpetuated an old liaison, but she felt left out. Why had he chosen not to tell her about this particular beautiful girl, in her high-collared coat?

To the left was fat Roger, grinning and blinking into the flashbulb, having raised his glass of wine to the nightclub camera: a man out on the town, celebrating, having a good time. "The jolly Roger": with his peculiar private irony Richard had sometimes called his brother that. On the right was skinny tortured Richard, who was staring at his brother with a gaze that was at the same time stern and full of an immoderate love. Between them, recessed into half shadow, was the long-necked beautiful dark girl, who was looking at Richard as though she thought he was either marvelous or crazy. Or perhaps she herself looked crazy. In the bright flat light her collar made an odd shadow on her cheek, and her eyes were a strange shape—very narrow and long, like fish.

Karen sighed heavily, and then sneezed from the dust. Although of German extraction she was a poor housekeeper, and did not like to be reminded of that fact, of which both the dust and the presence of that picture on an untouched shelf did remind her. Retreating from the closet, she put the picture on her husband's dressing table, meaning to ask him about it that night. She was a big dark handsome girl, descended from successful generations of Berlin bankers; her father, the last of the line, had come to San Francisco in the twenties, well before Hitler, and had been prominent in the founding of a local bank. Karen had already, in ten years of marriage to Roger, produced five sons, five stalwart big Washingtons who did not remember their difficult doomed Southern uncle, Uncle Richard, cartons of whose books were still unpacked in the basement.

Karen remembered Richard very well, and she thought of him for a great deal of that day as she moved about the enormous unwieldy and expensive house on Pacific Street, bought when Richard died and they inherited his money. The house from its northern windows had mammoth views of the Bay, and the bridge, Sausalito, the hills of Marin County. That day, that March, there were threatening rain clouds, a shifting kaleidoscope of them, an infinite variety of grays.

Karen had felt and still did feel an uncomfortable mixture of emotions in regard to Richard, one of which was certainly the guilty impatience of the healthy with the sick. Richard had been born with a defective heart, ten months after Roger's healthy and very normal birth, and had suffered greatly during his lifetime. But beyond his irremediable physical pain he had seemed, somehow, to choose to be lonely and miserable. He lived in a strange hotel even after he got his money; he was given to isolated, hopeless love affairs, generally with crazy girls. ("Affairs with psychopaths are a marvelous substitute for intimacy," he had been heard to say.) He only bought books and records; his clothes were impossible.

Like many very secure and contented people, Karen tended to be somewhat unimaginative about the needs, emotional and otherwise, of those who were not content, of those who were in fact miserable. To her credit she knew this, and so she sighed as she moved incompetently about her house with the vacuum cleaner; she sighed for Richard and for her own failure to have understood or in any way to have helped him.

Karen's deficiencies as a housekeeper were more than made up for by her abilities as a cook, or so her greedy husband and most of their greedy friends thought. That afternoon, as heavy dark rains enshrouded the city and the Bay, Karen made a superior moussaka, which was one of

Roger's favorites. It had also been a favorite of Richard's, and she was pleased to remember that she had at least done that for him.

Then, just as she had finished, from upstairs she heard the youngest child begin to whimper, waking up from his nap, and she went up to get him, to bathe and dress him before the older boys all tumbled home from school.

The maid would come at three and stay until after dinner, since Roger liked a formal evening meal.

Karen was dressing, and lost in a long skirt that she tried to pull down over big breasts, down over her increasing thighs, when Roger came in and asked her about the picture.

"What's that doing out here?" "Here" was "heah"; Roger had kept his Southern voice, though less strongly than Richard had.

Her head came out of the dress, and she bridled at the annoyance in his tone. "Why not? It was up on your top shirt shelf." At worst, in some atavistic Germanic way, Karen became coy. "Some old girl friend you haven't told me about?" she said.

Roger was holding the picture, blinking at it in the harsh light from Karen's makeup lamp, holding it closer and closer to the bulb as though he would burn it if the picture did not reveal all that he wanted to know. He was not thinking about Karen.

"She's beautiful," said Karen. She came to look over his shoulder, and pressed her cheek against his arm. She knew that he loved her.

"She was Richard's girl. Ellen. After that." He pointed unnecessarily at the picture. "We were celebrating his money, after he finally sold his land. That was the night he met her."

Karen was quiet, looking at the peculiar girl, and at Richard, whom no large sums of money had cheered, and at jolly Roger.

"What a creepy girl," Roger said. "Richard's worst. She finally had to be locked up. Probably still is."

"Oh." Karen shuddered.

Roger put the picture down with a heavy sigh. He was fatter now than when it was taken; his neck was deeply creased with fat, and his big cheeks drooped.

Then abruptly he turned around and embraced Karen with unaccustomed vigor. "What's for dinner?" he asked. "Did I smell what I think I did?"

. . .

Because Richard had been sick so much and had been tutored, he and Roger ended by finishing high school in the same June of 1943, and that July they entered Harvard together, two Southern 4-F's in giddy wartime Cambridge, fat Roger, who also had a punctured eardrum, and thin sick Richard. They both reacted to that scene with an immediate and violent loneliness. Together they were completely isolated from all those uniforms, from the desperately gay urgency of that war, that bright New England climate.

Roger's fat and Richard's illnesses had also isolated them in child-hood; they were unpopular boys who spent most of their afternoons at home, reading or devising private games. But to be isolated and unpopu-lar in a small town where everyone knows you is also to be surrounded— if not with warmth at least with a knowledge of your history. There is always the old lady approaching on the sidewalk who says, "Aren't you Sophie Washington's boys? I declare, the fat one is the living spit of your grandfather." Or the mean little girl in the corner grocery store who chants softly, "Skinny and fat, skinny and fat, I never saw two brothers like that."

They had too an enormous retreat from the world: that huge house full of books everywhere. And the aging pale parents, Josiah and Sophie Washington, who had been and continued to be surprised at finding themselves parents, who retreated from parenthood to long conversa-tions about the histories of other Southern families. "It was a perfect background for eccentrics of the future," Richard later told Ellen.

Both Roger and Richard had chosen history as their field of concen-tration at Harvard. During those summer afternoons, and into the gaudy fall, while R.O.T.C. units drilled in the Yard and pretty Radcliffe girls— in sloppy sweaters and skirts, white athletic socks and loafers—lounged on the steps of Widener Library, Richard and Roger studied furiously in their ground-floor rooms in Adams House, and at night they went to movies. Every night a movie, in suburbs as far-lying as the subway system would carry them, until one night when the only movie they had not seen twice was *I Wanted Wings,* in Arlington. So they stayed home and for a joke read chapters of *Lee's Lieutenants* aloud to each other, which was not one of the texts for History I but which was the only book in the room they had not already read. It had been an off-to-college present from their not very imaginative mother. In stage Southern accents they read to each other about Fredericksburg and Chickamauga, Appomattox and Antietam.

Roger had a photographic memory, of which Richard was wildly proud. His own memory was erratic; he easily memorized poetry but he had a lot of trouble with names and dates, with facts. As they walked across the Yard in the brilliant September air, Roger recited several pages from that book, still in that wildly exaggerated accent: ". . . and before the Northern armies could marshal their forces . . ." while Richard gamboled beside him, laughing like a monkey.

They were taking a course called Philosophic Problems of the Postwar World. With everyone else they stood around outside Emerson Hall, waiting for the hour to sound. Richard was overheard to say to Roger, in that crazy Southern voice, "As I see it, the chief postwar problem is what to do with the black people."

At the end of the summer Roger had four A's and Richard had two A's, a C and a D, the D being in Biology. They had no friends. Richard regarded their friendlessness as a sign of their superiority; no one else was as brilliant, as amusing, as his brother, and thus they were unappreciated. Roger didn't think much about that sort of thing then. He was solely concentrated on getting top grades.

Those Harvard years were, or perhaps became in memory, the happiest of Richard's life. Completely isolated from their classmates and from the war that for most people dominated the scene, he and Roger went about their scholarly pursuits; he had Roger's almost undivided attention, and it was a time when Roger laughed at all his jokes.

Aside from the Southern joke, which was their mainstay, they developed a kind of wild irony of their own, an irony that later would have been called sick, or black. Roger's obesity came into this. "You must have another hot dog, you won't last the afternoon," Richard would say as Roger wolfed down his seventh hot dog at lunch at the corner stand. And when Roger did order and eat another hot dog they both thought that wildly funny. Richard's heart was funny too. At the foot of the steps of Widener Roger would say, "Come on, I'll race you up to the top," and they would stand there, helplessly laughing.

That was how Richard remembered those years: big fat Roger, tilted to one side chuckling hugely, and himself, dark and wiry and bent double laughing, in the Cambridge sun. And he remembered that he could even be careless about his health in those years; he almost never hurt. They went for long walks in all the variously beautiful weathers of Cambridge. Years later, in seasonless California, Richard would sigh for some past Cambridge spring, or summer or fall. Roger remembered much less: for one thing he was in later life so extremely busy.

They were reacted to at Harvard for the most part with indifference; other people were also preoccupied, and also that is how, in general, Harvard is—it lets you alone. However, they did manage to be irritating: to the then current remark, "Don't you know there's a war on?" both Roger and Richard Washington had been heard to respond, "Sir, the War has been over for almost a hundred years." Also, those were very "liberal" years; racism, or what sounded like it, was very unpopular. No one made jokes about black people, no one but Roger and Richard.

Therefore, it is not too surprising that one night Roger and Richard came back from the movies (a revival of a *Broadway Melody* in Dorchester: Roger loved musicals) to find that someone had put a swastika in black chalk on the door to their room. Richard was absolutely enchanted; in a way it was the highest moment of his life. All his sense of the monstrosity of the outside world was justified, as well as his fondness for drama; he was persecuted and isolated with his brother. "Roger," he said very loudly and very Southernly, "do you reckon that's some kind of Indian sign they've gone and put on our door?"

Roger laughed too, or later Richard remembered Roger as laughing, but he recalled mainly his own delight in that climactic illuminated moment. They went into their room and shut the door, and after them someone yelled from down the stairwell, "Southern Fascists!" Richard went on chortling with pleasure, lying across the studio couch, while Roger walked thoughtfully about the room, that big bare room made personal only by their books and some dark curtains now drawn against the heady Cambridge spring night. Then Roger put a Lotte Lenya record on the player.

That was more or less that. The next day the janitor washed the chalk off, and Roger and Richard did not speculate as to who had put it there. Anyone could have.

But a week or so later Roger told Richard that he was tired of history; he was switching his field of concentration to economics. And then he would go to law school. "Fat makes you already eccentric," he said. "And eccentrics have to be rich."

"In that case I'll switch to Greek," Richard countered furiously, "and remain land poor."

And that shorthand conversation made perfect sense to both of them.

They both did what they said they would, except that soon after their graduation (Roger *summa cum laude* and Phi Bete) Richard had a heart attack that kept him in the hospital at home in Virginia, off and on for a couple of years, fending off his anxious mother and writing long funny letters to Roger, who seemed to be enjoying law school.

So it worked out that by the time Richard went back to Harvard for his master's in Greek literature, Roger had got out of law school and gone out to San Francisco, where he began to succeed as a management consultant to increasingly important firms. He was too busy even to come home for the funerals of his parents, who died within a month of each other during his first winter in San Francisco—Josiah and Sophie Washington, who had, they thought, divided their land equally between their two sons. Roger sold his immediately for thirty thousand, and thought he had done very well. He urged Richard to do the same, but Richard lazily or perversely held on to his, until the advent of a freeway forced him to sell, for a hundred thousand.

Richard did not enjoy his second time at Harvard, except in the sense that one does enjoy a season of mourning. He was terribly lonely, he missed Roger vividly, everywhere in Cambridge, and his heart hurt most of the time.

Thus it was not until the early fifties that Richard got his teaching job in the boys' school in San Francisco, and came out to see his brother again. And then came into his money, and met Ellen.

In those days, even after getting his money, Richard lived in a downtown hotel—his eccentricity. He had a large room that the maid was not allowed to enter. ("In that case why live in a hotel?" practical Roger had asked.) The room was stacked everywhere with books, with records and papers. Richard took most of his meals in the hotel dining room; after he came home from a day of teaching he rarely went out. He was not well; much of the time he felt dizzy, and he ached, but again it was hard to gauge the degree to which his loneliness was chosen. If Roger, for example, had had a bad heart he would undoubtedly have had it continually in the midst of a crowd.

Indeed, in the years since his Harvard isolation Roger had become extremely gregarious. Professionally he was hyperactive; his entire intelligence and energy were occupied. And a vivid social life grew out of professional contacts. People whose adviser he was in a legal economic sense also asked him to dinner, and he became known as a very courtly, if somewhat ponderous bachelor, as well as an astute businessman. Roger was greedy for company; he reveled in all his invitations, his cocktails and dinners and his girls.

Girls who fell in love with Richard were always girls with whom Roger had not been successful; that was how Richard met girls. In one of their rare conversations about relationships with women, Roger remarked on Richard's perfect score with women; Richard had never been turned down.

"But with how many ladies have I—uh—attempted to prove my valor?" Richard asked, in the parody Southern manner that he sometimes tried to continue with Roger. "Four, or is it three? I sometimes lose track of these—uh—astronomicals."

Ellen made five.

One March afternoon, a few months after they had met, Richard lay across some tufts of new grass on the bank of a duck pond in Golden Gate Park, watching Ellen, who was out wading among the ducks. Like a child, she held her skirt bunched up in front of her, at the top of her long thin childish legs. Water still had spattered the shabby gray flannel; Ellen visibly didn't care. She splashed out toward some brown ducks who were peacefully squatted on the surface of the pond. They fled, scuttering across the water, submarining under, as Ellen screamed out, "See! They know I'm here!"

Her long fish eyes that day were almost blue with excitement. When she was unhappy or simply remote they were gray. After she finally went mad they were gray all the time.

At the farther edge of the pond were willows, now thickly green with spring; they grew out into the water in heavy clusters. And all about the pond were tall eucalyptus, scenting the air with lemon, shedding their bark in long strips, as the breeze fluttered their sad green scimitar leaves above Richard's heavy head.

Out of the water, out of her element, Ellen became a detached and languorous girl who sat on the grass not far from Richard, clutching her arms about her knees and watching him curiously, listening to that tormented and violent Southern talk.

"Interest! *Interest!*" was what Richard was saying. "My own brother, my *heir,* and he offers me interest on a loan. My God, I told him, 'You're my brother, take all the money, but for God's sake don't offer me interest.'"

Above the trees pale-gray clouds drifted ceremoniously across the sky. Half closing her eyes, Ellen turned them into doves, flocks and flocks of pale soft gray doves.

"God, if I'd only sold the bloody land when Roger sold his," said Richard for the tenth or perhaps the hundredth time that day. "And got only thirty thousand like him instead of this bloody hundred."

Richard's wildness and the intensity of his pain had oddly a calming effect on Ellen. Unlike most people, who were frightened or impatient or even—like Roger—bored, Ellen experienced with Richard a reduction of the panic in which she normally lived. Rather reasonably she asked him what she had often been told but had forgotten: "Why didn't you sell it then?"

"I preferred to be land poor." This was in the old stage Southern voice. "Ah pruhfuhd." Then, "Christ, I didn't want the money. I still don't. If I could only just give it to him. Without dying, that is." And he laughed wildly.

By this time pain had deeply lined Richard's face. There were heavy lines across his forehead, lines down the sides of his nose and beside his wide, intensely compressed mouth. Many people, especially recent friends of Roger's, considered Richard to be crazy, but even they were aware that what sounded like madness could have been an outcry against sheer physical suffering.

"I may not even go to New York," Ellen said. "It takes so much nerve."

Ellen was a mathematician—"of all things," as most people said. Especially her Oakland–Baptist–John Birch Society mother said that, and often. Ellen was talented and had been offered a fellowship at Columbia.

"Stay here," Richard said. "Let me keep you. God, won't anybody take my money?"

The melodramatic note in that last told Ellen that Richard was going to talk about Roger again, and she sighed. She liked it better when he was reading poetry to her, or when he didn't talk at all and played records, Telemann and Boccherini, Haydn and Schubert, in his cluttered and most personal room.

But Richard said, "Roger wants to invest in some resort land at Squaw Valley, with some of his rich new German friends. Do you know the altitude at Squaw Valley? Six thousand feet. I wouldn't last a minute there. How to explain why his brother is never invited for weekends or summer vacations. I am socially unacceptable to my brother—isn't that marvelous?"

Richard's eyes were beautiful; they were large and clear and gray, in that agonized face. Those eyes exposed all his pain and anger and despair, his eyes and his passionate deep Southern voice. He was really too much for anyone, and certainly for himself. And there were times, especially when he ranted endlessly and obsessively about Roger, when even Ellen wanted to be away from him, to be with some dull and ordinary person.

Ellen had met Roger, who always retained a few intellectual friends, at a Berkeley cocktail party, and she had had dinner with him a couple of times before the night they celebrated Richard's money at the silly expensive restaurant, where the picture was taken. Ellen had not liked Roger very much. He was exceptionally bright; she recognized and responded to that, but she was used to very bright people, and all the money-power-society talk that Roger tried to impress her with alarmed her. "You could marry extremely well if you wanted to," Roger told her. "With your skin and those eyes and those long legs. And no one should marry on less than thirty thousand a year. It can't be done." Then he had laughed. "But you'd probably rather marry a starving poet, wouldn't you? Come and meet my crazy brother, though, even if he has just come into money."

And so Richard and Ellen met, and in their fashions fell in love.

Now, feeling dizzy, Richard lay back on the bright-green grass and stared up through the lowering maze of silvered leaves to the gray procession of clouds. Sickness sometimes made him maudlin; now he closed his eyes and imagined that instead of the pond there was a river near his feet, the Virginia James of his childhood, or the Charles at Harvard, with Roger.

Not opening his eyes but grinning wildly to himself, he asked Ellen, "Did I ever tell you about the night they put the swastika on our door?"

Of course Richard lent Roger the money, with no interest, and their dwindling relationship continued.

Sometimes even in the midst of his burgeoning social life Roger was lonely; he hated to be alone. Sometimes late at night he would telephone to Richard, who always stayed up late reading and playing records. These conversations, though never long, were how they kept in touch.

At some point, a couple of years after Richard had met Ellen, Roger began to talk about a girl named Karen Erdman, and Richard knew that she was the one he would marry. But Roger took a long time deciding—Karen was a patient girl. Richard did not meet Karen until the engagement party, but he was so intuitively attuned to his brother that he could see her and feel the quality of her presence: that big generous and intelligent girl who adored his brother. After all, Richard also loved Roger.

"The question seems to me," advised Richard, "as to whether you want to marry at all. If you do, obviously Karen is the girl you should marry."

"I have a very good time as a bachelor," Roger mused. "But it takes too much of my time. You break off with one girl and then you have to go looking for another, and at first you have to spend all that time talking to them."

"God, what a romantic view. In that case perhaps you should marry."

"But she wants children. I find it almost impossible to imagine children."

"Sir, what kind of a man would deplore the possibility of progeny?" Richard asked, in their old voice.

"I can't decide what to do," said Roger. Then, as an afterthought: "How is Ellen?"

"Marvelous. She has managed to turn down four fellowships in one year."

"She's crazy."

"You're quite right there."

"Well. Good night."

"Good night."

A heavy engraved invitation invited Richard to the Erdmans' engagement party for their daughter. "Oddly enough," Richard said to

Ellen. "Since they're being married at Tahoe I'm surprised they didn't do the whole thing up there. Or simply not mention it until later. God knows I don't read the society pages."

Richard was not asked to bring Ellen.

The Erdman house, in Seacliff, was manorial. Broad halls led into broader, longer rooms; immense windows showed an enormous view of the Bay. And the décor was appropriately sumptuous: satins and velvets and silks, walnut and mahogany and gilt. Aubusson and Louis XV. For that family those were the proper surroundings. They were big dark rich people who dressed and ate and entertained extremely well.

In those crowded, scented, overheated rooms Richard's pale lined face was wet. He went out so infrequently; the profusion and brilliance of expensive clothes, in all possible fabrics, of jewels—all made him dizzily stare. The acres of tables of incredibly elaborate food made him further perspire. He stood about in corners, trying to cope with his dizziness and wildly wondering what he could find to say to anyone there. Lunatic phrases of gallantry came to him. Could he say to the beautiful blonde across the room, "I just love the way you do your hair, it goes so well with your shoes"? Or, to the tall distinguished European, who was actually wearing his decorations, "I understand you're in money, sir. I'm in Greek, myself. Up to my ass in Greek." No, he could not say anything. He had nothing to say.

Roger's new circle included quite a few Europeans, refugees like his father-in-law to be, and Mr. Erdman's friends, and transients: visiting representatives of banks, commercial attachés and consuls. The rest were mainly San Francisco's very solid merchant upper class: German Jewish families who had had a great deal of money for a long time. They were very knowledgeable about music and they bought good paintings on frequent trips to Europe. Among those people Roger looked completely at home; even his heavy Southern courtliness took on a European flavor.

Mrs. Erdman was still a remarkably pretty woman, with smooth dark hair in wings and round loving eyes as she regarded both her husband and her daughter. Richard found this especially remarkable; he had never known a girl with a nice mother and he imagined that such girls were a breed apart. Ellen's mother had jumped under a train when Ellen was thirteen and miraculously survived with an amputated foot.

Mrs. Erdman was a very nice woman and she wanted to be nice to Richard, once it was clear to her who he was. The two boys were so unlike that it was hard to believe. "I'm so sorry that you won't be able to come up to the lake for the wedding," she said sympathetically.

"But who'd want a corpse at a wedding?" Richard cackled. "Where on earth would you hide it?" Then, seeing her stricken face and knowing how rude he had been, and how well she had meant, he tried again: "I just love the way you do your hair—" But that was no good either, and he stopped, midsentence.

Mrs. Erdman smiled in a vague and puzzled way. It was sad, and obvious that poor Richard was insane. And how difficult for poor Roger that must be.

Roger was beaming. His creased fat face literally shone with pleasure, which, for the sake of dignity, he struggled to contain. Having decided to marry, he found the idea of marriage very moving, and he was impressed by the rightness of his choice. People fall in love in very divergent ways; in Roger's way he was now in love with Karen, and he would love her more in years to come. He was even excited by the idea of children, big handsome Californian children, who were not eccentric. He stood near the middle of the enormous entrance hall, with Karen near his side, and beamed. He was prepared for nothing but good.

Then suddenly, from the midst of all that rich good will, from that air that was heavy with favorable omens, he heard the wild loud voice of his brother, close at hand. "Say, Roger, remember the night they put the swastika on our door?"

There was a lull in the surrounding conversations as that terrible word reverberated in the room. Then an expectant hum began to fill the vacuum. Feeling himself everywhere stared at, and hearing one nervous giggle, Roger attempted a jolly laugh. "You're crazy," he said. "You've been reading too many books. Karen, darling, isn't it time we went into the other room?"

It is perhaps to the credit of everyone's tact that Richard was then able to leave unobtrusively, as the front door opened to admit new guests.

And a month later, two months before the June wedding at Lake Tahoe, Richard had a severe heart attack and died at Mount Zion Hospital, with Ellen and Roger at his bedside.

They had been watching there at close intervals for almost the entire past week, and they were both miserably exhausted. Even their customary wariness in regard to each other had died, along with Richard.

"Come on, let me buy you some coffee," said Roger, fat and paternal. "You look bad."

"So do you," she said. "Exhausted. Thanks, I'd like some coffee."

He took her to a quiet bar in North Beach, near where she was then living, and they sat in a big recessed booth, in the dim late-afternoon light, and ordered espresso. "Or would you like a cappuccino?" Roger asked. "Something sweet?"

"No. Thanks. Espresso is fine."

The waiter went away.

"Well," said Roger.

"Well," echoed Ellen. "Of course it's not as though we hadn't known all along. What was going to happen."

The flat reasonableness of her tone surprised Roger. Ellen was never reasonable. So he looked at her with a little suspicion, but there was nothing visible on her white face but fatigue and sadness. The strain of her effort at reasonableness, at control, was not visible.

Roger said, "Yes. But I wonder if we really believed it. I mean Richard talked so much about dying that it was hard to believe he would."

The coffee came.

Stirring in sugar, regarding her cup, Ellen said, "People who talk about jumping under trains still sometimes do it. But I know what you mean. We somehow didn't behave as though he would die. Isn't that it?" She lifted her very gray eyes to his blinking pale blue.

He took the sugar, poured and stirred. "Yes, but I wonder what different we would have done."

In her same flat sensible tone Ellen said, "I sometimes wouldn't see him when he wanted to. I would be tired or just not up to it, or sometimes seeing someone else. Even if the other person was a boring nothing." She looked curiously at Roger.

But he had only heard the literal surface of what she had said, to which he responded with a little flicker of excitement. "Exactly!" he said. "He was hurt and complained when I went to boring dinners or saw business friends instead of him, but I had to do that. Sometimes for my own protection."

"Yes," said Ellen, still very calm but again with an oblique, upward look at Roger, which he missed.

"People grow up and they change." Roger sighed. "I could hardly remember all that time at Harvard and he always wanted to talk about it."

"Of course not," she said, staring at him and holding her hands tightly together in her lap, as though they contained her mind.

Roger was aware that he was acting out of character; normally he loathed these intimate, self-revelatory conversations. But he was extremely tired and, as he afterward told himself, he was understandably upset; it is not every day that one's only brother dies. Also, as he was vaguely aware, some quality in Ellen, some quality of her listening, drove him on. Her flat silence made a vacuum that he was compelled to fill.

"And remember that time a couple of years ago when I wanted to borrow the money?" Roger said. "He was so upset that I offered him interest. Of course I'd offer him interest. Otherwise it wouldn't have been fair."

"Of course not," said Ellen, looking deeply into his eyes. "Everyone has to pay interest," she reasonably said.

"It was the least I could do," Roger said. "To be fair to him. And I couldn't spend the rest of my life thinking and talking about how things were almost twenty years ago."

"Of course not," Ellen said again, and soon after that he took her home and they parted—friends.

But in the middle of that night Roger's phone rang, beside his wide bachelor bed, and it was Ellen.

"Pig pig pig pig pig pig pig pig pig!" she screamed. "Horrible fat ugly murdering pig, you killed him with your never time to see him and your wall of fat German business friends always around you and your everything for a purpose and your filthy pig-minded greed and your all-American pig success and your so socially acceptable ambitions. Richard was all Greek to you and you never tried to learn him, how lovely he was and suffering and you found him not socially acceptable to your new society and your new pig friends and I would even rather be thin and miserable and ugly me than fat you with your blubber neck and your compound interest and you couldn't believe his heart and now you can get filthy blubber fatter on his money—"

She seemed to have run down, and into the pause Roger asked, "Ellen, do you need money? I'd be more than happy—"

She screamed, but it was less a scream than a sound of total despair, from an absolute aloneness.

Then she hung up, and a few weeks later Roger heard that she had had a complete breakdown and was hospitalized, perhaps for good.

.   .   .

After the excellent dinner of moussaka, salad and strawberries in cream, Karen and Roger settled in the living room with strong coffee and snifters of brandy. It was an attractive, comfortable, if somewhat disheveled room, very much a family room. Karen's tastes were simpler than those of her parents. Her furnishings were contemporary; the fabrics were sturdy wools or linen; the broad sofa was done in dark-brown leather.

Roger leaned back; he blinked and then sighed, looking up to the ceiling. Karen could tell that he was going to say something about Richard.

"I sometimes wish," said Roger, "that I'd taken the time somewhere along the line to have learned a little Greek. It seemed to give Richard so much pleasure."

"But, darling, when would you ever have had the time?"

"That's just it, I never had the time." Roger's tone when talking about or in any way alluding to his brother was one of a softly sentimental regret; Karen gathered that he regretted both his brother's death and their lack of rapport in those final years.

Roger also sounded sentimentally regretful when he referred to anything cultural—those soft pleasures which he valued but for which he had never had time.

"I wonder what's ever happened to that girl. Ellen," said Karen.

"I'm not sure I'd even want to know," said Roger. "Did I ever tell you that she called me the night he died?"

"Really? No."

"Yes, she was quite hysterical. I think she was angry because she knew I was Richard's heir." By now Roger had come to believe that this was indeed the case. He was convinced that other people's motives were basically identical to his own. "Yes," he said. "She probably thought I should give her some of his money."

In the large safe room, beneath other large rooms where her sons were all sleeping, Karen shuddered, and together she and Roger sighed, for Richard's pain and death and for poor lost Ellen's madness.

"Here," said Karen, "have more coffee. Poor darling, you look as though you need it."

"You're right. I do." And Roger reached out to stroke his big wife's smooth dark cheek.

Flights

"Oh, yes, Valerie will like it *very much,*" said the energetic young man with blue-black hair and a sharply cleft chin, in an accent that was vaguely "English." He and Jacob Eisenman were standing in the large shabby room that overlooked the crashing Pacific, on Kauai, one of Hawaii's outermost and least populated islands.

Jacob later thought that the implications of his tone were a sort of introduction to Valerie, although at the time he had not entirely understood what was being implied. Jacob, the gaunt sardonic literary German who, incongruously, was the owner of this resort. Then he simply wondered why, why *very much?* The young man's clothes were pale, Italian, expensive; it was unlikely that he (or Valerie) would be drawn by the price, which was what drew most of the other guests: older people, rather flabby and initially pale, from places like North Dakota and Idaho and, curiously, Alaska—and a few young couples, wan tired families with children. These people stayed but were not enthusiastic; they would have preferred a more *modern* place. (Jacob was subject to radar intuitions.) And so this young man's eagerness to register for the room and pay in advance, which was unnecessary (with a hundred-dollar bill), made Jacob apprehensive, as though he were being invaded—a sense that he dismissed as paranoia, to which he was also subject. But before he could sort out reactions, the young man had swung out of the driveway in his orange Datsun, presumably to fetch Valerie from the nearby hotel, which he had said they did not like. "So loud, you know?"

In fact, for no reason Jacob found that his heart was beating in jolts, so that quite out of character he went to the bar, unlocked it and poured himself a shot of brandy.

The bar, a narrow slat-roofed structure, was ten winding steps up from the pool, between the rental units and Jacob's own office-apartment-library. Curiously, it was almost never used by the Alaskan–North Dakotans, the young couples. Nor was the neat functional built-in barbecue, which was adjacent. Most of the units had kitchenettes, but still wouldn't they sometimes want to cook outside? The barbecue was the last "improvement" that Jacob had given to his resort. He had spent most of his earlier years in California, going from Los Angeles up to International House at Berkeley; he later concluded that he had been misled by that background; only Californians liked barbecues, and no one from California seemed to come his way.

Except for a disastrous visit from his best friend, fat Otto from I. House days, and Otto's new wife—a visit which Jacob had determined not to think about.

The Datsun rushed back into the parking area, and "Valerie" got out. At first and somewhat distant glance, filtered through the bougain-villaea that hung about the bar, she was a delicately built young blonde. In dazzling white clothes. Huge dark glasses on a small face. An arrogant walk.

Jacob took a too large swallow of the rough brandy, which made him cough. So that both people turned to see him there at the bar, at eleven in the morning. ("You aroused *such* false expectations," Valerie said, later on.)

The young man, registered as Larry Cobb, waved, and Valerie smiled indefinitely. And a few minutes later, all the way from the room that he had rented them, Jacob heard a loud harsh voice that boomed, "But, darling, it's absolutely perfect."

Could that voice have come from such a delicate girl? He supposed it must. Jacob pulled on the large straw hat he always wore—he detested the sun—and hurried away from the bar.

The practical or surface reason for Jacob's presence in this unlikely setting was that he had inherited it from his parents. However, as Otto had pointed out more than once, he could have sold it when they died, when the place was still in good shape. Now he'd have to spend God knows how much to fix it up—assuming, as Otto did assume, that he wanted to sell.

The Eisenmans had fled Berlin in the early thirties, with their young son and a few remnants of their once-thriving rare-book business; following the terrible and familiarly circuitous route of the time (theirs had included Hong Kong), they finally reached Los Angeles, where they set up shop again and were (finally) successful enough to send their son to Berkeley. Later they were persuaded to invest in and retire to a warm island resort. It worked out well. They loved Kauai, where the sun warmed their tired bones and all around them magnificent flowers—flowers hitherto associated with expensive florists—effortlessly bloomed. Birds of paradise. Poinsettias, and of course everywhere the violent colors of bougainvillaea and hibiscus. They tended their property lovingly, and, a loving couple, they died peacefully within a week of each other. Jacob flew out to settle the estate and quixotically decided to stay. Well, why not? His Berkeley landlady could, and did, ship his books; besides, he was tired of graduate school, instructorships. And, as he wrote to Otto, "You know I have a horror of airplane flights. This way I avoid the return trip."

He promoted the woman who had been his parents' housekeeper to the position of manageress. Mrs. Wong, whom he then instructed to hire some local girls to help with the cleaning up. He was aware—his radar told him—that some of the local islanders imagined Mrs. Wong to be his mistress. He didn't mind; actually he liked her very much, but nothing could have been further from the truth.

Mrs. Wong was plain, round-faced, plump, and slovenly in her dress, and Jacob was sexually fastidious to the point of preferring celibacy to compromise. In fact in his entire life—he was almost fifty—he had had only three love affairs, and none of long duration; he was drawn to women who were violent, brilliant and intense, who were more than a little crazy. Crazy and extremely thin. "Basically I have a strong distaste for flesh," he had once confided to Otto.

"Which would explain your affection for myself." Otto had chuckled. "Pure masochism, of course."

Their kind of joke, in the good old lost days.

"It was like labor pains," Valerie loudly and accusingly said; she was speaking of the waves that later that afternoon had knocked her to the sandy bottom of the ocean, and from which the young man, Larry, had grabbed her out. "When Quentin was born, they kept coming back and back—"

She spoke furiously: why? From behind the bar where Jacob was making their drinks (he had never done this before, but the bar girl was sick and Mrs. Wong was somewhere else) he pondered her rage. At being a woman, forced painfully to bear children—blaming Larry for Quentin? No, they were not married; Larry certainly was not the father of Quentin, and she was not that silly. At Larry for having rescued her? No.

She was simply enraged at the sea for having knocked her down. It was an elemental rage, like Ahab's, which Jacob could admire; that was how he felt about the sun.

In the vine-filtered sunlight he could see that Valerie was older than he had thought, was somewhere in her thirties. All across her face, over the small nose, the slight rise of cheekbones, were tiny white tracings. Tiny scars. An exquisitely repaired face: Jacob did not want to imagine the accident involved, but then he did—driving too fast (in a convertible, it would have to have been a convertible) north of Boston, she had gone through a windshield. Her eyes were large and very dark, at first glance black, then perceived as an extraordinary midnight blue. Her voice was rasping, a whiskey voice, the accent crisply Bostonian. She was wearing something made of stiff white lace, through which a very small brown bikini was visible.

She gulped at her drink: straight gin, with a twist of lime. "God," she said, "I'm all scratched."

Larry asked her, "Does it hurt?"

"No, it just looks funny." She turned to Jacob. "You're so pale. Don't you go swimming at all?"

"No, I hate to swim."

She stared at him for an instant, and then seemed to understand a great deal at once; Jacob could literally feel her comprehension, which reached him like an affectionate hand.

She burst out laughing, a raucous, exhilarated laugh. "But that's absolutely marvelous!" she cried out. "I absolutely love it! You also hate the sun, right?"

Jacob nodded. But at the same time that he felt touched he also felt some part of his privacy invaded, which made him uneasy. He had been recognized.

"You must have a marvelous time here," said Larry, attempting a joke.

"I read a lot."

Larry did not like him.

"I need another drink," said Valerie, who probably had noted this too.

An impulse made Jacob say what he had not said before, to guests. "Look, I'm not always around. But if you want to drink that's where the key is," and he pointed to a spot at the top of a beam.

This was said to Larry (to make Larry like him better?), but it was Valerie who smiled and said, "That's really nice of you."

"We'll keep track" was what Larry said, and finally forgot to do.

Jacob left as soon as he could. He had decided to start rereading *Moby-Dick*.

Valerie liked his shabby place because she was rich, accustomed to grandeur. She was the opposite of upward ascendant: downward descendant? Was she that? Quite possible. Larry was somewhat younger than she, and rich in a different way: he had earned a lot of money, recently, in something trendy. A record company? TV? He resented Valerie's carelessness, her easy lack of ambitions.

Ahab said, "They think me mad, Starbuck does; but I'm demonic, I am madness maddened! that wild madness that's only calm to comprehend itself—"

Valerie had (probably) been married several times. Perhaps a husband had been with her when she smashed up the car? A now dead husband?

At about eleven the next morning, when Jacob approached the bar, Valerie was perched on a high stool, her long thin brown legs drawn up childishly. She had made herself a tall drink. "Won't you join me?"

"I don't drink much—no, thanks." Then, to her raised eyebrows, he added, "Yesterday was out of character."

"You aroused *such* false expectations." She let that go, and then asked, as though it were what they had been talking about for some time, "How do you feel about flying?"

"I hate it. That's one reason I'm here."

In an instant she had taken that in, and her riotous laugh broke out. "That's terrific!" Then she said, "But what do you do about it?"

"Obviously: I don't fly."

"If I could only understand why I'm so afraid. Larry has driven off to Koloa," she added, irrelevantly. "You'd think I'd be afraid to drive." And she told him then about her accident, the crashed convertible in which her second husband had been killed, the crash that in some sense he had already seen.

Jacob understood that they were communicating on levels that he could not fathom, that even made him somewhat uncomfortable. He could so vividly see and feel whatever she told him; apparently, in fact, even before she spoke.

"I have some idiot faith that if I could understand it I wouldn't be afraid anymore. Of flying," Valerie said. "I think that's what's called shrink-conditioning. I've even tried to 'associate' to the fear, and I do remember something weird: myself, but in a white wicker carriage, a *baby* carriage—how could I remember *that*? Anyway my nurse is push-ing it, a young Irish girl. And we're at the top of a hill in Magnolia, near the shore, and some older kids tell her to let it go—"

But she might as well have stopped talking, because Jacob could see it: a stone-fenced New England landscape, wild roses. A pretty dark maid with a tweed coat pulled over a white uniform. "But she didn't let go," he gently said.

"Of course not. But what in hell does that have to do with being afraid to fly?"

Larry arranged to go deep-sea fishing, near Lihue. Valerie sat by the pool, in a white bikini, with a stack of books. Seeing her there from above, as he conferred with Mrs. Wong about the necessity for a second visit from the plumber, Jacob was aware that he could go down to her and pull up a chair; they could talk all day. But that prospect was too much for him; it made his heart race. Instead he went back to the dim seclusion of his library; he went from *Moby-Dick* to Nerval, *"Je suis le Ténébreux—le Veuf—"* He went out into the sunlight.

He and Valerie had a brief conversation about Jane Austen, whom she was rereading. "I read her to regain some balance," said Valerie.

"You might try reading her on planes."

She gave him a long speculative look. "What a good idea."

Pretending busyness, Jacob went back to his office.

In fact all that day was punctuated with such brief conversations. Her nondemanding cool friendliness, her independence made this possible; they matched, or supplemented, his vast diffidence.

She asked, "How is it around Hanalei, the northern coast?"

"I don't know. I've never been there."

"You're absolutely marvelous."

"Do you think it's a fear that someone will throw you out of the sky—like God?"

"Alas, poor Icarus."

"Yes, that's sort of it. As though you shouldn't be up there, so high."

Sometime in the midafternoon he found her at the bar with a long drink.

"You know what I really like about this place?" she asked. "The whales. They're terrific, spouting out there."

"Yes." Her tan intensified the whiteness of her scars, making a sort of jigsaw of her face. Her eyes were dark and wild, and after a little while Jacob realized that she was drunk, or nearly so: like most people, he had trouble recognizing conditions foreign to himself. It had taken him a long time to see that Otto's wife, Joanne, was very stupid; at first he had thought her crazy, which was something he knew more about. In fact she was both.

He said, "A long time ago a woman came here who hated the whales, she was terrified of them."

"Really?" Valerie leaned forward, toward his face, so that he caught a whiff of exotic perfume, of musk.

"It finally turned out that she had them confused with sharks, and thought they would swim in and bite her."

"Good Christ."

"She was exceptionally stupid. My best friend's wife."

The first surprise had been Otto's extreme prosperity, as evidenced by the casual mention of buying several condominiums, on the peninsula south of San Francisco. "Well, I have to have them for tax shelters." In fact he had come to Hawaii to talk to a group of businessmen in Honolulu who were interested in some California coastal property. Not to see Jacob. The second surprise (probably not wholly unconnected with the first) was Joanne. Joanne from San Antonio, with her raven hair and milk-white skin, her rosebud mouth. (Otto's taste in women had never been original.) Big girlish breasts. A tiny well-focused mind. "Oh, I just think you're so *smart* not to waste your money on paint and fixing things up. I mean, who'd care?" And, "Oh, I just love all these darling yellow-brown people; they don't look a bit like darkies." Over her head Jacob had at first sought Otto's eyes, but Otto wasn't listening; in fact he had never (Jacob remembered too late) enjoyed talking or listening to women; he probably didn't hear a word she said. But Jacob heard it all, each abrasive idiocy, delivered in that nasal soprano. "Those are really whales out there? But how does anybody dare to go in swimming?"

One curious—to Jacob, incomprehensible—facet of Joanne's character was her imperviousness to coldness on another's part, to slights. Not that Jacob really slighted her, but surely his politeness came across coldly? Actually he couldn't stand her, and he found it hard to pretend otherwise. But she continued her bubbling smiles and winks (Christ, *winks*!) at him; on any pretext at all she stood so close that her glossy head touched his shoulder; she would introduce a sentence by touching his arm. Incredible! Jacob considered, and instantly dismissed, the insane possibility that she was sexually drawn to him; modesty aside, he found that unlikely. He had none of the qualities that would have drawn her to Otto, for example; he was not rich or ebullient or pleasure-loving (God knows, not that). Also he was bony, his dry skin was deeply lined, whereas Otto was sleek and fat. No, he decided, she was simply behaving as she always did with men.

Such was his estimate of Joanne, and of their situation up to the final terrible night of which he would not think: the knock at his door. (He had somehow known it was Joanne, and had frighteningly thought that Otto must be sick.) But, "You can't imagine how sound your old friend sleeps," she had said, pushing past him in her frilly thigh-length gown, beneath which unleashed fat breasts bounced. "I thought we could have a tiny drinkie together," she said. "I just feel as though I hardly know you at all." Her young face shone with joyous self-adulation.

Jacob couldn't believe it, not then or later (now) remembering. How had he got rid of her? He had muttered something about a strep throat, clutching at his neck. An insane impulse that had worked: Joanne was terrified of germs.

Most men of course would not have sent her away, and so friendship dictated that Jacob inform Otto. "You are married to a sub-moronic nymphomaniac. Even if you don't listen to her conversation. She is a bad person. She will do you harm." Of course the next day he said nothing of the sort, and for all Jacob knew Otto and Joanne were what is known as "happily married." Otto rarely mentioned her in his letters.

"One encouraging thing I recently read," said Valerie, beginning to slur a little, "is that if you fall from more than six thousand feet—or was it sixty thousand?—you die of a heart attack before you hit the ground. If you call that encouraging."

"I suppose you could."

"Well, I do. Christ, I'm sleepy. I'm going in for a nap."

She walked off unsteadily, between the clamorously brilliant blooms. Jacob heard the slam of her screen door.

That night, as he restlessly rebegan *The Wanderer* (he was slipping from book to book, a familiar bad sign), Jacob could hear them at the barbecue (its first use); in fact he could smell their steak. Valerie and Larry. Her rowdy laugh, his neat clipped voice.

Then it turned into a quarrel; Jacob caught the tone but not the words. Very quietly he got up and opened his door. Without a sound he went out, walking away from them through the dark until he could hear nothing at all. Down the small road, past all the oversized blooming plants, he walked, toward the small arc of beach, the surfers' beach, now coldly gray-white in the dark. There he stood on the mound of black lava rock, regarding the shining waves, their wicked curl before breaking, until one huge wave—as large, he imagined, as a giant whale—crashed near his rock and drove him back, and he started home. As he reached his door everything was still, no voices from the bar or anywhere. Only surf.

He didn't see Valerie (or Larry) all the next day until late afternoon when together they approached the bar, where Jacob had been talking to his liquor supplier, Mr. Mederious; he had needed to order more gin. Valerie and Larry were merry, friendly with each other, holding hands. Sand dried in their uncombed hair, his so dark, hers pale.

"We found the most fabulous beach—"

"—absolutely private, no one there at all."

"—really beautiful."

They had made love on the beach.

"I could stay here forever," said Valerie, dreamily.

"Baby, some of us have to work," Larry said, with some affection. But of course this was an issue between them. Also, Larry would have liked to marry her, and she didn't want to get married, having done it so often before.

Jacob knew everything.

Re-embarked on his own Jane Austen, he found that at last he was able to concentrate. He spent the next few days alone with *Emma, Persuasion, Northanger Abbey*—pure delight, a shining impeccable world, like Mozart, Flemish painting.

When next he saw Valerie, in still another bikini—beside the pool, Larry had gone fishing again—she was even browner. She looked clear-eyed, younger. "When we were in Honolulu," she told Jacob, "we saw the most amazing man on the sidewalk. Dressed in red, white and blue striped clothes, with an Uncle Sam hat. And sandwich boards with really crazy things written on them. Peace signs labeled 'Chicken Tracks of a Coward.' Something about abortion is murder. Really extraordinary— the superpatriot. I could not figure out what he was about."

Of course Jacob could see the man. Hunched over, lost.

"You know," she said, "I've got to get into some kind of work." Her harsh laugh. "I might even try to finish school. Last time around I got married instead."

"I think you should."

She laughed again. "Larry will die."

"He will?"

"He's not strong on intellectual women."

One night, as Jacob lay half asleep on his narrow hard bed (his monk's bed, as he thought of it), he heard what he imagined to be a knock on his door. At first he thought, Good Christ, Joanne? But of course Joanne was nowhere near, and his heart leaped up as he reached for the ancient canvas trench coat that served him as a robe, and he went to open the door.

No one there. But had there been?

He stood still in the starry flowering night, listening for any sound.

Someone was at the bar, and he walked in that direction.

Valerie. And at the instant that he saw her he also saw and heard the orange Datsun start up and swing out of the driveway, into the sleeping night.

Valerie, in a tailored red silk robe, was applying ice cubes to one eye, ice cubes neatly wrapped in a paper napkin; her performance was expert, practiced. She said, "You catch me at a disadvantage. I seem to have walked into the proverbial door."

"Can I—" He was not sure what he had meant to offer.

"No, I'll be all right. Care for a drink?"

She already had one, something dark on ice.

Jacob poured himself a shot of brandy.

She said, "You know, it's too bad that children are brought up so much with globes for toys. They see the world as a small ball full of oceans, with those insecure patches of land."

She spoke with great intensity, her visible dark eye huge. She was not drunk but Jacob sensed that earlier she had been. He wanted to ask her if she had, in fact, knocked on his door.

She said, "Tonight I was thinking about those old globes, and how these islands look on them, and I thought we might fall off into space. Do you think I'm going crazy?"

"No, I don't."

"God, I may never get back on a plane."

Jacob wanted to say, Don't. Don't go anywhere, stay with me. Read all my books, and then I'll send for more. Talk to me when you want to. Stay.

Valerie stood up, stretching. She still kept the side of her face that must by now be swollen and discolored turned away. She said, "Well, I think I can sleep now. See you in the morning."

In the morning he could say to her what he had meant to say.

Jacob went off to bed and while he was still reading (impossible then to sleep) he heard the Datsun return. Stop. Slam.

In the morning Valerie and Larry came to Jacob's office together, both dressed for travel—she in dark-blue linen, huge glasses covering whatever had happened to her eye, Larry in pale gray.

They had simply and suddenly decided to leave. They felt that they had to get back. Larry's new TV show. Quentin.

Jacob and Valerie shook hands—their only touch. Her hand was small and hard and strong, and she wore a lot of rings. "I'm absolutely terrified," she said, with a beautiful quick smile. "All those flights."

Jacob said, "You'll be all right," and he smiled too. Goodbye.

But he was not at all sure of what he said. All that day he was terrified of her flights.

Beautiful Girl

Ardis Bascombe, the tobacco heiress, who twenty years ago was a North Carolina beauty queen, is now sitting in the kitchen of her San Francisco house, getting drunk. Four-thirty, an October afternoon, and Ardis, with a glass full of vodka and melted ice, a long cigarette going and another smoldering in an almost full ashtray, is actually doing several things at once: drinking and smoking, of course, killing herself, her older daughter, Linda, has said (Ardis is no longer speaking to Linda, who owns and runs a health-food store), and watching the news on her small color Sony TV. She is waiting for her younger daughter, Carrie, who goes to Stanford but lives at home and usually shows up about now. And she is waiting also for a guest, a man she knew way back when, who called this morning, whose name she is having trouble with. Black? White? Green? It is a color name; she is sure of that.

Twenty years ago Ardis was a small and slender black-haired girl, with amazing wide, thickly lashed dark-azure eyes and smooth, pale, almost translucent skin—a classic Southern beauty, except for the sexily curled, contemptuous mouth. And brilliant, too: straight A's at Chapel Hill. An infinitely promising, rarely lovely girl: everyone thought so. A large portrait of her then hangs framed on the kitchen wall: bare-shouldered, in something gauzy, light—she is dressed for a formal dance, the Winter Germans or the May Frolics. The portrait is flyspecked and streaked with grime from the kitchen fumes. Ardis despises cleaning up, and hates having maids around; periodically she calls a janitorial service, and sometimes she has various rooms repainted, covering the grime. Nevertheless, the picture shows the face of a beautiful young girl. Also hanging there, gilt-framed and similarly grimed, are several family portraits; elegant and upright ancestors, attesting to family substance—

although in Ardis's messy kitchen they have a slightly comic look of inappropriateness.

Ardis's daughter Carrie, who in a couple of years will inherit several of those tobacco millions, is now driving up from the peninsula, toward home, in her jaunty brown felt hat and patched faded jeans, in her dirty battered Ford pickup truck. She is trying to concentrate on Thomas Jefferson (History I) or the view: blond subdivided hills and groves of rattling dusty eucalyptus trees that smell like cat pee. She is listening to the conversations on her CB radio, but a vision of her mother, at the table, with her emptying glass and heavy blue aura of smoke, fills Carrie's mind; she is pervaded by the prospect of her mother and filled with guilt, apprehension, sympathy. Her mother, who used to be so much fun, now looks as swollen and dead-eyed, as thick-skinned, as a frog.

Hoping for change, Carrie has continued to live at home, seldom admitting why. Her older sister, Linda, of the health-food store, is more severe, or simply fatalistic. "If she wants to drink herself to death she will," says Linda. "Your being there won't help, or change a thing." Of course she's right, but Carrie sticks around.

Neither Linda nor Carrie is as lovely as their mother was. They are pretty girls—especially Linda, who is snub-nosed and curly-haired. Carrie has straight dark hair and a nose like that of her father: Clayton Bascombe, former Carolina Deke, former tennis star, former husband of Ardis. His was a nice straight nose—Clayton was an exceptionally handsome boy—but it is too long now for Carrie's small tender face.

Clayton, too, had a look of innocence; perhaps it was his innocent look that originally attracted Ardis's strong instinct for destruction. In any case, after four years of marriage, two daughters, Ardis decided that Clayton was "impossible," and threw him out—out of the house that her parents had given them, in Winston-Salem. Now Clayton is in real estate in Wilmington, N.C., having ended up where he began, before college and the adventure of marriage to Ardis.

Ardis has never remarried. For many years, in Winston-Salem, as a young divorcée, she was giddily popular, off to as many parties and weekends out of town as when she was a Carolina coed. Then, after the end of an especially violent love affair, she announced that she was tired of all that and bored with all her friends. With the two girls, Ardis moved to San Francisco, bought the big house on Vallejo Street, had it fashionably decorated and began another round of parties with new people—a hectic pace that gradually slowed to fewer parties, invitations, friends. People became "boring" or "impossible," as the neglected house decayed. Ardis spent more and more time alone. More time drunk.

The girls, who from childhood had been used to their mother's lovers (suitors, beaux) and who by now had some of their own, were at first quite puzzled by their absence: Ardis, without men around? Then Linda said to Carrie, "Well, *Lord,* who'd want her now? Look at that face. Besides, I think she'd rather drink."

In some ways Ardis has been a wonderful mother, though: Carrie sometimes says that to herself. Always there were terrific birthday parties, presents, clothes. And there was the time in Winston-Salem when the real-estate woman came to the door with a petition about Negroes—keeping them out, land values, something like that. Of course Ardis refused to sign, and then she went on: "And in answer to your next question, I sincerely hope that both my daughters marry them. I understand those guys are really great. *Not,* unfortunately, from personal experience." *Well.* What other mother, especially in Winston-Salem, would ever talk like that?

Ardis dislikes paying bills—especially small ones; for instance, from the garbage collectors, although she loves their name. Sunset Scavenger Company. Thus the parking area is lined with full garbage cans, spilling over among all the expensively imported and dying rhododendrons and magnolia trees, the already dead azaleas in their rusted cans. Seeing none of this, Carrie parks her truck. She gets out and slams the door.

Five o'clock. Ardis will have had enough drinks to make her want to talk a lot, although she will be just beginning to not make sense.

Carrie opens the front door and goes in, and she hears her mother's familiar raucous laugh coming from the kitchen. Good, she is not alone. Carrie walks in that direction, as Ardis's deep, hoarse voice explains to someone, "That must be my daughter Carrie. You won't believe—"

Carrie goes into the kitchen and is introduced to a tall, thin, almost bald, large-nosed man. He is about her mother's age but in much better shape: rich, successful. (Having inherited some of her mother's social antennae, Carrie has taken all this in without really thinking.) In Ardis's dignified slur, his name sounds like Wopple Grin.

. . .

"Actually," Ardis tells Carrie later on, "Walpole Greene is very important in Washington, on the Hill." This has been said in the heavily nasal accent with which Ardis imitates extreme snobs; like many good mimics, she is aping an unacknowledged part of herself. Ardis is more truly snobbish than anyone, caring deeply about money, family and position. "Although he certainly wasn't much at Carolina," she goes on, in the same tone.

Tonight, Ardis looks a little better than usual, her daughter observes. She did a very good job with her makeup; somehow her eyes look O.K.—not as popped out as they sometimes do. And a gauzy scarf around her throat has made it look less swollen.

Walpole Greene, who is indeed important in Washington, although, as the head of a news bureau, not exactly in Ardis's sense "on the Hill," thinks how odd it is that Ardis should have such a funny-looking kid.

Carrie, reading some of that in his face, thinks, What a creep. She excuses herself to go upstairs. She smiles privately as she leaves, repeating, silently, "Wopple Grin."

In Chapel Hill, all those years ago, in the days when Walpole Greene was certainly not much—he was too young, too skinny and tall; with his big nose he looked like a bird—he was always acutely and enragedly aware of Ardis. So small and bright, so admired, so universally lusted after, so often photographed in the *Daily Tarheel* and *Carolina Magazine,* with her half-inviting, half-disdainful smile; she was everywhere. One summer, during a session of summer school, Walpole felt that he saw Ardis every time he left his dorm: Ardis saying "Hey, Walpole" (Wopple? was she teasing him?) in the same voice in which she said "Hey" to everyone.

He saw her dancing in front of the Y, between classes, in the morning—smiling, mocking the dance. He glimpsed her through the windows of Harry's, drinking beer, in the late afternoon. She was dressed always in immaculate pale clothes: flowered cottons, cashmere cardigans. And at night he would see her anywhere at all: coming out of the show, at record concerts in Kenan Stadium ("Music Under the Stars"), emerging from the Arboretum, with some guy. Usually she was laughing, which made even then a surprisingly loud noise from such a small thin girl. Her laugh and her walk were out of scale; she *strode,* like someone very tall and important.

Keeping track of her, Walpole, who had an orderly mind, began to observe a curious pattern in the escorts of Ardis: midmornings at the Y, evenings at the show, or at Harry's, she was apt to be with Gifford Gwathmey, a well-known S.A.E., a handsome blond Southern boy. But if he saw her in some more dubious place, like the Arboretum, late at night, she would be with Henry Mallory, a Delta Psi from Philadelphia.

Ardis always looked as if she were at a party, having a very good time but at the same time observing carefully and feeling just slightly superior to it all. And since his sense of himself and of his presence at Carolina was precisely opposite to that, Walpole sometimes dreamed of doing violence to Ardis. He hated her almost as much as he hated the dean of men, who in a conference had suggested that Walpole should "get out more," should "try to mix in."

It was a melancholy time for Walpole, all around.

One August night, in a stronger than usual mood of self-pity, Walpole determined to do what he had all summer considered doing: he would stay up all night and then go out to Gimghoul Castle (the Gimghouls were an undergraduate secret society) and watch the dawn from the lookout bench there. He did just that, drinking coffee and reading from *The Federalist Papers,* and then riding on his bike, past the Arboretum and Battle Park, to the Castle. The lookout bench was some distance from the main building, and as he approached it Walpole noted that a group of people, probably Gimghouls and their dates, were out there drinking *still,* on one of the terraces.

He settled on the hard stone circular bench, in the dewy pre-dawn air, and focused his attention on the eastern horizon. And then suddenly, soundlessly—and drunkenly: she was plastered—Ardis appeared. Weaving toward him, she sat down on the bench beside him, though not too near.

"You came out here to look at the sunrise?" she slurred, conversationally. "God, Wopple, that's wonderful." Wunnerful.

Tears of hatred sprang to Walpole's eyes—fortunately invisible. He choked; in a minute he would hit her, very hard.

Unaware that she was in danger, Ardis got stiffly to her feet; she bent awkwardly toward him and placed a cool bourbon-tasting kiss on Walpole's mouth. "I love you, Wopple," Ardis said. "I truly and purely do." The sun came up.

He didn't hate her anymore—of course he would not hit her. How could he hit a girl who had kissed him and spoken of love? And although after that night nothing between them changed overtly, he now watched her as a lover would. With love.

"Lord, you're lucky I didn't rape you there and then," says Ardis now, having heard this romantic story. She is exaggerating the slur of her speech, imitating someone even drunker than she is.

Walpole, who believes that in a way he has loved her all his life, laughs sadly, and he wonders if at any point in her life Ardis could have been—he backs off from "saved" and settles on "retrieved." Such a waste: such beauty gone, and brains and wit. Walpole himself has just married again, for the fourth time: a young woman who, he has already begun to recognize, is not very nice, or bright. He has little luck with love. It is not necessarily true that Ardis would have been better off with him.

She is clearly in no shape to go out to dinner, and Walpole wonders if he shouldn't cook something for the two of them to eat. Scrambled eggs? He looks around the impossibly disordered kitchen, at stacks of dishes, piled-up newspapers, a smelly cat box in one corner, although he has seen no cat.

He reaches and pours some more vodka into his own glass, then glances over at Ardis, whose eyes have begun to close.

By way of testing her, he asks, "Something I always wondered. That summer, I used to see you around with Gifford Gwathmey, and then later you'd be with Henry Mallory. Weren't you pinned to Gifford?"

Ardis abruptly comes awake, and emits her laugh. "Of course I was pinned to Giff," she chortles. "But he and all those S.A.E.s were almost as boring as Dekes, although he did come from one of the oldest and *richest* families in Charleston." (This last in her nasal snob-imitating voice.) "So I used to late-date on him all the time, mainly with Henry, who didn't have a dime. But the Delta Psis were *fun*—they had *style*—a lot of boys from New York and Philadelphia." She laughs again.

"Between dates, I'd rush back to the House and brush my teeth—talk about your basic fastidious coed. Henry teased me about always tasting of Pepsodent." For a moment Ardis looks extremely happy, and almost young; then she falls slowly forward until her head rests on the table in front of her, and she begins to snore.

Carrie, who has recently discovered jazz, is upstairs listening to old Louis Armstrong records, smoking a joint. "Pale moon shining on the fields below . . ."

She is thinking, as she often does, of how much she would like to get out of this house for a while. She would like to drop out of school for a term or two, maybe next spring, and just get into her truck with a few clothes and some money, and maybe a dog, and drive around the country. There is a huge circular route that she has often imagined: up to Seattle, maybe Canada, Vancouver, down into Wyoming, across the northern plains to Chicago—she knows someone there—New England, New York and down the coast to her father, in Wilmington, N.C.; Charleston, New Orleans, Texas, Mexico, the Southwest, L.A.; then home, by way of Big Sur. Months of driving, with the dog and the CB radio for company.

In the meantime, halfway through her second joint, she sighs deeply and realizes that she is extremely hungry, ravenous. She carefully stubs out the joint and goes downstairs.

Walpole Greene, whose presence she had forgotten, is standing in the pantry, looking lost. Ardis has passed out. Having also forgotten that she thought he was a creep, Carrie experiences a rush of sympathy for the poor guy. "Don't worry," she tells him. "She'll be O.K."

"She sure as hell doesn't look O.K.," says Walpole Greene. "She's not O.K. No one who drinks that much—"

"Oh, well, in the long run you're right," says Carrie, as airily as though she had never worried about her mother's health. "But I mean for now she's O.K."

"Well. I'd meant to take her out to dinner."

"Why bother? She doesn't eat. But aren't you hungry? I'm starved."

"Well, sort of." Walpole looks dubiously around the kitchen. He watches Carrie as she goes over to the mammoth refrigerator and extracts a small covered saucepan from its incredibly crowded, murky interior.

"She likes to make soup," says Carrie. "Lately she's been on some Southern kick. Nostalgia, I guess. This is white beans and pork. Just made yesterday, so it ought to be all right."

The soup, which Carrie has heated and ladled into bowls, is good but too spicy for Walpole's ulcer; the next day he will feel really terrible. Now he and Carrie whisper to each other, like conspirators, above the sound of Ardis's heavy breathing.

"Does she do this often?" asks Walpole.

"Pretty often. Well—like, every day."

"That's not good."

"No."

Having drunk quite a bit more than he usually does, Walpole feels that his perceptions are enlarged. Looking at Carrie, he has a sudden and certain vision of her future: in ten or so years, in her late twenties, early thirties, she will be more beautiful than even Ardis ever was. She will be an exceptional beauty, a beautiful woman, whereas Ardis was just a beautiful girl. Should he tell Carrie that? He decides not to; she wouldn't believe him, although he is absolutely sure of his perception. Besides, even a little drunk he is too shy.

Instead, in an inspired burst, he says, "Listen, she's got to go somewhere. You know, dry out. There's a place in Connecticut. Senators' wives—"

Carrie's bright young eyes shine, beautifully. "That would be neat," she says.

"You'd be O.K. by yourself for a while?"

"I really would. I'm thinking about getting a dog—our cat just disappeared. And there's this trip. But how would you get her there?"

"Leave that to me," says Walpole, with somewhat dizzy confidence.

Carrie clears the table—without, Walpole notices, washing any dishes.

Carrie goes back upstairs, her heart high and light.

She considers calling her sister, Linda, saying that Walpole Greene is taking their mother to Connecticut. But Linda would say something negative, unpleasant.

Instead, she puts on another record, and hears the rich pure liquid sound of Louis's horn, and then his voice. "Beale Street Blues,"

"Muskrat Ramble," "A Son of the South." She listens, blows more joints.

Downstairs, seated at the table, Walpole is talking softly and persuasively, he hopes, to Ardis's ear (her small pink ears are still pretty, he has noticed), although she is "asleep."

"This lovely place in Connecticut," he is saying. "A wonderful place. You'll like it. You'll rest, and eat good food, and you'll feel better than you've felt for years. You'll see. I want you to be my beautiful girl again—"

Suddenly aroused, Ardis raises her head and stares at Walpole. "I am a beautiful girl," she rasps out, furiously.

Home Is Where

In San Francisco there is apt to be no spring at all. During one such season of grayness, cold and wind, when everything else in my life was also terrible, I felt that I would die of longing for home—"home" being in my case a small Southern river town, not far inland from the Atlantic coast.

My problems were more serious than I could cope with or even think about: a husband, a lover and a landlady, all of whom I was terrified of, and a son for whose future, in those conditions, I greatly feared. And so, instead, I thought about hot river smells, jasmine and hyacinth and gardenias, caves of honeysuckle and live oaks festooned with Spanish moss.

And finally, in June (there was still no summer, no remission of cold and fog), against some better judgment, with my son I rushed back there—rushed toward what, in another frame of mind, I might have considered an origin of my troubles: alcoholic parents, a disapproving, narrow small town that still (probably) contained several former lovers (I had been a wild young girl) and some inimical former friends.

Exhilarated by a remembrance of steamy river afternoons, canoe trips down to small white beaches and summer night dances, I went and bought some light new clothes—cotton shorts, flouncy pastel dresses— such as out in San Francisco I hadn't needed for years. My married life had made me feel ugly—drained and discolored, old; and with the unerringly poor judgment of a depressed person I had found a lover who disliked me, who in fact was a little crazy, mean. Perhaps as much as anything else I needed to return to a place where I had been young and, if never beautiful, at least sought after.

And once my plans were made, my problems seemed somewhat to abate: the landlady herself went away on vacation, so that for a time there were no more of those harrowing, repeated phone calls about the noise of my son's running footsteps (Simon, at four, not a heavy or clumsy child); my lover was sympathetic (possibly relieved, since we had chosen each other out of angry needs?); my husband took Simon and me out for a pleasant, noncritical parting dinner, at a good Italian restaurant. He only said, "You won't be eating food like this for a while, will you, Claire," and I said that I supposed not.

Perhaps I did not have to go home after all? But by then I was committed. Letters written, tickets bought. And those clothes.

Only on the plane did some of the drawbacks inherent in my plan occur to me: my selfish parents' total indifference to children; the extreme heat, to which neither Simon nor I (now) was used; and the embarrassment (fear) of seeing certain people there—Mary Sue, my girlhood rival-friend-enemy; Dudley Farmer, with whom I had once had a violent and badly ending love; other friends.

And so I flew across the country in a wild mixture of fear and excitement, a state that was all too familiar to me: it was how I felt on getting married (rightly, as things turned out); how I felt each time I went to meet my lover. Often, when the phone rang I was afraid.

My apprehensive state increased in Washington—at the airport, where we were to change planes to go south, to go home. And by the time we were on that second plane, heading up through small puffy clouds in a pastel-blue sky, I was babbling to Simon, crazily: "Remind me to show you—take you—tell you about—"

He was fine, so far. Filled, perhaps, with nice kindergarten stories about little boys going to visit their grandparents, my volatile, difficult, demanding and adored young son sat buckled into his seat in seeming contentment. He listened to the ravings of his mother, himself at peace, sipping his diet cola (ludicrous, such a tall thin child, but having failed him in large ways I have tended to yield on small issues). I gulped vodka.

The plane landed and skidded along a red clay field—my part of the South is made almost entirely of red clay; the rest is dust. And we headed toward a one-story white clapboard building, the terminal. In front there was a high wire fence, next to which stood a portly, white-haired, red-faced man, very erect, in a white linen suit: my father. I would of course have known him anywhere, picked him out in any crowd, but what I first thought was: Oh! I'd forgotten how short he is. By reasonable standards he is not short, almost six feet, but I had been involved with unreasonably tall men: my husband, six two, and my lover, an impossible six four. My son too will be very tall.

We got out, Simon and I holding hands down the steps; for an instant I felt my father's eyes pass across and not recognize us. But then he did, and we were all upon each other, embracing and saying familiar blank words and smelling familiar smells: his cigarette-smoked clothes and breath, shaving lotion and mint (mints to kill the smell of bourbon). I don't know what about me seemed or smelled familiar: I switch perfumes a lot and drink scentless vodka—or Simon, whom he had only seen two or three times before, at widely spaced intervals.

Another thing I had forgotten about my father: he is impossible to understand until you have been with him for several days. He has a heavy Southern accent and he speaks extremely fast, generally with a cigarette in his mouth. And so, as we drove over the long flat white miles toward home, over swamps, past creeks and dried-out rutted farmland where the only shade was a single chinaberry tree, we did not exactly have a conversation. I said that my husband was fine but working too hard— "you know how he is" (which my father did not know). I didn't mention trouble with the landlady and certainly not my dangerous lover.

Between us, forgotten by us both, Simon sat forward on his seat and stared at everything.

As we approached our town, "New hospital!" my father cried out triumphantly, and he pointed toward a towering white mass of concrete and glass and steel that rose unrelatedly from a spreading pine grove. Its busy parking lot was islanded with buckets of thin young trees; the landscaping confirmed the newness of the place—to me it all looked raw and hostile. And so large: I had a quick image of all the inhabitants of our small town being sucked inside.

Just then my father was saying something about Dudley Farmer (I thought) and then (surely unconnectedly)—"psychoanalyst, from Boston, Harvard College, I believe, doing some sort of research"—but I really couldn't hear this either.

When we got to the house—a big, pillared box, imposingly back from the river—the sun was still high, yellow-hazed above the brown slow water, but actually it was five o'clock. "Time for a drink!" said my father, as he did each day at that time.

I was suddenly exhausted, and strangely inwardly tearful: a drink seemed a good idea. My mother was still asleep; she spends the afternoon sleeping off the lunchtime sherry, and then it's time to start again. And so we sat on the porch and waited for her entrance, while Simon ran down to the dock, where he took off his shoes and waded at the shallow muddy river edge.

My father was going on about the wonderful new hospital, the gift of a prominent (and dreadful right-wing rich red-neck, I thought) local family, and he mentioned again, with one of his curious jolting laughs, the psychoanalyst who had come down from Boston to do some work in the hospital, research. ("Artistic Negro children" is what my father said; I later learned he meant autistic—in his accent, impossible to tell.) And in a dreamy bleary way I thought, Good, I will have a summer romance with the Boston shrink. God knows I could use one, or both.

My mother is one of those women who, having been great beauties, forever retain that air; automatically people defer to and wait on her. All my life I had watched her performances with a defeated, angry envy, as I too deferred and waited on her. It was hard to believe that we belonged to the same sex, much less the same family. Now she came in, scarves floating around that faded golden head; my father and I stood up and she kissed us both, and we started getting things for her: a special drink, an ashtray and then another scarf that she had left upstairs in her bedroom.

I told her that I was fine, that it was good to be home. That she looked wonderful.

"Did Daddy tell you about poor Dudley Farmer?" she asked me next. "Has to have this terrible operation on his stomach, they say they're going to take out most of it. He's scared, I tell you. Supposed to lose a lot of weight."

"Is Dudley fat?" This seemed incredible: Dudley had been tall and lithe, a basketball star, with severe dark-blue eyes and an ironic mouth.

"Oh, very fat, you wouldn't recognize him, not any way. Got fat because of his ulcers, and now they have to operate."

The sun was lowering now; I watched it set over the river, as I had thousands of times before (but had it ever set into just those violet clouds, that pink?). And I thought, Oh, the strangeness of the intensely familiar, the wild confusions involved in coming home! It was truly as though I had never left, and at the same time as though I were a stranger, new to that place and to those people, my parents.

Forgetting Simon (as I'm sure they often forgot about me, at his age), they were getting a little drunk as we sat there in the barely cooling air, among fireflies and flowery smells from the shrubbery—until Simon came running up and said he was hungry. The maid had gone home—my parents were "good to the help"—and so my unmaternal mother said, "Why don't you go and see what's in the icebox?" just as she used to say to me, making me feel lonely and neglected. But Simon thought this was great—was freedom: no cross father telling him to eat his meat *first*. He came back after a while with an unbelievably messy sandwich, which looked to be made of chicken and peanut butter and chutney, which he had put together all by himself—and no one forced him to eat it.

The rest of us skipped dinner. I ate a hard-boiled egg on the way to bed, and slept hungrily, with agonizing dreams; I probably wept.

And the next day I fell in love with the Boston doctor.

Or, rather, the next afternoon. That morning, clutching Simon by the hand, wearing my new white shorts and hiding behind very large dark glasses, I wandered through the town—invisible.

The main street of our town is like that of so many small Southern towns: tacky, tawdry, unchanging. The Chatham Dairy Products, to which all of us in high school used to rush each afternoon, to pile around those tables, eating sundaes out of Dixie Cups, showing off for each other—the boys being funny, the girls laughing.

The Little Athens: a dark and dirty beer parlor, with high rickety curtained booths, where Dudley and I often began our evenings, began to kiss and grasp at each other, before we rushed out to his car, rushed down the highway to our small private clearing in a thicket of honey-suckle and crape myrtle, parked. (Adolescent sex, or, usually, non- or almost-sex: what a ghastly preparation for anything! How can anyone romanticize it? How can I?) Until Dudley dumped me and took up with Mary Sue, and then dumped her for a young married woman in another town.

Adolescent memories are not only the most recent and thus the most available, they are also the least subtle, the simplest. Below them stretch deeper, darker layers. However, instead of telling Simon about the time I lost my nickel on the way to Sunday school and hid under the giant magnolia tree (that one, *there*) feeling criminal, I took him to the dime store, where we bought two toy boats and a shovel and pail, and then we continued to the A&P, with my mother's shopping list—to which I added a pound of hamburger; I had decided on certain precautions against skipping dinner.

After that, since the groceries were to be delivered, we walked some more, Simon noticing and asking questions about things, as I remembered everything that had ever happened to me, my whole past assailing me like light continuously thrown stones.

Lunch, naps—for my half-drunk parents, my exhausted son. My father had muttered (I could still barely understand him) that the Boston doctor might come by with a book, and so I sat down out on the porch with a book of my own in my lap, in my short white shorts, in the glaring yellow afternoon sun. Waiting.

After a while I heard a car pull into our drive, behind the house; from the creaking sound of it, a very old car. (A doctor, with an old car? I thought, Terrific.) I heard the engine cut off, a door slam; I saw a tall man come around the corner. A man whom I got up and walked down the steps to greet.

Love at first sight is a silly feeling on one's face: standing there in the heavy sunlight, near a clump of hydrangeas, I looked up at his craggy reddish face, with large ears and sandy-grayish hair, and I knew that I was falling in love, and among other things I felt very foolish.

We said our names to each other: who would I be but Claire, the prodigal, as he later put it, and he of course was the Harvard-Boston shrink, the local prize and curiosity. Dr. C. S. Jones—Caleb Saltonstall— "My mother had some pretty embarrassing ambitions"—this too came later. Caleb.

Caleb and Claire.

We stood there laughing, like much younger, lighter-hearted people than we were.

I asked, "Do you want some iced tea, or something?" Why don't you touch me? We had not shaken hands.

He looked at his watch, and frowned unhappily. "I guess not, I've got a patient in twenty minutes." He looked at me.

And I, that formerly frightened, beaten down into self-hatred and ugliness—that young woman said, "Will you come back tonight? They all fall asleep about ten."

"Yes." We looked at each other again, but that quickly became too intense, my naked blue eyes into his dark brown, and we began to laugh—softly, this time, since we had just mentioned sleeping people. We wished that both now and tonight their sleep would be profound.

Hurriedly, I suppose to get things straight right away, I said, "I'm here with my son Simon. He's four. My husband's in San Francisco. Sort of a trial separation." I had not thought in those terms before, but those words, when said to Caleb, became true.

He hesitated for one instant. "Me too. Wife and kids in Boston. I keep so busy down here partly not to be besieged. God forbid I should be lonely. And I guess you'd call three thousand miles a separation, if not a trial."

We laughed, as all summer we were to laugh, at both the gravest and the most inconsequential matters. We laughed between our wildest encounters of love, and we talked almost not at all—and that, for that summer, for both of us was perfect.

He got up and we walked, touching shoulders in the accidental way that children might, toward his car. I said again, "You'll come around ten?"

"Of course."

By then he was sitting in his car, and I reached in, uncontrollably to touch his cheek.

Thus it was I who first invited, initiated, insisted—who first touched. And how lovely, with us, was the unimportance of that.

I went back into the house, where everyone was still asleep, where no one knew that anything important had occurred. Restless, elated and agitated, I walked through all those too-well-known overburdened rooms, staring at all the strange-familiar mahogany and silver, at heavy portraits of relatives who suddenly had a comical look of madness. At crazed mirrors which I considered crashing to the floor, so strong was my need for a commemorative gesture. At last in my wandering I came to the breakfast room (a room in which no one had ever had breakfast), where the phone was, and so, as though this had been my plan, I dialed my lover's San Francisco office, in itself a forbidden act. Collect.

Just after two, back there in San Francisco. He would quite possibly be just returned from lunch, possibly a little drunk.

He was, returned and drunk.

I said that I planned not to see him again, that it was all over. He said that he saw no reason whatsoever (a favorite lawyer word of his) for such a statement, nor for my call. I could imagine him sitting there, angrily twisting his too long legs—a way he has when exasperated. For good measure he threw in a few obscenities; I threw a few back, and hung up, feeling much better. Perhaps he did too? I would prefer to think not. But I had taken a step, my first for quite a while.

I took a long bath and put on a new light dress.

A little before six my father came downstairs, stretching and yawning and saying offhandedly, as though it were something I had already been told (this is an old trick of his), that Dudley Farmer and his wife and Mary Sue (my "old friend," the former belle who had inexplicably not yet married) were all coming by for drinks. In half an hour. I was thinking that in four more hours it would be ten, and Caleb would come; and so the impact of this information was less momentous than it might have been. I was not even frightened.

Dudley and his wife came first. She was a girl from another state, whom I had not met before, and for whom I felt an instant sympathy, a liking; it later occurred to me that we were somewhat alike.

But poor Dudley: my dangerous and violently handsome early love was muffled in fat, those terrific dark-blue eyes looked out, frightened, from folds of pale flesh. It was terrible: I wanted to hold him in my arms, to say, Don't worry, your operation won't be nearly as bad as you think it will be. Instead I embraced Simon, who had come in just then, so tardily awakened from his nap, and I introduced my son to my old friend.

They too liked each other on sight. My diffident difficult son told Dudley that he had never seen a cigarette lighter like the one Dudley had, and Dudley showed Simon how to use it, and how to light cigarettes for ladies, which Simon continued to do for the rest of that much too long cocktail hour.

(Three and a half more hours.)

Mary Sue arrived, and my first thought was: Well, she's got much better-looking, and at the same time I wondered if my brand-new feeling for Caleb would make me finally a kindly, charitable person. We greeted each other with that odd mixture of warmth and tentativeness which is seemingly the way of not quite old friends, and that odd brushing of cheeks that women do to each other, and I decided that yes, she did look better: thinner, a little sadder and certainly wiser than in her young and mindless, very popular days.

A thing to be said about Southern belles is that in fact they are often not very pretty. Mary Sue at an early age was plump and nearsighted, with mouse-colored hair. However, she laughed easily and often, she was friendly and nonassertive and she kept that mousy hair in perfect curls, her nails a perfect pink. My mother, seeing me moping around the house on Saturday nights, in the months after Dudley's defection, used to say, "I do not see what those boys see in that Mary Sue. Tacky! Dumb! You wait, when that girl is thirty she's going to weigh two hundred pounds. Claire, you are one hundred times prettier than that girl." Just not saying, So how come you're sitting at home and she's out with the best-looking boy in town? How come Dudley dumped you for her? But my mother is often wrong: I was never all that much prettier than Mary Sue, and at thirty, a few years hence, thin Mary Sue was to marry an extremely successful architect, from Atlanta.

We all sat around on that porch where I had seemingly spent half my life just sitting around, and we talked in the desultory way that I was used to. No one asked any but the most perfunctory questions about my life in San Francisco; I need not have worried. Actually they probably did not believe that such a place existed.

However, there were some things I wanted to know, and I did ask, although circuitously. Had the schools changed much? Jobs for black people? Bussing? Well, I was told, there had been a little trouble here and there, but not bad at all, nothing like what had gone on in Beaumont and Hilton. Meaning: we here have better manners, we act better than people in other, even neighboring places.

"Has your mother taught you about collecting fireflies in a fruit jar, to light up your room at night?" Dudley asked Simon. Of course I had not, and the three of us went into the kitchen to find some jars.

"You look really good," Dudley said to me. "Better than ever." His old grin.

"You look—" I began, not sure what I was going to say.

"I've got to get rid of fifteen more pounds before this lousy operation," he told me.

"When is it?"

"End of August."

"Well, worrying about operations is always the worst of them," I babbled. This may well be true, but I could not have known it was; I had only been hospitalized for the birth of Simon, to which I greatly looked forward. Having a child would win me favor with my husband, I then thought.

Back out on the porch everyone had more drinks, and Dudley, who was not drinking, took Simon down to the clumps of lilac at the edge of the lawn where the fireflies were, and he showed Simon how to capture them.

And at last everyone was gone, at last we had dinner and I put Simon to bed and my parents went upstairs to fall into their beds. And it was ten o'clock and I was out on the porch again, aware of veins that pulsed in my throat, and watching some fireflies that must have eluded Simon.

When I heard his car I wanted to run inside, upstairs and away from whatever was about to happen. Instead I sat there, as prim and proper (and as frightened) as I used to be when Dudley came to call. He—Caleb—came around the corner of the house and I got up and went down the stairs to meet him, and in a curious tense way we clasped each other, he a head taller than I—out there in the black sultry flower- and river-smelling night.

He said, "Let's go for a walk. I feel like walking."

That seemed a strange suggestion; I could have told him of lovely private places to drive to, but he had already started out, nervous and fast, and so I followed.

And it seemed strange that he should be nervous. "I hadn't planned to fall in love with anyone," he later explained. "I never had—just with ideas. I knew you were dangerous," and he laughed.

At first I thought that he would want to talk, that this walk was for self-revelations, but it was not like that at all. We just walked, and every now and then he would ask a question, but always an immediate one. What kind of flower makes that very sweet smell? How old is that house? And further down the river, are there places to swim?

Once a pair of twin black cats came toward us out of the darkness, the country night—two cats thin and sleek and moving as one, long legs interwoven with each other, sometimes almost tripping. At that we laughed and stopped walking and laughed and laughed, both wondering (I suppose) if that was how we looked, although we were so upright.

Then we walked on, hurrying, like people with a destination, talking less, simply sensing each other, until seemingly we had made a circle, and we were back at my parents' house. Where, near the camellia bushes, for the first time we kissed. I thought that was a beginning, that our first night would last until sometime near morning, but Caleb meant to kiss me good night.

He won. Over all my clinging and whispered pleas that he stay, he said that he had an early patient. He had to go; he would come back the next day, and that night. And he was gone.

He came back the next day just after lunch—I had told him about everyone's habits of naps.

It was a humid, hazy day. Everything looked heavier: the Spanish moss on the live oaks beside the river sagged lower toward the ground, wisteria vines hung heavily on their trellis.

He sat on the front steps, not having much time, my bare leg touching his bleached-out khaki pants. Caleb said, "I just can't believe this is happening to me. I'm a rational man—this is not my style at all."

I laughed, feeling amazingly light in the head and heart, unabashed, in the pounding sunshine. I said, "We have to go to a party this afternoon, but tonight? I'll see you tonight?"

We all went to the party, my parents and Simon and I—and there, of course, among the old family friends, were Dudley and his wife. I talked mostly to her; disliking large parties, I "circulate" poorly, tend to stay with one person with whom I can talk. A dark pretty girl, with a soft voice from somewhere further south. I recognized that the quality I had felt in common with her was fear, but whereas I had been nebulously frightened of looming, dangerous people (who had already become somewhat unreal), she was worried about Dudley, simply and specifically. She said, "I really hope you'll come over and see us while you're here. Bring Simon, of course. But, until August—" And I said that she mustn't fuss or worry, feeling as kindly toward her as though she were an oldest friend. In fact I could see the emergence in myself of a calmer, kinder person, and I could feel that person reflected in the eyes of the old people who had known me all my life: they were thinking, Why, for heaven's sake, she's *nice.*

My father was talking about the Vietnam War, which was still going on at that time. "Well, I'm neither a hawk nor a dove, but a *bustard,*" he said, as he was to say often over the summer (and I to cringe: my calm kindness had its limits). "Has anyone ever heard of that fabulous old bird? A native of Pakistan, I do believe."

That night in his beat-up car Caleb and I drove down the narrow tarred road, down along the river to a small clearing in the tropical tangle of Spanish moss and honeysuckle vines. We got out and in the heavy blackness we found the narrow beach, of coarse river sand, and there, at last, we made love. God knows what we said—I think not much at all.

That day, and that night began the pattern of my summer: days of walks and swims with Simon, frequent parties with my parents, old friends. Some encounters with Dudley and his wife, less frequently with Mary Sue. Nights with Caleb, plus a few infrequent daylight intervals; he was allowing himself to be overworked at the hospital, for reasons of his own. Also he was worried about his helpless charges. And working on a book.

I don't think that Caleb and I needed the excitement of illicitness; we simply wanted privacy, which was not easy in that town. But, "For secret lovers, we spend a lot of time outdoors, don't we?" Caleb remarked one night, as we lay on our tiny private beach in the dark. "I'm sure it's terribly healthy for us," he said, and we laughed like idiots.

Making love, laughing. That is what we did, that summer, both to excess; in both cases, having once started, we seemed unable to stop. Little talk, no plans—it was *marvelous.* I thought about Caleb all day; he was always in my mind, but with no anxiety, which I found amazing. Love and fear had always arrived together, for me, before.

I often forgot what Caleb did, his profession—or, rather, I didn't think about it. But he said a few things from such extraordinary insight that I thought, What an amazingly good doctor he must be. One thing that he said was "I think you're going to take a while getting used to being happy." That was true; it has taken years.

Sometimes—being already naked, Caleb and I—we slipped into the river and swam about in the warm black almost unmoving water. Remembered, this seems a dangerous thing to have done, for obvious reasons; at the time it seemed natural and easy—the river was there for us, as we were for each other.

Simon, too, thrived during that summer. He got taller, his hair lighter and his skin dark brown; and no one told him to be quiet or to finish his hamburger. With neighboring children he waded in the river and played with boats, his unaccented California voice mingling with their slower, softer speech.

I wrote to my husband and said that since this was, in fact, a separation, and it seemed to be working out (I cited Simon, his height and his happiness), perhaps we should consider a divorce. I had no clear plans involving Caleb, whose own life was obscure to me (it was one of the things we did not talk about), and I knew that in any case I would have to go back to San Francisco in the fall to straighten things out, as Caleb would have to go back to Boston. I wrote about a divorce simply to have it stated, to have something begun. My most definite plan was to move from that flat, with the live-in downstairs landlady. I would find a place with a wooded open setting, in a quiet neighborhood, perhaps on Twin Peaks or Potrero Hill, where Simon and I would feel at home. That seemed most important.

"We don't talk much, do we?" Caleb one night remarked, as, uncharacteristically, we sat in a booth in the New Athens, braving public opinion. Drinking beer. "Considering how much I think about us," he added.

"Do we have to? I love our not talking," I truthfully told him.

"I guess not." And then he said, "You know, sometimes you're so beautiful it hurts."

My husband responded rather tersely that he would talk to me when I got back to San Francisco; like so many lawyers, he hates to commit himself to the written word.

Looking back, I suppose it is surprising that I did not mention this exchange to Caleb; at the time it did not occur to me to do so.

And then without warning the summer began to rush toward fall. Even in that warm Southern air there was a hint of cooler days to come. It was almost the end of August, time for me to make reservations to go back (not "home") to San Francisco.

It was time for Dudley Farmer's operation.

The operation went well; Caleb called me from the hospital to tell me that. The surgeon was pleased. Of course Dudley would be in Intensive Care for a couple of days, but then I could go to see him.

I called the airline office and made our reservations. Twelve more days, which at the time seemed both infinite, a treasure, and like no time at all, like nothing.

Ten more days.

Because it is very late at night, Caleb and I are going for a walk instead of driving down to our beach. There is a light warm breeze that ruffles the dried-out, end-of-summer grasses at the edge of the road. And suddenly through the grasses come those two black cats—they are somewhat larger but they must be the same ones; surely no other two cats have this impossible way of walking, their legs weaving together.

Caleb and I stop walking and we begin to laugh, laughing softly, chokingly, in the black stirring night, until we are weak and we sit down in the field beside the road, and after a while, because it is so dark and we are lying there, we make love where we are.

Seven more days, a week. Over her third lunchtime sherry my mother has said that I may pick all the flowers I can find in the wilting garden, and I do just that; I make an enormous bouquet of overblown roses and crape myrtle and gardenias and camellias and I surround it all with magnolia leaves, and I take it to the hospital, to Dudley.

Walking through those greenish corridors, through swinging steel doors and forbidding alien smells, I am irrationally frightened, and I feel a lurch of sympathy for poor Dudley, incarcerated here, at the mercy of those brisk and stiffly uniformed people.

At the desk, on his floor, I am told that he cannot have visitors, not that day. My flowers are taken, will be given to him. I do not see his wife.

Six more days. Something has gone wrong, Caleb tells me. Dudley is bleeding internally. A hemorrhage.

Simon would like to write to all his new friends from San Francisco. He would like to send them cards of the Golden Gate Bridge, the cable cars, things like that. Will I help him? Could he learn to write? I say yes to both questions, and I note to myself that he is making more detailed plans for the winter than I am.

Dudley died two days before I was to fly West. Caleb came early in the afternoon to tell me that. Everyone was asleep and I was sitting on the steps, and it could have been the start of summer, except that it was not.

"It was one of those inexplicable medical horrors," Caleb said. "Why doctors feel basically helpless, or they should. A sudden infection, from nowhere."

I had begun to cry, for too many reasons. Caleb put his arms around me; if anyone passed and saw us we no longer cared. (I have since learned that everyone in town knew all—or almost all—about us anyway, of course.)

To me almost the worst of it was that Dudley had had to spend his last months so fat and frightened, dreading what he must darkly have known would happen.

Caleb had a staff meeting that night, and I a dinner party. Impossible to meet, although I had a dim sense that earlier in our heady, impetuous summer we would have worked it out.

"Reality has hit us," Caleb said, unhappily. "Christ, why can't we run backwards to June?"

In a brief exhausted way we talked about what to do the following night, our last; we even considered my saying, "I'm going out to dinner with Caleb Jones." But the prospect of saying those words was jarring; we would have felt invaded. And then there was the problem of Simon, whom (significantly) Caleb had never met.

We decided to do what we always did, to meet at ten.

And so the next night I had dinner with my parents, who got a little drunker than usual, I suppose out of a feeling that this was a festive occasion, and with Simon, who (I thought) was curiously callous about the end of his good summer, among new friends. He was excited about San Francisco.

That night Caleb and I talked far too much, and I especially said all the wild and impossible things that all summer I had managed not to say: I said that I had never loved anyone else, I never would, et cetera. Caleb responded reasonably enough that I was too young to predict my future feelings, that he could not accept such promises. Besides, he said, he was almost totally involved in his work, to an extent that I had not understood; also, he was basically not a terribly emotional person. Personal relationships were not, or had not been, of prime importance to him.

I wept, feeling abandoned and feeling too that I had managed to wreck the whole summer. In any case, that was our worst, our only bad time together. So that by the time we stopped talking and made love we were half asleep.

Back in San Francisco, not hearing from Caleb (I wrote him all the time, somewhat hysterically, trying to re-create our summer) and missing him, at first I was depressed; I felt almost as beaten down and helpless as before I had left.

But the weather that fall was cool and clear and lovely, and I seemed, somehow, to have acquired over the summer a more positive view, and some strength: I told my husband that I wanted a divorce, that I was going to find a new place to live, and a job.

And then, like a reward, a letter came from Caleb. Not at all a crazy impassioned one, as mine had been, but one that was rational and friendly, kind. He said that he had been too depressed to write before, and that sometimes, even, our summer seemed unreal to him. But I felt wonderful; reading his letter restored me. And, interestingly, the next day I found an apartment on a quiet wooded street, on the western slope of Twin Peaks.

My divorce, also, went astoundingly well; my husband made none of the trouble that I would have expected of him. (It later turned out that he wanted to marry his secretary—such an original man!)

Simon and I moved into our good new place; he went to a new school and I got a part-time job in a doctor's office. And I began to "go out," to have a good time.

Caleb and I continued to write to each other, I much more frequently than he, but that was all right; I assumed that he was busier, and in a curious way I did not expect certain things from Caleb. He did not say that he was living with his wife and children, but I assumed that to be the case. Why not? is how he would think of it.

Even when I eventually fell in love with someone else I continued to write to Caleb, not telling him about the other man (although somehow I felt that he would know, and not mind).

One night—I think in February: a cold swirling fog-bound night—during a lonely rift with the other man, I again wrote to Caleb, somewhat in my old tone. In part, I said to him, "I think you saved my life last summer, I will really always love you."

Home Is Where

And, the next morning, which was a cleared spring-suggesting day, I reread that letter and was surprisingly unembarrassed by it. I sent it off.

Caleb's book was successful. He became famous.

And later I married the other man, and later still I almost got used to being happy.

A Pale and Perfectly Oval Moon

Dying, for a time Penelope Moore behaved atrociously. To her husband, Van, who loved her (in his way), both the fact of her dying and her continuous, ferociously whispered accusations were intolerable.

She was supposed to have died early in the summer. "To be quite honest, old man, I'm surprised she lasted through the spring," the friendly internist whose charge she was had said to Van in June. But June had passed, July, August, September; and in the middle of October still she "lingered on," as the false old phrase would have it. As Penelope herself cried out, "My God, I'm lingering on—is that what *ma*lingering comes from, do you suppose? Have you thought of that? God, why am I still *here*?"

"Here," practically speaking, was the Moores' country weekend house, on a bend in a river, in California's High Sierras. It was a house that a local contractor had thrown together, somewhat hastily, on speculation—and which the Moores had bought on a hasty impulse. It was not well planned: some rooms, the master bedroom and the kitchen, were impractically large and drafty; the dining-living room was small and cramped. But outside the shingles had weathered beautifully, turning silver in the strong clear air, at that altitude, and Penelope had always loved the house's many-windowed openness, its proximity to the outdoors, and to the seasons. A New Englander, Penelope had remarked often before they bought this house that she literally could not bear the California lack of seasons. Windows gave either onto the meadow or the river, so that the house was full of rushing river sounds.

And now that she was so sick the too large bedroom did not seem an inconvenience: the table that held her drugs and other terrible accoutrements of her illness could be screened off, and a cot for Van had been placed beside the large old double bed, and on the other side a big comfortable chair. Although, should she "linger" through the winter, Van wondered how he could keep the house warm enough, could defend it against windows packed with snow. A neighbor, Miss Bird, a former nurse, had moved into the guest room to help with the care of Penelope. The local hospital was excellent, and near. (Everything might have been planned.)

Van was a lawyer with a small office in San Francisco—two partners, one harassed secretary. Therefore it was necessary for him to return to the city at intervals to keep things going, or to try to. Sometimes he drove the three hours there and back in a day; at other, less frequent times he stayed overnight in their Twin Peaks flat.

"Of course you have to spend the night," Penelope hissed on these occasions. "You have to get laid, and who would expect a man of your age to arise from some floozy's bed and drive for hours up into the mountains with a sick and thankless wife at the end of the trip?"

"Now, Pen, come on—"

Always pale, her pallor now had a cast that was almost blue—like moonlight on snow, Van uncharacteristically thought, but was unhappily not able to say, although he dimly knew that it was a thing she would like to have heard.

He also liked the floating pale scarves she wore, to hide the terribly thinning patchy hair, and he did not say that either.

"Tell me, will you tell me something I want to know?" asked Penelope furiously. "Do you really like those southern Italian girls, or Mexicans best? Oh, I know, as long as they're dark and sort of sleazy you don't much care. The most beautiful girl I ever knew was Corsican—thick, thick black hair and wild eyes and the sexiest mouth. My God, why couldn't you have met Maria? Why me? It's like the end of Proust, where Swann says that he's ruined his life for a woman who was not his type at all."

"I fell in love with you," said Van, quite truthfully.

"In love. Jesus. Well, have a divine time in the city. With whoever." She sighed, and in an instant had fallen into one of her short but deep and blessed sleeps.

Van went into the kitchen and told Miss Bird that he was going.

Outside Penelope's windows, the October landscape showed an

extraordinary spectrum of yellow: the wild-rose bush that grew beside the door was pinkish yellow, next to the brighter-yellow lilac leaves. Out in the meadow the grasses were yellow green, and the yellow yarrow bloomed there still. Beside the river, willow leaves had turned to rust; in the dark rapids ridiculous birds, called bobbers, dipped and swam, and across the water, from a stand of aspens, fluttered the most brilliant yellow of all, as clear and pure as sunlight.

Van's floozy—he both winced and was amused at Penelope's word—was in fact a pleasant and quite unspectacular girl named Joan, who had arrived in the office as a Kelly Girl, to help out the overburdened secretary. Neither Italian nor Mexican, in fact Scottish, Joan had pale-brown hair, more or less the color that Penelope's had been.

"What you don't understand," Van sometimes imagined saying to Penelope, as he drove the seemingly endless three-hour trip away from her, toward San Francisco and Joan, "what you don't understand is that I might stare at those big sexy dark girls, or I might make a pass at one of them at a party, if I'd had enough to drink. But ten years ago it was you, you with what you continue to call your dirty-blond hair, that I fell in love with. And now for quite another kind of love there is Joan." Impossible, of course, to say this to Penelope, and he found it harder and harder to talk to her at all. What can you say to someone who knows that she is dying, and who continuously rages at that deprivation?

In fact, Van had had one and only one affair with the sort of girl who Penelope insisted was his "type." She had been a woman of dazzling darkness, of a vast and careless voluptuousness. He had loved her wildly for a time, and the repeated failures of their acts of love had been to him a bitter and amazing disappointment. This was shortly before he met Penelope, who unfortunately remembered seeing him with his "dark prize" (her phrase) at a party some months earlier.

He had fallen in love at once with Penelope; she had been an enchantment to him, stirring all his senses—a wild delight.

She was at that time a thin young woman, divorced, with no children; she lived scantily on a part-time job in an art gallery. Her two manias, both unfamiliar to Van, were for chamber music and for conversation. When she wasn't listening to music—composers he hadn't heard of before: Telemann, Hummel, Boccherini—she was passionately talking, examining, commenting, then laughing a lot at it all. She read a lot of novels. They married rather hastily, they were often happy and sometimes they quarreled. And then she was sick—then dying.

Aside from the color of her hair, Joan, Van's Kelly Girl, his "floozy," was as unlike Penelope as one woman could be to another. Soft and plump, Joan was so passive, so vague and dreamy in manner that at first, hiring her, Van had nervously wondered if she was stupid—or possibly drugged. But as she sat at her typewriter, looking tranced, her fingers literally flew over the keys, and her work was perfect: the most abstruse words correctly spelled, the legal forms all exact, and all this was produced with a speed that was embarrassing to the other, regular secretary. Joan was not dumb. Eventually Van decided that she was concentrated on some unknown area of her own mind, which he was never to discover.

The "affair"—Van did not quite think of it as that; in fact he had no words for what went on between them, and tended to use Penelope's: "floozy," "getting laid," although he liked Joan, and meant no disrespect—whatever it was had begun predictably enough. On a certain evening last spring Van had an unavoidable dinner engagement with clients. Also, there was more immediately important work than Joan could finish by five—papers that Van had to take with him to court early the following morning. "No sweat," said Joan, in her pleasant passive way, lifting moony brown eyes to Van's darker brown. "I live sort of near you, on Ashbury, and I've got a machine like this at home. You could stop and pick up the stuff on your way by."

Somehow what came through to him as most odd in this statement was the fact that she had such an expensive piece of office machinery at home, an IBM Selectric, but being hard-pressed he accepted her offer without much thought.

The dinner with clients, at a "top" French restaurant, was carelessly seasoned and terribly expensive—was boring and unproductive. Driving away from it, having drunk an unnecessary final brandy, Van was assaulted by one of the awful and engulfing waves of self-pity that normally he was able to fight off. In that dark and rainy moment, driving through snarls of downtown night traffic, he saw himself as the hardworking husband of an ungratefully dying woman.

And it was more or less in that mood that he arrived at Joan's apartment, in the neighborhood that five years back had been loosely designated as "the Haight."

Concerned with himself, Van had not thought about Joan and her possible surroundings; probably he would have imagined plants and posters, what he thought of as the trappings of the young. Certainly he was not prepared for such visible luxury, so much soft pale leather, such a heavy bronze-bound glass coffee table, on which there was a huge jar of exotic flowers. In fact his look of surprise, on that first entrance, was enough to cause her to say, though softly, "I made a lot of money in the sixties, when anyone could." (Weeks later, in a moment of intimacy, he could ask how—how had she got so rich, so young? "Dealing, mostly." And when at first he did not understand she said, "Just grass, and sometimes acid. Never anything hard, and I don't deal at all anymore." She liked the variety of life as a Kelly Girl.)

Nor was he prepared for the mild and friendly pleasures of being in bed with Joan, which he was, rather soon, that first night. "Love," or whatever it was with Joan, was so totally unlike what love had been with Penelope that his guilt was decreased (a little); with Joan there were no wild sensual flights, there was no amazement. Ease and warmth and friendliness were what he felt with Joan. Some gratitude. Some guilt.

The guilt in fact went in both directions—or, rather, toward both women. Guilt toward Joan because he spent so little time with her, never more than an hour, sometimes less; even when he was staying overnight in town he left her scrupulously early and went back to his own place to sleep, back to his own phone.

Guilt toward Penelope because he was unable to keep her from dying.

Now, in the bright and boring sunshine, the relentless three hours of the trip to San Francisco, Van was mildly thinking of Joan, whom he expected to see that night. He even (improbably) imagined a conversation about her with Penelope. "Not quite your ordinary Kelly Girl," he imagined himself saying—to Penelope, who had sometimes accused him of being square. "She made a lot of money during the sixties selling dope. Sort of an interesting woman."

But, along with the too familiar smell of onions at Vacaville, an equally familiar depression settled into his mind. What, *really,* was so interesting about selling dope? Joan was not an interesting woman; Penelope was. Joan was simply very nice.

One of the things that Van most hated about this drive, both ways, was his obsessive fear that Penelope might die while he was on the highway, locked into speeding steel and burning rubber, into the screaming monotony of a superhighway. She could die while he was concentrated on passing a giant diesel freight truck, straining on the final lap of its cross-country haul—could die while he was passing the tollbooth at Vallejo and thinking, Thirty more miles.

Arrived at his office, in a converted Victorian house out on Pine Street, Van was informed by his secretary that his anticipated business lunch had been canceled—good: more uncluttered time for work. Miss Gibson had called—Joan, currently a Kelly Girl at an office somewhere in the Jack Tar Building. A court date had been shifted forward into December. A client had called to complain about his bill.

Van calculated: if he worked through lunchtime, ordering something, he could spend that extra couple of hours taking Joan out to dinner—a thing that he had never done, and felt badly about not doing. He could still go to bed early in his own Twin Peaks place, and be up early and back to work as planned.

But Miss Joan Gibson was unavailable on the phone, out of the office on an errand, or something, and it was midafternoon before Van reached her, and rather proudly invited her out for dinner.

"Wow, that sounds so nice," she said. "But of all the lousy breaks—my father's in town today."

"Your father?" She had never mentioned a father, and for a single instant it occurred to Van that she might be lying. But Joan wouldn't lie; she didn't need to. She would have said, as she had a couple of times before, "I'm really sorry, but I've got something else that I have to do."

And now she laughed, softly and pleasantly. "Yes, my father. He lives in Salt Lake; he's sort of a nice old guy. You'd like him. But I guess that's not such a neat idea."

"No, I guess not. Well, I hope I'll see you soon."

"Yes, really. And I'm sorry about tonight. Call me when you get back down, O.K.?"

Such was the friendly and casually intimate tone of their connection. Leaving the phone, Van was smiling to himself.

Then, recalculating his time and his work, he saw that if he again ordered something portable at his desk for dinner, and continued to work, he would be entirely through by nine or ten at the latest. He would not have to stay over; he could be back up in the mountains with Penelope by midnight or so.

He had a ham-and-cheese sandwich for dinner, and coffee, and he left the office at a little after nine.

And by eleven that night he had passed Auburn, and begun the third and final hour of his journey, the sixty miles or so of ascent into the mountains, from two to six thousand feet.

On either side of the highway, in the darkness, the black shapes of trees diminished as he climbed, and at last he was up in a barren and lonely landscape of rocks, of stretching waste.

Suddenly, near Donner Summit, the yellow edge of the rising moon appeared from behind an outcropping of rocks. A ridiculously shaped oval moon, a perfect egg—a Humpty-Dumpty moon that disappeared behind a rock as quickly, and as foolishly, as it had arisen.

Penelope was awake.

"Darling, what a lovely surprise," she said, in a voice from months or years ago. She was sitting up in bed, reading by lamplight, with something pale and floating about her head.

Van kissed her cheek, and then sat in the bedside chair. He told her about getting his work done, mentioning cases that he had talked about before. His trip home. The moon. "It was really a ludicrous moon. It looked just like Humpty-Dumpty," he said.

And Penelope laughed—her old light laugh that had once seemed to touch his skin like lace.

Remission. That was the word that Miss Bird whispered to Van as they both witnessed Penelope during the next few days, then weeks. But Van rejected the word; he knew that he was in the presence of a miracle.

Outside, in the bright cool October air, the leaves slowly darkened from yellow to burnished gold, and in the house the rooms were full of the sounds of flutes and clarinets, of violins and cellos—Brahms and Schubert, Boccherini, Telemann.

Which is not to say that Penelope was really *well:* when, as she infrequently did, she got out of bed and moved around the house, her movements were painfully, haltingly slow. But she talked a lot now—gently, amusingly, affectionately. She was so nearly her old self that it was hard for Van not to hope: perhaps she could be like this for years?

Only once—on the day, in fact, of the first snowfall of that season, a light white dusting that lay softly among the meadow grass—on that day, with the most terrible sadness, Penelope asked, "Do you know what this is like?" (She did not have to explain what she meant by "this.") "It's like having to separate from someone you're wildly in love with. When you desperately think that you'd give twenty years of your life for another hour together. I wonder if maybe that's what I've done. Taken extra hours. Made that bargain, somehow. Sometime."

Unbearably moved, at the same time Van experienced a spurt of jealousy. About whom had she felt such a desperate love? Not for him; their love affair had been passionate but without despair. No anguished separations. He himself had felt such desperation for his "dark prize," a feeling that he had forgotten, or that did not occur to him now.

But then smilingly Penelope said, "Van, darling, I do feel guilty about your staying up here so much, but of course it is lovely," and she reached to touch his hand with her white, white blue-veined hand.

She even looked, in a way, quite wonderful: the vague pale scarves about her head intensified the darkness of her eyes, the firm small structure of her nose. You look beautiful, he wanted to say, but he was afraid of a sound of mockery.

. . .

Early in the summer after Penelope died, Van married Joan. (Penelope died, as he had feared, while he was on the road, during one of those horrendously dull blurs between Auburn and San Francisco, early in November.) Van and Joan moved her expensive possessions up the hill from her Ashbury apartment to his Twin Peaks flat.

It all worked out quite well, including the furniture, which fit. Joan stopped being a Kelly Girl and took cooking lessons, and became a skillful cook. They made love often, and for the most part happily.

The only problem was—that Van was just slightly bored. As he had surmised some time ago, Joan was not a very interesting woman. But he didn't really mind this touch of boredom; it left him more time to himself. Since they talked rather little, Van began to read books that he had "always meant" to read. Novels, in fact, that Penelope had recommended. Proust, *Middlemarch, Anna Karenina* and, finally, *Wuthering Heights,* which made him weep—all alone, over a final brandy.

In fact, since Joan was a person who lived most vitally during the day (her favorite time for love was on waking, in the morning), and who often went to bed very early, Van took to drinking a little too much late at night, alone, confronted with his dark and sprawling city view of the light-scattered San Francisco hills. Penelope had been a night person; she had chosen this flat for its spectacular night view.

He had sold the mountain house soon after Penelope died, at a loss, because he was unable to imagine a stay up there without her. And now sometimes he dreamily imagined that he was back in the mountains, imagined that the actual sounds of traffic below his windows were river sounds, and that he was with Penelope.

Unhappily it was not always a loving and gentle Penelope that he believed he was with; he could remember Penelope the shrew quite accurately. (Had she been shrewish on purpose so that he would miss her less? He could believe that of complex Penelope.)

But now when she hissed that he didn't love her, that she was not his type—now he could say, and strongly enough to convince her, "You're the most remarkable and interesting woman I've ever known. I've never really loved anyone but you."

Roses, Rhododendron

One dark and rainy Boston spring of many years ago, I spent all my after-school and evening hours in the living room of our antique-crammed Cedar Street flat, writing down what the Ouija board said to my mother. My father, a spoiled and rowdy Irishman, a sometime engineer, had run off to New Orleans with a girl, and my mother hoped to learn from the board if he would come back. Then, one night in May, during a crashing black thunderstorm (my mother was both afraid and much in awe of such storms), the board told her to move down South, to North Carolina, taking me and all the antiques she had been collecting for years, and to open a store in a small town down there. This is what we did, and shortly thereafter, for the first time in my life, I fell permanently in love: with a house, with a family of three people and with an area of countryside.

Perhaps too little attention is paid to the necessary preconditions of "falling in love"—I mean the state of mind or place that precedes one's first sight of the loved person (or house or land). In my own case, I remember the dark Boston afternoons as a precondition of love. Later on, for another important time, I recognized boredom in a job. And once the fear of growing old.

In the town that she had chosen, my mother, Margot (she picked out her own name, having been christened Margaret), rented a small house on a pleasant back street. It had a big surrounding screened-in porch, where she put most of the antiques, and she put a discreet sign out in the front yard: "Margot—Antiques." The store was open only in the afternoons. In the mornings and on Sundays, she drove around the countryside in our ancient and spacious Buick, searching for trophies among the area's country stores and farms and barns. (She is nothing if not enterprising; no one else down there had thought of doing that before.)

Although frequently embarrassed by her aggression—she thought nothing of making offers for furniture that was in use in a family's rooms—I often drove with her during those first few weeks. I was excited by the novelty of the landscape. The red clay banks that led up to the thick pine groves, the swollen brown creeks half hidden by flowering tangled vines. Bare, shaded yards from which rose gaunt, narrow houses. Chickens that scattered, barefoot children who stared at our approach.

"Hello, there. I'm Mrs. John Kilgore—Margot Kilgore—and I'm interested in buying old furniture. Family portraits. Silver."

Margot a big brassily bleached blonde in a pretty flowered silk dress and high-heeled patent sandals. A hoarse and friendly voice. Me a scrawny, pale, curious girl, about ten, in a blue linen dress with smocking across the bodice. (Margot has always had a passionate belief in good clothes, no matter what.)

On other days, Margot would say, "I'm going to look over my so-called books. Why don't you go for a walk or something, Jane?"

And I would walk along the sleepy, leafed-over streets, on the unpaved sidewalks, past houses that to me were as inviting and as interesting as unread books, and I would try to imagine what went on inside. The families. Their lives.

The main street, where the stores were, interested me least. Two-story brick buildings—dry-goods stores, with dentists' and lawyers' offices above. There was also a drugstore, with round marble tables and wire-backed chairs, at which wilting ladies sipped at their Cokes. (This was to become a favorite haunt of Margot's.) I preferred the civic monuments: a pre-Revolutionary Episcopal chapel of yellowish cracked plaster, and several tall white statues to the Civil War dead—all of them quickly overgrown with ivy or Virginia creeper.

These were the early nineteen-forties, and in the next few years the town was to change enormously. Its small textile factories would be given defense contracts (parachute silk); a Navy preflight school would be established at a neighboring university town. But at that moment it was a sleeping village. Untouched.

My walks were not a lonely occupation, but Margot worried that they were, and some curious reasoning led her to believe that a bicycle would help. (Of course, she turned out to be right.) We went to Sears, and she bought me a big new bike—blue, with balloon tires—on which I began to explore the outskirts of town and the countryside.

The house I fell in love with was about a mile out of town, on top of a hill. A small stone bank that was all overgrown with tangled roses led up to its yard, and pink and white roses climbed up a trellis to the roof of the front porch—the roof on which, later, Harriet and I used to sit and exchange our stores of erroneous sexual information. Harriet Farr was the daughter of the house. On one side of the house, there was what looked like a newer wing, with a bay window and a long side porch, below which the lawn sloped down to some flowering shrubs. There was a yellow rosebush, rhododendron, a plum tree, and beyond were woods—pines, and oak and cedar trees. The effect was rich and careless, generous and somewhat mysterious. I was deeply stirred.

As I was observing all this, from my halted bike on the dusty white hilltop, a small, plump woman, very erect, came out of the front door and went over to a flower bed below the bay window. She sat down very stiffly. (Emily, who was Harriet's mother, had some terrible, never diagnosed trouble with her back; she generally wore a brace.) She was older than Margot, with very beautiful white hair that was badly cut in that butchered nineteen-thirties way.

From the first, I was fascinated by Emily's obvious dissimilarity to Margot. I think I was somehow drawn to her contradictions—the shapeless body held up with so much dignity, even while she was sitting in the dirt. The lovely chopped-off hair. (There were greater contradictions, which I learned of later—she was a Virginia Episcopalian who always voted for Norman Thomas, a feminist who always delayed meals for her tardy husband.)

Emily's hair was one of the first things about the Farr family that I mentioned to Margot after we became friends, Harriet and Emily and I, and I began to spend most of my time in that house.

"I don't think she's ever dyed it," I said, with almost conscious lack of tact.

Of course, Margot was defensive. "I wouldn't dye mine if I thought it would be a decent color on its own."

But by that time Margot's life was also improving. Business was fairly good, and she had finally heard from my father, who began to send sizable checks from New Orleans. He had found work with an oil company. She still asked the Ouija board if she would see him again, but her question was less obsessive.

The second time I rode past that house, there was a girl sitting on the front porch, reading a book. She was about my age. She looked up. The next time I saw her there, we both smiled. And the time after that (a Saturday morning in late June) she got up and slowly came out to the road, to where I had stopped, ostensibly to look at the view—the sweep of fields, the white highway, which wound down to the thick greenery bordering the creek, the fields and trees that rose in dim and distant hills.

"I've got a bike exactly like that," Harriet said indifferently, as though to deny the gesture of having come out to meet me.

For years, perhaps beginning then, I used to seek my opposite in friends. Inexorably following Margot, I was becoming a big blonde, with some of her same troubles. Harriet was cool and dark, with long gray eyes. A girl about to be beautiful.

"Do you want to come in? We've got some lemon cake that's pretty good."

Inside, the house was cluttered with odd mixtures of furniture. I glimpsed a living room, where there was a shabby sofa next to a pretty, "antique" table. We walked through a dining room that contained a decrepit mahogany table surrounded with delicate fruitwood chairs. (I had a horrifying moment of imagining Margot there, with her accurate eye—making offers in her harsh Yankee voice.) The walls were crowded with portraits and with nineteenth-century oils of bosky landscapes. Books overflowed from rows of shelves along the walls. I would have moved in at once.

We took our lemon cake back to the front porch and ate it there, overlooking that view. I can remember its taste vividly. It was light and tart and sweet, and a beautiful lemon color. With it, we drank cold milk, and then we had seconds and more milk, and we discussed what we liked to read.

We were both at an age to begin reading grown-up books, and there was some minor competition between us to see who had read more of them. Harriet won easily, partly because her mother reviewed books for the local paper, and had brought home Steinbeck, Thomas Wolfe, Virginia Woolf and Elizabeth Bowen. But we also found in common an enthusiasm for certain novels about English children. (Such snobbery!)

"It's the best cake I've ever had!" I told Harriet. I had already adopted something of Margot's emphatic style.

"It's very good," Harriet said judiciously. Then, quite casually, she added, "We could ride our bikes out to Laurel Hill."

We soared dangerously down the winding highway. At the bridge across the creek, we stopped and turned onto a narrow, rutted dirt road that followed the creek through woods as dense and as alien as a jungle would have been—thick pines with low sweeping branches, young leafed-out maples, peeling tall poplars, elms, brambles, green masses of honeysuckle. At times, the road was impassable, and we had to get off our bikes and push them along, over crevices and ruts, through mud or sand. And with all that we kept up our somewhat stilted discussion of literature.

"I love Virginia Woolf!"

"Yes, she's very good. Amazing metaphors."

I thought Harriet was an extraordinary person—more intelligent, more poised and prettier than any girl of my age I had ever known. I felt that she could become anything at all—a writer, an actress, a foreign correspondent (I went to a lot of movies). And I was not entirely wrong; she eventually became a sometimes-published poet.

We came to a small beach, next to a place where the creek widened and ran over some shallow rapids. On the other side, large gray rocks rose steeply. Among the stones grew isolated, twisted trees, and huge bushes with thick green leaves. The laurel of Laurel Hill. Rhododendron. Harriet and I took off our shoes and waded into the warmish water. The bottom squished under our feet, making us laugh, like the children we were, despite all our literary talk.

Margot was also making friends. Unlike me, she seemed to seek her own likeness, and she found a sort of kinship with a woman named Dolly Murray, a rich widow from Memphis who shared many of Margot's superstitions—fear of thunderstorms, faith in the Ouija board. About ten years older than Margot, Dolly still dyed her hair red; she was a noisy, biased, generous woman. They drank gin and gossiped together, they met for Cokes at the drugstore and sometimes they drove to a neighboring town to have dinner in a restaurant (in those days, still a daring thing for unescorted ladies to do).

I am sure that the Farrs, outwardly a conventional family, saw me as a neglected child. I was so available for meals and overnight visits. But that is not how I experienced my life—I simply felt free. And an important thing to be said about Margot as a mother is that she never made me feel guilty for doing what I wanted to do. And of how many mothers can that be said?

There must have been a moment of "meeting" Emily, but I have forgotten it. I remember only her gentle presence, a soft voice and my own sense of love returned. Beautiful white hair, dark deep eyes and a wide mouth, whose corners turned and moved to express whatever she felt—amusement, interest, boredom, pain. I have never since seen such a vulnerable mouth.

I amused Emily; I almost always made her smile. She must have seen me as something foreign—a violent, enthusiastic Yankee. (I used forbidden words, like "God" and "damn.") Very unlike the decorous young Southern girl that she must have been, that Harriet almost was.

She talked to me a lot; Emily explained to me things about the South that otherwise I would not have picked up. "Virginians feel superior to everyone else, you know," she said, in her gentle (Virginian) voice. "Some people in my family were quite shocked when I married a man from North Carolina and came down here to live. And a Presbyterian at that! Of course, that's nowhere near as bad as a Baptist, but only Episcopalians really count." This was all said lightly, but I knew that some part of Emily agreed with the rest of her family.

"How about Catholics?" I asked her, mainly to prolong the conversation. Harriet was at the dentist's, and Emily was sitting at her desk answering letters. I was perched on the sofa near her, and we both faced the sweeping green view. But since my father, Johnny Kilgore, was a lapsed Catholic, it was not an entirely frivolous question. Margot was a sort of Christian Scientist (her own sort).

"We hardly know any Catholics." Emily laughed, and then she sighed. "I do sometimes still miss Virginia. You know, when we drive up there I can actually feel the difference as we cross the state line. I've met a few people from South Carolina," she went on, "and I understand that people down there feel the same way Virginians do." (Clearly, she found this unreasonable.)

"West Virginia? Tennessee?"

"They don't seem Southern at all. Neither do Florida and Texas—not to me."

("Dolly says that Mrs. Farr is a terrible snob," Margot told me, inquiringly.

"In a way." I spoke with a new diffidence that I was trying to acquire from Harriet.

"Oh.")

Once, I told Emily what I had been wanting to say since my first sight of her. I said, "Your hair is so beautiful. Why don't you let it grow?"

She laughed, because she usually laughed at what I said, but at the same time she looked surprised, almost startled. I understood that what I had said was not improper but that she was totally unused to attentions of that sort from anyone, including herself. She didn't think about her hair. In a puzzled way, she said, "Perhaps I will."

Nor did Emily dress like a woman with much regard for herself. She wore practical, seersucker dresses and sensible, low shoes. Because her body had so little shape, no indentations (this must have been at least partly due to the back brace), I was surprised to notice that she had pretty, shapely legs. She wore little or no makeup on her sun- and wind-weathered face.

And what of Lawrence Farr, the North Carolina Presbyterian for whom Emily had left her people and her state? He was a small, precisely made man, with fine dark features. (Harriet looked very like him.) A lawyer, but widely read in literature, especially the English nineteenth century. He had a courtly manner, and sometimes a wicked tongue; melancholy eyes, and an odd, sudden, ratchety laugh. He looked ten years younger than Emily; the actual difference was less than two.

"Well," said Margot, settling into a Queen Anne chair—a new antique—on our porch one stifling hot July morning, "I heard some really interesting gossip about your friends."

Margot had met and admired Harriet, and Harriet liked her, too—Margot made Harriet laugh, and she praised Harriet's fine brown hair.

But on some instinct (I am not sure whose) the parents had not met. Very likely, Emily, with her Southern social antennae, had somehow sensed that this meeting would be a mistake.

That morning, Harriet and I were going on a picnic in the woods to the steep rocky side of Laurel Hill, but I forced myself to listen, or half listen, to Margot's story.

"Well, it seems that some years ago Lawrence Farr fell absolutely madly in love with a beautiful young girl—in fact, the orphaned daughter of a friend of his. Terribly romantic. Of course, she loved him, too, but he felt so awful and guilty that they never did anything about it."

I did not like this story much; it made me obscurely uncomfortable, and I think that at some point both Margot and I wondered why she was telling it. Was she pointing out imperfections in my chosen other family? But I asked, in Harriet's indifferent voice, "He never kissed her?"

"Well, maybe. I don't know. But of course everyone in town knew all about it, including Emily Farr. And with her back! Poor woman," Margot added somewhat piously but with real feeling, too.

I forgot the story readily at the time. For one thing, there was something unreal about anyone as old as Lawrence Farr "falling in love." But looking back to Emily's face, Emily looking at Lawrence, I can see that pained watchfulness of a woman who has been hurt, and by a man who could always hurt her again.

In those days, what struck me most about the Farrs was their extreme courtesy to each other—something I had not seen before. Never a harsh word. (Of course, I did not know then about couples who cannot afford a single harsh word.)

Possibly because of the element of danger (very slight—the slope was gentle), the roof over the front porch was one of the places Harriet and I liked to sit on warm summer nights when I was invited to stay over. There was a country silence, invaded at intervals by summer country sounds—the strangled croak of tree frogs from down in the glen; the crazy baying of a distant hound. There, in the heavy scent of roses, on the scratchy shingles, Harriet and I talked about sex.

"A girl I know told me that if you do it a lot your hips get very wide."

"My cousin Duncan says it makes boys strong if they do it."

"It hurts women a lot—especially at first. But I knew this girl from Santa Barbara, and she said that out there they say Filipinos can do it without hurting."

"Colored people do it a lot more than whites."

"Of course, they have all those babies. But in Boston so do Catholics!"

We are seized with hysteria. We laugh and laugh, so that Emily hears and calls up to us, "Girls, why haven't you-all gone to bed?" But her voice is warm and amused—she likes having us laughing up there.

And Emily liked my enthusiasm for lemon cake. She teased me about the amounts of it I could eat, and she continued to keep me supplied. She was not herself much of a cook—their maid, a young black girl named Evelyn, did most of the cooking.

Once, but only once, I saw the genteel and opaque surface of that family shattered—saw those three people suddenly in violent opposition to each other, like shards of splintered glass. (But what I have forgotten is the cause—what brought about that terrible explosion?)

The four of us, as so often, were seated at lunch. Emily was at what seemed to be the head of the table. At her right hand was the small silver bell that summoned Evelyn to clear, or to bring a new course. Harriet and I across from each other, Lawrence across from Emily. (There was always a tentativeness about Lawrence's posture. He could have been an honored guest, or a spoiled and favorite child.) We were talking in an easy way. I have a vivid recollection only of words that began to career and gather momentum, to go out of control. Of voices raised. Then Harriet rushes from the room. Emily's face reddens dangerously, the corners of her mouth twitch downward and Lawrence, in an exquisitely icy voice, begins to lecture me on the virtues of reading Trollope. I am supposed to help him pretend that nothing has happened, but I can hardly hear what he is saying. I am in shock.

That sudden unleashing of violence, that exposed depth of terrible emotions might have suggested to me that the Farrs were not quite as I had imagined them, not the impeccable family in my mind—but it did not. I was simply and terribly—and selfishly—upset, and hugely relieved when it all seemed to have passed over.

.   .   .

During that summer, the Ouija board spoke only gibberish to Margot, or it answered direct questions with repeated evasions:

"Will I ever see Johnny Kilgore again, in this life?"

"Yes no perhaps."

"Honey, that means you've got no further need of the board, not right now. You've got to think everything out with your own heart and instincts," Dolly said.

Margot seemed to take her advice. She resolutely put the board away, and she wrote to Johnny that she wanted a divorce.

I had begun to notice that these days, on these sultry August nights, Margot and Dolly were frequently joined on their small excursions by a man named Larry—a jolly, red-faced man who was in real estate and who reminded me considerably of my father.

I said as much to Margot, and was surprised at her furious reaction. "They could not be more different, they are altogether opposite. Larry is a Southern gentleman. You just don't pay any attention to anyone but those Farrs."

A word about Margot's quite understandable jealousy of the Farrs. Much later in my life, when I was unreasonably upset at the attachment of one of my own daughters to another family (unreasonable because her chosen group were all talented musicians, as she was), a wise friend told me that we all could use more than one set of parents—our relations with the original set are too intense, and need dissipating. But no one, certainly not silly Dolly, was around to comfort Margot with this wisdom.

The summer raced on. ("Not without dust and heat," Lawrence several times remarked, in his private ironic voice.) The roses wilted on the roof and on the banks next to the road. The creek dwindled, and beside it honeysuckle leaves lay limply on the vines. For weeks, there was no rain, and then, one afternoon, there came a dark torrential thunderstorm. Harriet and I sat on the side porch and watched its violent start— the black clouds seeming to rise from the horizon, the cracking, jagged streaks of lightning, the heavy, welcome rain. And, later, the clean smell of leaves and grass and damp earth.

Knowing that Margot would be frightened, I thought of calling her, and then remembered that she would not talk on the phone during storms. And that night she told me, "The phone rang and rang, but I didn't think it was you, somehow."

"No."

"I had the craziest idea that it was Johnny. Be just like him to pick the middle of a storm for a phone call."

"There might not have been a storm in New Orleans."

But it turned out that Margot was right.

The next day, when I rode up to the Farrs' on my bike, Emily was sitting out in the grass where I had first seen her. I went and squatted beside her there. I thought she looked old and sad, and partly to cheer her I said, "You grow the most beautiful flowers I've ever seen."

She sighed, instead of smiling as she usually did. She said, "I seem to have turned into a gardener. When I was a girl, I imagined that I would grow up to be a writer, a novelist, and that I would have at least four children. Instead, I grow flowers and write book reviews."

I was not interested in children. "You never wrote a novel?"

She smiled unhappily. "No. I think I was afraid that I wouldn't come up to Trollope. I married rather young, you know."

And at that moment Lawrence came out of the house, immaculate in white flannels.

He greeted me, and said to Emily, "My dear, I find that I have some rather late appointments, in Hillsboro. You won't wait dinner if I'm a trifle late?"

(Of course she would; she always did.)

"No. Have a good time," she said, and she gave him the anxious look that I had come to recognize as the way she looked at Lawrence.

Soon after that, a lot happened very fast. Margot wrote to Johnny (again) that she wanted a divorce, that she intended to marry Larry. (I wonder if this was ever true.) Johnny telephoned—not once but several times. He told her that she was crazy, that he had a great job with some shipbuilders near San Francisco—a defense contract. He would come to get us, and we would all move out there. Margot agreed. We would make a new life. (Of course, we never knew what happened to the girl.)

I was not as sad about leaving the Farrs and that house, that town, those woods as I was to be later, looking back. I was excited about San Francisco, and I vaguely imagined that someday I would come back and that we would all see each other again. Like parting lovers, Harriet and I promised to write each other every day.

And for quite a while we did write several times a week. I wrote about San Francisco—how beautiful it was: the hills and pastel houses, the sea. How I wished that she could see it. She wrote about school and friends. She described solitary bike rides to places we had been. She told me what she was reading.

In high school, our correspondence became more generalized, Responding perhaps to the adolescent mores of the early nineteen-forties, we wrote about boys and parties; we even competed in making ourselves sound "popular." The truth (my truth) was that I was some-times popular, often not. I had, in fact, a stormy adolescence. And at that time I developed what was to be a long-lasting habit. As I reviewed a sit-uation in which I had been ill-advised or impulsive, I would re-enact the whole scene in my mind with Harriet in my own role—Harriet, cool and controlled, more intelligent, prettier. Even more than I wanted to see her again, I wanted to *be* Harriet.

Johnny and Margot fought a lot and stayed together, and gradually a sort of comradeship developed between them in our small house on Russian Hill.

I went to Stanford, where I half-heartedly studied history. Harriet was at Radcliffe, studying American literature, writing poetry.

We lost touch with each other.

Margot, however, kept up with her old friend Dolly, by means of Christmas cards and Easter notes, and Margot thus heard a remarkable piece of news about Emily Farr. Emily "up and left Lawrence without so much as a by-your-leave," said Dolly, and went to Washington, D.C., to work in the Folger Library. This news made me smile all day. I was so proud of Emily. And I imagined that Lawrence would amuse himself, that they would both be happier apart.

By accident, I married well—that is to say, a man whom I still like and enjoy. Four daughters came at uncalculated intervals, and each is remarkably unlike her sisters. I named one Harriet, although she seems to have my untidy character.

From time to time, over the years, I would see a poem by Harriet Farr, and I always thought it was marvelous, and I meant to write her. But I distrusted my reaction. I had been (I was) so deeply fond of Harriet

(Emily, Lawrence, that house and land) and besides, what would I say—"I think your poem is marvelous"? (I have since learned that this is neither an inadequate nor in unwelcome thing to say to writers.) Of course, the true reason for not writing was that there was too much to say.

Dolly wrote to Margot that Lawrence was drinking "all over the place." He was not happier without Emily. Harriet, Dolly said, was traveling a lot. She married several times and had no children. Lawrence developed emphysema, and was in such bad shape that Emily quit her job and came back to take care of him—whether because of feelings of guilt or duty or possibly affection, I didn't know. He died, lingeringly and miserably, and Emily, too, died, a few years later—at least partly from exhaustion, I would imagine.

Then, at last, I did write Harriet, in care of the magazine in which I had last seen a poem of hers. I wrote a clumsy, gusty letter, much too long, about shared pasts, landscapes, the creek. All that. And as soon as I had mailed it I began mentally rewriting, seeking more elegant prose.

When for a long time I didn't hear from Harriet, I felt worse and worse, cumbersome, misplaced—as too often in life I had felt before. It did not occur to me that an infrequently staffed magazine could be at fault.

Months later, her letter came—from Rome, where she was then living. Alone, I gathered. She said that she was writing it at the moment of receiving mine. It was a long, emotional and very moving letter, out of character for the Harriet that I remembered (or had invented).

She said, in part: "It was really strange, all that time when Lawrence was dying, and God! so long! and as though 'dying' were all that he was doing—Emily, too, although we didn't know that—all that time the picture that moved me most, in my mind, that moved me to tears, was not of Lawrence and Emily but of you and me. On our bikes at the top of the hill outside our house. Going somewhere. And I first thought that that picture simply symbolized something irretrievable, the lost and irrecoverable past, as Lawrence and Emily would be lost. And I'm sure that was partly it.

"But they were so extremely fond of you—in fact, you were a rare area of agreement. They missed you, and they talked about you for years.

It's a wonder that I wasn't jealous, and I think I wasn't only because I felt included in their affection for you. They liked me best with you.

"Another way to say this would be to say that we were all three a little less crazy and isolated with you around, and, God knows, happier."

An amazing letter, I thought. It was enough to make me take a long look at my whole life, and to find some new colors there.

A postscript: I showed Harriet's letter to my husband and he said, "How odd. She sounds so much like you."

For Good

"How I hate California! God, no one will ever know how much I hate it here," cries out Pauline Field, a once-famous abstract-expressionist painter. It is lunchtime on a ferociously cold Sunday late in June—in a beach house near San Francisco: Pauline's house—and her lunch party that is assembled there in her enclosed patio, drinking sangrias. Almost no one (in fact only one person) pays any attention to Pauline, who tends to speak in an exaggerated way. She is a huge strong woman, dressed outrageously in pink; she has wild white hair and consuming dark-brown eyes. It is possible that she has made this impassioned complaint before.

The house is some three or four years old; those years (the years, incidentally, of Pauline's most recent marriage) and the relentless wind have almost silvered the shingled walls, and beach grass has grown up through the slats of the planked-over patio, where now all those guests, twenty or so, are standing with their cold fruity drinks, their backs to the wind and to the sea. The drive home, over steep winding hills and beside great wooded canyons, will be somewhat dangerous even for a sober driver; these weak drinks are the inspiration of Pauline's (third) husband, Stephen, a cautious former alcoholic.

The one person who paid attention to Pauline is also the only person who is looking out to the churning gray sea: a young girl, about twelve, Nell Ashbury, from New York; she is visiting her father and her stepmother. She listened to Pauline because her hostess has come across to her more vividly than any of the other adults present (discounting her father, Jason Ashbury, the writer, about whom she has the most passionate curiosity, not knowing him well at all). Pauline, to Nell, is more *present* than anyone else there. Her mother's Village circle includes a lot of writers, editors, agents; Nell is tired of literary people, who all talk too much. Perhaps she herself will be a painter, like Pauline? And Pauline listens; so many grown-ups (her mother's writers) ask questions and then don't wait to hear the answer. Pauline is kind; she has in fact wrapped reed-thin Nell in an old Irish sweater of her own, in which the girl now sits, enveloped—it comes down to her knees—looking out across a grass-tufted rise of sand to the turbulent sea, and thinking, Pacific?

But at Pauline's words—"I hate California"—Nell has turned to listen, and it occurs to her that she does not like it here much either; it is terribly windy and cold, not at all like a summer day at a real beach, not like Crane's Beach, at Ipswich, where she and her mother go for the month of August every summer. Nell has a tendency to take people at their word (she believes that Pauline hates California), and partly because she is so young, she believes that what is said is meant, for good.

Nell also (half-consciously) understands Pauline to mean that she does not like her party, her guests—and possibly she does not like her husband, the blond man, rather short, who is pouring out the reddish drinks.

"It's not a place that's fit for human beings," declaims Pauline, who has not had a show of her paintings for years, although she still works, if spasmodically, and who has unhappily become used to inattention. "Perhaps mountain lions," she continues. "Feel that wind, in *June.*"

Pauline's size is a further reason for Nell's instinct about her not liking her husband. "Women who hate their husbands always put on weight," Nell's mother has said, herself purposefully thin (and unremarried), and Nell has as yet found no evidence against this theory. Her stepmother, who visibly "adores" her father, is even trimmer than Nell's mother is. Given the ten years or so difference in their ages, they look rather alike, Nell thinks—and would of course not say to either of them. Brown-skinned blondes, blue-eyed, rather athletic. What her father likes?

In fact Nell has seen rather few fat women among the friends of either parent, and this too gives Pauline a certain interest: what *nerve,* to be so large. And her size is somehow sexy, all that energetic flesh. The other guests look vaguely alike and are dressed quite similarly: they are in stylishly good shape; they wear pants and expensive old sweaters.

Nell herself is physically a curious replica of her father: sandy-haired, with light-gray eyes. Everyone has remarked on the likeness, and Nell has sometimes wondered if this is one thing that makes him uneasy with her: it must be strange for Jason to see his coloring, his own long nose and impossibly high brow on a girl, a thin young girl. Sometimes Nell catches him staring at her in an unnerved way, and he seems not to know what to say to her. The phrase "pale imitation" has unfortunately stuck in her mind. They were divorced so long ago, Jason and her mother, when Nell was a baby and Jason a hugely successful novelist. On the heels of his greatest success—that rarity, a book that six or eight superior critics praised and that several hundred thousand people bought—he stopped writing entirely. He has lived a lot in Italy, in southern France and Greece.

Although she is the one complaining about the weather, Pauline has not dressed to defend herself from it: the long-sleeved pink cotton smock from which her spatulate-fingered, muscular brown hands extend is thin ("Fat women always love bright colors," Nell's mother has said, safe in navy or black); she is barefoot, and sand adheres to her large brown feet. She says, "I can't bear this wind!"

"Well, Pauline," says Jason, in his glancing, nonserious way that no one seems to know how to take (*is* he serious?), "you could chuck it all and run off to some warmer clime."

So, Nell thinks, he too has been listening to Pauline?

Pauline's great eyes flash across him; she says, "I just may."

But her husband, blond Stephen, has spoken much more loudly than she. "Pauline would rather stick around and make dramatic complaints," he says, sounding smug with his knowledge (and possession?) of Pauline.

Obviously these two men, Nell's father and Stephen, do not like each other much, and Nell begins to regard the party with slightly more interest. Just possibly something could happen? In general, her parents' friends do not make scenes, just talk, and she had sometimes thought that it would be more fun if they did.

"In fact I might join you there, wherever," Jason continues, as though Stephen had not spoken. "It is awfully goddam cold." He turns to his small blond wife. "And how would you like that, my love?"

Neither what he said nor his look has been clear: did he mean that he would take his wife or leave her there in the California cold? Nell's stepmother visibly does not know, but in a calm, controlled way she says,

"Well, in the meantime I think I'll go inside. It *is* terribly cold." She starts in, and everyone begins to follow her, as though an excuse or perhaps a leader was needed.

Jason laughs, as Nell wonders why: At what private joke?

"I need help!" wildly says Pauline as people are trooping past her into the house, and then, in a more rational way, she addresses Nell—who has taken her seriously and is staring in dismay. "Nell, do come in the kitchen with me. You look as though you were good at sorting things out."

The kitchen is farther away and thus more separate from the living room than is usual in the houses Nell has known. She and Pauline walk down a hall, past bedrooms, to what is the largest room in the house: a huge square, two stories high, with a backward-looking view of steep, ravined hills, all shades and shapes and varieties of green, here and there patched with sunlight, in other areas cloud-darkened, almost black. "There's only one painter out here who can do that," says Pauline (sadly? enviously? Nell can't tell). "I've never tried. Perhaps I should? This is my favorite room," she says. "I like to be alone here. I can't bear people who come out to try to help me—I can't be helped." She laughs, a short harsh definite sound. "Of course I don't mean you, little Nell—I asked you in." And Nell is then given a large handful of silver which, for a moment, she is afraid that she is supposed to polish; this has not been done for some time.

"Just sort it out into little piles," instructs Pauline. "You know, to be wrapped in a napkin. Something for everyone. And now tell me all about your mother."

"She's fine," Nell automatically says, and then asks, "Did you know her?"

"Oh, yes," says Pauline, sounding bored. "We all used to know each other. But that was terribly long ago. In the forties, in fact. Of course we were terribly young."

The *forties*. Wanting to know more (what was everyone like then? what was her father like?), Nell has understood that Pauline does not want to answer questions—she will talk more or less to herself.

Pauline is drinking vodka from a wineglass. "God, how I hate sangria," she abruptly says, in much her tone of hating California. And then she asks, "Are you very tired of conversations about why your father doesn't write anymore?"

Nell hesitates, at a loss. "No, we don't talk about that much," she honestly says, at last.

"Oh, I suppose not. Your mother would have lost interest, lucky for her. Out here it's quite a favorite topic, among his friends. That's partly what I mean about California. It's as vacuous as it is windy, in fact it's a chilly windbag of a place." And she laughs, in a pleased way—she will clearly say this again. "The truth is," she then continues, "Jason is scared. His last book was so good that it scared him to death, almost."

Nell smiles politely. She is the sort of child to whom adults often talk, perhaps in some (erroneous) belief that innocence prevents her understanding. She is by now used to nearly incomprehensible remarks that later make considerable sense, and so now she tucks away this notion of California, and of her father's work. And she wonders: Is Pauline talking about herself?

The salad that Pauline is making, in a huge wooden bowl on the large butcher-block table, also looks (at first) familiar to Nell: several kinds of lettuce, thinly sliced onion, parsley. But then other things from dishes in the giant refrigerator are added: fish-smelling things, pink, and indistinguishable in shape. "Mussels and clams," Pauline says. "*Fruits de mer.* They'll absolutely hate it. Everyone except your father. He loves all this stuff too."

Did Pauline once love her father? Did they have an affair, back in the forties? This thought, or question, has been slowly forming in Nell's mind. Nell's mother and her friends talk a lot about people having affairs, which Nell takes to mean making out with someone you're not married to. She is very interested, although she herself has so far only observed other kids at parties smoking grass, making out.

And she of course enjoys being talked to by adults, but only up to a point. She does not like it—is in fact frightened—when voices begin to slur, when eyes grow vague and at the same time wild. She now with alarm observes the onset of these symptoms in Pauline, as Pauline says, staring at Nell too intently, "If I could only get thin again, then I could work. It's all this fat that holds me."

Nell can no more imagine being fat than she can being dead, and she has only the vaguest ideas about work. But she has, still, a strong sense that Pauline even semi-drunk is someone to whom she should pay attention.

Pauline says, "The really important thing is never to marry."

Well, Nell had decided that for herself already, years ago.

Just then a dark man whom Nell has not much noticed before comes into the room, and Pauline embraces him in a way that Nell has seen before: grown-ups in a kitchen (usually) lurching at each other.

Pauline croons, "Ah, my long-lost love, why couldn't everything last?"

There are tears in her manic eyes that to Nell look real, but the man seems not to take them seriously. He pats her shoulder in a dismissing way; he even says, *"There,"* and he goes back out, looking embarrassed.

Pauline gives Nell a sober, calculating look of complicity; was she then pretending with that man to be drunk, or much drunker than she is, in order to make fun of him? What will she do next? Nell fully believes in Pauline's desperation.

Now Pauline goes over to the oven, and efficiently (undrunkenly) with asbestos gloves she removes a huge steaming garlic-smelling casserole. This and the salad and the napkin-wrapped silver are placed on a wire-wheeled cart, and propelled into the living room. Nell follows at a little distance in her wake.

People line up and help themselves. Not sure what to do, or where to be, Nell is surprised to see her father coming toward her, carrying two full plates, saying, "Come on, let's go over there."

And then, when they are seated, in a tone unusual for him, with her, he says, "I hope this isn't too bad a party for you? I didn't know there'd be so many people. And somehow I wanted you to meet Pauline. Anyway, sometimes it's easier to talk in the middle of a crowd, have you noticed that yet? And we haven't had much of a chance to talk, have we? Have I seemed preoccupied? The thing is—please, you won't mention this to anyone? I'm sure you won't. I wanted to tell you—"

Nell is to find that life often provides too much at once: just as her heart jumps with pleasure at her father's telling her something important, in confidence—just at that crucial moment they both hear Pauline shouting from across the room; they see Pauline wildly waving her arms—Pauline making a scene. "Well, goodbye, one and all. I'm off for a walk. Don't eat and run—I'll be gone for hours. Unless—would anyone like to come along?" There is a terrible pause, especially terrible for Nell, who believes that the invitation, or summons, was for her—who is frozen in her corner. "Well, then, O.K. Sorry I asked." A door is slammed, and Pauline is gone.

Nell looks at her father, and she sees her own feelings apparent on his face, written across his features so similar to her own: Jason looks stricken, deeply shocked, as she is. And Nell is aware of real panic: a friend of her mother's, a woman writer who often drank too much, committed suicide at last. What will happen to Pauline? Will she plunge drunkenly into that cold bleak ocean, that terrible Pacific?

She looks questioningly at her father, who only says, *"Well,"* in an exhausted way.

Unable not to, Nell asks him, "You wanted to tell me—"

He looks at her forgetfully. "Oh, just a novel. I've begun one."

Naturally enough, people do eat and run. In a flustered way Stephen serves coffee, which everyone seems to gulp, and then there is a general movement toward cars.

The drive home, to Nell, does not seem dangerous; she trusts her father's skill at the wheel. And the scenery is extraordinary: once they have left the beach, and the now golden glimpses of the sea, they climb steeply into what could be a rain forest, dense variegated vegetation, trees, giant ferns—into what must have been the view from Pauline's kitchen, and Nell remembers what Pauline said about its being a country for mountain lions. It smells of bay leaves.

Her stepmother is talking about Pauline. "Well, I never saw drink hit her quite like that. She has put on weight, hasn't she? Anyway, she always manages to put out a great lunch. Although I could have done without all those bits of seafood in the salad. I wonder why she ever married Stephen. She seems to fall in love with giants and marry pygmies. What do you suppose struck her, finally? Three ex-lovers all suddenly at the same party?"

Nell finds all this vaguely disturbing, less vaguely unpleasant. She is still worried about Pauline; why is no one else worried?

Her father makes a sound that for him is completely in character, that is brief and impossible to read. And Nell is suddenly aware of a rush of the most intense and private love for him.

A month or so later Nell and her mother are sitting on the beach—Crane's Beach, at Ipswich. A perfect beach, of fine white silk sand that squeaks underfoot. Dunes, grass. And a perfect hot still day. From time to time Nell has been thinking of Pauline. (She has gathered that nothing horrible happened to her; someone would have said.) Now she wonders if this was the way Pauline thought a beach should be, and that summers should produce this sort of day? Yes, probably, she decides, and then she experiences again a tiny pang of guilt-regret at not having gone for that walk with Pauline, Pauline leaving her own party, so furiously. Although, of course, it was impossible at the time; she was talking to her father.

These days Nell's mother is extremely happy, almost giddily so: a man she knows, in fact an old family friend, is getting a divorce, and he and Nell's mother are going to get married. He works for a firm that is moving to Houston, and that is where they will all live. Houston, Texas. "We can take wonderful trips to Mexico, and New Orleans," her mother has said, with her new young laugh. Nell wonders about parties in Houston, and what will happen to her there.

The sea is very calm today; the barest waves, translucent, lap the sand, where at the edge, on their crazy useless-looking legs, the sandpipers skitter past. And overhead white gulls wheel and dip, as though drunk with sunlight. Pauline would love it here, is what at that moment Nell thinks. She is also thinking that there are only about four more months until Christmas, which is when she can go to visit her father again. It has been agreed that she can now go more often.

Her mother, reading letters beside Nell on the sand, suddenly laughs. Nell has seen that this one is from her father, whose letters to his former wife do not usually make her laugh. "Well," her mother says, "everyone seems to be breaking up these days." (Does she mean Nell's father? Will she have a new stepmother? This quick notion is enough to make Nell queasy for an instant as her mother reads on.) "You met Pauline Field, didn't you, darling? Well, she's up and left poor old Stephen, and she's gone off to San Miguel de Allende, to study painting there."

Nell makes an ambiguous noise, not unlike her father's noncommittal sound. Then she asks, "That's probably good for her to do, isn't it?"

"I suppose. She was quite terrific, in her way." Nell's mother adds, "I never understood that marriage to Stephen. Or any of her marriages, for that matter."

Nell says what she has not said before: "She was sort of upset at her party that we went to. *She* said"—they both know that this "she" refers to Nell's stepmother—"something about three ex-lovers at the same party. Can a husband be counted as an ex-lover?"

Her mother laughs a lot. "Darling, what a marvelous question. Well, actually one of them would of course have been Jason. They had a tremendous love affair, just before me. Sometimes I thought he'd never get over it, and I used to wish he'd married her. Instead of me. Maybe he would have gone on writing, or at least got her out of his system."

Digesting this news, which is not news at all, but something deeply known or felt before, Nell experiences a kind of gladness. Things seem to fit, or to have sorted themselves out, after all.

And, later still, although she has been told that San Miguel is in the middle of Mexico, nowhere near the coast, and although she has not been told that her father and stepmother are separating, what she imagines is—Jason and Pauline (a Pauline brown and thin, renewed) on a bright hot windless tropical beach. For good.

Snow

On a trail high up in the California Sierra, between heavy smooth white snowbanks, four people on cross-country skis form a straggling line. A man and three women: Graham, dark and good-looking, a San Francisco architect, who is originally from Georgia; Carol, his girlfriend, a gray-eyed blonde, a florist; Susannah, daughter of Graham, dark and fat and now living in Venice, California; and, quite a way behind Susannah, tall thin Rose, Susannah's friend and lover. Susannah and Rose both have film-related jobs—Graham has never been quite sure what they do.

Graham and Carol both wear smart cross-country outfits: knickers and Norwegian wool stockings. The younger women are in jeans and heavy sweaters. And actually, despite the bright cold look of so much snow, this April day is warm, and the sky is a lovely spring blue, reflected in distant small lakes, just visible, at intervals.

Graham is by far the best skier of the four, a natural; he does anything athletic easily. He strides and glides along, hardly aware of what he is doing, except for a sense of physical well-being. However, just now he is cursing himself for having dreamed up this weekend, renting an unknown house in Alpine Meadows, near Lake Tahoe, even for bringing these women together. He had hoped for a diversion from a situation that could be tricky, difficult: a visit from Susannah, who was bringing Rose, whom he had previously been told about but had not met. Well, skiing was a diversion, but what in God's name would they all do tonight? Or talk about? And why had he wanted to get them together anyway? He wasn't all that serious about Carol (was he?); why introduce her to his daughter? And why did he have to meet Rose?

Carol is a fair skier, although she doesn't like it much: it takes all her breath. At the moment, with the part of her mind that is not concentrated on skiing, she is thinking that although Graham is smarter than most of the men she knows, talented and successful, and really nice as well, she is tired of going out with men who don't *see* her, don't know who she is. That's partly her fault, she knows; she lies about her age and dyes her hair, and she *never* mentions the daughter in Vallejo, put out for adoption when Carol was fifteen (she would be almost twenty now, almost as old as Graham's girl, this unfriendly fat Susannah). But sometimes Carol would like to say to the men she knows, Look, I'm thirty-five, and in some ways my life has been terrible—being blond and pretty doesn't save you from anything.

But, being more fair-minded than given to self-pity, next Carol thinks, Well, as far as that goes Graham didn't tell me much about his girl, either, and for all I know mine is that way, too. So many of them are, these days.

How can he possibly be so dumb, Susannah is passionately thinking, of her father. And the fact that she has asked that question hundreds of times in her life does not diminish its intensity or the accompanying pain. He doesn't understand anything, she wildly, silently screams. Stupid, straight blondes: *a florist. Skiing.* How could he think that I . . . that Rose . . . ?

Then, thinking of Rose in a more immediate way, she remembers that Rose has hardly skied before—just a couple of times in Vermont, where she comes from. In the almost noon sun Susannah stops to wait for Rose, halfheartedly aware of the lakes, just now in view, and the smell of pines, as sweat collects under her heavy breasts, slides down her ribs.

Far behind them all, and terrified of everything, Rose moves along with stiffened desperation. Her ankles, her calves, her thighs, her lower back are all tight with dread. Snow is stuck to the bottoms of her skis, she knows—she can hardly move them—but she doesn't dare stop. She will fall, break something, get lost. And everyone will hate her, even Susannah.

Suddenly, like a gift to a man in his time of need, just ahead of Graham there appears a lovely open glade, to one side of the trail. Two huge heavy trees have fallen there, at right angles to each other; at the far side of the open space runs a brook, darkly glistening over small smooth rocks. High overhead a wind sings through the pines, in the brilliant sunlight.

It is perfect, a perfect picnic place, and it is just now time for lunch. Graham is hungry; he decides that hunger is what has been unsettling him. He gets out of his skis in an instant, and he has just found a smooth, level stump for the knapsack, a natural table, when Carol skis up—out of breath, not looking happy.

But at the sight of that place she instantly smiles. She says, "Oh, how perfect! Graham, it's beautiful." Her gray eyes praise him, and the warmth of her voice. "Even benches to sit on. Graham, what a perfect Southern host you are." She laughs in a pleased, cheered-up way, and bends to unclip her skis. But something is wrong, and they stick. Graham comes over to help. He gets her out easily; he takes her hand and lightly he kisses her mouth, and then they both go over and start removing food from the knapsack, spreading it out.

"Two bottles of wine. Lord, we'll all get plastered." Carol laughs again, as she sets up the tall green bottles in a deep patch of snow.

Graham laughs, too, just then very happy with her, although he is also feeling the familiar apprehension that any approach of his daughter brings on: *will* Susannah like what he has done, will she approve of him, ever? He looks at his watch and he says to Carol, "I wonder if they're okay. Rose is pretty new on skis. I wonder . . ."

But there they are, Susannah and Rose. They have both taken off their skis and are walking along the side of the trail, carrying the skis on their shoulders, Susannah's neatly together, Rose's at a clumsy, difficult angle. There are snowflakes in Susannah's dark-brown hair—hair like Graham's. Rose's hair is light, dirty blond; she is not even pretty, Graham has unkindly thought. At the moment they both look exhausted and miserable.

In a slow, tired way, not speaking, the two girls lean their skis and poles against a tree; they turn toward Graham and Carol, and then, seemingly on a single impulse, they stop and look around. And with a wide smile Susannah says, "Christ, Dad, it's just beautiful. It's great."

Rose looks toward the spread of food. "Oh, roast chicken. That's my favorite thing." These are the first nice words she has said to Graham. (Good manners are not a strong suit of Rose's, he has observed, in an interior, Southern voice.)

He has indeed provided a superior lunch, as well as the lovely place—his discovery. Besides the chicken, there are cherry tomatoes (called love apples where Graham comes from, in Georgia), cheese (Jack and cheddar), Triscuits and oranges and chocolate. And the nice cold dry white wine. They all eat and drink a lot, and they talk eagerly about how good it all is, how beautiful the place where they are. The sky, the trees, the running brook.

Susannah even asks Carol about her work, in a polite, interested way that Graham has not heard from her for years. "Do you have to get up early and go to the flower mart every morning?" Susannah asks.

"No, but I used to, and really that was more fun—getting out so early, all those nice fresh smells. Now there's a boy I hire to do all that, and I'm pretty busy making arrangements."

"Oh, arrangements," says Rose, disparagingly.

Carol laughs. "Me, too, I hate them. I just try to make them as nice as I can, and the money I get is really good."

Both Rose and Susannah regard Carol in an agreeing, respectful way. For a moment Graham is surprised: these kids respecting money? Then he remembers that this is the seventies: women are supposed to earn money, it's good for them.

The main thing, though, is what a good time they all have together. Graham even finds Rose looking at him with a small, shy smile. He offers her more wine, which she accepts—another smile as he pours it out for her. And he thinks, Well, of course it's tough on her, too, meeting me. Poor girl, I'm sure she's doing the best she can.

"You all really like it down there in Hollywood?" he asks the two girls, and he notes that his voice is much more Southern than usual; maybe the wine.

"Universal City," Susannah corrects him, but she gives a serious answer. "I love it. There's this neat woman in the cutting room, and she knows I'm interested, so she lets me come in and look at the rushes, and hear them talk about what has to go. I'm really learning. It's great."

And Rose: "There's so many really exciting people around."

At that moment they both look so young, so enviably involved in their work, so happy, that Graham thinks, Well, really, why not?

Occasionally the wind will move a branch from a nearby tree and some snow will sift down, through sunlight. The sky seems a deeper blue than when they first came to this glade, a pure azure. The brook gurgles more loudly, and the sun is very hot.

And then they are all through with lunch; they have finished off the wine, and it is time to go.

They put on their skis, and they set off again, in the same order in which they began the day.

For no good reason, as he glides along, striding through snow in the early California afternoon, the heat, Graham is suddenly, sharply visited by a painful memory of the childhood of Susannah. He remembers a ferociously hot summer night in Atlanta, when he and his former wife, mother of Susannah, had quarreled all through suppertime, and had finally got Susannah off to bed; she must have been about two. But she kept getting up again, screaming for her bottle, her Teddy bear, a sand-wich. Her mother and Graham took turns going in to her, and then finally, about three in the morning, Graham picked her up and smacked her bottom, very hard; he can remember the sting on his hand—and good Christ, what a thing to do to a little baby. No wonder she is as she is; he probably frightened her right then, for good. Not to mention all the other times he got mad and just yelled at her—or his love affairs, the move to San Francisco, the divorce, more love affairs.

If only she were two right now, he desperately thinks, he could change everything; he could give her a stable, loving father. Now he has a nice house on Russian Hill; he is a successful man; he could give her— anything.

Then his mind painfully reverses itself and he thinks, But I was a loving father, most of the time. Susannah's got no real cause to be the way she is. Lots of girls—most girls—come out all right. At that overheated moment he feels that his heart will truly break. It is more than I can stand, he thinks; why do I have to?

Carol's problem is simply a physical one: a headache. But she never has headaches, and this one is especially severe; for the first time she knows exactly what her mother meant by "splitting headache." Is she going to get more and more like her mother as she herself ages? Could she be having an early menopause, beginning with migraines? She could die, the pain is so sharp. She could die, and would anyone care much, really? She's *lonely.*

Susannah is absorbed in the problem of Rose, who keeps falling down. Almost every time Susannah looks back, there is Rose, fallen in the snow. Susannah smiles at her encouragingly, and sometimes she calls back, "You're okay?" She knows that Rose would not like it if she actually skied back to her and helped her up; Rose has that ferocious Vermont Yankee pride, difficult in a fragile frightened woman.

It is breezier now than earlier in the morning, and somewhat cooler. Whenever Susannah stops, stands still and waits for Rose, she is aware of her own wind-chilled sweat, and she worries, thinking of Rose, of wet and cold. Last winter Rose had a terrible, prolonged bout of flu, a racking cough.

Talking over their "relationship," at times Susannah and Rose have (somewhat jokingly) concluded that there certainly are elements of mothering within it; in many ways Susannah takes care of Rose. She is stronger—that is simply true. Now for the first time it occurs to Susannah (wryly, her style is wry) that she is somewhat fatherly with Rose, too: the sometimes stern guardian, the protector. And she thinks, Actually, Graham wasn't all that bad with me; I've been rough on him. Look at the example he set me: I work hard, and I care about my work, the way he does. And he taught me to ski, come to think of it. I should thank him, sometime, somehow, for some of it.

Rose is falling, falling, again and again, and oh Christ, how much she hates it—hates her helplessness, hates the horrible snow, the cold wet. Drinking all that wine at lunchtime, in the pretty glade, the sunlight, she had thought that wine would make her brave; she knows her main problem to be fear—no confidence and hence no balance. But the wine, and the sun, and sheer fatigue have destroyed whatever equilibrium she had, so that all she can do is fall, fall miserably, and each time the snow is colder and it is harder for her to get up.

Therefore, they are all extremely glad when, finally, they are out of their skis and off the trail and at last back in their house, in Alpine Meadows. It is small—two tiny, juxtaposed bedrooms—but the living room is pleasant: it looks out to steeply wooded, snowy slopes. Even more pleasant at the moment is the fact that the hot-water supply is vast; there is enough for deep baths for everyone, and then they will all have much-needed before-dinner naps.

Carol gets the first bath, and then, in turn, the two younger women. Graham last. All three women have left a tidy room, a clean tub, he happily notices, and the steamy air smells vaguely sweet, of something perfumed, feminine. Luxuriating in his own full, hot tub, he thinks tenderly, in a general way, of women, how warm and sexual they are, more often than not, how frequently intelligent and kind. And then he wonders what he has not quite, ever, put into words before: what is it that women do, women together? What ever could they do that they couldn't do with men, and *why*?

However, these questions are much less urgent and less painful than most of his musings along those lines; he simply wonders.

In their bedroom, disappointingly, Carol is already fast asleep. He has not seen her actually sleeping before; she is always first awake when he stays over at her place. Now she looks so drained, so entirely exhausted, with one hand protectively across her eyes, that he is touched. Carefully, so as not to wake her, he slips in beside her, and in minutes he, too, is sound asleep.

Graham has planned and shopped for their dinner, which he intends to cook. He likes to cook, and does it well, but in his bachelor life he has done it less and less, perhaps because he and most of the women he meets tend to shy off from such domestic encounters. Somehow the implication of cooking *for* anyone has become alarming, more so than making love to them. But tonight Graham happily prepares to make pork chops with milk gravy and mashed potatoes, green peas, an apple-and-nut salad and cherry pie (from a bakery, to be heated). A down-home meal, for his girlfriend, and his daughter, and her friend.

From the kitchen, which is at one end of the living room, he can hear the pleasant sounds of the three women's voices, in amiable conversation, as he blends butter and flour in the pan in which he has browned the chops, and begins to add hot milk. And then he notices a change in the tone of those voices: what was gentle and soft has gone shrill, strident—the sounds of a quarrel. He hates the thought of women fighting; it is almost frightening, and, of course, he is anxious for this particular group to get along, if only for the weekend.

He had meant, at just that moment, to go in and see if anyone wanted another glass of wine; dinner is almost ready. And so, reluctantly he does; he gets into the living room just in time to hear Rose say, in a shakily loud voice, "No one who hasn't actually experienced rape can have the least idea what it's like."

Such a desperately serious sentence could have sounded ludicrous, but it does not. Graham is horrified; he thinks, Ah, poor girl, poor Rose. Jesus, *raped.* It is a crime that he absolutely cannot imagine.

In a calm, conciliatory way, Susannah says to Carol, "You see, Rose actually was raped, when she was very young, and it was terrible for her—"

Surprisingly, Carol reacts almost with anger. "Of course it's terrible, but you kids think you're the only ones things happen to. I got pregnant when I was fifteen, and I had it, a girl, and I put her out for adoption." Seeming to have just now noticed Graham, she addresses him in a low, defiant, scolding voice. "And I'm not thirty. I'm thirty-five."

Graham has no idea, really, of what to do, but he is aware of strong feelings that lead him to Carol. He goes over and puts his arms around her. Behind him he hears the gentle voice of Susannah, who is saying, "Oh Carol, that's terrible. God, that's *awful.*"

Carol's large eyes are teary, but in a friendly way she disengages herself from Graham; she even smiles as she says, "Well, I'm sorry, I didn't mean to say that. But you see? You really can't tell what's happened to anyone."

And Susannah: "Oh, you're right, of course you are. . . ."

And Rose: "It's true, we do get arrogant. . . ."

Graham says that he thinks they should eat. The food is hot; they must be hungry. He brings the dinner to them at the table, and he serves out hot food onto the heated plates.

Carol and Rose are talking about the towns they came from: Vallejo, California, and Manchester, Vermont.

"It's thirty miles from San Francisco," Carol says. "And that's all we talked about. The City. How to get there, and what was going on there. Vallejo was just a place we ignored, dirt under our feet."

"All the kids in Manchester wanted to make it to New York," Rose says. "All but me, and I was fixated on Cambridge. Not getting into Radcliffe was terrible for me—it's why I never went to college at all."

"I didn't either," Carol says, with a slight irony that Graham thinks may have been lost on Rose: Carol would not have expected to go to college, probably—it wasn't what high-school kids from Vallejo did. But how does he know this?

"I went to work instead," says Rose, a little priggishly (thinks Graham).

"Me too," Carol says, with a small laugh.

Susannah breaks in. "Dad, this is absolutely the greatest dinner. You're still the best cook I know. It's good I don't have your dinners more often."

"I'm glad you like it. I haven't cooked a lot lately."

And Rose, and Carol: "It's super. It's great."

Warmed by praise, and just then wanting to be nice to Rose (partly because he has to admit to himself that he doesn't much like her), Graham says to her, "Cambridge was where I wanted to go to school, too. The Harvard School of Design. Chicago seemed second-best. But I guess it's all worked out."

"I guess." Rose smiles.

She looks almost pretty at that moment, but not quite; looking at her, Graham thinks again, If it had to be another girl, why her? But he knows this to be unfair, and, as far as that goes, why anyone for anyone, when you come to think of it? Any pairing is basically mysterious.

Partly as a diversion from such unsettling thoughts, and also from real curiosity, he asks Carol, "But was it worth it when you got to the city?"

She laughs, in her low, self-depreciating way. "Oh, *I* thought so. I really liked it. My first job was with a florist on Union Street. It was nice there then, before it got all junked up with body shops and stuff. I had a good time."

Some memory of that era has put a younger, musing look on Carol's face, and Graham wonders if she is thinking of a love affair; jealously he wonders, Who? Who did you know, back then?

"I was working for this really nice older man," says Carol, in a higher than usual voice (as Graham thinks, *Ah*). "He taught me all he could. I was pretty dumb, at first. About marketing, arranging, keeping stuff fresh, all that. He lived by himself. A lonely person, I guess. He was—uh—gay, and then he died, and it turned out he'd left the store to me." For the second time that night tears have come to her eyes. "I was so touched, and it was too late to thank him, or anything." Then, the tears gone, her voice returns to its usual depth as she sums it up, "Well, that's how I got my start in the business world."

These sudden shifts in mood, along with her absolute refusal to see herself as an object of pity, are strongly, newly attractive to Graham; he has the sense of being with an unknown, exciting woman.

And then, in a quick, clairvoyant way, he gets a picture of Carol as a twenty-year-old girl, new in town: tall and a little awkward, working in the florist shop and worrying about her hands, her fingers scratched up from stems and wires; worrying about her darkening blond hair and then, deciding, what the hell, better dye it; worrying about money, and men, and her parents back in Vallejo—and *should* she have put the baby out for adoption? He feels an unfamiliar tenderness for this new Carol.

"You guys are making me feel very boring," says Susannah. "I always wanted to go to Berkeley, and I did, and I wanted to go to L.A. and work in films."

"I think you're just more direct," amends Rose, affectionate admiration in her voice, and in her eyes. "You just know what you're doing. I fall into things."

Susannah laughs. "Well, you do all right, you've got to admit." And, to Graham and Carol: "She's only moved up twice since January. At this rate she'll be casting something in August."

What Graham had earlier named discomfort he now recognizes as envy: Susannah is closer to Rose than she is to him; they are closer to each other than he is to anyone. He says, "Well, Rose, that's really swell. That's *swell.*"

Carol glances at Graham for an instant before she says, "Well, I'll bet your father didn't even tell you about his most recent prize." And she tells them about an award from the A.I.A., which Graham had indeed not mentioned to Susannah, but which had pleased him at the time of its announcement (immoderately, he told himself).

And now Susannah and Rose join Carol in congratulations, saying how terrific, really great.

. . .

Dinner is over, and in a rather disorganized way they all clear the table and load the dishwasher.

They go into the living room, where Graham lights the fire, and the three women sit down—or, rather, sprawl—Rose and Susannah at either end of the sofa, Carol in an easy chair. For dinner Carol put on velvet pants and a red silk shirt. In the bright hot firelight her gray eyes shine, and the fine line under her chin, that first age line, is just barely visible. She is very beautiful at that moment—probably more so now than she was fifteen years ago, Graham decides.

Susannah, in clean, faded, too tight Levi's, stretches her legs out stiffly before her. "Oh, I'm really going to feel that skiing in the morning!"

And Carol: "Me too. I haven't had that much exercise forever."

Rose says, "If I could just not fall."

"Oh, you won't; tomorrow you'll see. Tomorrow . . ." says everyone.

They are all exhausted. Silly to stay up late. And so as the fire dies down, Graham covers it and they all four go off to bed, in the two separate rooms.

Outside a strong wind has come up, creaking the walls and rattling windowpanes.

In the middle of the night, in what has become a storm—lashing snow and violent wind—Rose wakes up, terrified. From the depths of bad dreams, she has no idea where she is, what time it is, what day. With whom she is. She struggles for clues, her wide eyes scouring the dark, her tentative hands reaching out, encountering Susannah's familiar, fleshy back. Everything comes into focus for her; she knows where she is. She breathes out softly, "Oh, thank God it's you," moving closer to her friend.

Greyhound People

As soon as I got on the bus, in the Greyhound station in Sacramento, I had a frightened sense of being in the wrong place. I had asked several people in the line at Gate 6 if this was the express to San Francisco, and they all said yes, but later, reviewing those assenting faces, I saw that in truth they all wore a look of people answering a question they have not entirely understood. Because of my anxiety and fear, I took a seat at the very front of the bus, across from and slightly behind the driver. There nothing very bad could happen to me, I thought.

What did happen, immediately, was that a tall black man, with a big mustache, angry and very handsome, stepped up into the bus and looked at me and said, "That's my seat. You in my seat. I got to have that seat." He was staring me straight in the eye, his flashing black into my scared pale blue.

There was nothing of his on the seat, no way I could have known that it belonged to him, and so that is what I said: "I didn't know it was your seat." But even as I was saying that, muttering, having ceased to meet his eye, I was also getting up and moving backward, to a seat two rows behind him.

Seated, apprehensively watching as the bus filled up, I saw that across the aisle from the black man were two women who seemed to be friends of his. No longer angry, he was sitting in the aisle seat so as to be near them; they were all talking and having a good time, glad to be together.

No one sat beside me, probably because I had put my large briefcase in that seat; it is stiff and forbidding-looking.

I thought again that I must be on the wrong bus, but just as I had that thought the driver got on, a big black man; he looked down the aisle for a second and then swung the door shut. He started up the engine as I wondered, What about tickets? Will they be collected in San Francisco? I had something called a commuter ticket, a book of ten coupons, and that morning, leaving San Francisco, I'd thought the driver took too much of my ticket, two coupons; maybe this was some mysterious repayment? We lurched out of the station and were on our way to San Francisco—or wherever.

Behind me, a child began to shout loud but not quite coherent questions: "Mom is that a river we're crossing? Mom do you see that tree? Mom is this a bus we're riding on?" He was making so much noise and his questions were all so crazy—senseless, really—that I did not see how I could stand it, all the hour and forty minutes to San Francisco, assuming that I was on the right bus, the express.

One of the women in the front seat, the friends of the man who had displaced me, also seemed unable to stand the child, and she began to shout back at him. "You the noisiest traveler I ever heard; in fact you ain't a traveler, you an observer."

"Mom does she mean me? Mom who is that?"

"Yeah, I means you. You the one that's talking."

"Mom who is that lady?" The child sounded more and more excited, and the black woman angrier. It was a terrible dialogue to hear.

And then I saw a very large white woman struggling up the aisle of the bus, toward the black women in the front, whom she at last reached and addressed: "Listen, my son's retarded and that's how he tests reality, asking questions. You mustn't make fun of him like that." She turned and headed back toward her seat, to her noisy retarded son.

The black women muttered to each other, and the boy began to renew his questions. "Mom see that cow?"

And then I heard one of the black women say, very loudly, having the last word: "And I got a daughter wears a hearing aid."

I smiled to myself, although I suppose it wasn't funny, but something about the black defiant voice was so appealing. And, as I dared for a moment to look around the bus, I saw that most of the passengers were black: a puzzle.

The scenery, on which I tried to concentrate, was very beautiful: smooth blond hills, gently rising, and here and there crevasses of shadow; and sometimes a valley with a bright white farmhouse, white fences, green space. And everywhere the dark shapes of live oaks, a black drift of lace against the hills or darkly clustered in the valleys, near the farms.

All this was on our left, the east, as we headed south toward San Francisco (I hoped). To our right, westward, the view was even more glorious: flat green pasturelands stretching out to the glittering bay, bright gold water and blue fingers of land, in the late May afternoon sunshine.

The retarded boy seemed to have taken up a friendly conversation with some people across the aisle from him, although his voice was still very loud. "My grandfather lives in Vallejo," he was saying. "Mom is that the sun over there?"

Just then, the bus turned right, turned off the freeway, and the driver announced, "We're just coming into Vallejo, folks. Next stop is Oakland, and then San Francisco."

I was on the wrong bus. Not on the express. Although this bus, thank God, did go on to San Francisco. But it would be at least half an hour late getting in. My heart sank as I thought, Oh, how angry Hortense will be.

The bus swung through what must have been the back streets of Vallejo. (A question: why are bus stations always in the worst parts of town, or is it that those worst parts grow up around the station?) As our bus ground to a halt, pushed into its slot in a line of other Greyhounds, before anyone else had moved, one of the women in the front seat stood up; she was thin, sharply angular, in a purple dress. She looked wonderful, I thought. "And you, you just shut up!" she said to the boy in the back.

That was her exit line; she flounced off the bus ahead of everyone else, soon followed by her friend and the handsome man who had dislodged me from my seat.

A few people applauded. I did not, although I would have liked to, really.

This was my situation: I was working in San Francisco as a statistician in a government office having to do with unemployment, and that office assigned me to an office in Sacramento for ten weeks. There was very little difference between the offices; they were interchangeable, even to the pale-green coloring of the walls. But that is why I was commuting back and forth to Sacramento.

I was living with Hortense (temporarily, I hoped, although of course it was nice of her to take me in) because my husband had just divorced me and he wanted our apartment—or he wanted it more than I did, and I am not good at arguing.

Hortense is older than I am, with grown-up children, now gone. She seems to like to cook and take care; and when I started commuting she told me she'd meet me at the bus station every night, because she worried about the neighborhood, Seventh Street near Market, where the bus station is. I suppose some people must have assumed that we were a lesbian couple, even that I had left my husband for Hortense, but that was not true; my husband left me for a beautiful young Japanese nurse (he is in advertising), and it was not sex or love that kept me and Hortense together but sheer dependency (mine).

A lot of people got off the bus at Vallejo, including the pale fat lady and her poor son; as they passed me I saw that he was clinging closely to his mother, and that the way he held his neck was odd, not right. I felt bad that in a way I had sided against him, with the fierce black lady in purple. But I had to admit that of the two of them it was her I would rather travel with again.

A lot of new people began to get on the bus, and again they were mostly black; I guessed that they were going to Oakland. With so many people it seemed inconsiderate to take up two seats, even if I could have got away with it, so I put my briefcase on the floor, at my feet.

And I looked up to find the biggest woman I had ever seen, heading right for me. Enormous—she must have weighed three times what I did—and black and very young.

She needed two seats to herself, she really did, and of course she knew that; she looked around, but almost all the seats were taken, and so she chose me, because I am relatively thin, I guess. With a sweet apologetic smile, she squeezed in beside me—or, rather, she squeezed me in.

"Ooooh, I am so *big*," she said, in a surprisingly soft small voice. "I must be crushing you almost to death."

"Oh no, I'm fine," I assured her, and we smiled at each other.

"And you so thin," she observed.

As though being thin required an apology, I explained that I was not that way naturally, I was living with an overweight friend who kept me on fish and salads, mostly.

She laughed. "Well, maybe I should move in with your friend, but it probably wouldn't do me no good."

I laughed, too, and I wondered what she did, what job took her from Oakland to Vallejo.

We talked, and after a while she told me that she worked in Oakland, as well as lived there, not saying at what, but that she was taking a course in Vallejo in the care of special children, which is what she really wanted to do. " 'Special' mean the retards and the crazies," she said, but she laughed in a kindly way, and I thought how good she probably would be with kids.

I told her about the retarded boy who got off the bus at Vallejo, after all those noisy questions.

"No reason you can't tell a retard to quiet down," she said. "They got no call to disturb folks, it don't help them none."

Right away then I felt better; it was okay for me not to have liked all that noise and to have sided with the black woman who told the boy to shut up.

I did like that big young woman, and when we got to Oakland I was sorry to see her go. We both said that we had enjoyed talking to each other; we said we hoped that we would run into each other again, although that seemed very unlikely.

In San Francisco, Hortense was pacing the station—very worried, she said, and visibly angry.

I explained to her that it was confusing, three buses leaving Sacramento for San Francisco at just the same time, five-thirty. It was very easy to get on the wrong one.

"Well, I suppose you'll catch on after a couple of weeks," she said, clearly without much faith that I ever would.

She was right about one thing, though: the San Francisco bus station, especially at night, is a cold and scary place. People seem to be just hanging out there—frightened-looking young kids, maybe runaways, belligerent-looking drunks and large black men, with swaggering hats, all of whom look mysteriously enraged. The lighting is a terrible white glare, harsh on the dirty floors, illuminating the wrinkles and grime and pouches of fatigue on all the human faces. A cold wind rushes in through the swinging entrance doors. Outside, there are more dangerous-looking loiterers, whom Hortense and I hurried past that night, going along Seventh Street to Market, where she had parked in a yellow zone but had not (thank God) been ticketed.

For dinner we had a big chef's salad, so nutritious and slenderizing, but also so cold that it felt like a punishment. What I really would have liked was a big hot fattening baked potato.

I wondered, How would I look if I put on twenty pounds?

Early mornings at the Greyhound station are not so bad, with only a few drunks and lurching loiterers on the street outside, and it is easy to walk past them very fast, swinging a briefcase. Inside, there are healthy-looking, resolute kids with enormous backpacks, off to conquer the wilderness. And it is easy, of course, to find the right bus, the express to Sacramento; there is only one, leaving every hour on the hour. I almost always got to sit by myself. But somehow the same scenery that you see coming down to San Francisco is very boring viewed from the other direction. Maybe this is an effect of the leveling morning light—I don't know.

One day, though, the bus was more crowded than usual and a young girl asked if she could sit next to me. I said okay, and we started up one of those guarded and desultory conversations that travel dictates. What most struck me about her was her accent; I could tell exactly where she was from—upstate New York. I am from there, too, from Binghamton, although I have taken on some other accents along the way, mainly my husband's—Philadelphia. (I hope I do not get to sound like Hortense, who is from Florida.) Of course I did not ask the girl where she was from—too personal, and I didn't have to—but she told me, unasked, that she worked in an office in Sacramento, which turned out to be in the building next to mine. That seemed ominous to me: a girl coming from exactly where I am from, and heading in my same direction. I did not want her to tell me any more about her life, and she did not.

Near Sacramento, the concrete road dividers have been planted with oleander, overflowing pink and white blossoms that quite conceal oncoming traffic in the other lanes. It is hard to believe that the highway commissioners envisioned such a wild profusion, and somehow it makes me uneasy to see all that bloom, maybe because I read somewhere that oleander is poisonous. Certainly it is unnaturally hardy.

The Sacramento station is more than a little weird, being the jumping-off place for Reno, so to speak. Every morning there are lines for the Reno buses, lines of gamblers, all kinds: big women in bright synthetic fabrics, and seedy old men, drunks, with tired blue eyes and white indoor skin, smoking cigarillos. Gamblers seem to smoke a lot, I noticed. I also noticed that none of them are black.

A large elevated sign lists the departures for South Lake Tahoe and Reno: the Nugget express, which leaves at 3:40 a.m.; the dailies to Harrah's, starting at 9:05 a.m.; and on weekends you can leave for Reno any time between 2:35 a.m. and 11:15 p.m. I find it very hard to imagine going to Reno at any of those times, but then I am not a gambler.

Unfortunately, I again saw that same girl, Miss Upstate New York, the next few times that I took the correct bus, the express at five-thirty to San Francisco. She began to tell me some very boring things about her office—she did not like her boss, he drank—and her boyfriend, who wanted to invest in some condominiums at South Lake Tahoe.

I knew that Hortense would never believe that it was a mistake, and just possibly it was not, but a few nights later I took another wrong bus, really wrong: the local that stops everywhere, at Davis and Dixon and Fairfield, all down the line. Hortense was going to be furious. I began to work on some plausible lies: I got to the station late, this wrong bus left from the gate that the right bus usually leaves from. But then I thought, How ridiculous; and the very fact of Hortense's being there waiting for me began to seem a little silly, both of us being grown up.

Again most of the passengers were black, and I sensed a sort of camaraderie among them. It occurred to me that they were like people who have recently won a war, although I knew that to be not the case, not at all, in terms of their present lives. But with all the stops and starts the trip was very interesting; I would have been having a very good time if it were not for two things: one, I was worried about Hortense; and, two, I did not see again any of those people who were on my first wrong trip—

not the very fat black woman or the skinny one in purple, or the handsome man who displaced me from my seat.

Just in front of me were an elderly man and woman, both black, who seemed to be old friends accidentally encountered on this bus. They exchanged information about how they both were, their families, and then the woman said, "Well, the weekend's coming up." "Yep, jes one more day." "Then you can rest." "Say, you ever see a poor man rest?"

Recently I read an interview with a distinguished lady of letters, in which she was asked why she wrote so obsessively about the very poor, the tiredest and saddest poorest people, and that lady, a Southerner, answered, "But I myself am poor people."

That touched me to the quick, somehow. I am too. Hortense is not, I think.

Across the aisle from me I suddenly noticed the most beautiful young man I had ever seen, sound asleep. A golden boy: gold hair and tawny skin, large beautiful hands spread loosely on his knees, long careless legs in soft pale washed-out jeans. I hardly dared look at him; some intensity in my regard might have wakened him, and then on my face he would have seen—not lust, it wasn't that, just a vast and objectless regard for his perfection, as though he were sculptured in bronze, or gold.

I haven't thought much about men, or noticed male beauty, actually, since my husband left, opted out of our marriage—and when I say that he left it sounds sudden, whereas it took a long and painful year.

Looking back, I now see that it began with some tiny wistful remarks, made by him, when he would come across articles in the paper about swingers, swapping, singles bars. "Well, maybe we should try some of that stuff," he would say, with a laugh intended to prove nonseriousness. "A pretty girl like you, you'd do okay," he would add, by which he really meant that he thought he would do okay, as indeed he has—did, does. Then came some more serious remarks to the effect that if I wanted an occasional afternoon with someone else, well, I didn't have to tell him about it, but if I did, well, he would understand. Which was a little silly, since when I was not at my office working I was either doing some household errand or I was at home, available only to him.

The next phase included a lot of half-explained or occasionally overexplained latenesses, and a seemingly chronic at-home fatigue. By then even I had caught on, without thinking too specifically about what he must have been doing, which I could not have stood. Still, I was surprised, and worse than surprised, when he told me that he was "serious" about another woman. The beautiful Japanese nurse.

The golden boy got off at Vallejo, without our exchanging any look. Someone else I won't see again, but who will stay in my mind, probably.

Hortense was furious, her poor fat face red, her voice almost out of control. "One hour—one hour I've been waiting here. Can you imagine my thoughts, in all that time?"

Well, I pretty much could. I felt terrible. I put my hand on her arm in a gesture that I meant as calming, affectionate, but she thrust it off, violently.

That was foolish, I thought, and I hoped no one had seen her. I said, "Hortense, I'm really very sorry. But it's getting obvious that I have a problem with buses. I mix them up, so maybe you shouldn't come and meet me anymore."

I hadn't known I was going to say that, but, once said, those words made sense, and I went on. "I'll take a taxi. There're always a couple out front."

And just then, as we passed hurriedly through the front doors, out onto the street, there were indeed four taxis stationed, a record number, as though to prove my point. Hortense made a strangled, snorting sound.

We drove home in silence; silently, in her dining room, we ate another chef's salad. It occurred to me to say that since our dinners were almost always cold my being late did not exactly spoil them, but I forbore. We were getting to be like some bad sitcom joke: Hortense and me, the odd couple.

The next morning, as I got in line to buy a new commuter ticket, there was the New York State girl. We exchanged mild greetings, and then she looked at the old ticket which for no reason I was clutching, and she said, "But you've got one ticket left."

And she explained what turned out to be one more system that I had not quite caught on to: the driver takes the whole first page, which is why, that first day, I thought he had taken two coupons. And the back page, although another color, pink, is a coupon, too. So my first ride on the wrong bus to Vallejo and Oakland was free; I had come out ahead, in that way.

Then the girl asked, "Have you thought about a California Pass? They're neat." And she explained that with a California Pass, for just a few dollars more than a commuter ticket, you can go *anywhere in California.* You can't travel on weekends, but who would want to, and you can go anywhere at all—Eureka, La Jolla, Santa Barbara, San Diego; you can spend the weekend there and come back on an early Monday bus. I was fascinated, enthralled by these possibilities. I bought a California Pass.

The Sacramento express was almost empty, so I told the girl that I had some work to do, which was true enough. We sat down in our separate seats and concentrated on our briefcases. I was thinking, of course, in a practical way about moving out from Hortense's. That had to be next—and more generally I was considering the possibilities of California, which just then seemed limitless, enormous.

Actually, the Greyhound system of departure gates for buses to San Francisco is very simple; I had really been aware all along of how it worked. Gate 5 is the express, Gate 6 goes to Vallejo and Oakland before San Francisco and Gate 8 is the all-stop local, Davis, Dixon, everywhere. On my way home, I started to line up at Gate 6, my true favorite route, Vallejo and Oakland, when I realized that it was still very early, only just five, and also that I was extremely hungry. What I would really have liked was what we used to call a frappe in Binghamton, something cold and rich and thick and chocolate. Out here called a milkshake. And then I thought, Well, why not? Is there some law that says I can't weigh more than one-ten?

I went into the station restaurant, and at the counter I ordered a double-scoop milkshake. I took it to a booth, and then, as I was sitting there, savoring my delicious drink, something remarkable happened, which was: the handsome black man who so angrily displaced me on that first trip came up to me and greeted me with a friendly smile. "Say, how you, how're you doing this evening?"

I smiled back and said that I was fine, and he went on past with his cup of coffee, leaving me a little out of breath. And as I continued to sip and swallow (it tasted marvelous) I wondered: Is it possible that he remembers me from that incident and this is his way of apologizing? Somehow that seemed very unlikely, but it seemed even more unlikely that he was just a friendly sort who went around greeting people. He was not at all like that, I was sure. Even smiling he had a proud, fierce look.

Was it possible that something about me had struck him in just the right way, making him want to say hello?

In any case, I had to read his greeting as a very good sign. Maybe the fat young woman would get on the bus at Vallejo again. Maybe the thin one in purple. And it further occurred to me that traveling all over California on the Greyhound I could meet anyone at all.

By the Sea

Because she looked older than she was, eighteen, and was very pretty, her two slightly crooked front teeth more than offset by wheat-blond hair and green eyes, Dylan Ballentyne was allowed to be a waitress at the Cypress Lodge without having been a bus girl first. She hated the work—loathed, despised it—but it was literally the only job in town, town being a cluster of houses and a couple of stores on the northern California coast. Dylan also hated the town and the wild, dramatically desolate landscape of the area, to which she and her mother had moved at the beginning of the summer, coming down from San Francisco, where Dylan had been happy in the sunny Mission District, out of sight of the sea.

Now she moved drearily through days of trays and dishes, spilled coffee and gelatinous ash-strewn food, fat cross guests or hyper-friendly ones. She was sustained by her small paycheck and somewhat more generous tips, and by her own large fantasies of ultimate rescue, or escape.

The Lodge, an ornately Victorian structure with pinnacles and turrets, was on a high bluff two miles south of town, surrounded by sharply sloping meadows which were edged with dark-green cypresses and pines, overlooking the turbulent, shark-infested, almost inaccessible sea. (One more disappointment: talking up the move, Dylan's mother, self-named Flower, had invented long beach days and picnics; they would both learn to surf, she had said.)

Breakfast was served at the Lodge from eight till ten-thirty, lunch from eleven-thirty until two, in a long glassed-in porch, the dining room. Supposedly between those two meals the help got a break, half an hour for a sandwich or a cigarette, but more often than not it was about five minutes, what with lingering breakfasters and early, eager lunchers.

Dinner was at six, set up at five-thirty, and thus there really was a free hour or sometimes two, in the mid to late afternoon. Dylan usually spent this time in the "library" of the Lodge, a dim, musty room, paneled in fake mahogany. Too tired for books, although her reading habits had delighted English teachers in high school, she leafed through old *House Beautiful*s, *Gourmet*s or *Vogue*s, avidly drinking in all those ads for the accoutrements of rich and leisurely exotic lives.

Curiously, what she saw and read made her almost happy, for that limited time, like a drug. She could nearly believe that she saw herself in *Vogue,* in a Rolls-Royce ad: a tall thin blond woman (she was thin, if not very tall) in silk and careless fur, one jeweled hand on the fender of a silver car, and in the background a handsome man, dark, wearing a tuxedo.

Then there was dinner. Drinks. Wines. Specifics as to the doneness of steaks or roasts. Complaints. I ordered *medium* rare. Is this crab really *fresh*? And heavy trays. The woman who managed the restaurant saw to it that waitresses and bus girls "shared" that labor, possibly out of some vaguely egalitarian sense that the trays were too heavy for any single group. By eight-thirty or so, Dylan and all the girls would be slow-witted with exhaustion, smiles stiffening on their very young faces, perspiration drying under their arms and down their backs. Then there would come the stentorian voice of the manageress: "*Dylan,* are you awake? You look a thousand miles away."

Actually, in her dreams, Dylan was less than two hundred miles away, in San Francisco.

One fantasy of rescue which Dylan recognized as childish, and unlikely, probably, was that a nice older couple (in their fifties, anyway: Flower was only thirty-eight) would adopt her. At the end of their stay at the Lodge, after several weeks, they would say, "Well, Dylan, we just don't see how we're going to get along without you. Do you think you could possibly . . . ?" There had in fact been several couples who could have filled that bill—older people from San Francisco, or even L.A., San Diego, Scottsdale—who stayed for a few weeks at the Lodge, who liked Dylan and tipped her generously. But so far none of them had been unable to leave without her; they didn't even send her postcards.

Another fantasy, a little more plausible, more grown up, involved a man who would come to the Lodge alone and would fall in love with Dylan and take her away. The man was as indistinct as the one in the Rolls-Royce ads, as vaguely handsome, dark and rich.

In the meantime, the local boys who came around to see the other waitresses tried to talk to Dylan; their hair was too long and their faces splotchily sunburned from cycling and surfing, which were the only two things they did, besides drinking beer. Dylan ignored them, and went on dreaming.

The usual group of guests at the Lodge didn't offer much material for fantasy: youngish, well-off couples who arrived in big new station wagons with several children, new summer clothes and new sports equipment. Apart from these stylish parents, there were always two or three very young couples, perhaps just married or perhaps not, all with the look of not quite being able to afford where they were.

And always some very old people.

There was, actually, one unmarried man (almost divorced) among the guests, and although he was very nice, intelligent, about twenty-eight, he did not look rich, or, for that matter, handsome and dark. Whitney Iverson was a stocky red-blond man with a strawberry birthmark on one side of his neck. Deep-set blue eyes were his best feature. Probably he was not the one to fall in love and rescue Dylan, although he seemed to like her very much. Mr. Iverson, too, spent his late afternoons in the Lodge's library.

Exactly what Mr. Iverson did for a living was not clear; he mentioned the Peace Corps and VISTA, and then he said that he was writing; not novels—articles. His wife was divorcing him and she was making a lot of trouble about money, he said: a blow, he hadn't thought she was like that. (But how could he have enough money for anyone to make trouble about, Dylan wondered.) He had brought down a carload of books. When he wasn't reading in his room, or working on whatever he was writing, he took long, long walks, every day, miles over the meadows, back and forth to what there was of a town. Glimpsing him through a window as she set up tables, Dylan noted his stride, his strong shoulders. Sometimes he climbed down the steep perilous banks to the edge of the sea, to the narrow strip of coarse gray sand that passed for a beach. Perfectly safe, he said, if you checked the tides. Unlike Dylan, he was crazy about this landscape; he found the sea and the stretching hills of grass and rock, the acres of sky, all marvelous; even the billowing fog that threatened all summer he saw as lovely, something amazing.

By the Sea

Sometimes Dylan tried to see the local scenery with Whitney Iverson's eyes, and sometimes, remarkably, this worked. She was able to imagine herself a sojourner in this area, as he was, and then she could succumb to the sharp blue beauty of that wild Pacific, the dark-green, wind-bent feathery cypresses, and the sheer cliffs going down to the water, with their crevices of moss and tiny brilliant wild flowers.

But usually she just looked around in a dull, hating way. Usually she was miserably bored and hopelessly despondent.

They had moved down here to the seaside, to this tiny nothing town, Dylan and Flower, so that Flower could concentrate on making jewelry, which was her profession. Actually, the move was the idea of Zachery, Flower's boyfriend. Flower would make the jewelry and Zach would take it up to San Francisco to sell; someday he might even try L.A. And Zach would bring back new materials for Flower to use—gold and silver and pearls. Flower, who was several months behind in her rent, had agreed to this plan. Also, as Dylan saw it, Flower was totally dominated by Zach, who was big and dark and roughly handsome, and sometimes mean. Dylan further suspected that Zach wanted them out of town, wanted to see less of Flower, and the summer had borne out her theory: instead of his living with them and making occasional forays to the city, as Flower had imagined, it was just the other way around. Zach made occasional visits to them, and the rest of the time, when she wasn't working or trying to work on some earrings or a necklace, Flower sat sipping the harsh, local red wine and reading the used paperbacks that Zach brought down in big cartons along with the jewelry materials—"to keep you out of mischief," he had said.

Flower wore her graying blond hair long, in the non-style of her whole adult life, and she was putting on weight. When she wanted to work she took an upper, another commodity supplied by Zach, but this didn't do much to keep her weight down, just kept her "wired," as she sometimes said. Dylan alternated between impatience and the most tender sympathy for her mother, who was in some ways more like a friend; it was often clear to Dylan that actually she had to be the stronger person, the one in charge. But Flower was so nice, really, a wonderful cook and generous to her friends, and she could be funny. Some of the jewelry she made was beautiful—recently, a necklace of silver and stones that Zach said were real opals. Flower had talent, originality. If she could just dump Zach for good, Dylan thought, and then not replace him with someone worse, as she usually did. Always some mean jerk. If she could just not drink, not take speed.

From the start Flower had been genuinely sympathetic about Dylan's awful job. "Honey, I can hardly stand to think about it," she would say, and her eyes would fill. She had been a waitress several times herself. "You and those heavy trays, and the mess. Look, why don't you just quit? Honestly, we'll get by like we always have. I'll just tell Zach he's got to bring more stuff down, and sell more, too. And you can help me."

This seemed a dangerous plan to Dylan, possibly because it relied on Zach, who Dylan was sure would end up in jail, or worse. She stubbornly stuck with her job, and on her two days off (Mondays and Tuesdays, of all useless days) she stayed in bed a lot, and read, and allowed her mother to "spoil" her, with breakfast trays ("Well, after all, who deserves her own tray more than you do, baby?") and her favorite salads for lunch, with every available fresh vegetable and sometimes shrimp.

When she wasn't talking to her mother or helping out with household chores, Dylan was reading a book that Mr. Iverson had lent her— *The Eustace Diamonds,* by Trollope. This had come about because one afternoon, meeting him in the library, Dylan had explained the old *Vogue*s, the *House Beautiful*s scattered near her lap, saying that she was too tired just then to read, and that she missed television. The winter before, she had loved *The Pallisers,* she said, and, before that, *Upstairs, Downstairs.* Mr. Iverson had recommended *The Eustace Diamonds.* "It's really my favorite of the Palliser novels," he said, and he went to get it for her—running all the way up to his room and back, apparently; he was out of breath as he handed her the book.

But why was he so eager to please her? She knew that she was pretty, but she wasn't all that pretty, in her own estimation; she was highly conscious of the two crooked front teeth, although she had perfected a radiant, slightly false smile that almost hid them.

"I wonder if he could be one of *the* Iversons," Flower mused, informed by Dylan one Monday of the source of her book.

"The Iversons?" In Flower's voice it had sounded like the Pallisers.

"One of the really terrific, old San Francisco families. You know, Huntingtons, Floods, Crockers, Iversons. What does he look like, your Mr. Iverson?"

Dylan found this hard to answer, although usually with Flower she spoke very easily, they were so used to each other. "Well." She hesitated. "He's sort of blond, with nice blue eyes and a small nose. He has this birthmark on his neck, but it's not really noticeable."

Flower laughed. "In that case, he's not a real Iverson. They've all got dark hair and the most aristocratic beaky noses. And none of them could possibly have a birthmark—they'd drown it at birth."

Dylan laughed, too, although she felt an obscure disloyalty to Mr. Iverson.

And, looking at Flower, Dylan thought, as she had before, that Flower *could* change her life, take charge of herself. She was basically strong. But in the next moment Dylan decided, as she also had before, more frequently, that probably Flower wouldn't change; in her brief experience people didn't, or not much. Zach would go to jail and Flower would find somebody worse, and get grayer and fatter. And she, Dylan, had better forget about anything as childish as being adopted by rich old people; she must concentrate on marrying someone who really had *money*. Resolution made her feel suddenly adult.

"Honey," asked Flower, "are you sure you won't have a glass of wine?"

"My mother wonders if you're a real Iverson." Dylan had not quite meant to say this; the sentence spoke itself, leaving her slightly embarrassed, as she sat with Whitney Iverson on a small sofa in the library. It was her afternoon break; she was tired, and she told herself that she didn't know what she was saying.

Mr. Iverson, whose intense blue eyes had been staring into hers, now turned away, so that Dylan was more aware of the mark on his neck than she had been before. Or could it have deepened to a darker mulberry stain?

He said, "Well, I am and I'm not, actually. I think of them as my parents and I grew up with them, in the Atherton house, but actually I'm adopted."

"Really?" Two girls Dylan knew at Mission High had got pregnant and had given up their babies to be adopted. His real mother, then, could have been an ordinary high-school girl? The idea made her uncomfortable, as though he had suddenly moved closer to her.

"I believe they were very aware of it, my not being really theirs," Whitney Iverson said, again looking away from her. "Especially when I messed up in some way, like choosing Reed, instead of Stanford. Then graduate school . . ."

As he talked on, seeming to search for new words for the feelings engendered in him by his adoptive parents, Dylan felt herself involuntarily retreat. No one had ever talked to her in quite that way, and she was uneasy. She looked through the long leaded windows to the wavering sunlight beyond; she stared at the dust-moted shafts of light in the dingy room where they were.

In fact, for Dylan, Whitney's very niceness was somehow against him; his kindness, his willingness to talk, ran against the rather austere grain of her fantasies.

Apparently sensing what she felt, or some of it, Whitney stopped short, and he laughed in a self-conscious way. "Well, there you have the poor-adopted-kid self-pity trip of the month," he said. " 'Poor,' Christ, they've drowned me in money."

Feeling that this last was not really addressed to her (and thinking of Flower's phrase about the birthmark, "drowned at birth"), Dylan said nothing. She stared at his hands, which were strong and brown, long-fingered, and she suddenly, sharply, wished that he would touch her. Touch, instead of all this awkward talk.

Later, considering that conversation, Dylan found herself moved, in spite of herself. How terrible to feel not only that you did not really belong with your parents but that they were disappointed in you. Whitney Iverson hadn't said anything about it, of course, but they must have minded about the birthmark, along with college and graduate school.

She and Flower were so clearly mother and daughter—obviously, irrevocably so; her green eyes were Flower's, even her crooked front teeth. Also, Flower had always thought she was wonderful. "My daughter Dylan," she would say, in her strongest, proudest voice.

But what had he possibly meant about "drowned in money"? Was he really rich, or had that been a joke? His car was an old VW convertible, and his button-down shirts were frayed, his baggy jackets shabby. Would a rich person drive a car like that, or wear those clothes? Probably not, thought Dylan; on the other hand, he did not seem a man to say that he was rich if he was not.

In any case, Dylan decided that she was giving him too much thought, since she had no real reason to think that he cared about her. Maybe he was an Iverson, and a snob, and did not want anything to do with a waitress. If he had wanted to see her, he could have suggested dinner, a movie or driving down to Santa Cruz on one of her days off. Probably she would have said yes, and on the way home, maybe on a bluff overlooking the sea, he could have parked the car, have turned to her.

So far, Dylan had had little experience of ambiguity; its emerging presence made her both impatient and confused. She did not know what to do or how to think about the contradictions in Whitney Iverson.

Although over the summer Dylan and Whitney had met almost every day in the library, this was never a stated arrangement, and if either of them missed a day, as they each sometimes did, nothing was said. This calculated diffidence seemed to suit them; they were like children who could not quite admit to seeking each other out.

One day, when Dylan had already decided that he would not come, and not caring really—she was too tired to care, what with extra guests and heavier trays—after she had been in the library for almost half an hour, she heard running steps, his, and then Whitney Iverson burst in, quite out of breath. "Oh . . . I'm glad you're still here," he got out, and he sat down heavily beside her. "I had some terrific news." But then on the verge of telling her, he stopped, and laughed, and said, "But I'm afraid it won't sound all that terrific to you."

Unhelpfully she looked at him.

"The *Yale Review*," he said. "They've taken an article I sent them. I'm really pleased."

He had been right, in that the *Yale Review* was meaningless to Dylan, but his sense of triumph was real and visible to her. She *felt* his success, and she thought just then that he looked wonderful.

. . .

September, once Labor Day was past, was much clearer and warmer, the sea a more brilliant blue, than during the summer. Under a light, fleece-clouded sky the water shimmered, all diamonds and gold, and the rocky cliffs in full sunlight were as pale as ivory. Even Dylan admitted to herself that it was beautiful; sometimes she felt herself penetrated by that scenery, her consciousness filled with it.

Whitney Iverson was leaving on the fifteenth; he had told Dylan so, naming the day as they sat together in the library. And then he said, "Would it be okay if I called you at home, sometime?"

The truth was, they didn't have a phone. Flower had been in so much trouble with the phone company that she didn't want to get into all that again. And so now Dylan blushed, and lied. "Well, maybe not. My mother's really strict."

He blushed, too, the birthmark darkening. "Well, I'll have to come back to see you," he said. "But will you still be here?"

How could she know, especially since he didn't even name a time when he would come? With a careless lack of tact she answered, "I hope not," and then she laughed.

Very seriously he asked, "Well, could we at least go for a walk or something before I go? I could show you the beach." He gave a small laugh, indicating that the beach was really nothing much to see, and then he said, "Dylan, I've wanted so much to see you, I *care* so much for you— but here, there would have been . . . implications . . . you know . . ."

She didn't know; she refused to understand what he meant, unless he was confirming her old suspicion of snobbery: his not wanting to be seen with a waitress. She frowned slightly, and said, "Of course," and thought that she would not, after all, see him again. So much for Whitney Iverson.

But the next afternoon, during her break, in the brilliant September weather the library looked to her unbearably dingy, and all those magazines were so old. She stepped outside through the door at the end of the porch, and there was Mr. Iverson, just coming out through another door.

He smiled widely, said, "Perfect! We can just make it before the tide."

Wanting to say that she hadn't meant to go for a walk with him—she was just getting some air, and her shoes were wrong, canvas sandals—Dylan said neither of those things, but followed along, across the yellowing grass, toward the bluff.

He led her to a place that she hadn't known was there, a dip in the headland, from which the beach was only a few yards down, by a not steep, narrow path. Whitney went ahead, first turning back to reach for her hand, which she gave him. Making her way just behind, Dylan was more aware of his touch, of their firmly joined warm hands, than of anything else in the day: the sunlight, the sea, her poorly shod feet.

But as they reached the narrow strip of land, instead of turning to embrace her, although he still held her hand, Whitney cried out, "See? Isn't it fantastic?"

A small wave hit Dylan's left foot, soaking the fabric of her sandal. Unkissed, she stared at the back of his shirt collar, which was more frayed even than his usual shirts, below his slightly too long red-blond hair.

Then he turned to her; he picked up her other hand from her side, gazing intently down into her face. But it was somehow too late. Something within her had turned against him, whether from her wet foot or his worn-out collar, or sheer faulty timing, so that when he said, "You're so lovely, you make me shy," instead of being moved, as she might have been, Dylan thought he sounded silly (a grown man, shy?) and she stepped back a little, away from him.

He could still have kissed her, easily (she later thought), but he did not. Instead, he reached into one of the pockets of his jeans, fishing about, as he said, ". . . for something I wanted you to have."

Had he brought her a present, some small valuable keepsake? Prepared to relent, Dylan then saw that he had not; what he was handing her was a cardboard square, a card, on which were printed his name and telephone number. He said, "I just got these. My mother sent them. She's big on engraving." He grimaced as Dylan thought, Oh, your mother really is an Iverson. "The number's my new bachelor pad," he told her. "It's unlisted. Look, I really wish you'd call me. Any time. Collect. I'll be there." He looked away from her, for a moment out to sea, then down to the sand, where for the first time he seemed to notice her wet foot. "Oh Lord!" he exclaimed. "Will you have to change? I could run you home. . . ."

Not liking the fuss, and not at all liking the attention paid to those particular shoes (cheap, flimsy), somewhat coldly Dylan said no; the guests had thinned out and she was going home anyway as soon as the tables had been set up.

"Then I won't see you?"

She gave him her widest, most falsely shining smile, and turned and started up the path ahead of him. At the top she smiled again, and was about to turn away when Whitney grasped her wrist and said, with a startling, unfamiliar scowl, "*Call* me, you hear? I don't want to lose you."

What Dylan had said about being able to leave after setting up the tables was true; she had been told that she could then go home, which she did. The only problem, of course, was that she would earn less money; it could be a very lean, cold winter. Thinking about money, and, less clearly, about Whitney Iverson, Dylan was not quite ready for the wild-eyed Flower, who greeted her at the door: "We're celebrating. Congratulate me! I've dumped Zach."

But Dylan had heard this before, and she knew the shape of the evening that her mother's announcement presaged: strong triumphant statements along with a festive dinner, more and more wine, then tears. Sinkingly she listened as her mother described that afternoon's visit from Zach, how terrible he was and how firm she, Flower, had been, how final. "And we're celebrating with a really great fish soup," finished Flower, leading Dylan into the kitchen.

The evening did go more or less as Dylan had feared and imagined that it would. Ladling out the rich fish soup, Flower told Dylan how just plain fed up she was with men, and she repeated a line that she had recently heard and liked: "A woman without a man is like a mushroom without a bicycle."

Dylan did not find this as terrifically funny as Flower did, but she dutifully laughed.

A little later, sopping French bread into the liquid, Flower said, "But maybe it's just the guys I pick? I really seem to have some kind of instinct."

Flower had said that before, and Dylan always, if silently, agreed with her: it was too obvious to repeat. And then, maybe there really weren't any nice men around anymore, at her mother's age? Maybe they all got mean and terrible, the way a lot of women got fat? Dylan thought then of Whitney Iverson, who was only about ten years younger than Flower was; would he, too, eventually become impossible, cruel and unfaithful?

In a way that would have seemed alarmingly telepathic if Dylan had not been used to having her thoughts read by her mother, Flower asked, "What ever happened to your new friend, Mr. Iverson? Was he really one of *them*?"

"I don't know. I guess so," Dylan muttered, wishing that she had never mentioned Whitney to her mother.

Over salad, Flower announced that she was going on a diet. "Tomorrow. First thing. Don't worry, I'll still have the stuff you like around for you, but from now on no more carbohydrates for me."

At least, this time, she didn't cry.

At some hour in the middle of the night, or early morning, Dylan woke up—a thing she rarely did. Her ears and her mind were full of the distant sound of the sea, and she could see it as it had been in the afternoon, vastly glittering, when she had been preoccupied with her wet shoe, with Whitney's not kissing her. And she felt a sudden closeness to him; suddenly she understood what he had not quite said. By "implications" he had meant that the time and place were wrong for them. He was shy and just then not especially happy, what with his divorce and all, but he truly cared about her. If he had felt less he probably would have kissed her, in the careless, meaningless way of a man on vacation kissing a pretty waitress and then going back to his own real life. Whitney was that rarity her mother despaired of finding: a truly nice man. On her way back to sleep Dylan imagined calling him. She could go up to see him on the bus, or he could come down, and they could go out together, nothing to do with the Lodge. Could talk, be alone.

However, Dylan woke up the next morning in quite another mood. She felt wonderful, her own person, needing no one, certainly not a man who had not bothered, really, to claim her. Looking in the mirror, she saw herself as more than pretty, as almost beautiful; it was one of her very good days.

Flower, too, at breakfast seemed cheerful, not hung over. Maybe there was something in the air? Passing buttered English muffins to Dylan, Flower took none, although she loved them. "Tomato juice and eggs and black coffee, from here on in," she said. She did not take any pills.

Later, walking toward the Lodge, Dylan felt lighthearted, energetic. And how beautiful everything was! (Whitney Iverson had been right.) The sloping meadows, the pale clear sky, the chalky cliffs, the diamond-shining sea were all marvelous. She had a strong presentiment of luck; some good fortune would come to her at last.

At the sound of a car behind her she moved out of the way, turning then to look. She had had for a moment the crazy thought that it could be Whitney coming back for her, but of course it was not. It was a new gray Porsche, going slowly, looking for something. Walking a little faster, Dylan began to adjust her smile.

An Unscheduled Stop

Suddenly, on a routine flight between Atlanta and Washington, D.C., a young woman who has been staring intently out of her window bursts into violent tears. No turbulence can have upset her—the air is clear and blue and calm—but in an instant her eyes clench shut, her hands fly up to cover her face and her shoulders convulse in spasms.

She is seated near the front of the plane and the seat next to hers has not been taken. No one is aware of this outburst but the two men across the aisle from her. Because she is good-looking, in a dark, rather stylish way, these men have been observing her since she got on the plane with them in Atlanta; they like the somewhat old-fashioned smooth way her hair is knotted, although, good old Southern boys at heart, they are not so sure about the look on her face, what they could see of it, before she began to cry: wide-eyed and serious, she hardly smiled. One of those women too smart for their own good, they think.

The attention of the men has in fact been divided between the young woman and the landscape below, at which they, like her, have been intently peering: pinewoods, mostly; some exposed red clay, along winding white highways; a brown river; red fall leaves. Just before the woman began to cry, one of the men observed to the other, "Say, aren't we passing over Hilton right about now?"

"Sure looks like it. Yep, I bet you're right."

At that moment the woman's tears begin, and after a startled minute or two they start to whisper. "Say, whatever's eating her, do you reckon?" one of them asks.

"Haven't got the foggiest notion; she sure don't look drunk. Maybe some kind of a drug she took."

. . .

The young woman, Claire Williston, who is not on drugs, or drunk, has been deeply mortified by those tears, which came on her like a fit, a seizure. Generally she is a disciplined person; she behaves well, even under emotional stress. She does not make scenes, does not cry in public, and rarely cries alone. *Maudlin,* she is censoriously thinking, and, How could I have done this to myself? How could I take a flight that would go right over Hilton?

Vague about the specifics of geography, she had simply not realized what any map could have told her: flying from Atlanta to Washington of course you go right over Hilton, the small mid-Southern town where Claire was born and lived for the years until she went away to school up North. To which, except for one fatal summer and her father's funeral, she has not been back for years, and where, as she sees it, she cannot ever now go back. But here she is, directly overhead.

At last, gaining some control over the tears, she continues silently to castigate herself: for not having thought through the implications, geographic and otherwise, of flying all over the South except to Hilton. It is precisely the sort of "unconscious" mistake that people who pride themselves on rationality, on control, are most prone to make, she tells herself; it is how they do themselves in, finally.

In a professional way her own life is indeed rational, is even a moderate success. Based in San Francisco, she is the West Coast editor of a national magazine; she likes the work, and is paid fairly well. (A less successful side of her life, containing the unconscious mistakes of which she accuses herself, has to do with intemperate love affairs, occasional poor judgment as to friends. Flying right over the place you don't want to see or think about.) This is the last leg of a fact-finding trip in which she has thought in an abstract way about "the South," or "the new South," and has not thought about Hilton, or her on the whole painful upbringing there, or the searing love affair which took place on that last summer visit. Now, as a treat, she is on her way to see Susan, an old friend in Washington; she has filled a notebook with observations for the article she will write, but she has reserved some lighter conversational notes for Susan: her fantasy that all the food in New Orleans comes from a single subterranean kitchen with a gigantic black vat of béchamel; her dislike of the self-conscious, daily-manicured prettiness of Charleston; her encounter with the awful loudmouthed racist *(still)* cabdriver in Atlanta: "On Fridays, once they's had they lunch, they's no holding them till midnight, with they singing and they dancing and they razor fights." It was Susan who occupied her thoughts, until the land below began to look so overwhelmingly familiar and she heard the man across from her: "Say, aren't we passing over Hilton?"

At this altitude actual landmarks are impossible to recognize, but as she continues to look down, Claire feels the most powerful pull toward that land, as if there were some special gravity into whose range she has flown. And then a remarkable event occurs; over the loudspeaker comes this announcement: "Well, folks, we're going to be making a little unscheduled stopover right about now. Be landing down at Raleigh-Durham for a little adjustment in the oil-filter system. Won't take no more'n a minute."

Dear God, I do not deserve this, Claire thinks, and at the same time, crazily, she wonders if the plane has been compelled by the same pull that she felt, like an event in science fiction. Dabbing at her face, making a few cosmetic repairs (at which the men across from her sigh with relief: when a woman can tend to her face, she's pretty much all right, they think), she watches as the descending plane approaches the familiar pine-lined, long gray grass field. It bumps down; a few passengers applaud. The plane moves toward the bright beige terminal building.

Passengers get up and move along the aisle, murmuring to each other that they might as well get some air, maybe coffee; the men across from Claire, with a short glance at her, go out with new just-unwrapped cigars in their hands. She remains fixed in her seat; she watches as almost everyone else leaves, and then she turns to the window again. No longer crying, she has just realized that she is deeply afraid to go into the terminal; she might see someone she knows, or once knew. Maybe even Spencer Goddard, that summer's fatal lover, still living in nearby Hilton, presumably with his wife.

She looks toward the pinewoods, the lacing of bright fall leaves, and she thinks of something else that she will say to Susan, describing this last leg of her trip, her South revisited: "Seeing those woods made me actually burst into tears," she will say. "But you know how I always loved the woods down there. When I was a kid there I spent all my time outdoors."

Or maybe she won't tell anyone, ever, about crying in that awful way, at the sight of familiar woods.

The great thing about the woods, from a child's point of view, was that parents almost never came along; the woods were quite safe then, and there was a lot to do: you could dam up streams or build tepees, wade in the creek or swing on the heavy grapevines, or just run—race through dead leaves and overgrown corn furrows, in the smells of pine and dirt and sun.

Later, of course, the woods took on other meanings; they offered romantic shelter and privacy for kissing, touching—whatever forms early love took. Although actually (or so Claire thought) there was always something inherently sexual in that landscape: the lushness of it all, the white overflowing waterfalls and dense green caves of honeysuckle vines—and, in the fall, crimson leaves as bright as blood. The hiding and kissing, those heats and fears of love all came early for Claire, but for many years, all the years of her true childhood, she was busy with dams and Indian huts, with swinging out into the sky, wading and trying not to fall into the creek.

One afternoon, when she must have been five or six, a small dark skinny child, Claire did fall into the creek; she fell right off a log on which she and some other children had all been crossing to the other side—off, splash, into the water. Not hurt, she stood up, soaking wet, her pink dress streaked with brown. The other children, all older than Claire, began to point and laugh at her, and she laughed, too, enjoying all the attention and the drama. "Oh, my mother will kill me!" she cried out as the other kids went on laughing. And then one by one, accidentally on purpose, they all fell in, and stood around in their soaking wet clothes, in the hot, hot sun. It was a wonderful day, until it was time to go home, and then Claire began to get scared. Of course no one would kill her, but they would be very mad. Her mother, Isabel, would look at her and yell, because Claire was so careless, and her father, Bayard, might do almost anything, depending on how drunk he was; he might even yell at her mother for yelling at Claire, and hug Claire, but in a way that hurt. The only safe grown-up person was Lobelia, the maid, but there was no way to make sure of seeing Lobelia first, and Claire approached her parents' large stone hilltop house cold and heavy with fear.

There were five or six cars in the driveway, and then she remembered that they were having a party; good, she could go right into the kitchen, to Lobelia, and with luck they might forget all about her; she could sneak some food up the back stairs to her room, some ham and beaten biscuits, whatever.

But there right in the middle of the kitchen, of all places for her to be, was Claire's mother, with her head of wild red hair that everyone talked about (saying, "Too bad Claire didn't get your hair, Isabel honey"). She was laughing and telling Lobelia something that some new guests had said about her beaten biscuits, so that Lobelia was smiling, very happy. And Isabel had never looked so beautiful, blue eyes and white teeth flashing, wearing a yellow dress, something floating.

Claire's father, Bayard, must have thought she was beautiful, too; coming into the kitchen at just that moment, he stared at Isabel, and then a great smile broke across his red, usually melancholy face, and he went over and kissed her on the neck—a thing that Claire had never seen him do before.

Isabel must also have been surprised. "Well really, Bayard," she said, in her irrevocably Bostonian voice, frowning a little but very pleased.

And no one scolded Claire for her dirty dress, making it a most unusual evening for all of them. Claire took some chicken and biscuits up to her room, with the vague thought that maybe from now on her whole life would be patterned after this extraordinary day: happy hours of attention from the older kids, and smiles and kisses and happy getting-along-well parents at home.

Naturally enough, things did not continue in quite that way. Sometimes the older kids were nice to Claire and sometimes not, and most of the time Isabel and Bayard got along as badly as ever, and they drank, and drank.

And, like many couples whose mainstay is sheer rage, they kept on being married. Flamboyant Isabel had a couple of flagrant affairs (Claire gathered this from local gossip, later); they separated, reconciled; they both threatened suicide and got drunk together, instead.

Later, Claire escaped to a college in New England, where she was for the most part extremely happy: new friends, a turbulent emotional life, with boys—and no parents. She kept vacations at home to a minimum, often visiting New York or New England friends, instead.

And then, having graduated, she further escaped, to San Francisco, to the first of a series of impressive jobs (impressive to her friends; Isabel and Bayard always seemed a little vague as to what it was, exactly, that she did). But, writing letters back and forth, they got along quite well, Claire and her parents. Better than ever.

Which led to one of her more conspicuous errors in judgment: one June, having been told that her parents were going to Greece for a month, on an impulse Claire wrote and asked if (maybe, possibly) she could have—even rent—the house for that period; she was between jobs and had four weeks' vacation coming. She hadn't been home for so long, and she would really like to see them. Getting no answer at all to her letter, she was—well, hurt. And, characteristically, she castigated herself for that silly pain. How could she possibly, after a lifetime of evidence to the contrary, believe that her parents would behave in an ordinary "parental" way, would want to see her and maybe lend her a house?

However, at the very last minute—the week before they were to leave for Greece—Isabel wrote and said of course she could stay in the house; in fact, it would be quite helpful, since the latest maid had just quit; she was only sorry that their timing now worked out so that she and Bayard could not be there when Claire was, not even for a couple of days.

And so Claire rushed about getting tickets, packing—rushed back to Hilton and into love with Spencer Goddard, an impossible man, a local doctor, an allergist, whose wife and children were spending the summer in Vermont. And she fell in love despite several of Claire's private rules: against affairs with men who were married, with doctors and especially with Southern men, to whom she was not usually drawn (an unreliable lot, in regard to women, as she perfectly well knew). She later excused this lapse by concluding that it was not so much Spencer she had fallen in love with as it was the countryside, the land around Hilton. And that was very likely true.

The house itself was a little depressing that summer: floors long unpolished, certain necessary repairs not made to the tiles on the bathroom floors, the pantry shelves. There was even a smashed pane of glass in the sideboard, where the china and glassware were kept. The absence of a maid could explain some of this, or maybe Bayard and Isabel were drinking even more than usual? Claire was not much bothered by the state of the house, however; once she had fallen in love with Spencer Goddard she paid little attention to anything else.

They met at a party that someone gave for Claire the first week she was back in Hilton (gave out of sheer curiosity, she believed). Spencer was tall and lean, his blond hair almost gray, maybe twenty years older than Claire. Within ten minutes of their meeting he told her that he couldn't keep his eyes off her, that something about her face was haunting—if he never saw her again he would never forget her face. (Claire to Susan, later: "Only a submoron would fall for a man who came on like that.") And the next morning he was at her door with roses, saying that this was the most beautiful day, so far, that summer; wouldn't she come for a walk?

They walked down the white dirt road that led from her house to the woods, and turned off on the path that led to the waterfall and the small meadow of broomstraw, where the children used to build Indian huts.

The waterfall tumbled, still, from a flat ledge of slick black rock, between two densely rooted giant pines, down to an almost perfectly circular pool, dark and deep and always cold. Sometimes there were wild anemones in the crevices between the surrounding rocks, and below the pool the brook ran on through wild tangles of flowering honeysuckle vines—where, naturally enough, Spencer and Claire exchanged their first kiss.

After that day, and that night, Spencer came to her house, the big stone house, for the moment entirely hers, at all hours, several times a day and every night. He couldn't get enough of her, he said. And under such a barrage of apparent adoration, in the familiar June smells of roses and flowering privet and rich earth, the high singing of summer breezes in the pines, Claire began to think that she had, indeed, fallen in love; she had come home in order to find Spencer Goddard.

Actually, San Francisco was his favorite city, Spencer told her; he had often thought he would give anything to live there, and now that he had found her, lovely Claire, whom he could not live without—well, he would have to see. And Claire thought, Well, why not? Men do divorce their wives for younger women, sometimes; it can't be much of a marriage; maybe he will.

She said very little to Spencer along those lines. She said nothing at all until the day he took her to the airport (the airport in which she now sits, in an almost empty plane); on that last morning, sad and sleepless and slightly hung over, she said everything that she had not intended to say; she said that she did not see how she could get through the next few months without him, that if he came to Reno for a divorce she could join him there. And she cried, and for once Spencer said almost nothing at all.

He did not follow her to San Francisco, did not write or call. Once, having come in late from a party at which she had drunk too much wine, Claire called him—to hear him say, in a cold, very wide-awake voice, that she must have the wrong number.

She did hear quite a bit, however, from both Bayard and Isabel. In their version of her summer at home, she had wrecked their house and disgraced them both with her flagrant carryings-on, about which *everyone* was talking.

Almost as angry as she was wounded, Claire wrote back that they seemed to have forgotten that the house was in awful shape when she got there. Was she supposed to have waxed the floors and repaired the tiles and replaced the broken glass in the cabinet? And as for flagrant carryings-on, what about theirs?

A stalemate, no more letters.

And then Bayard died.

Claire went home for the funeral, dreading everything: what would have to be a maudlin, probably drunken reunion with her mother, and the likelihood of some glimpse or word of Spencer Goddard. And she was wrong, all around.

Isabel had stopped drinking entirely and, even more out of character, stopped dyeing her hair. What had been gloriously, if artificially, red was now plain and gray, and Isabel further announced that she was going back to the Catholic Church, from which, she now said, Bayard had stolen her away.

Bayard's funeral, however, was Episcopalian, and also, to Claire's even greater relief, it was not attended by Spencer; she saw and heard nothing of him on that visit.

There followed a period of friendship, or something like it, between Claire and her mother. Claire wrote letters about San Francisco and her job, never mentioning lovers; and Isabel wrote about her new happiness and peace, and her new friends, an order of nuns, cloistered nuns whom she was uniquely privileged to see.

And then quite suddenly Isabel died, and it turned out that she had left the house to the nuns. Which should not have surprised Claire in the least; it was very much an Isabel sort of gesture: attention-getting and absolute. But Claire was surprised, and hurt.

Having been left some money by her father, and being on the whole a fair-minded person, she could not object on material grounds; she could even see the appropriateness of a large stone hilltop house for a cloistered order. It was upsetting, though: the thought of those nuns, whom she envisioned as all clothed in white—white ghosts in all the rooms where Isabel and Bayard had shouted each other down, rooms where, all that summer, Claire and Spencer had violently made love; and the fact of those nuns made the house irrevocably alien, not only not hers but forbidden to her, forever.

"Well, you do look absolutely great" is the first thing that Susan says to Claire, at Dulles Airport, in Washington. "The trip's been a success?" Trim blond Susan, who does not look great; she looks tired and strained, too pale.

They are in the baggage area, waiting for Claire's suitcase. "Oh yes, on the whole," says Claire. "I learned a lot. I've got a suitcase full of notes." As an afterthought, she adds, "One funny thing—we landed at the Raleigh-Durham airport. An unscheduled stop."

Their eyes meet as Susan asks, "Oh, how did it look?"

"Shabby as ever. You know." Claire looks away for a tiny instant, then turns back to Susan as, smiling, she says, "And I really hated the food in New Orleans. I have this theory . . ." And, still smiling, she tells about the underground kitchen that supplies all the restaurants, and the black vat of béchamel.

Susan laughs, and then Claire asks, "Well, how's Jack?"

Three years ago, Susan was planning to leave Jack, her husband; she even came out to San Francisco, to get away and talk, and to be comforted, presumably. But then she went home and apparently decided not to go through with it. And now she says, "Oh, he's fine. Working too hard. You know."

The two women exchange a reassuring, quick smile, acknowledging that this is not to be a visit for serious conversation; neither of them is up to that, just now, but surely, some other time, they will talk again.

That night Susan and Jack give a party for Claire. Although she has met several of their friends before, people who know that she comes from Hilton, she does not explain, if they ask, how come she went almost all over the South but not to Hilton, and several people do ask that. "I just decided not to, this time," she says.

Nor does she drink too much, or urge anyone, particularly anyone's husband, to be sure to call her when he comes to San Francisco.

Nor, at this party, do Jack and Susan quarrel.

On the way to the airport with Susan, leaving Washington and heading for San Francisco, Claire remembers the story about the cab-driver in Atlanta, which she tells ("Once they's had they lunch . . ."). She and Susan laugh, and then Claire says, "It's curious, the ways in which it will absolutely never change."

"Yes—"

"On the whole I think I prefer the landscape to the people."

Susan laughs again. "Well, that's a good line. You could use it in your piece."

"Well, I just might."

Back in San Francisco, in her small house on the eastern slope of Telegraph Hill, her sanctuary, Claire, who at the moment has no ongoing love affair to disturb and distract her, begins to get to work on her article; she stays home from the office, and for long periods of time she turns off her phone. But not even a good title offers itself. In fact, from the beginning, the trouble that she has with this piece is an unwelcome surprise. Seated at her broad desk, before her window that looks out to the bay, Bay Bridge, Treasure Island and the Oakland hills—to water, boats and birds—in a laborious and quite unfamiliar way she lists possible topics, she tries for a plausible central thesis. At the desk, where she has so often worried and suffered acutely over love affairs, and at the same time managed to work quite hard and well, she now worries and begins to suffer over her work, over what has become an impossible assignment.

After a few such days it does begin to go a little better, but it is sheer labor; at no time does she feel the pleasure that she usually experiences in work, that lively joy in her own competence.

This is all very troubling to Claire, who has prided herself, always, on functioning in a highly professional manner, who has even been somewhat critical of those who do not.

Telegraph Hill is in many ways a small town, or perhaps several small towns; there are neighborhood feuds and passionate loyalties, complex and concentric circles of current and former lovers, husbands and wives, all of whom meet in the local restaurants and bars, the grocery stores and Laundromats along Grant Avenue, Green Street, Vallejo Street, Columbus Avenue. Many people who, like Claire, are for one reason or another alienated from where they grew up feel very much at home on Telegraph Hill.

One of Claire's long-standing, non-lover friends is a man named Dan Breckenridge, an aging, still-handsome bachelor, whose pattern with women is invariable, and unfortunate: a gambit going from heavy pursuit to a few weeks of heady love, quickly followed by elusiveness and distance—to, when he finds it necessary, downright meanness. But as a friend he is perfectly all right; he is amusing and generous and kind. From time to time he makes a semi-serious pass at Claire, a sort of sexual feint in her direction which is easy to head off, although (she has admitted to herself) she does find him attractive. They remain good friends, and their friendship is undoubtedly enhanced by this not-acted-out attraction.

Like many adoptive Californians (he is originally from Chicago), Dan is enthusiastic about California wine; he has usually just found something new and wonderful, from a small vineyard that no one else has heard of yet.

A week or so after her return from her trip, he invites Claire to dinner and he serves a nice dry Pinot Chardonnay—of which he and Claire both drink too much.

So that when he says, in his decisive Midwestern way, "There must be some reason for that article's hanging you up; I wish you'd really tell me about your trip," she does tell him.

She tells him about the cloying prettiness of Charleston; the more interesting beauty of Savannah; New Orleans food, and the vat of béchamel; the new architecture of Atlanta; the racist cabdriver.

And then she tells about flying from Atlanta to Washington. "I was looking down at the woods, and they looked so familiar," she said, "and then one of the men across from me said it must be Hilton—and, Dan, it was horrible, I burst into tears. I couldn't help it. God, it was awful."

Saying what she has so far said to no one, Claire feels the onset of tears, but this time she is able to control them, almost, as she hears Dan say, "Well, I don't think that's so terrible. Flying right over where you grew up, not expecting it. A lot of people would cry. And you really were exiled from there. Dispossessed."

Looking up at him, Claire sees that he is especially drawn to her at that moment (he likes women who cry?); and his kindness and empathy so move her that she is afraid of losing control. If she begins to cry seriously he will touch her, one thing will lead to another, and the last thing she needs, just then, is an affair with Dan Breckenridge. And so, with all the sobriety that she can muster, she gets up and says she's sorry she's so tired, the dinner was terrific—thanks.

Customarily, although affectionate in a verbal way with each other, Claire and Dan are not physically so; they almost never touch, and they do not do so now. They do not kiss good night after Dan has walked with her the two blocks from his house to hers, in the cool, very clear starred night. But at her door, he gives her a longer, more serious look than usual.

Can she have fallen in love with Dan? That is what some of the symptoms with which Claire wakes up the following morning suggest: a nervous lassitude, some fear of the oncoming day. However, she gets up and drinks a lot of tea; she concludes that she has a slight hangover; and she tries to get to work.

Around noon Dan telephones. That is not a usual time for him to call, and at first Claire thinks, Oh, I must have sounded terrible last night, and worried him.

He asks how things are going, and she tells him that, curiously enough, they seem to be going a little better. She is getting somewhere, at last, with whatever the problem was.

And then, in an odd, abrupt way, Dan says, "Well, how about tonight? Can we see each other?"

"Uh, sure. I'm not doing anything. Should I cook?"

"No, don't be silly. You're working. I want to take you out. Let's drive to Sausalito, okay?"

"Well, sure."

Claire hangs up, more puzzled than she is pleased. Nervous, apprehensive. She even thinks of calling Susan; she can hear herself saying, "Well honestly, now I've done something really dumb, I think. I've fallen in love with an old friend, Dan Breckenridge, and I think he feels that way too. And he's just my type, mean and selfish and elusive."

And Susan will laugh and say, "Well honestly, that's really too bad."

It is true, though, that she has begun to feel considerably better. After Dan's call she goes into the kitchen and heats up a can of tomato soup, with a lot of Parmesan, for nourishment. And she makes more tea.

Back at her desk, the beautiful bright familiar view is reassuring; this is, after all, where she has chosen to live—at the moment it seems a good choice.

However, instead of finally getting down to work on the serious article that is her assignment, in a dreamlike way Claire sits back in her chair, and she begins, rather, to recall the particularities of her trip. She remembers certain accents, heard on streets, in restaurants, in Atlanta and Charleston, Savannah and New Orleans—and gestures observed, both unique and indigenous to that region. And she sees again the colors of earth and leaves which, at certain times of the year, in a certain place, are absolutely unmistakable.

The Girl Across the Room

Yvonne Soulas, the art historian, is much more beautiful in her late sixties than she was when she was young, and this is strange, because she has had much trouble in her life, including pancreatic cancer, through which she lived when no one expected her to. Neither her doctor nor her husband, Matthew Vann, the musicologist-manufacturer, thought she would make it, such a small, thin woman. Make it she did, however, although she lost much of her hair in the process of treatment. Now, seated with Matthew on the porch of an inn on the northern California coast, her fine, precise features framed in skillfully arranged false white waves, she is a lovely woman. In the cool spring night she is wearing soft pale woolen clothes, a shawl and Italian boots, daintily stitched.

Matthew Vann is also a handsome person, with silky white hair and impressive dark eyes, and he, too, wears elegant clothes. His posture is distinguished. Yvonne has never taken his name, not for feminist reasons but because she thinks the combination is unaesthetic: Yvonne Vann? Matthew looks and is considerably more fragile than Yvonne, although they are about the same age: that is to say, among other things, of an age to wonder which of them will outlive the other. The question is impossible, inadmissible and crucially important. Matthew *is* frailer, but then Yvonne's illness could recur at any time.

They have been married for a little over thirty years, and they live, these days, in San Francisco, having decided that the rigors of New England winters and the overstimulation of Cambridge social life were, in combination, far too much for them. Trips to Europe, also, formerly a source of much pleasure, now seem, really, more strenuous than fun. And so Yvonne and Matthew have taken to exploring certain areas of California, beginning with the near at hand: Yosemite, Lake Tahoe and now this extraordinarily beautiful stretch of coast at Mendocino, where rivers empty into the sea between sheer cliffs of rock.

They are sitting at the far end of the white railed porch that runs the length of the building in which they are lodging. They have had an early dinner, hoping for quiet, and they are tired from a day of exploring the town and the meadows high above the vibrating sea. The other guests are almost all golfing people, since there is a course adjacent to the inn. They are people in late middle age, a little younger than Yvonne and Matthew, mostly overweight, tending to noise and heavy smoking and excessive drink. Not pleasant dinner companions. And Yvonne and Matthew were successful: they finished a quiet dinner of excellent abalone before the boisterous arrival of the golfing group. There was only one other couple in the dining room. That other couple had also been distinctly not a part of the golfing group, and they were as striking, in their way, as Yvonne and Matthew were in theirs. Yvonne had been unable not to stare at them—the girl so young and perfectly controlled in all her gestures, the man much older than the girl, so clearly and happily in love with her. It won't end well, Yvonne had thought.

Everything is fine as they sit now on the porch. This place to which they have come is very beautiful. The walks through wild flowers and the views back to the river mouth, the beaches, the opposite banks of green are all marvelous. Everything is fine, except for a nagging area of trouble that has just lodged itself somewhere near Yvonne's heart. But the trouble is quite irrational, and she is an eminently sensible woman, and so she pushes it aside and begins a conversation with Matthew about something else.

"A thing that I like about being old," she observes to him, at the same time as she reflects that many of their conversations have had just this beginning, "is that you go on trips for their own sake, just to see something. Not expecting the trip to change your life." Not hoping that the man you are with will want to marry you, she is thinking to herself, or that Italy will cure your husband of a girl.

"Ye-e-es," drawls Matthew, in his vague New Hampshire way. But he is a good listener; he very much enjoys her conversation. "Yvonne is the least boring person in the world," he has often said—if not to her, to a great many other people.

"When you're young, you really don't see much beyond yourself," Yvonne muses.

Then, perhaps at having spoken the word "young," thinking of young people, of herself much younger, the trouble increases. It becomes an active heavy pressure on her heart, so that she closes her eyes for a moment. Then she opens them, facing it, admitting to herself: That girl in the dining room reminded me of Susanna, in Cambridge, almost thirty years ago. Not long after we were married, which of course made it worse.

What happened was this:

In the late forties, in Cambridge, Yvonne was viewed as a smart, attractive but not really pretty French woman. A widow? Divorced? No one knew for sure. She had heavy dark hair, a husky voice and a way of starting sentences with an "Ah!" that sounded like a tiny bark. Some people were surprised to find her married to Matthew Vann, a glamorous man, admired for having fought in Spain as well as for his great good looks, a man as distinguished as he was rich. Then a beautiful young Radcliffe girl who wanted to become a dancer, and for all anyone knew eventually became one—a golden California girl, Susanna—fell in love with Matthew, and he with her. But Yvonne wouldn't let him go, and so nothing came of it. That was all.

Thus went the story that circulated like a lively winter germ through the areas of Cambridge adjacent to Harvard Square, up and down Brattle Street, Linnaean, Garden Street and Massachusetts Avenue, and finally over to Hillside Place, where Yvonne and Matthew then were living.

But that is not, exactly, how it was. It went more like this:

"You won't believe me, but I think a very young girl has fallen in love with me," Matthew said to Yvonne one night, near the end of their dinner of *lapin au moutarde,* a specialty of Yvonne's which she always thenceforward connected unpleasantly with that night, although she continued to make it from time to time. (Silly not to, really.) Then Matthew laughed, a little awkward, embarrassed. "It does seem unlikely."

"Not at all." Yvonne's tone was light, the words automatic. Her accent was still very French. "You are a most handsome man," she said.

"You might remember her. We met her at the Emorys'. Susanna something, from California. I've kept seeing her in Widener, and now she says she wants to help me with my research." He laughed, more embarrassed yet.

Yvonne experienced a wave of fury, which she quickly brought under control, breathing regularly and taking a small sip of wine. Of course she remembered the girl: long dark-gold hair and sunny, tawny skin; bad clothes, but not needing good clothes with that long lovely neck; a stiff, rather self-conscious dancer's walk; lovely long hands, beautifully controlled. Anyone would fall in love with her.

In those days, while Yvonne did her own work at the Fogg, Matthew was combining supervision of the factory he had inherited, in Waltham, with the musicologist's career that he had chosen. The research he had mentioned was for his book on Boccherini, for which they would later spend a year in Italy. They had married after a wildly passionate affair, during which Yvonne had managed to wrest Matthew away from poor Flossie, his alcoholic first wife, now long since dead in Tennessee.

And, thinking over the problem of Susanna, one thing that Yvonne said silently to her rival was: You can't have him; I've already been through too much for Matthew. Also, in her exceptionally clearheaded way, Yvonne *knew* Matthew, in a way that violent love can sometimes preclude. She knew that he would not take Susanna to bed unless he had decided to break with Yvonne—this out of a strong and somewhat aberrant New England sense of honor, and also out of sexual shyness, unusual in so handsome, so sensual a man. Yvonne herself had had to resort to a kind of seduction by force. But a young, proud girl could not know of such tactics.

Yvonne was right. Matthew did not have an affair with Susanna; he probably never saw her outside of Widener, except for an intense cup of coffee at Hayes-Bickford, where they were noticed together. However, Matthew suffered severely, and that was how Yvonne treated him—like someone with a serious disease. She was affectionate and solicitous, and very slightly distant, as though his illness were something that she didn't want to catch.

One March evening, after a bright, harsh day of intermittent sun, rain and wind, Matthew came home for dinner a little late, with a look on his face of total and anguished exhaustion. Handing him his gin—they were in the kitchen; she had been tasting her good lamb stew, a *navarin*—Yvonne thought, Ah, the girl has broken it off, or has given him an ultimatum; such a mistake. She thought, I hope I won't have to hear about it.

All Matthew said during dinner was "The Boccherini project is sort of getting me down. My ideas don't come together."

"Poor darling," she said carefully, alertly watching his face.

"I should spend more time at the factory."

"Well, why don't you?"

As they settled in the living room for coffee, Yvonne saw that his face had relaxed a little. Perhaps now he would want to talk to her? She said, "There's a Fred Astaire revival at the U.T. tonight. I know you don't like them, but would you mind if I go? Ah, dear, it's almost time."

Not saying: You unspeakable fool, how dare you put me through all this? Are you really worth it?

Alone in the crowded balcony of the University Theatre, as on the screen Fred and Ginger sang to each other about how lovely a day it was to be caught in the rain, Yvonne thought, for a moment, that she would after all go home and tell Matthew to go to his girl, Susanna. She would release him, with as little guilt as possible, since she was indeed fond of Matthew. *Je tiens à Matthew.*

Tenir à. I hold to Matthew, Yvonne thought then. And she also thought, No, it would not work out well at all. Matthew is much too vulnerable for a girl like that. He is better off with me.

Of course she was right, as Matthew himself must have come to realize, and over the summer he seemed to recover from his affliction. Yvonne saw his recovery, but she also understood that she had been seriously wounded by that episode, coming as it did so early in their life together. Afterward she was able to think more sensibly, Well, much better early than later on, when he could have felt more free.

That fall they left for Italy, where, curiously, neither of them had been before—Yvonne because her Anglophile parents had always taken her to the Devon coast on holidays, or sometimes to Scotland, Matthew because with drunken Flossie any travel was impossible.

They settled in a small hotel in Rome, in a large romantically alcoved room that overlooked the Borghese Gardens. They went on trips: north to Orvieto, Todi, Spoleto, Gubbio; south to Salerno, Positano, Ravello. They were dazed, dizzy with pleasure at the landscape, the vistas of olive orchards, of pines and flowers and stones, the ancient buildings, the paintings and statuary. The food and wine. They shared a mania for pasta.

A perfect trip, except that from time to time Yvonne was jolted sharply by a thought of that girl, Susanna. And, looking at Matthew, she wondered if he, too, thought of her—with sadness, regret? The question hurt.

She would have to ask Matthew, and deliberately she chose a moment of pure happiness. They were seated on a vine-covered terrace, at Orvieto, across the square from the gorgeously striped cathedral, drinking cool white wine, having made love early that morning, when Yvonne asked, "Do you ever wonder what happened to that girl, Susanna?"

Genuine puzzlement appeared on Matthew's distinguished face, and then he said, "I almost never think of her. I don't have time."

Knowing Matthew, Yvonne was sure that he spoke the truth, and she wryly thought, I undoubtedly think more often of that girl, that episode, than Matthew does.

And so she, too, stopped thinking of Susanna—or almost, except for an occasional reminder.

Leaving Rome, they traveled up to Florence, then Venice, Innsbruck, and Vienna.

That was the first of a succession of great trips.

Yvonne and Matthew remained, for the most part, very happy with each other, and over the years their sexual life declined only slightly. Then, in her late fifties, Yvonne became terribly sick, at first undiagnosably so. Surgery was indicated. On being told the probable nature of her illness—she had insisted on that—Yvonne remarked to her doctor, one of the chief surgeons at Massachusetts General, "Well, my chances are not exactly marvelous, then, are they?"

He looked embarrassed, and gazed in the direction of the Charles, just visible from his high office window. "No, not marvelous," he admitted.

After surgery, oppressively drugged, Yvonne was mainly aware of pain, which surged in heavy waves toward her, almost overwhelming her, and very gradually receding. She was aware, too, of being handled a great deal, not always gently, of needles inserted, and tubes, of strong hands manipulating her small body.

Sometimes, half conscious, she would wonder if she was dreaming. But at least she knew that she was alive: dead people don't wonder about anything, she was sure of that.

The first face that she was aware of was her surgeon's: humorless, stern, seeming always to be saying, No, not marvelous. Then there was the face of a black nurse, kind and sad, a gentle, mourning face. At last she saw Matthew, so gaunt and stricken that she knew she had to live. It was that simple: dying was something she could not do to Matthew.

"She's got to be the strongest woman I've ever seen, basically," the dubious surgeon remarked later on to Matthew, who by then could beamingly agree.

Chemotherapy worked; it took most of her hair but fortunately did not make her sick. Yvonne very gradually regained strength, and some health, and with a great effort she put back on a few of the many lost pounds. Matthew learned to make a superior fettuccine, and he served it to her often.

After her illness and surgery, they did not make love anymore; they just did not. Yvonne missed it, in a dim sad way, but on the other hand she could sometimes smile at the very idea of such a ludicrous human activity, to which she herself had once devoted so much time. She was on the whole amused and a little skeptical of accounts of very sexually active seventy- and eighty-year-olds: why did they bother, really?

While she was recuperating, Yvonne finished a study of Marie Laurencin that she had been working on for years, and her book had considerable acclaim, even reasonably good sales. Matthew did not finish his Boccherini study, but from time to time he published articles in places like the *Hudson Review,* the *Harvard Magazine.*

A year ago, they left Cambridge and moved to the pleasant flat on Green Street, in San Francisco.

Now, on the porch in Mendocino, thinking of the girl across the room at dinner, and remembering Susanna, all that pain, Yvonne has a vivid insight as to how it would have been if she had abandoned Matthew to Susanna all those years ago. Matthew would, of course, have married the girl—that is how he is—and they would have been quite happy for a while. He would have gazed dotingly upon her in restaurants, like the man in the dining room, with his Susanna. And then somehow it would all have gone bad, with a sad old age for Matthew, the girl bored and irritable, Matthew worn out, not understanding anything.

But what of herself? What would have happened to her? The strange part is that Yvonne has never inquired into this before. Now, with perfect logic, she suddenly, jarringly sees just what would have happened: for a while, considerable unhappiness for her, a slow recovery. And then she would have been quite herself again, maybe a little improved. She would have remarried—amazing, she can almost see him! He is no one she knows, but a man much younger than herself, very dark. In fact, he is French; they have many intimate things in common. He might be a painter. He is very unlike Matthew. Would she still have had her great illness? She is not sure; her vision ends with that man, her marriage to him.

Something in her expression, probably, has made Matthew ask a question never asked between them, a question, in fact, for adolescent lovers: "What were you thinking about, just now?"

And he is given, by Yvonne, the requisite response: "I was thinking, my darling, of you. At least in part."

The air on the porch is perceptibly chillier than when they first came out from dinner. Time to go in, and yet they are both reluctant to move: it is so beautiful where they are. In the distance, gray-white lines of foam cross the sea, beneath a calm pale evening sky; closer to hand are the surrounding, sheltering pines and cypresses.

Then, from whatever uncharacteristic moment of strong emotion, Matthew says another thing that he has not said before. "I was thinking," he says, "that without you I would not have had much of a life at all."

Does he mean if they had never met? Or does he mean if he had left her for that girl, for fair Susanna? Or if she had died? It is impossible to ask, and so Yvonne frowns, unseen, in the gathering dusk—both at the ambiguity and at the surprise of it. And she, too, says something new: "Ah, Matthew, what an absolute fool you are." But she has said it lightly, and she adds, "You would have got along perfectly well without me." She knows that out of her true fondness for Matthew she has lied, and that it is still necessary for her to survive him.

Lost Luggage

I can only explain my genuine lack of concern, when I first realized that my suitcase was missing, not coming up with the others off the plane, by saying that at that moment I was in a mood of more than usual self-approval; you could call it pride, or maybe hubris, even: I had just managed to enjoy a vacation alone—to come out unscathed, anyway—at a Mexican resort where I had often gone with my recently dead husband, a trip warned against by my children and well-meaning friends, of course. But it had been all right; I was glad that I had gone there. My other source of pride was sillier but forgivable, I think; it was simply that I was looking very well. I was tan, and the warm, gentle green Mexican water had been kind to my hair. I was brown and silver, like a weathering country house, and I did not mind the thought of myself as aging wood.

In any case, I watched the procession of luggage as it erupted from the maw of the baggage area in the San Francisco terminal, up from the Toltec Airlines plane that I had just got off; I watched each piece as it was claimed and lifted off the treadmill and taken away. With no sinking of my heart (that came much later), I waited until all the other bags were gone, as the empty treadmill moved in its creaking circle, and I realized that that was it: no more bags. An official-looking person confirmed that view: my suitcase was somewhere else, or lost, or irreparably smashed. And I was not at all upset.

I had not been so foolish as to take anything valuable (had I indeed owned anything of that sort of value) to a somewhat ratty resort, on a Mexican beach, and I even thought, Oh, good, now I won't have to wash out that robe with the suntan-lotion stains.

A pretty black girl in the uniform of the airline gave me a form to fill out, describing the suitcase, and giving my name, Janet Stone Halloran, my address and phone. She gave me a claim number, and she said, "You'll be given twenty-five dollars for makeup and drugs, you know, for tonight."

Good, is what I thought again. Very good. I can take a cab home and buy some toothpaste, a brush, astringent, cream. For various reasons, mostly having to do with pride and with my new role as a single woman, I had spent too much money in Mexico, paid for too many rounds of margaritas, so I was quite conscious of even small sums of money. I assumed then that a check for twenty-five would come to me automatically, probably tomorrow.

The truth is that I was quite broke; I needed to get a job as soon as possible, Walter not having believed in insurance, but I wasn't dealing with that problem yet. I had dealt as best I could with Walter's death, I had successfully gone to Mexico. I would think about money and jobs tomorrow; I would go out looking while I still was tan.

Actually, and this did not make his death any easier, Walter and I had not liked each other much lately. We had married young, for love (well, sex, really); in our day that is what you did when strongly attracted. And as the physical intensity calmed down, diminished, all our other energies seemed to go in opposite directions. A familiar story, I guess, but that made it no easier to bear.

Like many lonely women, I became bookish, an obsessive reader, my favorites being long Victorian novels. (Once, reading *The Egoist*—Meredith's best, I thought—I started to recommend it to Walter, such a wonderfully funny book. But then I recognized that Walter would not think it was funny at all.)

Walter's major passion, his obsession, turned out to be cars: even after professionally he went from selling Fords to selling life insurance, he was constantly buying, selling, trading, trading in, cars. We must have averaged four or five cars a year, and last year, the year he died, we went through seven. And always terrifically fancy ones; I now have a 1935 Franklin, in mint condition, up for sale. I hated to be unsympathetic, but I found all this car business scary, something we couldn't afford, and I sometimes said as much. But Walter, a fast-talking red-haired Irishman, a looker, a flirt, was not much of a listener, or not to me. He would frown distractedly, and go on with his dreams of cars.

None of which helped when he died. Along with natural grief and shock, I felt guilty as hell: why couldn't I have been nicer about a relatively harmless habit? He could have been "sleeping around," as we used to say; well, maybe he was doing that, too. In any case, his death was a dreadful—an appalling—event.

None of our friends knew how little money Walter and I had (no doubt misled by all those fancy cars), any more than they knew how little we liked each other. Neither fact had been something that I could ever speak of, or maybe I had long ago got used to not saying those things—a New England habit of reserve. And there was a connection between those conditions: if we had had money, especially if I had had a little of my own—that enviable condition—we could have split up; but no, we had children very early on (red-haired, all of them, of course), four children who seemed to stay young forever as we aged. Now they were all away at school, except our oldest daughter, who was married, and when I say that I had no money I mean that I had barely enough to keep them there, and not enough to live on much longer by myself. Probably we would all have to go to work. I didn't think it would hurt us much; more New England Puritanism, I guess.

And my choice of the Mexican beach had been connected with both of those unmentionable facts, lack of money and not getting along with Walter. It was extremely cheap, and it was where Walter and I had got along least well. I always loved it; he hated it there, and went along as a concession to my poor taste, if grudgingly. For one thing, there were no tennis courts within miles, and Walt was an impassioned tennis buff. (He died on the courts, in fact, after what I was told was a magnificent overhead smash. A good death, in that way, I guess you could call it.)

To a degree, naturally enough, my friends and children were right; it was lonely being there without even an unloved, quarrelsome Walter. And, as widows will, or anyone will just after a serious love affair, for a while I found it hard to remember anything but the good times between us, the early years when we both had jobs with conflicting schedules, his selling Fords, mine doing research for some lawyers; and so whenever we were even briefly at home together we would make love, as instantly and happily as mating birds.

Also, as I sat alone on my terrace, watching one of those incredible tropical sunsets, the whole sky covered with bright rags of clouds, I would feel really frightened, and not unreasonably so. There was not exactly a superabundance of jobs around, and suppose I couldn't find one, or not for years? I was well trained, I'd had occasional research jobs along the way, helping out with family money, and I knew a lot of people; still, I was quite a few years over twenty-five, or even thirty. What would I do? (I know, nowhere near the poverty level; but still a cause for concern, I thought.)

At other times, however, down there in the balmy breezes, I would experience an exhilarating sense of adventure. I knew myself to be a strong woman: surely I could turn my life around? I was not really dependent on a middle-class support system, on certain styles of dress and entertaining, on "safe" neighborhoods. I could even, I imagined, find a big house to share with some other working women, about my age—not exactly a commune but a cooperative venture. Such prospects excited and to a degree sustained me.

And there was always the extreme beauty of the place itself, the big horseshoe cove of lovely water, with its white, white beach and rocky promontories at either edge. The green tropical growth that rose from the outer edge of sand into hills. And the clear enormous sky, its brilliant blue, then gaudy sunsets, and, later, billions of stars. Not to mention the flowers spilling over everywhere—the profusion of bougainvillea, of every shade of pink and orange. I could feel it all seeping into me, with the stillness, the peace.

Fortunately, in a way, the last time Walt and I were in Mexico was by far our worst. Nothing dramatic or specific—just a miasma of incommunicable depression that settled on us both. What exactly was on Walt's mind I have no idea, just boredom and restlessness, perhaps—or he could have been having a "relationship" in San Francisco (I always at least half suspected that he was), with someone whom he missed. I myself was depressed at the changes that I saw in us, and in our bodies. Our slowing middle-aged flesh seemed to parody its former eager, quick incarnation, and I looked at the other couples, many considerably older than we were, who had come down to the tropics to warm their hardening bones—timorous people looking outward rather than toward each other, their flesh no longer joined. And I thought, Is that where we are going, Walt and I? Is the rest of our life together, if we stay together, to be such a process of attrition?

And so, in that sense, being there without Walt was better; I could remember the good days quite as easily as the bad—in fact, more easily;

I was no longer daily, hourly reminded by his presence that we no longer loved or even much liked each other. In a dignified way I could be sad about him, even. He had enjoyed his life, his tennis and skiing, parties, drinking, and, for the most part, he had enjoyed and liked our children. It was grossly unfair that he should be cut off from all that, so relatively young.

At the beach, then, I thought my own thoughts, and swam a lot, and read, and I let the gentle beauty of the place drift through my mind. And I observed, rather than actively participating in, what social life there was.

I saw a woman who, like myself, seemed to be traveling alone; some years older than I was, she could easily have been a widow also, or maybe divorced. And she was talking too much. I would see her with groups on the beach, or at the bar, talking and talking. I had earlier noticed such an impulse in myself; as though to compensate for Walter's lack, to say enough for us both, I had developed a new tendency to garrulousness. And now, in a distant, sympathetic way, I wanted to say to this woman, Please don't, you don't have to make up for being alone, in that way.

I further observed a young man, also alone, but seemingly having attached himself to a group of older people. He was not really as young as he felt that he was. He would be very good with old ladies, except for a certain kind of old lady (the kind I plan to be), who will suddenly wonder why she is paying for all his drinks, and will decide that he is not quite worth it. I watched as, each time someone in the group was due to sign for drinks, that aging boy would be engaged in animated conversation somewhere else—as, still unobserved by him, the smiles around him congealed and froze.

Which is one reason that whenever I fell in with a group at the bar I made a point of buying more than my share of drinks.

I looked, and thought, and observed, and I wrote down a great deal in a daybook that I had begun to keep, begun just after Walter died. Two friends had suggested this, women who did not know each other. A coincidence, possibly, but enough to make me listen—although I later concluded that they were both influenced by the fact that I write letters much more often than I telephone.

Also, like so many women of my generation (and I would hope some men and younger women, too), I had been powerfully moved by

Doris Lessing's *The Golden Notebook.* Not that I saw much connection between myself and her heroine, Anna (or with Lessing herself); still, for weeks and then months after Walter died, I made myself write everything down, like Anna in the Blue Notebook section, trying to understand.

And it did help, quite a lot. I could see a certain progress from the rage and despair of the first entries, the nightmare scene at the funeral parlor. I had not wanted to "view" Walter; I was talked into it—shamed into it, really—by my oldest daughter, the married one, and by, of course, the funeral-parlor person. How wonderful he looks, they both murmured, though in a questioning way; he looks asleep. Having spent many hours looking at Walter asleep—he always slept well, whereas I had occasional insomnia—I thought he did not look asleep; he looked dead, very dead, dead for good. I hated myself for breaking down and crying noisily in that place.

Well, all that was vividly in my notebook, and then there were some better days recorded, and a few more bad ones. Kind friends, insensitive friends, intuitive strangers.

It was encouraging on those bad days to look back to worse ones, earlier on, and when I actually felt well, restored to my old self, competent and strong—with what pride I recorded that sense.

It was not until I was in the taxi, heading home from the airport, and thinking with foolish pleasure about my check for twenty-five dollars, that I realized that my notebook was in the missing suitcase, along with the stained robe and the other things I didn't much care about. And in that moment of understanding that my notebook could be gone forever, I did not see how I could go on with my life. Everything within me sank. It was as though my respirator, whatever essential machine had kept me breathing, was cruelly removed. This is worse than Walter's death, I crazily thought, and then amended (I revised, as I had learned to do with crazy thoughts) so that in my mind it now read, I can deal with this less well than I did with Walter's death.

Arrived at my door, I paid for the taxi with several of my last vacation dollars, and I let myself into my small (though now too large) "safe" flat.

There was a pile of letters on the floor which, since I had no bag to unpack, I immediately sat down to read. And there, among the bills and circulars, the demands, were three letters which, had I been in a more normal mood, might have made me happy: two of them from two of my scattered children, both simply nice, kind and friendly—sounding like the sort of people I would have wanted them to turn out to be—and the third from a lawyer for whom I had once worked, offering sensible job-getting advice and strong encouragement. As I say, had it not been for my missing bag and my lost notebook, it would have been a good homecoming.

I lay awake planning phone calls.

Toltec Airlines, as it turned out the following morning, did not have its own Lost and Found (a bad sign right there, I thought); its losses and finds were reported to another airline, Griffith International. I described my bag to a cheerfully inattentive girl: a cheap make, I said, black vinyl, with a safety pin in the zipper. Yes, it was clearly marked with my name and address.

Had I reported its loss?

Yes, of course. Last night.

Well, most bags eventually turn up, she said, and I must believe that they were just as eager to return my bag to me as I was to get it.

I could not possibly believe that, I told her severely; it was simply untrue. And then, as though it were an afterthought, I asked about the twenty-five-dollar compensation check.

Oh, that's only for people just stopping over, she said.

Oh.

She suggested that I might want to call the night person at Toltec Airlines; he comes on every night at six, she said, and she gave me a number.

The man's name was Dick Parker—a too simple, forgettable name, but I managed to keep it in my mind all day; in fact I thought of nothing else.

He turned out to be both less interested and less optimistic than the morning girl. Well, sometimes bags did get stolen, he said. Nothing the airlines could do, thefts happen.

Even old shabby bags like mine?

Older, shabbier ones got ripped off. For all the thieves knew, there were diamonds inside, he picturesquely said.

After a long pause, during which I tried to digest his gloomy and irrefutable logic, I asked about compensation.

The airline pays three hundred dollars after two weeks, he said.

Oh.

The young woman who answered the Lost and Found number the next morning sounded Mexican, I thought, which I found irrationally cheering, as though national pride would encourage more strenuous efforts on her part. I again described my bag, and again she went off to look. Only later did it occur to me that she might—she *should* have had that description already filed.

No, she announced on her return; my bag was not there, I should immediately call Mr. Playa, Pablo Playa, who was in charge of Toltec Airlines, and she gave me a number.

This was encouraging—someone in charge—and I was charmed by the name Pablo Playa. The numbers that I dialed, however, felt familiar; just as Mr. Playa answered, I realized that it was the number of Dick Parker: Pablo Playa was the daytime Dick Parker.

But he had a mellifluous Latin voice, Pablo Playa did, and his tone was the most, if not the only, sympathetic official voice that I had heard. Of *course* I was upset, he said, and *everything* would be done to find my bag. I must believe him, the bag would be returned to me within days. And also, at the very worst, the airline paid five hundred dollars for lost bags, within fifteen days.

For a few minutes I felt vastly cheered—my automatic response to warmth and charm, to promises—and then, with a characteristic reversal, certain grim and obvious truths appeared, to rebuke my foolish optimism. First, none of those people knew what the others were doing; there was no one in charge. Second, there was no fixed policy about compensation. Third, there was no concentrated or even directed effort to retrieve my bag.

That night I again called Dick Parker, who instantly confirmed all those suspicions. How long had it been since I lost my bag, he wanted to know.

It was not I who had lost the bag, I reminded him; it was *them*. And maybe they should coordinate their files, as well as their efforts.

Thank you for telling me how to do my job, he said, in a furious way. I think we both hung up at the same moment.

Over the long haul of my life, I have noticed that even the most upsetting things get better with the simple passage of time; even deaths become less painful. But it was not so with my missing bag; it was, in many ways, like the aftermath of a robbery. Once, Walter and I had been burglarized, and for weeks I kept discovering more things that were not there: a set of silver grapefruit spoons, some pretty cocktail napkins, all the Beethoven quartets (a tasteful ripper-offer, that one was). And now, having thought everything but my notebook valueless, I began to remember a nice old pink cotton shirt, inexplicably becoming; some big white beads (cheap, from Cost Plus, but where would I find them again).

Far worse was my deranged sense of being crippled without my notebook, my notes; and my awareness that it made no sense was not much help. I considered, and discarded, the obvious theory that this was a substitute mourning for Walter, that it was actually Walter whom I could not live without; that explanation simply did not grip me in the way that a true insight invariably does. I also asked myself if the lost notebook was an excuse for postponing other tasks at hand, like scrubbing the open kitchen shelves. Looking for a job.

The next day, as though to refute that thought, I did scrub the shelves. I've read somewhere that all women have a least favorite household task, and that is mine: the irritation of putting those little spice jars and bottles somewhere else, displacing the adorable little keepsakes, spilling the cleaning stuff on the floor. Et cetera.

And then, like a reward, it came to me, something that probably anyone else would have thought of days before: I would go out and buy another notebook, I would write down all that I could remember from the former entries and then I would start in again. Obviously, I had become addicted to writing things down; that was the core of my problem.

A wonderful idea, a solution—but in the stationery store I hesitated. The lost notebook, whose duplicate was right there on the shelf before me, had been rather expensive, seven dollars, now up to eight-fifty. (I could measure the time since Walter's death by the rate of inflation,

I thought.) Maybe I would get the old notebook back? In that mood, I compromised on a much smaller, though matching, book; its spine was also stamped RECORD, and it cost two-fifty.

I took it home, and eagerly, right away, I began to record the newest chapter in my life, which I headed, of course, Lost Luggage.

By rights my suitcase should then have been returned—my reward for maturity and strength—and I superstitiously believed that it actually would be. It had been missing now for five full days. And, still expecting that it would reappear, I concentrated on writing. I stopped calling the Toltec people and, instead, I called my travel agent and told her of those troubles; she would take care of everything, she said.

I had imagined that I might try, as a sort of exercise, to record some of what I had felt and had written in my original book about the days and months just after Walter's death, but I did not. I wrote about the colors of Mexico, still lively and brilliant in my mind, and from there I moved farther back, much farther, to some childhood colors: the calm blue-black depths of a New Hampshire lake in summer; gray winter slush on Tremont Street, in Boston. I had no purpose, really; I only knew that the hour or so I spent writing every day was a happy time for me. I finished that notebook and I bought another small one, and probably I will keep on buying them. And, without really noticing it as something remarkable, I began to feel a great deal better.

Fate, as I should have recognized by now, tends to reward happiness rather than virtue: having to a large extent cheered up, in the same week I acquired both a paying guest and a good part-time job. The guest was a younger friend, Daisy, with whom I had worked on a couple of political campaigns; she had split with her most recent lover, and she wondered if maybe—now that—I would like to rent her a room. Well, knowing Daisy, it would not be for long, but she was entertaining, and kind, and reliable, in her way. And if this was not the cooperative venture I'd earlier dreamed of, it could be a step in that direction.

The job was with the lawyer for whom I'd worked before—a little less work than I needed, but, like the room arrangement, it seemed a strong step forward.

And, a month or so after that, I received, through my travel agent, a check for $343.79, from Toltec Airlines—a figure that I will never understand, but it paid a couple of bills.

I don't think much anymore about my lost notebook, or of those sad early days that it recorded, although I do occasionally wonder if Dick Parker, the night man at Toltec, could possibly have been right—if some misguided thief could have believed that I carried diamonds or cocaine in that shabby old bag, and found, instead, some well-worn summer clothes and the unhappy jottings of a very confused, a searching, woman.

I don't plan to go back to that particular Mexican resort; I believe that it has served its purpose in my life. But it has occurred to me that the next time I go on any trip, one of these new notebooks will fit easily into a carry-on bag, and that even if the book were to be lost, the loss would be minimal.

Berkeley House

Although Charlotte O'Mara lived in San Francisco, and her third and final stepmother, Blanche, in Berkeley, just across the bay, they traditionally communicated by postcard, an aversion to the telephone being one of the few things they had in common. Thus it was by way of a crowded card from Blanche that Charlotte first heard that the Berkeley house in which she had grown up was being sold.

That night, at dinner with her lover, Lyman Clay, a bookseller from Portland, Maine, a tall towheaded young man, Charlotte drank too much wine, and she cried out to Lyman, "You don't know how much I loved that house!"

Since theirs was a relatively recent friendship, a couple of months old, Charlotte had not, so far, talked much, if at all, about her parents, both now dead. And she had said nothing about the house other than that it was in the Berkeley hills. And so, although kind and intelligent, intuitive, Lyman was understandably puzzled at the extremity of her reaction. "It was a really great house?" he asked.

"No, actually it was pretty peculiar. Adobe, all sprawled out. It's just that—just that I always lived there," she told him hopelessly.

The next day, along with some gratitude for Lyman's kindness, and a slight hangover, Charlotte had an embarrassed sense of falseness. "Love" was too simple a word for her feelings about that house. She had reacted to its sale with rage and anguish, with an acute and wild sense of loss that she could not, for the moment, fathom, any more than she could get rid of the pain.

Charlotte was a painter, and in that precarious way she made her living—although that year, the year of the sale of the house, she had a very good fellowship. She thought she knew a lot about joy and grief, about broke and flush, failure and relative success. Still, she was surprised at the violence of her feelings about the house, about Blanche's selling it. Waking at three in the morning, she thought of crossing the Bay Bridge from Potrero Hill, where in their separate flats both she and Lyman lived, and going over to Grizzly Peak Boulevard, in Berkeley, where the house was. And burning it down. If I can't have it no one will, she wildly thought, at that most vulnerable predawn hour.

And she had no right to any of those emotions, any more than she had any "legal" right to the house. After all, her father, Ian O'Mara, had left the house to Blanche, his fourth wife, "to make her feel more secure." He had told Charlotte this in the same letter in which he first told about his will. But at that time Charlotte was living in Paris, studying, happily broke, and she hardly paid attention to what he said. She could not then focus on anything as distant and unlikely as her father's death.

She was aware, though, in a distant way, that Blanche, a fading tall blond Southern belle from Savannah, had not found much security in Berkeley, with those threatening academic people, or with Ian, who was inveterately mean to women: mean to Charlotte's mother, who had died young, and miserable; mean to his next, long-wooed wife, Pinky; and mean to Avis, the third. Mean to Blanche, often not speaking to her for days. In a way, leaving the house to Blanche was one of Ian's kinder gestures, although not exactly kind in regard to Charlotte.

Later, back from Paris and living in New York, very broke, nowhere near making it, Charlotte had remembered Ian's letter, and with uncharacteristic bravado—she was generally, and with good reason, quite frightened of her father—she wrote to him and said, "What exactly did you mean about leaving Blanche the house? Don't I get any of it?" And Ian, a smooth talker, wrote back reassuringly, "Of course Blanche will leave it to you. You'll get it all, eventually." But he did not say that in his will, and, what with taxes and repairs, the place probably was too much for Blanche, who was getting on. No surprise that she would have to sell the place, except that Charlotte was surprised; she was horrified.

A week or so after the postcard came, after Charlotte had begun to lie awake thinking always of the house, she had lunch with her friend Margery, an architect. Charlotte had formed the habit of telling Margery much, although never all, of what was on her mind. That day she talked for a while to Margery about Lyman, saying that it bothered her that he was five years younger, although why should that be a problem? She did not say that she really liked him enough to scare her, a little.

And then she tried to say what she felt about the house. She spoke, however, without much hope of comfort or understanding; she believed that because of her profession Margery would have a rather anatomical view of houses. To Margery, a house would be a shell for living in, designed and built in a certain way, in a certain state of repair.

Charlotte said, and she felt her breath tighten as she spoke, "It's crazy, the very idea of that house's being sold makes me feel dislodged. Deracinated." She tried to laugh, and coughed.

Margery laughed, too, and then she said, "Well, once I felt pretty much that way, when the house in Illinois that I grew up in was being sold. And then I thought, What's wrong with me? I spent the worst years of my life in that house, I was miserable there."

"Oh, Margery," Charlotte cried out. "It was horrible. My mother dying, and then Ian fighting with Pinky, and then Avis. Not speaking to Blanche."

Home from lunch, in her studio, from which on clear days she could see the Berkeley hills, Charlotte thought back to all the misery and unhappiness of the Grizzly Peak house. And maybe now, remembering, she would be all right?

But she was not all right. Lyman had gone to a convention of booksellers in Los Angeles, and that night, instead of sleeping, Charlotte argued ragingly with Ian, who had been dead for five years: "Why didn't you say in your will that I was supposed to have the house? What made you trust Blanche? You know she doesn't like me, none of them have. Why didn't you think of me when you made your will?"

And to Blanche: "If you're so broke why don't you go to work, for a change? You could try interior decoration, or real estate. I've always supported myself, one way or another, and if you think I liked being a waitress at Zim's . . ."

She got up in the morning scratchy-eyed, heavy in the head and heart, with no mind for work. She did work, though, on a stylized landscape, its tidiness possibly being a counter to the confusion in her mind:

a great flat yellow stretch of fields, hills nearly the same color and a paler-yellow sky.

One of the things that Charlotte did not tell Margery—and she hated to think what a shrink would make of this—was about her dreams: almost always, all her life, they had taken place in that pale adobe hilltop house, with its sprawling wings, in its high grove of redwood, and eucalyptus trees. Even in Paris, or New York, in her dream life, there she would be. This struck her as unbearably sentimental, not to mention infantile. Nevertheless, it was true.

For a time, then, Charlotte managed to get her worrying about the house down to ten or fifteen minutes a day; during those minutes she would still rave and rage, first at Ian, then at Blanche, but afterward she would get to work. She was working well, on that yellow landscape.

Also, she was getting along happily with Lyman Clay—surprisingly, since most of her love affairs had been marked by turbulence. Lyman was in fact such a gentle man, sensitive and keenly appreciative of her painting, and of her, that at times Charlotte wondered if he could be gay; no evidence pointed in that direction, it was just a way that living in San Francisco in those end-of-the-seventies years could make you think. She very much liked his unmanageable white-blond hair, his flat Maine voice and his Yankee wit.

A couple of weeks after getting the first postcard, in a mood of relative peace Charlotte decided that, in a simple and honest way, she would tell Blanche that she was indeed upset about her selling the house but that she now almost understood. She could almost stand it. After all, Blanche had been nicer than her two other stepmothers; once she had taken the trouble to polish and pack and deliver some old wineglasses of Charlotte's mother's (just in time, Charlotte was sure, to keep Ian from breaking them). But Charlotte forgot, as she thought of writing to Blanche, Blanche's deep suspicion of anything Charlotte did or said. Suspicion, Charlotte had to admit, not entirely unfounded. "I've tried to love Charlotte," Blanche had remarked one time to Ian, who reported this to Charlotte, in a concurring way—the effort of loving her being too much for anyone, it would seem.

And so, in answer to her postcard, Charlotte got back a long typed letter from Blanche, mainly to the effect that Charlotte had no legal right to the house. As if Charlotte didn't know her father's will by heart.

Even in her postcards, Blanche spoke what Charlotte thought of as "Southern," by which she meant the content as well as the accent. It was always necessary for Charlotte to shove aside a lot of words to get at what Blanche meant. That letter, translated, meant: Your father didn't care about you at all, he only cared for me. Which Charlotte had heard and even concluded on her own. Still, it hurt to have it pointed out.

In other, lighter moods, Charlotte could almost think of Blanche as funny; she was much a master, or mistress, of the velvet barb—as when she once remarked to Charlotte, "And I've always thought you were so pretty, even if no one else ever did." Well, Charlotte had never thought of herself as especially pretty—except maybe for a few minutes, sometimes. She no more needed to have that pointed out than she needed to be reminded of her father's non-caring. Still, the way Blanche got it across was fairly funny, Charlotte guessed.

Because Charlotte had been only six when her mother died, her memories of Eugenia, though clear, were brief, truncated. Eugenia had played the recorder, and she had gone to all the chamber-music concerts that came to Berkeley—a lot of concerts. Her erudition in both musical and literary areas was legendary. To this day she was talked about. She had had many friends in the academic community—professors, musicians, literary types, who no doubt disliked noisy, self-made Ian, as he probably disliked them back, and disliked Eugenia's friendships with them, and finally disliked Eugenia. And turned to beautiful, rich Pinky.

What Charlotte remembered best was lying in bed, her wing of the house juxtaposed to her mother's solitary wing, and hearing Eugenia weeping, weeping—hours of tears. Those terrible sounds were what Charlotte instantly, audibly remembered when her friend Margery said how miserable she had been in her parents' house. Eugenia's tears, her thick and heavy unhappiness had made the child Charlotte sick and heavy with unhappiness as Eugenia lay there crying over Ian—Ian the handsome, the unkind, the menace to women.

. . .

Given Ian, then, it is hardly surprising that Charlotte should have had her share of troubles with men. And maybe more. It sometimes seemed that way to Charlotte. She had been known to fall madly in love with the most impossible men—but a lot of women did that. What Charlotte also did, and what seemed even more dangerous, was: on the rare occasions when she was involved with a nice man, she would somehow induce him to behave in a cruel way. Or, even if she did not really succeed in that enterprise, she would somehow, nevertheless, begin to see the nice man as cruel.

The next Blanche postcard announced that since the house was for sale, and she was thinking of moving to Santa Barbara, she was putting the furniture in storage; if there was anything Charlotte wanted, would she please come over and get it right away, at least before next Tuesday. Well, "next Tuesday" was the day after Charlotte got the card, and for that and several other reasons she decided not to take Blanche up on her offer.

Other considerations being: if there was anything Charlotte really wanted, Blanche would come up with a strong justification for not giving it to her. That had been established when Ian died and the carved Spanish bench that Charlotte asked for turned out to have already been promised to a distant cousin.

"I just never would have known you wanted that little old bench," rambled Blanche, in her explanatory postcard. "You never once sat on it when you came here to visit, and I just knew it was too teeny and old-fashioned to be anything you'd ever want."

Of course I never sat there, not since I was a child, but I liked to look at it, it's so graceful and pretty—is what Charlotte despaired of trying to say to Blanche. Except for the bench, which would have been nice, furniture was actually the last thing Charlotte needed, her apartment being already crowded with canvases. Finally, and maybe most important, she could truly not bear the thought of going to the house, and going over all those remaining things, those silver and mahogany souvenirs of her past. With Blanche.

Any more than she could bear the house's being sold.

. . .

"It isn't so much the money that's involved," Charlotte had said to Margery when telling her of the house, "but it hurt my feelings, being disinherited." She had meant what she said, but as she listened to the echo of her words she heard an unexpected sanctimoniousness in them, a falseness, really. It was certainly true that her feelings had been hurt, badly hurt, but it was also true that she minded about the money. Her livelihood was precarious; certainly she could have used the proceeds from the sale of a large house.

"How much do you think she'll get for the house?" asked Margery, who had never seen it, Charlotte not being given to taking friends over to meet Blanche.

"I haven't any idea. I don't know about real estate," Charlotte said. "It's a big house, though. Sort of spread out."

"Well, anything in the Berkeley hills is worth at least two hundred grand," said Margery, who did know about those things.

Two hundred thousand dollars. With even half that, decently invested, Charlotte figured that she could live for the rest of her life. Not worry about selling paintings. Just paint.

But, in a way, the realization that something as concrete as money figured in her pain was comforting; it made her feel less blackly doomed—less crazy.

Margery mused, "It would be interesting to know what she'll get for it."

"I can't exactly ask her, though."

"Maybe I could find out."

As though things in her life were not difficult enough at that moment, Lyman Clay began to push Charlotte toward getting married. Or that is how Charlotte felt: pushed.

Typically, he presented his ideas in a literary way, over a dinner at his place. A dinner that he had cooked. And Lyman's cooking was another source of amazement and slight suspicion for Charlotte.

"A marriage is like the imposition of form on feeling in poetry," Lyman said. "Or in painting, for heaven's sake."

With a sharp leap of her heart, Charlotte saw what he meant; she felt it, but she was too disturbed—about the house, about Blanche, about Ian—to think in a serious way about what Lyman was suggesting.

And gloomily she foresaw that she and Lyman would eventually come to a parting over this issue, since he was clearly serious in what he said. A year or so later, when Lyman had married someone else (lots of women really want to marry, she knew, and Lyman was exceptionally nice), she, Charlotte, would wish that she were with him; then she would mourn for Lyman, as she had for various other departed men.

It was at Lyman's that Margery reached her—not wanting to wait to call Charlotte in the morning. She had to tell her the news.

"I can't believe this," said Margery over the phone. "The place is going for a hundred thousand. Honestly, Char, it must be a wreck."

Not grasping the sum of money, her mind instead wandering back to the actual house (a wreck?), Charlotte only said, "Well, it didn't use to be."

"Who ever would have thought that a hundred thousand could come to look like a bargain?" said Margery.

Vaguely offended at the word "bargain" being attached to her house, Charlotte murmured, "Not I."

An odd lapse, or confusion, of memory had been disturbing Charlotte, along with her other troubles, ever since first hearing from Blanche about the house: simply, she could not remember whether a giant pine that had been near the side porch had been cut down or not. In her earliest memories it was there; as a small child she had played with dolls and Dinky toys among its roots. And she could remember it when, as an older girl, she had sat there on the porch, making out with some boy. But then: had there been talk about cutting it down? Had Ian said it had to go, that it menaced the roof, or the porch? Possessed of an unusually active visual imagination, Charlotte could see the waving heavy-boughed pine, and she could also see its stump, raw and flat and new—or was she seeing the stump from another tree, somewhere else?

. . .

Without waiting to show it to Lyman or to Margery—to anyone—Charlotte took the yellow landscape to her gallery, a new one, in Embarcadero Center, and it was sold the next day, for more money than Charlotte could believe: enough to live on for five or six months, she thought.

To celebrate, and because, marriage or not, he was an extremely nice man, Charlotte took Lyman out to dinner, inviting him to a new French place, all polished brass and big mirrors and white linen, which they had sometimes walked past.

Exactly the kind of occasion that should be fun and won't be, Charlotte thought as she dressed, putting on an unaccustomed skirt and silk shirt and high sandals. Lyman will make some dumb scene about not letting me pay, and we won't have anything to talk about except the food, which will not be good.

The restaurant was attractive. And as they sat down, Lyman in a coat and tie, straw hair under control, Charlotte thought, Well, we do make a fairly handsome couple.

Easily, Lyman told the waiter to put the wine on a separate check, he would take care of that.

"Mais bien sûr, Monsieur."

As Charlotte thought, Well, so far so good.

The food, too, was good, but then after a while something in the tone of the restaurant, maybe, began to make them unfamiliar to themselves. Charlotte heard Lyman talking in a new and stilted way—indeed, discussing the food—and she began to think, I was right.

Mainly for something new to say, she asked, "How come you never talk about Portland?" more complainingly than she had meant to. "Did you like it, growing up there?"

He grinned, showing white, white teeth. "Well, I really did," he said. "It's still small enough to be comprehensible, sort of. There are even some cobbled streets left. And we lived out on Cape Elizabeth, right on the Atlantic."

He went on and on about Portland—the coast, the beaches, the rocks—and Charlotte could see it all vividly as he spoke.

But why was this conversation making her so sad? And then she knew: she was hearing the nostalgia in Lyman's voice; his missing the place he came from was making her miss her own place, her house.

. . .

She also took Margery out, for lunch, for further celebration.

"I honestly think I must be going crazy," Charlotte said. "Lyman could not be a nicer person; he's kind and smart, and being five years younger than I am is not important, really. But I keep making trouble. If I had better sense I could be perfectly happy with Lyman. I sometimes am."

Margery laughed. "If you had better sense you might not be a painter."

"Well, I guess."

Margery raised her wineglass in a toast, and then she asked, "What ever will you do with all that money?"

Charlotte frowned, her hands gestured helplessness. "I don't know, it's been worrying me. I should do something—sensible."

"What about our buying the Berkeley house?"

"*What?*"

"Your house in Berkeley. I have some money saved up . . . and I could . . . and you could . . . we could . . . rent . . . invest . . . property values."

Margery made the appointment and got the key from the real-estate agent—all the negotiations would have to be in her name, obviously—and on a bright October afternoon she and Charlotte drove over to Berkeley: two prospective buyers of an empty house.

They drove up Marin, and up and up, and then turned right on Grizzly Peak, at which point the sheer familiarity of everything she saw accelerated and heated the flow of Charlotte's blood: how she *knew* all those particular turns of the road, those steep sudden views of the bay. And then there it was, in a clump of tall waving eucalyptus: her house. Sand-colored adobe bricks and a red tiled roof, a narrow wooden porch stuck out to one side like an ill-advised whim, long one-storied wings seeming to wander off behind. Perhaps because of the five years' lapse since she had been there, or maybe because she was seeing it with Margery, Charlotte thought, What a nutty-looking house, it's crazy. But that was an affectionate thought; the house could have been an eccentric relative. In fact, it reminded her considerably of Ian: uncontrolled, given over to impulse. (An adobe house in the Berkeley hills had been itself an eccentric impulse, or a sentimental one: Ian and her mother had spent their honeymoon in Mexico.)

When Margery had parked the car, they got out and walked toward it, toward Charlotte's house. All the vines and shrubbery had increased considerably in the five years since her last visit; a green growth of wisteria almost covered the porch.

Like a thief, an accomplice in crime, Charlotte followed Margery up to the front door, which, with the real-estate agent's key, Margery opened, and they walked into an absolutely empty, echoing house.

But why was Charlotte so frightened? She could have been an actual intruder, even a thief, so violent was her apprehension as they walked from room to room, both of them on tiptoe. And along with this fear came a total disorientation: was this small stained room the one that had always been called the guest room but where Ian slept from one wife to another? And was this smaller room her own, in which she had lain and listened to Eugenia's weeping? Shivering, to Margery she whispered, "It all looks so small."

"Rooms do, without any furniture. Honestly, they weren't kidding about its being in bad shape."

"I'm going back outside," whispered Charlotte.

Outside was more familiar: the sweeping view of the bay—the water and sky, the darker skyline. The shrubs and trees and vines were all in their proper place, except for the big pine, which indeed was missing. Nor was there any stump where Charlotte thought the tree had been. Instead, in that spot Blanche (it must have been Blanche) had put in a bed of geraniums, her favorites; in the intense October sunlight they gave off a dusty, slightly rancid smell.

Margery came out at last, and together she and Charlotte walked around the house, Margery stopping to peer down at foundations, to mutter about dry rot.

Once back in the car, seemingly having put dry rot out of her mind, Margery began to talk animatedly about possible reconstruction of the house: "It really has marvelous potential; it needs a lot of work, but I could knock out walls . . . open up . . . a deck."

By this time they were on the bridge, crossing the shining water far below—that day an interesting slate blue, a color that wet stones sometimes are.

"Well, so what do you think?" asked Margery.

"I don't know. I guess it really doesn't seem my kind of thing," Charlotte said, with a certain effort.

"But I thought you wanted—I thought it would help." Although clearly intending kindness, sympathy, Margery sounded very slightly huffy: her professional imagination was being rebuffed.

Margery would get over her huffiness in time, Charlotte thought. And while Charlotte could not entirely "get over" her pain at the loss of what she continued to think of as her house, it would perhaps become bearable, little more than an occasional sharp twinge.

She began a new painting, this time all shades of blue, from slate to brightest azure.

When, a few weeks later, a postcard came from Blanche, in Santa Barbara, showing lots of palms and flowers, and announcing that she was going to marry the most wonderful (underlined) man with a lovely house on the ocean, near the Biltmore Hotel, Charlotte stuck the card in a box with letters that she meant to answer soon.

It was a few months after that, near Christmastime, that, waking with Lyman in his wide, eccentrically carved oak bed—their most recent decision had been to make no decision, no firm plans about legalities or moving in—in a wondering voice Charlotte said, "You know, it's curious, I don't dream that I live in Berkeley anymore. My dreams don't take place in that house."

"I didn't know they ever did," Lyman said.

Legends

Partly because she was so very plain, large and cumbersome, like her name, at first I liked Candida Heffelfinger better than any interviewer who had come around for years. Tall, almost gaunt, she had a big white pockmarked face, lank brown hair and beautiful dark eyes—have you ever noticed how many otherwise ugly women have lovely eyes? Also, she had that special, unassuming niceness that plain women often have; I should know, it was years before I dared to be as mean and recalcitrant, as harsh-mannered as I had always wanted to be.

I liked her as soon as I saw her awkwardly getting out of the red Toyota that she must have rented at the Raleigh-Durham Airport, and start up the pine-strewn path to my (Ran's) house. And I liked her although I knew that she would want to talk about my legendary love affair, about Ran, rather than about my work, the sculpture. I was used to that; it interested everyone, our "love," and besides, what can you say about structures almost twenty feet high, some weighing thousands of pounds?

In a welcoming way, and also as a surprise—I would not be the ogress that almost anyone in New York would have warned her about— I went to the door to greet her.

"Miss Phelps?" she puffed out. "Jane Phelps?"

Well, who in hell else would I be? But I said yes, and asked her to come in, and what would she like to drink?

In her dowdy-expensive gray flannel suit she followed me into the living room, and said that she drank bourbon-and-water.

I made the drinks, and we both settled down in that high-ceilinged, glassed-in living room; we stared out at the fading November sunset, against the black lace network of trees. We smoked our cigarettes, and drank, and we made friendly small talk about her flight, the drive from the airport to Hilton. This house, its view.

I not only liked Ms. Heffelfinger; I felt that I knew a lot about her. With that name, and that flat, unaccented voice, she would be Midwestern, as I am, from somewhere in Minnesota, or Wisconsin. I imagined a rural childhood for her, and I saw her as the eldest in a family of brothers, whose care would often fall to her. Then adolescence—well, we all know about the adolescent years of ugly girls: the furtive sexual encounters with boys who later don't speak to you in the halls at school, who invite small fluffy blondes to their parties. Then college, at a state university, where the social failure would be somewhat balanced by academic triumph, and maybe even a passingly satisfactory affair with a young instructor, although more likely an aging professor, paunchy and grimly married. Next the New York experience, the good job and the lonely love affairs: married men or alcoholics, or both, or worse.

You might ask why such an unattractive girl would be chosen in that way at all, but only if you had never heard the old saying that ugly women as lovers are fantastic. I remember the first time I heard that voiced, by a short, very truculent and quite untalented painter. I was entirely outraged, as though one of my most intimate secrets had been spoken aloud, for of course it is often true: a beautiful woman would expect to be made love to, we expect to make love.

Ms. Heffelfinger and I said what we could about the town—very old pre–Civil War—and the house, Ran's house, which was built in the twenties—and then considered very innovative, all that glass— with prize money from his first symphony. (Ran was once a famous composer.)

Perhaps by way of changing our direction, I asked her if she minded living alone in New York—and I was totally unprepared for her answer.

"Well, actually we don't live in the city," she said. "We live in a small town in northern New Jersey. It's very unchic, but it's great for the kids, they love it."

We? Kids? Perhaps unfairly I felt that I had been deceived, or at least misled. I tried to keep surprise and suspicion from my face but they must have shown (everything does), for she laughed and said, "I know, I don't look married, or much like a mother, but maybe that's just as well?" And then she said, "Well, we might as well start? It's okay to turn on the tape?"

I said yes as I noted what nice teeth she had, just then exhibited in her first smile. I thought too that I had better be on my guard, more than usually so.

Now the sky beyond all that naked glass was entirely black, and you would have thought that everything outside was stilled, unless you knew—as I, a night walker, knew—that in those depths of woods small leaves yet stirred, and tiny birds were settling for the night. Ms. Heffelfinger turned on her recorder, and she began to say what I had known that she would say: a small speech to the effect that she knew very little in a general way about sculpture, "although I am really moved by it, more so than any other visual form." (Was that true?)

I said I understood, and I gave the snort that over the years I had perfected. "Actually no one knows a damn thing about my work but me, and sometimes I'm not at all sure that I do," I told her.

She smiled, again those nice teeth, our smoke circled up to the arched, beamed ceiling, and then she made her second predictable speech; everyone said it, in one form or another. "Of course you realize that the main interest, prurient though it may be, is in your relationship with Randolph Caldwell."

I smiled, showing my tolerant indifference to prurience, to vulgar curiosity. "Of course, the legendary love affair," I said.

"By now I'm quite an expert on the legend," Ms. Heffelfinger assured me, looking off into a distance that might have contained her notes. "You came to Hilton not long after Lucinda Caldwell died, is that right? Mr. Caldwell at that time was still in mourning for his wife?"

"In his way. Yes. Mourning." I had never met Lucinda, of course, but I too, in my way, had sometimes mourned for her.

And while I had strayed off in that direction, poor Lucinda's, Ms. Heffelfinger slowly inserted her knife into my heart.

"One thing I don't quite understand," she said, beginning gently, so that I hardly felt it. Then, "About Gloria Bingham." *In.* "Just when was it that she first came here, and met Randolph Caldwell?"

All the books and articles, if they mention her at all, other than as a footnote, make it perfectly clear that Gloria Bingham was a totally unimportant figure in Ran's life, a girl who came after Lucinda, and before me, his major love. But I was unable just then to parrot the legend to Ms. Heffelfinger—or even, had I wanted to, to tell her that it was a bloody lie. I began to cough, passionately, as though I were trying to cough up my heart, that sudden cold stone in my chest.

Candida Heffelfinger looked alarmed, of course. She got up—for a moment I thought she meant to hit me on the back; fortunately she decided not to. She looked wildly about, and at last discovered the bar. She went over and brought me a glass of water, so helpful.

By then I could thank her, weakly. "But I really don't think I can talk anymore just now. I'll call you tomorrow," I told her. "You're staying at the inn?" In fact, I was not at all sure that I would call her—*why?*

She said yes, fine, and got up to go. I did not rise, I barely could have. I gave her a limp old lady's hand to shake, and I watched as she walked down the hall to the door, then turned to wave. Her suit was now rumpled, as though that brief encounter with me had messed up her clothes, as well as her good intentions.

It was the maid's night off, and so I decided not to bother with dinner. I made myself another drink, and then another, and later I had some cheese for nourishment. I watched the stars come out among the blackened pine and oak boughs, and then a waning moon come up, and I thought about life, and truth, and lies, as an old drunk person is very apt to do.

The true story, my—"our"—story, began a long time ago, in the thirties, my own late twenties, when I came to Hilton to begin an instructorship in the art department. I rented a tiny house, a cabin, on the road leading up to the Caldwell house, in the deepest, leafiest, most romantic Southern woods. And on that white road I first saw, driving fast in a snappy open car, a handsome man in early middle age, with thick gray hair, dark eyes and a bright red plaid wool shirt. Randolph Caldwell, the composer, I was told when I asked Dr. James, the head of the art department, about my conspicuous neighbor. (This was just after Lucinda Caldwell had died, and no one then had ever heard of Gloria Bingham. So you may conclude, Ms. Heffelfinger, that it was I, not Gloria, who formed the unimportant link, who came between Lucinda and Gloria.)

And later it was Dr. James who introduced me to Ran, in the A. & P., at the vegetable counter.

Legends

"I'm delighted to meet a near neighbor," he said as he took my hand, but his eyes glazed over in the automatic way of a man meeting a not pretty woman, a look I knew.

"I've admired your car," I told him, half-lying, and hoping that he would not imagine I knew anything whatsoever about cars.

But his voice and his eyes were beautiful. I loved him.

Actually I loved the whole town, the crazily heterogeneous architecture of the campus: cracked yellow plaster on its oldest buildings, with their ferociously clinging red Virginia creeper; and the newer brick additions, with their corny Corinthian pillars, which now, several generations later, look almost authentic. I loved my cabin in the woods, on a slope of poplars, looking out to early fall dusks, almost unpopulated hills of black, like a sea, the darkness stippled here and there with straight blue lines of smoke from other cabins, country people, mostly Negroes. The town and its surrounding hills, its woods, were exotic to me; I might have just arrived in Scotland, or East Africa. And, given my age and general inclinations, that excitement had to find a focus, a sexual object. I had to fall in love, and there was Ran, so handsome and seemingly unavailable, a man of the age I was used to choosing.

The next day I managed to be on the road just before he came by. I thought, even hoped, that he would wave in a friendly way, but he was much too Southern to let a lady walk; he stopped, and elaborately opened the door for me, and smiled, and instantly launched into a complicated monologue about the weather.

I soon worked out his schedule so that I could always be in his path. I would linger there in the smell of pines and leaves and dust and sunlight until I heard the sound of his car, and then I would move on briskly, until he should see me and stop. If he had passed me by, just waving, in a hurry, I would probably have died, my heart stricken and stilled then and there, and with a not pretty girl's dark imagination I always thought that would happen, but it never did—or never until he had Gloria with him in the car, and then they would both smile and wave, and hurry on.

Until Gloria, he would stop and open the door and I would clumsily get in; I was so dizzy, so wild with love, or lust, whatever, that I could hardly look at him. I am sure that he never noticed then, although much later, after we were lovers, of a sort, he claimed that he had always noticed everything about me. A typical Southern man's lie.

Now when I try to remember what we talked about, on those short important drives, I come up with nothing, The weather, the passage of time, the changing seasons. But that particular fall, I do remember, was extraordinarily beautiful, with vibrant, brilliant leaves against a vivid sky; it was more than worthy of our notice.

One problem in the way of talk was Ran's quite impenetrable accent. You think of a Southern accent as being slow, and lazy; Ran spoke more quickly than anyone I had ever known, and he constantly smoked—all those quick light Southern words arrived filtered through all that smoke. Half the time I hadn't the slightest idea what he was talking about, but I was excited by his voice, as I was by everything about him, his hair and his sad dark eyes, his cigarettes; his hunting shirts, his shabby tweeds, his snappy car. At worst, you could call it a crush.

Once in those early days he said to me, and this came out more distinctly than most of his sentences: "Lucinda never liked it here, you know. A Boston girl. She always said the woods down here were too *cluttered* for her taste," and he gestured with an elegant large white hand in the direction of the piny woods through which we passed, with their bright leaves, thick undergrowth.

For me just that luxuriance, that overplentitude of bush and wild grass and weed, was beautiful, was vaguely sexual. Still, I responded to her word, "cluttered," with the odd emphasis that Ran had given it; he had almost made me hear her Boston voice. I liked Lucinda's precision, and I felt a curious linkage with her, my dead rival.

Much later, during one of our more terrible drunken fights, Ran cried out, "You might as well be Lucinda, I can't stand it," and I countered, "You're just so stupid, you think all women are alike."

Still, he had a point; though I hadn't known her I sensed an affinity with Lucinda, as strong as my total antipathy to Gloria.

In early December of that year, that winter in Hilton, it suddenly snowed; one morning I woke to a white silent world, deep soft drifts everywhere, the road outside my house deeply buried in snow, the boughs of trees heavily ladened. Just after my second cup of coffee the telephone rang, and my heart leapt up, for I knew it could only be Ran.

"Well," he said, and I could hear the quick inhalation of smoke. "It looks like we both will be 'hoofing it' this morning. Nor man nor beast

could budge my car. How would it suit you if I knocked at your door in fifteen minutes or so?"

That would be the best thing in the world, I did not say. "I'll be ready, that's swell" is what I said.

Half an hour later he knocked at my door—the house that he had never seen inside. "Well, I can see you're very cozy here." He then asked, "It doesn't bother you, living all alone?"

"Oh no, I love it, the privacy," I lied.

"I don't love it," he announced, with a look almost of pain. I quickly regretted having sounded so silly and glib, but I could not say, as I wanted to, Please let me move into your house with you. I'll pay rent, or cook and sew, clean up, make love to you. Anything.

We exchanged a small smile, and set off through the snow.

We were becoming friends, and we continued in that process, over the winter. Occasionally we diverged from talking about the weather, noting changes in the colors and shapes of trees, leaves and underbrush, the early coming of spring in the woods that surrounded our lives, and Ran would talk about Lucinda, sadly, regretfully. I became, in a limited way, his comforter. In my life I have noticed that after a time of deep sorrow the greatest comfort may come from a person you do not know well, nor much care about. (God knows, Ran did not care much about me at that time, and you may even conclude, Ms. Heffelfinger, that he never did.) When Ran died I was comforted, a little, by a silly and very ambitious young art critic, in Westport, Connecticut, whom I did not like. Anyway, our most nearly intimate conversations were about Lucinda, her taste for Victorian novels and Elizabethan songs, her dislike of almost all Southern women. He never said what she died of, not then, and I assumed sheer misery.

I did not see Ran at the parties that I sometimes went to, graduate student, poor instructor parties. And for the most part I avoided them myself, those forlorn attempts at conviviality. I worked hard preparing for my classes, I was available for conferences with students and I had begun in a secret way to do some work of my own with wood, small sculptures. There was so much wood around, cheaply available, and I was fascinated by the variety of grains, of possible shapes. Also, my obsession with Ran took up considerable time, those daydreaming, fantasizing hours.

But late one night, in early April, I did see Ran at a party, at Dr. James's. I saw him across a very smoky room, looking handsome and sad and slightly drunk, and alone. I quickly divested myself of the philosophy instructor who was about to ask if he could take me home, and in my rush toward Ran I bumped into a sharp-cornered table, which happily he could not observe. I slowed down as I got to him, and assumed an expression of mixed surprise and pleasure, the latter at least being genuine. *"Well,"* I said, and it occurred to me that I had begun to sound like him. "Fancy meeting you here."

He said, "Well, fancy," and we both laughed again.

In my left hand was an empty glass that I had forgotten, but Ran noticed at once, with his Southern-hospitable-drunk instincts. "Well," he said, "you need more than a sweetening; you've got to have a real drink."

I did not—neither of us needed a drink—but of course I smiled, pleased and grateful, and I accepted a long dark glass of bourbon, barely iced. Our first drink together, and dear God, I hate to think how many others followed.

We began to talk, and in a quick excited way Ran told me about a trip that he was taking; he was leaving for Atlanta the next day, where a newly formed orchestra was to perform an early work of his. (The sad truth, as I had learned from local gossip, was that by now all Ran's work was "early"; for many years he had produced nothing new, beyond a short suite of songs, dedicated to Lucinda and often performed by the music department's chorus.) That night he looked, for the first time since I had known him, really happy, and, to me, most dazzlingly attractive. (A puzzle: did Ran ever know how handsome he was? Hard to miss, his good looks, but for such a deeply Presbyterian-Puritan it would have seemed a wicked thought. He certainly never dressed like a consciously handsome man.)

At last he said what I had been waiting to hear since I first spotted him across the room. He said, "Well now, don't you think it's high time we made our escape from here? I've got to get up and pack, and I wouldn't want to deprive a young woman of her necessary rest."

(I realize that Ran sounds silly, quoted literally, even pompous. I can only say that in his rich Southern voice, in the lightness and variety of tone, the actual effect was enchanting; certainly I was enchanted, and so was almost everyone who knew him.)

For years I have reviewed that spring night: driving home with Ran, in the scents of honeysuckle and wisteria, in his manic speeding open car. And in my mind I try to give that night a different ending, not its humiliating true one, and quite often I succeed, only thinking of flowers and scents of night. For even in a horticultural way, my memory of that whole April seems unlikely, but there it is: I remember that for several weeks all the flowers in bloom were white, dogwood and spirea, white Japanese quince, white roses, everywhere, luminous blossoms.

We raced down the highway, and then Ran turned off on the white dirt road, our road, leading to both our houses. We drove fast between the arching pines, the scented tall bent cedars, raced past my house, as I had somehow known or hoped we would. And suddenly there we were in a broad graveled parking area, just down from a hugely looming house, all its areas of glass reflecting shadows, the fabled house that I had so far never visited.

"Well," said Ran, in his characteristic tone that made everything almost, not quite, a joke. "I seem to have come a little too far—I seem to have taken you out of your way."

I laughed lightheartedly, excitedly, imagining that now we would go inside for the obligatory nightcap that neither of us needed, and that then we would go to bed, like grownups.

But no. Ran reached toward me, and at his touch I moved closer, and we kissed, passionately. And that is exactly how we spent the next hour or so, in kissing, like steamy adolescents, although I was close to thirty and Ran must have been almost fifty, or so. We writhed against each other, both violently aroused. Once or twice I reached for him in an explicit way—well, that's how plain girls are, aggressively sexual—and each time he stayed my hand.

(This amuses you, Ms. Heffelfinger? You find it hard to credit? In that case, it's clear that you've never tangled with a small-town, Southern white Protestant, a Presbyterian conscience.)

At last, in a moment of relative disengagement, Ran looked at his watch and exclaimed, "Good Lord, it's hours past a decent time for bed. You must forgive me, I'll take you right along home."

Still imagining that we were going to sleep together, as it were, I started to suggest that we stay at his house instead, my bed was so hard and narrow. Thank God I did not say that, but only smiled. I was worried about my face, which I knew at best to be unpretty, which must by now look ravaged, smeared, terrible.

Ran started his car, turned around in the driveway and headed toward my house, and for that short distance I was as happy as I have ever been, anticipating our long night hours together. He stopped the car, I in my eagerness hurrying out before he could be his usual chivalrous self and come around for me. Together we walked up to my door, and there, with a chaste kiss on my forehead, Ran murmured good night.

I was as horrified as I was surprised, as stricken, as frustrated. And although I may have been too upset to know what I was doing, I'm afraid I did know; in any case, I then forced a passionate kiss upon his unwilling mouth, I forced my whole body up against his as I said, "Come in with me, I want you."

"Well, my dear, I'm sure that would be delightful"—as though I had invited him in for cocoa—"but the fact is, it's just terribly late, and so I will have to bid you adieu."

He got away; he even waved as he got into his car and drove off, as I simply stood there.

Well, at least I didn't run up the road after him, and pound on his door, shouting; that would have been even worse to remember, and if I had been a little older, or a little more drunk, that is precisely what I would have done, what every instinct wanted me to do. It is in fact just what some years later I did do, after one of our nights of drunken fighting, tears and threats, departures. That night, I only went into my house and went to bed, where all my crying failed to soothe my rage and pain, where I could not sleep.

I did not see Ran for a couple of weeks after that, first because he was in Atlanta, and then, when I knew he must be back, because I avoided the time when I knew he would be driving by. However, one day either I had miscalculated or he had sought me out, for there he was, racing up from behind a few minutes after I had left my house, stopping, reaching to open the door for me.

He began talking his head off—I might have known that the next time I saw Ran he would distance me with conversation, "Well, my dear girl, I don't believe I've seen you since my recent sojourn in Atlanta." Et cetera, on and on about Atlanta: the heat, the ugliness of the local architecture, the too many parties—"Too much bourbon would be stating the case more accurately, I fear." The stupid hostesses who would not take no for an answer. "One of them even managed to wangle an invitation to come up here," he told me. "Can you imagine such a thing?"

This is the first I heard of Gloria Bingham, and I might have guessed then from Ran's excited tone exactly how it would all work out; I might also have guessed that Gloria was small and stupid-smart, in that special Southern way, and that she was beautiful. My total opposite, my natural enemy.

Gloria was "petite," dark-haired; a more just God, I thought, would have given her small dark eyes to match, but no, her eyes were exceptionally large and blue, unfairly brilliant. And her voice was remarkably low, for such a little person. "I'm so very glad to meet you; Ran's talked so much about his artistic neighbor," she told me, the first time we met. She managed, in the special way she pronounced "artistic," to combine awe with insult, a famous Southern-lady trick, at which Gloria was especially adept.

By the beginning of that summer two things were clear to me: first, that Gloria and Ran were embarked on a serious love affair, she would be coming up for lots of visits, if not to stay; and second, that I could not stand it, I really couldn't. I couldn't stand knowing that she was there, just up the road, with Ran, and I alone with my ugly, rampant fantasies— nor when they drove by, both waving, friendly and happy. Nor was it bearable to feel her presence in Ran's mind, the few times I saw him alone after the advent of Gloria.

Out of sheer desperation I did what I had sworn never to do: I telephoned my banker-father, in Milwaukee, and said that I had to have some money for a year in Italy. We had quarreled badly ten years back, when I had first mentioned art school, so that now he was so startled at hearing from me at all, and maybe even a little pleased, stonehearted bastard that he was, that he gave in after almost perfunctory resistance—just a few mutterings about my extravagance, which we both knew to be trumped up; I had always been the soul of thrift. There were also a few stern warnings about the dangers of Italy under Mussolini, about which he was not very well informed either.

Next I went to Dr. James; I asked for and was granted a year's leave of absence.

In early July I sailed for Genoa, on a cheap, rather small Greek freighter, during the course of which voyage I had an affair with a Greek sailor, who was very handsome, and I thought about Ran, obsessively.

In Italy I reverted to my old bad habit of affairs with married men, dark fat middle-aged Italians who spent pious afternoons in the museums, on the prowl for silly American girls; but these affairs were less lonely than their American counterparts; Italian men had more free time, their wives at home being more docile, less questioning. Among other things I learned to say "I love you" in Italian: *Ti voglio bene,* I wish you well. I thought considerably about the difference between that sentiment and what I felt for Ran, whom God knows I did not wish well—I often wished him dead—or, better still, painfully dying. I was obsessed with him in an ugly, violent way that seemed to preclude other softer, gentler feelings.

The most significant experience of my Italian year, by far, was that there for the first time I saw real Michelangelos, and it was as though I had never seen sculpture before. Later I said this to Ran, and he told me about the first time he heard a Beethoven symphony performed: he was very young, of course, and it was inevitably the Fifth, but he remembered thinking, Ah, so that's what music is. In the Bargello, in Florence, I was tremendously moved by the great unfinished marbles, the huge figures just emerging from the stone, and later, at the monumental sculptures in Rome, in the Vatican, I felt the most extraordinary excitement, exhilaration.

I had not in Hilton made any friendships that would warrant a correspondence; therefore, on the boat that took me back from Genoa to New York, a voyage on which I had no affairs with sailors, I did not know what to expect on my return. The strongest possibility was that by now Ran and Gloria would be married, given the extremely conventional habits of everyone involved. While I faintly hoped that they would have decided to live in Atlanta—maybe Gloria would have a family house down there, a "showplace"—I was also braced for their proximity in

Hilton; I even thought that occasional views of Ran, yoked to such a fatuous woman, might diminish him in my mind; I might recover from my crazed preoccupation, my ugly lust.

But no. On my first afternoon in Hilton, back in my small house in the woods, the tender bright green June trees that were leafed out all over the landscape, Dr. James informed me on the telephone, other business being out of the way, that a terrible misfortune had befallen my neighbor Randolph Caldwell: Ran had been engaged to marry Gloria Bingham, their wedding had been imminent; indeed it was on a shopping trip to New York for wedding and honeymoon clothes that Gloria had met a younger, much richer man, with whom she had run off out West. Phoenix, Tucson, some place like that. Poor Ran was in bad shape; he was said to be drinking too much, up there in his big glass house, all alone. Maybe, once I got settled, in a neighborly way I could call on him? I could tell him about my year in Italy? Ran had been there on his wedding trip with Lucinda, and later on a concert tour; he loved to talk about Italy, Dr. James assured me.

Hanging up, I digested this outrageous suggestion, a neighborly call from me, as best I could, along with the news of Gloria's defection. I found myself violently agitated, pacing about, unable to unpack, unable to do anything but smoke a lot of cigarettes and stare at nothing.

At last, in a mood of what-the-hell, or, what-have-I-got-to-lose, I did exactly what Dr. James had suggested: I went to the telephone and I dialed the number that I had memorized two years ago, which I still knew, although I had never used it before.

"This is Jane Phelps," I said in a clear strong voice, quite startling to my ears: who would have thought I could manage it? "I've just got back from Italy, and I thought—"

"Well, my dear Jane," he crashed into my sentence, as though he had been waiting to hear from me. "What an entirely delightful surprise, how quite wonderful to hear from you! And Italy, ah, how I would love to hear of your stay there, all of it. I don't suppose you could possibly—"

He was asking me up to his house for a bite of supper, as he put it, and I was saying yes. Yes, yes.

As we approached his door, Ran having gallantly driven down to pick me up at five-thirty—"Well, we might as well start with the cocktail hour, don't you agree?"—Ran seemed to have forgotten that I had never been to his house before, and I saw no reason to mention it. He did mumble as we entered that he was afraid it was a little messy, the "girl" got in his way; she hadn't been there for a while. I then walked into a huge room, the room that is now my own, to a scene of the most incredible squalor: spilled drinks and spilling-over ashtrays, scattered newspapers, magazines, unopened letters, face-down books. Dust rabbits at the edges of the rugs. Long grime-streaked windows that looked out to the lovely leaves, the hills, the gentle June twilight.

It was obviously the dwelling place of a person too miserable to function in a normal way, incapable of emptying an ashtray, of reading, finishing anything, probably of eating, and I wondered about the bite of supper. But mainly I was stricken with waves of pity for Ran, perhaps my first kindly emotion in his direction, which did nothing to diminish my other feelings. I sat down in a cleared space on a sofa as Ran went off for drinks. I knew that I would do well not even to think about the kitchen.

Sorrow, what he had recently been through, even too much bourbon had not made Ran less attractive; if anything, he looked better, leaner and sadder, his dark eyes larger and his hair, I thought, a shade more white. That night he was wearing, as I will (evidently) always remember, an old plaid wool shirt, probably from L. L. Bean, his favorite store.

We sat for a long time, there in the deepening dusk; from time to time Ran would get up and go and "sweeten" our drinks, not turning on any lights. And we talked, as Dr. James had more or less instructed, about Italy. Ran was upset that I had only gone to Florence and Rome; he didn't count Genoa. "But Siena," he said. "Bergamo. And Todi, Gubbio, Spoleto. Ravello! You can't believe the views of hills of olives. But after all you are so young, you can go many times to Italy." At that last I thought I heard a small quaver in his voice, but I could have been wrong. In truth I was barely listening; I was only looking at him, wanting to touch him, to be touched. And I was a little afraid: I knew that I could not stand another evening that ended as our last evening of intimacy had ended; this time I would behave very badly indeed.

Another fear was that he would get drunk and pass out: I didn't yet know that Ran was the stay-up-all-night sort of drinker.

He had been sitting on an armchair near my perch on the sofa. Coming back with what must have been our fifth or sixth drinks, he then sat down instead on the sofa, on another cleared space near mine, with only a pile of letters, bills, whatever, stacked between us. It was I who finally reached across, reached for Ran, but at least he was responsive; as though he had been waiting for just that gesture, and maybe in a way he had been, he grasped and kissed me, and at last, in the fumbling way of adolescents in a darkened room, on a cluttered family sofa, we managed to make love. And when Ran cried out, "Oh, my darling," although I partly knew that he did not mean me, my heart leapt gratefully anyway.

And that was the beginning of our legendary love affair, the great love of Jane Phelps and Randolph Caldwell. From then on we saw each other almost every day, one way or another, as the seasons changed around our separate houses on that road, in the deep beautiful woods. Wisely enough, we never even considered moving in together; after a night of love one or the other of us would return to his or her own dwelling. We both knew that we needed those hours apart, sometimes simply to gather more energy for love, at other, too frequent times to refuel a quarrel, to lick our wounds.

After the lush green summer, of honeysuckle, roses, wisteria everywhere, came an autumn landscape of the most brilliant leaves, crimson and gold against a blue, blue sky, in the brighter, colder air. Then winter, sometimes snow, or more often just cold, the woods full of thin crisp leaves, and the smell of wood smoke from the Negro cabins, far down the hill. As much as with Ran, I fell in love with that landscape, his countryside. Permanently.

One great shared pleasure, discovered early between us, was in talking about our work. It was the deep, extraordinary excitement between two people whose pursuits are quite separate, but whose dedication to these activities is similar, two people who can thus find areas of the most passionate affinity. These conversations occurred infrequently; like most "creative" people, neither of us was often moved to talk in that vein, but when we did it was entirely wonderful, talk that even now gives me the greatest joy to remember.

But a sad fact about these conversations, of course, was that for Ran it was all in the past; he was talking about how he used to feel, what he once had done. Whereas I had just begun to work in a serious way; I worked furiously, excited about what I was producing, what I dreamed of making in the future. In those early days I was just moving from small carved wooden sculptures to larger figures, and in my mind were even larger constructions, the sort of shapes that I eventually achieved.

What demons, then, drove us so frequently to ugly rages, unspeakable recriminations? We would goad each other on, until Ran would say that no, he did not love me at all, he never had, I did not know what real love was. Or I would go on and on about my great and numerous Italian lovers, exaggerating wildly, until Ran would get up and lurch toward me, and slap my face—this happened more than once, and then I would hit him back, of course.

Too much drink was certainly a cause of trouble between us, that endless succession of bourbons-and-water, but booze was not a necessary cause, I wouldn't think. Surely there must be at least a few blowsy alcoholic couples who get along affectionately, slurring their words of love?

No, with us there were at least two basic and seemingly irreparable causes of conflict, deep-rooted, unavailable to rational thought, or control.

To blame Ran first: one of our troubles was his basic mistrust-suspicion of sex, especially good sex, and ours was mostly excellent— hard to explain, but there it was, great sex. Although he never would have admitted it, being such a sophisticated man, a distinguished composer, Ran really believed all those Protestant-Puritan myths, especially strong in small-town Southern men, I think. He believed that sex weakened your intellectual processes: "Well, my dear, I fear that I must bid you an early adieu; I have to get a great deal done in the morning," he would say, over my impassioned protests, my threats, and this was not something that we could ever talk about. He believed too that nice women, good women, didn't really like sex; my evident sensual relish made me suspect, was probably proof of a bad character.

The other problem, maybe worse, was mine: my own unshakable, implacable self-dislike. Its causes no longer interest me; it was just a fact, like being tall. And we all know how it is with such people: anyone who claims to love us is either lying or soft in the head, inferior; at various times I accused Ran of both conditions, but mostly of lying. Even when he assured me, as he often did, that the happiest moments in his life had been with me, that he had never truly cared so much for any woman, and for so long, I was always sure that his heart and mind were still vividly inhabited by Gloria. I believed that even in our most tender moments he thought of her, and that to me he was simply being polite, saying what he felt the situation called for.

(But is it possible, Ms. Heffelfinger, that I was wrong, that I was indeed much loved by Ran? A heady thought: I can hardly take it in.)

The next phase of our "relationship" was mostly occupied with Ran's illness, and it was mostly terrible.

He had always coughed a lot, ever since I had known him, hardly surprising in such a perpetual smoker, although at the time I smoked as much as he and rarely coughed. We even joked sometimes about his smoker's hack, since he seemed to cough most violently in bed. Then, in a gradual way, we both noticed that the cough was getting worse, and worse and worse. He would be taken with terrible paroxysms, fits, during which he would seem to be trying to cough up his very lungs; he would clutch his arms together, his face an awful red, and wet with sweat.

I began to have secret fears of TB, then still relatively common, or of lung cancer, less prevalent, and not much known. At last I was so frightened that I dared his rage; I knew he would feel an imputation of illness as an accusation (one more!) but I said to him, "Ran, darling, that cough of yours is getting out of hand. You've got to get it seen to."

He answered so mildly that I was more alarmed than ever. "I know," he said, "I'm going up to Johns Hopkins next week."

My first thought, which I managed not to say, was: But I have to go to New York next week, I can't go with you. (I had begun, in the long course of my association with Ran, to enjoy some success, from a show in the small gallery of the Hilton art department, to several pieces in a statewide show, in the capital city, then moving north to a show in Washington, D.C. And then New York, Madison Avenue. The Whitney.)

I did say, "You'll give me a call? I'll be in New York. The Brevoort."

"Okay, if you're going to be such a silly bitch about it."

"Yes, I am, you dumb bastard."

That was how we often spoke to each other, affection concealed in abuse. I think Ran may even have felt rather daring, calling a woman a bitch right to her face, and God knows he often meant it.

. . .

Most of that trip to New York I spent on the phone, leaving messages as to my whereabouts: if Mr. Caldwell called I would be having a drink at the Plaza, in the Oak Room; I would be with Betty Parsons; I was back in the hotel, having dinner on the terrace, by myself.

By now we were in the early forties. Ran and I had been together for almost ten years, and the country was at war. New York, that bright October, was full of uniforms, arrivals and departures. Since the Brevoort was fairly expensive most of the uniforms there were officers', lots of brass and braid, ribbons and stars. I had just got rid of a very drunk colonel, who was insisting that he join me—how dare I have dinner alone, didn't I know there was a war on?—when there, where the colonel had been, was Ran, very dashing, very happy, almost drunk.

He kissed me lavishly, which was unusual: he disliked a public display. He sat down across from me, and he spoke the great news: "I thought I should tell you in person that I am a certified healthy man. Those gentlemen, with their innumerable tests, which were not at all pleasant—they all failed to turn up a single evil diagnosis. I have no infections, no malignancies."

Well. We celebrated with champagne and lobsters, and more champagne for breakfast. I took Ran around to some galleries, and he was very proud of me, I think. Later we met some old music friends of his for drinks, on Patchen Place, and more friends for dinner, at Luchow's. We had never had such a good time: how wonderful, Ran was not seriously sick.

What we both ignored, or failed for quite a while to see as significant, was that he was still coughing, badly.

Back in Hilton nothing else had changed much either. We drank and quarreled and talked as much as ever. I think we made love a little less, by then.

Sometime the following spring Ran announced that he had been offered a teaching job in the music department in Tucson, the University of Arizona. "Although I confess that the word 'emeritus' rather gives me pause," he said.

He rambled on, but I wasn't listening at all; I was thinking *Gloria.* Gloria had moved out to Phoenix or Tucson, to me almost the same place. Out West. Of course she must be Ran's true direction. That night we had one of our bad quarrels, about something else—naturally.

I went out to visit him in October, which was not one of our best times together.

For one thing, the place itself was so strange that it made us seem alien even to each other. Surrounded by the bizarre, inimical desert, the flat, palm-lined, unnaturally sunny town, Ran's apartment had the look of a motel: stucco, one-storied, part of a complex built around a large, much too blue swimming pool, in which it was never quite warm enough to swim.

Motels have always seemed somehow sexual to me, and I was unable to rid myself of fantasies involving Ran and Gloria: had she visited him there, did she maybe come for visits frequently? All morning, every day, when Ran was off teaching his classes, I would ransack his apartment (though tidily, a cautious spy), every cranny and corner, drawer and wastebasket, his desk, even the linen closet, in a search for Gloria, any trace of her—a quest that was as compulsive as it was humiliating, degrading. And it was also fruitless, yielding up nothing but a crick in my back, a broken fingernail and dust.

At night we went out and ate Mexican food and drank too much Mexican beer, and, out of character for us, we neither quarreled nor talked very much. I was afraid—in fact, I knew—that if we did talk much of it would lead to a fight, and any conversation might summon Gloria. And Ran had, seemingly, almost no energy. He coughed a lot, and we almost never made love.

(But then tonight, Ms. Heffelfinger, as I remembered that time, from such a long distance, and I recalled my desperate need to *know* about Gloria, I came to an odd conclusion: I thought, How strange of me to care, when really it didn't matter. What was the difference, finally, whether or not Gloria spent an afternoon or a weekend with Ran, within those garish stucco walls. Even whether or not they made love. I could almost hope they had; I could almost, if belatedly, halfheartedly, wish for a little almost final happiness for Ran. But not too much, and I was still consoled by the fixed idea that Gloria would have been uninteresting in bed.)

. . .

When he came back to Hilton, at the beginning of the following summer, I knew that Ran must be very sick indeed—his speech was so radically altered. Whereas before he had said everything so elaborately, with such a smoke screen of complicated verbiage, now he spoke very simply and directly, as though he had not much time or breath remaining. Which in fact he did not: he had what we now know as emphysema, he was dying of it.

That summer we spent most evenings in Ran's huge high glassed-in living room, watching fireflies and the lengthening shadows, among the barely stirring summer leaves, the flowering shrubbery.

"Sometimes I can't remember when you first came here," Ran said one night. "Was it before or after Lucinda killed herself?"

"Just after," I told him as I digested what I had only half known, or heard as rumor before, what he thought I already knew—Lucinda's suicide. And I sadly wished that he had been able to say this before; it might have eased some pain for him, I thought. And I thought about Lucinda, her long novels and small madrigals, her dislike of the "cluttered" landscape, and I cursed her for adding to a deeply guilty man's store of guilt. In the long run, really, Gloria had done him a lot less harm.

"I guess by now I think you've always been around," he said, with a new half-smile, so that my heart lurched with an aching, unfamiliar tenderness for him.

On another evening of that summer Ran told me that he was going to sell his house. "It's too big," he said. "Taxes. So many rooms. Maids. The windows." He had a new and alarming habit of quick breaths between almost each word, and deep difficult breaths between sentences. Now, after such a labored pause, he added, "I'm tired of it."

"You lying bastard." Fear made me rough; it was at about this time that I began to adopt my stance of gruffness, to perfect my just-not-rude snort. "You wouldn't know what to do without this house," I told him, and then I laughed. "But if you really want to sell it, I'll buy it from you."

That night was as close as we had come to quarreling for some time, but in the course of those hours we worked out a highly original real-estate deal, whereby I would buy Ran's house, but I would not take possession of it until I had paid for over half of it, by which time we both knew that Ran would be dead.

. . .

And that, Ms. Heffelfinger, in brief, is how it went. I bought Ran's house, and soon afterward, early that fall, he died, and I moved in. I sorted and labeled and stored away all his papers, his manuscripts, his library, as though it had all been infinitely valuable, which, to me, it was. (He had kept no letters from Gloria, which was both gratifying and frustrating.)

After so much heavy thought, and so much to drink, I should have awakened the next day in a state of hung-over exhaustion—a state that my poor guilty Presbyterian Ran used to describe as being "richly deserved." But I did not feel terrible, not at all. I got up and made myself a healthy breakfast, and then I telephoned the inn, for Candida Heffelfinger.

She came over promptly, in answer to my invitation (a summons, it must have sounded like), and she looked as I had imagined that she would: contrite and tired, and rumpled. Unlike me, she could not have slept well.

She told me that she had been walking around the town, and how much she liked it, and I agreed. Then we both admired, again, the bright fall view from my windows.

And then she said, "I've been thinking—and I hope this won't sound presumptuous, but would you mind if I shifted the focus of our talk a little? I mean, so many people have written about the legendary love affair."

This was irritating: she was saying to me exactly what I had meant to say to her.

I snorted. "I suppose you mean to take another tack, and zero in on our fights?"

"Oh no, of course not. I wouldn't—"

"In point of fact," I told her, "the written accounts are remarkably close to the truth. I was in Italy, and Gloria Bingham visited here for a while, and then she left. Ran and I both had our flings, but no one else mattered much to either of us."

Candida seemed to find that statement both moving and final, as I did myself. She was silent for a while, and then she said, "I really meant

about your work. It's interesting, your beginning with those small figures. The gain in scope."

"It undoubtedly had something to do with my physical size," I told
her, very dry.

"I can understand that," she said. Well, I believed that she could,
indeed; we are about the same height. Big ladies.

"What really happened," I then told her, "was in Italy, for the first
time, I saw real Michelangelos. In the Bargello, and in the Vatican,
St. Peter's—"

We talked for several hours, and I saw that I had been right all along
about Candida; my instincts still were fine. She was very nice indeed, and
smart. I liked her. Our talk went on all morning, and into the afternoon.

I had a marvelous time.

At the Beach

The very old couple, of whom everyone at the beach is so highly aware, seem themselves to notice no one else at all. Tall and thin, she almost as tall as he, they are probably somewhere in their eighties. They walk rather slowly, and can be seen, from time to time, to stop and rest, staring out to sea, or to some private distance of their own. Their postures, always, are arrestingly, regally erect; it is this that catches so much attention, as well as their general air of distinction, and of what is either disdain or a total lack of interest in other people.

Their clothes are the whitest at the beach; in the ferocious Mexican sun of that resort they both wear large hats, hers lacy, his a classic panama.

They look like movie stars, or even royalty, and for all anyone knows they are, deposed monarchs from one of the smaller European countries, world-wanderers.

Because there is not much to do at that resort, almost nothing but walking and swimming, reading or whatever social activities one can devise, most people stay for fairly short periods of time. Also, it is relatively expensive. The Chicago people, who have come as a group, will be there for exactly ten days. The couple who have the room just next door to that of the distinguished old couple will be there for only a week—a week literally stolen, since he is married to someone else, in Santa Barbara, and is supposed to be at a sales conference, in Puerto Rico.

But the old people seem to have been there forever, and the others imagine that they will stay on and on, at least for the length of the winter.

And while everyone else can be seen, from time to time, to wonder what to do next—the Chicago people, apparently committed to unity of action, were heard arguing in the dining room over whether, or when, to rent a boat for deep-sea fishing—the two old people have a clear, unwavering schedule of their own. After breakfast, to which they come in quite late, as they do to all meals, they sit out on their small porch for a couple of hours. The girl in the room next door, who is named Amanda Evers, is passionately curious about them, and she tries to look through the filagree of concrete that separates the two porches. But she discovers nothing. (She is in fact too curious about too many people; her lover, Richard Paxton, has told her so. Curiosity contributes to the general confusion of her life.)

The old man reads his newspapers, a Mexico City *News* that he has delivered to his table each morning, at breakfast, and sometimes he seems to be writing letters—or perhaps he keeps a journal? The woman does not read the paper; she seems to be doing nothing at all—a thing that Amanda, who is restlessly energetic, cannot imagine. (Amanda manages a travel agency, in Santa Cruz, California; she often considers other careers.)

The arrival of the elderly couple, down at the beach, at almost precisely noon each day, is much noticed; it is when they look, perhaps, most splendid. In trim dark bathing suits, over which they both wear white shirts, in their hats and large dark glasses, advancing on their ancient legs, they are as elegant as tropical birds—and a striking contrast to everyone else on the beach, many of whom wear bright colors. One woman in the Chicago group has a pea-green caftan that literally hurts Amanda's eyes.

The old people sit each day under the same small thatched shelter, a little apart from the others, at the end of the line. After a while they will rise and begin one of their long, deliberate walks, the length of the beach and back. Then, returned to their shelter, in a slow and careful way they divest themselves of the shirts, the hats and glasses; they walk down to the edge of the water, and slowly, majestically, they enter the lapping small green waves. After a not quite total immersion they return to the shelter, to rest. Even in such apparent repose, however, they both have a look of great attentiveness. They seem highly conscious of each moment, and very likely they are.

They take lunch quite late, and always, of course, alone, at one of the small restaurants down the beach. They are seen to chatter away to each other, and to eat rather little. But no one can ever overhear what they are saying, nor would anyone dare address them. *Her* accent, however, is recognizably "foreign"; his is English, probably—giving further credence to the theory that they are royalty, deposed.

And that notion is not entirely incorrect: those people are named Carlotta and Travis Farquhar, and once, if not royal, they were famous: Carlotta, originally Polish, as an actress, and Travis, a Scot, as an astronomer; an asteroid has his name. They both, simultaneously, reached their heights of achievement about forty years ago; since then, not entirely by choice, they have eased themselves into retirement. In Travis's case, what was then called a nervous breakdown took two years from his life; coming out of it, he was, or felt himself to be, too far behind, in terms of research. He could still teach, of course, but he tired of that, fairly early on. And Carlotta, who took care of him during those years, had never been truly dedicated to the stage; later she was happy enough to yield her place to younger actresses, or so she said.

They never had children, always traveled a lot.

One ostensible reason for the high cost of this resort is its extraordinary natural beauty—a beauty that most people seem to take some note of on arrival, and then, curiously, to forget.

The hotel is built on the downward slope of a hill above the beach, from which one faces a very large cove of bright, often glassy-green water. Far out across that water, at the mouth of the cove, there are two widely spaced but rather similarly shaped promontories of land; both slope gently down to the water, like great dark obedient beasts. Delicately feathered trees are silhouetted out there, at sunsets, which are almost always brilliant and violent, or in the first pale light of early mornings.

The beach, a wide white ribbon, encircles the cove; above the sand is the powerful, encroaching, mysterious green jungle—impenetrable, probably dangerous. It marks the start of a mountain range that extends almost to Mexico City.

The skies are nearly always clear and blue and pale, and the air is warm—subtle, moist, insinuating. Getting off the plane, their first night, still in her northern California clothes, Amanda gasped with pleasure at that tropical air and the smell of flowers that even at the airport hung in the slight evening breeze. "Oh, feel the air, it's so lovely," she cried out to

Richard, by which she meant: Our time here will be lovely. But then she forgot about the air, or stopped thinking about it.

Richard is usually foremost in Amanda's mind and consciousness; he is a difficult lover (although she has reflected that all her lovers have been difficult, in one way or another). Her obsession with Richard is so anxiety-ridden that she cannot sort out those emotions; indeed, it is hard for her to imagine love without anxiety. Richard is not only married, in an explosive off-and-on way, but he is exceptionally handsome, a golden southern California boy; he is spoiled, rather moody and seemingly fond of his moods—he has put in some time at Esalen. He is five years younger than she, which is not supposed to matter, but somehow, sometimes it does.

At this resort, though, he seems exceptionally cheery and calm. Before breakfast he runs on the beach, two lengths, and he has announced that the sand is superior. Amanda, whose discovery this place has been, is more than relieved; she is delighted. They swim far out into the cove together, in the clear warm green water; sometimes, looking down, they can see small stray brightly colored fish. At lunch they drink the excellent Mexican beer, and eat fresh garlicky seafood. They shower and sleep, they make love. They swim again, and shower again, and head up to the bar, which is cantilevered out into the open, starry, flowery night; they drink margaritas, toasting each other and the lovely, perfect place.

And the next day they repeat the pattern.

Perhaps for that reason, Richard's relatively "good mood," Amanda's attention wanders from him more than usual, and she finds herself acutely aware of the elderly, possibly royal couple next door: how long have they been married, she wonders. And who *are* they?

"You could ask them for autographs," Richard suggests. "Then you'd know."

It is just past noon. From their beach chairs Amanda and Richard are watching as the Farquhars slowly rise and start out on their walk, watching the slow progress of those erect, high, narrow bodies, on their thin brown wrinkled legs.

Choosing to ignore Richard's facetiousness (he enjoys teasing her), Amanda asks him, "Will your hair be white, do you think?"

He frowns a little. "Not any time soon, I hope." And then, as though taking her earlier question seriously, he says, "Why don't you ask those people to have a drink with us, if you really want to know something about them?"

"Oh, well. I really don't think so." Amanda says this calmly, but inwardly she has quailed at the very idea; of course it would have to be the other way around, the older people would have to ask them for a drink, which of course they never will do—but oh! if they should. To be with those people, to know them at all, Amanda feels, would itself confer distinction; in their presence one would find peace.

And then, as she contemplates the two tall, erect figures that gradually grow smaller, walking down the very white beach, slowly, near the bright green-blue water, for a moment Amanda's consciousness blurs; from behind closed eyelids she has a sudden vision of herself without Richard, without the chaos of his presence in her life: she sees herself in some new and calmer phase, even released from her frenetic occupation. She is running a bookstore, perhaps. There is one for sale in Aptos, a town next door to Santa Cruz but smaller and quieter, by far.

Opening her eyes, as though she had been asleep, she shakes her head, and drowsily, rather impersonally, she speaks to Richard: "It's so restful here, isn't it."

"Well, that's one thing we came for, I thought. Leave our old problems behind?" He grins in a familiar, challenging way; they both know what "problems" he means, and her usual fondness for discussing them.

But this time she does not take him up. "It's so beautiful. I could stay here forever" is all she says.

If the Farquhars are objects of Amanda's admiring curiosity, the Chicago group inspires opposite emotions: she finds them noisy, obtrusive, in their too bright clothes. One of them, a heavily mustached young man, even smokes a cigar, *all the time,* which you can smell all over the beach. Their loud, quite unself-conscious voices dominate the dining room or the bar when they are present—as they seemingly always are, and always together. Amanda cannot imagine herself, with or without Richard, as a part of any group at all.

"Wouldn't it be great if they'd leave before we do," she whispers to Richard.

"They look pretty settled in," he observes.

"That's probably how they'd look anywhere. Do you realize that there're actually only six of them? I just counted. They seem more like ten or twelve people."

Richard laughs. Her ability to amuse him is a thing that Amanda counts on; it almost makes up, she feels, for being older And less beautiful than he is, although by most standards she is pretty enough (which she sometimes forgets), in a thin, rather original way, with her heavy dark hair, narrow face and large pale-gray eyes.

Another object of Amanda's wayward curiosity is the hotel's manager, or manageress: a large blond strong-looking woman, who is unfailingly cheerful. A big happy woman, she walks about in old soft white pants and a blue work shirt. She is called, by everyone, Lisa, and she seems to have neither a last name nor a history; her accent, in English, is vaguely Central European. She also speaks German and Spanish, fluently.

She and the Farquhars appear to know each other, and this too, of course, draws Amanda's attention. Lisa is, in fact, the only person to whom the Farquhars are ever seen to speak.

Amanda wonders how Lisa happened to come to Mexico, and if she has ever been married. Mainly, though, she would like to know the secret of such level cheerfulness: how can Lisa cope with the whole hotel, the guests and the help, and answer everyone's questions and still smile like that? Her own work has taught Amanda more than a little about the irritations of travel.

In fact, Amanda is wrong about the people from Chicago: there are seven of them, not six, although she may have counted when one of them was missing. And they are not quite as homogeneous as, to Amanda, they appear. At least one of them, a recent widow, Natalie Barnes, is quite out of sorts with the rest. It was good of them to ask her along, without Herbert, but they all make too much noise, and she knows them well enough by now to have tired of all their jokes and stories. Besides, her skin is getting too old for all this sun.

Natalie, like Amanda, like everyone there, is fascinated by the Farquhars—especially that woman's skin, which is remarkable, so fine and smooth and white. Natalie wishes she knew what kind of sun block that woman uses.

And she wonders about their marriage, the Farquhars': have they always been married to each other, and got along as well as they now apparently do? Natalie and Herbert were actually separated at the time that he died, a fact known to none of their traveling friends, so that Natalie has been cast, by them, in a role that does not precisely suit her, that of Herbert's beloved, bereaved wife. But she is just as glad that none of them knew about the girl.

Did those old people ever quarrel and get back together? Would Herbert have come back, had he lived? Would he have tired of that girl? Natalie sighs, afraid that she will never have an answer to anything.

The bougainvillea, in that place, blooms with a wild extravagance; there is every shade of pink, of red, even violet and purple. Vines cling to the steep hillside, from which the gaudy blossoms foam. Brilliant colors lurk between the low white plaster buildings of the hotel; everywhere there are sudden bursts of flowers—on the way to the dining room, or going up to the bar, and flowers bloom all around the porch-balconies of the rooms. Just beyond the porch that Amanda and Richard share with the Farquhars (except for the intervening filagree) there is a bush of yellow angel's trumpets, and beside the bush a strangely branched small tree, reddish blossoms among its crooked limbs. Hummingbirds are drawn to the tree's red flowers, while among the trumpet flowers there often appear small yellow butterflies, almost indistinguishable from the yellow petals.

By their fourth day Amanda is acutely aware of just that: four days gone, only three remain. Less than half their time. And the four days seem to have passed as one, she feels. Just as the years of her life race faster and faster. Soon she will be middle-aged, then irretrievably old. In a discouraged way she looks around the beach, at so much exposed and aging flesh, the sags and wrinkles that painstakingly acquired suntans do not conceal.

Richard, though, is simply a darker shade of gold. The small fine patch of hair on his chest and the hairs on his arms and legs are all bleached out, pale, almost invisible. No wrinkles, anywhere. Amanda sighs, thinking of what they—or, rather, she—will be going back to: at work, days on the phone or at the computer, people either impatient or angry with her, or both, and most nights spent alone, either not hearing from Richard or hearing, via a hurried call, that they cannot meet, after all, wherever they had planned to.

For reassurance, or perhaps to answer some unformed question, she turns toward the elderly couple, who are resting beneath their small thatched shelter. He is lying back in his chair, his eyes closed against the sun and his mouth slightly open. But she, her white skin shaded by the lace-brimmed hat, sits intently forward; she is looking, looking—but at what? Following the direction of her gaze, Amanda sees, in the foreground, a small outcropping of rocks, spattered with a little white moss. Then sand, and then the water, bright and clear and green, rippling out in the dancing, dazzling sunlight, as far as the horizon. And the hot flat blue endless sky.

Further sadness for Amanda: after four days she and that couple, whose name she still does not know, are no closer to speaking or even nodding terms than they were on her arrival. They have never even seen her, Amanda believes.

That afternoon, after their siesta, Amanda goes up to the hotel desk to mail some postcards. Rounding a corner, she is confronted with a trailing vine, a cloud of peach-pink bougainvillea; she sees it against the soft blue midafternoon sky—she has never seen that particular color before.

Reaching the desk, she is surprised to find Lisa standing there, in a skirt and blouse, black pumps. Lisa looking older than usual, and tired. The change in her is so marked that Amanda assumes she is leaving for good, and she cries out, "Oh, Lisa, you're not going away?"—as though everything, lacking Lisa, would fall apart.

Lisa smiles, but her blue eyes remain worried. "I only go to Mexico City," she says. "Probably I return tomorrow. I go each other week."

"Oh. Well."

Several other people, Americans, come up to the desk just then, followed by two Mexican boys who carry the American luggage—unfortunately they are not the Chicago group, Amanda notes. The airport bus arrives, and they all get in, including Lisa.

Feeling abandoned, Amanda buys her stamps, and she sends off the cards to her friends; on all the cards she has written, "This is paradise!"

From the plane, on which Lisa and some of the former guests are flying to Mexico City, they can see, as it gains altitude, the whole great horseshoe cove: the white curve of beach, abrupt green jungle at the edge of the sand and even the clearing where the hotel is. Then the plane veers and heads directly inland, up over the huge sharp jungle-green mountains that are sometimes briefly, darkly shadowed with clouds.

Lisa is simply going to Mexico City on hotel business, but the prospect always unbalances her a little. Never married, a childless but strongly maternal Polish woman (nationality being her common bond with Carlotta Farquhar), she loves her work, finds it deeply satisfying.

She is genuinely concerned about the well-being of all the guests, and especially that of the Farquhars: she grew up on the romantic legend of Carlotta, who left the stage so relatively young. And she has worked it out that despite appearances the Farquhars do not have a great deal of money. She daringly hopes, on this trip, to persuade the owner of the hotel to give them a special rate, as long-term guests. In the meantime, she reminds herself to do their errands: a scientific magazine, in German, for Mr. Farquhar; for her a French cosmetic.

The next night, which is Amanda's and Richard's fifth, they decide to return to the bar for after-dinner drinks; once there, they are dismayed to find the Chicago people, who obviously have had the same impulse. But, feeling that they have not much choice, there being not much else to do, really, at nine-thirty, Amanda and Richard sit down anyway.

Early in the afternoon Richard spent a long time on the phone with his wife, or so Amanda believes; he only said that he had to go up to the desk. Unable to read, she lay waiting for him, all that time not doing any-thing—not knowing, wondering, what they could be saying to each other. For all she knew Richard could be telling his wife that he is bored at his "sales conference" and can't wait to see her again. It is harrowing to her, Amanda, not to know, and she feels that it is forbidden to ask; she would sound suspicious. When at last he came back to the room Richard looked cross, but that could have meant anything at all. At dinner he was pleasantly noncommittal: his usual self. But Amanda still feels anxious, vaguely apprehensive.

At the bar she is seated next to a woman whom she had not seen in that group: a surprisingly pleasant-looking woman, with short gray hair and a pretty dress. Amanda wonders why she has not noticed her before.

Natalie Barnes.

The two women exchange faint smiles of mutual approval.

Although the night is as clear and dazzlingly starred as all the nights have been, there are also, tonight, a few small drifting gray-white clouds, mysterious rags. Tattered ghosts.

Natalie, who will be at the resort with that group for another five days, has hitherto felt that since they invited her along, in spite of her widowed status, she was in some sense their guest. But just now, perhaps fortified by dinner, and some wine, she recognizes the untruth, even the unfairness of this theory: she is not their guest; she pays her own way. And she further thinks, Luther does not have to leave a cigar burning in the ashtray, constantly. Bracing herself, and trying for a pleasant voice, she says, "Luther, couldn't you please put those damn things out when you're not smoking them?"

They all stare at her; as a group they are not self-critical, but usually supportive, all the way. However, they are also dedicated to going along with each other's whims, all whims, and so Luther says, "Well, Nat, of course, I'll put it right out. Why didn't you tell me before, if they bothered you?" Everyone stares reproachfully at formerly good old Nat, who was so brave when Herbert died.

Turning away from them all, for a moment, Natalie finds the dark girl with the very handsome husband (or lover?), who is smiling and saying, or, rather, whispering: "Terrific. That smell has been driving me crazy."

Natalie whispers back, "I didn't sound too mean?"

"Heavens no."

Richard joins in, smiling charmingly. "Amanda has a thing about cigars."

Still whispering, Natalie admits, "Actually, so do I."

"Well: we were just going to have another drink. May I get you one?"

Natalie argues, and then accepts, and they introduce each other: Natalie, Amanda and Richard. The darkness and the loose, informal arrangement of the chairs at that bar make such regroupings easy. As Natalie glances back for a moment at her former companions, she even sees smiles of approval on several of their faces: good old Nat is out there making new friends; all *right*.

At some distance from everyone else, as usual, the Farquhars are seated, she in something long and pale and supple, dimly shining, he in an open white shirt, a dark ascot knotted at his throat. Their postures, as always, are perfectly erect. Her head moves slowly on her long and slender neck as she turns toward her husband.

"Do you think she could have been a dancer?" whispers Natalie to Amanda.

Richard answers, "That's a really good guess. I'll bet you're right."

Amanda suggests, "Or maybe an actress?"

"But what was he?" asks Natalie. She is thinking of Herbert, who was in business, but not on the scale that he originally intended.

"He could have been an actor," offers Richard, who has often heard that remark made of himself. On the whole, though, he is glad not to be an actor; he likes the challenge of investments, at which he is very good. And most actors burn out young, their looks gone.

"Somehow I don't think he was an actor," Amanda muses. "He looks more like an elder statesman. Or some Nobel Prize–winning scientist."

Just at that moment, though, Mrs. Farquhar is seen and heard, by those three observing her so closely, to cry out, in evident pain. With both hands she grasps her side, at her waist, and she says something short and urgent to her husband. They both stand up, she with what is obviously great difficulty; they leave the bar, presumably going toward their room.

Amanda feels cold waves of panic in her veins, in the warm tropical night—and so irrationally: she doesn't even know those people. "What can we do?" she asks of Richard and Natalie, and she hears a quaver in her own voice.

Richard, who thrives on emergencies (it is daily life that bores him), stands up. "I'll go down and ask," he says, and he is gone before the wisdom of his course can be questioned.

"Do you think it could be an appendix?" Amanda asks Natalie; she has somehow assumed that Natalie, being older than herself, would have more medical information.

Natalie does not, actually, but she makes a guess. "It looked a little high for an appendix, where she was clutching. But I don't know."

Richard, apparently, has done the right thing: within minutes he is back at the bar, with an errand. "I'm going up to the desk to get Lisa and phone for a doctor."

Amanda cries out, "But Lisa's in Mexico City."

"She's back." And, over his shoulder as he hurries off, "Their name is Farquhar." And he is gone.

In a helpless way Natalie and Amanda turn to each other.

And just then, behind Natalie, the other Chicago people begin to get up, making sounds of departure. Luther, without his cigar, is the one who says, "Well, good night, Nat," with only the slightest querulousness in his voice. "See you in the morning," says someone else.

She turns to say, "Yes, see you then."

And they are gone.

"At their age, almost any pain must be frightening" is the first thing that Amanda finds to say. It is understood that she refers to the Farquhars.

"Or maybe not? They must have had a lot of pains by now." As she says this, Natalie is rather surprised by what sounds like wisdom.

In a fairly short time Richard reappears, with Lisa—Lisa once again in her old pants and shirt; comfortable, competent Lisa, who says to Amanda, "The doctor comes. You could wait here? She knows where is the bar but not the room of the Farquhars. You could show her the way?"

"Oh, of course."

Lisa sighs vastly, and to all three of them she says, "Oh, how bad that she should be sick now. I come back from Mexico City with some good news," and she sighs again. "She come soon. The doctor. She is a friend to me."

And then she and Richard are gone, in the direction of the Farquhars' room, as well as of Richard's and Amanda's.

"A woman doctor?" Natalie asks Amanda.

"I guess. But how will we know her, or she us?" Amanda says.

She, the doctor, is immediately recognizable: a brisk young woman with a classic black doctor's satchel, who hurries down the steps toward

Amanda and Natalie. She smiles, in a shy, quick way. "It is you who will direct me to the lady not feeling well?"

"Yes, it's this way." And the three women, Amanda leading the doctor and Natalie, make their way down from the bar, down the series of dimly lit steps, past all the soft shapes of flowers, the colors now blotted out in the general dark. They reach the row of rooms, and go on to the room at the end, where Richard stands just outside the opened door.

As they arrive, through the door in one bright instant Amanda sees: two single beds, on one of which Mrs. Farquhar is stretched, immobile, her head back, chin raised, as on a bier. And beside her, bent toward her, is her husband. Lisa stands beside him.

Richard gestures the doctor inside, at which Lisa comes out, and the door is closed.

The four of them stand there, in the flowery darkness, Amanda and Richard, Lisa, Natalie.

"It is perhaps not something terrible," Lisa tells them all. "She kept saying she only wanted a shot. She said she could sleep off the pain."

Richard: "She looked awfully white."

"She's always white," Natalie tells him. And in a subdued way she laughs. "I only wish I knew her brand of sun block."

"I can tell you. I just bring it from Mexico," Lisa tells her, and she names the French cream.

"Well, thank you," Natalie murmurs, in surprise. And then, a few minutes later, she says, "Well, I think I'll go on up. After all, I don't really know them," and she says good night, and she leaves.

As though it would insure her safety, they all watch her as she walks slowly up the barely lit stairs.

Turning to Lisa, Amanda repeats what she had earlier said to Natalie, but as a question: "At their age almost any pain is frightening, isn't it?"

Clearly thinking of something else, or possibly a little frightened herself, Lisa is slightly brusque. "At any age—no pain is good." And then, "You two should go in. There is no need for you also to wait. I know them a long time."

Dismissed, Amanda and Richard go into their room next door, from which they can hear nothing. Nevertheless they continue to address each other in whispers.

"Another drink? Some brandy?"

"Oh, thanks. I could use some."

"Here. It's a little full."

Later they hear the subdued sounds of the doctor coming out of the room adjacent, some murmurs of conversation, the door softly closed. Nothing more.

Later still they undress, and wash; they get into bed and make love. They are comforting to each other.

But, lying there in the hot unmoving night, Amanda is terrified. The beautiful, old and almost totally unknown Mrs. Farquhar could die, and that possibility is intolerable to Amanda.

In the morning, Carlotta Farquhar is perfectly well; the shot administered by the young doctor put her out for about nine hours, as she, Carlotta, knew that it would. Sitting out on the porch, propped against a small pillow, she breathes deeply, feeling only slightly sluggish from the morphine. Needing air.

Travis has made the tea; they always travel with a small kit. He hands her the cup, and he says, "Drink up. You look half asleep."

Carlotta smiles. "But, darling, I am." And then she says, "How kind of Señor Blumenthal. Our new rate."

"Oh yes, that." He frowns, just slightly embarrassed. And then he lowers his voice as he says to her, "The young couple next door, they were most kind, do you know? He went up to get Lisa, and to phone. They showed such concern, when they don't even know us. Don't you think—suppose we invite them for a drink?"

"Oh, darling, absolutely yes. We'll speak to them after breakfast. Or I'll write a note."

But just then Carlotta, who has been looking out to the early morning sea, and the bright pale sky, when she has not been turned to Travis, leans suddenly forward: there on the yellow bush at the edge of their terrace is the largest, the loveliest white butterfly that she has ever seen. She gasps with pleasure. There is nothing in her mind but the butterfly, on its flower.

Truth or Consequences

This morning, when I read in a gossip column that a man named Carstairs Jones had married a famous former movie star, I was startled, thunderstruck, for I knew that he must certainly be the person whom I knew as a child, one extraordinary spring, as "Car Jones." He was a dangerous and disreputable boy, one of what were then called the "truck children," with whom I had a most curious, brief and frightening connection. Still, I noted that in a way I was pleased at such good fortune; I was "happy for him," so to speak, perhaps as a result of sheer distance, so many years. And before I could imagine Car as he might be now, Carstairs Jones, in Hollywood clothes, I suddenly saw, with the most terrific accuracy and bright sharpness of detail, the schoolyard of all those years ago, hard and bare, neglected. And I relived the fatal day, on the middle level of that schoolyard, when we were playing truth or consequences, and I said that I would rather kiss Car Jones than be eaten alive by ants.

Our school building then was three stories high, a formidable brick square. In front a lawn had been attempted, some years back; graveled walks led up to the broad, forbidding entranceway, and behind the school were the playing fields, the playground. This area was on three levels: on the upper level, nearest the school, were the huge polished steel frames for the creaking swings, the big green splintery wooden seesaws, the rickety slides—all for the youngest children. On the middle level older girls played hopscotch, various games, or jumped rope—or just talked and giggled. And out on the lowest level, the field, the boys practiced football, or baseball, in the spring.

To one side of the school was a parking space, usually filled with the bulging yellow trucks that brought children from out in the country in to town: truck children, country children. Sometimes they would go back to the trucks at lunchtime to eat their sandwiches, whatever; almost always there were several overgrown children, spilling out from the trucks. Or Car Jones, expelled from some class, for some new acts of rebelliousness. That area was always littered with trash, wrappings from sandwiches, orange peel, Coke bottles.

Beyond the parking space was an empty lot, overgrown with weeds, in the midst of which stood an abandoned trellis, perhaps once the support of wisteria; now wild honeysuckle almost covered it over.

The town was called Hilton, the seat of a distinguished university, in the middle South. My widowed mother, Charlotte Ames, had moved there the previous fall (with me, Emily, her only child). I am still not sure why she chose Hilton; she never much liked it there, nor did she really like the brother-in-law, a professor, into whose proximity the move had placed us.

An interesting thing about Hilton, at that time, was that there were three, and only three, distinct social classes. (Negroes could possibly make four, but they were so separate, even from the poorest whites, as not to seem part of the social system at all; they were in effect invisible.) At the scale's top were professors and their families. Next were the townspeople, storekeepers, bankers, doctors and dentists, none of whom had the prestige nor the money they were later to acquire. Country people were the bottom group, families living out on the farms that surrounded the town, people who sent their children in to school on the yellow trucks.

The professors' children of course had a terrific advantage, academically, coming from houses full of books, from parental respect for learning; many of those kids read precociously and had large vocabularies. It was not so hard on most of the town children; many of their families shared qualities with the faculty people; they too had a lot of books around. But the truck children had a hard and very unfair time of it. Not only were many of their parents near-illiterates, but often the children were kept at home to help with chores, and sometimes, particularly during the coldest, wettest months of winter, weather prevented the trucks' passage over the slithery red clay roads of that countryside, that era. A child could miss out on a whole new skill, like long division, and fail tests, and be kept back. Consequently many of the truck children were overage, oversized for the grades they were in.

In the seventh grade, when I was eleven, a year ahead of myself, having been tested for and skipped the sixth (attesting to the superiority of Northern schools, my mother thought, and probably she was right), dangerous Car Jones, in the same class, was fourteen, and taller than anyone.

There was some overlapping, or crossing, among those three social groups; there were hybrids, as it were. In fact, I was such a crossbreed myself: literally my mother and I were town people—my dead father had been a banker, but since his brother was a professor we too were considered faculty people. Also my mother had a lot of money, making us further élite. To me, being known as rich was just embarrassing, more freakish than advantageous, and I made my mother stop ordering my clothes from Best's; I wanted dresses from the local stores, like everyone else's.

Car Jones too was a hybrid child, although his case was less visible than mine: his country family were distant cousins of the prominent and prosperous dean of the medical school, Dean Willoughby Jones. (They seem to have gone in for fancy names, in all the branches of that family.) I don't think his cousins spoke to him.

In any case, being richer and younger than the others in my class made me socially very insecure, and I always approached the playground with a sort of excited dread: would I be asked to join in a game, and if it were dodge ball (the game I most hated) would I be the first person hit with the ball, and thus eliminated? Or, if the girls were just standing around and talking, would I get all the jokes, and know which boys they were talking about?

Then, one pale-blue balmy April day, some of the older girls asked me if I wanted to play truth or consequences with them. I wasn't sure how the game went, but anything was better than dodge ball, and, as always, I was pleased at being asked.

"It's easy," said Jean, a popular leader, with curly red hair; her father was a dean of the law school. "You just answer the questions we ask you, or you take the consequences."

I wasn't at all sure what consequences were, but I didn't like to ask.

They began with simple questions. How old are you? What's your middle name?

This led to more complicated (and crueler) ones.

"How much money does your mother have?"

"I don't know." I didn't, of course, and I doubt that she did either, that poor vague lady, too young to be a widow, too old for motherhood. "I think maybe a thousand dollars," I hazarded.

At this they all frowned, that group of older, wiser girls, whether in disbelief or disappointment, I couldn't tell. They moved a little away from me and whispered together.

It was close to the end of recess. Down on the playing field below us one of the boys threw the baseball and someone batted it out in a long arc, out to the farthest grassy edges of the field, and several other boys ran to retrieve it. On the level above us, a rutted terrace up, the little children stood in line for turns on the slide, or pumped with furious small legs on the giant swings.

The girls came back to me. "Okay, Emily," said Jean. "Just tell the truth. Would you rather be covered with honey and eaten alive by ants, in the hot Sahara Desert—or kiss Car Jones?"

Then, as now, I had a somewhat literal mind: I thought of honey, and ants, and hot sand, and quite simply I said I'd rather kiss Car Jones.

Well. Pandemonium: Did you hear what she said? Emily would kiss Car Jones! *Car Jones.* The truth—Emily would like to kiss Car Jones! Oh, Emily, if your mother only knew! Emily and Car! Emily is going to kiss Car Jones! Emily said she would! Oh, Emily!

The boys, just then coming up from the baseball field, cast bored and pitying looks at the sources of so much noise; they had always known girls were silly. But Harry McGinnis, a glowing, golden boy, looked over at us and laughed aloud. I had been watching Harry timidly for months; that day I thought his laugh was friendly.

Recess being over, we all went back into the schoolroom, and continued with the civics lesson. I caught a few ambiguous smiles in my direction, which left me both embarrassed and confused.

That afternoon, as I walked home from school, two of the girls who passed me on their bikes called back to me, "Car Jones!" and in an automatic but for me new way I squealed out, "Oh no!" They laughed, and repeated, from their distance, "Car Jones!"

.   .   .

The next day I continued to be teased. Somehow the boys had got wind of what I had said, and they joined in with remarks about Yankee girls being fast, how you couldn't tell about quiet girls, that sort of wit. Some of the teasing sounded mean; I felt that Jean, for example, was really out to discomfit me, but most of it was high-spirited friendliness. I was suddenly discovered, as though hitherto I had been invisible. And I continued to respond with that exaggerated, phony squeal of embarrassment that seemed to go over so well. Harry McGinnis addressed me as Emily Jones, and the others took that up. (I wonder if Harry had ever seen me before.)

Curiously, in all this new excitement, the person I thought of least was the source of it all: Car Jones. Or, rather, when I saw the actual Car, hulking over the water fountain or lounging near the steps of a truck, I did not consciously connect him with what felt like social success, new popularity. (I didn't know about consequences.)

Therefore, when the first note from Car appeared on my desk, it felt like blackmail, although the message was innocent, was even kind. "You mustn't mind that they tease you. You are the prettiest one of the girls. C. Jones." I easily recognized his handwriting, those recklessly forward-slanting strokes, from the day when he had had to write on the blackboard, "I will not disturb the other children during Music." Twenty-five times. The note was real, all right.

Helplessly I turned around to stare at the back of the room, where the tallest boys sprawled in their too small desks. Truck children, all of them, bored and uncomfortable. There was Car, the tallest of all, the most bored, the least contained. Our eyes met, and even at that distance I saw that his were not black, as I had thought, but a dark slate blue; stormy eyes, even when, as he rarely did, Car smiled. I turned away quickly, and I managed to forget him for a while.

Having never witnessed a Southern spring before, I was astounded by its bursting opulence, that soft fullness of petal and bloom, everywhere the profusion of flowering shrubs and trees, the riotous flower beds. Walking home from school, I was enchanted with the yards of the stately houses (homes of professors) that I passed, the lush lawns, the rows of brilliant iris, the flowering quince and dogwood trees, crape myrtle, wisteria vines. I would squint my eyes to see the tiniest pale-green leaves against the sky.

My mother didn't like the spring. It gave her hay fever, and she spent most of her time languidly indoors, behind heavily lined, drawn draperies. "I'm simply too old for such exuberance," she said.

"Happy" is perhaps not the word to describe my own state of mind, but I was tremendously excited, continuously. The season seemed to me so extraordinary in itself, the colors, the enchanting smells, and it coincided with my own altered awareness of myself: I could command attention, I was pretty (Car Jones was the first person ever to say that I was, after my mother's long-ago murmurings to a late-arriving baby).

Now everyone knew my name, and called it out as I walked onto the playground. Last fall, as an envious, unknown new girl, I had heard other names, other greetings and teasing-insulting nicknames, "Hey, Red," Harry McGinnis used to shout, in the direction of popular Jean.

The next note from Car Jones said, "I'll bet you hate it down here. This is a cruddy town, but don't let it bother you. Your hair is beautiful. I hope you never cut it. C. Jones."

This scared me a little: the night before I had been arguing with my mother on just that point, my hair, which was long and straight. Why couldn't I cut and curl it, like the other girls? How had Car Jones known what I wanted to do? I forced myself not to look at him; I pretended that there was no Car Jones; it was just a name that certain people had made up.

I felt—I was sure—that Car Jones was an "abnormal" person. (I'm afraid "different" would have been the word I used, back then.) He represented forces that were dark and strange, whereas I myself had just come out into the light. I had joined the world of the normal. (My "normality" later included three marriages to increasingly "rich and prominent" men; my current husband is a surgeon. Three children, and as many abortions. I hate the symmetry, but there you are. I haven't counted lovers. It comes to a normal life, for a woman of my age.) For years, at the time of our coming to Hilton, I had felt a little strange, isolated by my father's death, my older-than-most-parents mother, by money. By being younger than other children, and new in town. I could clearly afford nothing to do with Car, and at the same time my literal mind acknowledged a certain obligation.

Therefore, when a note came from Car telling me to meet him on a Saturday morning in the vacant lot next to the school, it didn't occur to me that I didn't have to go. I made excuses to my mother, and to some of the girls who were getting together for Cokes at someone's house. I'd be a little late, I told the girls. I had to do an errand for my mother.

It was one of the palest, softest, loveliest days of that spring. In the vacant lot weeds bloomed like the rarest of flowers; as I walked toward the abandoned trellis I felt myself to be a sort of princess, on her way to grant an audience to a courtier.

Car, lounging just inside the trellis, immediately brought me up short. "You're several minutes late," he said, and I noticed that his teeth were stained (from tobacco?) and his hands were dirty: couldn't he have washed his hands, to come and meet me? He asked, "Just who do you think you are, the Queen of Sheba?"

I am not sure what I had imagined would happen between us, but this was wrong; I was not prepared for surliness, this scolding. Weakly I said that I was sorry I was late.

Car did not acknowledge my apology; he just stared at me, stormily, with what looked like infinite scorn.

Why had he insisted that I come to meet him? And now that I was here, was I less than pretty, seen close up?

A difficult minute passed, and then I moved a little away. I managed to say that I had to go; I had to meet some girls, I said.

At that Car reached and grasped my arm. "No, first we have to do it."

Do it? I was scared.

"You know what you said, as good as I do. You said kiss Car Jones, now didn't you?"

I began to cry.

Car reached for my hair and pulled me toward him; he bent down to my face and for an instant our mouths were mashed together. (Christ, my first kiss!) Then, so suddenly that I almost fell backward, Car let go of me. With a last look of pure rage he was out of the trellis and striding across the field, toward town, away from the school.

For a few minutes I stayed there in the trellis; I was no longer crying (that had been for Car's benefit, I now think) but melodramatically I wondered if Car might come back and do something else to me—beat me up, maybe. Then a stronger fear took over: someone might find out, might have seen us, even. At that I got out of the trellis fast, out of the vacant lot. (I was learning conformity fast, practicing up for the rest of my life.)

I think, really, that my most serious problem was my utter puzzlement: what did it mean, that kiss? Car was mad, no doubt about that, but did he really hate me? In that case, why a kiss? (Much later in life I once was raped, by someone to whom I was married, but I still think that counts; in any case, I didn't know what he meant either.)

Not sure what else to do, and still in the grip of a monumental confusion, I went over to the school building, which was open on Saturdays for something called Story Hours, for little children. I went into the front entrance and up to the library where, to the surprise of the librarian, who may have thought me retarded, I listened for several hours to tales of the Dutch Twins, and Peter and Polly in Scotland. Actually it was very soothing, that long pasteurized drone, hard even to think about Car while listening to pap like that.

When I got home I found my mother for some reason in a livelier, more talkative mood than usual. She told me that a boy had called while I was out, three times. Even before my heart had time to drop—to think that it might be Car, she babbled on, "Terribly polite. Really, these *bien élevé* Southern boys." (No, not Car.) "Harry something. He said he'd call again. But, darling, where were you, all this time?"

I was beginning to murmur about the library, homework, when the phone rang. I answered, and it was Harry McGinnis, asking me to go to the movies with him the following Saturday afternoon. I said of course, I'd love to, and I giggled in a silly new way. But my giggle was one of relief; I was saved, I was normal, after all. I belonged in the world of light, of lightheartedness. Car Jones had not really touched me.

I spent the next day, Sunday, in alternating states of agitation and anticipation.

On Monday, on my way to school, I felt afraid of seeing Car, at the same time that I was both excited and shy at the prospect of Harry McGinnis—a combination of emotions that was almost too much for me, that dazzling, golden first of May, and that I have not dealt with too successfully in later life.

Harry paid even less attention to me than he had before; it was a while before I realized that he was conspicuously not looking in my direction, not teasing me, and that that in itself was a form of attention, as well as being soothing to my shyness.

I realized too, after a furtive scanning of the back row, that Car Jones was *not at school* that day. Relief flooded through my blood like oxygen, like spring air.

Absences among the truck children were so unremarkable, and due to so many possible causes, that any explanation at all for his was plausible. Of course it occurred to me, among other imaginings, that he had stayed home out of shame for what he did to me. Maybe he had run away to sea, had joined the Navy or the Marines? Coldheartedly, I hoped so. In any case, there was no way for me to ask.

Later that week the truth about Car Jones did come out—at first as a drifting rumor, then confirmed, and much more remarkable than joining the Navy: Car Jones had gone to the principal's office, a week or so back, and had demanded to be tested for entrance (immediate) into high school, a request so unprecedented (usually only pushy academic parents would ask for such a change) and so dumbfounding that it was acceded to. Car took the test and was put into the sophomore high-school class, on the other side of town, where he by age and size—and intellect, as things turned out; he tested high—most rightfully belonged.

I went to a lot of Saturday movies with Harry McGinnis, where we clammily held hands, and for the rest of that spring, and into summer, I was teased about Harry. No one seemed to remember having teased me about Car Jones.

Considering the size of Hilton at that time, it seems surprising that I almost never saw Car again, but I did not, except for a couple of tiny glimpses, during the summer that I was still going to the movies with Harry. On both those occasions, seen from across the street, or on the other side of a dim movie house, Car was with an older girl, a high-school girl, with curled hair, and lipstick, all that. I was sure that his hands and teeth were clean.

.   .   .

By the time I had entered high school, along with all those others who were by now my familiar friends, Car was a freshman in the local university, and his family had moved into town. Then his name again was bruited about among us, but this time as an underground rumor: Car Jones was reputed to have "gone all the way"—to have "done it" with a pretty and most popular senior in our high school. (It must be remembered that this was more unusual among the young then than now.) The general (whispered) theory was that Car's status as a college boy had won the girl; traditionally, in Hilton, the senior high-school girls began to date the freshmen in the university, as many and as often as possible. But this was not necessarily true; maybe the girl was simply drawn to Car, his height and his shoulders, his stormy eyes. Or maybe they didn't do it after all.

The next thing I heard about Car, who was by then an authentic town person, a graduate student in the university, was that he had written a play which was to be produced by the campus dramatic society. (Maybe that is how he finally met his movie star, as a playwright? The column didn't say.) I think I read this item in the local paper, probably in a clipping forwarded to me by my mother; her letters were always thick with clippings, thin with messages of a personal nature.

My next news of Car came from my uncle, the French professor, a violent, enthusiastic partisan in university affairs, especially in their more traditional aspects. In scandalized tones, one family Thanksgiving, he recounted to me and my mother, that a certain young man, a graduate student in English, named Carstairs Jones, had been offered a special sort of membership in D.K.E., his own beloved fraternity, and "Jones had *turned it down*." My mother and I laughed later and privately over this; we were united in thinking my uncle a fool, and I am sure that I added, Well, good for him. But I did not, at that time, reconsider the whole story of Car Jones, that most unregenerate and wicked of the truck children.

But now, with this fresh news of Carstairs Jones, and his wife the movie star, it occurs to me that we two, who at a certain time and place were truly misfits, although quite differently—we both have made it: what could be more American dream-y, more normal, than marriage to a lovely movie star? Or, in my case, marriage to the successful surgeon?

And now maybe I can reconstruct a little of that time; specifically, can try to see how it really was for Car, back then. Maybe I can even understand that kiss.

Let us suppose that he lived in a somewhat better than usual farm-house; later events make this plausible—his family's move to town, his years at the university. Also, I wish him well. I will give him a dignified white house with a broad front porch, set back among pines and oaks, in the red clay countryside. The stability and size of his house, then, would have set Car apart from his neighbors, the other farm families, other truck children. Perhaps his parents too were somewhat "different," but my imagination fails at them; I can easily imagine and clearly see the house, but not its population. Brothers? sisters? Probably, but I don't know.

Car would go to school, coming out of his house at the honk of the stained and bulging, ugly yellow bus, which was crowded with his sup-posed peers, toward whom he felt both contempt and an irritation close to rage. Arrived at school, as one of the truck children, he would be greeted with a total lack of interest; he might as well have been invisible, or been black, *unless* he misbehaved in an outright, conspicuous way. And so he did: Car yawned noisily during history class, he hummed dur-ing study hall and after recess he dawdled around the playground and came in late. And for these and other assaults on the school's decorum he was punished in one way or another, and then, when all else failed to curb his ways, he would be *held back,* forced to repeat an already insuf-ferably boring year of school.

One fall there was a minor novelty in school: a new girl (me), a Yan-kee, who didn't look much like the other girls, with long straight hair, instead of curled, and Yankee clothes, wool skirts and sweaters, instead of flowery cotton dresses worn all year round. A funny accent, a Yankee name: Emily Ames. I imagine that Car registered those facts about me, and possibly the additional information that I was almost as invisible as he, but without much interest.

Until the day of truth or consequences. I don't think Car was around on the playground while the game was going on; one of the girls would have seen him, and squealed out, "Oooh, there's Car, there *he is*!" I rather believe that some skinny little kid, an unnoticed truck child, overheard it all, and then ran over to where Car was lounging in one of the school buses, maybe peeling an orange and throwing the peel, in spirals, out the window. "Say, Car, that little Yankee girl, she says she'd like to kiss you."

"Aw, go on."

He is still not very interested; the little Yankee girl is as dumb as the others are.

And then he hears me being teased, everywhere, and teased with his name. "Emily would kiss Car Jones—Emily Jones!" Did he feel the slightest pleasure at such notoriety? I think he must have; a man who would marry a movie star must have at least a small taste for publicity. Well, at that point he began to write me those notes: "You are the prettiest one of the girls" (which I was not). I think he was casting us both in ill-fitting roles, me as the prettiest, defenseless girl, and himself as my defender.

He must have soon seen that it wasn't working out that way. I didn't need a defender, I didn't need him. I was having a wonderful time, at his expense, if you think about it, and I am pretty sure Car did think about it.

Interestingly, at the same time he had his perception of my triviality, Car must have got his remarkable inspiration in regard to his own life: there was a way out of those miserably boring classes, the insufferable children who surrounded him. He would demand a test, he would leave this place for the high school.

Our trellis meeting must have occurred after Car had taken the test, and had known that he did well. When he kissed me he was doing his last "bad" thing in that school, was kissing it off, so to speak. He was also insuring that I, at least, would remember him; he counted on its being my first kiss. And he may have thought that I was even sillier than I was, and that I would tell, so that what had happened would get around the school, waves of scandal in his wake.

For some reason, I would also imagine that Car is one of those persons who never look back; once kissed, I was readily dismissed from his mind, and probably for good. He could concentrate on high school, new status, new friends. Just as, now married to his movie star, he does not ever think of having been a truck child, one of the deprived, the disappointed. In his mind there are no ugly groaning trucks, no hopeless littered playground, no squat menacing school building.

But of course I could be quite wrong about Car Jones. He could be another sort of person altogether; he could be as haunted as I am by everything that ever happened in his life.

To See You Again

Like so many acutely dreaded moments, this one arrived and passed in an unanticipated fashion: the moment after which I would not again see my most brilliant and beautiful student, Seth. I looked up from the group of girl students—ironically, the ones I had least liked—who were asking me silly questions; I looked toward his seat, and was confronted with his absence, his absolute loss.

Considerably older than these kids, and especially, cruelly, older than Seth, I had envisioned quite another scene: I had imagined and feared a moment at which the students would recognize, collectively, that it was over, that this was my last class, the end of my temporary and quite accidental presence in their lives. They would never see me again, any of them. At that instant of recognition, I thought, I would have to smile and say something like "Well, it's been very nice knowing all of you. I've enjoyed this time at Cornford."

(Of course I would look at Seth as I spoke, but could I do it with no break in my voice, no catch?)

And what would they all do, my students, including Seth, I had wondered: would they smile back and maybe clap? What sort of expression would Seth wear, on that most entrancing face?

But that is not how it went at all. The class—it was in freshman composition—simply ended as it had every day of my time there. Across the campus some clear bells chimed; in the classroom books were gathered from the floor; slowly the kids began to get up and move toward the door. And some of the silliest, noisiest girls gathered at my desk, not to say goodbye or anything so formal, just to be told again what they already knew: that their final papers were to be collected from the English office. And then I looked up to the total absence of Seth.

One of the things I first thought was: If I ever see him again he'll be older. Still handsome, probably, but he won't look quite like *that*.

Seth: red-gold curls, a wild never-combed tangle, curls that shadowed remarkably white unfreckled skin. Narrow green eyes; a small childish nose; and a wide, somehow unformed mouth—a young mouth. And an incongruous, scruffy reddish beard. Just a messy red-haired kid was how someone else might have seen him. Whereas to me: perfect poignant beauty. And what he wrote was extraordinary—weird wild flashes of poetry, flaming through the dullest assignments. At times I considered the possibility that he was in some way crazy, at others the possibility of genius. But how can you tell with anyone so young? He might be, or might become, anything at all. Anything, in his case, except ugly or ordinary.

Not quite anguished—I had had worse losses in my life (I have them still)—but considerably worse than "let down" was how I felt as I began the drive from Cornford west to San Francisco. To my house, and Gerald, my sad fat husband, a distinguished architect—and my most precariously balanced, laboriously achieved "good life."

Cornford is about forty miles east of San Francisco, near Vallejo, in the tawny, oak-shadowed foothills. It is on Interstate 80, the main east-west thoroughfare; after Vallejo and Cornford, the highway continues past Sacramento to Tahoe, Reno, Salt Lake City, the East. Going anywhere in that direction, and Gerald and I often spend time at Tahoe, we will pass right by Cornford, again and again. Next fall Seth will be there, after a summer of hitchhiking in Spain. How will it feel, I wonder, to drive right past where Seth is, in the fall and following winter?

Or suppose he should move to San Francisco. Kids do, all the time. Just what would I do with him? What, really, do I want of him? I have asked myself that question, repeatedly, at terrible sleepless predawn hours, and have come up with no answer. The obvious ones do not apply.

Meaning that it is nowhere near as simple as sex (Christ! as if sex were ever simple). If my strong feelings in his direction do have an object, it is not the act of love—I find the very idea both terrifying and embarrassing, and oh! how horrified he would be if he knew that I had even, ever, considered that. How old I must seem to him! Revolting, really, although I am in very good shape "for my age." But to him revolting—as I sometimes am to myself; as often I feel that I am to Gerald.

I reread *Death in Venice,* and, with all due respect, I do not think that Aschenbach knew what he wanted of Tadzio, either.

In an earnest way I have tried to see Seth as objectively as possible—to catalogue him, as it were. I began, for whatever reason, with his voice, and right away I was balked. I could not decide whether the sound was high or deep, and I concluded that it is simply young, a little rough. Some softness in the lines of his face might suggest a plump body, but the actual body that I saw in his daily, worn, taut jeans is thin, a thin boy's body; maybe in middle age he will be heavy? I wistfully considered that. His facial expressions, too, are elusive, escaping definition—a shade of defiance, sometimes a slow smile; he is far less ready than the rest of the class to show amusement. A wary, waiting look, perhaps—is that it?

And so I was left with nothing clear, no definitions, only the weight of my own meticulous observations. And his face in my heart.

Spring and summer at Cornford, so near the Sacramento Valley, are hot and dry—a heat and dryness inversely proportional to the cold gray wet San Francisco fog, one set of weather pushing out the other. And the transition from one climate to another struck me as symbolic as I drove back and forth, in May and then in June, between the two areas. The heat of Cornford was like an adolescent summer—urgent, flushed—and San Francisco's cold like middle age. Resignation. Disappointment. Grief.

Approaching the hill where the fog always began, on my last drive home from Cornford, when everything was over, I shivered, thinking of my own, known, familiar life: Gerald, our cold clean flat. And no Seth. Ridiculously, I thought, I can't live without seeing him—what shall I do?

Gerald and I know an older man—considerably older than ourselves, that is: Larry Montgomery. As I crested that hill, for no reason that I could immediately understand Larry came into my mind. And in the next instant I saw that he had arrived there for a very clear reason: Larry is exactly as much older than I am as I am older than Seth. He has what Gerald describes as a crush on me. Larry looks at least ten years younger than he is, trim and tan, with lively blue eyes and fine silver-white hair. A forties dandy, he hums snatches from Gershwin, Rodgers and Hart, Cole Porter; he wears gold-buttoned navy blazers. His blue eyes widen and deepen, always, when I come into a room. He makes excuses to stand very near me; sometimes he touches me, but in a serious, respectful way.

Once, though, finding ourselves alone at a party, instead of beginning a romantic or even an affectionate conversation, we got into a silly argument—or, rather, he led me into it, baiting me, really. Which, as I thought back to times when I was curt with Seth, almost pushing him out of my office, I now understood: Larry was terrified that whatever he felt would show.

Once I even asked Gerald, though very idly, "What do you think Larry would do if I propositioned him?"

Surprisingly—I had supposed he would laugh—Gerald gave me a serious, considered answer. He said, "I think he would be scared to death, but very polite about how he put you off." I thought Gerald was right; whatever Larry wanted was not an affair with me; a stray motel afternoon with Larry was as unimaginable as it would be with Seth. Larry just likes to see me, to be near me, sometimes—and very likely that is what I feel for Seth, pretty much?

The accident of my teaching at Cornford came about because my friend Amy, who teaches there regularly, was suddenly, between terms, summoned to the side of her ailing mother, in New Hampshire.

"But, Amy, I've never taught," I said.

"It's easy, there're just a few tricks to it. I'll teach you."

"But credentials—"

"Private junior colleges don't much care. They'll be so impressed that you've got a master's—"

"But that was just to stay on in Cambridge another year." To stay on and be with Gerald, as Amy already knew.

"How would they know that? And you got it, didn't you? Besides, Laura, it'll be a good change for you. You need . . ." For a moment Amy faltered at prescribing for my needs, then finished, lamely, "You need to get out more."

However, getting out more was surely among the things that I did need, and partly for that reason I began the twice-a-week drive, back and forth to Cornford College. I began to teach, and there was Seth, in the second row, nearest the door. Red curls, green eyes.

At first, despite the handsomeness that I noted in passing, Seth was simply one among fifteen surprisingly nice, clean young California kids—much nicer and more civil, all of them, than the Cornford faculty, none of whom ever bothered to speak to me, the substitute teacher. However, I had been warned by Amy that this might be the case. "They're incredibly rude," she had said, knowing how thin-skinned I tended to be. I managed not to mind; I told myself that I wouldn't be there for long, and that the kids were what mattered.

The first assignment I gave was a physical description of something encountered outdoors. "You want very simple, specific assignments," Amy had cautioned. "Anything else only confuses them." The papers ranged from the outrageously illiterate to the adequate; they were mostly misspelled descriptions of lakes and mountains, mountain streams and sunsets. But Seth wrote about an abandoned truck, come upon, surprisingly, in a small eucalyptus grove: the heavily stained windshield, the drifts of leaves all over, and their smell. Rotted tires, rust. A dead truck. His style was flat, specific, and yet the total effect was haunting. I, who have almost no feeling for cars, and surely none for trucks, was haunted by this mechanical death, this abandonment. I began to look closely, even wonderingly, at Seth. And I saw that he was more beautiful than I had seen at first, as well as possibly, probably, brilliant.

In fact, as my short time at Cornford passed, my feelings in regard to all my students polarized—as I might have known they would, given my propensity for extremes of feeling. Some fairly silly girls who at first I thought were just that, fairly silly, after three weeks and then four I found intolerably fatuous—the very ones who were to block out my last view of Seth. About one student other than Seth I became enthusiastic: a dark shy girl, who seemed to have read everything, discerningly, with real intelligence. And always there was Seth, about whom my feelings were strongest—were inexplicable, and impossible.

. . .

But when I was midway across the Bay Bridge, suddenly the perfect solution to those unruly feelings came to me; in effect I would domesticate them, just as, years back, I had tamed my wild mania for Gerald. Quite simply, I would make him a friend of our family: I will write him a note next fall, inviting him for dinner. With some other friends, of course, maybe people with kids of Seth's own age. In that setting, my own home ground, Seth will seem a kid like any other, perhaps slightly handsomer, a touch more brilliant, but not noticeably so to anyone else, and surely not remarkable to Gerald, my sad, successful husband. And Gerald and I will present one of our best, our most convincing surfaces to the group at large, and especially to Seth: we will portray a very adult couple, stringently amusing: Gerald and generous-to-guests Laura. I'll cook something wonderful. The two of us mildly, fondly bantering with each other.

And after dinner Gerald will say, a little chillingly, "Well, my dear Laura, I do congratulate you on your springtime of patience with the young." And then, "When would you imagine that boy last combed his hair—care to place a bet?"

And slowly, gradually, Seth will disappear from my mind—or Seth as the author of violent feelings will go, to be replaced by the messy kid I first saw, of whom I will never think.

In that good mood, having even begun to plan the menu, I drove into the city and arrived at our house on Edgewood, Gerald's and mine. And I saw Gerald's car parked in front of the house, although it was much too early for him to be at home.

My stomach and heart seemed simultaneously to clench tight. Not out of fear. I did not wonder what was wrong; I knew. One and only one condition would have brought Gerald home so early—a new depression. His depressions are as severe and as invariably recurrent as they are apparently incurable. "My sweet old Melancholia, my maiden aunt, my child, my baby Melancholia," I once heard him say, babbling his way out of the shock treatment that didn't help.

I knew what was wrong, but not why, never why, or why now—and one problem about living with someone who is depressed is that inevitably you think it has to do with you, your fault, although you are told that it is not. And I knew exactly what I would find on entering the house: heavy Gerald immobilized, immobile, on the wicker settee in the entrance hall, unable to go comfortably into the living room, or upstairs to bed. Unable to leave the house, or the marriage, as I have thought that he must, sometimes, want to do.

He has explained to me how he feels, depressed. "As heavy as boulders," he has said. "I can't open my mouth, it's so heavy. Much less move." I can feel what Gerald feels—and can do nothing about it.

And there he was, slumped down, gray-faced, barely looking up as I opened the door and then closed it behind me. I went over and placed a light kiss on his forehead—the lightest kiss—but he flinched, a little.

"I'll call," I told him.

Something crossed his face; some shadow of relief, perhaps. Not hope.

The phone is in the kitchen. As I dialed, I thought, How immaculate it is, this room. How sterile. Could I paint it red? Would that help?

"Dr. Abrams, please," I said to the voice on the other end. "Right now, if I can." And then, "Hi, Ed. It's Laura. I'm bringing him over, okay?"

Passing Gerald in the hall, I prevented myself from touching his shoulder.

Upstairs, I packed his small bag: pajamas, toiletries, a sweater, one change of clothes.

I got him up and through the front door, and out to my car. I drove north this time, toward the Golden Gate Bridge. Marin. The small hospital in Larkspur. Yellow fog lights lined the approach to the bridge, and it was fogged in already—summer fog, gray and billowing between the dim masses of the headlands, and swirling below the bridge, obscuring the dangerous black water. Beside me, as far from me as possible, Gerald sat, heavy as cement and as unmoving.

I turned off the highway, past developments, shopping centers, schools, playing fields, jogging courses and a few small untouched areas of land—rough, with scattered small shabby houses.

Larkspur. The hospital is one-story, white, ranch style. It could be a motel, and there is even a swimming pool in back, for the more mobile, less desperate patients.

And there was Dr. Abrams, Ed, waiting, having recognized our car. Kind Ed, kind enough not to be hearty, or to pretend that this was a social occasion. He knows, too, not to touch Gerald. Gerald allowed me to help him from the car, and then for an instant Ed touched my hair; he must know that I love touching, any gesture of affection.

Although, driving over, I had not been aware of it, had not thought of weather, I now noticed that the day was still clear in Larkspur, a blue summer day, just fading.

The checking-in process was of course familiar, and minimal. We left Gerald in his room, and Ed Abrams and I walked toward my car, and although in a way we like each other, and surely wish each other well, we had little to say.

"Well, let's hope it won't be for very long this time," he said.

"Yes."

Then, remembering some prior conversation, he asked, "How was the teaching? You liked it okay?"

"It went pretty well. A couple of the students were terrific."

"Oh, good. Well, all done with that now?"

"Yes. Done. Today was my last day."

"Well, good."

I backed out of the driveway and headed back toward the almost invisible bridge, and the darkened, fog-shrouded city.

In Cambridge, a long time ago, I thought Gerald was so beautiful, so dark and thin, so elegant, so elusive that I used to trail him around the Yard: me, a silly undergraduate with a crush on a future architect who was studying at the School of Design. We had met a couple of times—I had seen to that, quizzing everyone I knew who might know him, and finally coming up with a girl with a brother who knew Gerald. But Gerald hardly had time to speak to me.

But there I always was, in St. Clair's, out of breath from following him on my bike but saying hello; and in Hayes-Bickford, or the Wursthaus. Late one afternoon I found him alone, on the steps of Widener, and with my heart in my mouth I asked him to a dance at Whitman Hall, where I lived. He came late, stayed a very short time and left, with an abstracted frown. But the next time he saw me, standing in his way, again on the steps of Widener, he asked me up for tea, in his room, at Dunster House, and instead of tea we drank a lot of gin, and fell into bed together—for me, the consummation of a major passion; for Gerald, the onset of a habit. I stayed on in Cambridge for a master's in English literature while Gerald finished his degree, and we married; we moved out to San Francisco and we bought and remodeled the house near Twin Peaks, and we had no children. Gerald began to be a considerable success. And sometimes to be sad, then seriously depressed. Recurrently. Ed Abrams says that with age the cycle may well lengthen, and the severity of each attack will decrease. A sort of flattening out of the curve. But age could take forever; I'm not sure I have that much time.

Driving back to the city, across the bridge, I did not think in symbolic terms about my re-entry into dark and fog; I hardly had to, having made that trip from Marin so many times before. I thought about supper, a glass of wine and getting into bed to watch TV, which I don't do with Gerald at home. And in a cautious way I wondered how long it would be this time.

As always, I made it home perfectly all right. But once I was inside, the idea of cooking anything in the impeccable kitchen was so discouraging that I just nibbled on a piece of cheese—a halfhearted graying mouse.

I even thought, in a lonely way, of calling Larry Montgomery, for a friendly conversation, God knows, not meaning to proposition him. But I am not really sure that we are friends.

I washed and got into bed. I turned on the TV, and I watched one foolish thing after another—until, at about ten, a play was announced, with an actress I liked, and so I propped myself up for that.

And then, Seth, there you were. A great deal older, of course, even older than I am now, curls all gone gray but the same narrow, unmistakable green eyes. It was absolutely extraordinary. In the play, Seth, you were a workman, a sort of handyman, which I suppose is one of the things you could become. The actress, funnily enough, was a schoolteacher. After a tremendous, wrenching love affair, you gave each other up, you and she, because you were married, and responsible. But, Seth, the resemblance was so striking that I thought, Oh, so that is how he will look: gray, slightly overweight but *strong,* with a brilliant smile, and those eyes.

I waited for the credits at the end of the play; for all I knew, your father could be an actor, that actor—I know so little about you—but he had another name, and besides, he looked more like you than like a possible father.

In any case, that sight of you was strangely cheering to me. I turned off the TV and contented myself with visions of my own.

I imagined a time when you will really be as old as that man, and as gray—when, much older still than you, I can say to you, "Ah, Seth, at last you begin to lose your looks. Now you are merely handsome, whereas before you were so beautiful that I could hardly look at you." We both will laugh.

And at that time, your prime and our old age, Gerald's and mine, Gerald will be completely well, the cycle flat, no more sequences of pain. And maybe thin again. And interested, and content.

It's almost worth waiting for.

Alaska

Although Mrs. Lawson does not drink any more, not a drop since New Year's Day, 1961, in Juneau, Alaska, she sometimes feels a confusion in her mind about which husband she will meet, at the end of the day. She has been married five times, and she has lived, it seems to her, almost everywhere. Now she is a cleaning lady, in San Francisco, although some might say that she is too old for that kind of work. Her hair, for so many years dyed red, is now streaky gray, and her eyes are a paler blue than they once were. Her skin is a dark bronze color, but she thinks of herself as Negro—black, these days. From New Orleans, originally.

If someone came up and asked her, Who are you married to now, Lucille Lawson? of course she would answer, Charles, and we live in the Western Addition in San Francisco, two busses to get there from here.

But, not asked, she feels the presences of those other husbands—nameless, shadowy, lurking near the edges of her mind. And menacing, most of them, especially the one who tromped her in Juneau, that New Year's Day. He was the worst, by far, but none of them was worth a whole lot, come to think of it. And she was always working at one place or another, and always tired, at the end of her days, and then there were those husbands to come home to, and more work to do for them. Some husbands come honking for you in their cars, she remembers, but usually you have to travel a long way, busses and street cars, to get to where they are, to where you and them live.

These days Mrs. Lawson just cleans for Miss Goldstein, a rich white lady older than Mrs. Lawson is, who lives alone in a big house on Divisadero Street, near Union. She has lots of visitors, some coming to stay, all funny-looking folk. Many foreign, but not fancy. Miss Goldstein still travels a lot herself, to peculiar places like China and Cuba and Africa.

What Mrs. Lawson is best at is polishing silver, and that is what she mostly does, the tea service, coffee service, and all the flatware, although more than once Miss Goldstein has sighed and said that maybe it should all be put away, or melted down to help the poor people in some of the places she visits; all that silver around looks boastful, Miss Goldstein thinks. But it is something for Mrs. Lawson to do every day (Miss Goldstein does not come right out and say this; they both just know).

Along with the silver polishing she dusts, and sometimes she irons a little, some silk or linen shirts; Miss Goldstein does not get dressed up a lot, usually favoring sweaters and old pants. She gets the most dressed up when she is going off to march somewhere, which she does fairly often. Then she gets all gussied up in a black suit and her real pearls, and she has these posters to carry, NO NUKES IS GOOD NUKES, GRAY PANTHERS FOR PEACE. She would be a sight to behold, Mrs. Lawson thinks: she can hardly imagine Miss Goldstein with all the kinds of folks that are usually in those lines, the beards and raggedy blue jeans, the dirty old sweat shirts, big women wearing no bras. Thin, white-haired Miss Goldstein in her pearls.

To help with the heavy housework, the kitchen floor and the stove, bathtubs and all like that, Miss Goldstein has hired a young white girl, Gloria. At first Mrs. Lawson was mistrustful that a girl like that could clean anything, a blonde-haired small little girl with these doll blue eyes in some kind of a white pants work outfit, but Gloria moves through that big house like a little bolt of white lightning, and she leaves everything behind her *clean.* Even with her eyesight not as good as it was Mrs. Lawson can see how clean the kitchen floor and the stove are, and the bathtubs. And she has *looked.*

Gloria comes at eight every morning, and she does all that in just two hours. Mrs. Lawson usually gets in sometime after nine, depending on how the busses run. And so there is some time when they are both working along, Mrs. Lawson at the sink with the silver, probably, or dusting off Miss Goldstein's bureau, dusting her books—and Gloria down on her knees on the bathroom floor (Gloria is right; the only way to clean a floor is on your knees, although not too many folks seem to know that, these days). Of course they don't talk much, both working, but Gloria has about twenty minutes before her next job, in that same neighborhood. Sometimes, then, Mrs. Lawson will take a break from her polishing, dusting, and heat up some coffee for the both of them, and they will talk a little. Gloria has a lot of worries, a lot on her mind, Mrs. Lawson can tell, although Gloria never actually says, beyond everyone's usual troubles, money and rent and groceries, and in Gloria's case car repairs, an old VW.

The two women are not friends, really, but all things considered they get along okay. Some days they don't either of them feel like talking, and they both just skim over sections of the newspaper, making comments on this and that, in the news. Other times they talk a little.

Gloria likes to hear about New Orleans, in the old days, when Mrs. Lawson's father had a drugstore and did a lot of doctoring there, and how later they all moved to Texas, and the Klan came after them, and they hid and moved again, to another town. And Gloria tells Mrs. Lawson how her sister is ashamed that she cleans houses for a living. The sister, Sharon, lives up in Alaska, but not in Juneau, where Mrs. Lawson lived. Gloria's sister lives in Fairbanks, where her husband is in forestry school.

However, despite her and Gloria getting along okay, in the late afternoons Mrs. Lawson begins to worry that Gloria will find something wrong there, when she comes first thing in the morning. Something that she, Mrs. Lawson, did wrong. She even imagines Gloria saying to Miss Goldstein, Honestly, how come you keep on that old Mrs. Lawson? She can't see to clean very good, she's too old to work.

She does not really think that Gloria would say a thing like that, and even if she did Miss Goldstein wouldn't listen, probably. Still, the idea is very worrying to her, and in an anxious way she sweeps up the kitchen floor, and dustmops the long front hall. And at the same time her mind is plagued with those images of husbands, dark ghosts, in Juneau and Oakland and Kansas City, husbands that she has to get home to, somehow. Long bus rides with cold winds at the places where you change, or else you have to wait a long time for the choked-up sound of them honking, until you get in their creaky old cars and drive, drive home, in the dark.

Mrs. Lawson is absolutely right about Gloria having serious troubles on her mind—more serious in fact than Mrs. Lawson could have thought of: Gloria's hideous, obsessive problem is a small lump on her leg, her right leg, mid-calf. A tiny knot. She keeps reaching to touch it, no matter what she is doing, and it is always there. She cannot make herself not touch it. She thinks constantly of that lump, its implications and probable consequences. Driving to work in her jumpy old VW, she reaches down to her leg, to check the lump. A couple of times she almost has accidents, as she concentrates on her fingers, reaching, what they feel as they touch her leg.

To make things even worse, the same week that she first noticed the lump Gloria met a really nice man, about her age: Dugald, neither married nor gay (a miracle, these days, in San Francisco). He is a bartender in a place where she sometimes goes with girlfriends, after a movie or something. In a way she has known Dugald for a long time, but in another way not—not known him until she happened to go into the place alone, thinking, Well, why not? I'm tired (it was late one afternoon), a beer would be nice. And there was Dugald, and they talked, and he asked her out, on his next night off. And the next day she discovered the lump.

She went with Dugald anyway, of course, and she almost had a very good time—except that whenever she thought about what was probably wrong with her she went cold and quiet. She thinks that Dugald may not ever ask her out again, and even if he did, she can't get at all involved with anyone, not now.

Also, Gloria's sister, Sharon, in Fairbanks, Alaska, has invited her to come up and stay for a week, while Sharon's forestry-student husband is back in Kansas, visiting his folks; Sharon does not much like her husband's family. Gloria thinks she will go for ten days in June, while Miss Goldstein is in China, again. Gloria is on the whole pleased at the prospect of this visit; as she Ajaxes and Lysols Miss Goldstein's upstairs bathroom, she thinks, *Alaska,* and she imagines gigantic glaciers, huge wild animals, fantastic snow-capped mountains. (She will send a friendly postcard to Dugald, she thinks, and maybe one to old Lawson.) Smiling, for an instant she makes a small bet with herself, which is that at some point Sharon will ask her not to mention to anyone, *please,* what she, Gloria, does for a living. Well, Gloria doesn't care. Lord knows her work is not much to talk about; it is simply the most money she can get an hour, and not pay taxes (she is always afraid, when not preoccupied with her other, more terrible worries, that the IRS will somehow get to her). On the other hand, it is fun to embarrass Sharon.

At home though, lying awake at night, of course the lump is all that Gloria thinks about. And hospitals: when she was sixteen she had her tonsils out, and she decided then on no more operations, no matter what. If she ever has a baby she will do it at home. The hospital was so frightening, everyone was horrible to her, all the doctors and nurses (except for a couple of black aides who were sweet, really nice, she remembers). They all made her feel like something much less than a person. And a hospital would take all her money, and more, all her careful savings (someday she plans to buy a little cabin, up near Tahoe, and raise big dogs). She thinks about something being cut off. Her leg. Herself made so ugly, everyone trying not to look. No more men, no dates, not Dugald or anyone. No love or sex again, not ever.

In the daytime her terror is slightly more manageable, but it is still so powerful that the very idea of calling a doctor, showing him the lump, asking him what to do—chills her blood, almost stops her heart.

And she can feel the lump there, all the time. Probably growing.

Mrs. Lawson has told Gloria that she never goes to doctors; she can doctor herself, Mrs. Lawson says. She always has. Gloria has even thought of showing the lump to Mrs. Lawson.

But she tries to think in a positive way about Alaska. They have a cute little apartment right on the university campus, Sharon has written. Fairbanks is on a river; they will take an afternoon trip on a paddleboat. And they will spend one night at Mount McKinley, and go on a wild life tour.

"Fairbanks, now. I never did get up that way," says Mrs. Lawson, told of Sharon's invitation, Gloria's projected trip. "But I always heard it was real nice up there."

Actually she does not remember anything at all about Fairbanks, but for Gloria's sake she hopes that it is nice, and she reasons that any place would be better than Juneau, scrunched in between mountains so steep they look to fall down on you.

"I hope it's nice," says Gloria. "I just hope I don't get mauled by some bear, on that wild life tour."

Aside from not drinking and never going to doctors (she has read all her father's old doctor books, and remembers most of what she read)

Mrs. Lawson believes that she gets her good health and her strength—considerable, for a person of her years—from her daily naps. Not a real sleep, just sitting down for a while in some place really comfortable, and closing her eyes.

She does that now, in a small room off Miss Goldstein's main library room (Miss Goldstein has already gone off to China, but even if she were home she wouldn't mind about a little nap). Mrs. Lawson settles back into a big old fat leather chair, and she slips her shoes off. And, very likely because of talking about Alaska that morning, Gloria's trip, her mind drifts off, in and out of Juneau. She remembers the bitter cold, cold rains of that winter up there, the winds, fogs thicker than cotton, and dark. Snow that sometimes kept them in the little hillside cabin for days, even weeks. Her and Charles: that husband had the same name as the one she now has, she just remembered—funny to forget a thing like that. They always used to drink a lot, her and the Charles in Alaska; you had to, to get through the winter. And pretty often they would fight, ugly drunk quarrels that she couldn't quite remember the words to, in the mornings. But that New Year's Eve they were having a real nice time; he was being real nice, laughing and all, and then all of a sudden it was like he turned into some other person, and he struck her. He grabbed up her hair, all of it red, at that time, and he called her a witch and he knocked her down to the floor, and he tromped her. Later of course he was sorry, and he said he had been feeling mean about not enough work, but still, he had tromped her.

Pulling herself out of that half dream, half terrible memory, Mrs. Lawson repeats, as though someone had asked her, that now she is married to Charles, in San Francisco. They live in the Western Addition; they don't drink, and this Charles is a nice man, most of the time.

She tries then to think about the other three husbands, one in Oakland, in Chicago, in Kansas City, but nothing much comes to mind, of them. No faces or words, just shadows, and no true pictures of any of those cities. The only thing she is perfectly clear about is that not one of those other men was named Charles.

On the airplane to Alaska, something terrible, horrible, entirely frightening happens to Gloria, which is: a girl comes and sits in the seat next to hers, and that girl has—the lower part of her right leg missing.

Cut off. A pretty dark-haired girl, about the same size as Gloria, wearing a nice blazer, and a kind of long skirt. One boot. Metal crutches.

Gloria is so frightened—she knows that this is an omen, a sign meant for her—that she is dizzy, sick; she leans back and closes her eyes, as the plane bumps upward, zooming through clouds, and she stays that way for the rest of the trip. She tries not to think; she repeats numbers and meaningless words to herself.

At some point she feels someone touching her arm. Flinching, she opens her eyes to see the next-seat girl, who is asking, "Are you okay? Can I get you anything?"

"I'm all right. Just getting the flu, I think." Gloria smiles in a deliberately non-friendly way. The last thing in the world that she wants is a conversation with that girl: the girl at last getting around to her leg, telling Gloria, "It started with this lump I had, right here."

Doctors don't usually feel your legs, during physical examinations, Gloria thinks; she is standing beside Sharon on the deck of the big paddleboat that is slowly ploughing up the Natoma River. It would be possible to hide a lump for a long time, unless it grew a lot, she thinks, as the boat's captain announces over the bullhorn that they are passing what was once an Indian settlement.

Alaska is much flatter than Gloria had imagined its being, at least around Fairbanks—and although she had of course heard the words, midnight sun, she had not known they were a literal description; waking at three or four in the morning from bad dreams, her nighttime panics (her legs drawn up under her, one hand touching her calf, the lump) she sees brilliant sunshine, coming in through the tattered aluminum foil that Sharon has messily pasted to the window. It is all wrong—unsettling. Much worse than the thick dark fogs that come into San Francisco in the summer; she is used to them.

In fact sleeplessness and panic (what she felt at the sight of that girl with the missing leg has persisted; she knows it was a sign) have combined to produce in Gloria an almost trancelike state. She is so quiet, so passive that she can feel Sharon wondering about her, what is wrong. Gloria does not, for a change, say anything critical of Sharon's housekeeping, which is as sloppy as usual. She does not tell anyone that she, Gloria, is a cleaning person.

A hot wind comes up off the water, and Gloria remembers that tomorrow they go to Mount McKinley, and the wild life tour.

Somewhat to her disappointment, Mrs. Lawson does not get any postcards from Gloria in Alaska, although Gloria had mentioned that she would send one, with a picture.

What she does get is a strange phone call from Gloria on the day that she was supposed to come back. What is *strange* is that Gloria sounds like some entirely other person, someone younger even than Gloria actually is, younger and perfectly happy. It is Gloria's voice, all right, but lighter and quicker than it was, a voice without any shadows.

"I'm back!" Gloria bursts out, "but I just don't think I want to work today. I was out sort of late—" She laughs, in a bright new way, and then she asks, "She's not back yet, is she?"

Meaning Miss Goldstein. "No, not for another week," Mrs. Lawson tells her. "You had a good trip?"

"Fabulous! A miracle, really. I'll tell you all about it tomorrow."

Hanging up, Mrs. Lawson has an uneasy sense that some impersonator will come to work in Gloria's place.

But of course it is Gloria who is already down on her knees, cleaning the kitchen floor, when Mrs. Lawson gets there the following day.

And almost right away she begins to tell Mrs. Lawson about the wild life tour, from Mount McKinley, seemingly the focal point of her trip.

"It was really weird," says Gloria. "It looked like the moon, in that funny light." She has a lot to say, and she is annoyed that Mrs. Lawson seems to be paying more attention to her newspaper—is barely listening. Also, Mrs. Lawson seems to have aged, while Gloria was away, or maybe Gloria just forgot how old she looks, since in a way she doesn't act very old; she moves around and works a lot harder than Sharon ever does, for one example. But it seems to Gloria today that Mrs. Lawson's skin is grayer than it was, ashy-looking, and her eyes, which are always strange, have got much paler.

Nevertheless, wanting more attention (her story has an important point to it) Gloria raises her voice, as she continues, "And every time someone spotted one of those animals he'd yell out, and the man would stop the bus. We saw caribou, and these funny white sheep, high up on the rocks, and a lot of moose, and some foxes. Not any bears. Anyway, every time we stopped I got real scared. We were on the side of a really steep mountain, part of Mount McKinley, I think, and the bus was so wide, like a school bus." She does not tell Mrs. Lawson that in a weird way she liked being so scared. What she thought was, if I'm killed on this bus I'll never even get to a doctor. Which was sort of funny, really, now that she can see the humor in it—now that the lump is mysteriously, magically gone!

However, she has reached the dramatic disclosure toward which this story of her outing has been heading. "Anyway, we got back all right," she says, "and two days after that, back in Fairbanks, do you know what the headlines were, in the local paper?" She has asked this (of course rhetorical) question in a slow, deepened voice, and now she pauses, her china-blue eyes gazing into Mrs. Lawson's paler, stranger blue.

"Well, I don't know," Lawson obliges.

"They said, BUS TOPPLES FROM MOUNTAIN, EIGHT KILLED, 42 INJURED. Can you imagine? Our same bus, the very next day. What do you think that means?" This question too has been rhetorical; voicing it, Gloria smiles in a satisfied, knowing way.

A very polite woman, Mrs. Lawson smiles gently too. "It means you spared. You like to live fifty, sixty years more."

Eagerly Gloria bursts out, "Exactly! That's just the way I figured it, right away." She pauses, smiling widely, showing her little white teeth. "And then, that very same afternoon of the day we saw the paper," she goes on, "I was changing my clothes and I felt the calf of my leg where there'd been this lump that I was sort of worried about—and the lump was gone. I couldn't believe it. So I guess it was just a muscle, not anything bad."

"Them leg muscles can knot up that way, could of told you that myself," Mrs. Lawson mutters. "Heavy housework can do that to a person." But Gloria looks so happy, so bright-faced and shiny-eyed, that Mrs. Lawson does not want to bring her down, in any way, and so she adds, "But you sure are right about that bus accident. It's a sure sign you been spared."

"Oh, that's what I think too! And later we saw these really neat big dogs, in Fairbanks. I'm really thinking about getting a dog. This man I know really likes dogs too, last night we were talking." Her voice trails off in a happy reminiscence.

Later in the day, though, thinking about Gloria and her story, what she and Gloria said to each other, Mrs. Lawson is not really convinced about anything. The truth is, Gloria could perfectly well get killed by a bus in San Francisco, this very afternoon, or shot by some sniper; it's been saying in the paper about snipers, all over town, shooting folks. Or Gloria could find another lump, some place else, somewhere dangerous. Missing one bus accident is no sure sign that a person's life will always come up rosy, because nobody's does, not for long. Even Miss Goldstein, in China, could fall off of some Chinese mountain.

In a weary, discouraged way Mrs. Lawson moved through the rest of her day. It is true; she is too old and tired for the work she does. Through the big street-floor windows she watches the cold June fog rolling in from the bay, and she thinks how the weather in California has never seemed right to her. She thinks about Charles, and it comes to her that one Charles could change into the other, the same way that first Charles in such a sudden way turned violent, and wild.

That thought is enough to make her dread the end of her work, and the day, when although it is summer she will walk out into streets that are as dark and cold as streets are in Alaska.

Return Trips

Some years ago I spent a hot and mostly miserable summer in an ugly yellow hotel on the steep and thickly wooded, rocky coast of northern Yugoslavia, not far from the island of Rab. I was with a man whom I entirely, wildly loved, and he, Paul, loved me, too, but together we suffered the most excruciating romantic agonies, along with the more ordinary daily discomforts of bad food, an uncomfortable, poorly ventilated room with a hard, unyielding bed, and not enough money to get away. Or enough strength: Paul's health was bad. Morosely we stared out over the lovely clear, cool blue water, from our pine forest, to enticing islands that were purplish-gray in the distance. Or else I swam and Paul looked out after me.

Paul's problem was a congenital heart condition, now correctable by surgery, but not so then; he hurt a lot, and the smallest walks could cause pain. Even love, I came to realize, was for Paul a form of torture, although we kept at it—for him suicidally, I guess—during those endless sultry yellow afternoons, on our awful bed, between our harsh, coarse sheets.

I wanted us to marry. I was very young, and very healthy, and my crazy, unreal idea of marriage seemed to include a sort of transfer of strength. I was not quite so silly as to consciously think that marrying me would "cure" Paul, nor did I imagine a lifelong nurse role for myself. It was, rather, a magic belief that if we did a normal thing, something other people did all the time, like getting married, Paul's heart would become normal, too, like other, ordinary hearts.

Paul believed that he would die young, and, nobly, he felt that our marriage would be unfair to me. He also pointed out that whereas he had enough money from a small inheritance for one person, himself, to live on very sparingly, there was really not enough for two, and I would do well to go back to America and to the years of graduate study to which my professor mother wanted to stake me. At that time, largely because of Paul, who was a poet, I thought of studying literature; instead, after he died I turned to history, contemporary American. By now I have written several books; my particular interest is in the Trotskyite movement: its rich history of lonely, occasionally brilliant, contentious voices, its legacy of schisms—an odd choice, perhaps, but the books have been surprisingly popular. You might say, and I hope Paul would, that I have done very well professionally. In any case you could say that Paul won our argument. That fall I went back to graduate school, at Georgetown, and Paul died young, as he said he would, in a hospital in Trieste.

I have said that Paul loved me, and so he did, intensely—he loved me more, it has come to seem to me, than anyone since, although I have had my share, I guess. But Paul loved me with a meticulous attention that included every aspect. Not only my person: at that time I was just a skinny tall young girl with heavy dark hair that was fated to early gray, as my mother's had been. With an old-fashioned name—Emma. Paul loved my hair and my name and whatever I said to him, any odd old memory, or half-formed ambition; he took all my perceptions seriously. He laughed at all my jokes, although his were much funnier. He was even interested in my dreams, which I would sometimes wake and tell him, that summer, in the breathless pre-dawn cool, in the ugly hotel.

And so it is surprising that there was one particular dream that I did not tell him, especially since this dream was so painful and troubling that I remember it still. Much later I even arranged to reënact the dream, an expurgatory ritual of sorts—but that is to get far ahead of my story.

In the dream, then, that I dreamed as I slept with Paul, all those years ago in Yugoslavia, it was very hot, and I was walking down a long, intensely familiar hill, beside a winding white concrete highway. In the valley below was the rambling white house where (long before Yugoslavia) my parents and I had lived for almost five years, in a small Southern town called Hilton. I did not get as far as the house, in the dream; it was so hot, and I was burdened with the most terrific, heavy pain in my chest, a pain that must have come from Paul's actual pain, as the heat in the dream would have come from the actual heat of that summer.

"Oh, I had such an awful dream!" I cried out to Paul, as I burrowed against his sharp back, his fine damp skin.

"What about?" He kissed my hair.

"Oh, I don't know," I said. "I was in Hilton. You know, just before my parents' divorce. Where I had such a good time and my mother hated everything."

Against my hair he murmured, "Your poor mother."

"Yes, but she brings it on herself. She's so difficult. No wonder my father . . . really. And I don't want to go to graduate school."

And so I did not tell Paul my dream, in which I had painfully walked that downhill mile toward the scene of our family's dissolution, and the heady start of my own adolescence. Instead, in a familiar way, Paul and I argued about my future, and as usual I took a few stray shots at my mother.

And Paul died, and I did after all go to graduate school, and then my mother died—quite young, it now seems to me, and long before our war was in any way resolved.

A very wise woman who is considerably older than I am once told me that in her view relationships with people to whom we have been very close can continue to change even after the deaths of those people, and for me I think this has been quite true, with my mother, and in quite another way with Paul.

I am now going back to a very early time, long before my summer with Paul, in Yugoslavia. Before anyone had died. I am going back to Hilton.

When we arrived in Hilton I was eleven, and both my parents were in their early forties, and almost everything that went so darkly and irretrievably wrong among the three of us was implicit in our ages. Nearly adolescent, I was eager for initiation into romantic, sensual mysteries of which I had dim intimations from books. For my mother, the five years from forty-two or forty-three onward were a desolate march into middle age. My father, about ten months younger than my mother—and looking, always, ten years younger—saw his early forties as prime time; he had never felt better in his life. Like me, he found Hilton both romantic and exciting—he had a marvelous time there, as I did, mostly.

My first overtly sensual experience took place one April night on that very stretch of road, the graveled walk up above the highway that wound down to our house, that I dreamed of in Yugoslavia. I must have been twelve, and a boy who was "walking me home" reached for and took and held my hand, and I felt an overwhelming hot excitement. Holding hands.

About hands:

These days, like most of my friends, I am involved in a marriage, my second, which seems problematical—even more problematical than most of the marriages I see—but then maybe everyone views his or her marriage in this way. Andreas is Greek, by way of Berkeley, to which his parents immigrated in the thirties and opened a student restaurant, becoming successful enough to send their promising son to college there, and later on to medical school. Andreas and I seem to go from friendliness or even love to rage, with a speed that leaves me dizzy, and scared. However, ambivalent as in many ways I am about Andreas, I do very much like—in fact, I love—his hands. They are just plain male hands, rather square in shape, usually callused and very competent. Warm. A doctor, he specializes in kidneys, unromantically enough, but his hands are more like a workman's, a carpenter's. And sometimes even now an accidental meeting of our hands can recall me to affection; his hands remind me of love.

I liked Paul's hands, too, and I remember them still. They were very smooth, and cool.

Back in Hilton, when I was twelve, my mother violently disapproved of my being out at night with boys. Probably sensing just how exciting I found those April nights that smelled of privet and lilacs, and those lean, tall, sweet-talking Southern boys, she wept and raged, despairing and helpless as she recognized the beginning of my life as a sensual woman, coinciding as it probably did with the end of her own.

My feckless father took my side, of course. "Things are different down here, my dear," he told her. "It's a scientific fact that girls, uh, mature much earlier in the South. And when in Rome, you know. I see no harm in Emma's going to a movie with some nice boy, if she promises to be home at a reasonable hour. Ten-thirty?"

"But Emma isn't Southern. She has got to be home by ten!"

My mother filled me with a searing discomfort, a longing to be away from her. Having no idea how much I pitied her, I believed that I hated her.

My father was not only younger than my mother, he was at least a full inch shorter—a small man, compactly built, and handsome. "Has anyone ever told you that you took like that writer fellow, that Scott Fitzgerald?" asked one of the local Hilton ladies, a small brunette, improbably named Popsie Hooker. "Why no, I don't believe anyone ever has," my father lied; he had been told at least a dozen times of that resemblance. "But of course I'm flattered to be compared to such a famous man. Rather a devil, though, I think I've heard," he said, with a wink at Popsie Hooker.

"Popsie Hooker, how remarkably redundant," hopelessly observed my academic mother, to my bored and restless father. They had chosen Hilton rather desperately, as a probably cheap place to live on my father's dwindling Midwestern inheritance; he was never exactly cut out for work, and after divorcing my mother he resolved his problems, or some of them, in a succession of marriages to very rich women.

Popsie Hooker, who was later to play a curious, strong role in my life, at that time interested me not at all; if I had a view of her, it was closer to my mother's than I would have admitted, and for not dissimilar reasons. She was ludicrous, so small and silly, and just a little cheap, with those girlish clothes, all ribbons and bows, and that tinny little laugh. And that accent: Popsie out-Southerned everyone around.

"It's rather like a speech defect," my mother observed, before she stopped mentioning Popsie altogether.

Aside from her smallness and blue-eyed prettiness, Popsie's local claim to fame was her lively correspondence with "famous people," to whom she wrote what were presumably letters of adulation, the puzzle being that these people so often wrote back to her. Popsie was fond of showing off her collection. She had a charming note from Mr. Fitzgerald, and letters from Eleanor Roosevelt, Norma Shearer, Willa Cather, Clare Boothe Luce. No one, least of all my mother, could understand why such people would write to dopey Popsie, nor could I, until many years later, when she began to write to me.

However, I was too busy at that time to pay much attention to my parents or their friends, their many parties at which everyone drank too much; my own burgeoning new life was much more absorbing.

My walks at night with various boys up and down that stretch of highway sometimes came to include a chaste but passionate kiss; this would take place, if at all, on the small secluded dirt road that led down from the highway to our house.

One winter, our fourth year in Hilton, when I was fifteen, in January we had an exceptionally heavy fall of snow, deep and shadowed in the valley where our house was, ladening boughs of pine and fir and entirely covering the privet and quince and boxwood that edged the highway. For several days most of the highway itself lay under snow. Cars labored up and down the hill, singly, at long intervals, wearing unaccustomed chains.

Those nights of snow were marvelous: so cold, the black sky broken with stars as white as snow. My friends and I went sledding; that winter I was strongly taken with a dark boy who looked rather like Paul, now that I try to see him: a thin, bony face, a certain Paul-like intensity. On a dare we sledded down the highway, so perilously exciting! We lay on the sled, I stretched along his back.

We went hurtling down past the back road to my house, past everything. At last on a level area we stopped; on either side of us fields of white seemed to billow and spread off into the shadows, in the cold. Standing there we kissed—and then we began the long slow ascent of the highway, toward my house. He was pulling the sled, and we stopped several times to kiss, to press our upright bodies warmly together.

As we neared and then reached the back road to my house, we saw a car stopped, its headlights on. Guiltily we dropped hands. Dazzled by the light, only as we were almost upon it could I recognize our family car, the only wood-panelled Chrysler in town. In it was my father, kissing someone; their bodies were blotted into one silhouette.

If he saw and recognized us, there was no sign. He could easily not have seen us, or, knowing my father, who was nothing if not observant, I would guess it's more likely he did see us but pretended to himself that he did not, as he pretended not to see that my mother was miserably unhappy, and that I was growing up given to emotional extremes, and to loneliness.

"Stricken" probably comes closest to how I felt: burning rage, a painful, seething shame—emotions that I took to be hatred. "I hate him" is what I thought. Oblivious of the tall boy at my side, I began to walk as fast as I could, clumping heavily through the snow; at the door of my house I muttered what must have been a puzzlingly abrupt good night. Without kissing.

By the time we left Hilton, the summer that I was sixteen, my parents were entirely fed up with Hilton, and with each other. My father thought he could get a job in the Pentagon, in Washington—he knew someone there; and my mother had decided on New York, on graduate school at Columbia; I would go to Barnard.

I was less upset about my parents' separation than I was about leaving Hilton, which was by now to me a magic, enchanted place. In the spring and summer just preceding our departure there were amazing white bursts of dogwood, incredible wisteria and roses.

I wept for my friends, whom I would always love and miss, I thought.

I hated New York. The city seemed violent and confusing, ugly and dirty, loud. Voices in the streets or on subways and busses grated against my ears; everyone spoke so stridently, so harshly. Until I met Paul I was lonely and miserable, and frightened.

I would not have told him of my unease right away, even though Paul and I began as friends. But he must have sensed some rural longings just beneath my New York veneer. He would have; almost from the start Paul felt whatever I felt—he came to inhabit my skin.

In any case, our friendship and then our love affair had a series of outdoor settings. Paul, melancholy and romantic, and even then not well, especially liked the sea, and he liked to look out to islands—which led us, eventually, to Yugoslavia, our desolate summer there.

Not having had an actual lover before, only boys who kissed me, who did not talk much, I was unprepared for the richness of love with Paul—or, rather, I assumed that that was how love was between true intimates. Paul's sensuality was acutely sensitive, and intense; with him I felt both beautiful and loved—indescribably so. You could say that Paul spoiled me for other men, and in a way that is true—he did. But on the other hand Paul knew that he was dying, gradually, and that knowledge must have made him profligate with love. We talked and talked, we read poetry; Paul read Wallace Stevens and Eliot aloud to me, and his own poems, which I thought remarkable. We made jokes, we laughed, we made love.

Since Hilton was only twelve hours from New York by train, and we both liked travel, and trains, in a way it is odd that Paul and I did not go down to Hilton. I know he would have said yes had I suggested a trip. His curiosity about me was infinite; he would have wanted to see a place that I cared so much about. I suppose we would have stayed at the inn, as I was to do later on, when finally I did go back to Hilton. We could have taken a taxi out to what had been my house.

However, for whatever reasons, Paul and I did not go to Hilton. We went to upstate New York and to Connecticut, and out to Long Island.

And, eventually, to Yugoslavia.

Our unhappiness there in the ugly yellow hotel on the beautiful rockbound coast was due not only to Paul's declining health and my unreal but urgent wish to marry. Other problems lay in the sad old truth, well known to most adults but not at that time to us, that conducting a love affair while living apart is quite unlike taking up residence together, even for a summer. In domestic ways we were both quite impossible then—and of course Paul did not get time to change.

I could not cook, and our arrangement with the hotel included the use of a communal kitchen, an allotted space in the refrigerator and time at the stove; my cooking was supposed to save us money, which my burned disasters failed to do. Neither could I sew or iron. I even somehow failed at washing socks. None of this bothered Paul at all; his expectations of me did not run along such lines, but mine, which must have been plucked from the general culture rather than from my own free-thinking mother, were strong, and tormenting.

Paul had terrible troubles with the car, a Peugeot that we had picked up in Paris, on our way, and that had functioned perfectly well all across the Italian Alps, until we got to Trieste, where it began to make inexplicable noises, and sometimes not to start. Paul was utterly incapable of dealing with these *crises;* he would shout and rant, even clutch melodramatically at his thin black hair. I dimly sensed that he was reacting to the car's infirmities instead of to his own, which of course I did not say; but I also felt that men were supposed to deal with cars, an insupportable view, I knew even then, and derived from my father, who possessed remarkable mechanical skills.

We were there in Yugoslavia for almost three months in all, from June to September. It was probably in August, near the end of our stay, that I had my dream of going back to Hilton, and walking down the highway to our house—in the heat, with the pain in my heart that must have been Paul's pain. The dream that I did not tell Paul.

And in the fall I went back to America, to Washington, D.C., to study at Georgetown.

And Paul moved up to Trieste, where shortly after Christmas he went into a hospital and died.

Sheer disbelief was my strongest reaction to the news of Paul's death, which came in the form of a garbled cablegram. I could not believe that such an acute and lively intelligence could simply be snuffed out. In a conventional way I wept and mourned his loss: I played music that he had liked—the Hummel trumpet concerto, of which he was especially fond—and I reread "Sunday Morning" and "Four Quartets." But at the same time I never believed that he was entirely gone (I still do not).

Two years after Paul's death, most unexpectedly my mother died, in a senseless automobile accident; she was driving to see friends in Connecticut and swerved on a wet highway to avoid an oncoming truck. I was more horrified, more devastated, really, than I could have believed possible. I went to an analyst. "I haven't even written her for a month!" I cried out, during one dark fifty-minute hour. "How many letters does it take to keep a mother alive?" was the gentle and at least mildly helpful answer. Still, I wrestled with my guilt and with the sheer irresolution of our connection for many, many years.

In my late twenties I married one of my former professors: Lewis—a large, blond, emphatically healthy, outgoing man, as much unlike Paul as anyone I could have found; this occurred to me at the time as an ironic twist that only Paul himself could have appreciated. We lived in New York, where we both now taught.

To sum up very complicated events in a short and simple way: my work prospered, while my marriage did not—and I present these as simultaneous conditions, not causally linked. A happier first marriage could have made for even better work on my part, I sometimes think.

During those years, I thought of my mother with increasing sympathy. This is another simplification, but that is what it came to. She did her best under very difficult, sometimes painful circumstances is one way of putting it.

And I thought of Paul. It was his good-friend aspect that I most missed, I found, in the loneliness of my marriage. I felt, too, always, the most vast regret for what seemed the waste of a life.

And Hilton was very much in my mind.

Sometimes I tried to imagine what my life would have been like if I had never left: I could have studied at the university there, and married one of those lean and sexy sweet-talking boys. And often that seemed a preferable way to have taken.

I divorced Lewis, and I had various "relationships." I wrote and published articles, several books—and I began getting letters from Popsie Hooker. Long, quite enthralling letters. They were often about her childhood, which had been spent on a farm in Illinois—southern Illinois, to be sure, but, still, I thought how my mother would have laughed to hear that Popsie, the near-professional Southerner, was really from Illinois. Popsie wrote to me often, and I answered, being compulsive in that way, and also because I so much enjoyed hearing from her.

Some of her letters were very funny, as when she wrote about the new "rest home" in Hilton, in which certain former enemies were housed in adjacent rooms: "Mary Lou and Henrietta haven't spoken for years and *years,* and there they are. Going over there to visit is like reading a novel, a real long one," Popsie wrote, and she added, "They couldn't get me into one of those places if they carried me there on a stretcher." I gathered that Popsie was fairly rich; several husbands had come and gone, all leaving her well endowed.

We wrote back and forth, Popsie and I, she writing more often than I did, often telling me how much my letters meant to her. Her letters meant a great deal to me, too. I was especially moved when she talked about the seasons down there in Hilton—the weather and what was in bloom; I could remember all of it, so vividly. And I was grateful that she never mentioned my parents, and her own somewhat ambiguous connection with them.

· · ·

During some of those years, I began an affair with Andreas, the doctor whom I eventually married: a turbulent, difficult, and sometimes rewarding marriage. Andreas is an exceptionally skilled doctor; he is also arrogant, quick-tempered, and inconsiderate, especially of other people's time—like all doctors, I have sometimes thought.

Our conflicts often have to do with schedules: his conference in Boston versus mine in Chicago; his need for a vacation in February versus mine for time to finish a book, just then. And more ordinary arguments: my dislike of being kept waiting, his wish that I do more cooking. Sometimes even now his hot, heavy body next to mine in bed seems alien, unknown, and I wonder what he is doing there, really. At other times, as I have said, I am deeply stirred by an accidental touching of our hands.

At some of our worst moments I think of leaving Andreas; this would be after an especially ugly quarrel, probably fuelled by too much wine, or simply after several weeks of non-communication.

In one such fantasy I do go back to Hilton, and I take up the rest of my life there as a single woman. I no longer teach, I only do research in the library, which is excellent. And I write more books. I imagine that I see a lot of Popsie Hooker; I might even become the sort of "good daughter" to her that I was so far from being to my own mother. And sometimes in this fantasy I buy the house that we used to live in, the rambling house down the highway, in the valley. I have imagined it as neglected, needing paint, new gutters, perhaps even falling apart, everything around it overgrown and gone to seed.

Last June, when I had agreed to give a series of lectures at Georgetown, Andreas and I made reservations in a small hotel where we had stayed before, not far from the university. We both like Washington; we looked forward to revisiting favorite galleries and restaurants. It was one of the many times when we needed a vacation together, and so, as I might have known would happen, this became impossible: two sick patients got sicker, and although I argued, citing the brilliance and the exceptional competence of his partners (an argument that did not go over very well), Andreas said no, he had to stay in New York, with the kidneys of Mrs. Howell and old Mr. Rosenthal.

I went to Georgetown and to our hotel alone. I called several times, and Andreas and I "made up" what had been a too familiar argument.

In Georgetown, the second day, as I walked alone past those elegantly maintained houses, as I glanced into seductively cloistered, luxuriantly ferned and flowered gardens, some stray scent of privet or a glimpse of a yellow rosebush in full bloom—something reminded me strongly, compellingly of Hilton, and I thought, Well, why not? I could take the train and just stay for a couple of days. That much more time away from Andreas might be to the good, just now. I could stay at the Hilton Inn. I could visit Popsie. I could walk down the highway to our house.

And that is what I did, in more or less that order, except that I saved the visit to Popsie for the last, which turned out to be just as well. But right away I stopped at a travel agency on Wisconsin Avenue, and I bought a ticket to Raleigh, treating myself to a roomette for the five-hour trip; I felt that both ceremony and privacy were required.

I had thought that on the train I would be struck by the deep familiarity of the landscape; at last, that particular soil, that special growth. But actually it was novelty that held me to my window: the wide flat brown shining rivers that we crossed, with their tacky little marinas, small boats, small boys on the banks. Flooded swamps, overgrown with kudzu vines and honeysuckle. I had the curious illusion that one sometimes gets on trains, of traversing an exotic, hitherto untraveled land. I felt myself to be an explorer.

That night I had an unmemorable dinner alone at the inn—which, having been redone, was all unfamiliar to me. I went to bed early, slept well.

Sometime in the night, though, I did wake up with the strange and slightly scary thought that in a few years I would be as old as my mother was when she died, and I wondered what, if anything, that fact had to do with my coming back to Hilton, after all these years.

The next morning's early air was light and delicate. Dew still shone on the heavy, dark-green shrubbery around the inn, on silver cobwebs, as

I set out for my walk—at last! The sky was soft and pale, an eggshell blue. Walking along the still graveled sidewalk, beside the tarred road that led from the inn out to the highway, I recognized houses; I knew who used to live in almost all of them, and I said those names to myself as I walked along: Hudson, Phipps, Zimmerman, Rogerson, Pittman. I noticed that the old Pittman place was now a fraternity house, with an added sun porch and bright new paint, bright gold Greek letters over the door. In fact, the look of all those houses was one of improvement, upgrading, with their trim lawns, abundant boxwood, their lavish flower beds.

I reached the highway, still on the graveled walk, and I began the long descent toward my house. The air was still light, and barely warm, although the day to come would be hot. I thought of my dream in Yugoslavia, of this walk, and I smiled, inexplicably happy at just that moment—with no heat, no pain in my heart.

I recognized more houses, and said more names, and I observed that these houses, too, were in splendid shape, all bright and visibly cared for. There was much more green growth than I remembered, the trees were immense, and I thought, Well, of course; they've had time to grow.

No one seeing me as I walked there could know or guess that that was where I used to live, I thought. They would see—a tall thin woman, graying, in early middle age, in a striped gray cotton skirt, gray shirt. A woman looking intently at everything, and smiling to herself.

And then, there before me was our house. But not our house. It, too, had been repainted—all smartened up with bright white paint and long black louvred shutters, now closed against the coming heat and light. Four recent-model sports cars, all imported, were parked in the driveway, giving the place a recreational, non-familiar air. A group of students, I thought; perhaps some club? The surrounding trees were huge; what had been a small and murmurous pine grove at one side of the house now towered over it, thickly green and rustling slightly in a just-arisen morning breeze. No one came out while I stood there, for not very long, but I was sure that there was not a family inside but some cluster of transients—young people, probably, who liked each other and liked the house, but without any deep or permanent attachment.

I continued on my walk, a circle of back roads on which I was pleased to find that I still knew my way, which led at last back to the highway, and up the hill, to the inn.

I had called Popsie Hooker from Washington, and again from the inn, when I got there. She arose from her nap about four in the afternoon, she said, and if I could come out to her house along about then she would be thrilled, just simply thrilled.

By midafternoon it was too hot for another walk, and so I took a taxi out to Popsie's house, in the direction opposite to mine. I arrived about four-thirty, which I assumed to be along about four in Southernese.

Popsie's house, the fruit of one of her later marriages, was by far the most splendid I had yet seen in town: a Georgian house, of ancient soft red brick smartly trimmed in black, with frequent accents of highly polished brass. Magnificent lawns, magnolias, rhododendrons. By the time I got to the door I half expected to be greeted by an array of uniformed retainers—all black, of course.

But it was Popsie herself who opened the door to me—a Popsie barely recognizable, so shrunken and wizened had she become: a small woman withered down to dwarf size, in a black silk dress with grosgrain at her throat, a cameo brooch. She smelled violently of gardenia perfume and of something else that at first I could not place.

"Emma! Emma!" she breathed up into my face, the old blue eyes filming over, and she caught at both my arms and held them in her weak tight grasp. I recognized the second scent, which was sherry.

"You're *late,*" she next accused me. "Here I've been expecting you this whole long after*noon.*"

I murmured apologies, and together we proceeded down the hallway and into a small parlor, Popsie still clutching my arm, her small fierce weight almost tugging me over sideways.

We sat down. The surfaces in that room were all so cluttered with silver and ivory pieces, inlay, old glass, that it could have been an antique shop, or the parlor of a medium. I told Popsie how happy I was to be there, how wonderful Hilton looked.

"Well, you know, it's become a very fancy place to live. Very *ex-*

pensive. Lots of Yankees retiring down here, and fixing up the old houses."

"Uh, where do the poor people live?"

She laughed, a tiny rasp. "Oh, there you go, talking *liberal,* and you just got here. Well, the poor folks, what's left of them, have moved out to Robertsville."

Robertsville was the adjacent town, once predominantly black, and so I next asked, "What about the Negroes?"

"Well, I guess they've just sort of drifted back into the countryside, where they came from. But did you notice all the fancy new stores on Main Street? All the restaurants, and the *clothes*?"

We talked for a while about the new splendors of Hilton, and the rudeness of the new Yankees, who did not even go to church—as I thought, This could not be the woman who has been writing to me. Although of course she was—the same Popsie, half tipsy in the afternoon; she probably spent her sober mornings writing letters. This woman was more like the Popsie of my early years in Hilton, that silly little person, my mother's natural enemy.

Possibly to recall the Popsie of the wonderful letters, I asked about the local rest home. How were things out there?

"Well, I have to tell you. What gripes me the most about that place is that they don't pay any taxes" was Popsie's quick, unhelpful response. "Tax-*free,* and you would not believe the taxes I have to pay on this old place."

"But this place is so beautiful." I did not add, And you have so much money.

"Well, it is right pretty," she acknowledged, dipping her head. "But why must I go on and on paying for it? It's not fair."

Our small chairs were close together in that crowded, stuffy room, so that when Popsie leaned closer yet to me, her bleary eyes peering up into mine, the sherry fumes that came my way were very strong indeed. And Popsie said, "You know, I've always thought you were so beautiful, even if no one else ever thought you were." She peered again. "Where did you get that beauty, do you think? Your mother never was even one bit pretty."

More stiffly than I had meant to, I spoke the truth. "Actually I look quite a lot like my mother," I told her. And I am not beautiful.

Catching a little of my anger, which probably pleased her, Popsie raised her chin. "Well, one thing certain, you surely don't favor your daddy."

"No, I don't. I don't favor him at all." My father had recently moved to La Jolla, California, with another heiress, this one younger than I am, which would have seemed cruel news to give to Popsie.

After a pause, during which I suppose we both could have been said to be marshalling our forces, Popsie and I continued our conversation, very politely, until I felt that I could decently leave.

I told her how much I liked her letters, and she said how she liked mine, and we both promised to write again, very soon—and I wondered if we would.

On the plane to New York, a smooth, clear, easy flight, I was aware of an unusual sense of well-being, which out of habit I questioned. I noted the sort of satisfaction that I might have been expected to feel on finishing a book, except that at the end of books I usually feel drained, exhausted. But now I simply felt well, at peace, and ready for whatever should come next.

Then Paul returned from nowhere to my mind, more strongly than for some time. In an affectionate way I remembered how impossible he was, in terms of daily life, and how much I had loved him—and how he had loved me.

Actually he and Andreas were even more unlike than he and Lewis were, I next thought, and a little wearily I noted my own tendency to extremes, and contrasts. Andreas likes to fix and mend things, including kidneys, of course. He is good with cars. "I come from strong Greek peasant stock" is a thing that he likes to say, and it is true; clearly he does, with his powerful black hair, his arrogant nose. His good strong heart.

We were planning a trip to Greece the following fall. Andreas had gone back as a boy to visit relatives, and later with both his first and second wives. And he and I had meant to go, and now we would.

We planned to fly to Rome, maybe spend a few days there; we both like Rome. But now another route suggested itself: we could fly to Vienna, where we have never been, and then take the train to Trieste, where we could pick up a car and drive down to Greece by way of Yugoslavia. We would drive past the ferry to the island of Rab, and past the road that led to our yellow hotel. I did not imagine driving down to see it; Andreas would be in a hurry, and my past does not interest him much. He would see no need to stop on such an errand.

Nor do I. And besides, that particular ugly, poorly built structure has probably been torn down. Still, I very much like the idea of just being in its vicinity.

La Señora

The grand hotel is some kilometres beyond the village, on a high road that winds between the jungle and the sea. It has been there for years now, standing taller than the palm trees that surround it, the fat-trunked palms all wrapped with flower vines.

The face of this hotel has many balconies with small fringed awnings, and everywhere windows, all wide and open to the air. Even the dining room, the largest of all rooms and by far the most grand, looks out openly to the sea.

Some of the village girls work there as waitresses. They are very pretty girls, but silly, most of them, and not serious in their work. Older women, if they still are strong, with luck may obtain positions as room maids. Those maids have in their care the rows of large and very beautiful rooms where the hotel guests come to live—the gringos, from everywhere up north. The room maids also have charge of all the sheets and towels, each day supplying more to each room, all fresh and clean. They dust out the rooms, those maids, even sweeping under the beds, if they choose to do so.

The room maids in most respects are more fortunate than the dining room girls. The work of the girls is harder, which is just, since they are much younger, and their wages are somewhat higher; but often the room maids have closer associations with the guests, some of whom are especially kind, in terms of tips and presents. Many guests come year after year and often to their exact same rooms, each year, and they remember the names of the maids—though often pronouncing them strangely, and confusing Teodola with Teodora, for example. Naturally some other guests are not at all sympathetic, with their floors full of wet towels and sand, their strong-smelling bottles and broken glasses, their stains of lipstick, dark smudges on sheets, pillowcases.

There is one guest, a very thin and now very old North American, a woman who came there always with her husband and then for a time alone, a lady always referred to by the maids and even the silliest dining room girls as La Señora, always said in a certain way, "La Señora," so that only this lady is meant.

She is very white, the señora, everything white, her skin and her hair like white silk and almost all of her clothes. She is white, but with great dark eyes, like Mexican eyes. Despite all her years this lady moves very swiftly, and with great smoothness; she might balance a jug of water on her head, and never spill. She is kind, this lady, but at times she can be fiercely angry, when she feels that what has been done is not quite right. Many of the maids greatly fear her, and dread her coming; she was even heard to raise her voice in a harsh way with her husband.

With Teodola, though, the oldest room maid, the one who has been there longest, the lady has never been angry. To Teodola it seems that they have a way of understanding each other. She, Teodola, understands that it is important to the lady that the floors of the room all be dusted, even under the beds; that the sheets on the bed be stretched tight; and that all of the white parts of the bathroom be washed many, many times. And the lady understands that Teodola does not like to be called Teodora, and that inquiries as to her health are received as great courtesies. The lady brings large boxes of chocolates to Teodola; Teodola does not eat candy any longer but she enjoys handing it out to her grandchildren.

Each year the lady brings her dictionary of Spanish words, and each year she speaks more, and she seems better able to understand Teodola. In the mornings after taking her breakfast the lady always sits for a time on the terrace of her room, in former years with her husband (whom now Teodola has almost forgotten, as even her own dead husband has dimmed in her mind), in recent years alone. She reads from books, she writes in another small book, she writes on postcards. But she seems for most hours just to rest there, to regard the flowers that border her terrace, the bushes and vines; the pink, red, purple blossoms, white butterflies, black hummingbirds. The far-off sea.

In her own late years Teodola is often unclear as to seasons, except to observe that the weather, which should never change, now does so; there is rain, even coolness, quite unexpectedly. There is thus no seasonal way for her to know precisely the day of the arrival of the lady, except that she does know: her dreams inform her. She begins to dream of the lady, several nights of such dreams, and then there will come a morning when she knocks on a certain door—and there is La Señora, the very white lady in her light white clothes, embracing Teodola—a small quick light kiss on each cheek, like the kiss of a bird—and the lady saying, "Ah, Teodola, well, here I am again. I never believe I'm going to make it ever again, but here I am. And how happy I am to see you! You look very well—you have had a good year? Your health has been good—and your children? Tell me, how many grandchildren by now? Please, I want you to say all their names to me."

And Teodola will begin to recite: "Ernesto, Felipe, Sara, Elvira, Carlos, Eva. And the infant Jiménez, Jimmy." Then both she and the lady will laugh from sheer happiness, Teodola being happy to see the lady again, the lady who now will be there for quite a while; and the lady, who is every year more white, and smaller in her bones, is happy to be resting in the warm bright days, to be watching her birds and flowers, and the gold-blue ocean waves.

There must come a year when the lady does not appear; this is something that Teodola has considered. The lady is very old: one day she must die. What Teodola does not know is in what way she herself will receive this information. It is possible that she will simply dream of the death of the lady, but even if such a dream did come she would not quite trust it, for lately she has received information from dreams that is quite unreliable. She has seen her husband alive again, and wanting more sons, wanting ever more sons, and she has dreamed of her grandchildren old and dying in wars—all craziness.

But someday the lady will be permanently gone, and in the meantime Teodola's own days go faster and faster, always less time between dawn, the moment of leaving her hut just outside the village, and sunset, the long tired downhill homeward trudge.

Teodola is much respected by the other room maids. They respect her right to private naps, sometimes, in an unused room just next to the storeroom of linens. They do not ask that she carry the largest stacks of clean sheets, or full trays of new glasses. They even (usually) obey her when Teodola says that a certain floor must be dusted yet once again, especially in the room of the señora, who at any moment could still reappear. The maids and the girl waitresses too all respect Teodola, but they do not have true friendship for her; to them Teodola seems just a woman alone, become old and strange. Teodola knows of their feelings, but such isolation is a part of becoming old that one must accept, she believes.

However, on a certain day all the waitress girls and the hotel maids together decide to play a trick on Teodola, a trick that is at last too much for her.

It begins quite early one morning, when Teodola is walking slowly up the steep dirt road, all crevassed and full of holes, toward the main hotel road, and on her way she encounters a very young and pretty waitress girl, Elisabeta, who says to her, "Oh Teodola, have you heard the news? La Señora does not come this year. She has died up in the north, in New York."

Teodola experiences a sharp sudden pain, but she frowns, refusing to be teased in this way, and by this particularly foolish girl, who is always much too familiar with the manager. "You know nothing," she tells the girl. "You are so silly, believing whatever a man says to you!"

Elisabeta makes an angry face, but she hurries away without more lying.

But later on that same day when Teodola insists that one of the room maids, Margarita, again dust the floor of the room of the lady, Margarita simply stares at Teodola and asks her, "But why, Teodola? Why dust the floor? You know that we have heard that the lady is dead."

Although it is not yet noon the sun is especially hot, and Teodola already is very tired; she had just been thinking of her coming nap. Perhaps for those reasons she is crosser than she intended to be with Margarita. "Enough of your teasing and laziness!" she cries out. "You say anything that arrives in your head to avoid doing work. You tell lies!"

Margarita shakes her head in an angry way, as Teodola recalls that she, Margarita, is the aunt of Elisabeta: of course, it is a story that the two of them together have concocted, for tormenting Teodola.

Teodola herself then sets about dusting the floor in the room of the lady, and that work is a comfort to her. As always, she feels the presence of the lady there; she can almost smell the flower-sweet scent of the lady's clothes, can almost hear the sound of the lady's voice, as she tries new Spanish words.

In the afternoon of that day two other maids try the same trick on Teodola, both of them saying, "Teodola, did you hear? La Señora has died." But by now Teodola knows not to say anything whatsoever, not to gratify them by her anger, nor to show that she knows that they lie. She ignores them; she does her work of making the beds and arranging the flowers in all the bedside tables. Those words have given her a queasy feeling, though, an inner blackness.

At the end of the day, the huge red sun slipping down below the line of the darkening sea, Teodola starts home. The walk seems much longer and harder than usual, but at last she arrives at her hut. Too tired to eat, she lies down on her mattress, and is soon fast asleep.

Night comes without her waking, and with it strange dreams. In one of them the señora has indeed arrived at the hotel but she herself, Teodola, has died. Very strange indeed: within the dream Teodola knows that she is dreaming, and that nothing in the dream is true—of course if she were dead she would not be dreaming. Yet when she struggles very hard to wrest herself from sleep and from the dream, she cannot. She is powerless against her sleep, against the dream.

New Best Friends

"The McElroys really don't care about seeing us anymore—aren't you aware of that?" Jonathan Ferris rhetorically and somewhat drunkenly demands of his wife, Sarah Stein.

Evenly she answers him, "Yes, I can see that."

But he stumbles on, insisting, "We're low, *very* low, on their priority list."

"I *know.*"

Jonathan and Sarah are finishing dinner, and too much wine, on one of the hottest nights of August—in Hilton, a mid-Southern town, to which they moved (were relocated) six months ago; Jonathan works for a computer corporation. They bought this new fake-Colonial house, out in some scrubby pinewoods, where now, in the sultry, sulfurous paralyzing twilight no needle stirs, and only mosquitoes give evidence of life, buzz-diving against the window screens.

In New York, in their pretty Bleecker Street apartment, with its fern-shaded courtyard, Sarah would have taken Jonathan's view of the recent McElroy behavior as an invitation to the sort of talk they both enjoyed: insights, analyses—and, from Sarah, somewhat literary speculations. Their five-year marriage has always included a great deal of talk, of just this sort.

However, now, as he looks across the stained blond maple table that came, inexorably, with the bargain-priced house, across plates of wilted food that they were too hot and tired to eat—as he focusses on her face Jonathan realizes that Sarah, who never cries, is on the verge of tears; and also that he is too drunk to say anything that would radically revise what he has already said.

Sarah does begin to cry. "I know we're low on their list," she chokes. "But after all we only met them a couple of months before they moved away. And they'd always lived here. They have family, friends. I've always accepted that. I even said it to you. So why do you have to point it out?"

If he could simply get to his feet, could walk around the table and say, I'm sorry, I didn't mean it—then at least temporarily there would be an improvement in the air between them, a lifting of the heavy night's burden. But Jonathan cannot move; it is so hot his shirt is still stuck to his back, as it has been all day. And he is exhausted.

Besides, what he just said about the McElroys (who at first seemed an instrument of salvation; Sarah was crazy about them) is all too true: Hugh and Hattie McElroy, who moved to Santa Fe in June, now are back for the wedding of a son, and Sarah has barely seen them. And she used to see Hattie almost every day. On this visit, though, the McElroys have come to Sarah and Jonathan's once for dinner, and Sarah saw Hattie at a large lunch party (given by Hattie's old friend Popsie Hooker).

Of course, having lived here forever, the McElroys are indeed involved with family and friends, as Sarah has just said. But really, Jonathan now furiously thinks (as Sarah must have thought), at least they could call her; they could meet for tea, or something.

Weeping, Sarah looks blotchy, aged, distorted; her fine, just-not-sharp features are blurred. "Piquant" is the word that Jonathan's mother has found for Sarah's face. "Well, I wouldn't call her pretty, in any conventional way, but her face is so intelligent, so—piquant." To Jonathan, her face is simply that, her own; he is so close to her that he rarely thinks about it, except that a sudden, unexpected sight of her can deeply move him still. She simply looks like a young woman who is crying, almost any young woman.

Thinking this, it occurs to Jonathan that he has never seen another man cry, and he himself would like to weep, at this moment; it is so hot, they are both so unhappy, everything seems lost. He pulls himself together, though, after this frightening thought, and then he remembers that in fact he did see his own father in tears, as he lay dying, in Mass. General Hospital; big heavy tears ran down his father's long lined white face.

"You must think I'm really stupid," Sarah gets out.

No, you're the brightest girl I ever met, Jonathan does not say. Nor does he add, But that was a stupid remark.

Stupid is the last thing that Sarah is, actually, and during their New York married life (before *this*) she had no trouble getting the part-time editorial jobs that she liked, or books to review. Those occupations used to absorb much of Sarah's time, and her plentiful energy, and Jonathan knows that lack of any such work down here contributes to her unhappiness; it is not just disappointment with the McElroys.

In New York, in a vague, optimistic way (they have been generally happy people, for these times), as they discussed the projected move to Hilton, Sarah and Jonathan assured each other that since it was a university town, not just any old backward Southern city, there would be work of some sort available to her, at the university press, or somewhere. Saying which they forgot one crucial fact, which is that in or around any university there are hundreds of readily exploitable bright students' wives, or students, who grasp at all possible, however low-paying, semi-intellectual work.

And so for Sarah there has been little to do, in the too large, uncharming house, which (Jonathan has unhappily recognized) Sarah has been keeping much too clean. All her scrubbing and waxing, her dusting and polishing have a quality of desperation, as well as being out of character; his old busy Sarah was cheerfully untidy, which was quite all right with Jonathan, who did not mind housework.

Unsteadily, they now clear the table and wash up. They go upstairs to bed; they try to sleep, in the thick damp heat.

Sarah and Jonathan's first month in Hilton, February, was terrible for them both. Cold, dark and windy, and wet, a month of almost unrelenting rains, which turned the new red clay roads leading out to their house into tortuous slicks, deeply rutted, with long wide puddles of muddy red water, sometimes just frozen at the edges. Cold damp drafts penetrated their barnlike house; outside, in the woods, everything dripped, boughs sagged, and no birds sang.

March was a little better: not yet spring, none of the promised balmy Southern blue, and no flowers, but at least the weather cleared; and the blustery winds, though cold, helped to dry the roads, and to cleanse the air.

And, one night at dinner, Sarah announced that she had met a really wonderful woman, in a bookstore. "My new best friend," she said, with a tiny, half-apologetic laugh, as Jonathan's heart sank, a little. They both knew her tendency toward somewhat ill-advised enthusiasms: the charming editor who turned out to be a lively alcoholic, given to midnight (and later) phone calls; the smart young film critic who made it instantly clear that she hated all their other friends. The long line of initially wonderful people, the new best friends, who in one way or another became betrayers of Sarah's dreams of friendship.

However, there was another, larger group of friends she'd had for years, who were indeed all that Sarah said they were, smart and loyal and generous and fun. Jonathan liked those friends, now his friends, too. Life with Sarah had, in fact, made him more gregarious, changing him from a solitary, overeducated young man with a boring corporation job, despite an advanced degree in math, into a warmer, friendlier person. Sarah's talkative, cheery friends were among her early charms for Jonathan. He simply wondered at her occasional lapses in judgment.

Hattie McElroy, the new best friend (and the owner, it turned out, of the bookstore where they had met), was very Southern, Sarah said; she was from Hilton. However, except for her accent (which Sarah imitated, very funnily), she did not seem Southern. "She reads so much, I guess it gives her perspective," Sarah said. And, with a small pleased laugh, "She doesn't like it here very much. She says she's so tired of everyone she knows. They're moving to Santa Fe in June. Unfortunately, for me."

After that, all Sarah's days seemed to include a visit to Hattie's bookstore, where Hattie served up mugs of tea, Sarah said, along with "super" gossip about everyone in town. "There's an old group that's unbelievably stuffy," Sarah reported to Jonathan. "People Hattie grew up with. They never even want to meet anyone new. Especially Yankees." And she laughed, happy to have such an exclusive connection with her informative and amusing new friend.

"Any chance you could take over the bookstore when they leave?" asked Jonathan, early on. "Maybe we could buy it?" This was during the period of Sarah's unhappy discovery about the work situation in Hilton, the gradually apparent fact of there being nothing for her.

"Well, the most awful thing. She sold it to a chain, and just before we got here. She feels terrible, but she says there didn't seem any other way out, no one else came around to buy it. And the chain people are even bringing in their own manager." Sarah's laugh was rueful, and her small chin pointed downward as she added, "One more dead end. And damn, it would have been perfect for me."

The next step, Jonathan dimly imagined, would be a party or dinner of some sort at the McElroys', which he could not help mildly dreading, as he remembered the film critic's party, at which not only was almost everyone else gay (that would have been all right, except that some of the women did seem very hostile, to him) but they all smoked—heavily, some of them pipes and cigars—in three tiny rooms on Horatio Street.

However, it was they who were to entertain the McElroys at dinner, Sarah told him. "And I think just the four of us," she added. "That way it's easier, and I can make something great. And besides, who else?"

All true: an imaginative but fluky cook, Sarah did best on a small scale. And, too, the only other people they knew were fellow-transferees, as displaced and possibly as lonely as themselves, but otherwise not especially sympathetic.

The first surprise about Hattie McElroy, that first April night, was her size: she was a very big woman, with wild bleached straw-looking hair and round doll-blue eyes, and about twenty years older than Jonathan would have imagined; Sarah spoke of her as of a contemporary. Hugh McElroy was tall and gray and somewhat dim.

And Hattie was a very funny woman. Over drinks, she started right in with a description of a party she had been to the night before. "I was wearing this perfectly all-right dress, even if it was a tad on the oldish side," Hattie told them, as she sipped at her gin. "And Popsie Hooker— Can you imagine a woman my age, and still called Popsie? We went to Sunday school together, and she hasn't changed one bit. Anyway, Popsie said to me, 'Oh, I just love that dress you're wearing. I was so sorry when they went out of style five years ago.' Can you imagine? Isn't she marvelous? I just love Popsie, I truly do."

For such a big woman, Hattie's laugh was small, a little-girl laugh, but Jonathan found himself drawn to her big friendly teeth, her crazy hair.

Sarah, it then turned out, had met Popsie Hooker; early on in their stay in Hilton she had gone to a luncheon that Popsie gave for the new corporation wives. And, Sarah told Hattie, "She made a little speech that

I didn't quite understand. About how she knew we were all very busy, so please not to write any thank-you notes. It was odd, I thought."

Hattie's chuckle increased in volume. "Oh, you don't understand Southern talk, not at all! I can tell you don't. That meant you were all supposed to write notes, and say you just couldn't resist writing, even if she said not to, since her lunch party was just so lovely."

Sarah laughed, too. "Well, dumb me. I took her at her word, and didn't write."

"Well, honey, you'll larn. But I can tell you, it takes near 'bout a lifetime."

Dinner was not one of Sarah's more successful efforts: veal Orloff, one of her specialties, but this time a little burned.

Hattie, though, seemed to think it was wonderful. "Oh, the trouble you must have gone to! And you must have a way with your butcher. I've just never seen veal like this—not down here."

Jonathan felt that she was overdoing it, but then chided himself: Hattie was Southern, after all; that was how they talked. He must not be negative.

"These mushrooms are truly delicious," Hugh McElroy put in. In Jonathan's view, a truer remark. Hugh was a kind and quiet man, who reminded Jonathan of someone; in an instant, to his mild surprise, he realized that it was his own father, whose shy manner had been rather like Hugh's.

A good evening, then. Jonathan could honestly say to Sarah that he liked her new best friends; they could even laugh over a few of the former candidates for that title.

Their return invitation, to a party at the McElroys', was less fun all around: too many people, in a cluttered but surprisingly formal house, on a too hot night in May. But by then it was almost time for the McElroys to leave, and Hattie had explained to Sarah that they just had to have all those people.

"They're really so loved around here," Sarah somewhat tipsily remarked, as they drove home from that party. "It just won't be the same town."

"It's still very pretty," Jonathan reminded her. "Smell the flowers."

The spring that had finally arrived, after so much rain, had seemed a reward for patience, with its extraordinary gifts of roses, azaleas, even gardenias, everywhere blooming, wafting sweetness into the light night air. And out in the woods white lacings of dogwood had appeared.

For some reason ("I can't think why! I must be going plumb crazy!" Hattie had confided to Sarah), Hattie and Hugh had agreed to be photographed over local TV on the day of their departure, and that night, on a news program, there they were: big Hattie, in her navy linen traveling suit, her white teeth all revealed in a grin for the camera, as she clutched an overflowing tote bag and tried to pin on a cluster of pink camellias; and tall Hugh, a shy smile as he waved an envelope of airline tickets.

As, watching, Sarah, who never cried, burst into tears.

And then they were gone, the McElroys. Moved out to New Mexico.

Sarah moped around. Indifferent housekeeping, minimal efforts. She made thrifty, ordinary meals, so unlike her usual adventurous, rather splashy culinary style, and she lost all interest in how she looked. Not that she was ever given to extravagance in those matters, but she used to wash and brush her hair a lot, and she did something to her eyes, some color, that Jonathan now recognized as missing, gone.

She often wrote to the McElroys, and Hattie answered, often; Sarah produced the letters for Jonathan to read at dinner. They contained a lot about the scenery, the desert, and fairly amusing gossip about what Hattie referred to as the Locals. "You would not believe the number of painters here, and the galleries. Seems like there's an opening most every night, and the Local Folk all come out in their fancy silver jewelry and their great big silver belts. Whole lots of the men are fairies, of course, but I just don't care. They're a lot of fun, they are indeed gay people." Funny, longish letters, with the sound of Hattie's voice, always ending with strong protestations of love and friendship. "Oh, we love you and miss you so much, the both of us!" cried out Hattie, on her thin flowered writing paper.

Jonathan observed all this with dark and ragged emotions—Sarah's deep sadness and the occasional cheer that Hattie's letters brought. He cared about Sarah in a permanent and complex way that made her pain his; still, what looked like true mourning for the absent McElroys gave him further pain. He had to wonder: was he jealous of the McElroys? And he had to concede that he was, in a way. He thought, I am not enough for her, and at the same time he recognized the foolishness of that thought. No one is "enough" for anyone, of course not. What Sarah needs is a job, and more friends that she likes; he knew that perfectly well.

And then one night at dinner, near the first of August, came the phone call from Hattie; Jonathan overheard a lot of exclamations and shouts, gasps from Sarah, who came back to the table all breathless, flushed.

"They're here! The McElroys are back, and staying at the Inn. Just for a visit. One of their boys suddenly decided to marry his girlfriend. Isn't that great?"

Well, it turned out not to be great. There was the dinner at Jonathan and Sarah's house, to which the McElroys came late, from another party (and not hungry; one of Sarah's most successful efforts wasted), and they left rather early. "You would not believe the day we have ahead of us tomorrow! And we thought marrying off a son was supposed to be easy." And the luncheon at Popsie Hooker's.

Jonathan and Sarah were not invited to the wedding, a fact initially excused (maybe overexcused) by Sarah: "We're not the Old Guard, not old Hiltonians, and besides, it's the bride's list, not Hattie's, and we don't even know her, or her family."

And then two weeks of the McElroy visit had passed, accurately calculated by Jonathan. Which calculation led to his fatal remarks, over all that wine, about the priorities of the McElroys.

On the morning after that terrible evening, Jonathan and Sarah have breakfast together as usual, but rather sombrely. Hung over, sipping at tea, nibbling at overripe late-summer fruit, Jonathan wonders what he can say, since he cannot exactly deny the truth of his unfortunate words.

At last he brings out "I'm really sorry I said that, about Hattie and Hugh."

Sarah gives him an opaque, level look, and her voice is judicious as she says, "Well, I'm sure you were right."

One of the qualities that Jonathan has always found exciting in Sarah is her ability to surprise him; she rarely behaves in ways that he would have predicted. Nevertheless, having worried intermittently during the day over her sadness, her low spirits and his own recent part in further lowering them, he is delighted (ah, his old astonishing Sarah) to find her all brushed and bright-eyed, happy, when he comes in the door that night.

"Well, I decided that all this moping around like an abandoned person was really silly," she tells him, over cold before-dinner glasses of wine, in the bright hot flower-scented dusk. "And so I just called Hattie, not being accusatory or anything. I just said that I'd really missed seeing her—them."

"Well, *great.*" Jonathan is thinking how he admires her; she is fundamentally honest, and brave. And so pretty tonight, her delicately pointed face, her lively brown hair.

"Hattie couldn't have been nicer. She said they'd missed us, of course, but they just got so caught up in this wedding business. It's next Saturday—I'd lost track. They truly haven't had one minute, she told me, and I can believe her. Anyway, they're coming for supper on Sunday night. She said a post-wedding collapse would be just the best thing they could possibly think of."

"Well, great," Jonathan repeats, although some dim, indefinable misgiving has edged into his mind. How can one evening of friends at dinner be as terrific as this one will have to be? That question, after moments, emerges, and with it a darker, more sinister one: suppose it isn't terrific at all, as the last one was not?

By mid-August, in Hilton, it has been hot for so long that almost all the flowers have wilted, despite an occasional thundershower. Many people are away at that time, and in neglected gardens overblown roses shed fat satin petals onto drying, yellowing grass; in forgotten orchards sweet unpicked fruit falls and spatters, fermenting, slowly rotting, among tall summer weeds, in the simmering heat.

The Saturday of the McElroy son's wedding, however, is surprisingly cool, with an almost New England briskness in the air. That familiar-feeling air gives Jonathan an irrational flutter of hope: maybe the next night, Sunday, will be a reasonable evening. With the sort of substantive conversation that he and Sarah are used to, instead of some nutty Southern doubletalk. With this hope, the thought comes to Jonathan that Hattie imitating Popsie Hooker is really Hattie speaking her own true language. Dare he voice this to Sarah, this interesting perception about the nature of mimicry? Probably not.

Sarah spends a lot of Saturday cooking, so that it can all be served cold on Sunday night; she makes several pretty vegetable aspics, and a cold marinated beef salad. Frozen lemon soufflé. By Saturday night she is tired, but she and Jonathan have a pleasant, quiet dinner together. He has helped her on and off during the day, cutting up various things, and it is he who makes their dinner: his one specialty, grilled chicken.

Their mood is more peaceful, more affectionate with each other than it has been for months, Jonathan observes (since before they came down here? quite possibly).

Outside, in the gathering, lowering dusk, the just perceptibly earlier twilight, fireflies glimmer dimly from the pinewoods. The breeze is just barely cooler than most of their evening breezes, reminding Jonathan of the approach of fall—in his view, always a season of hope, of bright leaves on college campuses, and new courses offered.

Having worked so much the day before, Sarah and Jonathan have a richly indolent morning; they laze about. Around noon the phone rings, and Sarah goes to answer it. Jonathan, nearby, hears her say, "Oh, Hattie. Hi."

A very long pause, and then Sarah's voice, now stiff, all tightened up: "Well, no, I don't see that as a good idea. We really don't know Popsie—"

Another long pause, as Sarah listens to whatever Hattie is saying, and then, "Of course I understand, I really do. But I just don't think that Jonathan and I—"

A shorter pause, before Sarah says again, "Of course I understand. I do. Well, sure. Give us a call. Well, bye."

As she comes out to where Jonathan stands, waiting for her, Sarah's face is very white, except for her pink-tipped nose—too pink. She says, "One more thing that Hattie, quote, couldn't get out of. A big post-wedding do at Popsie Hooker's. She said of course she knew I'd been working my head off over dinner for them, so why didn't we just put it all in a basket and bring it on over there. They'd come and help." Uncon-sciously, perhaps, Sarah has perfectly imitated Hattie's inflections—even a few prolonged vowels; the effect is of a devastating irony, at which Jonathan does not smile.

"Jesus" is all he says, staring at Sarah, at her glistening, darkening eyes, as he wonders what he can do.

Sarah rubs one hand across her face, very slowly. She says, "I'm so tired. I think I'll take a nap."

"Good idea. Uh, how about going out to dinner?"

"Well, why not?" Her voice is absolutely level, controlled.

"I'll put some things away," Jonathan offers.

"Oh, good."

In the too small, crowded kitchen, Jonathan neatly packages the food they were to have eaten in freezer paper; he seals up and labels it all. He hesitates at marking the date, such an unhappy reminder, but then he simply writes down the neutral numbers: 8, 19. By the time they get around to these particular packages they will not attach any significance to that date, he thinks (he hopes).

He considers a nap for himself; he, too, is tired, suddenly, but he decides on a walk instead.

The still, hot, scrubby pinewoods beyond their house are now a familiar place to Jonathan; he walks through the plumy, triumphant weeds, the Queen Anne's lace and luxuriant broomstraw, over crum-bling, dry red clay. In the golden August sunlight, he considers what he has always recognized (or perhaps simply imagined that he saw) as a par-ticular look of Sundays, in terms of weather. Even if somehow he did not know that it was Sunday, he believes, he could see that it was, in the motes of sunlight. Here, now, today, the light and the stillness have the same qualities of light and stillness as in long-past Sundays in the Boston suburb where he grew up.

Obviously, he next thinks, they will have to leave this place, he and Sarah; it is not working out for them here, nothing is. They will have to go back to New York, look around, resettle. And to his surprise he feels a sort of regret at the thought of leaving this land, all this red clay that he would have said he hated.

Immersed in these and further, more abstract considerations (old mathematical formulas for comfort, and less comforting thoughts about the future of the earth), Jonathan walks for considerably longer than he intended.

Hurrying, as he approaches the house (which already needs new paint, he distractedly notes), Jonathan does not at all know what to expect: Sarah still sleeping (or weeping) in bed? Sarah (unaccountably, horribly) gone?

What he does find, though, on opening the front door, is the living room visibly pulled together, all tidied up: a tray with a small bowl of ice, some salted almonds in another bowl, on the coffee table. And Sarah, prettily dressed, who smiles as she comes toward him. She is carrying a bottle of chilled white wine.

Jonathan first thinks, Oh, the McElroys must have changed their minds, they're coming. But then he sees that next to the ice bowl are two, and only two, glasses.

In a friendly, familiar way he and Sarah kiss, and she asks, "How was your walk?"

"It was good. I liked it. A real Sunday walk."

Later on, he will tell her what he thought about their moving away—and as Jonathan phrases that announcement he considers how odd it is for him to think of New York as "away."

Over their first glass of wine they talk in a neutral but slightly stilted way, the way of people who are postponing an urgent subject; the absence of the McElroys, their broken plans, trivializes any other topic.

At some point, in part to gain time, Jonathan asks her, "Have I seen that dress before?" (He is aware of the "husbandliness" of the question; classically, *they* don't notice.)

Sarah smiles. "Well, actually not. I bought it a couple of months ago. I just haven't worn it." And then, with a recognizable shift in tone, and a tightening of her voice, she plunges in. "Remember that night when you were talking about the McElroys? When you said we weren't so high on their priority list?"

Well, Jesus, of course he remembers, in detail; but Jonathan only says, very flatly, "Yes."

"Well, it's interesting. Of course I've been thinking about them all day, off and on. And what you said. And oh dear, how right you were. I mean, I knew you were *right*—that was partly what I objected to." Saying this, Sarah raises her face in a full look at him, acknowledging past pain.

What can he say? He is quiet, waiting, as she continues.

"But it's interesting, how you put it," she tells him. "How accurately. Prophetic, really. A lot of talk, and those letters! All about wonderful us, how great we are. But when you come right down to it—"

"The bottom line is old friends," Jonathan contributes, tentatively.

Pleased with him, Sarah laughs, or nearly; the sound she makes is closer to a small cough. But "Exactly," she says. "They poke a lot of fun at Popsie Hooker, but the reality is, that's where they are."

He tries again. "Friendships with outsiders don't really count? Does that cut out all Yankees, really?" He is thinking, Maybe we don't have to leave, after all? Maybe Sarah was just settling in? Eventually she will be all right here?

Grasping at only his stated question, about Yankees, Sarah gleefully answers, "Oh, very likely!" and she does laugh. "Because Yankees might do, oh, almost anything at all. You just can't trust a one of them."

As she laughs again, as she looks at Jonathan, he recognizes some obscure and nameless danger in the enthusiastic glitter of her eyes, and he has then the quite irrational thought that she is looking at him as though he were her new best friend.

However, he is able quickly to dismiss that flashed perception, in the happiness of having his old bright strong Sarah restored to him, their old mutually appreciative dialogue continuing.

He asks her, "Well, time to go out to dinner?"

"Oh yes! Let's go," she says, quickly getting to her feet.

A Public Pool

Swimming

Reaching, pulling, gliding through the warm blue chlorinated water, I am strong and lithe: I am not oversized, not six feet tall, weighing one eighty-five. I am not myself, not Maxine.

I am fleet, possessed of powerful, deep energy. I could swim all day, swim anywhere. Sometimes I even wonder if I should try the San Francisco Bay, that treacherous cold tide-wracked water. People do swim there, they call themselves Polar Bears. Maybe I should, although by now I like it here in the Rossi Pool, swimming back and forth, doing laps in the Fast Lane, stretching and pulling my forceful, invisible body.

Actually the lane where I swim is not really Fast. I swim during Recreational Swimming, and during Rec. hours what was Fast during Laps is roped off for anyone to use who does laps—Slow, Medium, or genuinely Fast, which I am not.

Last summer I started off in Slow, and then I could not do many lengths at a time, 16 or 18 at most, and only sidestroke. But I liked it, the swimming and the calm, rested way it seemed to make me feel. And I thought that maybe, eventually I might get thinner, swimming. Also, it takes up a certain amount of time, which for an out-of-work living-at-home person is a great advantage. I have been laid off twice in the past five years, both times by companies going out of business; I have a real knack, my mother says. And how many hours a day can a young woman read? That is a question my mother often asks. She is a downtown saleslady, old but blonde, and very thin.

So—swimming.

After a month or so I realized that I was swimming faster than most of the people in Slow, and that some people who could barely swim at all were in my way. For another two or three weeks I watched Medium, wondering if I dare try to swim in there. One day I forced myself, jumping into Medium, the middle lane. I felt very anxious, but that was hardly an unfamiliar or unusual sort of emotion; sometimes shopping for groceries can have the same effect. And actually Medium turned out to be okay. There were a few hotshots who probably belonged in Fast but were too chicken to try it there, but quite a few people swam about the same as I did, and some swam slower.

Sometime during the fall—still warm outside, big dry yellow sycamore leaves falling down to the sidewalks—the pool schedule changed so that all the lap swimming was geared to people with jobs: Laps at noon and after five. Discouraging: I knew that all those people would be eager, pushy aggressive swimmers, kicking big splashes into my face as they swam past, almost shoving me aside in their hurry to get back to their wonderful jobs.

However, I found out that during Rec. there is always a lane roped off for laps, and the Rec. hours looked much better: mid to late afternoon, and those can be sort of cold hours at home, a sad end of daytime, with nothing accomplished.

In any case, that is why I now swim my laps during Rec., in the Fast lane. In the rest of the pool some little kids cavort around, and some grownups, some quite fat, some hardly able to swim at all. Sometimes a lot of school kids, mostly girls, mostly black, or Asian. A reflection of this neighborhood, I guess.

To Meet Someone

Of course I did not begin swimming with any specific idea that I might meet someone, any more than meeting someone is in my mind when I go out to the Ninth Avenue Library. Still, there is always that possibility: the idea of someone is always there, in a way, wherever I go. Maybe everywhere everyone goes, even if most people don't think of it that way?

For one thing, the area of the Rossi Recreation Center, where the pool is, has certain romantic associations for me: a long time ago, in the sixties, when I was only in junior high (and still thin!), that was where all the peace marches started; everyone gathered there on the Rossi playing field, behind the pool house, with their placards and flags and banners, in their costumes or just plain clothes. I went to all the marches; I loved them, and I hated LBJ, and I knew that his war was crazy, wicked, killing off kids and poor people, mostly blacks, was how it looked to me. Anyway, one Saturday in May, I fell in with a group of kids from another school, and we spent the rest of that day together, just messing around, walking almost all over town—eating pizza in North Beach and smoking a little dope in the park. Sort of making out, that night, at one of their houses, over on Lincoln Way. Three guys and a couple of girls, all really nice. I kept hoping that I would run into them somewhere again, but I never did. Or else they, too, underwent sudden changes, the way I did, and grew out-of-sight tall, and then fat. But I still think of them sometimes, walking in the direction of Rossi.

Swimming, though: even if you met someone it would be hard to tell anything about them, beyond the most obvious physical facts. For one thing almost no one says anything, except for a few superpolite people who say Sorry when they bump into you, passing in a lane. Or, there is one really mean-looking black woman, tall, and a very fast swimmer, who one day told me, "You ought to get over closer to the side." She ought to have been in East, is what I would like to have said, but did not.

The men all swim very fast, and hard, except for a couple of really fat ones; most men somersault backward at the end of each length, so as not to waste any time. A few women do that, too, including the big mean black one. There is one especially objectionable guy, tall and blond (but not as tall as I am), with a little blond beard; I used to watch him zip past, ploughing the water with his violent crawl, in Fast, when I was still pushing along in Medium. Unfortunately, now he, too, comes to swim in Rec., and mostly at the same times that I do. He swims so fast, so roughly cutting through the water; he doesn't even know I am there, nor probably anyone else. He is just the kind of guy who used to act as though I was air, along the corridors at Washington High.

I have noticed that very few old people come to swim at Rossi. And if they do you can watch them trying to hide their old bodies, slipping down into the water. Maybe for that reason, body shyness, they don't come back; the very old never come more than once to swim, which is a great pity, I think. The exercise would be really good for them, and personally I like very old people, very much. For a while I had a job in a home for old people, a rehabilitation center, so-called, and although in many ways it was a terrible job, really exhausting and sometimes very depressing, I got to like a lot of them very much. They have a lot to say that's interesting, and if they like you it's more flattering, I think, since they have more people to compare you with. I like *real* old people, who look their age.

People seem to come and go, though, at Rossi. You can see someone there regularly for weeks, or months, and then suddenly never again, and you don't know what has happened to that person. They could have switched over to the regular lap hours, or maybe found a job so that now they come very late, or early in the morning. Or they could have died, had a heart attack, or been run down by some car. There is no way you could ever know, and their sudden absences can seem very mysterious, a little spooky.

Garlic for Lunch

Since my mother has to stay very thin to keep her job (she has to look much younger than she is), and since God knows I should lose some weight, we usually don't eat much for dinner. Also, most of my mother's money goes for all the clothes she has to have for work, not to mention the rent and the horrible utility bills. We eat a lot of eggs.

However, sometimes I get a powerful craving for something really good, like a pizza, or some pasta, my favorite. I like just plain spaghetti, with scallions and garlic and butter and some Parmesan, mostly stuff we have already in the house. Which makes it all the harder not to yield to that violent urge for pasta, occasionally.

One night there was nothing much else around to eat, and so I gave in to my lust, so to speak. I made a big steaming bowl of oniony, garlicky, buttery spaghetti, which my mother, in a worse than usual mood, ate very little of. Which meant that the next day there was a lot left over, and at noontime, I was unable not to eat quite a lot of it for lunch. I brushed my teeth before I went off to swim, but of course that doesn't help a lot, with garlic. However, since I almost never talk to anyone at Rossi it didn't much matter, I thought.

I have worked out how to spend the least possible time undressed in the locker room: I put my bathing suit on at home, then sweatshirt and jeans, and I bring along underthings wrapped up in a towel. That way I just zip off my clothes to swim, and afterward I can rush back into them, only naked for an instant; no one has to see me. While I am swimming I leave the towel with the understuff wrapped up in it on the long bench at one side of the pool, and sometimes I have horrible fantasies of someone walking off with it; however, it is comforting to think that no one would know whose it was, probably.

I don't think very much while swimming, not about my old bra and panties, nor about the fact that I ate all that garlic for lunch. I swim fast and freely, going up to the end with a crawl, back to Shallow with my backstroke, reaching wide, stretching everything.

Tired, momentarily winded, I pause in Shallow, still crouched down in the water and ready to go, but resting.

Just then, startlingly, someone speaks to me, a man's conversational voice. "It's nice today," he says. "Not too many people, right?"

Standing up, I see that I am next to the blond-bearded man, the violent swimmer. Who has spoken.

Very surprised, I say, "Oh yes, it's really terrific, isn't it. Monday it was awful, so many people I could hardly move, really terrible. I hate it when it's crowded like that, hardly worth coming at all on those days, but how can you tell until you get here?" I could hear myself saying all that; I couldn't stop.

He looks up at me in—amazement? disgust? great fear, that I will say even more. It is hard to read the expression in his small blue blood-shot eyes, and he only mutters, "That's right," before plunging back into the water.

Was it my garlic breath or simply my height, my incredible *size* that drove him off like that? In a heavy way I wondered, as I continued to swim, all the rest of my laps, which seemed laborious. It could have been either, easily, or in fact anything about me could have turned him off, off and away, for good; I knew that he would never speak to me again. A pain which is close to and no doubt akin to lust lay heavily in my body's lower quadrant, hurtful and implacable.

Sex

The atmosphere in the pool is not exactly sexy, generally, although you might think that it would be, with everyone so stripped down, wearing next to nothing, and some of the women looking really great, so slim and trim, high-breasted, in their thin brief bathing suits.

Once, just as I was getting in I overheard what looked like the start of a romance between a young man, fairly good-looking, who was talking to a very pretty Mexican girl.

The girl said, "You're Brad?"

"No. Gregory."

"Well, Greg, I'll try to make it. Later."

But with brief smiles they then both plunged back into doing their laps, seeming not to have made any significant (sexual) contact.

I have concluded that swimming is not a very sexual activity. I think very infrequently of sex while actually swimming. Well, all sports are supposed to take your mind off sex, aren't they? They are supposed to make you miss it less?

The lifeguards, during swimming hours, usually just sit up on their high wooden lifeguard chairs, looking bored. A couple of youngish, not very attractive guys. Every now and then one of the guys will walk around the pool very slowly, probably just to break his own monotony, but trying to look like a person on patrol.

One afternoon I watched one of those guys stop at Shallow, and stare down for a long time at a little red-haired girl who was swimming there. She was a beautiful child, with narrow blue eyes and long wet red hair, a white little body, as lithe as a fish, as she laughed and slipped around. The lifeguard stared and stared, and I knew—I could tell that sex was on his mind. Could he be a potential child molester?

I myself think of sex more often, in spite of swimming, since the day Blond Beard spoke to me, the day I'd had all that garlic for lunch. I hate to admit this.

The Shrink

An interesting fact that I have gradually noticed as I come to Rossi, to swim my laps, is that actually there is more variety among the men's trunks than among the bathing suits the women wear. The men's range from cheap, too-tight Lastex to the khaki shorts with thin blue side stripes that they advertise at Brooks, or Robert Kirk. Whereas, as I noted early on, all the women wear quite similar-looking dark suits. Do the men who are rich, or at least getting along okay in the world, not bother to hide it when they come to a cheap public pool, while the women do? A puzzle. I cannot quite work it out. Blond Beard wears new navy Lastex trunks, which might mean anything at all.

Most people, including a lot of the men, but not Blond Beard, wear bathing caps, which makes it even harder to tell people apart, and would make it almost impossible, even, to recognize someone you knew. It is not surprising that from time to time I see someone I think I know, or have just met somewhere or other. At first, remembering the peace march kids, I imagined that I saw one or all of them, but that could have been just hope, a wishful thought. I thought I saw my old gym teacher, also from junior-high days. And one day I saw a man who looked like my father, which was a little crazy, since he split for Seattle when I was about five years old; I probably wouldn't know him if I did see him somewhere, much less in a pool with a bathing cap on.

But one day I saw an old woman with short white hair, swimming very fast, who I really thought was the shrink I went to once in high school, as a joke.

Or, going to the shrink started out to be a joke. The school had a list of ones that you could go to, if you had really "serious problems," and to me and my girlfriend, then, Betty, who was black, it seemed such a ludicrous idea, paying another person just to listen, telling them about your sex life, all like that, that we dreamed up the idea of inventing some really serious problems, and going off to some fool doctor and really putting him on, and at the same time finding out what it was like, seeing shrinks.

Betty, who was in most ways a lot smarter than me, much faster to catch on to things, chickened out early on; but she kept saying that I should go; Betty would just help me make up some stuff to say. And we did; we spent some hilarious afternoons at Betty's place in the project, making up lists of "serious problems": heavy drugs, of course, and dealers. And stepfathers or even fathers doing bad sex things to you, and boys trying to get you to trick. All those things were all around Betty's life, and I think they scared her, really, but she laughed along with me, turning it into one big joke between us.

I made the appointment through the guidance office, with a Dr. Sheinbaum, and I went to the address, on Steiner Street. And that is where the joke stopped being a joke.

A Public Pool

A nice-looking white-haired lady (a surprise right there; I had expected some man) led me into a really nice-looking living room, all books and pictures and big soft comfortable leather furniture. And the lady, the doctor, asked me to sit down, to try to tell her about some of the things that upset me.

I sat down in a soft pale-colored chair, and all of the funny made-up stuff went totally out of my mind—and I burst into tears. It was horrible, great wracking sobs that I absolutely could not stop. Every now and then I would look up at the doctor, and see that gentle face, that intelligent look of caring, and for some reason that made me cry much harder, even.

Of course I did not tell Betty—or anyone—about crying like that. All I said about going to the shrink was that it was all right, no big deal. And I said about the good-looking furniture. Betty was interested in things like that.

But could the fast-swimming older woman be that shrink? Well, she could be; it seemed the kind of thing that she might do, not caring what anyone thought, or who might see her. But she would never remember or recognize me—or would she?

Looking for Work

The job search is something that I try not to think about, along with sex, general deprivation. It is what I should be doing, naturally; and in theory that is what I do all day, look for work. However, these days I seldom get much further than the want ads in the paper, those columns and columns of people saying they want secretaries, or sales people. And no one, not in a million years, would think of hiring me for either of those slots. Secretaries are all about the same size, very trim and tidy-looking, very normal, and so are people in sales—just ask my mother.

Sometimes an ad for a waitress sounds possible, and that is something I've done; I had a part-time waitress job the summer I got out of Washington High. But in those days I was thinner, and just now my confidence is pretty low. In my imagination, prospective employers, restaurant owners take one look at me and they start to sneer: "We don't even have the space for a person your size," or some such snub.

Instead I swim, and swim, swim—for as long as I can, every day. I can feel my muscles stretching, pulling, getting longer, in the warm strong water.

Hello

An odd coincidence: on a Tuesday afternoon—short Rec. hours, one-thirty to three—both Blond Beard *and* the big black woman who told me to swim closer to the side, so crossly—both those people on that same day said Hello to me, very pleasantly.

First, I had just jumped down into the pool, the shallow end of the lap section, when Blond Beard swam up and stood beside me for a minute. Looking up at me, he said Hello, and he smiled. However, his small pale eyes were vague; very likely he did not remember that we sort of talked before (hopefully, he did not remember the garlic).

I concentrated on not making too much of that encounter.

Later, when I had finished swimming and was drying off and dressing in the locker room, I was half aware that someone else was in there, too, on the other side of a row of lockers. Hurrying, not wanting to see anyone (or anyone to see me!), I was about to rush out of the room when at the exit door I almost bumped into the big black woman. In fact, it was a little funny, we are so nearly the exact same size. We both smiled; maybe she saw the humor in it, too? And then she said, "Say, your stroke's coming along real good."

"Oh. Uh, thanks."

"You're a real speeder these days."

I felt a deep pleasure in my chest. It was like praise from a teacher, someone in charge. We walked out of the building together, the black woman going up across the playground, where the peace marches gathered, maybe toward Geary Boulevard. And I walked down Arguello, out into the avenues. Home.

Warmth

The water in the pool is warm. In our cold apartment, where my mother screams over the higher and higher utility bills and keeps the heat down, I only have to think about that receiving warmness, touching all my skin, to force myself out into the cold and rain, to walk the long blocks to Rossi Pool, where quickly undressed I will slip down into it.

And swim.

In January, though, the weather got suddenly warmer. The temperature in the pool also seemed to have suddenly changed; it was suddenly cooler. Distrustful, as I guess I tend to be regarding my perceptions, I wondered if the water only seemed cooler. Or, had they turned it down because of the warmer weather, economizing, as my mother does? In any case it was disappointing, and the pool was much less welcoming, no matter how falsely spring-like the outside air had turned.

"Do you think the water's colder?" It was Blond Beard who asked this of me one day; we were standing momentarily in the shallow end. But although I was the person he had chosen to ask, I was still sure that for him I was no one; he remembers nothing of me from one tiny, minor contact to another. I am a large non-person.

I told him, "Yes, it seems a little colder to me" (not wanting to say too much—again).

"They must have turned it down."

Swimming

Since the pool is 100 feet long, a half mile is 26 lengths, which is what I try to do every day. "I swim three miles a week," would sound terrific, to anyone, or even, "I swim a little over two miles a week." Anyone would be impressed, except my mother.

On some days, though, I have to trick myself into swimming the whole 26. "I'm tired, didn't sleep too well, 16 lengths is perfectly okay, respectable," I tell myself. And then, having done the 16, I will say (to myself) that I might as well do a couple more, or four more. And if you get to 20 you might as well go on to 26, as I almost always do.

On other, better days I can almost forget what I am doing; that is, I forget to count. I am only aware of a long strong body (mine) pulling through the water, of marvelous muscles, a strong back, and long, long legs.

The Neighborhood

Sometimes, walking around the neighborhood, I see swimmers from the pool—or, people I think I have seen in swimming; in regular clothes it is hard to be sure.

Once, passing a restaurant out on Clement Street I was almost sure that the waitress with her back to the window was the big black woman, formerly cross but now friendly and supportive. Of course I could go in and check it out, even say Hello, but I didn't want to do that, really. But I was pleased with just the idea that she might be there, with a waitress job in such a nice loose-seeming coffee place. I even reasoned that if they hired that woman, big as she is, mightn't someone hire me, about the same size? (I think swimming is making me more optimistic, somehow.) Maybe I should look harder, not be so shy about applying for waitress jobs?

However, one day in late June, there is no mistaking Blond Beard, who comes up to me on Arguello, near Clement: I am just coming out of the croissant place where I treated myself to a cup of hot chocolate. I am celebrating, in a way: the day before I had pulled all my courage together and went out to a new "rehabilitation place" for old people, out in the Sunset, and they really seemed to like me. I am almost hired, I think. They would give me a place to live—I could leave home!

"Hey! I know you from swimming, don't I? In Rossi?" Blond Beard has come up close to me; he is grinning confidently up into my face. His clothes are very sharp, all clean and new, like from a window at Sears.

"You look so good, all that swimming's really trimmed you down," he tells me. And then, "This is a coincidence, running into you like this when I was needing a cup of coffee. Come on back in and keep me company. My treat."

He is breathing hard up into my face, standing there in the soft new sunlight. I am overwhelmed by the smell of Juicy Fruit—so much, much worse than garlic, I suddenly decide. And I hate sharp clothes.

Stepping back I say, "Thanks, but I have to go home now," and I move as smoothly as though through water.

I leave him standing there.

I swim away.

Waiting for Stella

Actually it is Jimmy, Stella's fourth and final husband (Stella died a month ago), for whom everyone is waiting, all these old people, in this large sunny clearing in a grove of ancient redwoods. It is high noon, on a bright October day, and time for lunch, but Rachel, the hostess, has delayed serving the food, because of Jimmy's lateness. This will be everyone's first sight of him since Stella's death; he took off for Santa Barbara just afterward to visit a sister there, and presumably to recuperate, traveling in Stella's old car. Perhaps the car is making him late this morning? The guests, old friends, sip nervously at tomato juice or club soda, while a few of the hardier ones have white wine; they are all in their seventies or eighties, except for a young dark, vividly pretty girl, Day, a visiting friend of Rachel's, who will help with lunch.

Everyone, including Rachel and her husband, Baxter, and Day, the visiting girl, is seated at a long bandanna-cloth-covered table, on benches. Not far from the table is a small oval concrete swimming pool, its unused murky water now flat and still. Here and there in the grove are clumps of huge thick-fronded ferns, a dusty gray green, quite motionless, in the moted sunlight.

They are all waiting for Jimmy, of course, but it is Stella whose lively absence dominates the mood, so that several people, especially Rachel and Baxter, have to remind themselves that they are waiting for Jimmy, not for Stella.

Rachel and Baxter's house is up on a knoll, invisible from the pool, among tall thick eucalyptus trees, gray thickets of manzanita. It is a big house, though cheaply and somewhat flimsily constructed of clapboard, now nicely weathered to silver. It was a great bargain forty years ago when Rachel and her first husband had it built. Now it is probably worth a lot of money, as she and Baxter wryly say to each other from time to time, and they add, "but only if we sell it." (Baxter is Rachel's third husband, and surely her last, she thinks.) Near the house, a little way down toward the pool, is the guest cabin, slatted, green.

All the houses in this small enclave, in the Santa Cruz Mountains, are somewhat similar, as, not quite accidentally, are their owners; friends, they all were professional people, "liberals," mildly intellectual. Rachel was a doctor, a professor of medicine, rather distinguished; Baxter, although he inherited money, was an art critic. Stella was a painter.

What once were vacation homes now house their retirements.

In those younger, summer days, feelings sometimes ran high: dissensions occurred over love affairs, real or imagined; opposing political views split their ranks. But now old feuds are quieted, if not forgotten—especially today, as in an almost unified way they think about Stella, the first of them to die, and they think about Jimmy, who is *very* late.

Now, conferring with Day, Rachel decides to go ahead and serve the first course, a gazpacho, which has already been brought down and is sitting there on the table, in its huge green-glazed tureen. And so Rachel ladles out the soup, and Day takes the bowls around to everyone.

Actually, Stella has always been a sort of unifying principle for this group, in that they have generally been united in opposition to whatever she was doing. Not actual opposition to her views, but Stella always, somehow, went too far. Wonderful of her to march in Selma at already sixty-odd, but did she have to get arrested, so purposefully, and spend a week in that jail? Or, more recently, was it necessary, really, that she scale the fence at Diablo Canyon, protesting nuclear power? Not to mention the fact that she often drank too much, and almost always talked too much, with her proud white tooth-flashing grin; she had too many husbands and lovers (though fortunately, it was sometimes remarked, no children).

Her final marriage to Jimmy Scott, a former alcoholic, former film director (not important), was hard to understand, the other husbands having been, in their ways, almost predictable: Jack, a Communist, and Jewish (this was daring, in 1922, for a New England girl of "good"—

Republican, Unitarian—family); Horace, a black longshoreman; and Yosh, a Japanese painter, whom she married just after Pearl Harbor (of course). But—Jimmy?

During the illness preceding Stella's death, however, the mercifully short three months, Jimmy's behavior toward her was observed to be exemplary. It was hardly a time when anyone would have behaved badly, but still his patience was remarkable. He searched for out-of-print books that Stella mentioned wanting to reread, for out-of-season flowers for her bedroom (they were not rich people, not at all), for special delicate foods, rare fruits to tempt her waning appetite.

In the last awful month of her life, although she stayed at home, in the house up the road from Rachel and Baxter's, Stella refused (through Jimmy, of course) to let anyone visit her; not even Rachel, a doctor, was allowed to see her then, which no one quite understood, except, just possibly, Rachel.

Of the dozen people there—thirteen, counting Day—only Day is not thinking in a concentrated way about Stella. Day is thinking painfully, obsessively of Allen, the lover whom she came to California to see, but with whom things did not work out; they just broke up in San Francisco, where Allen lives. Scenes and quarrels, all terrible to recall. Passing breadsticks, Day considers the phrase "to break up." It is odd, she thinks, that people always say "break up *with*," since the whole point of breaking up is that you are no longer *with* but alone.

In order not to think about Allen, and then, too, because it seems appropriate, Day makes a conscious effort to think about Stella, whom she met fairly often, over the years, at Rachel's. (Day's mother, also a doctor, a friend of Rachel's, named Day for her heroine, Dorothy Day, who was also much admired by Rachel.) Stella was perfectly all right, Day thinks, but she talked so much. And that hair. Bright red hair, for a woman in her seventies or (probably) eighties? More generously, Day then admits to herself that you can't tell what you'll do that far ahead. She herself at eighty might dye her hair purple, or green, a one-person revival of punk, in the year two thousand and whatever, out of sheer boredom with living that long.

Stella never seemed bored with her old age—you had to give her that. And even if Jimmy bored her she never let it be known. ("Jimmy was actually more interesting as an alcoholic," Baxter has remarked. "Poor Stella! No luck at all with men.")

Day, who in her grief is not even aware of how pretty she is, now sits down with her own cold bowl of soup, next to Baxter, who must have been extremely handsome, a long time ago, Day imagines.

Baxter, who dislikes gazpacho (the peppers seem to disagree with him, or perhaps the cucumbers), looks for diversion at Day's long thin brown legs, now exposed beneath her loose flowered skirt, in high rope clogs. Day's legs, which Baxter much admires, lead him back to a sensual dream of Stella. He sees a room in the Sherry Netherland, in New York (he has just married Rachel; she is waiting for him, up in Connecticut— she is giving a seminar at Yale). Gold coverlets drawn back on sumptuous beds, in the half-light of an August afternoon. Champagne in a silver bucket, two chilled glasses. And Stella: all that pink-gold flesh (she was fairly plump in those days), all that flesh, half revealed, half concealed. Silk, rows of lace. That flesh, breasts, and that brilliant hair, spread on her pillow, his pillow.

But even in his dream he, Baxter, is actually sitting there alone, and fully dressed. And he never saw any flesh of Stella's beyond that revealed in a modest bathing suit. For Stella, if the truth were known, and he trusts that it is not—Stella had stood him up. There he was, expecting her, in that room, with champagne, and the next day she had the consummate gall to say, "But Baxter, darling, I can't believe you were serious." And that awful laugh. What a bitch, when you came right down to it—really surprising that more people didn't see through her. He wonders if Rachel did; he has never been sure just how Rachel felt about Stella. Well, there's no possibility of understanding women, as he has always said.

More crossly than he meant to, Baxter whispers to Day, "Why do you think Rachel serves this damned soup so often?"

Startled, Day answers him literally. "She thinks it's good in hot weather, I guess." And then she says the next thing that enters her grief-dulled mind: "And it seems a more leftist sort of soup than vichyssoise."

Baxter emits a loud cackling laugh. "Oh, very good," he tells Day, who has not meant to be funny, especially. "A leftist soup. That's *very good.*"

Baxter's laugh and some words of this small exchange have caught everyone's attention, so that it all has to be repeated several times, and explained, many of those old ears not being quite what they once were. No one seems to think "leftist soup" is quite as funny as Baxter did. (Rachel especially, in the way of wives, did not find it awfully funny. Why did she marry Baxter, she wonders. But even if she knew, it is much too late to reconsider.) However, at least a diversion was created, from so many sad thoughts of Stella, and such anxiety as how to deal with Jimmy: how will he be?

This October day is unseasonably hot; everyone has agreed on that, and commented at length. Even in this shaded glen, where usually it is cool, often cold, almost always too cold for swimming in the dark green-ish pool, today it is very warm, so that swimming is at least discussed. Warm shafts of light fall dustily between the redwoods, on the thick still tessellated fronds of ferns.

Stella, of course, would have been in hours ago, flopping around like a porpoise and exhorting everyone else to come in, too. No one has remarked on this probability, but what Stella would have been doing has occurred to everyone there. They will continue to think, in other con-texts, of what Stella would have done.

However, the heat is actually a relief to so many old bones; they bask and relax in it. And the warm weather seems a reprieve of sorts, to these old people. The fact is that their location, in these mountains south of San Francisco, is not an ideal spot for the retired, for the very old. They are vulnerable to such extremes of cold, and to floods, from moun-tain streams, as well as to spectres of isolation, loneliness, helplessness. Danger. They have all thought and talked from time to time of moving somewhere else, but where? And for them to move would seem a sort of giving up, giving in, a yielding to old age and infirmity.

This day, though, is reassuring; they are still all right, exactly where they are.

And, as no one says, and perhaps no one is really aware, it is rather a relief not to have Stella around, loudly splashing in the pool, and always urging them all to exceed themselves, somehow.

· · ·

Although they were very close friends, as far as anyone knew, and were almost exactly the same age, Rachel's and Stella's personal styles were very different. Rachel's low-key, toned-down quiet mode could almost have been developed in opposition to Stella's flamboyance. All three of Rachel's husbands, including Baxter, have affectionately compared her to a wren, a coincidence that tactful Rachel has mentioned to no one, surely not to Baxter, who despite his money and good looks is quite insecure.

Rachel is small, with neat gray-brown hair and finely lined lightly tanned skin. When Baxter came home to her that time in Connecticut, just mentioning that he had "caught a glimpse" of Stella in New York, Rachel quite accurately surmised what had happened: Baxter had made a pass, of some sort, and Stella in some way had turned him down. Curiously, at first she was a little annoyed at Stella: poor Baxter, aging is hard on such a handsome man. But it soon came to her, causing a wry, inward smile, that after all if Stella had said yes, she, Rachel, would have been considerably more annoyed.

Standing just off from the group, near the end of the table, Day and Rachel now consult with each other, Rachel saying, "Well, I just don't know. Jimmy's usually so punctual," and she frowns.

"He might feel worse if we waited," Day offers. "Worse about everything, I mean."

Rachel gives Day an attentive, interested look. (Rachel listens to what other people say.) "Well, of course you're absolutely right," she says. "Besides, it's making everyone nervous. We'll just go ahead with the salmon."

"He might always call and say that he isn't coming after all," Day further contributes. She is thinking: Allen might call.

"Oh, right," says Rachel.

It is true that the prolonged absence of Jimmy is nervously felt, all around. People speculate about what could have happened. Flat tires are mentioned, as well as being out of gas, or lost. What no one voices is the fear, felt by almost all of them, that he could have started drinking again. Stella was believed to have helped get him off the bottle.

Someone, more mean-spirited than the rest, has just said, "I hope our dear Jimmy hasn't stopped off at some bar," when fortunately Rachel and Day arrive with their platters of cold salmon, the glistening silvery pink surrounded by various shades of green—parsley and several sauces—so that everyone can exclaim over the beauty of the food.

One moment after everyone is served, there comes the sound and then a quick flashed glimpse in the driveway above of a hastily braked and parked red sports car.

What an odd car for a man whose wife has just died is what everyone instantly, simultaneously thinks—everyone but Day, who has recognized the car. It is not Jimmy's car but Allen's, and she begins to run back up the path that she has just come down with her platter, now going several times as fast as before: she is almost flying.

Behind her, a guest who has not yet understood that it is not Jimmy's car after all, and who has apparently not forgotten some ancient political feud, is heard to mutter, "Perfect car for a red-haired Communist!"

Half an hour later (still no sign of Jimmy), a few people are on their second helpings of salmon. Rachel keeps an experienced-hostess eye on all the plates; she is hoping for not much left over, Baxter not being overly fond of salmon (hard to think what he does like, really), and she cannot bear waste. It is sad, she thinks, the loss of appetite suffered by the old, and she remembers her own gnawing hungers as a scrawny Brooklyn girl. It is far worse than the diminution of sexual appetite, one's lessening interest in food. After all, most people eat three times a day, most not truly poor Americans.

She is allowing her mind to wander foolishly. Rachel looks across the table at Day and Allen, who appear to be absolutely, heedlessly absorbed in each other. She looks at her watch, unobtrusively, she hopes, and frowns.

It is so strange, Day is thinking, her feelings on being with Allen. Now. He is so near that she can smell him, his known scents of clean skin and recent soap, clean cotton work shirt just slightly perspired on. He is so near, so known and loved (she supposes) and still so strange, unreal to her. Their quarrels, too, are unreal, all suddenly dissolved. "Whatever was that all about?" Allen asked her, after their long greeting kiss, as hand in hand they walked down to the shaded dell together, and Day said, "Oh, I don't *know.*"

Now, though, it is as if she had known all along that Allen would come to her here; she has been waiting for Allen, as everyone else waited for Jimmy, and thought about Stella.

But, most curiously, she is aware in some depth of herself of the faintest disappointment that he has come, after all. She feels the lack of her recent misery; weirdly, she misses its bite; the very sharpness of that anguish seems a loss.

Then quite suddenly everything that is happening is interrupted, all the eating and serving and clearing, all the intense thoughts of everyone there, all rudely broken into by the sharp repeated blast of a horn, the country sound of a very old Ford. Stella's car: it is Jimmy at last, of course.

Straining to look up through the immense, thick trees, enormous trunks of the venerable redwoods, the smaller eucalyptus, manzanitas, they can just see the old rattletrap that Stella always drove, as shabby and dusty as though she drove it still. The door slams three, then four times (it is remembered that Stella never could get that door shut), and from way up there comes the jaunty sound of Jimmy calling, "Halloo, hallooo!"

"Oh dear, he must be drunk," someone says.

"Oh, I hope not," says Baxter eagerly, clearly hoping that he is.

"He is not drunk," Rachel fiercely tells them both.

What Day first sees of Jimmy, and maybe the others, too, is the bright stripes of the sweater he is wearing, a brilliant orangy red, on a darker background. What Day thinks is: How amazing, his sweater is striped with the color of Stella's hair.

In a curious way, Jimmy looks both smaller and livelier than usual. He fairly runs down the path toward them all.

Watching him, as everyone is, several people seem to decide that perhaps so much attention paid to his arrival will be awkward, and small attempts are made at conversation, here and there. However, none succeed, and by the time Jimmy, quite out of breath, arrives at the end of the table, Rachel's end, they are all staring, and smiling welcomes in his direction.

"Well," Jimmy at last gets out, "you all look like you'd been waiting for somebody more important. Or bigger, anyway," and with an odd quirky smile he actually turns to look behind him, as though the larger, more important person had followed him down the path.

"Jimmy dear, don't be silly," Rachel chides him. "But what ever happened? You're so late."

"Well, it's that damned old car of Stell's, of course. Damned old thing wouldn't start, and then I had to wait for the tow truck."

"Well, fortunately everything's cold, and there's lots left. Here's a plate, just sit right here by me." A small catch can be heard in Rachel's voice, as she speaks to Jimmy, and tears are seen in her eyes. But since all these people are so old, and given to emotional moments, no one wonders why at this particular moment of first seeing Jimmy Rachel should be so moved.

Across the table from Rachel and Jimmy, Baxter has been struck by a new thought, one that makes him very happy. Alcoholics are almost always impotent, he thinks; that fellow Jimmy very likely never had her, either, the poor dumb sod.

Vastly cheered (and quite wrong: Stella and Jimmy enjoyed a spirited sexual rapport), Baxter thinks again of Stella, her often imagined, forever inaccessible flesh—ah, no one now! And he smiles in a warm, comradely way in Jimmy's direction.

Jimmy is talking about his labors with Stella's papers. "So much!" he tells everyone, with a pixieish widening of his old bright blue eyes. "So many papers! She wrote to everyone, you know, and they always wrote her back, and she kept everything. Even foolish letters from me. I was proud to come upon them." With a look of surprise he beams at his audience, then stops for a bite of salmon.

They are all regarding Jimmy as though he were a brand-new person, some visitor of charm and distinction. (It is Baxter who makes this observation to himself, and quite without pleasure.)

"It's going to take me a good ten years to get through it all," announces Jimmy (as though he could count on living ten more years). Everyone smiles at him with happy approval (as though they, too, could live that long).

Almost from one moment to the next, the day that seemed so unseasonably warm has turned cool—a sudden chill in the air, and a breeze, reminding everyone that the season is actually autumn, that summery warmth at noon was delusional. And they are none of them as young as they once were.

"I could go up and get some sweaters," Rachel offers. "Day and I—"

But they all decline. They have all been there long enough, they almost say.

It is somehow assumed that when everyone leaves Rachel will have some time alone with Jimmy, which they no doubt need—they will want to talk about Stella—and that Day will go off with that fellow, that young Allen (well, off to bed). And that Baxter will take a nap, by himself.

All these things do take place, but not quite as anyone would have expected.

In bed, after a brief interval of love, Day and Allen take up their argument again.

Allen believes that they should marry. In a fast-disintegrating world, a personal commitment is almost all that is left, he thinks. Let us love one another or die, he says. Ah, love, let us be true. Besides, he is making a lot of money in San Francisco, in real estate.

Well, Day does not see marriage as an ultimate commitment. She does love Allen, and she is true. But still. And she has hopes of being accepted at law school, in New Haven.

Well, if she must, then why not Stanford, or Berkeley, or Davis?

In the waning late-afternoon light, the cool fall end of that golden October day, their words rise in the air, in circles and patterns that then, like smoke, dissolve, and Day and Allen fall asleep, in the high narrow guest bed, in the flimsily slatted green-stained cabin.

.   .   .

In the kitchen, clearing up, Rachel and Jimmy do not fall into a conversation having to do with Stella; they do not even mention Stella. Instead, they discuss Santa Barbara, and Jimmy's plans to go there, to live with his sister.

"It's a most charming place," he tells Rachel, as he polishes glasses (remembering that Stella thought they came out brighter with paper than with linen. "Such an affectation, linen towels," she used to say). "And the flowers," Jimmy now tells Rachel, quickly. Well, the flowers. And it's interesting, he continues, how some people seem to mellow with age: his sister, who for years was such a terror, now is very nice, a kind and pleasant person.

"I suppose that must be true," murmurs Rachel, who is wondering if either of those adjectives, kind and pleasant, would ever apply to Baxter, and if so, when.

"When I'm settled there, you've got to come and visit," Jimmy says.

Baxter goes off to bed, alone, of course, but despite the huge new down quilt and the lowered blinds and all the soothing books (his favorites, Ruskin and Swinburne, odd tastes, perhaps somewhat misleading, having to do with his mother), despite all the available comforts of the bedroom, poor Baxter is quite unable to sleep, even to doze for a minute or two.

He is thinking of Day and Allen, rancorously, uncontrollably. His are not exactly personal thoughts; he is simply thinking of youth, of obviously taken-for-granted health and sensuality. The condition of youth now seems to Baxter a club from which he has abruptly and most unfairly been excluded.

A couple of hours later Jimmy has gone. Outside, the night has turned black and cold, and a wind has come up, rattling leaves, shaking windowpanes, but Rachel remains in the small bright kitchen. Everything is clean and put away, and she is tired. She has made herself a small pot of tea, and she sits sipping, at the kitchen table. She thinks, How wonderful not to be talking to anyone, not even thinking of people.

However, this is not to last, as she might have known that it would not: light footsteps in the passageway hurry toward her, someone else with something to say, or ask.

And of course it is Day.

"Well," Day begins, with a smile of pure pleasure at the sight of Rachel which almost dissolves Rachel's wish that she not be there. "Oh, I hoped I'd find you," says Day. "I slept for a while, and I had such an odd dream, about Stella. So vivid." She smiles again, disarmingly. "In the dream, I asked her point-blank how come she married Jimmy, and she told me, but what's terrible is that I can't remember what she said!"

"Would you like some tea? The cups are right there behind you."

Day sits down with her tea. In her old loose blue cotton robe, with her just-washed face, she looks even younger than she is. She says, "Well, it was really a nice lunch party?"

What was intended as a statement has come out as a question, at which Rachel smiles. "I guess," she says. "I wanted Jimmy to have a good time, and to feel that everyone liked him, after all. I wish that damned old car hadn't made him so late. On the other hand . . ."

She has left her thought dangling, but Day takes it up. "On the other hand, maybe just as well? Time enough?" she asks, in her clear young voice.

"Could be. Enough of all of us. We don't really make up for Stella." She adds, after the smallest pause, "And I thought Baxter was especially cross. Men are so much less forgiving than women are, don't you think?" She sighs, at this quite unintended afterthought.

"Oh really, how do you mean?"

Day is so eager that Rachel regrets her observation. "Well, maybe it's not even true."

But Day is relentless. "What does Baxter have against Jimmy, do you think?" she pursues.

"Well, basically just his marrying Stella. It was Stella that Baxter had it in for, so to speak."

Day asks, "Because of her politics, you mean?"

"Well, that among other things. Actually, a lot of men didn't like her, not at all. It was odd, I always thought. Men are supposed to like beautiful women." Rachel's voice is reedy, low and rather tired, an old thrush.

"You mean, men fell in love with her but really didn't like her much?" Day's tone is that of someone zeroing in—perhaps a lawyer's tone.

Rachel smiles. With exhausted emphasis she says, "Exactly. That's just what Stella said, in fact. I think it made her lonely, a lot of the time."

"Especially since no one would see what was going on. Oh, I can see that," Day improvises.

"And Jimmy liked her very much, it's that simple," Rachel concludes. "She said she could hardly believe it." And she adds, as though it were irrelevant, "I think everyone is a little mad at Stella now for having died."

Ignoring that last (could she not have heard it? did Rachel not actually say it, only think it?), Day smiles; she is in love with this conversation. She now asks, "Did you notice Jimmy's sweater? Those stripes?"

"Exactly the color of Stella's hair. I saw that too."

"Do you think he thought of it?" Day is very serious.

"When he bought the sweater?" Rachel pauses before she answers. "No, I'm sure the choice was quite unconscious. But still."

"Yes, still. He did buy it." And Day smiles again, as though they had, together, understood and settled everything.

And Rachel, who feels that almost nothing has been understood, or settled, who herself does not see how she can get through the coming winter, much less the rest of her life—Rachel smiles back at her.

Barcelona

In the darkened, uneven cobbled square, in the old quarter of Barcelona, the Barrio Gótico, the middle-aged American couple who walk by appear to be just that: American, middle-aged. The man is tall and bald; his head shines dimly as he and his wife cross the shaft of light from an open doorway. She is smaller, with pale hair; she walks fast to keep up with her husband. She is wearing gold chains, and they, too, shine in the light. She carries a small bag in which there could be—more gold? money? some interesting pills? They pass a young Spaniard lounging in a corner whose face the man for no reason takes note of.

Persis Fox, the woman, is a fairly successful illustrator, beginning to be sought after by New York publishers, but she sees herself as being in most ways a coward, a very fearful person; she is afraid of planes, of high bridges, she is overly worried by the illnesses of children—a rather boring list, as she thinks of it. Some years ago she was afraid that Thad, her husband, who teaches at Harvard, would take off with some student, some dark, sexily athletic type from Texas, possibly. More recently she has been frightened by accounts everywhere of muggings, robberies, rapes. She entirely believes in the likelihood of nuclear war. She can and does lie awake at night with such thoughts, for frozen hours.

However, walking across these darkened cobbles, in the old quarter of Barcelona, toward a restaurant that Cambridge friends have recommended, she is not afraid at all, only interested in what she is seeing: just before the square, an arched and windowed walk up above the alley, now crenellated silhouettes, everywhere blackened old stones. Also, she is hungry, looking forward to the seafood for which this restaurant is famous. And she wishes that Thad would not walk so fast; by now he is about five feet ahead of her, in an alley.

In the next instant, though, before she has seen or heard any person approaching, someone is running past her in the dark—but not past; he is beside her, a tall dark boy, grabbing at her purse, pulling its short strap. Persis' first instinct is to let him have it, not because she is afraid—she is not, still not, afraid—but from a conditioned reflex, instructing her to give people what they want: children, her husband.

In the following second a more primitive response sets in, and she cries out, "No!"—as she thinks, Kindergarten, some little boy pulling a toy away. And next thinks, Not kindergarten. Spain. A thief.

He is stronger, and with a sudden sharp tug he wins; he has pulled the bag from her and run off, as Persis still yells, "No!"—and as (amazingly!) she remembers the word for thief. "LADRÓN!" she cries out. *"Ladrón!"*

Then suddenly Thad is back (Persis has not exactly thought of him in those seconds), and almost before she has finished saying "He took my bag!" Thad is running toward the square, where the thief went. Thad is running, running—so tall and fast, such a sprint, as though this were a marathon, or Memorial Drive, where he usually runs. He is off into the night, as Persis yells again, *"Ladrón!"* and she starts out after him.

Persis is wearing low boots (thank God), not heels, and she can hear Thad's whistle, something he does with two fingers in his mouth, intensely shrill, useful for summoning children from ski slopes or beaches as night comes on. Persis, also running, follows the sound. She comes at last to a fairly wide, dimly lit street where Thad is standing, breathing hard.

She touches his arm. "Thad—"

Still intent on the chase, he hardly looks at her. He is not doing this for her; it is something between men. He says, "I think he went that way."

"But Thad—"

The street down which he is pointing, and into which he now begins to stride, with Persis just following—this street's darkness is broken at intervals by the steamy yellow windows of shabby restaurants, the narrow open door of a bar. Here and there a few people stand in doorways, watching the progress of the Americans. Thad sticks his head into the restaurants, the bar. "I don't see him," he reports back each time.

Well, of course not. And of course each time Persis is glad—glad that the boy is hidden somewhere. Gone. Safe, as she and Thad are safe.

They reach the end of the block, when from behind them a voice calls out, in English, not loudly, "Lady, this your bag?"

Thad and Persis turn to see a dark, contemptuous young face, a tall boy standing in a doorway. Not, Thad later assures Persis, and later still their friends—not the thief, whom he saw as they first crossed the square, and would recognize. But a friend of his?

The boy kicks his foot at something on the cobbles, which Thad walks over to pick up, and which is Persis' bag.

"I can't believe it!" she cries out, aware of triteness, as Thad hands over the bag to her. But by now, now that everything is over, she is seriously frightened; inwardly she trembles.

"Well, we got it." Thad speaks calmly, but Persis can hear the pride in his voice, along with some nervousness. He is still breathing hard, but he has begun to walk with his purposeful stride again. "The restaurant must be down here," he tells her.

Astoundingly, it is; after a couple of turns they see the name on a red neon sign, the name of the place they have been told about, where they have made a reservation.

The kitchen seems to be in the front room, next to the bar: all steam and steel, noisy clanging. Smoke and people, glasses rattling, crashing. "I really need a drink," Persis tells Thad, as instead they are led back to a room full of tables, people—many Americans, tourists, all loud and chattering.

At their small table, waiting for wine, with his tight New England smile Thad asks, "Aren't you going to check it? See what's still there?"

Curiously, this has not yet occurred to Persis as something to be done; she has simply clutched the bag. Now, as she looks down at the bag on her lap, it seems shabbier, a battered survivor. Obediently she unsnaps the flap. "Oh good, my passport's here," she tells Thad.

"That's great." He is genuinely pleased with himself—and why should he not be, having behaved with such courage? Then he frowns. "He got all your money?"

"Well no, actually there wasn't any money. I keep it in my pocket. Always, when I go to New York, that's what I do."

Why does Thad look so confused just then? A confusion of emotions is spread across his fair, lined face. He is disappointed, somehow? Upset that he ran after a thief who had stolen a bag containing so little?

Upset that Persis, who now goes down to New York on publishing business by herself, has tricks for self-preservation?

Sipping wine, and almost instantly dizzy, light in her head, Persis tries to explain herself. "Men are such dopes," she heedlessly starts. "They always think that women carry everything they own in their bags. Thieves think that, I mean. So I just shove money and credit cards into some pocket. There's only makeup in my bags."

"And your passport." Stern, judicious Thad.

"Oh yes, of course," Persis babbles. "That would have been terrible. We could have spent days in offices."

Gratified, sipping at his wine, Thad says, "I wonder why he didn't take it, actually."

Persis does not say, "Because it's hidden inside my address book"— although quite possibly that was the case. Instead, she says what is also surely true: "Because you scared him. The last thing he expected was someone running after him, and that *whistle.*"

Thad smiles, and his face settles into a familiar expression: that of a generally secure, intelligent man, a lucky person, for whom things happen more or less as he would expect them to.

Persis is thinking, and not for the first time, how terrible it must be to be a man, how terrifying. Men are always running, chasing something. And if you are rich and successful, like Thad, you have to hunt down anyone who wants to take away your possessions. Or if you're poor, down on your luck, you might be tempted to chase after a shabby bag that holds nothing of any real value, to snatch such a bag from a foreign woman who is wearing false gold chains that shine and glimmer in the dark.

Separate Planes

In the Mexico City airport, in the upstairs bar adjacent to the waiting room for planes to various Mexican cities—Oaxaca, Ixtapa, Mérida—three highly conspicuous Americans are having a drink together, attracting considerable attention from other, mostly Mexican travelers. They are a young man and a somewhat older married couple; in some indefinable way the couple look long married, which they are. The young man, who is actually in early middle age, still appreciably younger than the other two—this man is the most conventionally dressed of the three: khaki pants, navy blazer, white shirt. Sheer physical beauty is what draws so many looks to him, especially in Mexico, among dark people: his sleek flat blond hair shines, even in this ill-lit room; his narrow eyes are intensely blue, his teeth of a dazzling whiteness. He is a tennis instructor at a small college in Southern California, and he is going from Oaxaca, where all three of these people just have been, on to Ixtapa, where there is to be a tournament at the Club Med. His name is Hugh Cornelisen.

Of the older two, who are headed for Mérida, the man is the more flamboyant, as to costume. Tall, excessively thin, with thinning, grayish hair and a reddish face, he is wearing a pink linen suit, an ascot of darker pink silk. His gestures are slightly overanimated. Behind heavy horn-rimmed glasses his dark eyes blink a lot. His face is deeply furrowed; deep lines run down his cheeks and across his forehead—perhaps from a lifetime of serious thought, deep contemplation, and possibly more than his share of conflicts, sharp torments of the heart. He is Allen Rodgers, a lawyer, from New Haven.

His wife, Alexandra, is a woman of considerable size—a wonderful size, actually; her height and her general massiveness convey strength and power. She is unaware, though, of the impression she makes—she wishes she were smaller. She has great dark, golden eyes, and black, gray-streaked hair pulled into a knot. A long time ago, in the forties, she was studying Greek literature at Yale; she and Allen met at various New Haven parties—an older (ten years) man, a tall, uneasy girl. And actually she looks better now than she did as a very young woman; then she was awkward with her size, shy, and overeager in her mania for knowledge, her greed for love. Now, especially in her brown, loosely woven dress, with her big purple beads, big gold earrings, Alexandra looks majestic—but at this moment she is thinking that she would give everything she has if she could be young again, even for just a couple of days; then, just possibly, she would be going off to Ixtapa with Hugh, instead of to Mérida with Allen. At this moment she does not see how she can bear the rest of her life with Hugh's face absent from it.

On second thought, though, she does not really wish that she could go to Ixtapa with Hugh—complications, embarrassments. She would only like him to kiss her, preferably in the dark, where she is invisible.

Alexandra's quest for love did not end after her marriage to Allen, although she had hoped (they both hoped) that she would change. At first there were just a few excited flurries, kitchen kisses, some passionate gropings in cars, after summer parties in Vermont, where they and many of their friends had lakeside cottages. Then there was a serious, real affair with a younger colleague of Allen's, cautiously, rather guardedly begun as a summer romance but continued with frenzied meetings in New York hotels, in motels along the turnpike. This left everyone involved raw and shaken (Alexandra had been forced or felt herself forced to tell Allen almost all about it). After that she "drifted into," as she put it to herself, a couple of not very serious dalliances; she found the very contrast between these connections and the high seriousness of her first affair depressing, and she resolved not to do that again. But then she did. All of which was at least suspected by Allen, if unclearly.

Her Greek studies have more or less lapsed, although she still tries an occasional translation; some of her translated poems have been published in literary journals.

In what Allen describes as his own "declining years" he has experienced a series of critically painful "crushes" on young women, usually students, always beautiful. Analysis of these feelings has been a source of further pain, a scalpel applied to a wound, but he has achieved a certain understanding of his feelings: he has come to understand that all he wants of these young women is sometimes to *see* them, but "want" is an imprecise word for his wild craving, his need.

The most recent object of this "surely most unwanted affection," as Allen might say, were he able to talk about it—the most recent "crush" has been on a tall, pale red-haired girl, Mona, from Colorado. Mona, with milk-white, unfreckled skin, wide light-blue eyes, and endless legs, which she carelessly, restlessly crossed and recrossed, all summer long, in her white tennis shorts. Mona was in New Haven visiting the daughter of friends, making everything worse, more "social." A feminist, she planned to go to law school, and she liked to talk to Allen about law. "I think she has a sort of crush on you," Alexandra imperceptibly remarked, at the start of summer. "Well, feminists get crushes too," he limply countered.

Later, seeming to catch some hint of his actual feelings, Alexandra stopped mentioning Mona altogether.

Alexandra and Allen met Hugh because they were all staying in the same hotel in Oaxaca—a beautiful converted convent, with open court-yards full of flowers, lovely long cloisters, and everywhere birds. Arriving there on an early-morning plane from Mexico City, registering at the desk, as they were led toward their room, Alexandra and Allen ex-changed smiles of pure pleasure at the beauty of it all, the sweet fresh-ness of the air, such a contrast to Mexico City or New Haven. They liked their room, which was white-plastered, very clean, with a low slant ceil-ing, a window looking out to an ancient well, of soft gray stone. As they stood there just within the doorway, taking everything in, a young blond American in khaki walking shorts passed by; he looked in, smiled quickly in their direction.

After a little unpacking Alexandra and Allen walked up to the neighboring church, whose annex was a museum of costumes and arti-facts, and there was the blond young man again, before a display of fero-cious armaments, feathered headdresses. Seeing them, he gave another smile; they all smiled, acknowledging the coincidence.

At lunch, in the sunny, vine-hung courtyard, a haven for butterflies and hummingbirds, there he was again, but at a table some distance from theirs. More smiles.

And late in the afternoon, after more walking about, a little shopping, sightseeing, the blond young man was just across the pool, sunning himself, as he glanced through a magazine. He waved in their direction; they returned the gesture.

"Odd that he's alone," Alexandra murmured. "He's really quite *beau.*"

"Oh, he's probably saving himself for something. He looks athletic."

"I wonder what."

Allen speculated. "Well, something graceful. Something not, as the kids say, gross. Golf? Maybe tennis?"

That night, after a fairly long siesta—though they were both troubled sleepers, often restless—Alexandra and Allen came into the bar rather late to find almost all the tables occupied, and there *he* was, standing up at the sight of them, saying, "Well, we seem to be on the same schedule, don't we? Won't you folks join me for a drink?"

Close up, even in that darkish bar, Hugh turned out to be somewhat less young than they at first had thought; still, he was considerably younger than they were, and his general air was boyish—to Alexandra, privately, he remained "the young blond." As they exchanged names and certain identifying facts—home bases, previous trips to Mexico, next destinations—professions were brought out last, and Hugh seemed impressed by theirs: a lawyer and a scholar, of Greek! He was very pleased at Allen's guess as to tennis for himself.

"Allen's terrifically intuitive," explained Alexandra.

"Oh, I believe you!" A flash of teeth.

"Mostly I'm very observant." Dry Allen.

They passed a pleasant, noncommittal evening together, going off early to their separate rooms.

And, the next morning, there was Hugh, arriving for breakfast at the exact moment of their arrival.

Unlike either Allen or Alexandra, Hugh was an intensely physical person, a man much at home in his body, exuding animal energy. He even looked at things in a total, physical way, as animals do, all his muscles at attention, along with his depthless, clear blue eyes. On their one planned excursion together, in a rented car, out to the ruins at Monte Albán, the ancient pyramids, instead of looking at the stones Alexandra mostly watched Hugh, as he paced and bent and stopped to look, turned and bent down again. (And Allen watched Alexandra, watching.)

And their odd synchroneity continued. Even when Allen and Alexandra slept somewhat late and were late coming in to breakfast, there would be Hugh, saying ruefully that he had overslept. They laughed about it, this coincidence of inner timing, but even as they did so Alexandra felt a tiny chill of fear: suppose they should come into a room, as they surely would, sooner or later, and not find Hugh? Coming into the bar and finding him there at night, smiling and standing up at the sight of them, saying, "This is my first Margarita, honest"—coming on Hugh in that way became for Alexandra like finding a sudden brilliant light, in anticipated darkness.

Now they are drinking what are probably their last Margaritas, in this huge, dingy, crowded area, among their own and other people's piles of luggage, these somewhat unlikely, not quite friends (although not unlikely to the mostly shabby Mexicans who are with them in the waiting room, who stare and find it perfectly reasonable that these three Hollywood-looking Americans should be together).

In a summing-up way Hugh says, "Well, it certainly was lucky for me, running into you folks down there."

"Oh, lucky for us!" Allen responds very quickly, with a lively smile.

"Oh, lucky!" Alexandra echoes, her own smile a little uncertain.

Hugh's face is bright as, having covered that topic, he moves on to more urgent matters. "I guess planes are always late getting out of here?" he questions. "No counting on schedules?"

Allen answers, "Probably not. Schedules are, uh, almost irrelevant."

Hugh's plane for Ixtapa was originally scheduled to leave an hour after that of Allen and Alexandra for Mérida; however, both schedules have continuously changed, so that now the question of who leaves when is quite "up in the air," as Allen has put it, to a dutiful smile from Alexandra, a brief but appreciative chuckle from Hugh.

Now, though, as they regard the shifting numbers on the elevated blackboard, it appears that Hugh will leave first. Alexandra has all along known that this would be the case.

And, finally, his plane is announced. Boarding time.

In a suddenly awkward cluster the three of them stand up, not quite facing each other.

Allen, as he always uncontrollably does when ill at ease, begins to talk. "Well, I hope your tournament—this short flight—not too late," he says, almost unheard in the general mounting confusion of people moving toward a just forming, straggling line, Spanish voices raised in prolonged farewells, bodies momentarily clutched in parting embraces.

Hugh grasps Allen's hand, and presses it for an instant. What he indistinctly says is *"Swell."*

Turning to Alexandra, so large and helpless, Hugh seems to see or simply to feel some nuance that moves him, somehow. Quickly bending toward her, he kisses her lightly on each cheek (a most un-Hugh-like gesture, Allen thinks) as he says, "Like the French! Well, Alexandra, so long!" and he turns and walks quickly, jauntily, into the crowd, toward the now moving line, in the huge and dingy, barely illuminated room.

Leaving them there.

Molly's Dog

Accustomed to extremes of mood, which she experienced less as "swings" than as plunges, or more rarely as soarings, Molly Harper, a newly retired screenwriter, was nevertheless quite overwhelmed by the blackness—the horror, really, with which, one dark pre-dawn hour, she viewed a minor trip, a jaunt from San Francisco to Carmel, to which she had very much looked forward. It was to be a weekend, simply, at an inn where in fact she had often stayed before, with various lovers (Molly's emotional past had been strenuous). This time she was to travel with Sandy Norris, an old non-lover friend, who owned a bookstore. (Sandy usually had at least a part-time lover of his own, one in a series of nice young men.)

Before her film job, and her move to Los Angeles, Molly had been a poet, a good one—even, one year, a Yale Younger Poet. But she was living, then, from hand to mouth, from one idiot job to another. (Sandy was a friend from that era; they began as neighbors in a shabby North Beach apartment building, now long-since demolished.) As she had approached middle age, though, being broke all the time seemed undignified, if not downright scary. It wore her down, and she grabbed at the film work and moved down to L.A. Some years of that life were wearing in another way, she found, and she moved from Malibu back up to San Francisco, with a little saved money, and her three beautiful, cross old cats. And hopes for a new and calmer life. She meant to start seriously writing again.

In her pre-trip waking nightmare, though, which was convincing in the way that such an hour's imaginings always are (one sees the truth, and sees that any sunnier ideas are chimerical, delusions) at three, or four a.m., Molly pictured the two of them, as they would be in tawdry, ridiculous Carmel: herself, a scrawny sun-dried older woman, and Sandy, her wheezing, chain-smoking fat queer friend. There would be some silly awkwardness about sleeping arrangements, and instead of making love they would drink too much.

And, fatally, she thought of another weekend, in that same inn, years back: she remembered entering one of the cabins with a lover, and as soon as he, the lover, had closed the door they had turned to each other and kissed, had laughed and hurried off to bed. Contrast enough to make her nearly weep—and she knew, too, at four in the morning, that her cherished view of a meadow, and the river, the sea, would now be blocked by condominiums, or something.

This trip, she realized too late, at dawn, was to represent a serious error in judgment, one more in a lifetime of dark mistakes. It would weigh down and quite possibly sink her friendship with Sandy, and she put a high value on friendship. Their one previous lapse, hers and Sandy's, which occurred when she stopped smoking and he did not (according to Sandy she had been most unpleasant about it, and perhaps she had been), had made Molly extremely unhappy.

But, good friends as she and Sandy were, why on earth a weekend together? The very frivolousness with which this plan had been hit upon seemed ominous; simply, Sandy had said that funnily enough he had never been to Carmel, and Molly had said that she knew a nifty place to stay. And so, why not? they said. A long time ago, when they both were poor, either of them would have given anything for such a weekend (though not with each other) and perhaps that was how things should be, Molly judged, at almost five. And she thought of all the poor lovers, who could never go anywhere at all, who quarrel from sheer claustrophobia.

Not surprisingly, the next morning Molly felt considerably better, although imperfectly rested. But with almost her accustomed daytime energy she set about getting ready for the trip, doing several things simultaneously, as was her tendency: packing clothes and breakfast food (the cabins were equipped with little kitchens, she remembered), straightening up her flat and arranging the cats' quarters on her porch.

By two in the afternoon, the hour established for their departure, Molly was ready to go, if a little sleepy; fatigue had begun to cut into her energy. Well, she was not twenty any more, or thirty or forty, even, she told herself, tolerantly.

Sandy telephoned at two-fifteen. In his raspy voice he apologized; his assistant had been late getting in, he still had a couple of things to do. He would pick her up at three, three-thirty at the latest.

Irritating: Molly had sometimes thought that Sandy's habitual lateness was his way of establishing control; at other times she thought that he was simply tardy, as she herself was punctual (but why?). However, wanting a good start to their weekend, she told him that that was really okay; it did not matter what time they got to Carmel, did it?

She had begun a rereading of *Howards End,* which she planned to take along, and now she found that the book was even better than she remembered it as being, from the wonderful assurance of the first sentence, "One may as well begin with Helen's letters to her sister—" Sitting in her sunny window, with her sleeping cats, Molly managed to be wholly absorbed in her reading—not in waiting for Sandy, nor in thinking, especially, of Carmel.

Just past four he arrived at her door: Sandy, in his pressed blue blazer, thin hair combed flat, his reddish face bright. Letting him in, brushing cheeks in the kiss of friends, Molly thought how nice he looked, after all: his kind blue eyes, sad witty mouth.

He apologized for lateness. "I absolutely had to take a shower," he said, with his just-crooked smile.

"Well, it's really all right. I'd begun *Howards End* again. I'd forgotten how wonderful it is."

"Oh well. *Forster.*"

Thus began one of the rambling conversations, more bookish gossip than "literary," which formed, perhaps, the core of their friendship, its reliable staple. In a scattered way they ran about, conversationally, among favorite old novels, discussing characters not quite as intimates but certainly as contemporaries, as alive. *Was* Margaret Schlegel somewhat prudish? Sandy felt that she was; Molly took a more sympathetic view of her shyness. Such talk, highly pleasurable and reassuring to them both, carried Molly and Sandy, in his small green car, past the dull first half of their trip: down the Bayshore Highway, past San Jose and Gilroy, and took them to where (Molly well remembered) it all became beautiful. Broad stretches of bright green early summer fields; distant hills, grayish-blue; and then islands of sweeping dark live oaks.

At the outskirts of Carmel itself a little of her pre-dawn apprehension came back to Molly, as they drove past those imitation Cotswold cottages, fake-Spanish haciendas, or bright little gingerbread houses. And the main drag, Ocean Avenue, with its shops, shops—all that tweed and pewter, "imported" jams and tea. More tourists than ever before, of course, in their bright synthetic tourist clothes, their bulging shopping bags—Japanese, French, German, English tourists, taking home their awful wares.

"You turn left next, on Dolores," Molly instructed, and then heard herself begin nervously to babble. "Of course if the place has really been wrecked we don't have to stay for two nights, do we. We could go on down to Big Sur, or just go home, for heaven's sake."

"In any case, sweetie, if they've wrecked it, it won't be your fault." Sandy laughed, and wheezed, and coughed. He had been smoking all the way down, which Molly had succeeded in not mentioning.

Before them, then, was their destination: the inn, with its clump of white cottages. And the meadow. So far, nothing that Molly could see had changed. No condominiums. Everything as remembered.

They were given the cabin farthest from the central office, the one nearest the meadow, and the river and the sea. A small bedroom, smaller kitchen, and in the living room a studio couch. Big windows, and that view.

"Obviously, the bedroom is yours," Sandy magnanimously declared, plunking down his bag on the studio couch.

"Well," was all for the moment that Molly could say, as she put her small bag down in the bedroom, and went into the kitchen with the sack of breakfast things. From the little window she looked out to the meadow, saw that it was pink now with wildflowers, in the early June dusk. Three large brown cows were grazing out there, near where the river must be. Farther out she could see the wide, gray-white strip of beach, and the dark blue, turbulent sea. On the other side of the meadow were soft green hills, on which—yes, one might have known—new houses had arisen. But somehow inoffensively; they blended. And beyond the beach was the sharp, rocky silhouette of Point Lobos, crashing waves, leaping foam. All blindingly undiminished: a miraculous gift.

Sandy came into the kitchen, bearing bottles. Beaming Sandy, saying, "Mol, this is the most divine place. We must celebrate your choice. Immediately."

They settled in the living room with their drinks, with that view before them: the almost imperceptibly graying sky, the meadow, band of sand, the sea.

And, as she found that she often did, with Sandy, Molly began to say what had just come into her mind. "You wouldn't believe how stupid I was, as a very young woman," she prefaced, laughing a little. "Once I came down here with a lawyer, from San Francisco, terribly rich. Quite famous, actually." (The same man with whom she had so quickly rushed off to bed, on their arrival—as she did not tell Sandy.) "Married, of course. The first part of my foolishness. And I was really broke at the time—*broke,* I was poor as hell, being a typist to support my poetry habit. You remember. But I absolutely insisted on bringing all the food for that stolen, illicit weekend, can you imagine? What on earth was I trying to prove? Casseroles of crabmeat, endive for salads. Honestly, how crazy I was!"

Sandy laughed agreeably, and remarked a little plaintively that for him she had only brought breakfast food. But he was not especially interested in that old, nutty view of her, Molly saw—and resolved that that would be her last "past" story. Customarily they did not discuss their love affairs.

She asked, "Shall we walk out on the beach tomorrow?"

"But of course."

Later they drove to a good French restaurant, where they drank a little too much wine, but they did not get drunk. And their two reflections, seen in a big mirror across the tiny room, looked perfectly all right: Molly, gray-haired, dark-eyed and thin, in her nice flowered silk dress; and Sandy, tidy and alert, a small plump man, in a neat navy blazer.

After dinner they drove along the beach, the cold white sand ghostly in the moonlight. Past enormous millionaire houses, and blackened windbent cypresses. Past the broad sloping river beach, and then back to their cabin, with its huge view of stars.

In her narrow bed, in the very small but private bedroom, Molly thought again, for a little while, of that very silly early self of hers: how eagerly self-defeating she had been—how foolish, in love. But she felt a certain tolerance now for that young person, herself, and she even smiled as she thought of all that intensity, that driven waste of emotion. In many ways middle age is preferable, she thought.

Molly's Dog

.   .   .

In the morning, they met the dog.

After breakfast they had decided to walk on the river beach, partly since Molly remembered that beach as being far less populated than the main beach was. Local families brought their children there. Or their dogs, or both.

Despite its visibility from their cabin, the river beach was actually a fair distance off, and so instead of walking there they drove, for maybe three or four miles. They parked and got out, and were pleased to see that no one else was there. Just a couple of dogs, who seemed not to be there together: a plumy, oversized friendly Irish setter, who ran right over to Molly and Sandy; and a smaller, long-legged, thin-tailed dark gray dog, with very tall ears—a shy young dog, who kept her distance, running a wide circle around them, after the setter had ambled off somewhere else. As they neared the water, the gray dog sidled over to sniff at them, her ears flattened, seeming to indicate a lowering of suspicion. She allowed herself to be patted, briefly; she seemed to smile.

Molly and Sandy walked near the edge of the water; the dog ran ahead of them.

The day was glorious, windy, bright blue, and perfectly clear; they could see the small pines and cypresses that struggled to grow from the steep sharp rocks of Point Lobos, could see fishing boats far out on the deep azure ocean. From time to time the dog would run back in their direction, and then she would rush toward a receding wave, chasing it backward in a seeming happy frenzy. Assuming her (then) to live nearby, Molly almost enviously wondered at her sheer delight in what must be familiar. The dog barked at each wave, and ran after every one as though it were something new and marvelous.

Sandy picked up a stick and threw it forward. The dog ran after the stick, picked it up and shook it several times, and then, in a tentative way, she carried it back toward Sandy and Molly—not dropping it, though. Sandy had to take it from her mouth. He threw it again, and the dog ran off in that direction.

The wind from the sea was strong, and fairly chilling. Molly wished she had a warmer sweater, and she chided herself: she could have remembered that Carmel was cold, along with her less practical memories. She noted that Sandy's ears were red, and saw him rub his hands together. But she thought, I hope he won't want to leave soon, it's so beautiful. And such a nice dog. (Just that, at that moment: a very nice dog.)

The dog, seeming for the moment to have abandoned the stick game, rushed at a just-alighted flock of sea gulls, who then rose from the wet waves' edge and with what must have been (to a dog) a most gratifying flapping of wings, with cluckings of alarm.

Molly and Sandy were now close to the mouth of the river, the gorge cut into the beach, as water emptied into the sea. Impossible to cross—although Molly could remember when one could, when she and whatever companion had jumped easily over some water, and had then walked much farther down the beach. Now she and Sandy simply stopped there, and regarded the newish houses that were built up on the nearby hills. And they said to each other:

"What a view those people must have!"

"Actually the houses aren't too bad."

"There must be some sort of design control."

"I'm sure."

"Shall we buy a couple? A few million should take care of it."

"Oh sure, let's."

They laughed.

They turned around to find the dog waiting for them, in a dog's classic pose of readiness: her forelegs outstretched in the sand, rump and tail up in the air. Her eyes brown and intelligent, appraising, perhaps affectionate.

"Sandy, throw her another stick."

"You do it this time."

"Well, I don't throw awfully well."

"Honestly, Mol, she won't mind."

Molly poked through a brown tangle of seaweed and small broken sticks, somewhat back from the waves. The only stick that would do was too long, but she picked it up and threw it anyway. It was true that she did not throw very well, and the wind made a poor throw worse: the stick landed only a few feet away. But the dog ran after it, and then ran about with the stick in her mouth, shaking it, holding it high up as she ran, like a trophy.

Sandy and Molly walked more slowly now, against the wind. To their right was the meadow, across which they could just make out the cottages where they were staying. Ahead was a cluster of large, many-windowed ocean-front houses—in one of which, presumably, their dog lived.

Once their walk was over, they had planned to go into Carmel and buy some wine and picnic things, and to drive out into the valley for lunch. They began to talk about this now, and then Sandy said that first he would like to go by the Mission. "I've never seen it," he explained.

"Oh well, sure."

From time to time on that return walk one or the other of them would pick up a stick and throw it for the dog, who sometimes lost a stick and then looked back to them for another, who stayed fairly near them but maintained, still, a certain shy independence.

She was wearing a collar (Molly and Sandy were later to reassure each other as to this) but at that time, on the beach, neither of them saw any reason to examine it. Besides, the dog never came quite that close. It would have somehow seemed presumptuous to grab her and read her collar's inscription.

In a grateful way Molly was thinking, again, how reliable the beauty of that place had turned out to be: their meadow view, and now the river beach.

They neared the parking lot, and Sandy's small green car.

An older woman, heavy and rather bent, was just coming into the lot, walking her toy poodle, on a leash. *Their* dog ran over for a restrained sniff, and then ambled back to where Molly and Sandy were getting into the car.

"Pretty dog!" the woman called out to them. "I never saw one with such long ears!"

"Yes—she's not ours."

"She isn't lost, is she?"

"Oh no, she has a collar."

Sandy started up the car; he backed up and out of the parking lot, slowly. Glancing back, Molly saw that the dog seemed to be leaving too, heading home, probably.

But a few blocks later—by then Sandy was driving somewhat faster—for some reason Molly looked back again, and there was the dog. Still. Racing. Following them.

She looked over to Sandy and saw that he too had seen the dog, in the rearview mirror.

Feeling her glance, apparently, he frowned. "She'll go home in a minute," he said.

Molly closed her eyes, aware of violent feelings within herself, somewhere: anguish? dread? She could no more name them than she could locate the emotion.

She looked back again, and there was the dog, although she was now much farther—hopelessly far behind them. A small gray dot. Racing. Still.

Sandy turned right in the direction of the Mission, as they had planned. They drove past placid houses with their beds of too-bright, unnatural flowers, too yellow or too pink. Clean glass windows, neat shingles. Trim lawns. Many houses, all much alike, and roads, and turns in roads.

As they reached the Mission, its parking area was crowded with tour busses, campers, vans, and ordinary cars.

There was no dog behind them.

"You go on in," Molly said. "I've seen it pretty often. I'll wait out here in the sun."

She seated herself on a stone bench near the edge of the parking area—in the sun, beside a bright clump of bougainvillea, and she told herself that by now, surely, the dog had turned around and gone on home, or back to the beach. And that even if she and Sandy had turned and gone back to her, or stopped and waited for her, eventually they would have had to leave her, somewhere.

Sandy came out, unenthusiastic about the church, and they drove into town to buy sandwiches and wine.

In the grocery store, where everything took a very long time, it occurred to Molly that probably they should have checked back along the river beach road, just to make sure that the dog was no longer there. But by then it was too late.

They drove out into the valley; they found a nice sunny place for a picnic, next to the river, the river that ran on to their beach, and the sea. After a glass of wine Molly was able to ask, "You don't really think she was lost, do you?"

But why would Sandy know, any more than she herself did? At that moment Molly hated her habit of dependence on men for knowledge—any knowledge, any man. But at least, for the moment, he was kind. "Oh,

I really don't think so," he said. "She's probably home by now." And he
mentioned the collar.

Late that afternoon, in the deepening, cooling June dusk, the river
beach was diminishingly visible from their cabin, where Molly and
Sandy sat with their pre-dinner drinks. At first, from time to time, it was
possible to see people walking out there: small stick figures, against a
mild pink sunset sky. Once, Molly was sure that one of the walkers had a
dog along. But it was impossible, at that distance, and in the receding
light, to identify an animal's markings, or the shape of its ears.

They had dinner in the inn's long dining room, from which it was by
then too dark to see the beach. They drank too much, and they had a silly
outworn argument about Sandy's smoking, during which he accused her
of being bossy; she said that he was inconsiderate.

Waking at some time in the night, from a shallow, winey sleep,
Molly thought of the dog out there on the beach, how cold it must be, by
now—the hard chilled sand and stinging waves. From her bed she could
hear the sea's relentless crash.

The pain that she experienced then was as familiar as it was acute.

They had said that they would leave fairly early on Sunday morning
and go home by way of Santa Cruz: a look at the town, maybe lunch, and
a brief tour of the university there. And so, after breakfast, Molly and
Sandy began to pull their belongings together.

Tentatively (but was there a shade of mischief, of teasing in his
voice? Could he sense what she was feeling?) Sandy asked, "I guess we
won't go by the river beach?"

"No."

They drove out from the inn, up and onto the highway; they left
Carmel. But as soon as they were passing Monterey, Pacific Grove, it
began to seem intolerable to Molly that they had not gone back to the
beach. Although she realized that either seeing or *not* seeing the dog
would have been terrible.

If she now demanded that Sandy turn around and go back, would he do it? Probably not, she concluded; his face had a set, stubborn look. But Molly wondered about that, off and on, all the way to Santa Cruz.

For lunch they had sandwiches in a rather scruffy, open-air place; they drove up to and in and around the handsome, almost deserted university; and then, anxious not to return to the freeway, they took off on a road whose sign listed, among other destinations, San Francisco.

Wild Country: thickly wooded, steeply mountainous. Occasionally through an opening in the trees they could glimpse some sheer cliff, gray sharp rocks; once a distant small green secret meadow. A proper habitat for mountain lions, Molly thought, or deer, at least, and huge black birds. "It reminds me of something," she told Sandy, disconsolately. "Maybe even some place I've only read about."

"Or a movie," he agreed. "God knows it's melodramatic."

Then Molly remembered: it was indeed a movie that this savage scenery made her think of, and a movie that she herself had done the screenplay for. About a quarrelling, alcoholic couple, Americans, who were lost in wild Mexican mountains. As she had originally written it, they remained lost, presumably to die there. Only, the producer saw fit to change all that, and he had them romantically rescued by some good-natured Mexican bandits.

They had reached a crossroads, where there were no signs at all. The narrow, white roads all led off into the woods. To Molly, the one on the right looked most logical, as a choice, and she said so, but Sandy took the middle one. "You really like to be in charge, don't you," he rather unpleasantly remarked, lighting a cigarette.

There had been a lot of news in the local papers about a murderer who attacked and then horribly killed hikers and campers, in those very Santa Cruz mountains, Molly suddenly thought. She rolled up her window and locked the door, and she thought again of the ending of her movie. She tended to believe that one's fate, or doom, had a certain logic to it; even, that it was probably written out somewhere, even if by one's self. Most lives, including their endings, made a certain sort of sense, she thought.

The gray dog then came back powerfully, vividly to her mind: the small heart pounding in that thin, narrow rib cage, as she ran after their car. Unbearable: Molly's own heart hurt, as she closed her eyes and tightened her hands into fists.

"Well, Christ," exploded Sandy, at that moment. "We've come to a dead end. Look!"

They had; the road ended abruptly, it simply stopped, in a heavy grove of cypresses and redwoods. There was barely space to turn around.

Not saying, "Why didn't you take the other road?" Molly instead cried out, uncontrollably, "But why didn't we go back for the dog?"

"Jesus, Molly." Redfaced with the effort he was making, Sandy glared. "That's what we most need right now. Some stray bitch in the car with us."

"What do you mean, stray bitch? She chose us—she wanted to come with us."

"How stupid you are! I had no idea."

"You're so selfish!" she shouted.

Totally silent, then, in the finally righted but possibly still lost car, they stared at each other: a moment of pure dislike.

And then, "Three mangy cats, and now you want a dog," Sandy muttered. He started off, too fast, in the direction of the crossroads. At which they made another turn.

Silently they traveled through more woods, past more steep gorges and ravines, on the road that Molly had thought they should have taken in the first place.

She had been right; they soon came to a group of signs which said that they were heading toward Saratoga. They were neither to die in the woods nor to be rescued by bandits. Nor murdered. And, some miles past Saratoga, Molly apologized. "Actually I have a sort of a headache," she lied.

"I'm sorry, too, Mol. And you know I like your cats." Which was quite possibly also a lie.

They got home safely, of course.

But somehow, after that trip, their friendship, Molly and Sandy's, either "lapsed" again, or perhaps it was permanently diminished; Molly was not sure. One or the other of them would forget to call, until days or weeks had gone by, and then their conversation would be guilty, apologetic.

And at first, back in town, despite the familiar and comforting presences of her cats, Molly continued to think with a painful obsessiveness of that beach dog, especially in early hours of sleeplessness. She imagined going back to Carmel alone to look for her; of advertising in the Carmel paper, describing a young female with gray markings. Tall ears.

However, she did none of those things. She simply went on with her calm new life, as before, with her cats. She wrote some poems.

But, although she had ceased to be plagued by her vision of the dog (running, endlessly running, growing smaller in the distance) she did not forget her.

And she thought of Carmel, now, in a vaguely painful way, as a place where she had lost, or left something of infinite value. A place to which she would not go back.

Mexican Dust

Four North American tourists are walking through the interior of a small church, near Oaxaca: one square room, shabby but strictly decorous, with its white lace altar cloth and intricate silver candlesticks; its outsize, bright floppy flowers, and vague, dark holy pictures. Single file, the tourists tiptoe: three large fair-haired people, a woman and two men, followed by another woman, who is small and dark, named Miriam. Miriam lags slightly behind the others, in the gray stone shadows.

The group of three which Miriam trails is led by Eric, her husband, a doctor. Next comes Eric's twin sister, Joan, also a doctor, and after Joan bearded Russell, a physicist, husband of Joan. Earlier that morning the two couples visited a splendid cathedral, very near the pretty hotel where they are all staying. This little church seems drab, comparatively. "It's sort of dreary, for a church," Joan whispers ahead to her brother Eric. Eric laughs, very quietly.

The group is all related, then, although Miriam is aware that the others are more related to each other than to her; and they look so alike, those three, so blond and full-fleshed. Before she met them (they were all at Stanford together), Miriam imagined them to be a family, two brothers with their sister, and she thought she had never seen such glamorous, such quintessentially *California* people. Small dark Miriam, from Quincy, Mass., on a scholarship, was dazzled, and she remained dazzled after they met—or, rather, after she met Eric (at a swimming party at Lake Lagunitas, of all odd circumstances; Eric said she looked like a goldfish, in her small yellow bathing suit). She and Eric fell in love, and he introduced her to his twin sister, Joan, in medical school along with him and married. And she met Joan's husband, Russell, studying physics.

And so, in addition to their similar looks, those three have science in common. Miriam, who studied English, now does volunteer work at the public library in Seattle, where she and Eric have moved. However, it is Miriam who has, just then, in the church, a weird science-fiction thought: she thinks that all the dust particles in Mexico could be silicon chips, programmed for some violence. She thinks that anything at all could happen there, and she is suddenly afraid.

Still tiptoeing behind the others, Miriam then notices a small crucifix, in a deeply recessed niche. Even in those dark shadows, though, she can see that the sagging figure of the Christ is lined with blood; red blood (well, paint, of course) seeps down from the gaping wound, just below his ribs.

Or did Miriam's peripheral vision catch that image, that blood, just before her strange, quite uncharacteristic thought about dust and violence? She is not sure, not then or later on, when she considers everything.

Usually—almost always, really—Miriam finds it wonderful to be associated with those others, to be with them. When she is with them she has, even, a sense of being assimilated by them, with them, into them. It is as if by sufficiently gazing up at them, at Eric, Joan, and Russell, she could absorb—could take on their qualities, even their blondness and height.

And in their separate and collective ways they cherish her, too, Miriam feels; even her differences from themselves are appreciated. "How small you are!" Eric sometimes laughingly, lovingly remarks, even now, after eight years of marriage. And Joan: "What heaven it must be to shop for size-3 clothes!"

It has sometimes occurred to Miriam, though, that she could do with fewer remarks about her size; so much attention to it makes her feel rather like their mascot. She is simply small, a fact not terribly interesting to herself.

And she does have to argue with them all, when the four are together, about her library volunteer work, her arguments being the obvious ones: tax cuts are killing the libraries, libraries need all the help they can get. And, she adds, with only a B.A. in English lit., what sort of job could she get these days? Also, Eric's cardiology practice brings in plenty of money. Everything she says is true, they have to agree. Still, they all—especially Joan (who earns more than either Eric or Russell)—seem to wish that she did something else. That she had a career.

Being alone with Eric is not at all the same as being with Eric and Joan and Russell; of course not. Alone, in Seattle, Miriam and Eric have domestic conversations: what needs to be fixed (their house is old, and large). And food: big Eric eats a lot, and on her way home from the library Miriam often stops to shop at the Pike Place Market (she loves it there, the beautiful open displays); Eric likes to hear about that, what she saw, what looked best. Their dinners are the high points of their days.

She occasionally feels, though, that Eric is more himself when they are with Joan and Russell than when there are only the two of them. With Joan and Russell, Eric talks more, expresses opinions, makes jokes. Mostly medical jokes. (Russell collects dirty limericks; he knows thousands.)

However, since Eric and Miriam have been in Seattle, they see Joan and Russell considerably less, Joan's practice being in Palo Alto; Russell works on the linear accelerator, at Stanford.

But they still have these trips: by tradition the four of them take vacations together. Joan and Russell do not come up to Seattle; they have let it be known that they really can't stand the Northwest. Miriam has not let it be known that she is not truly fond of San Francisco, where they sometimes meet. Everything so pretty, so "cute," she thinks, and does not say. She also thinks (silently) that cable cars are dangerous. But: one year a barge trip in France, another the small towns of Umbria and Tuscany. Last year Scotland, this year Mexico.

Miriam's features are rather small, and her face has a curious flatness to it. A small mask. Dark eyes in shallow sockets, freckles across unprominent cheekbones. Small pointed nose, small mouth. Longish black-brown hair, which she sometimes knots up, to give herself more height.

Miriam.

On the day after she has her curious intimation of violence in the dusky church, Miriam and the others go out to the ruins at Monte Albán in a hired car, with a guide. Magnificently preserved flattened stone pyramids, rising up from the broad flat plain, at mystical intervals.

On their way home, driving along the Pan-American highway, approaching the city of Oaxaca, they see an ambulance stopped just ahead of them, and a small cluster of people. Miriam begins to hold her breath.

"A woman and a baby, both killed," their guide mutters. He is sitting in front, next to the driver—but how did he know this, Miriam later wonders. He could see ahead? See the feet?

The car slows down, and Miriam, who is closest to the window on the left, looks out and sees: on the ground, a white cover of some sort pulled over two human shapes, one medium-sized, one tiny. Two thin brown ankles protruding from the larger shape. Dusty brown feet. Red streams coming from underneath the cover. Blood.

Sadness, misery on all the dark surrounding faces, the clustered onlookers. Their driver is very upset, although he goes on driving, slowly, as though in a mourning procession. To the guide, or perhaps to himself, he speaks in a low, continuous way, very softly, in Spanish.

Miriam also speaks to herself, but inwardly, with no sound. People are killed every day, in one way or another, somewhere, she tells herself; you must not sentimentalize these two, they are out of pain now. You did not know them.

Joan says, "That's absolutely horrible." Her mouth twists, and tightens.

And Eric, in a bitter voice: "They think God will get them across highways." He is looking anxiously at Miriam. To reassure him she smiles, and touches his hand.

Ten or fifteen minutes later, Joan speculates, "It could have been an older sister carrying a baby. There seem to be a lot of them—older kids helping. Family support systems."

Eric: "Sometimes it's hard to tell who's the mother, girls having babies at fifteen or sixteen." Eric is in favor of zero population growth, generally. Miriam would like to have one child. Early on in their marriage she was pregnant, accidentally, and she had a miscarriage: a lot of pain, blood. She still hopes for a child, eventually, but they no longer talk about it.

. . .

During the rest of that day Miriam, anyway, thinks often of the family of those killed people. She imagines a small funeral parlor, too many bright flowers. People sitting around, moaning, crying. She can see it all quite clearly.

Their ultimate destination is Ixtapa, for a rest, but they will get there by way of Puerto Escondido, a smaller, less well known resort. (It was Miriam who came up with the idea of Escondido: a young woman she knows in Seattle, a weaver with a stall in the Pike Place Market, has said it is beautiful, wonderful, undiscovered.) On maps it looked as though both those laps—Oaxaca to Escondido, Escondido to Ixtapa (skirting Acapulco)—were possible by car; their travel agent also believed that they could drive, although she cautioned them about bad roads. However, it turns out in Oaxaca that the only way to Escondido is by plane. A DC-3.

Miriam, of course, is the nervous flier of the group. It is explained to her that although the DC-3s are small and old, from the Second World War, they are (undoubtedly) kept in very good shape; after all they make the trip every day. Russell, who was a Navy pilot, cannot resist teasing; he says, "I can't imagine a trip on a DC-3 with no parachute. We always had parachutes."

Joan and Russell laugh, watching Miriam. She laughs, too, though unconvincingly.

However, as a farewell to their Oaxaca hotel, they have Margaritas in the bar, just before departure. Miriam has two, purposefully, and she loves that plane trip.

They fly very low over sharp green mountains that are crisscrossed with tiny, narrow perilous roads, so low that each tree is visible, and occasionally there is a small village, a scattering of shacks. Tiny people are walking around—she can even see them as they look up at the plane.

"Oh, it's really beautiful!" says Miriam, several times; she is a little drunk.

"Miriam thinks that flying low is safer: it's closer to the ground," Eric explains to the others, who laugh. But that is just what Miriam does think, and she continues to believe it.

The view from their hotel room is exceptionally beautiful: a long broad white beach, deserted, beside the glittering, bright blue-green sea. Some strange greenish-gray vegetation and, at the far end of the beach, some white cliffs, or dunes—high, deeply ridged.

"Oh, how lovely," Miriam breathes; she is feeling the Margaritas, a little.

Behind her, Eric is saying, "This is the dirtiest room I've ever seen."

Miriam turns to see that he is right: an unmade bed, glasses with inches of dark liquid at their bottoms, floating cigarette stubs. A smeared mirror (lipstick? blood?), deep dust on the floor.

They both are right, about the view and the condition of the room.

It is quite a while before a maid comes in to clean it up, although Eric goes out to the desk to make a fuss.

For whatever reasons—fatigue, drinks, the flight—Miriam has a headache as she and Eric go to bed that night. But women cannot say that anymore, she knows, when they are not in the mood to make love. "I have a headache": a sitcom joke. And so she does not say it, and they do, happily—a happy surprise.

Downstairs in the hotel, and outside, some sort of fiesta seems to be going on. A rock band, as well as mariachis. Amplified.

All night.

The hotel is up on a high bluff above the sea—as they did not quite realize the day before, on their arrival. Its broad grassy grounds stretch to an edge, a dropping off. There is a round blue swimming pool and a thatch-roofed bar. A romantic situation for the central building, which is itself romantic, with its balconies and long arched windows, its heavy growth of bougainvillea—brilliant blossoms, delicate green vines.

However, the fiesta of the night before has left an incredible litter everywhere—piles of empty bottles: Scotch, French champagne, Mexican beer. Heaped-up ashtrays. Dirty plates.

Observing all this, around noon, Russell severely remarks, "Do you realize that no one has touched this since last night?"

And Joan: "Ugh. They're probably all home sleeping off hangovers. They just don't give a damn."

Perversely, Miriam finds something appealing, romantic even, in all that mess (although she does not say so, of course). So much champagne everywhere—what an incredible time they all must have had! It is how Gatsby's lawns must have looked after one of his parties, before the servants came.

But at that hotel, in Puerto Escondido (not West Egg), no one comes to clean up, not all day.

The ocean water—which holds, surrounds, embraces Miriam as she swims, and dives down to explore beneath its surface—is like no other water in her life; surely not the New England ponds of her childhood, or the harsh Atlantic waves that pound the Northeastern coast. This clear and lightly cool green water seems another element—enchanted water—and, swimming there, in the gentle waves, Miriam feels herself transformed, her body as quick and light as a minnow. As small and brown.

The others, Eric and Joan and Russell, are swimming there, too, but they are off somewhere else; Miriam hears them, distantly. She feels most splendidly, luxuriantly alone in the lovely water. And she is alone, except for a little Mexican boy, a child, who from time to time swims up to her; he smiles shyly, darkly, and as quickly disappears, another fish.

"Miriam, come on, we're getting out now," she hears someone call.

"I think I'll stay in for a while. I'll meet you up at the room."

"Well—"

She dives down as far as she can, in the watery green silence.

Late that afternoon, they learn that there are no rental cars available, and anyway it is not allowed to drive rented cars from Escondido to Ixtapa, or even to Acapulco.

Airplanes do not fly to Ixtapa, or to Acapulco. Only backward to Oaxaca.

There is only the second-class bus to Acapulco, and from there they may take a first-class bus to Ixtapa. One must travel from the second- to the first-class bus station, a matter of no distance. First class is called Estrella de Oro. A good sign.

"But, uh, couldn't we possibly just stay on here? It's really nice, don't you think? And second-class busses—" It is of course Miriam who has said all this.

She is answered by a chorus: "Oh Miriam, of course not, we have reservations, Ixtapa . . ."

Because they get there early, well before nine in the morning, they all have good seats on the bus, Miriam and Eric across the aisle from Joan and Russell, the two women at the windows.

They are the only North Americans on the bus.

The Mexicans who crowd into the other seats, and who, at the first and all subsequent stops, begin to fill the aisles, are not the poorest Mexicans—after all, they are traveling second class, not third—but they are considerably less rich than the four *norte-americanos*. Their clothes, the Mexicans', are bright and cheap and new, possibly bought for this trip, in some cases, whereas the North Americans wear old jeans and old cotton shirts; their leather bags are hidden in the luggage compartment, under the bus.

Miriam wishes that she were wearing something else. In these circumstances the jeans seem an affectation, besides being too hot. In a bright cotton dress, for instance (there are several in her suitcase, old summer favorites), she could look like any other passenger. She feels not liked by the Mexicans.

In addition to stops at all the small villages for new passengers, the bus is often forced to stop for sheep and cattle, or goats that appear in small herds or scattered at roadsides, evidently just emerged from the rich green tropical growth that lines the way. At moments, through the thick palm trunks, a portion of the sea is visible, sharp blue, as quickly gone; mostly the road wanders up small hills and down into dried-out creek beds. A burdened beast, the heavy, packed bus lumbers and creaks over potholes as large as moon craters.

At the village stops the windows are opened, things to eat and drink passed back and forth; shouts, laughter, money exchanged. To Miriam it all looks very good: the fruit, dark meats, strange pastries. But no one, not her husband or friends, would approve of such exotic fare; she knows this perfectly well.

Joan has brought some soda crackers in a package, from some restaurant; she passes them across to Miriam and Eric. Miriam is actually quite hungry, and the crackers help a little, although they are stale.

The bus is supposed to arrive at Acapulco at three, but it does not—not until four—and so the six-hour trip has taken seven.

"Seven hours on a second-class bus! No one will believe this story," Russell says, once they have got out and are standing there, stretching, breathing in the hot, murky city air. But he is laughing; Miriam can tell that it will be a good story for him, later on. They will all laugh about it on later trips together—probably.

They are standing in an incredible area of broken paving, refuse, dirt, over which hordes of shabby people are rushing with their battered luggage, packages.

Now they pick up their own suitcases (easy to recognize) from the pile outside their bus; they head for the street, where taxis can be seen cruising by. At some distance, in another direction, they can also see a large building, which is probably the station. And Miriam cannot resist saying, "We'd probably do just as well to get on another bus right here."

"Miriam, you've got to be kidding."

"Another second-class bus? Come *on*."

However, as soon as they have piled into a taxi and told the driver that they want the first-class station, Estrella de Oro, to Ixtapa, he tells them that they will have much trouble. Many crowds, he says gloomily; they may not get to Ixtapa.

They all look at each other. "But we have to get to Ixtapa," Eric mutters. "We have reservations for tonight."

. . .

Downstairs in the Estrella de Oro station a large crowd surrounds the ticket counter that is marked Zihuatanejo-Ixtapa—all kinds of people, mostly Mexican. It seems impossible that so many people would want to go in just that direction at that moment, but there they are.

"I suppose some people live and work there," Miriam suggests.

The waiting rooms and restaurant are on the second floor. "Why don't you girls go back upstairs? No point in all of us waiting in line," Eric says.

By now, it is six o'clock, and there is, in theory, a bus that leaves at seven-thirty. But will there be room on it for all these people, plus four North Americans? Quite possibly not.

The upstairs restaurant is closed, it seems, for repairs, and so Miriam and Joan simply wander about, in an idle though nervous way.

At one point they go out to the front entrance and stand there, observing the garish, tropical, and infinitely dirty scene, the broken-down cars and the beggars, dark withered women with sleeping children in their arms. "I think Acapulco is the bottom of the world." Miriam shudders as she says this, in the thick infested heat.

"Oh, I've seen worse," Joan says. She has recently been to India—a medical conference—which is presumably what she means.

Looking up at Joan, who is visibly tired, her light hair straggling down, her face dirt-streaked, lipstick gone, Miriam hopelessly thinks that Joan is still very beautiful, and then she wonders (not for the first time), But does Joan like me, really?

And then (a new thought), Oh, I just don't care!

After a while, they go back downstairs to see what has happened to Eric and Russell.

What has happened is that they have been given numbers and moved to another line.

"It's like a lottery?" asks Miriam.

Eric frowns. "Jesus, I hope not."

. . .

By about eight it is clear that they have missed the seven-thirty bus, but it is said that there is another at ten. Everything is shouted in Spanish, though, which they only partially understand, and they never actually see the busses as they come in or depart.

"Miriam was absolutely right," Eric concedes, in a rueful way. "We should have just gone into the second-class station and got on another bus."

Miriam does not quite remember having said that, but she supposes that she did.

Clear information comes through at ten-fifteen: they have indeed missed the ten-o'clock bus, but there is another at eleven. However, there are still many people who wait for the bus; that is evident.

"Eleven. Jesus, that gets us to Ixtapa about three, or *four.*" Russell fumes.

"Terrific, that's what we really need right now. Five more hours on a bus. Even if it is first class." Eric is muttering, as though to himself.

In a low, very reasonable voice, Joan asks, "Do we have a choice, though? We'd never get into a hotel. Or could we?"

At which Miriam cries out, "Oh, no, God, not a hotel here—it's so horrible! Why not just take a bus back to Escondido?"

She has spoken heedlessly, an outburst; still, she is unprepared for the silent, stony rage on those three so similar faces, looking down at her from their impressive heights. Joan's mouth is taut; Russell's eyes are wild, they glare as he says, "That's crazy."

At which Eric turns from Miriam to Russell, as he says, very quietly and furiously, "That's enough, now, Russ. Just shut up, will you?"

As though they had always hated each other, the two men glare at each other for a moment that lasts forever, in the throbbing, crowded, filthy alien room, in Acapulco.

At eleven, having hardly spoken, any of them, for the past forty-five minutes, in a blind exhausted way the four of them pile into the bus that has mysteriously appeared, out of the night. There are, strangely, just enough seats for everyone.

Miriam has stumbled into a window seat, on the left of the bus, next to the ocean, as they wind northward, up the coast. If anything were to be seen, through the heavy darkness—if there were a view, hers would be the best, and she feels a miserable guilt over even that nonexistent advantage. She also (miserably) feels responsible for their quarrel. Eric and Russell never fight.

The road seems very smooth, on this stretch of the coast. No potholes, but there are curves, which the driver takes at top speed, so that several passengers, Miriam among them, gasp aloud. Miriam thinks it quite possible that he could be drunk. Why not, at this dangerous, unreal hour? They will all be killed, she thinks, and then, so total is her discomfort, so deep her unhappiness, she further thinks that she does not care if they are. But please don't let me be the sole survivor, she earnestly prays, to someone.

Most people have fallen instantly, noisily asleep, despite the danger, Beside Miriam, Eric sleeps lightly, restlessly.

The dawn is dirty, yellowish, menacing. In the coconut-palm plantations, just now barely, grayly visible, the heavy fronds are too still, and the ocean, glimpsed at intervals, is flat and black, dangerous-looking.

"Does it ever storm down here?" Russell has leaned across the aisle to ask this question of Eric, just awake.

Miriam watches Eric as he frowns and speaks impatiently. "I don't know. Probably."

If any of them spoke Spanish it would all have been different, Miriam thinks. They would have understood what was being said in the station about the busses, and even, maybe, have grasped a little more about the terrible accident on the road: how the guide knew so quickly what had happened, and what their driver was saying to himself—so sadly, so brokenly.

She will study Spanish, she then swiftly decides. There is a night course at the library branch at which she works; she will sign up as soon as they get home.

. . .

At about five a.m. they arrive at Ixtapa: a cluster of thick pale high buildings (an eruption of poisonous growths, Miriam thinks) in the sulfurous light. Across the way an endless golf course spreads, the smooth grass now all silverish gray.

They enter a building; there are red tiles, wooden arches hung with cut-tin ornaments.

From behind the desk a sleepy clerk hands out room keys.

In a heavily carpeted, perfectly silent elevator they all ascend.

Miriam and Eric's room has a gigantic bed, thickly quilted in red and orange. Two big chairs, and on the walls several huge garish paintings, of improbable bright flowers. A mammoth mirror, all shining.

Beyond exhaustion, they each in a perfunctory way wash up; they remove a few clothes and fall into bed.

Lying there, in the yellowish semi-dark, Miriam has a vivid sense of having arrived at last in hell. Beside her, Eric has gone instantly to sleep; his heavy breath rasps, regularly. She closes her eyes, but then uncontrollably re-sees, with perfect clarity, that tragic roadside scene—the covered bodies, blood, the protruding brown bare dusty feet.

Quickly opening her eyes, she feels that all her senses are conspiring to make sleep out of the question; she is so overtired, so hungry, so afraid. She lies there for a while, eyes wide.

When she closes her eyes once more, however, Miriam has quite another vision: she sees herself on the second-class bus again, but she is headed back toward Escondido, and this time she's wearing a cotton dress, her bright blue, and she is alone. The bus rumbles along, much faster this trip, although from time to time it stops for passengers, and once more windows are opened, food passed through. And Miriam eats, everything she wants! Spicy aromatic meats and flaky pastries, pulpy fruits and tall sweet, colored fruity drinks. All exotic, delicious. And at Puerto Escondido the grounds have been all cleaned up; here and there are clumps of tropical vegetation, flowering bushes, small trees. And then the hotel itself, with its lovely bright covering bougainvillea.

Her room is clean and bright. She puts her bag down, undresses quickly, puts on her bathing suit and sandals. Grabs up a towel.

And she rushes, at last, down the winding rooted pathway, almost stumbling in her hurry—to the beach! She runs across the sand, to the gently lapping, warm clear water.

Half waking from what she recognizes as a dream (but how real it was, the water against her skin), Miriam tries, and fails, to read its meaning. Further awake, she realizes, too, that she is refreshed, as though she had indeed dipped into the ocean, or certainly had slept for more than the couple of hours which is actually the case.

Eric is still asleep. Carefully she slips out of bed and goes over to the window; she parts the heavy gold-threaded draperies and looks out. The menacing dawn has become an overcast, gray day, with strange dark clouds at the horizon. Closer in, on the beach, dozens of people are lying out on towels, body to body almost, all oiled as though there were sun— or as though they were dead.

Miriam unpacks some toilet things and goes into the bathroom, into further garish opulence: thick green towels, glistening green tile. And everything is scented, so sickly sweet that she hurries through washing.

Distantly, from the bedroom, she hears a knock at their door, in Russell's familiar rhythm—then Eric's sleepy voice, and Russell's. The closing door.

When she reënters the room Eric is sitting on the edge of the bed. He is still mostly unwashed, of course, his face blue-shadowed, blond stubble on his chin and his cheeks. But he looks cheerful, restored to himself. "A great place, huh?" he asks her. "Finally." And then he says, "Well, Joanie and Russ think a swim might be just the thing."

"Let them go swimming, then." Miriam has spoken with a calm, an assurance, that is absolute. "I think it looks dangerous." Let them drown, she does not say.

In her blue robe she goes over to stand beside him. She says, "I have to leave here." At that moment she is taller than he is.

He looks up at her, worriedly, uncomprehending. "You mean, just us?"

"I don't care. I have to leave."

Intelligent Eric has almost understood her, though. Reaching for the phone, he says, "I'll try for an afternoon plane," and he smiles, his old blond dazzling smile. "In the meantime, you don't want a swim?"

"No, I don't. But you go on, if you want to," and she smiles back.

Miriam. A small woman, who can suddenly, vividly see her husband Eric's body washed up on a beach, blond hair spread against cold sand, and long pale legs crookedly stretched down to the murky, turbulent sea.

Elizabeth

For every reason, including conventional wisdom's dictates that one should not go back to the scene of exceptional past happiness, I did not at all want to return to the Mexican beach at which I had not only been happy, my whole inner balance had seemed restored to me there, there at the extraordinarily lovely beach, with Elizabeth, my friend who now was dying and whom I could in no way restore, or save.

Since Elizabeth is—was about thirty years older than I am, you say that her role in my life was maternal; my mother, a psychoanalyst, as my father is, does say just that; she is also aware of her own jealousy of Elizabeth—of course she is, both jealous and aware. To me that is not how it seemed at all; I did not see Elizabeth as "mother"; I simply liked her, and I admired her more than anyone I knew. For a long time I wondered whether my feelings for Judson, to whom I now am married, were colored by the fact that I first met him in her house. I have concluded that yes, they were, and are; after all, they loved each other too. Elizabeth and Judson.

In any case I did not at all want to go back to Mexico, to the beach and to Elizabeth's house, where now my friend lay miserably dying, of emphysema. And I knew at last that I had to go, although of course Elizabeth did not say so—Elizabeth, the most elegantly tactful, most graceful of all people. I had been conscientiously writing her at least a couple of times a week, since she had allowed me to know of her illness, and for a while I managed to convince myself that that was better; many warm "interesting" letters might be less disturbing to her than an actual visit.

Then Judson, with whom I was not exactly in touch at that time— our connection was tentative, indefinite, perhaps anomalous—Judson telephoned me from Iowa, where he was living and teaching that year

Elizabeth

(Judson is a poet; I am a lawyer and I live—we live in Oakland, California). Judson said that I had better go down to see Elizabeth.

"It's simple, Minerva," he said. "If you don't you won't see her again."

Judson's poetry is minimalist, nor in personal conversation does he tend to waste words. I probably waste most things, certainly time and energy. Sometimes friendship, or love.

I asked him, "Will you go too?"

"If I can."

Judson and I had talked a lot, becoming friends, that first summer at San Angel, and once we had kissed. Not what anyone would term an affair, or even a "relationship"; still, the kiss took it a little out of the pure friendship class.

But I think I should begin with meeting Elizabeth, all those years back, the August when I was house-sitting for my parents in the hills of Berkeley. Being shrinks they both always took August off, and they usually rented a house in Wellfleet, Mass., where they got to see a lot of other shrinks. Then as now I was living in Oakland, and at that time I was going to law school, at U.C., in Berkeley. And so it made sense to stay in my parents' big house during August, to take care of their plants and the pool. They even offered to pay me, which I proudly refused.

At some point, along with various instructions, in an afterthought-sounding way my father said, "Oh. Your mother and I met an interesting woman at the Garsons'. An art historian. Originally Viennese, I think. She's renting the Jefferson cottage up the street and we told her to come use the pool if she ever felt like it." Piously he added, "Of course we told her to call you first."

"Dad. Really." My father knew perfectly well that I was having a relationship with a lawyer who was married but who spared me an occasional afternoon.

"Well, as you know it'll probably be cold all August anyway. How often we wonder whatever made us dream of putting in a pool. She might very well never call. Anyway you might like her."

If anyone else talked like that my father would call it "cross-signalling," which I believe is supposed to be "schizophrenogenic," but in himself he does not, of course. And in fact I am not especially schizy, more given to depression, unfortunately—although schizes probably don't much like their condition either.

"Her name is Elizabeth Loewenstein," my father added, and he repeated, "I really think you might like her. She has a very beautiful voice."

Only that last statement came as a surprise. Funnily enough, in view of his trade, my father is not at all a good listener, and so I was struck by the notion of a voice so beautiful that he would listen to it.

As things turned out, he was wrong only about the weather of that August, which was record-breakingly warm and clear, amazing and beautiful. From my parents' giant picture windows I watched the sun set over San Francisco and the bay, all implausibly gold and glistening.

Elizabeth Loewenstein, the possibly garrulous nuisance whom I had feared, never phoned, and it is hard to recall on just what impulse I finally called her and asked her over for a swim. Partly it was because I was lonely—were I a believer, though, I would say that God had instructed me. As it is I see my call to her as a piece of sheer good luck, for me. In any case, I did call, and she said that yes, she would like to come over for a swim.

Elizabeth was small and dark, with short, graying curly hair and gray-green eyes. Lightly lined pale skin, a bony nose. Her manner was tentative, rather shy—and she had the most attractive voice that I had ever heard. (It was almost annoying, to have my father proved so accurate.) A low voice, slightly hoarse, and very slightly accented. A voice with great range: warm brightness, and a complicated depth of shadows. "Your voice has chiaroscuro," I once said to Elizabeth, and she laughed, of course, but she was pleased. She had a certain, highly characteristic way of saying "Ah!" like a tiny bark. That "Ah" was one of her responsive, listening sounds; she listened more actively than anyone, I thought—I think so still. She smoked a lot.

God knows what we talked about, that first afternoon. I only remember liking her very much and urging her to stay. She left after less than half an hour, and I told her please to come back whenever she could.

Nor do I remember much of the content of later conversations; it is rather the quality of being with Elizabeth that I remember. And her voice, and that tiny barked "Ah!" And her just-hoarse laugh.

Rather little of our talk was personal. Elizabeth almost never talked about herself, and so I was not encouraged to do so—which, that summer, was quite all right with me; I was tired of talking or even thinking about my troublesome, somewhat sordid love affair. Elizabeth often talked about places, her passion for Venice, and for the hill towns of Umbria and Tuscany. And she told me about the extravagant, wildly impractical (not even quite legal) gesture of buying a house in Mexico, near the beach.

Once I talked to a Berkeley woman who also admired and liked Elizabeth, and that woman said, "Oh, Elizabeth is so wonderful. You can do absolutely anything you want around her. Say anything."

Well, that was entirely to miss the point of Elizabeth, I thought. I would never knowingly have expressed a trivial or mean-spirited thought to Elizabeth; her own elegant, supremely intelligent demeanor forbade it. And actually one of the reasons that I so much liked Elizabeth was that she, as the phrase goes, "brought out my best." With her I was less trivial and mean, and much more intelligent, more finely observant than usual, and if not elegant at least restrained. Judson and I have talked about this, and he says that he felt the same. "Elevated," is a word he used. "Ennobled, even," Judson said.

This is the much abbreviated story of Elizabeth's life, as I pieced it together from stray remarks, tiny glimpses over our years of conversation, and all our letters.

She was born not in Vienna but in Paris, and later, before the Anschluss, she had studied in Vienna. Her parents were deported to camps in Germany, where they died (very little about this from Elizabeth). After the war she studied in Florence, in Bologna, and at Oxford. In addition to those places she had lived in Lisbon and in Cuernavaca, and in her Mexican beach town, San Angel. And in New York and Boston. She had been married three times, twice divorced, once widowed—but of those relationships I know nothing. Once she spent some time at Lake Tahoe with a man who was trying to get a divorce in Reno but did not (out of character, this intimate glimpse arrived in a letter, like a present, when she knew that I was having some troubles of that nature). When I first knew her she was living in Boston, out in Berkeley on a studying visit. Later she moved down to New York. And later still, she moved to San Angel, to her small house in the manzanita thickets. For good.

That first summer in Berkeley Elizabeth and I saw each other mostly for late afternoon swims. We also went to the Berkeley and the Oakland art museums. Elizabeth looked as actively as she listened, as intently. I can see her: a small woman in something elegantly plain, gray linen, maybe brown, bending forward to see yet more clearly, her eyes narrowed in the effort, as she stands before a big canvas of some enormous, primitive animals, by Joan Brown.

Elizabeth was especially fond of that Oakland museum; to my great pleasure she preferred it to the San Francisco MOMA. "So much less pretentious," she remarked, quite accurately, I thought. "A more *real* museum, and architecturally it is marvelous, a beauty."

I have said that most of my talk with Elizabeth was impersonal; however, I do remember one conversation which became intimate, oddly enough having to do with our noses.

I had spent too many hours the week before just lying beside the pool, ostensibly studying for the bar, actually worrying about my life, as I enjoyed the sun. As a reward for that self-indulgence my nose first blistered, then peeled (I have inherited my mother's white Irish skin, my father's Polish-Jewish nose).

"I wish it would peel away," I said to Elizabeth, as though joking. "Peel down to a tiny snub nose, like my mother's. Why did I just get her skin?"

Elizabeth laughed, accepting my joke, but she said, "You're too tall for a tiny snub nose, Minerva. Besides, yours is distinguished, like an Italian Renaissance lady." And then she sighed. "But I know about hating noses. For years I despaired of mine. And Minerva, I had more reason, you will admit. I am a very small woman with a very large nose."

"But yours is beautiful!"

"Ah! There, you see?"

We both laughed then, in the end-of-August almost cooling air, an hour or so before the sun would set.

Elizabeth

.   .   .

In September Elizabeth went back to Boston. My parents came home, and I moved back into my own small Oakland apartment; I studied hard, I spent time with friends and with my lover, with whom I quarrelled a lot—on whom I made, according to him, impossible demands.

And I began what was to become a rich and wonderfully gratifying correspondence with Elizabeth. (I have it still, now boxed and tied up with heavy string. I always mean to take it out for rereading, but so far I have not.) It turned out that for us both letters were a form of conversation. I have sometimes even thought letters more satisfactory and God knows safer than most human contact, and it is possible that Elizabeth felt so too. In any case we wrote to each other quite often, and generally at some length. Only on trips Elizabeth might confine herself to postcards, with beautiful pictures: Venice, Spoleto, Siena.

And even cards from Elizabeth had the unique, quite unmistakable sound of her voice. I have sometimes had quite the opposite experience, very likely everyone has: the stiff, ungiving letters from friends who in person are both warm and amusing; dull letters from people one thought bright. Elizabeth's letters and her cards were exactly like herself, including her very slight, to-me-delightful mistakes in English.

Then, over the next months and the following years everything in my life went black, and wrong. I had passed the bar, and got a job with an okay firm in Oakland, specializing in labor law; but I felt that I was overworked, too many sudden trips to Chicago or Los Angeles, for depositions. Worse, I began to have serious doubts about the law itself, or rather about its current practice, its practitioners. My lover left for New Haven, with his wife. I got along with my parents even less well than usual, and I quarrelled in a serious way with a couple of longstanding friends. I was very tired. I imagined myself as a piece of old elastic, all gone gray, all the stretch and give worn out.

Well, a classic depression, but no one's depression seems "classic" to the person enduring it. And in my case, such overexposure to shrinks made it hard for me even to think, This is a depression, this too will pass. I did not even consider the possible aid of some therapy.

The very weather that year seemed inimical: a long fall and winter of cold rain, ferocious winds, followed by a spring of no respite but more cold and winds, a perpetual black-gray fog, looming up from the bay.

I had not written to Elizabeth that I was depressed, or whatever I was, but she may of course have sensed it. I did write about the frightful summer weather, the dark fog and cold, the perpetual wind.

Elizabeth wrote back that she would be in her house in Mexico for all of November, and that I must get some time off and come to visit her then. "I know how it is with long cold summers," she wrote. "You believe them to last forever, as sometimes they do. But maybe the idea of a warm white beach and many flowers will help a little to get you through the next few months." She further explained that she had already promised "such guest quarters as there are" to another friend—"a poet, Judson Venable, you might sometime have read him?" I had not.

But that is how I came to spend two weeks of that November in Mexico, my first trip to Elizabeth's house. Which in many ways changed my life.

As though to test my stamina, even September and October, which are often the nicest months in Northern California, that year were terrible; black heavy rains, and more rains, with dangerous flooding, mudslides near the coast. Dark, relentless winds. I packed for Mexico in a state of disbelief, jamming the light cottons recommended by Elizabeth into my seabag. And I boarded the plane that dark November morning still unconvinced that weather anywhere would be welcoming, and warm.

After seven hours that were alternately boring and turbulent (more tests!), including a frantic, high-stress changing of planes in Mexico City, in a smaller plane we flew toward a range of sharp green mountains, between perilously rocky peaks and over jungles, leveling at last toward a flat blue sea, and beaches. A white airstrip surrounded by green jungle growth.

Getting off that plane and walking down the ramp was like entering another atmosphere; I swam into warm, moist, delicately scented air, into an embrace of warmth and flowers. I began to smile, and for most of the time that I was there I felt that smile, which was interior as well—that

November, and sometimes I did think how strange that it should be indeed November, the dark, funereal month of death and sorrow and ashes, especially in Mexico.

And—there was Elizabeth, small and lightly tanned, reaching up to kiss me on both cheeks, saying, "Ah! Minerva, how good it is that you are here. But how thin, how pale! We must work to change you—"

I was embarrassingly close to tears, and only murmured that I was glad to see her too. I was grateful for the activity involved in stowing my bag into her improbably pink jeep. "I had not before driven a jeep, perhaps it is fortunate that it comes in so ridiculous a color," Elizabeth laughed, very happily.

We jolted over a deeply potholed road, through a shaded stretch of jungle, all wildly, diversely green, toward a small, shabby cluster of buildings, a town at which I barely looked, for there ahead of us was the sea: glinting, green and blue, white-waved, dancing out to a pale-blue sky. And everywhere flowers, bougainvillea, hibiscus, vines and bushes blooming in all possible shades, pinks and reds and purples, other blossoms of the smallest, most delicate yellow white. And butterflies, and birds.

"The place where you stay may not be entirely to your taste," Elizabeth was saying. "But you will be so little there. Mostly, it is very close to where I am."

She was right about my hotel, Del Sol: a cluster of bright new cottages around a pool and bar-restaurant—less than entirely to my taste. It was garish and sometimes noisy, populated as it was by young Texans and Germans. None of which mattered at all, as I was almost never there. That first day Elizabeth dropped me off with brief instructions. "You must take what time you need to collect yourself. Then walk out to the beach and turn left. Not too many yards to the end is a road leading up into the woods, and there you find my small house. It is brown, with a porch."

I collected myself for fifteen or twenty minutes, washing and changing to my lightest cotton dress, wrapping a bathing suit in a towel, and then I walked out to the beach and turned left. It is not too much to say that I already felt myself another person, in that air—Elizabeth's air.

Her house was not quite as easy to find as she had said. I hesitated in front of a couple of shacky cottages, and then I walked on up into some dark manzanita woods, the trees here and there overhung with heavy moss, thick vines. And there was Elizabeth's house—it had to be: a small square brown structure, over half its space a generous porch, the wall that faced the sea entirely of glass.

On the porch was a broad woven hammock on which someone obviously had slept ("Judson"?); there were rumpled pillows, a thrown-aside light blanket. Next to the hammock some big dark leather sling chairs.

And Elizabeth, coming out to greet me. "Ah, good Minerva to have brought your bathing suit. Always we have a little swim before our drinks and dinner."

Going inside, I saw that a large area between the house and the beach had been cleared, giving a branch-framed picture of the sea: sand, small birds, waves and distant headlands. The other walls were filled with pictures, narrow-framed line drawings, a few photographs. A wide low sofa, Elizabeth's bed (where sometimes she slept with Judson Venable?). Big bright wool pillows. A low tile table. Lamps.

I changed into my suit in the bathroom and we went down to the beach and swam, and I was entirely enchanted. Magic water, I thought, magically light and clear, of a perfect coolness.

I am aware, speaking of Elizabeth and of her surroundings, in San Angel, that I am presenting a possibly implausible perfection. As to Elizabeth herself, I can only say that for me she did seem that impossibility, a perfect person. To put it negatively, she was a person about whom I never felt even slightly troubled, I was never bored with her—reactions that I have experienced at one time or another with almost everyone else I have known very well (beginning, I guess, with my parents). And as for San Angel itself, and the beach there, it was at first perfect, perfectly quiet and beautiful. Later it did change considerably, but that is the later part of my story, of my return visit to Elizabeth, in her illness.

Back in the house, while I dressed Elizabeth began several processes in the kitchen. "My good Aurelia comes later to serve our dinner," she explained. "And Judson. He will very soon be back, I think." She added, "I hope that you will like him, as I do."

Actually I did not like Judson very much, at first. That was in part because I assumed him to be Elizabeth's young lover, and he seemed neither sufficiently young nor dashing for that role. Also, he speaks very softly, and infrequently, with an almost impenetrable Southern accent, which at the time I took to be a bad sign, suggestive of bigotry, if not downright stupidity.

Also, Judson is more than a little odd to look at. Tall, very thin, with a big nose and big floppy-looking ears (curiously we look somewhat alike, except for the ears; mine, like my mother's, are quite small), as he shambled up to the porch that first night I thought, Oh, surely not. I even thought, Elizabeth, how could you?

I also distrusted Judson's protestations as to "their" pleasure at my arrival. He said, "We've been most looking forward to your visit," and the words sounded false and stilted to me: the proverbial Southern good manners. I am not notably trusting, in my reactions to people.

Aurelia, the Mexican helper ("maid" does not seem the proper word, nor did Elizabeth ever refer to her as such), next arrived, and I did like her. She was tall and dark and beautiful, evidently deeply fond of Elizabeth; she smiled a great deal and spoke almost not at all. (It turned out later that it was through Aurelia that Elizabeth had bought the house; it was actually in Aurelia's name, a legal necessity, for beach-front property, but also generous on Elizabeth's part. Aurelia's life was to be transformed.)

The sunset that was just then commencing over the far eastern rim of the Pacific was the most splendid that I had ever seen, the wildest range of color; gorgeous, brilliant rags of color hung across the sky.

Judson made Margaritas which he served to us out on the porch, as we watched the sunset remnants slowly fade—and then Aurelia brought out our dinner, the first of many wonderfully garlicky fish.

But mainly, for me, there was Elizabeth's lovely voice to listen to— although for the first time I began to wish she would not smoke so much; I don't especially mind cigarette smoke, not outside on a porch, but it obviously made her cough a lot.

Elizabeth and I talked and talked, and talked and laughed, and she smoked, and coughed. Judson said rather little, but I had already begun to like him a little better. He had a good, responsive smile, and his occasional laugh seemed warm.

After dinner Elizabeth looked tired, I thought; actually I was too, and I got up to leave.

"Ah! Then Judson will walk with you," Elizabeth announced.

"Oh no, how silly, it's no distance—"

"Minerva, there could be banditos." Elizabeth laughed, then a tiny cough. "But I expect you back here for breakfast, which we eat all through the morning."

And so Judson did walk back to Del Sol with me, along the shadowy, gray-white sand, beside the black sea. In perfect silence. At my cottage door we stopped, and he touched my shoulder very lightly. Not quite looking at me (a habit of his) he said, "I'm glad you came down." Adding, "She's really been looking forward to you." Long speeches, coming from Judson.

I was smiling as I went inside to bed.

Although I should admit to being quite as prurient as the next person, that November I did not subject the Elizabeth-Judson relationship to serious scrutiny, having to do with sex. I assumed some form of love to exist between them, and I did not concern myself with determining its exact nature. I saw that Elizabeth's bright gray eyes were often watching Judson thoughtfully, and that when he spoke she listened with her intensely attentive semi-smile. But then she watched me too, and listened when I spoke, with extreme attention.

My parents (the shrinks) would have said and probably did say that I had fallen into an ideal—or rather, an idealized situation: I was the loved child of loving parents, whose sexual lives I did not think about.

Another explanation for my relative lack of curiosity about them is that I was simply too happy there in Mexico, during that beautifully, caressingly warm November stay, for serious thoughts about other people's lives. (An extreme of happiness can make you just as self-absorbed as misery can; witness people happily in love.) With Elizabeth and sometimes with Judson too I swam three or four times a day, in the marvelous, buoyant water; we walked, and walked and walked along the beach, in the direction of the tiny town, San Angel, or sometimes, more adventurously, we took the other direction: a walk that involved scrambling across small cliffs of sheer sharp rock, clutching in our passage at thin manzanita boughs, until we reached another beach, where we swam and sometimes picnicked.

An abundance of sheer physical exertion, then, was clearly contributing to my new and entire well-being, but I think quite as significant was the extraordinary beauty of the place, the white, white beach with its background of wild, brilliant jungle growth, interspersed with bright flowers. And the foreground of a brighter, greener sea.

And Elizabeth.

And Judson, whom I continued increasingly to like. I even began to think him good enough for Elizabeth, almost. I began to see the attractiveness of his long slow supple legs, as he ambled along the sand, or swam, or led the way across the difficult stretch of rocks, often waiting to extend a hand to me, or to Elizabeth, who lagged behind. As she sometimes said (perhaps too often?) she simply could not keep up with young folks such as we. She was in fact quite often out of breath; she required a lot of rest, which at the time I put down simply to her age, and to smoking so much. But I thought Judson was very good to her.

One of the pleasures of those first, enchanted November weeks in Mexico (as opposed to my second visit, four years later)—a considerable joy for Elizabeth and for me was our shopping from the occasional vendors: Indian-looking, mostly, both men and women of all ages, sometimes with small children. They would hold out bright flimsy dresses to us, trays of silver and jade; they smiled at our greed, and our inability to make up our minds. And at our very faulty Spanish, Elizabeth's considerably better than mine. Judson watched, and smiled, and seemed to enjoy the spectacle.

Elizabeth bought a long dark blue dress, the blue unusually rich and deep; I bought something white, long and lacy, and we both wore our new dresses that night at dinner.

In those idle, happy ways our days ran past. Sunsets succeeded each other, each brilliant panoply of clouds seemed new, original and splendid. We watched those displays each night as we drank our salty-sweet Margaritas, served by Judson with his particular Southern ceremoniousness, his semi-bow as he handed either of us our glass. Later, in the near-dark shadows, we had our dinner. Later still, in the true dark, the heavy tropical night, Judson would walk down to my cottage with me. Sometimes we talked a little, more often not. He would say good night, perhaps with a quick touch to my arm, or my shoulder; I would go inside, get ready for bed, and read for a little while. And Judson would hurry back to Elizabeth—or so I for the most part imagined.

On my next-to-last night there, the end of my November weeks, at my door Judson turned to me; he took my shoulders in his hands and then, quite simply, we kissed. Or, not simply; it was a complicated kiss, containing as it did so much unspoken between us. In the next instant, that of our separation, I felt dizzied, almost unreal.

Judson touched my face. "You're lovely."

"But—" Meaning, as he knew, But what about you and Elizabeth?

"I think you've got things a little wrong," was all he said. So like him; talk about minimalism.

One of the things I had wrong was the time of Judson's departure, which took place quite early the next day; he was gone by the time I arrived for breakfast.

Actually I was glad, happier to have a final day alone with Elizabeth, and I did not want to face possible complications with Judson. I wanted to thank Elizabeth, to say how happy my time there had made me. And that is how it went; Elizabeth and I talked and talked all day, she in her lovely, amazing voice. And she listened as I talked, with her wide, calm, amused gray eyes.

And the next day I went back to California.

Not quite predictably (I myself would not have predicted it) things went well with me, over the next months and then years that followed that November visit to Elizabeth. I was on an unusually even keel, for me. I had no major love affairs, nothing marvelous, but then no disasters either, just a couple of pleasant "relationships" with very nice men. I switched law firms, moving to a new one, still in Oakland, but a firm with a feminist–public good orientation.

Elizabeth and I wrote many letters to each other; I'm afraid mine were mostly about myself (Ah, the joys of a good correspondent as a captive audience!). Elizabeth wrote about everything except herself—or Judson, for that matter.

This went on until what must have been a couple of years later, when I got a letter from her that seemed more than a little alarming, though it was couched in Elizabeth's habitual gentle language. First, the good news that she had stopped smoking. And then this sentence: "Judson was here for a visit, and as I had not seen him for some time I fear he was alarmed by my not-so-good health."

Violently alarmed myself, I immediately telephoned Elizabeth; she was out at first, it was hours before I could reach her, and then, in character, she apologized for having upset me. "It is just this emphysema that I have," she said, but I could hear her labored breath. "Nature's punishment for heavy smokers." She tried to laugh, and gasped, and coughed.

After that I wrote to her much more often, and I tried to think of presents for her—not an easy task with elegant, apparently self-sufficient Elizabeth, but sometimes I succeeded, I think. I understood that she would write more briefly now, and less often, and that was true; she sent notes and postcards, thanking me for my letters, for whatever book or small Berkeley trophy I had sent (a paper cat, some Mexican-looking straw flowers). She said very little about how she was, but when I pressed her in a specific way ("Please tell me how you are") she admitted to not feeling very well. "I have so little strength, much discomfort. At times it seems cruel and unusual, at other times deserved." She would spend the winter in Mexico. "I hope there to breathe more easily."

This was the period I mentioned at the start, during which I believed, or perhaps succeeded in convincing myself that my frequent letters and small attentions were more beneficial than an actual visit from me would be.

And that was the theory broken by Judson's phone call, from Iowa, telling me that I should go to Mexico. "It's simple, Minerva. If you don't, you won't see her again."

"Will you go too?"

"If I can."

Those were the first sentences to pass between us since the night of that kiss, I later thought.

Of course I would go, and of course for every reason I did not want to. I made reservations, plane tickets and a cottage at Del Sol. Since Elizabeth had no phone down there I tried calling Del Sol myself, remembering that she received an occasional message through them. At last I reached a person who seemed to know that a Señora Loewenstein lived nearby, but I had no faith in the message, and I wrote to her too.

It was only as I boarded the plane, early one foggy, chilly morning at the San Francisco airport, that it occurred to me that this too was the month of November, that an almost exact four years had passed since my first visit.

However, disembarking at San Angel, the air was as moist, as caressing and fragrant as I remembered, and I began to think or hope that this trip might be all right.

I was surprised to find Aurelia in the terminal waiting room—tall, beautifully smiling Aurelia, who in answer to my quick question told me that Elizabeth was not well at all. "She lay down, she not get up," Aurelia said.

My first strong and confused reaction to this shocking news was anger: how could Elizabeth be so ill and not say so? Or, really, *how could Elizabeth be so ill?*

In Elizabeth's old pink jeep Aurelia drove me through the turbulent, violent green jungle, to the glittering sea, waves dancing in the bright mid-afternoon sunlight—to my cottage at Del Sol. I threw my bag onto the bed, threw water on my face and combed my hair, and ran back out to Aurelia, in the jeep.

How like Elizabeth (as Judson and I said later) to have arranged that my first sight of her should be reassuring. She lay on her hammock (Judson's hammock, as I thought of it), Elizabeth, in something pale blue, gauzy, very pretty. At my approach she half sat up, she reached out her hands to me. "Ah! Minerva. How good that you have come." And she smiled, and said all the rest with her eyes.

I bent or rather knelt to kiss her cheeks, thinking, How could I have blamed her for her illness? as I fought back tears. I asked, "You don't feel so well?"

"Not too." Another smile.

We had both begun to sound like Judson, I thought just then; our speech was as stripped down, as minimal as his was.

Elizabeth next asked, "Judson called you?"

"Uh, yes. He did."

She coughed. "He will come also?"

"He said if he could. He's really busy there, I think."

Elizabeth

Her eyes blazed at me then, gray fire, for a full moment before she spoke, and when she did her damaged voice was wild. "He must come. You will call to him," she said.

I was too pummelled by violent emotion to understand, quite. I only said, "Of course. Tomorrow."

Elizabeth smiled, and she lay back and closed her eyes. When she opened them again, after a short moment, it was as though that passionate exchange had not taken place. She said, "Ah, Minerva. Now you must tell me all about your life."

Much later, Judson in his way explained, or nearly. "Yes, in love. I think we were," he said. "But never lovers."

"But, why not?"

He smiled, not looking at me but at some private interior vision, probably Elizabeth. "Too risky, for one thing. A good friendship at stake."

By then of course Elizabeth had died, and Judson and I in our own curious ways had "fallen in love" and married. Which is what we both thought quite possibly she had wanted us to do. In a sense I had been "offered up" to Judson, that first November: Elizabeth's insistence that I visit her just then, her always making Judson walk home with me. Perhaps she thought that if he and I became lovers she would love him less? I don't know, surely not, nor does Judson. It is only clear that Elizabeth was an immeasurably subtle woman, and a passionate one.

Now, more or less repeating things already said in letters, I told Elizabeth that on the whole my life seemed very good. I was happy in my new law firm, I was even getting along better with my parents (possibly because they had separated and were in that way getting along much better with each other).

Elizabeth listened, and smiled, saying very little. Then Aurelia reappeared, to arrange Elizabeth's pillows and to say to me, "She very tired now, I think."

(Aurelia, soon to be the owner of that house; perhaps something of that showed in her just perceptibly less shy bearing? Elizabeth must have liked to think of her there, of the difference in her life.)

I got up to go, but Elizabeth's thin hand detained me. "Dinner at eight," she said, with a smile and a small choked laugh.

It was still not late, not sunset time, and so instead of turning in at Del Sol I walked on down the beach, toward town. And I knew at once that this was a mistake: seemingly overnight (although actually there had been four years), big gaudy condominiums had sprung up, and a couple of huge hotels, towering and bright and hideous, where before there had been jungle green, and flowers, and space. Bodies crowded the beach; even had I wanted to walk much farther that would have been impossible. And vendors: I was almost instantly accosted by a swarm of them, sad-eyed little boys selling Chiclets, thin old men with bags of peanuts, women with the same butterfly-colored dresses as before, some trays of silver and jade, but I thought they all looked suddenly sad and thin, and too eager to sell, whereas before a certain diffidence had prevailed. The town's so-visible prosperity had not trickled down to these natives, I thought.

And so I turned back to Del Sol, and it was from my tiny sea-front cottage there that I watched the glorious sunset of that first night, and in fact of all the nights of my stay at San Angel—as from the bar loud hard rock music blared, hits from the States of ten or so years back. I could not decide whether the place had got much noisier in the years of my absence or if it was simply that I had spent so little time there, before.

At dinner Elizabeth looked rested, animated, though her color was so bad, yellowish, sallow. "I am glad you have come!" she said to me several times—an unnecessary expense of breath; I knew she was glad.

I went back to my cottage early, and read for a couple of hours, despite the clamorous music—and I tried not to think very deeply about Elizabeth.

The next morning was overcast, gray. I went in to the office to put in the call to Judson, in Iowa, and I was told that it would probably rain before noon. A surprise: I had thought it never rained in San Angel.

A further surprise, and a better one, was that I got through to Judson almost at once, with a perfect connection.

"I really think Elizabeth wants to see you," I told him. "I think you should come down."

A small pause, during which I could hear him thinking, almost.

"Not right now," he said. "I can't. But tell her I'll be there before Christmas."

"Good," I told him. "She'll feel better with something definite." I added, "She's pretty bad."

"I know." Another pause, before he asked, "You're okay?"

"Oh, sure. But it's raining here."

He made an effort which I could feel to say, "Give my love to Elizabeth."

"Oh, I will."

"Good-by, Minerva. I thank you."

"Good-by!"

In fact Elizabeth was to die before the end of November. She had what I tried hard to think of as a merciful heart attack a week after I had gone back to Oakland; Aurelia called to tell me. As Judson and I said to each other, how perfectly in character, how exquisitely polite of her to wait for death (for which she must have longed, she was so miserably uncomfortable) until after I had come and gone, and to spare Judson even making the trip.

Her death, I suppose, is what began to bring me and Judson together, though actually a teaching stint at Stanford was what brought him to California, and to me. Here we began to talk less about Elizabeth, more of ourselves. Very cautiously we began to be in love.

But that morning in Mexico, when I went to see Elizabeth, walking across the damp gray sand in the gentle rain—when I gave her the message from Judson she smiled as though she had all the time in the world for future visits, for receiving and giving love.

"Ah! Good," she said. And, in almost Judson's words, "I thank you, Minerva. You are good to me, you and Judson."

Sintra

In Lisbon, Portugal, on a brilliant October Sunday morning, an American woman, a tourist, experiences a sudden rush of happiness, as clear and pure as the sunshine that warms the small flowers near her feet. She is standing in the garden of the Castelo de São Jorge, and the view before her includes a great spread of the city: the river and its estuary, the shining new bridge; she can see for miles!

Her name is Arden Kinnell, and she is a journalist, a political-literary critic, sometimes writing on films; she survives somewhat precariously, although recently she has begun to enjoy a small success. Tall and thin, Arden is a little awkward, shy, and her short blonde hair is flimsy, rather childlike. Her face is odd, but striking in its oddity: such wide-spaced, staring, yellow-green eyes, such a wide, clearly sensual mouth. And now she is smiling, out of sheer pleasure at this moment.

Arden and her lover-companion—Gregor, the slightly rumpled young man at her side—arrived the night before from Paris, and they slept long and well, after only a little too much wine at their hotel. Healthy Californians, they both liked the long, rather steep walk up those winding, cobbled streets, through the picturesquely crumbling, red tile–roofed old quarter, the Alfama, up to this castle, this view of everything. Arden is especially struck by the sight of the distant, lovely bridge, which she has read was dedicated to the revolution of April, 1974, the so-called Generals' Revolution that ended fascism in Portugal.

The air is so good, so fresh and clear! Breathing in, Arden thinks, Ah, Lisbon, how beautiful it is. She thinks, I must tell Luiz how much I like his city.

Madness: in that demented instant she has forgotten that at a recent party in San Francisco a woman told her that Luiz was dying (was "terminal," as she put it). Here in Lisbon. Now.

And even stranger than that friendly thought of Luiz, whom she once loved wildly, desperately, entirely—dear God, friends is the last thing they were; theirs was an adversary passion, almost fatal—stranger than the friendly impulse is the fact that it persists, in Arden, generally a most disciplined woman; her mind is—usually—strong and clear, her habits of work exemplary. However, *insanely,* there in Lisbon, that morning, as she continues to admire and to enjoy the marvelous sweep of city roofs, the graceful bridge above the shining water, she even feels the presence of Luiz, and happily; that is the incredible part. Luiz, with whom she experienced the wildest reaches of joy, but never the daily, sunny warmth of happiness.

Can Luiz possibly just that day have died? Can this lively blue Portuguese air be giving her that message, and thus causing her to rejoice? Quickly she decides against this: Luiz is not dead, he cannot be—although a long time ago she surely wished him dead, believing as she then did that only his death could release her from the brutal pain of his absence in her life.

Or, could the woman at the San Francisco party (a woman whom she did not like at all, Arden now remembers—so small and tautly chic), could that woman have been mistaken? Some other Luiz V. was dying in Lisbon? But that was unlikely; the woman clearly meant the person that Arden knew, or had known—the rich and well-connected, good, but not very famous painter. The portraitist.

Then, possibly Luiz was ill but has recovered? A remission, or possibly a misdiagnosis in the first place? Everyone knows that doctors make such mistakes; they are often wrong.

Arden decides that Luiz indeed is well; he is well and somewhere relatively nearby, in some house or apartment that she can at least distantly see from where she is standing, near the crenellated battlements of the castle, on the sun-warmed yellow gravel. She looks back down into the Alfama, where Luiz might be.

Gregor, the young lover—only five years younger than Arden, actually—Gregor, a photographer, "knows" about Luiz. Friends before they became lovers (a change in status that more than once has struck Arden as an error), in those days Arden and Gregor exchanged life stories, finding that they shared a propensity for romantic disaster—along with their similarly precarious freelance professions (and surely there is some connection? both she and Gregor take romantic as well as economic risks?).

"Can you imagine a woman dumb enough to believe that a Portuguese Catholic would leave his wife and children just for her?" Arden asked, in the wry mode that had become a useful second nature to her. "Oh, how stupid I was!" she lamentingly laughed. And Gregor countered with his own sad love adventure; she was a model, Lisa. "Well, can you imagine a photographer who wouldn't know not to take up with a model?" This was when Gregor, just out of art school, was trying to get a start in New York; Lisa, though younger than he, was already doing quite well. But Lisa's enchanting liveliness, and her wit, as well as her lovely thin body, turned out to be coke-maintained. "No one then was doing anything but plain old dope and a little acid," was Gregor's comment. "I have to hand it to her, she was really ahead of her time. But *crazy.*"

Gregor too can be wry, or does he imitate Arden? She sometimes has an alarmed sense that he sounds like her, or tries to. But he is fun to talk to, still, and often funny. And he is smart, and sexy. Tall and light-haired, he is not handsome but very attractive, with his huge pale Russian eyes, his big confident body. A good photographer, in fact he is excellent.

At moments, though, Arden feels a cold enmity from Gregor, which is when she wishes that they were still "just friends." And is he an alcoholic, really? He drinks too much, too often. And does he love her?

Oh, *love,* Arden thinks. How can I even use that word.

Gregor and Arden do not in fact live together, and although she sometimes tells friends that she considers this an ideal arrangement, often she actually does not. Her own house in Larkspur is small, but hardly too small for two, and it is pleasantly situated on a wooded knoll, no other houses in sight. There is a pool, and what Arden considers her recreational garden, an eccentric plot all crowded with squash and nasturtiums and various lettuces. Gregor spends much of his time there with her; he likes to swim, although gardening does not interest him—

but he also keeps a small place of his own on a rather bleak street near Twin Peaks, in San Francisco, high up in the fog and winds. And his apartment itself is bleak: three small rooms, monastically clean and plain and white. There is also a darkroom, of course, where he often works late at night. No personal traces anywhere, no comfortable mess. Forbidding. Arden has only been there twice. Even when they are in the city it always seems better to drive on back to Larkspur, after the movie or concert, whatever. But Arden thinks of him there, in those rooms, on the nights that he stays in town, and her thoughts are uneasy. Not only the existence of that apartment, an alternative to her house, as well as to herself, but its character is threatening to Arden, reminding her of aspects of Gregor himself: a sensed interior coldness, an implacable emptiness. When she thinks of Gregor's house she could be imagining an enemy.

She has never seen any food around, for instance: does he only drink there, alone, in his white, white rooms? She does not imagine that he sees other women, but certainly he could. He could go out to bars, bring women home. This though seems less likely, and therefore possibly less threatening than just drinking alone, so grimly.

At the end of Arden's love affair with Luiz there were hints in local gossip columns that he had a "somewhat less than professional relationship" with a few of the subjects of his portraits, and the pain of this information (explaining so much! so plausible!) was a further unbearable thrust to Arden.

In any case, since Gregor knows about Luiz, including the fact of Lisbon, home of Luiz (but not the possible mortal illness; Arden has not been able or perhaps not seen fit to mention this), does Gregor think it strange that so far in Lisbon Arden has not mentioned Luiz, whom she used sometimes to talk about? Here she has not once said his name, in any context. She herself does not quite know why she has not.

Still, just now she is happy, looking down to small balconies of flowers, of vines that climb up on intricate iron grillwork. She wonders: possibly, is that where Luiz lives, that especially handsome, long-windowed apartment? with the dark-gray drapery?

Arden is happy and well and suddenly very hungry. She says to Gregor, "Isn't that a restaurant over there? Shouldn't we try it? It looks nice, and I can't bear to leave this view."

"Well, sure." Gregor's look in Arden's direction is slightly puzzled—as well it might be, Arden thinks. She too is puzzled, very. She loves Lisbon, though, and her blood races dizzily.

They go into the restaurant; they are quickly seated at a white-clothed table, with the glorious Lisbon view.

"Had you ever, uh, heard about this place before?" asks Gregor, once their wine has come. This is his closest—if oblique—reference to Luiz, who surely might have mentioned to Arden a favorite restaurant, with its marvelous view. But as though realizing what he has done Gregor then covers up. "Or did you read about it somewhere? a restaurant guide?"

"No, actually not. It just looked good. The doors—" The front door is of heavy glass, crossed with pitted, old-looking iron bars. "An interesting use of glass, don't you think?"

"Yes," says Gregor.

Their eyes regard each other suspiciously.

Remembering Luiz, Arden sees flat smooth black hair, that shines, in bedside lamplight. She watches him as he dresses, while she lies there spent and languid; she watches everything shining, his hair and his bright black eyes, their dark glitter. He comes over to kiss her good-by, for that day, and then he cannot, does not leave.

"This is an illness, this endless craving that I have for you. A mania—" Luiz more than once remarked, with an accuracy that Arden could not then admit to herself. She did not feel ill, only that all her nerves had been touched, involved.

Luiz is (or was) an excellent portraitist. His paintings were both elegant and penetrating, often less than flattering; on the other hand, on occasion, very flattering indeed. He was at his best with women (well, of course he was, Arden has thought). Once she went to an exhibit of his paintings at a Sutter Street gallery—though not, naturally, to the opening, a social event much reported in the papers.

In fact they first met at a gallery opening. From across the room Luiz found Arden (that is how he put it, "I *found* you there"), coming over to talk to her intently for a while (about what? later she could never remember). He called the next day; he called and called, he would not be put off.

This was in the early sixties. Arden, then much involved in the peace movement, saw his assault on her life as an incursion, an invasion. He attacked with superior weapons, and with the violence of his passion for her. And he won. "I think that you have fallen in love with my love for you," he once (again accurately) remarked.

Out of her depth, and dismayed by everything about Luiz—the wife and family at home in Portugal, a fascist country—Arden found some small comfort in the fact that all his favorite writers seemed to be of the Left: Silone, Camus—and that his favorite movie director was Pasolini.

She pointed this out, rather shyly—the shyness of an essentially defeated person.

"My darling, I have a horror of the Right, of *fascismo.*" (But in much the same tone he also said, "I have a horror of *fat,*" as he stroked her thin thigh, then cupped the sharp crest with his wise and skillful hand.)

You could simply look at his eyes, or his mouth, Arden thinks now, and know that Luiz was remarkable.

She remembers his walk. The marvelous confidence in that stride. During all the weeks of suffering so acutely from his absence in her life (classically, Luiz did not get the promised divorce, nor did he defect from the fascist government he railed against; he went back to Lisbon, to his wife, to that regime)—during all that time of suffering, it was the thought of his walk that caused Arden the most piercing pain: that singular, energetic motion of his body, its course through the world, without her.

After lunch, much more slowly than earlier they had climbed the streets, Arden and Gregor start down. The day is still glorious; at one point they stop at a small terrace where there are rounded cypresses, very small, and a lovely wall of soft blue tiles, in an intricate, fanciful design— and a large and most beautiful view of sky and majestic, glossy white clouds, above the shimmering water of the sea. From this distance the commemorative suspension bridge is a graceful sculpture; catching the sunlight, it shines.

Arden is experiencing some exceptional, acute alertness; as though layers of skin had peeled away, all her senses are opened wide. She sees, in a way that she never has before. She feels all the gorgeous day, the air, and the city spread below her.

She hardly thinks of Gregor, at her side, and this is something of a relief; too often he is a worrying preoccupation for her.

Their plan for the afternoon has been to go back to their hotel, where they have left a rental car, and to drive north to Cascais, Estoril, and Sintra. And that is what they now proceed to do, not bothering to go into the hotel, but just taking their car, a small white Ford Escort, and heading north.

As they reach the outskirts of the city, a strange area of new condominiums, old shacks, and some lovely, untouched woods—just then, more quickly than seemed possible, the billowing clouds turn black, a strong wind comes up, and in another minute a violent rainstorm has begun, rains lashing at the windshield, water sweeping across the highway.

Arden and Gregor exchange excited grins: an adventure. She thinks, Oh, good, we are getting along, after all.

"Maybe we should just go to Sintra, though," he says, a little later. "Not too much point in looking at beach resorts?"

Yielding to wisdom, Arden still feels a certain regret. *Cascais.* She can hear Luiz saying the word, and "Estoril," with the sibilant Portuguese *s*'s. But she can also hear him saying *Sintra,* and she says it over to herself, in his voice.

A little later, looking over at her, Gregor asks, "Are you okay? You look sort of funny."

"How, funny?"

"*Odd.* You look odd. And your nose. It's so, uh, pink."

Surprising them both, and especially herself, Arden laughs. "Noses are supposed to be pink," she tells him.

Normally, what Arden thinks of as Gregor's lens-like observations make her nervous; they make her feel unattractive, and unloved. But today—here in Portugal!—her strange happiness separates her like a wall, or a moat from possible slights, and she thinks, How queer that Gregor should even notice the color of my nose, in a driving rainstorm—

here, north of Lisbon, near Sintra. As, in her mind, she hears the deep, familiar, never-forgotten voice of Luiz saying, "I adore your face! Do you *know* how I adore it? How lovely you are?" She hears Luiz, she sees him.

Then quite suddenly, as suddenly as it began, the storm is over. The sky is brilliantly blue again, and the clouds are white, as Arden thinks, No wonder Luiz is more than a little erratic—it's the weather. And she smiles to herself.

Suppose she sent him a postcard from Lisbon? *Ego absolvo te.* Love, Arden. Would he laugh and think fondly of her, for a moment? *Is* he dying?

In Sintra they drive past a small town square, with a huge, rather forbidding municipal building, some small stores. The wet stone pavement is strewn with fallen wet yellow leaves. They start up a narrow road, past gates and driveways that lead to just-not visible mansions, small towered castles. (The sort of places that Luiz might visit, or own, for weekends, elegant parties.) As they climb up and up in the small white car, on either side of the road the woods become thicker, wilder, more densely and violently green—everything green, every shape and shade of green, all rain-wet, all urgently growing. And giant rocks, great dead trees lying beside them. Ferns, enormously sprouting. Arden is holding her breath, forgetting to breathe. It is crazy with green, she thinks, crazy growth, so old and strong, ancient, endless and wild, ferocious. Like Luiz. Like Portugal, dying.

Gregor is making some odd maneuver with the car; is he turning around, mid-road? Trying to park, among so many giant rocks, heavy trees, and brilliant, dripping leaves?

In any case he has stopped the car. On a near hill Arden can see the broken ruins of a castle, jagged black fragments of stone, and in the sky big clouds are blackening again.

Willing calm (though still having trouble with her breath), Arden says, "I think it's going to rain again."

Huge-eyed, pale, Gregor is staring across at her. He says, "You cut me out—all the way! You might as well be here alone!"

He is right, of course; she is doing just that, pretending he is not there. So unfair—but his staring eyes are so light, so *blue*. Arden says, "I'm sorry, really—" but she can feel her voice getting away from her, can feel tears.

Gregor shouts, "I don't know why we came here! Why Portugal? What did you expect? You could have just come by yourself!"

But Arden can hardly hear him. The rain has indeed begun again; it is pelting like bullets against the glass, and wind is bending down all the trees, flattening leaves.

And suddenly in those moments Arden has understood that Luiz is dead—and that she will never again feel for anyone what she felt for him. Which, even though she does not want to—she would never choose to feel so much again—still, it seems a considerable loss.

In fact, though, at that particular time, the hour of that passionate October storm (while Arden quarrelled with Gregor), Luiz is still alive, although probably "terminal." And she only learns of his death the following spring, and then more or less by accident: she is in Washington, D.C., for some meetings having to do with grants for small magazines and presses, and in a hasty scanning of the *Post* she happens to glance at a column headed "Deaths Elsewhere."

Luiz —— —— V. (There were two intervening names that Arden has not known about.) Luiz V. had died a few days earlier in Lisbon, the cause of death not reported. Famous portraitist, known for satire, and also (this is quite as surprising to Arden as the unfamiliar names)—"one of the leading intellectuals in Lisbon to voice strong public support for the armed forces coup in April 1974 that ended half a century of right-wing dictatorship."

Curiously—years back she would not have believed this possible, ever—that day Arden is too busy with her meetings to think about this fact: Luiz dead. No longer someone whom she might possibly see again, by accident in an airport, or somewhere. No longer someone possibly to send a postcard to.

That day she is simply too busy, too harried, really, with so many people to see, and with getting back and forth from her hotel to her meetings, through the strange, unseasonable snow that has just begun, relentlessly, to fall. She thinks of the death of Luiz, but she does not absorb it.

That quarrel with Gregor in Sintra, which prolonged itself over the stormy drive back to Lisbon, and arose, refuelled, over dinner and too much wine—that quarrel was not final between them, although Arden has sometimes thought that it should have been. They continue to see each other, Arden and Gregor, in California, but considerably less often than they used to. They do not quarrel; it is as though they were no longer sufficiently intimate to fight, as though they both knew that any altercation would indeed be final.

Arden rather thinks, or suspects, that Gregor sees other women, during some of their increasing times apart. She imagines that he is more or less actively looking for her replacement. Which, curiously, she is content to let him do.

She herself has not been looking. In fact lately Arden has been uncharacteristically wary in her dealings with men. In her work she is closely allied with a lot of men, who often become good friends, her colleagues and companions. However, recently she has rather forcibly discouraged any shifts in these connections; she has chosen to ignore or to put down any possible romantic overtones. She spends time with women friends, goes out to dinner with women, takes small trips. She is quite good at friendship, has been Arden's conclusion, or one of them. Her judgment as to lovers seems rather poor. And come to think of it her own behavior in that area is not always very good. Certainly her strangeness, her removal in Lisbon, in Sintra, was quite enough to provoke a sensitive man, which Gregor undoubtedly is.

On that night, the night of reading the news item (Deaths Elsewhere) containing the death of Luiz—that night Arden is supposed to meet a group of friends in a Georgetown restaurant. At eight. In character, she gets there a little early, and is told that she will be seated as soon as her friends arrive; would she like to wait in the bar?

She would not, especially, but she does so anyway, going into a dark, panelled room, of surpassing anonymity, and seating herself in a shadowed corner from which new arrivals in the restaurant are visible. She orders a Scotch, and then wonders why; it is not her usual drink, she has not drunk Scotch for years.

By eight-ten she has begun to wonder if perhaps she confused the name of the restaurant. It was she who made the reservation, and her friends could have gone to some other place, with a similar French name. These friends like herself are always reliably on time, even in snow, strange weather.

The problem of what to do next seems almost intolerable, suddenly—and ridiculously: Arden has surely coped with more serious emergencies. But: should she try to get a cab, which at this crowded dinner hour, in the snow, would be difficult? And if she did where would she go?

In the meantime, at eight-twenty, she orders another drink, and she begins to think about the item in the paper. About Luiz.

Odd, she casually thinks, at first, that she should have "adored" a man—have planned to marry a man whose full name she did not know. And much more odd, she thinks, that he should have publicly favored the '74 revolution, the end of dictatorship. Opportunism, possibly, Arden first thinks. On the other hand, is she being unfair, unnecessarily harsh? He did always describe himself as anti-fascist. And perhaps that was true?

Perhaps everything he said to her was true?

Arden has finished her second drink. It is clear that her friends will not come; they have gone somewhere else by mistake, and she must decide what to do. But still she sits there, as though transfixed, and she is transfixed, by a sudden nameless pain. Nameless, but linked to loss: loss of Luiz, even, imminently, of Gregor. Perhaps of love itself.

Understanding some of this, in a hurried, determined way Arden gets to her feet and summons the bill from her waiter. She has decided that she will go back to her hotel and order a sandwich in her room. Strange that she didn't think of that before. Of course she will eventually get a cab, even in the steadily falling, unpredicted snow.

My First and Only House

Because of my dreams, I have begun to think that in some permanent way I have been imprinted, as it were, by the house in which I spent my first sixteen years. I have never owned another house (one could also say that I did not own that house either), and since this is true of almost none of my contemporaries and close friends in real-estate-crazed California, it would seem to deserve some explanation. Circumstances aside, is it possible that I have never bought or seriously thought of buying another house because of the strength of that imprinting, and if so, just why has it been so dominant, so powerful, in my life?

In more than half of my dreams I live there still, in that house just south of Chapel Hill. I am visited there in dreams by the present-day population of my life, people who in fact have never been to that hilltop where the house was—where it *is;* I saw it there last summer.

I also, though very rarely, dream of my former—my first and only—husband. But since this occurs only when I am angry with the man with whom I now live, the reasons for those dreams seem fairly clear. However, as with not buying another house, it also seems possible that I have not remarried because of that early impression of marriage. Californians, or some of them, might say that I avoid commitment, but that is not true. I do not. In fact, I seem to seek it out. I simply feel that first marriages, like the first houses in which we live, are crucially important, that in one way or another we are forever marked by them.

The Chapel Hill house, as my parents first found and bought it in the early twenties, a few years before I was born, was a small, possibly run-down and isolated farmhouse on a lovely broad hilltop. Very likely it was a good buy, cheap even for those pre-boom days; my father, as a just-hired professor at the university, would certainly not have had much money. In any case, my mother and father must have been drawn to all that space, a couple of acres; they may have already been planning the gardens, the tennis court and the grape arbors they were to put in later. And they must have fallen in love with the most beautiful view of farther gentle hills and fields, and a border of creek. They would have placed those aesthetic advantages above the convenience of a smaller lot, a tidier house in town. And along with the space and the view, they chose an unfashionable direction (which would have been characteristic; my parents—especially my mother, a snobbish Virginian—were always above such considerations).

Although in those days Chapel Hill was an extremely small town, there was already a row of fairly grand houses on Franklin Street, which continued on to become the Durham Road; whereas the highway running down past our house went on to Pittsboro, which was then a very déclassé town. And although our house became rather grand too in its way, there was always the Pittsboro connotation. "Oh, you live almost to Pittsboro," early non-driving beaux used to say to me by way of complaint about the distance they had to walk to get to my house, then back into town for a movie or whatever, back home with me, then back to wherever they lived, maybe Franklin Street.

By the time I was born, a small wing had been added to the old farmhouse, with a large upstairs bedroom for my parents and a small living room below. And that is what I first remember, that slightly lopsided house with the narrow front porch, a new wing on one side and on the other the tiny separate building that housed my father's study. In early snapshots the house looks bare, rather naked on its hilltop, with new, spindling trees out in front.

But what I most remember is flowers—everywhere. Roses, pink and white ones, climbed up a trellis and over the roof of the porch, entangled there with thick wisteria vines; rose petals and heavy lavender blossoms brushed the roof's green shingles and the ground. Over an arbor, next to the red-clay tennis court, more wisteria mingled with the gray-green grapevines—and then there was the garden itself: terraced beds of more rosebushes, crape myrtle and Japanese quinces, tall hollyhocks, sunflowers, cowslips, sweet william and lilies of the valley. Below the garden proper, beyond a green wooden fence, was a small apple orchard. Our family laundry was hung out there, billowing white sheets among the whiter apple blossoms.

In the side yard grew rows of irises and a bed of jonquils, a flowering plum tree, more quinces. That yard sloped down to a small, much steeper area of pinewoods above the swimming pool that my father put in during the early thirties with his World War I bonus. In those woods bloomed white dogwood and wildflowers—tiny, amazing wild irises and yellow dogtooth violets—nestled down among the dead pine needles and rotting leaves that covered the earth.

Of course it is highly unlikely—impossible, even—that all those flowers and shrubs and trees came to blossom at anywhere near the same time or even within a single season. But that is what I remember: the flowers all in bloom and as taken for granted (by me) as the grass, as the sweeping view of hills and fields, of everything green—a view that no longer exists from that house.

I am writing, then, at least in part, about the vagaries of memory and about the house that in dreams I permanently inhabit—or, it might be more accurate to say, the house that inhabits me.

Indoors, even before the final ungainly additions to the house, some strangeness prevailed, some awkwardness as to proportion and transition from one room to another. Upstairs, there was even a dead-end hall and several completely nonfunctional closets. The final, large addition to the house was built where my father's study had been. This new wing included a big living room and a big new study for my father, a prominent feature of which was a locked liquor closet (Verlie, who worked for us, was thought to drink). Upstairs was a double bedroom for my parents, a guest room and a sleeping porch. In actual fact, my mother slept in the guest room and my father out on the sleeping porch, an arrangement that seemed perfectly normal to me at the time.

Other people, though, did remark on the size of that house for just three people. "Don't you all get lost in all these rooms?" was the standard question. I did not exactly see us as lost, but I do remember a not-quite-conscious feeling that my parents were too far away from where I slept; that they were also far from each other did not strike me as strange until sometime later.

Below us, in a small house down the hill (even closer to tacky Pittsboro), lived a family of six: two parents, four small children. Very likely they were truly needy people. I somehow learned, or heard, that they all slept together in one bed. And I felt the most passionate envy of that condition, that bodily family warmth. As I imagined it, they would all lie cuddled like puppies, with the mother and father on the outside edges, protectively.

For reasons I can no longer remember, I was moved about among those oddly shaped bedrooms in the old part of the house. I slept alone, of course, and was generally frightened at night—until I learned to read. Then, as now, books served to keep the terrifying world at bay for a while.

Downstairs was generally more cheerful than up; the house was splendid for parties, for bringing people home to. Everyone admired its impressive size and the splendid view. And we three difficult, isolated people got along much better when there were others around. Even Verlie, she who supposedly drank (my own view is that my father simply thought she might if tempted; it is what he thought Negro servants did), liked cooking for parties more than for just us three. So my parents entertained a lot, and later I was encouraged to also. "We love to have your friends here," I was always told.

Downstairs was better, but outside was better yet. Once we had the pool, that was where most of the parties were. People were always invited to "come by for a dip," drinks were brought down, and then the guests were probably encouraged to stay on for supper. At one end of the pool, a privet hedge shielded us from the road, and it flowered, intensely sweet.

Still, it is strange to me that I am so fixed, so literally rooted in a house of which my memories are not of a very positive nature on the whole, and standard psychological explanations of fixation by trauma seem both simplistic and uninteresting. Last summer, as I have said, I went to see the house, "my house," which I had not seen for twenty-five years, not since my father died and my stepmother, who had inherited it outright, put it up for sale (a serious trauma, that: it was made clear that indeed I had never owned the house, nor had my mother, who might as well have been a guest). And what is curious is that I cannot now, six months later, recall just how it looked. It had been repainted a new color. But was it gray? Pale yellow? I have no idea. (I recently saw my former husband in a local bank, and for one fleeting instant I did not know who he was, but I know very clearly how he looked thirty years ago.) Across the road from the house, though, I am sure that there was a total obstruction to the view. Huge trees, I think.

But that freshly painted, viewless house is non-existent in my mind; it is not where I live. I live in a huge, mad house with the loveliest view. With everything in bloom.

1940: Fall

"Hasn't anyone noticed those clouds? They're incredibly beautiful." These words were spoken with some despair, for indeed no one had noticed, by a woman named Caroline Gerhardt, on a late evening in September, 1940. Caroline Coffin Gerhardt, actually, or so she signed the many letters that she wrote to newspapers, both local and further afield: the *Capitol Times,* right there in Madison, Wisconsin, and Colonel McCormick's infamous (Caroline's word) Chicago *Tribune.*

The ponderously shifting, immense white clouds contemplated by Caroline were moving across an enormous black sky, above one of Madison's smaller lakes. This house, Caroline's, was perched up on a fairly high bluff, yielding views of the dark water in which the reflected clouds were exaggerated, distorted by the tiny flicker of the waves. There was also a large full moon, but full moons—at least to Caroline—seemed much less remarkable than those clouds.

No one else in the room noticed anything remarkable, because almost all of them, all much younger than Caroline, were dancing slowly, slowly, body to body, to some slow, very sexy recorded music. The "children," as Caroline thought of these steamy adolescents, especially her own two girls, have only taken romantic notice of the moon. Beautiful raven-haired Amy Gerhardt, who resembles her absent father rather than smaller, pale, and somewhat wispy Caroline—Amy's perfectly painted lips have just grazed her partner's ear as she whispered, "You see? Another full moon. That makes seven since February." The boy pressed her more tightly into his own body. All those tall boys and smooth-haired, gardenia-smelling girls danced too closely, Caroline had observed, with pain. Hardly dancing at all. Six or eight couples, two or three stags, in the big, low-ceilinged, pine-paneled room—the game room. Dancing, their eyes half closed, not looking out to the lake, to the moon and sky.

Caroline's letters to the papers had to do with the coming war, with what Caroline saw as its clear necessity: Hitler must be stopped. The urgency of it possessed her, what Hitler was doing to the Jews, the horror of it always in her mind. And the smaller countries, systematically devastated. There in the isolationist Midwest she was excoriated as a warmonger (small, gentle, peaceable Caroline). Or worse: more than once—dirty toilet paper in the mail.

She also received from quite other sources pictures that were just beginning to be smuggled out of the camps. Buchenwald, Dachau.

She was actively involved in trying to help the refugees who had begun to arrive in Madison, with housing, jobs, sometimes at the university.

There was in fact a refugee boy at the party in Caroline's game room that night. Egon Heller, the son of an anti-Nazi editor, now dead in Auschwitz. Egon and his mother had arrived from England. Hearing of them, going over to see them, and liking the mother (able actually to help her with a translator job), Caroline impulsively invited the boy. "If you're not busy tonight, there's a little party at my house. My daughters—about your age. They're both at Wisconsin High. Oh, you too? Oh, good."

Egon seemed more English than German. "The years of formation," his mother explained. Tall and shy, long-nosed and prominent of tooth, he seemed much younger than he was—younger, that is, than American boys his age. Not adolescent, more childlike. One of the three young people not dancing just then, Egon stood near the record player, in the proximity of Caroline's younger daughter, Julie—plump and brilliant and not yet discovered by boys (Caroline's idea being that she surely would be, and soon)—although Julie was extremely "well liked," as the phrase then went, in high school. By boys and girls, and teachers.

Caroline's secret conviction about her daughter was that within Julie's flesh were embedded her own genes, her sensuality. The intense dark impulses that had enmeshed her with Arne Gerhardt and landed her with three children—the youngest, now upstairs asleep, born embarrassingly only a year ago, when Caroline was already over forty.

Caroline felt with Julie a sensual kinship and consequent cause for alarm far more than with more overtly sexy Amy, the oldest. Caroline too had once been plump and brilliant and shy.

Maybe this Egon will be the one, romantic Caroline thought, looking toward the corner to Egon and Julie, who so far seemed to have in common only the fact of not dancing. He's so tall and thin and toothy, Julie now so unsmiling, so matter-of-fact. Still, it would be very nice, thought Caroline. English–Jewish–New England–Swedish grandchildren—she would like that very much.

The other young person not dancing in the early part of that evening was a new girl in town, from Julie's class, invited by Julie (who would later be strongly maternal, Caroline knew). A strange-looking girl from Oklahoma, with an odd accent and a funny name: Lauren. Most striking of all about Lauren, right off, was her hair—very pale, more white than blond, it stood out all over her head in tiny fine soft ringlets.

She looked younger than the rest of the girls, perhaps partly because she did not wear lipstick. Her mouth was long and finely drawn, and pale, in that roomful of girls. Even Julie had dark blood-red lips. A very tall, very thin girl, her neck was long and she moved her head about uncertainly, watching the dancers. Her smile was slightly crooked, off.

Someone should ask her to dance, thought Caroline. How rude these children are, how entirely selfish. Perhaps Egon will, that would be very nice, two strangers finding each other. But maybe he is too polite to ask Lauren with Julie standing there; he doesn't know that Julie wouldn't mind in the least being left alone. She will probably be going up soon to see about Baby.

Seeing no way out of this social dilemma, but fated always to feel responsible, Caroline herself began to move in Lauren's direction—not easy, as the music had become more lively, people hopping about and arms and legs thrust out. Slowly making her way, Caroline tried to think of social-welcoming-maternal conversation.

"So you and Julie are taking Latin together?" Reaching Lauren at last, this breathless, silly remark was all she had been able to summon up finally.

"Yes. Cicero. There's only five of us in the class." Lauren laughed apologetically, as though abashed at the small size of the Latin class. But then, her huge eyes on Caroline, she said earnestly, "This is the most beautiful room I've ever seen. The view—"

Unprepared for intensity, Caroline was flustered. "Well, it's a funny old house. Not exactly practical. But it is nice, being here on the lake."

"I love it in Madison." Lauren's voice was rapt, those huge pale eyes burned. Caroline sensed that the girl had not said this before, to anyone. It was not a remark to be made to contemporaries, other children.

"Well, yes, it is a very nice town," Caroline agreed. "Especially the lakes, and the university." Some flicker of intelligent response across Lauren's face made her add, "A very conservative place, though, on the whole."

"Try Enid, Oklahoma," Lauren laughed quickly. "More backward than conservative. But I know what you mean. The whole Midwest. Especially now."

Was the girl simply parroting remarks overheard at home, or were those ideas of her own? Impossible to tell, but in any case Caroline found herself liking this Lauren, wanting to talk to her.

However, just at the moment of Caroline wanting to speak, forming sentences in her mind, the two of them were interrupted by a tall, fair, thin boy—Caroline knew him, knew his parents, but could not for the moment recall his name. Thick light hair, distinctively heavy eyebrows above deepset dark blue eyes. To Lauren he said, "Care to dance this one?" And then, somewhat perfunctorily (still, he did say it), "Okay with you, Mrs. Gerhardt?" He was staring at Lauren.

And they were gone, off and out into the room, lost among other couples, Lauren and Tommy Russell (his name had just come to Caroline, of course). And before she could collect herself or even could turn to watch them, from far upstairs she heard Baby's urgent cry. Bottle time. Glancing toward Julie, observing that she and Egon had at last begun to talk, Caroline signaled to her daughter that she would go up. "I want to get to bed early anyway," Caroline mouthed above the music, smiling, as she headed for the kitchen. For milk, a clean bottle, a heating saucepan.

Good Baby, the easiest child of the three, subsided as soon as she heard her mother's footsteps on the stairs. Smiling up from her crib, she grasped the proffered bottle, clamped it into her mouth as Caroline settled into the adjacent battered easy chair.

From here, upstairs, she had an even better view of the lake, and the moon and the marvelous white clouds, and Caroline then felt an unaccustomed peace possess her. She thought, It *is* easier with Arne away (a fact hitherto not quite acknowledged). Generally his absences were only troubling: *would* he come back? That year he had a visiting professorship at Stanford, two years before at Virginia.

Now, as she peacefully crooned to the milk-smelling, half-asleep fair child, she thought that this time even if Arne decided to take off for good, she would really be all right, she and her three girls, who themselves were more than all right—they were going to be great women, all three. She could cope with the house, the good big lakefront place bought so cheaply ten years back. They would all be perfectly okay, Amy with her heady romances and her disappointing grades, Julie with her perfect grades, and perhaps a new beau in this nice English-German boy, this Egon. And maybe a nice new friend in this Lauren Whitfield, from Enid, Oklahoma. And Baby will always be fine, thought Caroline, sleepily.

And Roosevelt will win the election and declare war on Germany within the year, and we will win that war in a matter of months. Hitler defeated. Dead. Maybe tortured in a concentration camp.

Caroline thought all that, still crooning to Baby, and smiling secretly, somnolently to herself.

Lauren Whitfield, the new girl with the funny hair, and Julie Gerhardt did indeed become friends, though not quite of the sort that Caroline had envisioned. They began going to lunch at the Rennebohm's drugstore across from the school, and Julie, sensing Lauren's extreme interest in what was to her a glamorous new place, became a sort of balladeer, a chronicler of high-school love affairs, past and present. Disastrous breakups, the occasional betrayal. Along with a detailed rundown on the current situation, who was going with whom as this new season began, this warm and golden fall.

Over thick chocolate malteds and English muffins, Julie told Lauren everything she wanted to know, or nearly, including the story of Julie's own sister, Amy the beautiful, with whom boys quite regularly fell in love. "She was just having a good time, her sophomore year, really getting around. But the phone calls! Arne threatened to have the phone cut off, he has a pretty short temper. And then during spring vacation she met Nelson Manning, he was home from Dartmouth, much too old for her, about nineteen. But they fell madly in love, flowers all the time, and after he went back to school those letters. And more flowers, and phone calls! Poor Amy spent that whole spring fighting with Caroline and Arne. But she sort of won, I think mostly just wearing them down. So that when Nelson came home in June she got to see him. Under certain conditions. Well, she sneaked out and saw him a lot more than they ever knew about. Nelson was entirely insane over Amy, he wanted to quit school and get married right away. But of course Amy wasn't about to do that, and so in the fall he went back to Dartmouth and she moped around and then suddenly no more letters. No flowers. Another girl back there, probably someone at Vassar or one of those places, we're sure it must have been. Caro and I were truly worried about her. Moping all day, not eating. But gradually she began to go out a little, and then over Christmas she got sort of serious about Jeff, and they started going steady in February. Full-moon time. But there are still certain songs she can't hear without crying, 'All the Things You Are' is one. She's not *really* over Nelson."

Nothing like that had ever gone on in Enid, not that Lauren had ever heard about.

And then, "I think Tommy Russell is really interested in you," Julie told Lauren.

So much for the intellectual friendship that Caroline Gerhardt had envisioned between her brilliant middle daughter and Lauren Whitfield, the bright new girl in town. But even had she been aware of the content of those endless conversations Caroline would really not have cared, so entirely absorbed was she in her own despair: her desperation over what was going on, still, in Germany.

Even the Midwestern press had by now conceded that Roosevelt would win the election, and would get the country into that European war—wasteful, unnecessary. But Caroline often felt that it would be too late, too late for murdered Jews, for devastated Poland. Holland. Fallen France.

She continued her impassioned but well-reasoned letters to the press, along with occasional gay (she hoped for gaiety) small notes to Arne, in response to his occasional cards from California.

Caroline Coffin, from Vermont, and Arne Gerhardt, from northern Wisconsin, Door County, met at Oberlin College in the early twenties, and both at that time were filled with, inspired by, the large-spirited ideals of that institution. Big, dark, clumsy (but very brilliant, Caroline thought) Arne, enthusiastic about the new League of Nations, and smaller, fairer Caroline, who was then, as now, dedicated to peace, the abolition of war. Young and passionately in love, together they read Emma Goldman, Bertrand Russell—and moved into an apartment together. Caroline became pregnant, and a week before the birth of Amy they yielded to their parents and got married.

"Lauren Whitfield is going steady with Tommy Russell," Julie reported to her mother at breakfast on Saturday morning. They were both feeding Baby, alternating spoonfuls of cereal with scrambled eggs, which was Baby's preferred method. Amy slept upstairs, on into the day.

"Isn't that rather sudden?" Caroline was a little surprised at the censoriousness with which she herself spoke.

"Oh yes, everyone thinks it's terribly romantic. He asked her on their first date."

Impossible for Caroline to gauge the content of irony in her daughter's voice. "I somehow thought she was more—" Caroline then could not finish her own sentence, and she realized that she had to a considerable degree already lost interest in this conversation, a thing that seemed to happen to her far too often.

"You thought she was more intelligent?" Knowing her mother well, Julie supplied the missing bias. "Actually she's extremely smart, but she's sort of, uh, dizzy. Young. Her parents are breaking up, that's why she's here with her grandparents. They drink a lot, her parents."

"Poor girl."

"Yes. Well, anyway, she's bright but she's not all intellectual. Yet."

Julie herself did not go out a lot with boys that year. But she seemed both busy and contented. She studied hard and read a lot, at home she helped Caroline with Baby. She also functioned as a sort of occasional secretary for her mother, opening mail and often shielding Caroline from extreme isolationist vituperation.

And Julie and Egon Heller, the German-English refugee boy, did become friends, of sorts, if not in the romantic way that Caroline had hoped. Their friendship was in fact remarked upon, so unusual was it in those days of rigidly coded adolescent behavior. Simply, they spent a lot of time together, Egon and Julie. They could be seen whispering over their books in study hall, though very possibly about assignments. Never holding hands, no touching, nothing like that. Sometimes they went to the movies together, but usually on a Saturday afternoon, sometimes with Baby along. Not at night, not a date.

Very odd, was what most people observing them thought. But then exceptionally bright children were often odd; psychologists said so.

Caroline heard from Arne in a somewhat longer than usual postcard that he would not, after all, be coming home to Madison for Christmas, for a number of reasons; money, time, and work were cited. Nothing very original by way of an excuse.

But Caroline, who had painful premonitions of just this announcement, reacted with a large sense of relief. To her own great surprise. Oh, *good,* is what she thought. I won't have to make a lot of Christmas fuss— or not Arne's kind of fuss. No big parties, and I won't have to try to look wonderful all the time. And worry that he's drinking too much and making passes at undergraduate girls. I can just do the things I like, that he thinks are dumb. I can bake cookies, maybe run up a new formal for Amy. (Caroline had a curious dramatic flair for making certain clothes. Highly successful with evening things, she had never done well with the small flannel nightgowns, for example, that other women did in no time.) I can read a lot, she thought. And I'll go for a lot of walks in the snow.

The snows had come somewhat earlier than usual to Madison that year. Soon after the first of November (just after the election), serious snowfalls began, blanketing the steeply sloped university campus, causing traffic trouble in the streets—and making life far more wonderful for all children, including those in high school.

Couples on dates went tobogganing on the vast golf course of the Black Hawk Country Club, an endless hill, just dangerous enough to provide a long intensely satisfying thrill. And couples who had parked on other hills to neck, in the marvelous privacy of deep snowbanks, could emerge to observe a curious pink light on all the surrounding miles of white, reflected in all the lakes.

Lauren Whitfield and Tommy Russell spent considerable time in his car, in that way. They marveled both at each other (so much in love) and at the loveliness of snow, which Lauren had never really seen before.

Caroline's kitchen was hung with rows of copper pots, enthusiastically bought in Paris, in the flea market, on Arne and Caroline's honeymoon (with baby Amy in tow). Never polished, they were now all dark and dull, black-grimed. The blue Mexican tile around the sink, from an attempted second honeymoon, this time without Amy but on which Julie was conceived—the tile had fared somewhat better; though cracked, it retained a bright brave color.

On the afternoon that Caroline had chosen for Christmas-cookie baking, by the time the children arrived from school there were already smells of burned sugar, and spilled flour on the floor into which Baby continually crawled. Julie had brought both Lauren Whitfield and Egon Heller.

"Egon, and Lauren! How very nice to see you. These days I hardly ever." Floury, flustered Caroline made effusive welcoming gestures, to which Egon responded with one of his curious stiff bows (he actually bowed), and a smile.

Julie took over the problem of keeping Baby out of the general mess, and Caroline divided her attention between the cookies, which she judged still salvageable, and an intense old argument with Egon, about Roosevelt.

"But he's always—"

"But what you fail to grasp—"

"People of his social class—"

Lauren seemed quiet, preoccupied and sad, Caroline observed, with a certain impatience. Adolescents are simply very, very self-absorbed, she thought.

To Egon she said, positively, "Roosevelt will soon declare war on Germany, and he will be able to win it very quickly. And I know a man who's in a position to know things who tells me that the Nazi-Soviet pact can't last, not possibly. The Russians will come in on our side. Our strongest allies."

· · ·

"Lauren and Tommy Russell have broken up," Julie told her mother one night in February as together they did the supper dishes, Baby being asleep and Amy out.

"Wasn't that rather quick? You just told me, I thought . . ." Caroline heard her own voice trail off into vagueness.

"Quick and strange. She can't quite say what happened, or she won't. She just cries a lot. Like when Amy and Nelson broke up."

"That's too bad," Caroline began to say, and then did not, as she recognized that in truth she had almost no sympathy for the broken hearts of the very young. "That girl seems to be rushing through her life at quite a rate" was her more sincere comment.

"I think she'll be okay eventually. It may just take a while." Judicious Julie.

"When I think of Tito's brave Partisans," wrote Caroline to the *Capitol Times* (Madison), with copies to the Chicago *Tribune,* the Des Moines *Register,* and the Moline *Dispatch.* She thought of the San Francisco *Chronicle* or even the Palo Alto *Times* (where Arne was) but she censored that impulse as frivolous. Also, they would probably not print letters from an unknown woman in Wisconsin. And anyway, California went for Roosevelt.

Actually, Caroline was managing considerable detachment from Arne these days, this early and acutely beautiful spring.

Long walks were a reliable cure for her troubled sleep, she found, and so every afternoon for an hour or so she walked around the lake, noting pussywillows at the muddy edges of the water, where small gentle waves lapped, very slowly. And sudden secret wildflowers in what had been a small neglected meadow. And at the bottom of her garden (also neglected) early iris, wild and bright.

She began to sleep better. Or if she should wake up she could read. One of the joys of singleness, she told herself; you don't have to worry about the other person's sleep, along with your own.

June 22, 1941, was the day on which Hitler's troops attacked Soviet Russia. No more Nazi-Soviet pact. The Russians were now our valiant allies. (It was also Lauren Whitfield's last day in Madison. Back to Enid, Oklahoma.)

Possibly more than anyone else in Madison, Caroline Coffin Gerhardt was moved to celebrate this clear beginning of the end of Hitler. She wanted a party, but from the beginning nothing worked out in terms of this festive impulse. No one even remotely appropriate was available. Vacations had begun, varieties of other plans. Even her children failed her: Amy was off dancing with her beau, and Julie was to have an early farewell supper with Lauren and her grandparents.

Caroline's happy day was further marred by news from Arne: a postcard (so typical) announcing his imminent arrival. "I've missed all my girls." Well, I'll bet he has, was Caroline's sour reaction. Who else would put up with such a selfish bastard?

We will have to work out a much more independent life from each other, Caroline thought, over the small steak that she had bought for her solitary celebration (*not* black market: her month's ration), as she sipped from the split of Beaujolais, an even greater treat.

I should not have Arne so continually in my mind, she told herself. That's what the children do, they think only of themselves and their impassioned sexual lives.

The important fact is that the end of Hitler's evil has now begun.

Epilogue: San Diego, California. The middle eighties.

The man at the next table at this almost empty semi-Polynesian restaurant is not even slightly interested in her, thinks Lauren Whitfield, now a tall, gray-blond, very well dressed woman, a psychologist, well known for several books.

She is in fact on a tour for her latest book, having to do with alcoholic co-dependency. She reached San Diego a day early, hoping for a rest. On her way to her room, across a series of tropically planted lawns she observed an Olympic pool, and she thought, Oh, very good. And seated next to the pool, though fully dressed, she saw this same tall man, whom she had also seen at the reservation desk. Coming into the dining room just now, he smiled very politely, if coldly, acknowledging these small accidental encounters.

Lauren is quite used to book tours, by now. Living alone in New

York after the lengthy demise of her second marriage, she rather likes the adventure of trips, the novelty of unfamiliar scenery, new faces. She quite often falls into conversation with other single travelers, such encounters providing at the worst only a few bored hours. More frequently she has felt warm stirrings of interest, of possible friendship. On far rarer occasions, sex.

But this tall, too thin, nearsighted, and not well dressed European intellectual keeps his large nose pushed clearly into his book. Lauren has observed him with some care, over all of their small encounters, and is quite sure that they could find areas of common interest, some shared opinions. Their political views, she would bet, would be similar.

Sex is out; in a sexual way she is not drawn to him in the least. But so often men are slow to perceive that overtures of any sort are not necessarily sexual in nature. Lauren ponders this sad and trouble-causing human fact as she also thinks, Well, hell, I'd really like an hour or so of conversation. Coffee. Damn his book.

And then, as she stares (he is so entirely unaware of her that she is able to stare with impunity), a small flash goes off within the deep recesses of her mind, so that she is able, with great confidence, and a smile that she knows is appealing, slightly crooked and not *too* self-assured, to tap his elbow and to say, "Excuse me, but aren't you Egon Heller?"

Perfectly calm, as though used to being thus accosted (possibly he is somewhat famous too, used to being recognized? or a professor, with old students sometimes showing up? or both?), Egon lowers his book very patiently, and very politely he tells her that yes, that is his name. And then, with the very slightest English-German accent, he asks her, "But have we met?"

"Yes, but terribly long ago. At the Gerhardts'. In Madison, Wisconsin."

Now Egon does look quite startled, and confused, so much so that he drops his book as he stands and extends a smooth cool strong hand to Lauren. "At the Gerhardts'! Extraordinary."

"Yes, in the fall of 1940. You'd just got there, I think, and I had just moved to Madison. But do sit down. Coffee?"

"Yes, thank you." He does sit down, now smiling warmly, attractively.

Lauren asks him, right off, "Do you ever go back to Madison? I always wonder what happened to Julie Gerhardt. My favorite friend."

At this, quite startlingly Egon begins to laugh, in a choking, ratchety way that reddens his face, and it is some minutes before he is able to say, "Well, one of the things that happened to her is that she married me, in 1947. And another thing, or five other, is our children. We have five, the last one thank God just out of graduate school. And another—I know I should have said this first—she has her doctorate in math. From the University of Chicago. Very hard on her, doing all that at once." Egon smiles with such sympathy, such unambivalent admiration that Lauren is more than a little envious (neither of her husbands had much use for her work). As well as touched.

She says, "Well, I love that news, that's wonderful. And it's so amazing that I ran into you. By the way, I'm Lauren Whitfield, I just lived in Madison that one year."

Obviously not remembering her (if he noticed her at all, he must have thought her just another blond, boy-crazy American girl, which Lauren will now concede that she was), Egon politely says, "Oh, of course," and proceeds to tell her more Gerhardt news.

Amy has been married three times but seems at last to have settled down with a man whom Egon describes as a really nice fellow (Lauren has the sense, though, that Egon, so visibly nice himself, has said that about all the husbands). Baby—and now Egon's face lengthens and saddens—Baby died in the early sixties. Drugs.

Lauren: "Oh dear. So in a way Baby was always Baby." She has been unable not to say that.

"Quite." Egon frowns, and then his face brightens as he asks, "You remember Caroline, the mother?"

"Of course, she was wonderful. I always wanted to know her more."

Caroline, still very much alive at eighty-something, is even more wonderful now, Egon tells Lauren. She still writes letters to papers, to congressmen and senators, and she goes to demonstrations, *still:* for disarmament, against military involvement, anywhere. She has been honored by national peace organizations; he names several. "Most of the time she feels quite well," Egon says. "A little trouble with her back, some other small problems, but she is for the most part all right."

Arne died a long time ago, in the fifties.

Digesting all this news, which has mostly made her smile with pleasure, Lauren is quiet for a while, stirring and drinking her coffee very slowly, before she asks him, "Tell me, do you happen to know anything about someone named Tommy Russell?"

"No, I don't think so. But the name, something comes. A football star, in high school?"

"Basketball. He was very thin. Blond."

Egon frowns. "No. Now nothing comes."

Surprised at the depth of her disappointment, and afraid that it will show, Lauren tells him, "I, uh, went steady with him for a while that year. And then one night he got really drunk, and I was really scared, and I couldn't tell anyone. And my parents—"

She sees that she has completely lost his interest. A polite glaze has replaced the animation with which Egon described the new-old Caroline and the accomplishments of Julie. And Lauren senses that actually they do not have a great deal more to say to each other. "Such ancient history!" she comments.

"But you must come to see us," Egon next (somewhat surprisingly) says to her. "Julie would be so pleased, I know, and Caroline. Did I say that we are all still there in that same house on the bluff? The house you remember?"

"No, you didn't but that's really great. I will come, what a wonderful idea."

And, sitting there among the fake South Sea Island masks and the real but derelict, neglected tropical plants, Lauren tries to reimagine that house in Madison. How the lake looked at night.

The End of the World

Zelda Hoskins, a pretty, light-haired young woman from Toronto, is seated on the balcony of her hotel room, far south, in the Mexican tropics. At the moment, she is contemplating the small quick black butterflies in the shrubbery next to her terrace: an occasional monarch, and a couple of large, very fluttery pure white ones. She watches as a tiny green-black hummingbird zooms from nowhere to the bush of red flowers, ignoring the amber-yellow bougainvillea that Zelda especially admires. She has thought of that particular color in Canada. Would it be there still? During all the heavy-ended, frozen Canadian months that preceded this trip she has imagined the yellow bougainvillea, and butterflies, hummingbirds.

And even now that she is here, those long leaden cold days are very much in Zelda's mind. A Toronto winter. She sees herself there, dreaming of Mexico, of here. Dreams of flowers and warmth and the glittery sea.

Or perhaps this is still the dream? Perhaps actually she is now in Toronto, only dreaming of Mexico? In the unreal warmth she shivers. She finds such speculations interesting, though slightly scaring. And dangerous, really. She knows that she should simply savor being here. She should concentrate on these given moments, even try to slow their passage. After all, they will only be here for a week.

But it is very hard to accept the fact of being where you have dreamed of; Zelda begins to see that. Like the troubles of love, the difficulty of actually being with the longed-for person, when you have spent so many hours imagining how it will be.

Yes, that is exactly what it is like. Like love, an extremity of love. Zelda sighs, and yields to thoughts of her lover, a young man whom

Zelda loves extremely. Who is now in Toronto, or maybe he is back in New York, where he lives. In any case, not with her.

Inside their room Abe Hoskins is almost ready to go to breakfast, to which he very much looks forward: the piles of fresh fruit, and the Mexican rolls, *bolillos,* that he especially likes.

Abe in fact relishes the whole episode of breakfast, the walk from their room on the narrow pathway, with the view of the beach and the ocean, sometimes boats. And the other view, to their right, of banks of flowers. And then the look of the dining room itself, the sea seen through heavy waving palms, and the waiting white beach below.

He even enjoys bargaining for newspapers with the small, wiry brown Mexican newsboys, one especially—Gabino, an appealing, very quick-witted kid with an odd, twisted, reluctant smile. Last winter, with considerable trouble, Abe mailed the pair of tennis shoes (high, white) that Gabino had made it clear he very much wanted (with pictures and sign language: the Hoskinses do not speak Spanish). Abe drew all around Gabino's foot on some writing paper, and took the drawing to the store in Toronto. Bought, packaged, mailed, and he never heard from Gabino. He wonders if Gabino will show up this year, and if he ever got the package.

"It's really clouded over," Zelda and Abe say to each other as together they emerge from their room and begin the walk toward breakfast.

"Look," Zelda says next.

She means the rising, arching plants that now line their pathway. Feathery greenery, against what had been a bare embankment. An archway of green, making a ceremony of their progress that first day.

But above them the sky is hung with clouds, pale, cottony, in a sky that is always simply clear and blue.

"It never rains?" says Zelda.

"It could. But more likely a fantastic sunset," Abe assures her.

Evelyn Fisk, from Washington, D.C., also comes to this hotel for a week each winter, and although her weeks often overlap with those of the Hoskinses, they have so far exchanged only the most tentative looks of recognition. Evelyn, Mrs. Fisk, is a large middle-aged woman, her face broad and pleasant, her short white hair shaped smoothly to her head. She is always alone on these trips, but something about her prohibits the sort of overtures that such "single" people can invite, a look of self-sufficiency, perhaps, or of sheer absorption in private concerns—of which she has in fact a great many: a large and demanding family, and more recently an involvement with the sanctuary movement.

This annual trip to Mexico is actually a sort of present she has awarded to herself for years of service: thirty-odd years of marriage to Grantly Fisk, a Midwestern senator prominent in Washington. A busy liberal: Evelyn supports his views, although very much disliking the public life that his work requires. Grantly refers to these trips as Evelyn's "time off for good behavior," by which she is only half amused. She no longer gives much thought to her actual feelings about her husband. At this point, as she sees it, what could possibly be gained by such a dissection?

In Washington she usually manages to avoid the press, which by this time is not very much interested in her.

Already seated in the dining room, she is looking down to the beach, where she sees a few runners near the edge of the waves, and a bunch of dogs, of various colors and sizes, that have gathered there at a small outcropping of rocks, as though deciding something. A conference of dogs.

There used to be a lot of cats wandering about the dining room at mealtimes—though careful to keep out of the way of the quick-footed young maids and especially of Oscar, an unpleasant Russian, the manager of the hotel. Evelyn Fisk used to like giving the cats bits of bacon at breakfast, and pieces of meat, or fish, whatever, at night. She was in fact extremely fond of those cats.

Observing that Oscar has just come into the room on some errand, she frowns to herself, and hopes that he won't come over to speak to her.

It must have been Oscar who in some way got rid of the cats.

Oscar, of White Russian parents, is in his own view an aristocrat. No one much likes him. He is erroneously described as a Communist by certain guests; educated in Germany, he is labeled "that Nazi" by another sort of guest. He is very thin and sun-withered, inattentive except for occasional fits of concentrated and usually inappropriate emotion, often rage. He gives an impression of disliking all of Mexico, including the hotel and its guests.

For several years there was a Polish woman of a certain age, named Marya, always there with Oscar and assumed to be his wife. A lean, faded blonde, who simply seems to be no longer around, and no one has asked about her.

Oscar himself does not appear to know who is there from one year to the next, and he has been known to greet an already tanned mid-stay guest as though that person were a new arrival. Today he speaks to no one but a certain maid, who has done some wrong. Oscar scolds her at length, very sharply. He shakes one long finger much too close to her face, so that the girl shrinks and cowers.

"Oh, there's the woman who used to feed the cats," Zelda says to Abe as they settle into their stiff, uncomfortable chairs and look about the room.

"She must miss them." Abe and Zelda have two dogs at home, whom Abe secretly misses very much. He would like to have children, but Zelda postpones even discussions of this possibility with vague remarks about how young they are (how young she is), plenty of time.

"She doesn't took to me as though she missed anyone, or anything," Zelda tells him. "Do you suppose she's married, or what?"

"If she were married, she wouldn't always come here alone, would she?" Logical Abe is often wrong.

"Oh, she might." Zelda does not take trips alone, although she has thought that she would like to, especially now, with the presence of a lover in her life. In Toronto for the last few years she has managed a travel agency—no reason for her not to travel now. "I miss the cats a lot," she says to Abe. "And there's horrible Oscar. I wonder whatever happened to Marya?"

No newsboys come into the dining room that morning. Possibly they will be down on the beach later on.

. . .

Now, in midwinter, and because this bay is surrounded by high mountains, a range extending almost to Mexico City, the sun comes up late and slowly above the eastern ridge, a yellow haze, shafts of light that at last reach the sea.

By midmorning, though, beachtime, the sunlight is well established: heavy, powerful, almost overwhelming. The hotel guests sit beneath their thatched *palapas,* shielded and sunblocked, emerging occasionally to walk toward or run into the sea. To move through waves, in the warm-cool caressing water.

On this particular day the waves are higher than usual, the undertow strong. Good swimmers, like Abe Hoskins, treat the water with some respect, gauging the sizes of waves, waiting before diving through. Deciding not to bodysurf that day.

Abe thinks he read about an odd, unusual conjunction of planets taking place just now, along with a full moon. All that would surely affect the tides?

Looking at the sky, at the unfamiliar thickening gray banks of clouds, Abe thinks that indeed it could rain. Even if it never does.

Zelda is up in their room putting the final touches to their unpacking. Or maybe talking to the room maid, by now an old friend.

Abe wishes he had a Mexico City *News,* the only available English-language paper.

And he wonders about Gabino.

Evelyn Fisk, several *palapas* away from that of Abe Hoskins, also wishes for a newspaper, but her wish is mild, and she manages to content herself for the moment with her thick paperback, a new Iris Murdoch.

On this first day, though, her attention wanders. In particular, her eye is caught by the vendors who trudge slowly up and down, barefoot, on the hot white sand. Selling their awful wares. It seems to Evelyn that this year their faces are longer and sadder than usual, which could well be the case, the Mexican economy being what it is: splendid for tourists, over two thousand pesos to the almighty dollar—and dreadful, punitive for Mexicans, especially of course for the poor.

Evelyn notices—or, rather, she thinks of something new today, which is that the women's wares are generally much better than the men's, and she ponders this fact: vending is women's work, finally? (This might be something to include in a letter to Grantly; on the other hand, perhaps not. Grantly's "liberalism," of a somewhat old-fashioned sort, does not seem to extend itself to feminist issues.)

The shabbiest, saddest-looking vendors of all are those who sell peanuts. All men, mostly old. The younger and relatively more prosperous men have terrible carved birds for sale. Or, so unappealing in this heat, woven woolen rugs.

Many of the women wear a sort of costume: full dark blue skirts with layers of petticoats, and modestly ample white blouses with long sleeves and big floppy lace collars. Perhaps an Indian tribe? They are selling jewelry: armloads of colored glass or plastic beads, all in lovely colors, dark blues and greens, pinks and amethysts.

And silver, endless streams of silver. Necklaces, bracelets, earrings.

Later, Evelyn will buy presents for all her daughters and her daughters-in-law. Her female grandchildren.

Zelda Hoskins is neither talking to the maid nor unpacking, but writing a secret letter. One that she has written quite often before, and sometimes mailed but more often not. A letter in which she tells her lover, Evan, that they simply must break off. Seeing him makes her feel too terribly guilty with Abe, who after all is so *nice.* No more Evan, never again.

Evan is a computer salesman based in New York who occasionally comes to Toronto, to stay in the Harborfront Hotel, where Zelda has her travel office. These letters of hers never seem to affect him in the slightest; he shows up anyway, no more or less frequently than before. Looking shy, he comes into her office, saying couldn't they at least have a drink in the bar? Maybe lunch? And there they soon are, back in bed again. In love.

Evan does not look at all the part that he plays with Zelda. A worried, chronically rumpled young man, light-skinned (well, sallow) and too thin, he looks more like the other things that he is, a husband and father, with a heavy mortgage in Douglas, Long Island. A salesman. With Zelda, though, as he has often told her, he is someone else, a strong, confident, often laughing man. "Lord, I even feel handsome," he once half-jokingly confided.

"Darling, you are" was of course what Zelda said (with the odd thought that actually of the two men Abe is better-looking, just a little older).

However, today she is not getting far with her letter. "My darling," she has written. And then she is distracted by a rustle of large black birds, just settling in the bush beyond her terrace. Three of them, a family. Their sleek wings shine, with hints of darkest blue, blue-black velvet. "This time I absolutely," Zelda writes before crumpling up her paper.

Abe too has been watching the vendors, and he, like Evelyn Fisk, sees the peanut vendors as the saddest of all. Even their voices are sad, and their faces are so long. Trickle-down economics, Abe thinks. Poverty trickles down very fast to these poorest of the poor.

Just then, though, a group of small boys appears, bearing newspapers. Abe watches as Evelyn (whom he thinks of as the cat woman) buys a paper. But when the boy reaches him, Abe waves him off, saying, "No, Gabino." Meaning, I'm waiting to buy a paper from Gabino.

The child looks puzzled, whether as to Abe's meaning or the identity of Gabino, Abe can't tell, and so he asks, "Gabino. *Dónde?*" (He does know a very few words of Spanish.)

The small boy shrugs and goes off, leaving Abe with no paper. With nothing.

He probably should have bought one, what the hell? A few pesos here or there won't mean much even to Gabino. However, to the next boy with a bunch of papers who cries "English language! Mexico City *News!*" Abe hears himself repeating, "No, Gabino."

This child, though, seems to understand. And he speaks some English. He asks Abe, "You wait Gabino?"

"*Sí!*" Enthusiastically. And then, "Gabino. *Dónde?*"

The small brown monkey face scrutinizes Abe's much larger, paler face before he says, "*Gabino está muerto.* Dead."

"*No.*"

The devil-child begins to laugh. "*Sí, Gabino está muerto!*" and he runs off after the others, down the beach.

There in the heavy heat Abe sits frozen, immobilized. *Muerto.* Does it mean just dead, or killed? Slain, murdered. How awful for there to be just the one word. And how plausible a violent end would be for Gabino, an artful, ambitious little boy, a Mexican street child. It is entirely horrible. Abe has no words, no way of dealing with this.

And should he tell Zelda? Such a shadow over their trip, and Zelda tends to be superstitious.

Easy enough not to tell her, Abe decides.

Perhaps she will buy all her silver presents today, thinks Evelyn Fisk. Get it over with and simply not consider presents again. She decides this as a very young, dark, Indian-looking girl approaches her *palapa,* a girl with lovely, luminous black eyes and terrible teeth, too large for her face, askew, protuberant. But a radiant smile.

Evelyn, whose Spanish is excellent, asks her name.

Lupe.

Evelyn. Eva.

Lupe has a small brown briefcase of silver things, plus the pretty glass necklaces held over her arm. In a random way Evelyn begins to choose. Later she will sort them out, considering their recipients. In the meantime she talks to Lupe.

Is this her first year on the beach selling silver? Evelyn does not believe she has seen her before.

No, Lupe came before with her mother, Carmelita. However, at that time she was still in school for much of the day. Next year Lupe will have for sale tapes, instead of these, and in a deprecating way she indicates her jewels.

Tapes? Evelyn at first does not understand.

Tapes! Music! All kinds of music. All the latest hits. Music, on tapes.

Zelda, passing the *palapa* of Evelyn Fisk to get to her own, to reach Abe, sees Lupe there with her silver, her bright glass, and on an impulse she stops. She smiles, and by way of greeting to Evelyn she says, "Oh, it's all so pretty."

"I'm afraid I've been very extravagant." Evelyn Fisk smiles back. "But I have all these grandchildren. Not to mention daughters."

"Oh, then you are married." Zelda had not meant to say this. The words rushed out, unbidden.

"Oh indeed. Very much so. But I need a little time off, now and then."

"Oh, *really.*"

"Lupe has been telling me that next year she'll have tapes for sale," Evelyn Fisk says firmly, putting an end to further personal conversation.

"You must miss the cats this year," persists Zelda. Her curiosity has been intensely aroused by this woman, whom she sees close up to be much more interesting-looking than from a distance. For one thing, the white pants, dark shirt, and straw hat that across the dining room look like everyone else's clothes are actually extremely smart. Unusual. Working within a hotel has taught Zelda something about such distinctions. She knows at a glance which guests at the Harborfront are rich, or European, or from the States, as opposed to Canadians, rich or medium rich, from Ottawa or Calgary. Evelyn Fisk is very rich, and from the States.

"I try not to think about the cats," says Evelyn Fisk somewhat dismissingly, turning back to Lupe.

Abe, out in the water, has observed Zelda's arrival at the beach, and he has noted with some surprise her stop at the cat woman's *palapa.* He waves, but she probably can't see him, can't tell him from any other bather out there in the surf. Nearsighted Zelda is vain about her large dark blue eyes: no glasses. He watches as she settles down with her magazines and lotions in their own *palapa,* and he thinks, What a pretty woman. He decides again not to mention Gabino.

The quality of that water, in that particular bay, is amazing, extraordinary. Abe concentrates on his sense of the water, its lively, active buoyancy, its blue-green clearness. Its perfectly embracing warmth. It is quite unlike any other water, Abe believes. A unique experience of water.

Up on the beach, Zelda is talking to a young Mexican. A news vendor, but considerably taller than the rest. Abe watches as she buys a paper from this boy. She seems in fact to engage him quite unnecessarily in some sort of conversation; even at this distance, out in the waves, Abe sees them laugh, notes their friendly postures. And he experiences a flush of jealous blood—so ridiculous, a Mexican child. Still, there have been times with Zelda when she has given him good cause for jealousy. If not actual, at least approximate.

With a jaunty wave to Zelda, the boy heads down the beach with his armload of papers, and after a calculated minute or two Abe starts in. Swimming, not riding waves. Until he stands up and begins to wade.

He can see Zelda, now smiling and waving in his direction. It is probably the stripes on his new bathing suit that she recognizes.

What Evelyn Fisk absolutely must not think about, she now reminds herself, is just how Oscar got rid of the cats. No speculations along those lines. *None.* Never.

There were quite a lot of cats. Several families.

Oscar must have—

Someone must have—

NO.

"Well, of course it was Gabino," insists Zelda, at lunch, over Abe's continuing incredulity. "I told you, he wanted to thank you for the shoes. Only he's outgrown them and he'd like another pair." She laughs. "Some con man, that kid. I'm sure he'll go far."

"I can't get over hearing *muerto,*" Abe tells her. "It just seemed so plausible for a kid like Gabino. For really any Mexican kid, these days."

"But it wasn't true," Zelda reminds him. "I keep telling you, he's fine. Just suddenly looking adolescent, not a cute little boy anymore. With acne, poor guy."

Abe can less easily imagine Gabino with acne than he was able to imagine him dead.

"Some nerve he has demanding more shoes." Zelda laughs. And she says again, "He'll go far."

"It seems to me that the prawns were better here last year, don't you think?" Abe recognizes his own reluctance to talk about Gabino as he says this. As Zelda sometimes points out, he tends to avoid issues. A male characteristic, according to Zelda.

She now regards him somewhat narrowly, but she seems willing to leave the topic of Gabino. "Maybe," she says of the prawns. "I don't know, it's all still so beautiful here. I don't much notice flaws."

"On the other hand," says Abe, somewhat later in their meal, "why blame Gabino for trying to get anything he can? Lord knows what his life is like. Where he lives. In what. I may send him three more pairs of shoes. Why in hell not?"

By midafternoon, which is still beachtime for most people, between lunch and their long siestas, the color of the sky is a queer bright ocher, unnaturally intense. And the heavy hot still air is rippled by occasional small spasmodic winds. Out at sea, the color is dark and strange.

No one knows what will happen next.

Many guests start up toward their rooms.

Finding themselves together on the path, Evelyn Fisk and Zelda and Abe all smile, murmuring at the oddity of the weather. Abe insists on carrying Evelyn's rather large book bag—at which they exchange a small laugh.

Pausing for a moment—the path is fairly steep—they turn, the three of them simultaneously, for a backward look at the menacing sky, the beach.

And down there beside the water is Oscar, striding along as though rain were out of the question, were expressly forbidden by himself.

Evelyn. "He really is dreadful."

Zelda. "Horrible. I wonder whatever happened to his wife. Remember Marya?"

"Yes, actually I do. Well, it's not hard to cast him as a sort of Bluebeard."

Perhaps from some automatic impulse of male solidarity (women tend to go too far, almost always), Abe demurs. "Well, come on now. But he is a mean S.O.B., that's for sure."

At the top of the path he hands Evelyn her books, they separate and go off to their own rooms, to bed.

And then the rains begin. A heavy roar of water, pounding down. Water slapping against the concrete walkways. Attacking the roof like bullets. A ferocious rain, that goes on and on, and on.

Believing Abe to be asleep, Zelda pulls the light blanket from the end of the bed to cover his shoulders and her own. And then, that small wifely task completed, she burrows down, breathing the unexpectedly new cool air. For her the sounds of rain are a summer sound, any winter rains in Toronto being muffled by snow. But of course it is summer down here, a perpetual summer. That's why they come here.

Zelda then begins to think of a small trip alone somewhere. Maybe to San Francisco. Well, why not? This is something that women do all the time these days. She could get tickets through the agency, and she could see the city, San Francisco! (She notes with some interest that she is not thinking of New York, or Evan.)

Dozing off, Zelda dreams of freedom. Somewhere else.

Beside her, Abe, who is not asleep, is thinking somewhat resentfully of Gabino, who after all could have written a note when he got the shoes. Abe very carefully included his own name and address, both inside and outside the package. A postcard, any sort of acknowledgment would have done. And today he didn't even wait for Abe to come up from swimming. Surely Zelda would have said that that was where he was.

Or would she?

The intensity of the downpour, the extreme heaviness of that deluge suggests that it won't last long, the rainstorm. But it seems to go on and on, heavy water pouring from the sky.

It could cause some very bad flooding, Abe thinks next, as he envisions the dry riverbeds, the eroded sloping fields that they pass on their way from the airport to this hotel. And in his mind he can also see a cluster of shacks, the floorless dwellings of the very poor. Small and fragile, hardly shelters at all, precariously perched on the crumbling hillside earth.

Where Gabino might well come from.

His resentment vanished as though washed away in the rain, Abe determines that tomorrow he will go and find Gabino. He will find out just where he lives (he has kept the address), what the circumstances of his family are.

Evelyn Fisk, alone in her wide lumpy hard bed, is thinking that if the cats were still around she would at this moment be worried about where they were now, in the drenching, unaccustomed rain. However, she derives small solace from the fact that there are no cats for her to worry about. Really no solace at all.

In a terrible and permanent way she misses all of them, with their long skinny graceful bodies, their blue-green-yellow wise watchful eyes.

Unspeakable Oscar.

And Grantly, never allowing cats in their house. She has never seen him sneeze or turn red, no true allergic symptoms. He simply doesn't like them.

Well, thinks Evelyn, warm beneath her covers, taking in cool air, Well, there's more than one solution to that problem.

And she smiles.

Fog

On an unspeakably cold and foggy night one November in San Francisco, something terrible happens to a woman named Antonia Love. She is a painter, middle-aged, recently successful, who has invited some people to her house for dinner (one of whom she has not even met, as yet). But in the course of tearing greens into the salad bowl and simultaneously shooing off one of her cats—the old favorite, who would like to knead on one of her new brown velvet shoes—Antonia, who is fairly tall, loses her balance and falls, skidding on a fragment of watercress and avoiding the cat but landing, *bang,* on the floor, which is Mexican-tiled, blue and white. Hard. Antonia thinks she heard the crack of a bone.

Just lying there for a moment, shocked, Antonia imagines herself a sprawled, stuffed china-headed doll, her limbs all askew, awry. How incredibly stupid, how dumb, she scolds herself; if I didn't want people to dinner, I could just have not asked them. And then: Well, useless to blame myself, there are accidents. The point is, what to do now?

As she tries to move, it is apparent that her left arm indeed is broken; it won't work, and in the effort of trying to move it Antonia experiences an instant of pain so acute that she reels, almost faints, and only does not by the most excruciating effort of will.

The problem of what to do, then, seems almost out of her hands. Since she can't for the moment get up, she also can't call her doctor, nor 911. Nor, certainly, can she go on with making dinner.

Fortunately her coming guests are old close friends (except for the very young man she doesn't know, although he seems to think he has met her somewhere). And, further luck, she is sure that she unlocked the front door, its bell being hard to hear, back here in the kitchen. And so her friends will arrive and they will come on in, calling out to her, and she to them. They will find her ludicrously positioned, they will help—although possibly she is really quite all right, and will manage to get up by herself any minute now.

A new flash of pain as she tries to move convinces Antonia that her arm is really broken, and again she castigates herself for clumsiness, for evident ill will toward her friends, determined self-defeat. For steady progress toward no progress at all—oh, for everything!

In addition to which she has probably scared her cat quite badly. He is nowhere around, although she calls out to him, "Baron! Baron?"

No cat, then, and no live-in lover either, since Reeve is at the moment off on one of his restless trips somewhere; Reeve who in an off-and-on way lives there with Antonia, the arrangement being that both are "free." And just as well he is gone, thinks Antonia; he so hates debility, hates bodily things going wrong. (But in that case why has he chosen to live, more or less, with an "older woman," whose body must inevitably decline?) Antonia wonders if Reeve is alone on this trip (she knows that he sometimes is not), but she finds that she lacks just now the stamina for jealous speculation.

Her arm really hurts badly, though; she wishes someone would come, and she wonders who will be the first—who will come in to find her in this worse than undignified position? Will it be her old friend from school days, Lisa, who is bringing the strange young man? Or will it be Bynum and Phyllis, who are old friends—or Bynum is. He is a sculptor, and Phyllis, his latest wife, a very young lawyer. Antonia believes they are not getting along very well.

Or (at this new notion Antonia grimaces to herself) it could always be tall, thin, sandy Reeve himself, who is given to changing his mind, to turning around and away from trips, and people. Reeve, a painter too, is more apt to come home early from trips on which he is accompanied than from those he takes alone; but even that is not a formulation on which anyone, especially Antonia, should count.

Antonia is aware that her friends wonder why she "puts up" with Reeve, his absences, his occasional flings with young art students. And she considers her private view of him: an exceptional man, of extreme (if occasional) sensitivity, kindness—a painter of the most extraordinary talent. (On the other hand, sometimes she too wonders.)

Fog

Antonia knows too that her friends refer to Reeve as "Antonia's cowboy" . . .

Reeve is from Wyoming.

She tries next to lie down, believing that some rest might help, or ease the pain, which now seems to have become a constant. Never mind how appalling the spectacle of herself would be, her oversized body sprawled across the floor. However, she can't get down, can't reach the floor; the broken arm impedes any such changes of position. Antonia finds that the most she can achieve is leaning back against table legs, fortunately a heavy, substantial table.

Perry Loomis, the unmet guest, is a journalist, just getting started, or trying to in New York. He could surely sell an article about such a distinguished, increasingly famous woman, especially since Antonia never gives interviews. Now, having cleverly engineered this meeting, and being driven in from Marin County by Antonia's old friend Lisa, Perry is overexcited, unable not to babble. "It said in *Time* that a lot of speculators are really grabbing up her stuff. Even at thirty or forty thousand per. She must hate all that, but still."

"It's hard to tell how she does feel about it," Lisa responds. "Or anything else, for that matter. I think success has been quite confusing to Antonia."

The bay is heavily fogged, slowing their progress from Mill Valley into town, to Antonia's small house on Telegraph Hill. Not everyone slows, however; an occasional small, smart sports car will zoom from nowhere past Lisa's more practical Ford wagon. Scary, but she does not even think of asking this young man to drive. They met through friends at a recent gallery (not the opening) at which Antonia's work was being shown. Perry described himself as a "tremendous Antonia Love fan" and seemed in his enthusiasm both innocent and appealing. Which led Lisa fatally to say, "Oh, really, I've known her almost all my life." Which was not even quite true, but which, repeated to Antonia, led up to this dinner invitation. "Well, why don't you bring him along when you come next Thursday? I'm almost sure Reeve won't be here, and poor Bynum must be tired of being the token man."

"And she's so beautiful," rattles Perry. "Was she always such a beauty?"

"Well, no," says Lisa, too quickly. "In fact, I don't quite see—but you know how old friends are. As a young woman, she was just so—big. You know, and all that hair."

"But I met her," Perry reminds her firmly. "At that thing in New York. She had on the most marvelous dress, she was ravishing, really."

"Oh yes, her green dress. It is good-looking. I think she paid the earth for it. That's one of the points about darling Antonia, really. Her adorable inconsistencies. A dress like that but never a sign of a maid or even a cleaning person in her house." And just why is she sounding so bitchy? Lisa wonders.

"Maybe she thinks they'd get in her way?" Perry's imagination has a practical turn. As a schoolboy, which was not all that long ago, he too meant to be an artist, and was full of vague, romantic plans. However, during college years, in the late seventies, he came to see that journalism might better serve his needs, a judgment seemingly correct. However, his enthusiasm for "artists," in this instance Antonia, is a vestige of that earlier phase.

"Well, she's in any case a marvelous cook," Lisa promises warmly. And then, somewhat less charitably, "Her cooking is surely one of those things that keeps young Reeve around."

"But isn't he a painter too?" Saying this, with an embarrassed twinge Perry realizes that he has imagined Reeve, described in Antonia Love articles as her "young painter companion" as a slightly older version of himself. He had looked forward to seeing just what of himself he would find in Antonia's Reeve.

"Of course he's a painter, that's nine-tenths of the problem right there. Reeve's from Wyoming, we call him 'Antonia's cowboy.' But they should never—Oh, look. *Damn.* There must be an accident on the bridge. Damn, we'll never get there."

Before them, on the downward, entirely fog-shrouded approach to the Golden Gate Bridge, what now seems heavy traffic is halted, absolutely. Red brake lights flicker as thick cold moisture condenses and drips in rivulets down windshields, windows, as somewhere out in the depthless, dangerous bay the foghorns croak, and mourn.

"Oh dear," says Perry Loomis. Although this attractive, rather interesting "older woman" was kind enough to bring him to his object, the desired Antonia, he thinks he really doesn't like her very much. (Are she and Antonia Love the same age? he wonders. This one looks younger, he thinks.)

"Indeed," says Lisa. On the whole an honest woman, she now admits to herself that she agreed to bring this Perry along not entirely out of kindness; there was also (she confesses to herself) some element of fantasy involved, specifically a romantic fantasy of herself with a younger lover (Lisa has been twice divorced, most recently two years back, from an especially mean-spirited lawyer). And then: Oh God, she thinks. Do I have to spend my life trying to be Antonia?

Reeve, who did indeed start out for Oregon, and alone, has now made a wide detour via the Richmond–San Rafael Bridge and is headed for Berkeley. Where, as Antonia might have guessed, had she the energy, there is a girl, Sharon, in whom Reeve is "interested." At this moment, heading along the foggy freeway toward the Berkeley exits, he longs to talk to Sharon, talking being so far about all they have done.

It's very difficult living with Antonia, he would like to tell Sharon. Here she is so successful, everything people work for, and she doesn't believe it. In her mind she's still starving and probably lonely. I mean, it's very hard to live with someone whom nothing can convince that she's all right. Nothing can convince her that people love her, including me.

Sharon is one of the most beautiful young women that Reeve has ever seen; he rather suspects that she was hired in the Art Department, where she works, on that basis—she was formerly a model. A darkly creamy blonde, with dreamy, thick-lashed blue-green eyes, Sharon holds her perfect body forward like a prize; she moves like a small queen—and she would not understand a single word of all that Reeve would like to say. To Sharon it would all be the ancient complaints about a wife.

In fact, the only person who could make the slightest sense of his ravings is Antonia herself. Reeve, a somewhat sardonic, self-mocking young man, comes to this conclusion with a twisting, interior smile. And, on an impulse, passing Sharon's exit, which is University, and heading toward the fog-ladened Bay Bridge, he speeds up the car.

. . .

"Phyllis and Bynum, Lisa. Perry. I'll be back soon. Sorry. Stew and risotto in the oven. Salad and wine in refrig. Please take and eat. Love, Antonia."

This note, taped to Antonia's door, was found by Phyllis and Bynum, one of whose first remarks to each other then was "Who on earth does she mean by Perry?"

"Oh, some new young man of Lisa's, wouldn't you say?"

"But what could have happened to Antonia?"

"One of her meetings, wouldn't you imagine? One of her good works." This last from Bynum, Antonia's oldest friend, who has very little patience with her, generally.

That exchange takes place on the long stairs leading up to the small, shabby-comfortable living room in which they soon sit, with glasses of wine, engaged in speculations concerning their hostess.

"Something could be wrong?" Phyllis ventures. A small, blond, rather pretty woman, she is much in awe of Antonia, whom she perceives as exceptionally *strong,* in ways that she, Phyllis, believes herself not to be.

"I doubt it." Big, gnarled Bynum frowns.

This room's great feature—to some its only virtue—is the extraordinary view afforded of the city, even now, despite the thick fog. City lights still are faintly visible, everywhere, though somewhat muffled, dim, and the looming shapes of buildings can just be made out against the lighter sky.

Phyllis, who is extremely tired (a grueling day in court; but is she also tired of Bynum, as she sometimes thinks?), now lounges across a large, lumpy overstuffed chair, and she sips at the welcome cool wine. (The very size of Antonia's chair diminishes her to almost nothing, Phyllis feels.) She says, "Obviously, the view is why Antonia stays here?"

"Contrariness, I'd say," pontificates Bynum, himself most contrary by nature. "I doubt if she even notices the view anymore."

A familiar annoyance tightens Phyllis's throat as she mildly says, "Oh, I'll bet she does." She is thinking, if Bynum and I split up, I'll be lucky to get a place this nice, he doesn't have to keep putting it down. This could cost, oh, close to a thousand.

"Besides, the rent's still so low," continues Bynum, as though Phyllis had not spoken, perhaps as though he had read her mind.

A pause ensues.

"God, I'm so hungry," says Phyllis. "Do you think we should really go ahead with dinner?"

"Baby, I sure do." Bynum too is tired, a long sad day of not being able to work. And he too is hungry. "Antonia could be forever, and Lisa and her young man lost somewhere out in the fog."

The immediate prospect of food, however, serves to appease their hunger. They smile pleasantly at each other, like strangers, or those just met. Phyllis even thinks what a handsome man Bynum is; he looks wonderful for his age. "Was Antonia good-looking back when you first knew her?" she asks him.

"Well, she was odd." Bynum seems to ruminate. "She varied so much. Looking terrific one day, and really bad the next. But she was always, uh, attractive. Men after her. But the thing is, she doesn't know it."

"Oh, not even now?" Phyllis, disliking her own small scale, her blond pallor, admires Antonia's larger, darker style. Antonia is so emphatic, is what Phyllis thinks.

"Especially not now." Bynum's smile and his tone are indulgent.

"Do you remember that really strange thing she said, when she told a reporter, 'I'm not Antonia Love'?" asks Phyllis. She has wanted to mention this before to Bynum, but they have, seemingly, no time for conversation.

"I think she meant that she could only view herself as created," Bynum explains authoritatively.

Phyllis is not sure whether he is speaking as a fellow artist or simply as an old friend. She asks, "Do you mean by the media?" She is aware of enjoying this conversation, perhaps because it is one, a conversation.

"Oh no, so much more sinister," Bynum assures her. "By herself. She thinks she's someone she's painted." He chuckles a little too loudly.

And loses the momentary sympathy of his young wife. Declining to comment, though, and remembering how hungry she is, Phyllis gets up to her feet. "Well, I don't care how lost Lisa and what's-his-name are. I'm heating up dinner."

She goes out into the kitchen as Bynum calls after her, "I'll be there in a minute."

But several minutes pass, during which Bynum does not follow

Phyllis. Instead he stares out the window, out into the dark, the enveloping, thickening fog. Into dimmed yellow lights.

He is fairly sure that Phyllis will leave him soon; he knows the signs—the ill-concealed small gestures of impatience, the long speculative looks, the tendencies to argument. How terribly alike they all seem, these girls that he marries. Or is it possible that he sees none of them very sharply, by herself—that he can't differentiate? One of them made this very accusation, referring to what she called his "myopia." In any case, he will probably not miss Phyllis any more than he missed the others, and in a year or so he will find and marry a new young woman who is very much like Phyllis and the rest. He knows that he must be married.

A strong light wind has come up, rattling the windowpanes. Standing there, still looking out, Bynum has a brand-new thought—or, rather, a series of thoughts. He thinks, Why do they always have to be so goddam young? Just who am I kidding? I'm not a young man. A woman of my own age or nearly might at last be a perfect companion for me. A woman artist, even, and he thinks, Well, why not Antonia? This place is a dump, but she's so successful now we could travel a lot. And I've always liked her really, despite our fights. This Reeve person must surely be on the way out. She won't put up with him much longer—so callow.

"Bynum, come on, it's all ready," Phyllis then calls out as at that same instant the doorbell rings.

It is of course Lisa and the new young man, Perry, who looks, Bynum observes, far too smugly pleased with himself.

Introductions are made, warm greetings exchanged: "But you look marvelous! Have you been here long? Yes, I'm sure we met at the gallery. How very like Antonia not to be here. But whatever could have happened?"

"Actually, it is not at all like Antonia not to be here," Bynum announces. He is experiencing a desire to establish himself as the one of them who knows her best.

Over dinner, which indeed is excellent—a succulent veal stew, with a risotto—Bynum scrutinizes Lisa, and what looks to be her new friend. Lisa is looking considerably less happy than the young man is, this Perry, in Bynum's view. Could they possibly have made it in the car, on the way over here, and now Lisa is feeling regrets? Even to Bynum's somewhat primitive imagination this seems unlikely.

Fog

What Lisa regrets is simply having talked as much as she did to Perry as on the way over they remained locked in the fogbound traffic. She not only talked, she exaggerated, overemphasized Antonia's occasional depression, even her worries over Reeve.

And even while going on and on in that way, Lisa was visited by an odd perception, which was that she was really talking about herself. She, Lisa, suffers more than occasional depressions. It is her work, not Antonia's (well, hardly Antonia's), that seems to be going nowhere. And Lisa, with no Reeve or anyone interesting in her life at the moment, is worried that this very attractive young man will not like her (she has always liked small, dark, trimly built men like Perry). Which is really why she said so much about Antonia—gossip as gift, which is something she knows about, having done it far too often.

The truth is—or one truth is—that she is deeply, permanently fond of Antonia. And another truth is that her jealous competitiveness keeps cropping up, like some ugly, uncontrolled weed. She has to face up to it, do something about it, somehow.

"What a superb cook Antonia is," she now says (this is true, but is she atoning?). "Her food is always such a treat."

"The truth is that Antonia does everything quite well," Bynum intones. "Remember that little spate of jewelry design she went into? Therapy, she called it, and she gave it up pretty quickly, but she did some lovely stuff."

"Oh, Bynum," Lisa is unable not to cry out. "How can you even mention that junk? She was so depressed when she did it, and it did not work as therapy. You know perfectly well that she looked dreadful with all those dangles. She's too big."

Perry laughs as she says this, bur in a pleasant, rather sympathetic way, so that Lisa thinks that maybe, after all, he understood? understood about love as well as envy?

Below them on the street now are the straining, dissonant, banging sounds of cars: people trying to park, trying to find their houses, to get home to rest. It is hard to separate one sound from another, to distinguish, identify. Thus, steps that must be Antonia's, with whomever she is with, are practically upon them before anyone has time to say, "Oh, that must be Antonia."

It is, though: Antonia, her arm in its bright white muslin sling thrust before her, in a bright new shiny plaster cast. Tall Antonia, looking triumphant, if very pale. And taller Reeve, somewhat disheveled, longish sandy hair all awry, but also in his own way triumphant, smiling. His arm is around Antonia's shoulder, in protective possession.

First exclamations are in reaction to the cast. "Antonia, how terrible! However did you? How lucky that Reeve— How awful, does it still hurt? Your *left* arm, how lucky!"

Reeve pulls out a chair for Antonia, and in an already practiced gesture with her good, lucky right arm she places the cast in her lap. In a somewhat embarrassed way (she has never been fond of center stage), she looks around at her friends. "I'm glad you went on with dinner" is the first thing she says. "Now you can feed us. God, I'm really starving."

"I came home and there she was on the floor—" Reeve begins, apparently about to start a speech.

"The damn cat!" Antonia cries out. "I tripped over Baron. I was making the salad."

Reeve scowls. "It was very scary," he tells everyone present. "Suppose I hadn't come home just then? I could have been traveling somewhere, although—"

This time he is interrupted by Bynum, who reasonably, if unnecessarily, states, "In that case, we would have been the ones to find Antonia. Phyllis and I."

"I do wish someone would just hand me a plate of that stew," Antonia puts in.

"Oh of course, you must be starved," her friends all chorus. "Poor thing!"

It is Lisa who places the full, steaming plate before Antonia, Lisa asking, "You can eat okay? You want me to butter some bread?"

"Dear Lisa. Well, actually I do, I guess. God, I hope I don't get to like this helplessness."

"Here." Lisa passes a thick slice of New York rye, all buttered. "Oh, and this is Perry," she says. "He's been wanting to meet you. You know, we drove down from Marin together."

Antonia and Perry acknowledge each other with smiles and small murmurs, difficult for Antonia, since she is now eating, ravenously.

.   .   .

"Real bastards in the emergency ward," Reeve is telling everyone; he obviously relishes his part in this rescue. "They let you wait forever," he says.

"Among bleeding people on gurneys," Antonia shudders. "You could die there, and I'm sure some people do, if they're poor enough."

"*Does* it hurt?" asks Lisa.

"Not really. Really not at all. I just feel so clumsy. Clumsier than usual, I mean."

She and Lisa smile at each other: old friends, familiar irony.

Now everyone has taken up forks again and begun to eat, along with Antonia. Wine is poured around, glasses refilled with red, or cold white, from pitchers.

Reeve alone seems not to be eating much, or drinking—for whatever reasons of his own: sheer excitement, possibly, anyone who thinks about it could conclude. He seems nervy, geared up by his—their recent experience.

The atmosphere is generally united, convivial, though. People tell their own accident stories, as they will when anyone has had an accident (hospital visitors like to tell the patient about their own operations). Bynum as a boy broke his right arm not once but twice, both times falling out of trees. Lisa broke her leg on some ice. "You remember, Antonia, that awful winter I lived in New York. Everything terrible happened." Perry almost broke his back, "but just a fractured coccyx, as things turned out," failing off a horse, in New Mexico (this story does not go over very well, somehow; a lack of response can be felt around the room). Phyllis broke her arm skiing in Idaho.

Reeve refrains from such reminiscences—although he is such a tall, very vigorous young man; back in Wyoming, he must have broken something, sometime. He has the air of a man who is waiting for the main event, and who in the meantime chooses to distance himself.

In any case, the conversation rambles on in a pleasant way, and no one is quite prepared to hear Antonia's end-of-meal pronouncement. Leaning back and looking around, she says, "It's odd that it's taken me so long to see how much I hate it here."

This is surely something that she has never said before. However, Antonia has a known predilection for the most extreme, the most emotional statement of any given feeling, and so at first no one pays much serious attention.

Lisa only says, "Well, the city's not at its best in all this fog. And then your poor arm."

And Bynum? "You can't mean this apartment, I've always loved it here." (At which Phyllis gives him a speculative, not quite friendly look.)

Looking at them all—at least she has everyone's attention—Antonia says, "Well, I do mean this apartment. It's so small, and so inconvenient having a studio five blocks away. Not to mention paying for both. Oh, I know I can afford it, but I hate to." She looks over at Reeve, and a smile that everyone can read as significant passes between the two of them.

One of Antonia's cats, the guilty old tabby, Baron, has settled on her lap, and she leans to scratch the bridge of his nose, very gently.

And so it is Reeve who announces, "I've talked Antonia into coming back to Wyoming with me. At least to recuperate." He smiles widely (can he be blushing?), in evident pleasure at this continuation of his rescuer role.

"I'm so excited!" Antonia then bursts out. "The Grand Tetons, imagine! I've always wanted to go there, and somehow I never dared. But Reeve has this whole house, and a barn that's already a studio."

"It's actually in Wilson, which is just south of Jackson," Reeve explains. "Much less touristic. It's my folks' old place."

If Antonia expected enthusiasm from her friends about this project, though, she is disappointed.

Of them all Bynum looks most dejected, his big face sags with displeasure, with thwarted hopes. Phyllis also is displeased, visibly so (but quite possibly it is Bynum of whom she disapproves?).

Lisa cries out, "But, Antonia, what'll I do without you? I'll miss you so, I'm not used to your being away. It'll be like New York—"

To which Antonia smilingly, instantly responds, "You must come visit. Do come, we could start some sort of colony. And, Bynum, you can use this place while I'm gone if you want to."

Perry of course is thinking of his article, of which he now can envision the ending: Antonia Love off to the wilds of Wyoming, putting fog-bound, dangerous San Francisco behind her. He likes the sound of it, although he is not quite sure that Jackson or even Wilson would qualify as "wilds." But there must be a way to find out.

In any case, he now sees that he has been quite right in his estimate of Antonia: she is beautiful. At this moment, radiantly pale, in the barely candlelit, dim room, her face is stylized, almost abstract, with her broad, heavy forehead and heavy dark brows, her wide-spaced large black eyes and her wide, dark-painted mouth. It will be easy to describe her: stylized, abstract.

She is of course not at all his type (he actually much prefers her friend Lisa, whom he has decided that he does like, very much; he plans to see her again)—nor does Perry see himself in Reeve, at all. He senses, however, some exceptional connection between the two of them, some heightened rapport, as though, already in Wyoming, they breathed the same heady, pure, exhilarating air.

Antonia is talking about Wyoming now, her imagined refuge. "Mountains, clouds, water. Wildflowers," she is saying, while near her side Reeve smiles, quite privately.

And Perry believes that he has struck on the first sentence of his article: "Antonia Love these days is a very happy woman."

Tide Pools

For some years I lived alone in a small white clapboard house, up on a high wooded bluff above the Mississippi River, which I could hardly see—so far down, glimpsed through thick vines and trees, and so narrow just there.

This was near Minneapolis, where I was an assistant professor at a local college. Teaching marine biology. And I thought quite a lot about the irony of my situation—a sea specialty in the landlocked Midwest. (I am from Santa Barbara, California, originally, which may explain quite a bit.)

During those Minnesota years, despite professional busyness, a heavy teaching load, labs, conferences, friends, and a few sporadic love affairs, I was often lonely, an embarrassing condition to which I would never have admitted. Still, and despite my relative isolation, at that time I regarded the telephone as an enemy, its shrill, imperative sound an interruption even to loneliness. When my phone rang, I did not anticipate a friendly chat. For one thing, most of my friends and lovers were also hard-working professionals, not much given to minor social exchange.

Thus, on a summer night about a year ago, a rare warm clear twilight, reminding me of Southern California, I was far from pleased at the sound of the telephone. I had just taken a bath and finished dressing; I was going out to dinner with a man I had met recently, whom I thought I liked. (Was he calling to break the date? Native distrust has not helped my relationships with men, nor with women.) We were going out to celebrate my birthday, actually, but I did not imagine that the ringing phone meant someone calling with congratulations, my birthday not being something that I generally talk about.

What I first heard on picking up that alien instrument was the hollow, whirring sound that meant a long-distance call, and I thought, How odd, what a strange hour for business. Then, as I said hello, and hello again, I heard silence. At last a female voice came on, very slurred. But then words formed. "Judith? Have I got Miss Judith Mallory? *Dr.* Mallory?"

"Yes—"

"Judy, is that you, truly? Truly, Jude? Judy, do you know who this is?" An excited, drunken voice, its cadence ineradicably familiar to me— and only one person has ever called me Jude. It was Jennifer Cartwright, my closest early-childhood friend, my almost inseparable pal—whom I had not heard from or about for more than twenty years, not since we both left Santa Barbara, where we grew up together, or tried to.

I asked her, "Jennifer, how are you? Where are you? What are you doing now?"

"Well, I'm back in our house, you know. I've come back home. I've been here since Mother died, and I guess I'm doing okay. Oh, Judy, it's really you! I'm so happy . . ."

Happy was the last thing that Jennifer sounded, though; her voice was almost tearful.

"Oh, Jennifer." I was assailed by an overwhelming affection for my friend, mixed with sadness over whatever ailed her just now, including being so drunk. I had not even known that her mother was dead. Nicola—Nickie Cartwright, whom I had also cared about a lot.

My own parents had both been dead for some time, which is one reason I had had no news from Santa Barbara. Also, since they died of so-called alcohol-related ailments, I was perhaps unreasonably alarmed at Jennifer's condition. A nervous stomach, which is no stomach at all for booze, had kept me, if unwillingly, abstemious.

"And oh!" Jennifer's voice sounded indeed much happier now. "I forgot to say happy birthday. Judy, Jude, happy happy birthday! Every year I think of you today, even if I haven't ever called you."

"You're so good to remember," I told her. "But really, tell me how you are."

"Oh, you tell me! First off, you tell me just what you have on." Such a perfect Jennifer question—or Nickie: Nickie too would have asked me what I was wearing, in order to see me, and to check on how I was.

To please Jennifer, I should have described a beautiful, colorful dress, but a lack of imagination, I believe, has kept me honest; I tend to tell the truth. My former (only) husband observed that I had a very literal mind, and he might have been right, as he was with a few other accurate accusations. In any case, I told Jennifer, "Just a sweater and some pants. My uniform, I guess. But they're both new. Black. Actually, I'm going out to dinner. This man I met—"

Jennifer began to laugh, her old prolonged, slow, appreciative laugh, and I thought, Well, maybe she's not so drunk. Just a little tipsy, maybe, and overexcited.

"Oh, Jude." Jennifer was laughing still. "You're going out on a date, and we're so old. But you sound like you're about sixteen, and wearing something pink and gauzy."

Rational, sober person that I am, I could have cried.

But Jennifer went on in a conversational, much less drunken way. "I think about you so much," she said. "And everything back then. All the fun we had. Of course, since I've moved back here it's all easier to remember."

"I'm really sorry to hear about Nickie," I told her.

"Well, just one more terrible thing. Everyone gets cancer, it seems like to me. Honestly, Jude, sometimes I think being grown up really sucks, don't you? To use a word I truly hate."

"Well, I guess."

"Your parents die, and your husbands turn out bad. And your kids—oh, don't even talk to me about kids."

Her voice trailed off into a total silence, and I thought, Oh dear, she's fallen asleep at the telephone, out there in California, in that house I know so very well. The house right next door to the house where my parents and I used to live—in fact, its architectural twin—on what was called the Santa Barbara Gold Coast, up above the sea. I wondered what room Jennifer was in—her own room, in bed, I hoped. I called out "Jennifer!" over all that space, Minnesota to California. Calling out over time too, over many years.

Her laugh came on again. "Oh, Jude, you thought I'd gone to sleep. But I hadn't, I was just lying here thinking. In Mother and Dad's big old bed. You remember?"

"Oh, of course I do." And with a rush I remembered the Sunday morning when Jennifer and I had run into the Cartwrights' bedroom, I guess looking for the Sunday papers, and there was blond Scott and blonder Nickie in their tousled nightclothes, lying back among a pale-blue tangle of sheets. Not making love, although I think we must have caught them soon after love. They may have moved apart as we came in; Scott's hand still lingered in Nickie's bright, heavy uncombed hair. At the time, I was mostly struck by their sleepy affection for each other, so clearly present. I can see it now, those particular smiles, all over their pale morning faces.

The room, with its seascape view, was almost identical to my parents' bedroom, and their view. My parents slept in narrow, separate beds. They were silent at home except when they drank, which loosened them up a little, though it never made them anywhere near affectionate with each other.

In any case, I surely remembered the Cartwrights' broad, blue-sheeted carved-mahogany bed.

I asked Jennifer, "Your father—Scott died too?" Although I think I knew that he must have. But I used to see Scott Cartwright as the strongest man I ever knew, as well as the most glamorous, with his golfer's tan, and his stride.

"Just after your mother died. They were all so young, weren't they? Dad had a stroke on the golf course, but maybe that's the best way to go. Poor Mother was sick for years. Oh, Judy, it's all so scary. I hate to think about it."

She had begun to trail off again, and partly to keep her awake, in contact, I asked her if she had married more than once; I thought I had heard her say "husbands," plural, but it was hard to tell, with her vagueness, slurring.

But "Oh, three times!" Jennifer told me. "Each one worse. I never seem to learn." But she sounded cheerful, and next she began to laugh. "You will not believe what their names were," she said. "Tom, Dick, and Harry. That's the truth. Well, not actually the whole truth—I can't lie to my best old favorite friend. The whole truth is, the first two were Tom and Dick, and so when I went and got married the third time I had to call him Harry, even if his name was Jack."

I laughed—I had always laughed a lot with Jennifer—but at the same time I was thinking that people from single, happy marriages are supposed to marry happily themselves. They are not supposed to make lonely, drunken phone calls to old, almost forgotten friends.

Mostly, though, I was extremely pleased—elated, even—to have heard from Jennifer at all, despite the bad signs, the clear evidence that she was not in very good shape. As we hung up a few minutes later, I was aware of smiling to myself, the happy recipient of a happy birthday present. And like most especially welcome, sensitive presents, this gift from Jennifer was something that I had not known I needed, but that now I could no longer do without: a friend for talking to.

I went out for dinner with my new beau in a rare lighthearted mood, but I may have seemed more than a little abstracted. I was thinking of Jennifer, her parents, and California.

When Jennifer and I were friends, all that time ago, I truly loved her, but I also coveted almost everything about her: her golden curls, small plump hands, her famously sunny disposition, but most especially and most secretly I envied her her parents. I wanted them to be mine.

I have since learned (hasn't everyone?) that this is a common fantasy; Freud tells us that many children believe they have somehow ended up with the wrong set of parents. But at the time I naturally did not know this; guiltily I felt that only I had such an evil wish, to be rid of my own parents and moved in with another set. If it could somehow be proved, I thought, that I had been stolen by this dark and somber couple with whom I lived, while all along I was really a Cartwright child—then I would be perfectly happy. And if Jennifer's parents were mine, then of course Jennifer and I would be truly sisters, as so often we spoke of wishing that we were.

From the moment I saw them, even before seeing Jennifer, I was drawn to Scott and Nickie Cartwright, a tanned couple getting out of a new wood-paneled station wagon to look at a house for sale, the house next door to our house. I liked their bright splashy clothes, and the easy, careless way they walked and laughed; I wanted them to be the people to buy that house.

I thought that they looked too young to be parents; that they turned out to have a little girl just my age was a marvelous surprise, a bonus, as it were.

My own parents did not like the look of the Cartwrights, at first. "Lots of flash" was my Vermont mother's succinct summation. And my father's: "That garden they're buying needs plenty of solid work. I hope they know it." But fairly soon the four grown-ups took to dropping in on each other for a cup of coffee or a Coke, maybe, during the day; and at night they all got together for drinks. The Cartwrights, from St. Louis, had a sort of loose-style hospitality to which even my fairly stiff-mannered parents responded.

What must initially have won my stern parents' approval, though, was the Cartwrights' total dedication to their garden. Even before actually moving in, they began to spend their weekends digging among the dahlias, pruning hibiscus, trimming orange blossoms, and probing the roots of ivy. And once they lived there, all during the week beautiful Nickie in her short red shorts could be observed out clipping boxwoods, often mowing the lawn. And watering everything.

On weekends, around dusk if not sooner, the four of them would start in on their Tom Collinses, gin rickeys, or fruity concoctions with rum. Eventually one of the grown-ups (usually Nickie Cartwright) would remember that Jennifer and I should have some supper, and the two men (probably) would go out for some fried clams or pizza. Later on they would pretty much forget all about us, which was fine with Jennifer and me; we could stay up as long as we liked, giggling and whispering.

All the grown-ups that I knew at that time drank; it was what I assumed grown-ups did when they got together. Jennifer and I never discussed this adult habit, and "drunk" is not a word we would have used to describe our parents, ever. "Drunk" meant a sort of clownish, TV-cartoon behavior.

My parents as they drank simply talked too much; they told what seemed to me very long dull stories having to do with Santa Barbara history, early architects, all that. The Cartwrights, being younger, listened politely; Nickie laughed a lot, and they sat very close together.

Certainly my parents were never clownish or even loud; God knows they were not. In a bitter, tight-mouthed way they might argue at breakfast; a few times (this was the worst of all) I could hear my mother crying late at night, all by herself.

Because I had never heard them do so, I believed that the Cartwrights never argued, and I was sure that beautiful happy Nickie Cartwright never cried, and maybe she did not.

.   .   .

In the days that succeeded that first phone call from Jennifer, I thought considerably about her, about her parents, and mine. With terrible vividness I remembered the strength of my yearning for the Cartwrights, and I was assailed—again!—by the sheer intensity of all that childhood emotion, my earliest passions and guilts and despairs.

Quite as vividly, though, I also remembered the simple fun that we used to have, Jennifer and I, as children, especially on the beach. Since I had always lived there in Santa Barbara, on the California coast, and the Cartwrights were originally from inland Missouri, I was Jennifer's guide to the seashore. Bravely kicking our sneakers into tide pools, Jennifer and I uncovered marvels: tiny hermit crabs, long swaying seaweed, all purple. Anemones. Jennifer would squeal at dead fish, in a high, squeamish way, as I pretended not to mind them.

I also showed Jennifer the more sophisticated pleasures of State Street, the ice-cream parlors and the hot-dog stands. As we both grew up a little, I pointed out the stores. Tweeds & Weeds, my mother's favorite, was always too conservative for the Cartwright ladies, though. Nickie loved frills and lots of colors; she dressed herself and Jennifer in every shade of pink to tangerine. My mother ordered almost all of my clothes from the Lilliputian Bazaar, at Best & Company.

Undoubtedly the tide pools and my happy fascination with them to a great extent determined my later choice of a career, although a desire to displease and / or shock my parents must have figured largely also. Biology to them connoted sex, which in a general way they were against.

And possibly in some way of my own I made the same connection. In any case, I am forced to say that so far I have shone neither professionally nor in a romantic way. I did achieve a doctorate, and some years later an assistant professorship, at relatively early ages, but I do not feel that I will ever be truly distinguished.

As one of my more kindly professors put it, my interest in marine biology could be called aesthetic rather than scientific. I excel at drawing—urchins, starfish, snails.

As to my romantic history, it got off to a shaky start, so to speak, with my marriage to a fellow biologist, a man who after two years of me announced that colleagues should not be married to each other. (This could be true, but it had been his idea, originally.) He left me for a kindergarten teacher in Chicago, where his next teaching job happened to be. I became involved with an elderly musicologist, who was married; later with a graduate student in speech and drama, who, I came to believe, used coke, a lot of it.

Three men, then—my husband and two subsequent lovers—who presented certain problems. However, surely I do too? I am hardly "problem-free" or even especially easy to get along with. I am moody, hypersensitive, demanding.

In any case, these days as far as men are concerned I am running scared.

After that first birthday call, Jennifer telephoned again, and again. She seemed to have an unerring instinct for the right time to call, not an easy feat with me. (I once knew a man who always called me when I was brushing my teeth; I used to think that if I really wanted to hear from him I had only to get out my toothbrush.) In Jennifer's case, though, it may have been that I was simply so glad to hear from her.

I gathered that her present life was quite reclusive; she did not seem to know where anyone else whom we had known was now. I gathered too that she was quite "comfortably off," to use an old phrase of my mother's. My mother thought "rich" a vulgar word, and perhaps it is. Anyway, I was very glad that Jennifer was comfortable.

As I got used to talking to Jennifer again, sometimes I would find myself scolding her. You should get out more, take walks, get exercise, I would say. Go swimming—there must be a pool around. And what about vitamins? Do you eat enough? And Jennifer would laugh in her amiable way, and say she was sure I was absolutely right.

Jennifer's memory for long-gone days was extraordinary, though. She reminded me of the day we decided that to be kidnapped would be a thrilling adventure. We put on our best dresses and paraded slowly up and down State Street, conversing in loud voices about how rich (we liked the word) our parents were. Yachts, Spanish castles, trips on the *Queen Mary,* penthouses in New York—we mentioned all the things the movies had informed us rich people had, and did.

"You had on your striped linen," Jennifer perfectly recalled, "and I was wearing my lavender dotted swiss." She laughed her prolonged, slow chuckle. "We just couldn't understand why no one picked us up. Rich and adorable as we were. You remember, Jude?"

Well, I would not have remembered, but Jennifer brought it all back to me, along with our beach walks, the beautiful tide pools, the white sand, the rocks.

I began to look forward to those phone calls. I felt more and more that my connection with Jennifer was something that I had badly missed for years.

I believe I would have enjoyed talking to Jennifer under almost any circumstances, probably, but that particular fall and winter were bad times for me—and seemingly the rest of the world: Ethiopia, Nicaragua. In the American Midwest, where I was, unemployment was rife, and terrible. And to make everything worse the snows came early that year—heavy, paralyzing.

In a personal way, that snowed-in, difficult winter, things were especially bad: I was not getting along at all with my latest beau, the man who came to take me out to dinner on the night of Jennifer's first phone call. This was particularly depressing since we had got off to a very, very good start—not fireworks, not some spectacular blaze that I would have known to distrust, but many quiet tastes in common, including cats (he had five, an intensely charming fact, I thought, and they all were beautiful tabbies). The truth was that we were quite a lot alike, he and I. Not only our tastes but our defects were quite similar. We were both wary, nervy, shy. Very likely we both needed more by way of contrasting personality—although his former wife had been a successful actress, flamboyant, a great beauty, and that had not worked out too well, either. In any case, we further had in common the fact of being veterans of several mid-life love affairs, both knowing all too well the litany of the condition of not getting along. We exhibited a lessening of interest in each other in identical ways: an increase in our courtesy level. We pretended surprise and pleasure at the sound of each other's voice on the phone; with excruciating politeness we made excuses not to see each other. (At times it occurred to me that in some awful way I was becoming my parents—those super-polite role models.) And then we stopped talking altogether, my lover and I.

The next year was to be my sabbatical from the college, and none of my plans seemed to be working out in that direction, either. Nothing available at Woods Hole, nothing in San Diego. Or Berkeley, or Stanford.

Around March, with everything still going bad and no signs of spring, I realized that I had not heard from Jennifer for several weeks. Some instinct had all along advised me that I should wait to be called, I should not call Jennifer. Now, however, I did; I dialed the number in Santa Barbara. (Easy enough to come by: Jennifer, an unlikely feminist, had returned to her maiden name.)

It was not a good conversation. Jennifer was very drunk, although it was only about six at night, California time. She was drunk and sad and apologetic, over everything. She was extremely polite, but I felt that she was not even certain who I was; I could have been almost anyone. Any stranger, even, who happened to call, selling magazine subscriptions or offering chances to buy tax-free municipal bonds.

I was seriously worried, and after a little time I came to certain serious decisions.

I did the following things, in more or less this order:

I made an appointment and went to see the head of my department, and after some conversation, some argument, we struck up a bargain, of sorts. I would be granted a year's leave of absence (this involved less pay than a sabbatical, which was one of my selling points), and in return for this great favor I would teach an extra section of the general-science course for freshmen on my return.

I put up a notice on the bookstore bulletin board about renting out my house; from a great many applicants (probably I should have asked for more money) I selected a nice young couple from the Music Department. The only problem was that two people in the house would need all my small space; I would have to store everything but the furniture.

Through a national real-estate outfit I located a real-estate agent in Santa Barbara, who (this seemed an omen, a sure sign that I was on the right track) had a listing just a couple of houses down from Jennifer's—a garage apartment, mercifully cheap.

I called Jennifer, and as though it were a joke I said that I was coming out for a year, to take care of her.

. . .

And that is where I am now, and what I am doing. My apartment is in an alley half a block from Jennifer's house, the Cartwright house—and of course from my parents' house, too, the house that I sold when they died: my money for graduate school. My apartment is tiny, but since I am not there much, no matter. I have room for my drawing board, shelves of books and stacked papers; and outside there is a tiny scrap of a yard, where a neighbor cat comes to visit occasionally (he is beautiful—a pale-gray, long-eared, most delicate-footed creature).

I am beginning to run into a problem with space for clothes, though. When I first got here, Jennifer was so depressed, she said, by the darkness of my wardrobe ("Judy, you can't go around like that, not out here, in those professor clothes") that we have done a lot of State Street shopping, by way of brightening up my look. "But you're wonderful in that red silk," Jennifer insisted.

Jennifer herself, for a person who drinks or who has drunk that much, looks remarkably well. Needless to say, I was more than a little nervous about seeing her again. How would she look? I was so scared, in fact, that I gave very little thought to how I would look to her, and I think actually I am the one who has aged more. Jennifer is thin, a little frail and shaky on her feet, that is true, but her skin is still good, fine and pink, and her eyes are blue and clear. She just looks like a very, very pretty woman, of a certain age.

The first few weeks of my stay I made all the obvious suggestions having to do with drink: the Betty Ford place, or A.A., or just a plain good doctor. Well, Jennifer refused to go to anything, as I might have known she would—she has always been extremely stubborn. She even says that her doctor says she is perfectly all right. Two explanations for that last occur to me: one, she does not tell her doctor, or did not, how much she really drinks; or, two, the doctor himself is an alcoholic; I've heard that a lot of them are.

I have made a couple of strong advances, though. One is in terms of nutrition. I have instituted a heavy regimen of vitamins, and also I do most of the shopping and cooking. I go down to the docks for fresh fish, and on Saturday mornings there is a Farmers' Market, with lovely California vegetables and fruits. We eat very well, and I am sure that Jennifer eats a lot more with me around.

Another considerable advance is that Jennifer has entirely given up hard liquor, and now only drinks wine, white wine. In her big blue Ford station wagon we drive down to the new liquor store just off State Street. A handsome, bright-brassy, airy space. We walk around among the wooden crates and bins and shelves of bottles. This particular store deals mostly in California wines, and there are always some interesting new labels. New wineries keep turning up all over the state, even in very unlikely places, like San Luis Obispo or San Diego. We laugh at some of the names, which are often a little outlandish: Witches' Wish? And we admire the designs of the labels. We have even come to conclude that there is a definite correlation between beautiful labels and first-rate wines. Vichon, for example, one of our favorites, has an especially pretty picture on its bottle.

One of the best aspects of this whole venture for me is my discovery that after all I really can drink wine, with no ill effects. When I first came out, I would have one glass of wine at dinner, to keep Jennifer company, as it were. Then sometimes two, then sometimes another at home.

And now, in the late afternoons, though still too early to start over to the Cartwrights'—to Jennifer's house—I begin to think how nice a cool dry glass of wine would taste, and then I think, Well, why not? This is, after all, a sort of vacation for me. And so I pour myself one. I take the wine outside. I sit in one of the half-collapsed but still quite comfortable rattan chairs, in my tiny yard with its minute view of the evening sea, the sky, the burning sun. I sip, and in a peaceful way I contemplate my return to Santa Barbara.

I almost never think about my parents, or those old unhappy days spent here with them, growing up. Our family house has been remodeled almost beyond recognition, for which I am grateful. Only very infrequently do I feel its presence as that of a ghost, looming there just next to the Cartwright house.

I do not worry in the way that I used to about my career—that career, teaching at Minnesota. Marine biology. Sometimes I think I could stay right here forever (someone else could take on the freshman sections), and maybe get into something entirely new. I could walk on the beach and make sketches. (I do that already, of course; I mean I could do it in a more programmatic way.) Maybe someday I would be good enough to have a show, and maybe sell some. Or I could give drawing lessons at some local school. I might even, as we say, *meet someone.* Some nice young bearded man, with leftist views and a fondness for cats. A farmer, maybe; he might wander into the market some Saturday morning, with some lovely artichokes.

Jennifer and I have agreed that I should be the one to keep our store of wine, despite my small quarters. The bottles are stacked in silly places—all over my rooms—some under the bed, for example. When I start over to Jennifer's house at dinnertime, I just bring along one bottle; in that way I can keep a check on Jennifer's intake. Which is now down to a couple of glasses a day, I believe.

It is interesting and to me a little spooky to see how entirely unchanged the Cartwright house is. Everything is just the same, but since it all looks, as always, brightly new—the fabrics on the upholstered furniture, for instance, the cushions and draperies—everything must in fact *be* new. Jennifer must have gone out and found duplicates to replace all the worn-out stuff—and with such precision. What trouble she must have gone to, getting everything just right, getting Nickie's look! Including the flourishing garden, now tended by a nice Japanese couple.

All I said was that it looked really great, what a relief it was to see so little changed—which I know must have pleased Jennifer. She would not have wanted the extreme nature of her pursuit to be mentioned.

As I thought in Minneapolis about coming out here, one of my many conscious or semiconscious fears (worries about Jennifer's looks and her general health naturally being foremost) was a nagging, shadowy worry that as Jennifer and I talked it would somehow come out that Nickie and Scott had been less than the happy, fair, affectionate couple I used to see, and to long for. Heaven knows we would talk a lot, endless talk, and without (probably) coming out and saying so (Jennifer is unusually discreet) she might let me know that sometimes they, like my own parents, used to have recriminatory breakfasts, silences, bitterness. Maybe, even, handsome Scott had affairs, and Nickie cried. That would be a more usual, contemporary ending to their story—and in some circles it would "explain" Jennifer.

But from what Jennifer did say, that sad version would seem not to have taken place; according to her, the sadness was of quite another sort. "My mother was so upset when Dad died she just never got over it, never at all" is what Jennifer said. "Never even looked at anyone else, and you know how pretty she always was."

Well, I do remember how pretty Nickie was, and I can accept that version of her life, I guess. In fact, I would rather; it is what I thought I saw.

"I sometimes wonder if I got married so many times to be just the opposite," Jennifer once mused. "Not to depend on any one person in that way."

"Well, maybe" was all I could contribute. But then I added, "And my parents didn't get along, so I only dared try it once?"

"Lord, who knows?" Jennifer laughed.

Often, as we talked, new memories would assail one or the other of us.

"Do you remember the surprise you planned for Scott one time, on his birthday? The *real* surprise?" I asked Jennifer one night.

She seemed not to, and so I told her: "You led him on into the house when he got home from work, and you told him that you'd found what he'd like better than anything in the world. You brought him to the door of the back-hall closet, and when he opened it up, there was Nickie, laughing and jumping out to hug and kiss you both."

"Oh *yes!*" cried Jennifer. "I'd forgotten that, and how could I forget? But you see what I mean, Judy, Jude? Who could ever come up with a relationship like that?"

Who indeed? Most surely not I, I reflected.

But mostly Jennifer and I are not so serious. Our dinners are fun. We remember school friends, boys, our teachers; we go over and over the people we knew and the times we had back then, just remembering and laughing. Not deeply, intellectually scrutinizing, as I might have with other friends, at another time.

Jennifer subscribes to all the fashion magazines, and sometimes sitting there at dinner we may just leaf through a couple. Most of the newest styles are quite ugly, if not downright ludicrous, we are agreed. But every now and then there will be something really pretty; we will make a note to check it out in the downtown stores.

Jennifer has not taken a newspaper for years, and since I have been out here I have not really read one, either. I find it a great relief, in fact, not to know just how awful things have become. How entirely out of control the whole terrifying world is.

We did at first go over some of the unfortunate events of both our marriages, and in a discreet way I told her about my love affairs. I found that, recounting them to Jennifer, I could make them really funny. She liked the story about the man who always called when I was brushing my teeth, and she appreciated my version of my most recent relationship, the man and I becoming more and more polite as we liked each other less. She told me a couple of funny stories about her husbands, though I think their names are what she most likes to remember.

Jennifer does not talk about her children, except to say that she has three of them, all moved East. Three girls. Two work in New York, one lives on a farm in Vermont—no grandchildren that she has mentioned—and since she never seems to hear from her daughters I would guess that they don't get along. But I never ask.

By the time we have finished our dinner, our bottle of wine, we are both rather sleepy. We get up from the table, and together we walk out to the front hall. Jennifer opens the door, we say good night; we kiss, and I go outside and listen for the sound of the lock behind me.

I walk the short, safe distance down the road to my apartment.

If the weather is nice, a warm night, I may sit outside for a while, something I could almost never have done in Minnesota. Maybe I will have one more glass of wine. Maybe red, a good zinfandel, for sleep.

Just sitting there, sipping my wine, I think a lot, and one of my conclusions has been that, all things considered, even living alone, I really feel better and better out here, and I think I have never been so happy in my life.

The visitor cat must by now be on to my habits, for sometimes at these moments I will feel the sudden warm brush of his arching back against my leg. I reach to stroke him. He allows this, responding with a loud purr—and then, as suddenly as he appeared, with a quick leap out into the dark he is gone.

Favors

July that year is hotter, the air heavier and more sultry than is usual in Northern California, especially up in the Sierras, near Lake Tahoe. Along the Truckee River, which emanates from that lake, mosquitoes flourish in the thick green riverside bushes and grass. Even in the early mornings—most unusual—it is already warm and damp. An absolute stillness, a brooding quiet.

"If this were Maine, there would be a thunderstorm," remarks Maria Tresca, an elderly political activist, just released from jail. By profession she is an architect. A large-boned, heavy woman, with gray-brown hair and huge very dark eyes, she is addressing the much younger couple who are with her on the terrace of her river house. The three of them have just finished a light breakfast in the dining room, inside; they now sit on old canvas deck chairs.

Having spoken, Maria closes her eyes, as though the effort involved in keeping them open were more than she could manage in the breeze-less heat, the flat air.

The two young people, the couple, are Danny Michaels, a small, gray-blond young man, rather lined for someone his age, serious, bookish-looking; and thin, bright-red-haired Phoebe Knowles, Danny's very recent wife.

"That would be wonderful, a storm," says Phoebe, who seems a little short of breath.

And Danny: "We sure could use the rain."

"Actually, I'd be quite terrified," Maria opens her eyes to tell them. "I always used to be, in Maine. We had the most terrific summer storms." She recloses her eyes.

Danny has known Maria for so long (almost all the thirty-odd years of his life) that nearly all questions seem permitted; also they like and trust each other. However, so far his evident sympathetic interest in her recent experience has been balked. About Pleasanton, where the jail was, Maria has only said, not quite convincingly, "It wasn't too bad. It's minimum security, you know. I felt rather like a Watergate conspirator. The clothes they gave me were terribly uncomfortable, though. Just not fitting, and stiff."

Only Maria's posture suggests discouragement, or even age. On the old rattan sofa she slumps down in a tired way among the cushions, her large hands clasped together on the knees of old corduroys.

And goes on about Maine. "The chipmunks there were much bigger than the ones out here," she tells Phoebe and Dan. "Or maybe they only seemed bigger because I was very small. I haven't been back there since I was a child, you know."

Phoebe and Dan are in the odd position of being both Maria's hosts and her guests: it is her house—in fact, very much her house, designed by Maria for her own use. But it was lent to Danny and Phoebe by Ralph Tresca, Maria's son and a great friend of Danny's. This was to be their wedding present, two weeks alone in this extraordinary, very private house. For which they had both arranged, with some trouble, to take off from their jobs. Phoebe and her best friend, Anna, run a small restaurant on Potrero Hill; Danny works in a bookstore, also on Potrero, of which he is part owner.

Danny and Ralph have been friends since kindergarten, and thus Danny has known Maria for all that time. He and Phoebe have known each other for less than four months; theirs was a passionate, somewhat hasty marriage, indeed precipitated by Ralph's offer of the house. Danny called Ralph in Los Angeles, where Ralph is a sometime screenwriter, to say that he had met a girl about whom he was really serious. "I think we might get married." To which Ralph responded, "Well, if you do it this summer you can have the house for two weeks at the end of July. It's rented for most of the rest."

Not the reason, surely, but an impetus. Danny has always loved the beautiful, not entirely practical house, at which he has often been a guest. A wonderfully auspicious beginning to their marriage, Danny believed those weeks would be.

But after the first week of their time at the house had passed, there was suddenly the phone call from Ralph, asking if it would be all right for Maria to come up and stay with them; Maria was about to be released, after fourteen days in jail. Danny had known about Maria's sentencing; he and Phoebe had talked about it, early on—so severe for an antinuclear protest, and for a woman of Maria's age. But they had not been entirely clear as to when Maria started to serve, nor when she was to get out. And it had certainly not occurred to Danny that Maria might want to come from jail to her house on the Truckee River. However: *Of course,* he told Ralph.

Hanging up the phone, which is in the kitchen, and walking across the long living room toward their bedroom, where he and Phoebe had been taking a semi-nap, Danny considered how he would put it to Phoebe, this quite unforeseen interruption to their time. Danny knows that he is crazy about Phoebe, but also acknowledges (to himself) some slight fear; he suspects that she is perceptibly stronger than he is. Also, it was he who insisted on marriage and finally talked her into it, mentioning their ages ("we're not exactly kids") plus the bribe of the house. But the real truth was that Danny feared losing her—he had indecisively lost a couple of other really nice women; now he wanted to settle down. In any case, although he feels himself loved by Phoebe, feels glad of their marriage, he worries perhaps unduly about her reactions.

"You see, it was such a great favor that I couldn't not do it" was one of the things he decided to say to Phoebe, approaching their room. "All that time in jail, a much longer sentence than anyone thought she would get. I think her old protest history worked against her. I know it was supposed to be our house for these two weeks, Ralph kept saying that. He really felt bad, asking me to do this," Danny meant to add.

What he did not mean to say to Phoebe, in part because he did not know quite how to phrase it, was his own sense that if Maria were to come up to them, Ralph should come too. Ralph's presence would make a better balance. Also, Ralph's frenetic nervous energy, his offbeat wit—both qualities that made Danny smile, just to think about—would have lightened the atmosphere, which so far has been more than a little heavy, what with the weather and Maria's silences, her clearly sagging spirits.

However, Dan had barely mentioned to Phoebe that Maria was getting out of jail on July 19 when Phoebe broke in, "Oh, then she must come right up. Do you think we should leave, or stay on and sort of take care of her? I could cook a lot, prison food has to be horrible. Tell Ralph not to worry, it'll be fine." All of which led Danny to think that he does not know Phoebe well at all.

Phoebe herself has had certain odd new problems on this trip: trouble eating, for one thing; she who generally eats more than her envious friends can believe, scrawny Phoebe of the miraculous metabolism now barely manages a scant first helping of the good cold rice salads, the various special dishes she planned and made for this first leisurely time alone with Dan. And she is sometimes short of breath. Also, despite long happy nights of love, she has trouble sleeping. All these problems clearly have to do with the altitude, six thousand feet, Phoebe knows that perfectly well; still, does it possibly have something to do with being married—married in haste, as the old phrase used to go?

By far her worst problem, though, is sheer discomfort from the heat, so much heavy sun all day. Like many redheads, Phoebe does not do well in very warm weather, the affliction being an inability to perspire. Instead, out in the sun her skin seems to wither and burn, both within and without. Very likely, she thinks, if it cooled off even a little, all her troubles would disappear; she could eat and sleep again, and enjoy being married to Dan.

However, she reminds herself, there would still be the house. Danny talked about it often; he tried to describe Maria's house, and Phoebe gathered that it was beautiful—impressive, even. Still, she was unprepared for what seems to her somewhat stark: such bare structural bones, exposed textures of pine and fir, such very high, vaulted ceilings. Phoebe has never been in a house with so definite a tone, a stamp. In fact, both the house's unfamiliarity and the strength of its character have been more than a little intimidating. (Phoebe is from a small town in New Hampshire of entirely conventional, rather small-scale architecture.)

Even the bookcases have yielded up to Phoebe few clues of a personal nature, containing as they do a large, clearly much used collection of various field guides, to birds, wildflowers, trees, and rocks; some yellowed, thumbed-through Grade-B detective fiction; and a large, highly eclectic shelf of poetry—Rilke, Auden, Yeats, plus a great many small volumes of women poets. Marianne Moore, Elizabeth Bishop, Louise Bogan, Katha Pollitt, Amy Clampitt. Clues, but to Ralph or to Maria? Ralph's father, Maria's husband, died young, Dan has said; he has spoken admiringly of Maria's uncompromising professionalism, her courage— never a shopping center or a sleazy tract. The poetry, then, might belong to them both? There are no inscriptions.

Thus, occupying the house of two very strong, individualistic people, neither of whom she has met, fills Phoebe with some unease, even a sort of loneliness.

The site of the house, though, is so very beautiful—magical, even: that very private stretch of clear brown river, rushing over its smoothly rounded, wonderfully tinted rocks. And the surrounding woods of pine and fir and shimmering gray-green aspens, and the lovely sky, and clouds. The very air smells of summer, and earth, and trees. In such a place, Phoebe thinks, how can she not feel perfectly well, not be absolutely happy?

Indeed (she has admitted this to herself, though not to Dan), she welcomed Maria at least in part as a diversion.

Though since her arrival Maria has seemed neither especially diverting, as Phoebe had hoped, nor heroic—as they both had believed.

"It would be a lot better if Ralph were here too, I know that," Dan tells Phoebe, later that morning, as, barefoot, they pick their way back across the meadow to the house; they have been swimming in the river— or, rather, wading and ducking down into the water, which is disappointingly shallow, slow-moving, not the icy rush that Danny remembers from previous visits.

Phoebe, though, seems to feel considerably better; she walks along surefootedly, a little ahead of Dan, and her tone is reassuring as she says, "It's all right. I think Maria's just really tired. I'm doing a vitello tonnato for lunch, though. Remember, from the restaurant? Maybe she'll like that. God, I just wish I could eat!"

Avoiding sharp pinecones and sticks and skirting jagged rocks requires attention, and so they are quiet for a while as they walk along. But then, although he is in fact looking where he is going, Dan's foot hits something terrible and sharp, and he cries out, "Damn!"

"What's wrong?"

"My foot, I think a stone."

"Oh dear." Phoebe has stopped and turned to ask, "Shall I look?"

"No, it's okay, nothing," Dan mutters, striding on past her.

But he is thinking, Well, really, how like Ralph to saddle me with his mother on my honeymoon. And with Maria just out of jail, for God's sake. So politically correct that I couldn't possibly object. Damn Ralph, anyway.

Never having met Ralph, who has been in Los Angeles for all the time that Dan and Phoebe have known each other (the long, not long four months), Phoebe has no clear view of him, although Dan talks about him often. What has mostly come across to Phoebe is the strength of the two men's affection for each other; so rare, in her experience, such open fondness between men. She has even briefly wondered if they could have been lovers, ever, and concluded that they were not. They are simply close, as she and her friend-partner, Anna, are close. Danny would do almost anything for Ralph, including taking in his mother at a not entirely convenient time.

In fact, his strong, evident affections are among the qualities Phoebe values in Dan—and perhaps Ralph is more or less like that? His closeness to his mother has had that effect? Although so far Maria herself has not come across as an especially warm or "giving" person.

Early common ground, discovered by Dan and Phoebe on first meeting, was a firm belief in political protest. They had both taken part in demonstrations against the Nicaraguan embargo, against South African racism; both felt that there was, generally, a mood of protest in their city, San Francisco, that spring. By which they were encouraged.

And they had had serious talks about going to jail. Taking part in demonstrations is not the same as being locked up, they are agreed.

"It's hard to figure out just how much good it does. Jail."

"Especially if you're not famous. Just a person. Ellsberg going to jail is something else."

"Do famous people get lighter sentences?"

"I'd imagine. In fact, I'd bet."

"So hard to figure. Is it better to go to jail, or to stay out and do whatever your work is and send money to your cause?"

Impossible to decide, has been their conclusion.

However, someone probably has to go to jail; they think that too. So why not them?

Working in the kitchen, making lunch, Phoebe feels better than she has for several days. Good effects of the dip into the river seem to last, a lively sense of water lingers on her skin. Carefully, thinly slicing the firm moist white turkey (she is good at this, a good carver), Phoebe feels more in control of her life than she has in days just past, no longer entirely at the mercy of weather and altitude. She even feels more at peace with the house. Here in the kitchen, its bareness and extreme simplicity seem functional; the oversized butcher-block table with its long rack for knives is a great working space.

She is happily breaking an egg into the blender, reaching for oil, when she hears the sound of slow footsteps approaching the kitchen. It must be Maria, and the distress that Phoebe then experiences is both general and particular: she likes best to cook alone; in fact, she loves the solitary single-mindedness of cooking. Also, none of her conversations with Maria have been very successful, so far.

Hesitantly, distractedly, Maria comes to stand outside the kitchen doorway. Vaguely she says, "I'm sure I can't help you." She is not quite looking at Phoebe but rather out the window, to the river. "But I did wonder—you're finding everything you need?"

"Oh yes, it's a wonderful kitchen." Working there, it has become clear to Phoebe that Maria herself must be a very good cook; this is the working space of a dedicated person. "I feel bad displacing you this way," she says to Maria.

This earns the most direct and also the most humorous look from Maria yet seen. "You're good to say that. But actually I could use a little displacement, probably."

Phoebe ventures, "Do you have trouble letting people help you, the way I do?"

A wide, if fleeting, grin. "Oh, indeed I do. I seem to believe myself quite indispensable, in certain areas."

They smile, acknowledging some kinship.

"Well, I won't keep you." Maria begins to leave; then, from whatever inner depths of thought, she remarks, "I do wish Ralph were here too. It would be nice for you to meet him here."

"It would have been," agrees Phoebe. "But sometime."

Lunch, though, is no better than breakfast, conversationally, and in Phoebe's judgment even the food is not entirely successful.

They are gathered again on the terrace above the river, joined at the too large round table—scattered around it.

However, partly because he knows that Phoebe is genuinely curious, as he is himself, Danny persists in asking about Maria's time in jail. (Also, he is convinced that talking about it will help Maria.) "What does Pleasanton look like?" he asks her. "I can't even imagine it."

"Oh—" At first Maria's vague, unfocused glance goes out to the river, as though for help, but then she seems to make an effort—for her guests. "It's quite country-club-looking," she tells them. "Very clean and bland." In a tantalizing way, she adds, "It's rather like the White House."

"Really? How?" This has been a chorus, from Dan and Phoebe.

Maria sighs, and continues to try. "Well, externally it's so clean, and behind the scenes there's total corruption." Having gone so far, though, she leans back into her chair and closes her eyes.

Dan looks at Phoebe. On her face he sees both blighted curiosity and genuine if momentary helplessness. He sees too her discomfort from the increasing heat. Her skin is so bright, dry, pink. The sultry air has curled her hair so tightly that it looks uncomfortable. At that moment Danny believes that he *feels* all Phoebe's unvoiced, unspoken sensations; her feelings are his. And he further thinks, I am married to Phoebe permanently, for good.

And, looking at his wife, and at Maria, whom he has always known, Danny thinks how incredibly complex women are. How *interesting* they are.

"In Maine the air never felt exactly like this air," Maria tells them, as though Maine had been under discussion—again. "A little like it, fresh and clean, but not exactly. It's interesting. The difference, I mean. Though hard to describe," she trails off.

"I know what you mean, though," comments Phoebe. "In the same way that all the colors are different, but you can't exactly say how."

"Phoebe grew up in New Hampshire," Danny tells Maria, wondering why this fact had not emerged earlier, or did it?

"Oh, did you really." But Maria has returned to her own privacy, her thoughts.

The heat has gathered and intensified. Phoebe feels that she will burst, her skin rent apart, the way a tomato's skin will split in heat. What she also feels is a kind of rage, though she tries to tell herself that she is simply hot, that she feels so ill-tempered only because of the weather, the temperature. And, knowing herself, certain bad tendencies, she determines that she will not *say* how angry she is, and especially she will not take it out on Danny.

I love Dan. The weather is not his fault—nor, really, is absent Ralph. Gross, inconsiderate, totally selfish Ralph. Some friend, thinks Phoebe.

She and Dan are lying across their bed, ostensibly napping, although the turgid air seems entirely to forbid real sleep. Naked, they still do not touch, although earlier Dan has asked, "Can I douse you with some cold water, or maybe an alcohol rub?"

"No thanks, but really, thanks." (It was at that moment that Phoebe determined not to vent her ire on Dan, who is genuinely kind, well-meaning.)

They have both been whispering, although no one could conceivably hear them, the rooms being so spread apart; Maria's is several rooms away. "Maria simply clutches that prison experience to herself, doesn't she?" now whispers Phoebe. "Not that she much wants to talk about anything else either."

"Except Maine." Danny tries a small laugh. "Lots of Maine."

"And the way she eats," complains Phoebe bitterly. "Just bolting down a few bites and then a dead stop. It's not exactly flattering. Not that I really care, I mean. Did she always eat like that?"

"I sort of can't remember. Maybe not. I didn't notice, really."

"I have to say, though," announces Phoebe, "I really think this is a very selfish move on Ralph's part."

Dan very lightly sighs, just shifting in bed. "I'm afraid I agree. But people change, I think. Maybe he's pure L.A. these days. More selfish than he used to be. He's been seeing some shrink down there for years."

"That whole culture's so selfish. Crass."

"Oh, *right.*"

Feeling a little better, Phoebe reaches her fingers just to graze the top of Danny's hand. They look at each other; they smile.

Dinner that night, which again is out on the terrace, is in many ways a repeat of lunch, except of course for the menu; provident Phoebe has made a nice cold pasta, with garlicky brandied prawns. But Maria again eats very little, and that most rapidly.

And again she talks about Maine. "The soil was so rocky around our house it was hard to grow flowers," she says. "I've never even tried to plant anything out here."

The night is densely dark, pitch black; in an absolute and final way it is still. And heavy; the air seems weighted. Oppressive, stultifying.

"I do wish Ralph could have been here." It is Dan who has said this, not having at all intended to. It simply slipped out, like a sigh, and now he feels tactless. "But it's great that he has so much work down there," he feebly amends.

"I suppose so." Unhelpful Maria puts her fork down and stares out into the black.

Going about the house, as every night he has—checking door locks, turning off lights—for the first time on this visit Danny has a sad sense of spuriousness: this is not his house, he is much more guest than host. And he recalls now that this place has always been somewhat daunting; its proportions make him feel even less tall than in fact he is. And very possibly Phoebe's deepest reactions have been similar? She too has been made uncomfortable by the house, in addition to the appalling heat, her enemy? None of these facts augur poorly for their marriage, though, Danny believes. Once they are back in San Francisco, in the cool foggy summer weather, in their own newly painted rooms, then they will be fine.

He admits to himself, however, some real disappointment over what he feels as the failure of connection between Maria and Phoebe. When Ralph called about Maria's coming up, just out of jail, along with disappointment at the curtailment of their privacy, Danny experienced a small surge of happy expectation. Maria and Phoebe, despite obvious differences of age, career, could become great friends, a complement to his own friendship with Ralph. And now that this rapport seems entirely unlikely, Danny recognizes the strength of his hope—his conviction, even—that it might have taken place.

Before starting his tour of the house, Dan urged Phoebe to go and take a long cool bath. "Do you a world of good," he told her. And that presumably is where Phoebe is now, in the bathroom down the hall. (The distance between bathrooms and bedrooms in this house seems an almost deliberate inconvenience.)

As Dan gets into bed, he hears nothing, no sound from anywhere. Outside the window the air is motionless, still; the river is soundless, slow. And although he knows that in a few minutes Phoebe will be there with him, Danny experiences a solitude that seems entire, and final.

And then, around midnight, everything breaks. Brilliant flashes of lightning split open the sky, thunder roars—a sound of huge rocks falling down a mountainside. Slits of light, crashing noise.

Entirely awake, and a little scared, Phoebe abruptly remembers Maria this morning as she talked about thunderstorms in Maine. "Actually, I'd be quite terrified, I always used to be" is what Maria said.

To Dan, who is much less fully awake (he seemed to have trouble going to sleep at all), Phoebe whispers, "I'm just going down to see if Maria's all right."

Slipping into her sandals, pulling on her light cotton robe—in the new blessed cool!—Phoebe begins to feel her way down the narrow, pine-smelling hall to Maria's room at the end, the room nearest the river.

Seeing no light beneath the door, she hesitates, but then very gently she knocks, at the same time saying firmly and loudly enough to be heard across the thunder crashes, "It's Phoebe."

For a moment there is no response at all; then some faint sound comes from Maria that Phoebe chooses to interpret as assent.

Entering, she sees Maria upright in bed, sitting erect but pressed back, braced against the headboard. "Oh" is all she says to Phoebe.

Coming over to stand beside her, Phoebe asks, "Should I turn the light on?" and she reaches toward the bedside lamp, on its table.

Maria stops her, crying, "Electricity—don't!"

Recognizing true panic, Phoebe quietly tells her, "I'll just stay here for a minute, if you don't mind."

In the strange half-light between crashes, Maria reaches for her hand. She says, "Thank you," and can just be seen to smile before quickly releasing Phoebe.

Outside, a heavy pounding rain has now begun, but the thunderstorm seems suddenly to be over; there is only the hard drumbeat of rain on the shingled roof, the thud of water on windowpanes.

Phoebe pulls the small bentwood chair from Maria's desk over to the bed, and sits down.

Maria says, "It was good of you to remember."

"I was a little scared," admits Phoebe.

"The thing about prison," Maria takes this up as though prison had just then been under discussion, "is that they do everything to wreck your mind. 'Mind-fuck,' some of the younger women called it." A faint, tight smile. "But they do. Rushing you all the time. Starting you in to do something, and then right away it's over. Even eating, even that horrible food I never got to finish. And they mix up everyone's mail so you think it must be on purpose. And the noise. Radios. And people smoking."

"Jesus" is all Phoebe can manage to say.

Maria is leaning forward now, her eyes luminous, deep, immense. "At my age," she says. "I mean, I often wonder where my mind is going anyway, without all that."

"That's frightful. Terrible."

"Well, it was terrible. I didn't want to admit it to myself. I got just so plain scared. The truth is I'm still scared."

"Well, of course. Anyone is scared of jail. I'm not even sure I could do it."

Maria's gaze in the semi-dark seems to take all of Phoebe in. "I think you would if you had to, or thought you had to," she says.

"I hope so."

"But I'm worried about going back there," Maria tells her. "If for some reason I had to. Again."

At that moment, however, a new sound has begun, just audible through the steady, heavy rain. And lights can be seen to approach the house, very slowly.

Lights from a car, now visible to them both. Unnecessarily, Phoebe announces, "Someone's coming. A small sports car. Whoever—?"

"It must be Ralph," says Maria, smiling. And she exclaims, "Oh, I do think things will be better now. It's even got cool, do you feel it?" But in an anxious way her face still searches Phoebe's. "Do you want to turn on the light?"

Phoebe reaches to touch Maria's hand, very quickly, lightly—before she pushes the switch.

Standing up, then, in the sudden brightness, smiling, as Phoebe moves toward the door she turns back to Maria; she tells her, "I'll get Danny. We'll go make sandwiches—some tea? Poor Ralph, all that driving. We'll celebrate!"

Ocracoke Island

Tall and too thin, sometimes stooped but now bent bravely forward into the wind, old Duncan Elliott heads southward in Central Park, down a steep and cindery path—his scattered, shamed, and tormented mind still alert to the avoidance of dangerously large steel baby carriages, and of runners (he must not be run down by babies or by runners, he cautions himself). But most of his thoughts are concentrated on the question of comparative evils: of all that has befallen him lately, and particularly today, what is worse—or, rather, which is worst of all? To have been abandoned by one's fourth and one had hoped final wife, or to have made a total fool of oneself discussing that event—even trying, as it were, to explain it away.

Duncan is a distinguished professor, now an emeritus at a large Midwestern university (for all the good that is doing him now); his wife Cath left the month before, in hot September. Disconsolately traveling to New York, in part to cheer himself up, along with some publishing business, Duncan forgot the possibility of chill late October breezes.

Or—he continues his plaintive litany—is the worst thing of all to have broken off and lost an old, much filled and refilled tooth, leaving what must be a conspicuously ugly black hole in the forefront of one's mouth? Oh, what matter which is worse! thinks Duncan then. All of these things have happened (the most recent being the tooth, which only came to his attention out here in the cold) and he can stand none of them.

The runners that Duncan encounters along his way are grim-faced, red, and sweaty, and the young mothers pushing those carriages are scruffy, sloppily dressed; and the babies are—well, babies. Where are the handsome, glamorous pairs of lovers that one used to glimpse in New

York, in Central Park? Duncan asks this wistful question of himself, and then he answers (insanely!): On Ocracoke Island. For it is to Ocracoke that Cath has run off with her poet, and in his mind Duncan has just seen the two of them, Cath and Brennan O'Donahue (of all corny, false-literary names), Brennan as handsome and fair as Cath herself is—he sees Brennan and Cath and scores of other couples, all young and blond, all healthy and beautiful, and running, running like horses, on a wild and endless beach.

Cath's gesture—if you call running off to an island with a poet a gesture—was made even less bearable for Duncan by the publicity it drew; she had to choose a famous poet, a Pulitzer Prize–winning, brawling media hero of a poet. A small item in *Newsweek* (Newsmakers) described O'Donahue as having run off to Ocracoke Island "like a pirate, a professor's wife his plunder." Very poetic for a newsmagazine, Duncan thought. Perhaps Brennan himself had written the item? In any case, a lot of people seemed to know whose wife was meant.

At times Duncan feels literally murderous: he will go there to Ocracoke and shoot them both, and then himself. He has found the place on a map, and it looks as though you had to take a ferry from a town called Swan Quarter. *Swan Quarter?* But surely murder would be a more respectable, even a nobler act than a lot of talk, so deeply embarrassing, so sickly humiliating to recall.

Nearing his hotel, and the promise of some comfort, Duncan begins, though, to dread the coming night. He is to dine with Emily, his second wife: his briefest marriage, that to Emily, and perhaps for that reason they have stayed in touch, have remained almost friends. Emily and Cath have even met, Duncan now recalls, on a trip to New York that he and Cath took just before their marriage. Emily is a painter, beginning to be quite successful. She is, as they all have been, considerably younger than Duncan.

(Younger and in one way or another very talented, the first three of them, Duncan reflects. More talented than he? That was surely a problem with Jessica, the first wife, a poet who took a very low view of criticism. Less so with Emily, perhaps because painting is—well, not literary, and they were not together very long. The worst was Janice, herself a professor, a literary critic. Undoubtedly, Janice in her way was responsible for Cath, who is talentless, a born appreciator.)

But unless he exercises the utmost caution, for which he feels himself much too tired, devoid of resources, Duncan fears that he will simply repeat the follies of the day, with Emily, tonight. He will talk again—perhaps even more ridiculously—about Cath; obviously he will do so, since she and Emily have met. Emily by now is probably—is undoubtedly a feminist; she could finish him off entirely.

At the hotel desk Duncan looks longingly toward the cubbyholes of messages. If only there were a pink phone slip from Emily, canceling, for whatever reason. (Or a slip saying Cath had called?) But there is nothing, and heavily now Duncan walks over to the elevator. He rings, ascends.

This making a fool of himself began for Duncan at breakfast, in the somewhat dingy dining room of his hotel, as he talked (or tried to explain) to Jasper Wilkes, a former student, and began to babble. "In point of fact I actually encouraged her to have an affair—or affairs; one can't say I wasn't generous. Ironically enough, she could be said to be doing just what I told her to do. In a sense."

Jasper repeated "In a sense" with perhaps too much relish. A highly successful advertising executive since abandoning academe, Jasper is a prematurely, quite shiningly bald young man, with clever, hooded eyes.

"After all," Duncan continued, long fingers playing with his croissant's cold buttery remains, "I'm very busy. And besides . . ." He smiled briefly, sadly, implying much.

"Of course." Jasper's eyes closed, but his voice had an agreeing sound.

Gulping at strong lukewarm coffee—he had just sent back for fresh—Duncan had a nervously exhilarated sense that this was not how men talked to each other, or not usually. Or perhaps these days they do? They are "open" with each other, as women have always been? In any case, he hoped that he had not got out of his depth with Jasper. The coffee had made him feel a little drunk.

And at the word "depth" his mind stopped totally, and replayed, *depth, depth.* He had suddenly, involuntarily seen Atlantic waves, brilliant and mountainous, quite possibly fatal. He had imagined Ocracoke Island. Again.

But could Jasper be in a hurry? Off somewhere? Duncan was conscious of wanting to prolong (oh! all day) this relieving, if highly unusual, conversation. "Precisely," he hastened to agree with what he imagined

Jasper just had said. "I intended something discreet and, I suppose I also hoped, something minor. A dalliance more or less along my own lines. My old lines, I suppose I should say." He attempted a modest laugh, but the sound was bleak.

"Right," Jasper agreed. "Something to take up a certain amount of her time and energy. Rather like going to a gym."

"Oh, precisely."

The two men exchanged looks in which there was expressed some shock at their complicitous cynicism, but more pure pleasure—or so Duncan for the moment believed.

The coffee arrived, at which Jasper frowned, conclusively proving to Duncan that he was after all in a hurry; he did not even want more coffee.

"The point is," said Jasper, in a summing-up way, "whether or not you want her back. One. And, two, if you do, how to get her."

Unprepared for this précis, Duncan felt quite dizzied.

Nor was he prepared for what came next, which was Jasper's efficient departure: a smooth rise to his feet, and a firm, sincere handshake. Lots of eye contact. Murmurs of friendship. And then Jasper was gone, last glimpsed as a narrow, animated back departing through the door that led out to the lobby.

Quite disconcerted, and alone with his hot, unconsoling coffee, Duncan looked around. This room had got uglier, he thought, trying to recall what he used to like about it. Surely not the pictures, the big bright oils that all looked like copies of famous works, giving the room a spurious look of "taste"? Never the pictures, he concluded, and surely not the inferior coffee, and fake croissants. Dismally he reminded himself that he had always chosen this hotel for reasons of economy, never for charm.

Now everything seemed to disturb him, though: the room with its awful art, the bad coffee, and particularly his just ended conversation with Jasper Wilkes. And why? Rerunning that conversation, he succeeded in finding nothing truly objectionable. (Unless that crack about going to gyms—would that have been a "put-on"?) Bright Jasper, though. All agreement, stating and restating Duncan's own views in a clear succinct way. But perhaps that very succinctness was the problem? Especially at the end, just before Jasper hurried off to wherever?

Leaning back into the once pneumatic banquette, for reassurance

Duncan stroked his hair, now white but still gratifyingly thick and fine. How Jasper must envy his hair! That in itself could explain quite a lot.

Duncan thought then of the old days, when Jasper as a student came petitioning with his poetry. In conference with Jasper, Duncan might sneak a quick took at his large grandfather clock while pretending to allow his gaze to wander. And apprised of the time, he, Duncan, might then too brusquely sum up his view of Jasper's poem, or poems: Jasper had been all too prolific. And as Jasper at last got up reluctantly to leave, the also departing Duncan, a man in early middle age, might well be off to visit some pert-breasted, ambitious literary girl, for something "discreet," and "minor."

As though Jasper had encouraged him—seduced him, even—into all that talk about Cath, Duncan felt a pained resentment. Especially he resented Jasper's just getting up and leaving him like that—all at sea, almost drowned in ungovernable feelings.

But at lunchtime Duncan could be said to have done it again.

"It was really the way she left that I so much minded," he remarked to his lunch companion, Marcus Thistlethwaite, an English critic, a very old friend. They were seated in a corner of a pretty new Upper West Side restaurant, banks of fall flowers in the windows, filtered sunshine. "I would have given a maid more notice," Duncan added, and then reflected that his analogy had been slightly confused: just who did he mean was whose maid, and who gave notice? He hoped that Marcus had not observed this, but naturally no such luck.

"I'm not sure just who was whose maid," said Marcus, with his ratchety, cropped-off laugh. "But I believe I rather catch your drift, as it were." And then, "Is this quite the proper thing to do with lobster claws?"

"Oh yes, you just crack them like nuts," instructed Duncan, who had just wondered why on earth he had ordered something he had never much liked, and that was at best quite difficult to eat. (And that reminded him inevitably of the seacoast.)

Marcus's hair is thin and silvery, like tinsel; draped across his bright impressive skull, it ornaments his head. Duncan has always been somewhat in awe of Marcus, of his erudition and his cool, uncluttered, passionless judgments. And so why on earth did he have to make that silly remark about Cath, and the dismissal of maids? "Say what you like about

New York," he then attempted, striving for an even tone despite a certain pressure in his chest, "the autumns here are wonderful. You know, I walked up through the park from my hotel, and the air—so brisk! And the color of the sky, and those flowers."

Marcus just perceptibly inclined his head, acknowledging flowers, and weather. And then he launched into one of the mini-speeches to which he is given. "An interesting fact, and one that I've made note of"—to those who know Marcus, a familiar beginning, very likely boding no good to his audience, be it plural or singular—"and of which you, my dear Duncan, have just furnished further proof, in any case so interesting, is the human tendency in times of distress at some ill-treatment by a fellow human to complain of the method of treatment, the form it took, rather than the actuality. The cruel event itself is not mentioned, even. A man who is fired from his job invariably sounds as though a little more tact would have made it perfectly acceptable. And a fellow whose mistress has taken off—well, I'm sure you quite see what I mean."

"In my own case, I do think even some slight warning might have been in order," Duncan bravely, if weakly, managed to say. "And she was not my mistress—my *wife*. We'd been married for almost three years."

"My dear fellow, naturally I was speaking in a general way, and you know how I tend to run on. Well, I don't think I much care for these lobsters of yours. What's our next course? I seem already to have forgotten."

What an old bore Marcus has become, so opinionated, so—so insensitive, thought Duncan, once they parted and he began his walk. However, irritation soon gave way to the sound of darker voices, which asked if he himself was not almost as old, and as boring. And perhaps Marcus was less insensitive than he, Duncan, was hypersensitive, an open wound.

At which point he made—or, rather, his probing tongue made—the most unwelcome discovery about his missing tooth.

Back at last in his hotel room, that cold and perilous park walk done with, behind him, Duncan picks up the phone and almost instantly he succeeds (the day's first small piece of luck) in reaching his dentist. Who is reassuring. Nothing to worry about, the dentist tells Duncan, happens all the time. He adds that it probably does not look as unsightly as Duncan thinks it does; and gives him an appointment for the following week.

The bathroom mirror informs Duncan that his missing tooth, his "black hole," is unsightly only when he very broadly grins, which he can surely see no reason for doing at any foreseeable time.

Lying at last across his oversized bed, eyes closed, Duncan attempts to generalize about his situation; particulars are what finally do you in, he has found—and so he will not think about Cath's pretty shoulders, not her odd harsh mountain consonants. He strives instead for abstraction, beginning some mental notes on jealousy in an older person, as opposed to what is experienced by the young.

When one is young, he thinks, the emotion of jealousy is wracking, torturous, but at the same time very arousing (he has to admit), an almost delicious pain. Whereas when one is older, and jealous, there is only deep, irremovable sadness, deprivation, hopelessness.

(So much for notes.)

Cath: just a pallid, slightly gangling, easily blushing, mild-tempered girl from the land of the Great Smoky Mountains, from whence those consonants, those vowels. But a girl with an amazing ear for poetry, and a passion for it. Cath was (she *is,* oh, surely she still is) literally crazy about the verse of Andrew Marvell, Herrick, Donne. Wallace Stevens (Duncan's own particular enthusiasm) and more recently some women whose names he now forgets. And most recently of all, Mr. Brennan O'Donahue.

Though at first she did not even want to go to his reading. "It's too hot to go anywhere," she complained.

"But you're crazy about O'Donahue," Duncan (oh irony!) reminded her, and he added, "He's just back from Nicaragua, remember? Besides, I do think one of us should go." Duncan sniffed to emphasize the bad summer cold from which he was suffering (and he now remembers that self-pitying, self-justifying sniff with such shame, such regret). "I'm sure the Taylors would come by for you," he added, naming a younger, obsequious colleague, with a silly wife.

Cath sighed. "Oh, I'll go by myself. That way I can come home early. And Bipsy Taylor is such a nerd." Another sigh. "If I can work out what to wear in this weather."

It was an especially hot September, everything limp and drooping, or fallen to the ground. Bleached rose petals on yellow lawns, and out in the woods where Duncan liked to walk the silence was thick and heavy, as though even the birds were prostrate, drugged with heat.

Cath chose to wear her barest dress that night, which seemed sensible, if slightly inappropriate for a poetry reading. But Duncan felt that it would not do to object: he was making her go there, was he not? And so she went out alone, bare-armed and braless, in her loose black cotton; her sun-bleached hair loosely failing, her small round shoulders lightly tanned.

You look almost beautiful, is what Duncan thought of saying, and fortunately or not forbore; too often he said things to Cath that he later lived to regret. His suggestion—half-joking, actually—that she could have an affair had aroused real rage. An obscene suggestion, she seemed to take it as; clear evidence of lack of love. Whereas he was not even really serious (God knows he was not). And so as she left that night Duncan only said, "I hope it won't be too dull for you, my love."

"Oh no, don't worry. But you take care of your cold, now. I put the bottle of C pills right next to your bed."

She came home very late, explaining at breakfast that there had been a party at the Taylors', who lived out of town. She had not wanted to wake Duncan with a phone call. She had driven O'Donahue back to the Hilton, where he was staying. The reading was good. He was nice. She thought she would go downtown to do some shopping. Would probably not be back before Duncan's afternoon seminar.

And Duncan returned late that afternoon, after the seminar that included a sherry hour, to find her note. Gone off to Ocracoke Island, with Brennan O'Donahue.

The Village restaurant in which Duncan meets Emily for dinner is a comforting surprise, however; a most unfashionable homey old-bohemian decor, checkered tablecloths and multicolored candles in fat dark green wine bottles, a look dearly familiar to Duncan, who spent feckless youthful years in this neighborhood. Then he was a handsome young man, very easy with women—with a great deal to say about literature, he thought.

Emily, at least at first, seems determinedly nice. "It's wonderfully corny, don't you think?" she says of the restaurant. "But with our luck this look will come back and be madly fashionable. Oh dear, do you suppose it has, and we're the last to know?" And she laughs companionably. "I'm taking you to dinner," she tells him. "We're celebrating a grant I just got."

"You look splendid, my dear, you really do," Duncan tells her gratefully as they are seated; he has never been taken to dinner by a woman before, and he rather enjoys the sensation. This is feminism? And it is true that Emily in early middle age, or wherever she is, has never looked better. A tall woman, she had put on a little weight, in her case very becoming (but can you say that to a woman?). Short curled gray hair, gray eyes, and very white teeth. She looks strong, and immensely healthy. "You look so—so very *fit,*" Duncan says to her. "Do you, er, jog, or something?"

Emily laughs again. "Well, I have, but I didn't like it much. Now I just walk a lot."

"Well, I must say, I'm glad to hear that. I find runners such a grim group, they quite scare me," Duncan confesses.

"Oh, me too, they never smile. But, dear Duncan, why are you smiling in that somewhat odd way?"

"I've lost a tooth."

"Well, we all do," Emily tells him. "But you don't have to twist your mouth that way. It's only a gap."

Quite amiably then she talks about her work: painting, teaching, a summer workshop in Provincetown—until Duncan suspects that she is being consciously nice to him, that she is purposefully not mentioning Cath (whom he himself has determined not to talk about).

Well, if that is the case he surely does not mind; nice is perfectly okay with him, Duncan decides, and then he wonders, *Are* women after all really nicer than men are? (He does not voice this question, however, not just then wanting to hear Emily too strongly agree.)

But Emily does at last bring up the subject of Cath, though gently. "I am sorry about Cath," she says. "That must be rough for you."

"Well, yes, it is. But it's nice of you to say so." Which it was.

"I'm sure your literary friends have been enormously comforting, though," Emily in a changed tone goes on, her irony so heavy that Duncan is quite taken aback until he remembers just how much she disliked his "literary" friends, especially Jasper Wilkes, who was still a poet when Emily knew him.

Duncan can only be straightforward with her now. "You're right," he says. "The friends I've talked to have succeeded in making me feel much worse. I had it coming, seems to be the general view."

Emily smiles, her eyes bright. "Oh, you could say that to almost anyone, I think. It's even said to cancer patients. But it really doesn't seem to me that you've been any worse than most men are."

Grasping at even this dubious compliment, Duncan smiles, and then he further complains, "You know, even well-deserved pain is painful."

"Of course it is."

Why did he ever leave Emily, who is as intelligent as she is kind—and attractive? But he did not leave Emily, Duncan then recalls; Emily left him, with sensible remarks about not being cut out for marriage, either of them. Which did not stop her from marrying an Indian painter a few years later, and a sculptor soon after that—nor did it stop Duncan from marrying Janice, and then Cath.

In any case, kind or not, right or wrong, Emily is far better to talk to than Jasper or Marcus. Duncan feels safe with Emily—which leads him to yet another confession. "I did one really dumb thing, though. At some point I told Cath that she should have an affair. Of course I spoke in jest, but can she have taken me seriously?"

Emily frowns. "Well, jesting or not, that's really worse than dumb. That's cruel. It's what men say to wives they want to get rid of."

"Oh, but I surely didn't mean—" Crestfallen Duncan.

Fortunately just at that moment the food arrives, and it is after some silence between them that Emily asks, "You do know that she'll be back?"

"Oh no, no, of course I don't know that at all." Duncan feels dizzy.

"Well, she will. She's basically very sensible, I think. She'll see that Brennan O'Donahue is no one to live with. Running off with poets is just something young women do. Or some of them do."

"Oh? They do?"

"She'll come back, and if you want her to stick around you'd better be very kind. Just remember, a lot of women have been really nice to you. Be understanding. Sensitive. You're good at that."

He is? Entirely flustered, Duncan gulps at wine, hitherto untouched in his swirled dark blue glass. "I find it extremely hard to believe that you're right," he tells Emily, "that she's coming back."

"You just wait." She gives a confident flash of her regular, somewhat large teeth, and then she frowns. "The real problem may be whether or not you really want her back."

"Oh, that's more or less what Jasper said."

Emily's frown becomes a scowl. "*That* expert. Well, probably you shouldn't listen to anyone, really. Just see what happens, and then see what you feel like doing about it. But I'll bet she does come back. And quite soon, I'd imagine."

Once more picking up his key at the hotel desk, as he notes the absence of any phone message, nothing pink, Duncan's tremulous, wavering heart informs him that he has actually feared as much as he has been hoping for a message from Cath. He is so tired, so extraordinarily tired; he has neither the stamina for Cath's return nor for her continued absence. Which is worse? Oh, everything is worse!

In his room, in bed (so depressing, the great size of hotel beds, when you travel alone), feeling weakened rather than tipsy from the moderate amount of wine that he has drunk, nevertheless Duncan's imagination begins to wander quite wildly, and he thinks again of assaulting Ocracoke—oh, the whole bloody island, all those couples, the tall blond lovers, all racing around. As waves crash, as winds hurl sheets of sand, maybe even a hurricane.

Sleepless, disoriented, Duncan feels the sharp anguish of someone very young—of a young man whose beautiful wife has been stolen away. The forsaken merman.

He feels in fact as though he had been forsaken by everyone—by Jasper and by Marcus, even by Emily, with her great superior health and all her hoards of female wisdom. By Cath especially of course, and by Brennan O'Donahue. By all the people on Ocracoke Island—that most beautiful, isolated and imperiled scrap of ground, the one place to which he can never, ever go, and for which Duncan's whole tormented land-locked soul now longs.

Your Doctor Loves You

After her husband, Sebastian, had left her, all alone in their beautiful, entirely impractical house (drafty, leaking, often cold and dark), Holly Jones felt loss as something sharp in the cavity of her chest. Her pain was severe, and in those terrible days, and weeks, then months, Holly, a basically friendly, chatty young woman, sought to ease that pain, somewhat, by talk. By trying to talk it out.

Those obsessive conversations went on continuously, like tapes. Some were entirely silent, going on in her head, and those were with—or, rather, to—Sebastian. Sebastian, a handsome, old-family-rich, nonviolent alcoholic, often impotent—an unsuccessful though talented painter (so he and Holly thought)—had gone off to New York, it seemed for good. He often used to go there, on gallery or family business, but this time he had been gone for three months, during the last of which he had not communicated with Holly.

These Sebastian talks were a terrible mix of cold analysis and warm vituperation, often with more than a little scalding lust thrown in; Holly had always wanted Sebastian, she did still. But gradually she came to see that all this quiet talk to him, these silent screams did her no good, and she made a serious effort to stop all that. (And she called a lawyer.)

Her actual, voiced conversations were mostly with her friend Mary, a sculptor, a somewhat older and at least temporarily happier woman, married to a pediatrician. These real conversations were frequent; kindly Mary made a lot of time for Holly. And generally they were helpful, though sometimes not. Sometimes just a heavy dose of Sebastian-talk could throw Holly backward, into tears or worse, back into her wide unshared bed, in the lovely glassed-in bedroom that now, in January, was often freezing cold. In Ross, California, just north of San Francisco.

Occasionally, in a deliberate way, both Holly and Mary tried to shift the focus of their talk away from Sebastian and onto almost anything else: the weather, Reagan, the contras, the Democratic candidates. Clothes, old friends, gossip. Their friendship predated both marriages. It went back to the days when they lived in North Beach, in San Francisco, and were fairly broke, working at odd jobs. Holly, a leggy blonde, did mostly modeling while she took courses at the Art Institute; and Mary, who cooked in an Italian restaurant, also studied sculpture at the Institute. They had always liked each other, although "when I first met you I thought you were so pretty you had to be some kind of a bubble head," Mary had confessed. In stages, Mary first, both women had moved to Marin. With husbands. Their social lives had diverged (Sebastian did not much like Mary; as some men will, he suspected the "best friend" of sharing evil confidences concerning himself). But they still knew enough people in common to talk about.

One of the people they knew and mentioned from time to time was a man named Jonathan Green, Dr. Green, an internist in Mill Valley, to whom they both went as patients. Jonathan was tall and dark and heavy, a serious, kindly-looking man in his middle fifties (Sebastian's age). Even today, in Marin County, Jonathan made house calls; he seemed to care incredibly for his patients. Some time ago Mary had heard (through Mark, her husband) that Jonathan was getting a divorce.

And one morning, the day after her annual checkup with Jonathan, Mary remarked rather carelessly to Holly, "You know, I get the impression that Jonathan's really interested in you."

"Oh, come on."

"I really think so. You're all he talks about, he knows we're friends. He wanted to know if you felt better now. Really, Holly, he could be in love." She laughed. "Why not give it a whirl? Why not call him and ask him to dinner?"

"Oh. Well. Well, really, it seems so unlikely. I mean, I know Jonathan likes me, but I think he likes all his patients. Love! Honestly, Mary."

But Holly's heart, like an uncaged bird, had begun to soar into higher air as ancient, buried hopes revived.

Just suppose it were true, she thought. Just suppose. Jonathan Green. Well, why not? He was not as handsome or fun as Sebastian at his best could be, but on the other hand not an alcoholic, not vain or irresponsible or mean. A caring person, a man unlikely to hurt her. Someone serious. A doctor.

Indeed, why not ask him for dinner?

She telephoned Jonathan, one of whose virtues was phone-availability to patients. She heard his pleasant, soft, somewhat tentative voice almost right away. "Well, I hardly know what to say. How nice" was Jonathan's response.

But then a certain amount of trouble set in: finding an evening that would work out for them both. Jonathan was on call a lot, it seemed, he had a medical society meeting, an evening with his kids. Holly had only one date, with an old friend up from L.A. She never broke dates, although this time she was tempted. But at last a night was established, ten days off. Jonathan would come over to her house for dinner.

"It's too far off," Holly complained to Mary. "Too much time for me to think and get nervous. God, a date. I haven't had a date in ten years."

"You already sound better, though. It'll be good for you."

It was true that Holly felt better.

Married to Sebastian, she had always been aware of his acute, censorious, controlling eye. The look of the house could never be quite right, nor the meals. Nor, God knows, Holly's opinions. Unstated but heavily, coldly present was the fact that Holly had grown up in a trailer park near Tucson; her father was a Yugoslavian metalworker, a drunk, whose awful name, Jewerelsky, Holly had happily given up for Jones—and for Sebastian. Holly could thus not be expected to do things, anything, correctly, although Sebastian did expect things of her, actually. He expected everything.

However, there was no reason to believe that Jonathan Green was at all like that. A busy doctor, he might not even notice how his house looked, or not notice in the meticulous, cruel way that Sebastian did.

Holly went about in a happy flurry of straightening up, cleaning, and polishing. Even rearranging, putting a vase of flowers on the hearth, daring to remove a couple of Sebastian's paintings (stark steel girders, flying freeways), and substituting an old one of her own, of flowers.

Sebastian married Holly and bought this house on what now seemed (to Holly) a single impulse, a manic summer whim. "Oh, you're the prettiest girl in the world. You know what you are? You're cute, you're a living doll," he had crooned to her, that first summer (drunk-enly, but you had to know Sebastian very well indeed to know when he was drunk. He "drank like a gentleman"). And "I'll have to buy you the prettiest house in Marin. It's all wonderful wood, all windows and sky-lights, and everything around it green, all flowing." And Holly, tipsy her-self on champagne (she did not drink much and, according to Sebastian, did not know how), Holly was charmed into love with Sebastian, and later with the house.

Sebastian then was in his mid-forties, his dark blond handsomeness in its ripest phase. "My autumn," he said of himself, one long finger caressing the cleft in his chin. "If I grew a beard it would come out gray. You should have known me when I was young and gorgeous, baby doll."

"You're gorgeous enough. I mean, you're plenty gorgeous."

In those days she could usually make him laugh.

And Holly did fall in love with the house, along with Sebastian. It was a lovely summer house, built as such near the turn of the century by some San Francisco people seeking escape from the city's summer fog. There was a single, very large high-beamed room; as Sebastian said, all wood and windows and skylights. A small glassed-in bedroom to one side, surrounded by ancient, giant ferns and live oaks, cypress, man-zanita. The house was a dream that Holly herself could have had, in the trailer, in the desert, a dream of hills and greenery, of polished wooden spaces, and no sand, anywhere, to sweep.

Lovingly, Sebastian chose all the furniture, their bed with its intri-cate brass headboard was his especial pride, and the track lights installed to illuminate his paintings. His house. And for ten years Holly went along with all that, yielding to his superior taste and wisdom. Wishing he would drink less and make love to her more often.

Holly was literally crazy about Sebastian, she knew that. She thought he was the most beautiful person she had ever seen. Or touched. These days, she wept to remember the exceptional smoothness of all his body skin, the perfect small patch of hair on his chest, so soft and fine. In the night, when they were together, she used sometimes to reach to stroke his back—to no avail, he almost never turned to her. Or if he did it was with a reluctant sigh.

His presence became a tease to Holly; he was constantly tantalizing, simply being there. And once he had gone, his absence, especially in bed, was horrible.

So fixated was she on Sebastian ("A true addiction," she had said more than once to Mary. "So that now I'm in withdrawal") that she had not thought much about herself. A slight, fair girl when they married, when Sebastian found her so pretty, *cute,* Holly as a neglected wife had felt herself grow heavier. She thought she sagged all over.

And in that neglected phase, to make her feel even uglier, some ugly physical things began to go wrong with her. Pain, colitis. It was all very neurotic, probably (Sebastian said she was being neurotic. "Slavic," he called her behavior). But still her symptoms had to be checked out. (Mary insisted that she go to someone.) And so she went to Jonathan Green, who took everything she said very seriously, listening with his great dark sympathetic eyes. Jonathan, who seemed to like her and not think that she was crazy, even having heard and seen all the worst of her. Her rejected body.

Now anticipating Jonathan as a lover (well, of course she was, of course that was what she was doing), Holly thought that if Jonathan loved her, or even just liked her a lot, it would mean she was all right. An okay person. Even, once more, possibly, cute.

"It's great, the house is getting to look a lot more like you. Less Sebastian." Mary, arrived for a drink, had been looking around.

"Well, that's what I had in mind. He always wanted everything so bare. But you know, this is really a little sick. I'm doing it all for Jonathan Green. And that's crazy, that's as bad as doing everything for Sebastian."

"Not quite. Jonathan is a much nicer person."

"We hope." Holly had begun to see herself as chasing a rainbow named Jonathan Green, and all from an idea of Mary's that could easily be wrong ("I think Jonathan Green is interested in you"). She was in a sort of frenzy, she recognized that.

Mary now said, "As a matter of fact I will have another glass of wine. What the hell, I'm getting so fat it hardly matters."

"Oh Mary, you're not." Mary, a tall, dark, strong woman looked more or less the same to Holly, always. However, looking now more closely, she saw that Mary had indeed put on a few pounds. And she thought, Oh dear, I've been so upset, so self-absorbed that I haven't really looked at Mary.

However, over their second drinks Mary seemed okay, her old self. "Actually, you and Jonathan could get married right in this house," she said. "And I'll take pictures and send them along to Sebastian, that'll really thrill him. And I'll make the cake and the wedding food, and Mark will give you away, and I'll be friend of honor."

"Mary, come on, that's not even funny."

"Yes, it is. And after the wedding we'll all live very happily ever after. Take trips together, all that nerdy middle-aged stuff. Cruises, when we get really old. How would you feel about having children with Jonathan?"

"Mary, cut it out!" But Holly was laughing too, and actually, she was also thinking, why not? She could marry again, if her lawyer ever pulled himself together and had papers served on Sebastian, as he was supposed to be doing. And she could have children. Why not with Jonathan Green? So handy, his being a doctor.

"Maybe you're right, I need a doctor around the house," she said to Mary.

"Well, I think Jonathan should be really grateful that we've got his life all worked out for him," said Mary finally.

Five more days, still, until the famous date. And Holly found that instead of talking to Sebastian in her head, or to Mary, she was having very long, silent, and extremely interesting (to her) conversations with Jonathan Green.

"So typical, his leaving me with this stupid name," Holly in her mind told Jonathan. "Holly Jones, of all the plain-Jane names. Whereas Sebastian Jones has a lot of style, don't you think? I should have kept my old name, but is Jewerelsky really any better? I don't know. Maybe it doesn't matter, after all."

And she told him, "I think I'm sort of like a convalescent person. Getting better from something serious. I do okay and then I have a kind of relapse. Isn't that what people do when they're getting well?" She liked the medical analogy, something Jonathan would appreciate, she thought.

She did not tell Jonathan about the form of those relapses: the crying. Hours, sometimes whole days, it seemed, of tears. Unable to stop, she found it impossible too to phone for help, not even to Mary. Holly hated those tears, she hated crying. It was like some loathsome disease, incapacitating, shameful.

She wondered if she would ever be able to make love to another man without weeping for Sebastian. Sometimes she thought that she could not, and she despaired.

Preparing for Jonathan, their date, she tried not to think of tears, of crying. She concentrated on household tasks, her house.

"In summer it's really wonderful," she told Jonathan Green, in her mind. "All the flowers outside in bloom, the breezes, the cool. And it's great having so much space." But what was this, an advertisement for her house? Did she want him to come and live there?

In the two days immediately preceding the date, Holly changed her mind several dozen times on the two crucial issues of what to serve for dinner, and what to wear.

"Make something really simple, obviously," Mary counseled. "A good make-ahead stew, I could give you a new recipe I've been doing. And have lots of flowers all over. You might as well wear something pretty, maybe one of those long silk numbers?"

Good advice, but it still left considerable latitude for obsessive thought, which Holly gave it. Which stew? What kind of flowers? And which long silk dress, the blue or the black?

· · ·

And Holly knew, intelligent, streetwise Holly knew all along that she was making (dangerously) too much of this. Much too much. She was asking for trouble, begging for it, she knew that she was.

She almost began to hope that Jonathan would have to break the date, or forget it.

Jonathan not only did not forget, he arrived quite promptly at seven. Hearing his car, a new Porsche, then observing his approach as he walked up the path to her house and came across the porch, Holly half-consciously made two notes: one, he looks nervous, his shoulders are tight. And, two, why is he wearing that pink sweater? She herself was wearing the long black silk, much too dressed up but too late now to change.

At her door they shook hands, both said how nice to see each other, as though it were accidental. And in a quick agitated way Jonathan took in her house.

"What a nice big place," he said, with what looked like a tiny shiver, as Holly thought, He doesn't like it. Well, neither do I, actually.

Seated, he accepted a glass of Perrier.

"A nice big house," he repeated, once they were settled with drinks.

He is wearing that sweater to make himself look younger, was what Holly was thinking. At a certain point Sebastian had begun to wear a lot of pink.

"Where are you living now?" Holly asked Jonathan.

"Well, it's a little complicated. I'm still in what was the family house. My wife, the children, school . . ." He said all this at some length, managing curiously to omit saying where he lived.

Jonathan was fairly handsome, better-looking than Holly had previously observed. However, she reminded herself, I was so hung up on the beauty of Sebastian that I didn't notice any male attractiveness, only his. I only saw Sebastian.

Jonathan's eyes were large and very dark. Very unlike Sebastian's narrow, gold-brown eyes.

"Does it feel better when a divorce is sort of finalized?" Holly attempted, thinking that divorce or separation was actually what they most had in common, at that time.

Rather defensively Jonathan told her, "Mine's nowhere near final. In fact, we're still in the very early stages. Thrashing things out. Kicking the ball around." He grinned, as though to assure her of the non-seriousness of his divorce.

His face was better in its serious phase, Holly decided. The grin was too much just that, a grin. So many large healthy white teeth that you missed his eyes, by far his best feature.

It was impossible now to imagine the long easy fluid talk that Holly had silently enjoyed with him, all those conversations in her head. Whatever had they talked about? She could no longer remember, even.

"How about dinner?" she asked. "It's not too early? It's all sort of ready, won't take a minute."

Jonathan looked at his watch and they both saw: 7:30. "Fine by me," he said.

Mercifully alone in her kitchen, Holly faced or tried to face the fact of this awkward evening. She was pleased at the degree to which she could accept its semi-failure. Not her fault, and it meant nothing, really. Just two people shy with each other, in an unaccustomed situation. Jonathan as a doctor, her doctor, was of course considerably more assured. Good at his work, always knowing what to say.

And Holly herself could be fairly animated, talkative, although it felt like rather a long time since she had been so.

Steak-and-kidney pie. A favorite of Sebastian's, and received enthusiastically by Jonathan, at first. "What a great crust!"

But Holly next noticed that he was picking out pieces of steak, avoiding the kidney. She supposed that she should have asked, but still she would not have expected that sort of squeamishness from a doctor. On the other hand, why not? Maybe doctors are more squeamish, really, than other people are? And with considerably more reason, so much exposure to visceral ugliness.

"This house can get awfully cold in the winter, though," Holly found herself babbling (obviously they would do well not to talk about the food). "Drafts everywhere. Damp."

"It feels very comfortable." Courteous Jonathan. And then, conversationally, "In your settlement, you get the house?"

"Uh?"

"The house. It's yours now?"

"Well, not exactly. I mean, I'm not sure yet. My lawyer—"

"Oh. Lawyers." Jonathan's mouth curled.

Are they really so much worse than doctors? Holly did not ask this.

Jonathan chose not to have dessert. "Got to stay in shape." He grinned, and then, "Help you with the dishes?"

"Oh, no. Just go on in the living room. I'll bring coffee. Decaf?"

"Please."

Holly brought in the coffee, which was unaccountably cool. They sat sipping at it as Holly thought again, Well, so much for that. How silly I was. And whenever will he go?

Instead of going, though, Jonathan Green moved closer to her, on the sofa where they sat. Very gently he put one arm around her, and then still very gently he began to kiss her. Their mouths were open, but not in an urgent way. Just kissing, hungrily (at least Holly kissed hungrily, she had not kissed anyone for so long), but the hunger seemed for more kissing. No question of anything further.

At some point Jonathan murmured near her ear, half laughing, "High school."

"Yes." And Holly thought, This is perfect, this is what I really wanted. All this tender kissing, this is what I've missed. Much more than sex. To his ear she whispered, "Jonathan, I really like you."

It went on and on, this gentle semi-greedy kissing, along with mild back-stroking caresses. Touching Jonathan's shoulders, which were broad, strong-feeling, Holly was intensely aware of maleness, such very male shoulders. Another quality she had missed.

After what could have been an hour of this occupation (impossible to tell about the time), Jonathan, still gentle, began to start to disentangle himself. He still clung to her—or was it that he allowed her to cling? No way to remember that, later on.

At last they stood kissing at the door. Good night.

"I must see you very soon" was what Jonathan said. "I'll call you."

And Holly went off happily to bed, leaving the dishes and thinking, How nice, that was just right. How nice Jonathan is, after all. I was right about him, sort of.

But the next day, on waking, Holly's first thought was that Jonathan would not call. She knew this as surely as she had always known, in her bones, that eventually Sebastian would leave her.

Her bedroom that morning was fiercely cold. Sharp winds blew through as outdoors, beyond the shuddering French windows, rain dripped from everything, from heavy rhododendron leaves, from ferns and winter weeds.

If Jonathan had stayed over, had slept there with her, there would now be another warm body in her bed. Sometimes Holly had thought that was what she most missed of Sebastian, simple bodily warmth. On the other hand, perhaps it was just as well that Jonathan had not stayed; he would not like this awakening to cold drafts, probably.

I hate this house, Holly thought as she forced herself up and out of bed. Off to do last night's dishes, to make her small breakfast.

"It was, well, sort of nice" was how Holly described the evening to Mary, who of course called to see how things had gone. "No big deal, in fact he's not the easiest guy in the world to talk to. But at the end it was, well, nice. Affectionate."

"Well, that's nice. I don't see why you're so sure you won't hear from him."

"I just am." For one thing, it's after noon, he must have been up for hours by now, he could have called. Holly did not say this, although it was much in her mind.

"Well, in any case he's a start," said Mary ambiguously.

At least we didn't actually make love, Holly also later thought. Or would that in a way have been better? Would Jonathan be more apt to call if we had? And come to think of it, why didn't we? Does he go out with a lot of women, and only make love to one, or maybe two? Is he into safe sex, scared of AIDS?

Over the years, in waiting rooms and on planes, Holly had seen articles about men who take you to bed and then never call, no matter what they said. But she could not remember any proposed solutions. Especially not after just kissing.

Should you call him, pretending that it doesn't matter who calls whom?

"Oh, Holly. Well, I should have called you yesterday" was available Jonathan's instant response, the next morning (Holly had told his nurse that this was a "social" call, and was nevertheless put through right away).

"Well, I decided it didn't matter who called whom," Holly lied. "But I was thinking about this weekend. I sort of feel like cooking again." (Another lie, she did not feel at all like cooking. She felt like more kissing, perhaps a long slow progress into bed.)

"Well, this weekend. Not good at all. I'm on call, beeper always going off. Such a nuisance. Seeing my kids on Sunday. But next week, first thing. I'll call you."

Hanging up from that conversation, on Thursday morning, Holly thought, I really cannot bear this. I cannot get through until Monday. Anxiety is the worst of all, worse even than grief. And, as she sometimes used to do, in the early days of knowing Sebastian was gone, Holly took to her bed, with a pile of magazines. Getting up from time to time to heat a can of soup, or make tea.

She cried, so that even calling Mary was out of the question.

And whether she wept for Sebastian or for Jonathan seemed hardly to matter.

On Friday her lawyer called. "You sound terrible" was his comment.

"Well yes, this cold. I can't seem to shake it." Not an inventive lie, but it served.

"Well, there's a lot of flu around. Have you called your doctor?"

"No."

"You should. Anyway, I have some news that may cheer you up."

His good news was that Sebastian, in New York, had signed papers: a quitclaim to the house, in return for assurances (elaborate, binding) of no further claims, ever, on him or his estate. No alimony. No-fault divorce.

"He must be planning to marry someone else." Holly had only dimly thought of this before.

"Sounds like it. Well, I guess you're in no mood for a visit. I have to be in Marin, and I thought—"

"No. Thanks."

For Holly that Saturday represented a sort of nadir, given over to pain. Bad thoughts. Self-pity. Solitude.

On Sunday, Mary called, and she too commented, "You don't sound very good."

"I don't feel too great." Holly then described her conversation with Jonathan, and finished by asking, "Why am I so sure he was lying?"

"Maybe because he was," Mary contributed (too quickly? had she seen him somewhere, with someone?). And then, possibly to change the subject, she continued, "You really sound bad. Have you considered taking your temperature?"

She told Holly about a party in Sausalito the night before, mainly colleagues of Mark's, at which, Holly thought, she could easily have seen Jonathan Green. With whoever.

On Monday, Holly conceded that actually something physical could be wrong with her; she had chills, aches in all her joints, and an entire sense of bodily weakness. She did take her temperature, which was 102 degrees.

The fact of an actual illness with a probable diagnosis, flu, was cheering. To go back to bed would be sensible, a yielding to the superior claims of illness rather than to sheer self-indulgence.

Quite early on Monday night the phone rang, and there was Jonathan Green, right on schedule—as he had said, first thing in the week.

"Odd you should call," Holly told him. "I have a sort of high fever, a hundred and two degrees. Flu, I guess."

"Well, that is pretty high. More of a child-sized fever than one we see in adults. What do you have around, medicine-wise?"

Having ascertained that she had nothing in the house beyond aspirin and cough drops, Jonathan said he would be right over.

"Okay, but Jonathan, I feel really terrible. I mean, I don't feel up to getting dressed." No long black silk, she added to herself.

"Oh, that's okay. Consider this a house call." He chuckled.

Holly changed into a prettier nightgown (cotton, nothing sexy), a good robe, and settled in the living room to wait for him.

By this time she had taken down most of Sebastian's paintings and stacked them in a closet, and had put books up on the shelves (eccentric Sebastian was fond of bare bookcases, empty shelves). There was a sheaf of magazines on the table, and flowers. Still, the room looked bare and cold, Holly thought. So large, it dwarfed every effort at warmth, and color.

She heard the car, and then the footsteps of Jonathan Green. A somewhat distant handshake at the door would be right, she thought, getting up.

Going to the door, extending her hand as she had intended, Holly found herself instead embraced. Chastely, perhaps paternally, but still, there she was, enfolded in the arms of Jonathan. For one moment.

In the living room, though, he seated himself quite apart from her, choosing the chair adjacent to the sofa where she sat (where they had spent all that time necking, before). And in a kindly, interested way, he listened to her description of her symptoms. He had even brought along some magic remedies, which he took out from a pocket: samples of antibiotics, Tylenol, cough medicine.

Holly was touched by what seemed simple human kindness. He was nice, after all.

Their medical business over, Jonathan even seemed inclined to stick around. He was looking forward to the end of winter, he told her, stretching long legs before him. Spring skiing, sailing. Baseball. His wife had not been very interested in those pursuits, and so he hoped that this year he could put in more time in that way. He grinned.

Had he guessed that Holly was not exactly a sports fan either? She rather imagined that he had, and even that she was forgiven. But she also imagined, or perceived, that he no longer saw her as a woman to kiss on a sofa. However, to some degree Holly dismissed all her crowding intuitions regarding Jonathan. After all, she was sick.

It was, though, all around a pleasant conversation, far easier than their halting, strained attempts at dinner. And then Jonathan got up to go.

At the door he embraced her again, more briefly than before. "I'll call you tomorrow," he said.

About what? Holly wondered, as she shivered in bed a short time later. And then she answered her own question, About my flu, that's what. That's what he finds interesting in me. What he likes best, now.

She was then assailed by familiar, painful thoughts of Sebastian. His beauty, and his terrible, implacable indifference to her. But she did not, as she so often had before, engage in imagined conversations with Sebastian. Perhaps she had said it all already? Nor did she cry.

Jonathan called the next day to see how she was.

"My fever's gone down. Your magic pills seem to work."

"Good. Well, I'll call you tomorrow."

On the night that he came to dinner, when they had sat there necking, why had he not gone on to take her to bed? This was something that Holly pondered, in her illness. Something that she could discuss with no one. Not even with Mary.

Because she was old and fat, was that it? And Jonathan knew just how old and fat she was, he had seen her, everything about her was down in his charts. That could be the explanation, but in that case why kiss her at all? He didn't have to, under the circumstances, he could have just been a very polite, onetime dinner guest.

Or was it because he did not want to commit himself to that extent? In a rational way, this made more sense. It was even a little too rational for Holly, who after all had the flu.

.   .   .

A day or so later, kind Mary came over with mushroom soup and some home-baked bread, and a basket of fruit, grapes and peaches and papayas. They sat in Holly's living room, in some rare February sunshine, a brief false spring. They talked.

And at last Holly asked her friend, "I really wonder whatever gave you the idea that Jonathan liked me."

"Well—" To Holly's surprise, Mary, who never blushed, now did so, a slow red flush that rose on her neck. "Well," Mary said, "that may have been a small case of wishful thinking on my part. And a little simplistic. You know, someone nice to replace mean Sebastian. And there was Jonathan, just getting a divorce, and nice. I thought."

"He is nice, in a way." He had called every day about Holly's flu, which was considerably better. Now she was just a little weak, and slightly light-headed. "I still don't quite see why Jonathan," she persisted, for no good reason. Giddily, perhaps.

"Well." Amazingly, Mary's flush deepened. "I have to admit I had the smallest crush on him myself. He is sort of, uh, cute."

"I guess." They both laughed nervously.

"And then," Mary went on, "there is this sexual fix we all seem to have on doctors. Little kids playing doctor, all that. Even before Mark, I always liked doctors, remember?"

"Yes." But Holly found herself uncomfortable in this conversation. It had gone far enough, she felt. She did not want to discuss Mary's possible crushes—nor, in a general way, sexuality.

Mary may well have felt the same, for she next asked, "What you have to do now is put on a little weight. Do you know how skinny you are? You look like that model we used to use, remember? Miss Anorexia?"

"But me? You've got to be kidding."

"I'm not, take a look at yourself."

Restored to their more usual tone, both women were happier. "I'll start by eating that whole loaf of bread you brought," Holly told Mary. "It smells fantastic."

Late one night in March, Holly's phone rang—shrill, an alarm that cut into her already unsettled sleep.

"Hello." A male voice that she did not instantly recognize, but that in a moment she knew could only be Sebastian's voice.

"Oh. Hi." Sitting up in bed, Holly pulled the covers around her shoulders. It was spring, but the nights were still very cold, and damp.

"Well, you don't sound too welcoming, but I really can't say that I blame you. Or not very much. I don't blame you very much." The slightest slur informed Holly that Sebastian was very drunk—of course he was, at three in the morning, New York time.

He laughed, and Holly heard the familiar contempt in his laugh. "I just wondered how you were," he said. "You and my house."

"I'm okay," Holly told him. "And I guess I'm going to put the house up for sale." Strangely, she had not known this was her plan until she said it to Sebastian.

He exploded, as she may have meant him to do. "Christ, do you have any idea how dumb that is? A valuable house, more valuable— Christ, how stupid can you get?"

"I need the money," she told him. "And I really don't like it here."

"You don't even know what you like! Ignorant Slavs—"

Holly replaced the receiver into its cradle, then reached down to unplug the cord. She was trembling, but only a little.

Several times later that night, in the course of her troubled sleep, she heard the dim sound of the living-room phone, which rang, and rang.

Nevertheless, in a way that she could not quite understand, the next day Holly felt considerably better. Even rested.

"I'm definitely going to move back to the city," she told Mary, over the phone. "Maybe back to our old neighborhood. I want to go back to school."

"North Beach is impossible now." Unenthusiastic Mary.

"Well, with the money from this house I could even go to Pacific Heights. Then I'd be close to the bridge. To Marin."

Mary laughed. "You're right. I just don't want you to leave. But I agree that's what you should do."

For no particular reason—she had not been thinking of their doctor—Holly next asked, "What do you hear these days about Jonathan Green?"

"Oh, we sort of see him around. Mark and I do. You know, doctor parties."

Mary's tone had been rather studiedly vague, Holly thought, and so she pursued it. "With whom?" she asked Mary. "Surely not his wife?"

"Oh no, I think that's all over. But Jonathan seems to be into the very young. Lord, the last one looked about sixteen."

"She's probably really forty but works out all the time. Plays baseball."

They both laughed.

"What men don't know," Mary told Holly, "or one of the things they don't know is how old those kids make them look. The contrast can be cruel."

"I wonder if that's what Sebastian is up to."

"The dumb shit, I wouldn't put it past him."

That conversation took place around noon, a time of day when they often made contact, Holly and Mary.

In the course of that afternoon, Holly gave somewhat fleeting thought both to Jonathan and to Sebastian.

Of Sebastian she thought, I haven't cried for a couple of weeks. I wouldn't dare say that the pain is absolutely gone, very likely it won't ever be. It's something I have to live with, probably, the way some people have bad backs or trick knees. Ten years is just not a dismissible part of my life.

Of Jonathan she thought, How crazy that all was, pinning all those fantasies on him when he's just a plain ordinary doctor. But what did he imagine that I would be, she wondered, that I wasn't? Rich, possibly, in a house that was more to his liking? Better at talking, funnier? God knows he can't have thought I'd be younger or prettier, Jonathan already knew what I looked like.

In the later afternoon, near dinnertime, as though telepathically summoned, Jonathan called Holly. She had not heard from him since the end of her flu, a couple of weeks ago.

And that is what he asked about. "How's your flu?"

"Well, it seems to be all better. Just a little cough sometimes."

"You'd better be careful, if you're still coughing. I've seen some people down with it for a second or even a third time."

"Oh, how terrible." But why tell me about them? Holly wondered.

"And then there's a brand-new strain of flu that we're seeing. A really bad one. But if you come down with that we've got a pill that works."

"Jonathan, I don't understand what you're saying."

"I just meant, if you get this new flu we have a specific for it."

"Oh." Is that what you called about? she wanted to ask. Instead she ventured, "Well, how've you been, otherwise?" Was this a social call? Was she supposed to make small talk?

Apparently not. Very briskly Jonathan told her, "Fine, really great in fact. Well, I just wanted to be sure you're okay."

"Well, I seem to be. As far as I know, I don't have the new flu. Yet."

He seemed to grasp that a small joke had been intended, and gave her a little laugh. "So far so good," he said.

And minutes after that they said goodbye.

It was nice to hear from you, I guess, is what Holly thought.

And for some minutes she wondered just what had motivated that call. Simple curiosity as to how she was? A medical need to warn her about relapses and the dangerous new kind of flu? Or had he wanted to find her sick, and needing him in that way?

Any answer to any of those questions was possible, Holly decided, and she thought that Jonathan himself did not know, really, why he had called. In his own mind, probably, he was just a doctor checking on a patient who had been quite sick, with a child-sized fever.

Fleetingly, she wondered whether he would send her a bill.

He did. It arrived, perhaps by coincidence, the following day. House call and follow-up treatment. One hundred dollars.

After You've Gone

The truth is, for a while I managed very well indeed. I coped with the house and its curious breakages, and with the bad nights of remembering you only at your best, and the good days suddenly jolted by your ghost. I dealt with the defection of certain old friends, and the crowding-around of a few would-be new best friends. I did very well with all that, in the three months since your departure for Oregon, very well indeed until I began to get these letters from your new person (I reject "lover" as too explicit, and, knowing you, I am not at all sure that "friend" would be applicable). Anyway, Sally Ann.

(You do remember encouraging me to write to you, as somewhat precipitately you announced your departure—as though extending me a kindness? It will make you feel better, you just managed not to say. In any case, with my orderly lawyer's mind, I am putting events—or "matters," as we say—in order.)

The house. I know that it was and is not yours, despite that reckless moment at the Trident (too many margaritas, too palely glimmering a view of our city, San Francisco) when I offered to put it in both our names, as joint tenants, which I literally saw us as, even though it was I who made payments. However, your two-year occupancy and your incredibly skillful house-husbanding made it seem quite truly yours. (Is this question metaphysical, rather than legal? If the poet-husband of a house is not in fact a husband, whose is the house?) But what I am getting at is this. How could you have arranged for everything to break the week you left? Even the Cuisinart; no one else even heard of a broken Cuisinart, ever. And the vacuum. And the electric blanket. The dishwasher and the Disposal. Not to mention my Datsun. "Old wiring, these older flats," the repair person diagnosed my household problems, adding, "But you've got a beautiful place here," and he gestured across the park—green, pyramidal Alta Plaza, where even now I can see you running, running, in your eccentric non-regular-runner outfit: yellow shorts, and that parrot-green sweatshirt from God knows where, both a little tight.

My Datsun turned out simply to need a tune-up, and since you don't drive I can hardly blame that on you. Still, the synchronism, everything going at once, was hard not to consider.

Friends. Large parties, but not small dinners, my post-you invitations ran. Or very small dinners—most welcome, from single women friends or gay men; unwelcome from wives-away husbands, or even from probably perfectly nice single men. I am just not quite up to all that yet.

People whom I had suspected of inviting us because of your poet fame predictably dropped off.

Nights. In my dreams of course you still are here, or you are leaving and I know that you are, and there is nothing to do to stop you (you have already told me, so sadly, about Sally Ann, and the houseboat in Portland). Recently I have remembered that after my father died I had similar dreams; in those dreams he was dying, I knew, yet I could not keep him alive. But those father dreams have a guilty sound, I think, and I truly see no cause for guilt on my part toward you. I truly loved you, in my way, and I did what I could (I thought) to keep us happy, and I never, never thought we would last very long. Isn't two years a record of sorts for you, for maybe any nonmarrying poet? Sometimes I thought it was simply San Francisco that held you here, your City Lights–Tosca circuit, where you sought out ghosts of Beats. Well, in my dreams you are out there still, or else you are here with me in our (my) bed, and we awaken slowly, sleepily to love.

Once, a month or so ago, I thought I saw you sitting far back in a courtroom; I saw those damn black Irish curls and slanted eyes, your big nose and arrogant chin, with that cleft. A bad shock, that; for days I wondered if it actually could have been you, your notion of a joke, or some sort of test.

In all fairness, though—and since I mention it I would like to ask you something. Just why did my efforts at justice, even at seeing your side of arguments, so enrage you? I can hear you shouting: "Why do you have to be so goddam *fair,* what *is* this justice of yours?"

But as I began to say, in all fairness I have to concede that I miss your cooking. On the nights that you cooked, that is. I really liked your tripe soup and your special fettuccine with all those wild mushrooms. And the Sunday scrambled eggs that we never got to till early afternoon.

And you are a marvel at fixing things, even if they have a tendency not to stay fixed.

And, most importantly, a first-rate poet; Yale and now the Guggenheim people seem to think so, and surely as you hope the MacArthur group will come around. Having read so little poetry other than yours, I am probably no judge; however, as I repeatedly told you, to me it was magic, pure word-alchemy.

I do miss it all, the house-fixing and cooking, the love and poetry. But I did very well without it all. Until recently.

The letters. The first note, on that awful forget-me-not paper, in that small, tight, rounded hand, was a prim little apology: she felt badly about taking you away from me (a phrase from some junior high school, surely) but she also felt sure that I would "understand," since I am such a fair-minded person (I saw right off that you had described my habits of thought in some detail). I would see that she, a relatively innocent person, would have found your handsomeness-brilliance-sexiness quite irresistible (at that point I wondered if you could have written the letter yourself, which still seems a possibility). She added that naturally by now I would have found a replacement for you, the natural thing for a woman like me, in a city like San Francisco. That last implication, as to the loose life-styles both of myself and of San Francisco, would seem to excuse the two of you fleeing to the innocence of Portland, Oregon.

A couple of false assumptions lay therein, however. Actually, in point of fact, I personally might do better, man-wise, in Portland than down here. The men I most frequently meet are young lawyers, hard-core yuppies, a group I find quite intolerable, totally unacceptable, along with the interchangeable young brokers—real-estate dealers and just plain dealers. Well, no wonder that I too took up with a poet, an out-of-shape man with no CDs or portfolio but a trunk full of wonderful books. (I miss your books, having got through barely half of them. And did you really have to take the *Moby-Dick* that I was in the middle of? Well, no matter; I went out to the Green Apple and stocked up, a huge carton of books, the day you left.)

In any case, I felt that she, your young person, your Sally Ann, from too much evidence had arrived at false conclusions. In some ways we are more alike, she and I, than she sees. I too was a setup, a perfect patsy for your charm, your "difference."

But why should she have been told so much about me at all? Surely you must have a few other topics; reading poems aloud as you used to do with me would have done her more good, or at least less harm, I believe. But as I pondered this question, I also remembered several of our own conversations, yours and mine, having to do with former lovers. It was talk that I quite deliberately cut short, for two clear reasons: one, I felt an odd embarrassment at my relative lack of what used to be called experience; and, two, I did not want to hear about yours. You did keep on trying, though; there was one particular woman in New York, a successful young editor (though on a rather junky magazine, as I remember), a woman you wanted me to hear all about, but I would not. "She has nothing to do with us," I told you (remember?). It now seems unfortunate that your new young woman, your Sally Ann, did not say the same about me.

Next came a letter which contained a seemingly innocent question: should Sally Ann go to law school, what did I think? On the surface this was a simple request for semi-expert advice; as she went on and on about it, though, and on and on, I saw that she was really asking me how she could turn herself into me, which struck me as both sad and somewhat deranged. Assuming that you have an ideal woman on whom Sally Ann could model herself, I am hardly that woman. You don't even much like "lady lawyers," as in some of your worst moments you used to phrase it.

Not having answered the first note at all (impossible; what could I have said?), I responded to this one, because it seemed required, with a typed postcard of fairly trite advice: the hard work involved, the overcrowding of the field, the plethora of even token women.

And now she had taken to writing me almost every day; I mean it, at least every other day. Does she have no other friends? No relatives, even, or old school ties? If she does, in her present state of disturbance they have faded from her mind (poor, poor Sally Ann, all alone with you, in Portland, on a Willamette River houseboat), and only I remain, a purely accidental, non-presence in her life.

The rains have begun in Portland, and she understands that they will continue throughout the winter. She does not really like living on a houseboat, she finds it frightening; the boat rocks, and you have told her that all boats rock, there is nothing to be done. (You must be not exactly in top form either. I never heard you admit to an inability to remedy anything—even my Datsun; you said you could fix it and you did, temporarily.)

You have found some old friends over at Reed College, she tells me; you hang out a lot over there, and you tell her that she would be very much happier with a job. Very likely she would, but you have taken her to an extremely high unemployment area.

She doesn't understand your poetry at all, and doesn't know what to say when you read it to her. Well, this is certainly a problem that I too could have had, except that I dealt with it head-on, as it were, simply and clearly saying that I didn't understand poetry, that I had not read much or ever studied it. But that to me your poems sounded marvelous—which they did; I really miss the sound of them, your words.

You talk about me more and more.

You are at home less and less. And now Sally Ann confesses to me that she used to be a waitress at the Tosca; on some of the nights when I was at home, here in San Francisco (actually I used to be grateful for a little time to catch up on work), when I assumed you were just hanging out in North Beach, you were actually courting Sally Ann, so to speak. Well, at this point I find this new information quite painless to absorb; it simply makes me miss you even less. But Sally Ann wonders if I think you could possibly be seeing someone else now? She says that you've mentioned a French professor at Reed, a most talented woman, you've said. Do I think—?

Well, I most certainly do think; you seem to prefer women with very respectable professions, poor Sally Ann representing the single rule-proving exception, I suppose. Some sort of lapse in calculation on your part—or quite likely Sally Ann had more to do with me than with herself, if you see what I mean, and I think you will. In any case, a fatal error all around.

Because it is clear to me that in an emotional sense you are battering this young woman. She is being abused by you. I could prove it to a jury. And, unlike me, she is quite without defenses.

You must simply knock it off. For one thing, it's beneath you, as you surely in your better, saner, kinder moments must clearly see (you're not all bad; even in my own worst moments I recall much good, much kindness, even). Why don't you just give her a ticket to somewhere, along with some gentle, ego-preserving words (heaven knows you're at your best with words), and let her go? Then you can move in your Reed College French professor and live happily there on your houseboat—almost forever, at least until the Portland rains let up and you feel like moving on.

As for myself, it seems only fair to tell you that I have indeed found a new friend—or, rather, an old friend has reappeared in my life in another role. (*Fair.* As I write this, I wonder if in some way, maybe, you were right all along to object to my notion of fairness? There was always a slightly hostile getting-even element in my justice? Well, I will at least admit that possibility.) In any case, I am taking off on a small trip to Jackson, Wyoming, day after tomorrow, with my old-new friend. About whom I can only at this moment say so far so good, in fact very good indeed—although I have to admit that I am still a little wary, after you. However, at least for me he is a more known quality than you were (we were undergraduates together, in those distant romantic Berkeley days), and I very much doubt that you'll be getting any letter of complaint regarding me. He already knows what he's getting, so to speak.

And so, please wish me well, as I do you (I'll keep my fingers crossed for the MacArthur thing).

And, I repeat, let Sally Ann go. All three of us, you, me, and Sally Ann, will be much better off—you without her, and she without you. And me without the crazy burden of these letters, which, if I were *really* fair, I would send on to you.

His Women

"I think we should try it again. You move back in," says Meredith, in her lovely, low, dishonest Southern voice.

Carter asks, "But—Adam?"

"I'm not seeing him anymore." Her large face, not pretty but memorable, braves his look of disbelief. Her big, deep-brown eyes are set just too close; her shapely mouth is a little too full, and greedy. Big, tall, dark, sexy Meredith, who is still by law his wife. She adds, "I do see him around the campus, I mean, but we're just friends now."

That's what you said before, Carter does not say, but that unspoken sentence hangs there in the empty space between them. She knows it as well as he does.

They are sitting in the garden behind her house—their house, actually, joint ownership being one of their central problems, as Carter sees it. In any case, now in early summer, in Chapel Hill, the garden is lovely. The roses over which Carter has labored in seasons past—pruning, spraying, and carefully, scientifically feeding—are in fragrant, delicately full bloom: great bursts of red and flame, yellow and pink and white. The beds are untidy now, neglected. Adam, who never actually moved in (Carter thinks), is not a gardener, and Meredith has grown careless.

She says, with a pretty laugh, "We're not getting younger. Isn't it time we did something mature, like making our marriage work?"

"Since we can't afford a divorce." He, too, laughs, but since what he says is true, no joke, it falls flat.

And Meredith chooses to ignore it; they are not to talk about money, not this time. "You know I've always loved you," she says, her eyes larger and a warmer brown than ever.

Perhaps in a way she has, thinks Carter. Meredith loves everyone; it is a part of her charm. Why not him, too? Carter and Adam and all her many friends and students (Meredith teaches in the music department at the university), and most cats and dogs and birds.

She adds, almost whispering, sexily, "And I think you love me, too. We belong together."

"I'll have to think about it," Carter tells her, somewhat stiffly.

The brown eyes narrow, just a little. "How about Chase? You still see her?"

"Well, sort of." He does not say "as friends," since this is not true, though Carter has understood that the presence of Chase in his life has raised his stature—his value, so to speak—and he wishes he could say that they are still "close."

But four years of military school, at The Citadel, left Carter a stickler for the literal truth, along with giving him his ramrod posture and a few other unhelpful hangups—according to the shrink he drives over to Durham to see, twice a week. Dr. Chen, a diminutive Chinese of mandarin manners and a posture almost as stiff in its way as Carter's own. ("Oh, great," was Chase's comment on hearing this description. "You must think you're back in some Oriental Citadel.") In any case, he is unable to lie now to Meredith, who says, with a small and satisfied laugh, "So we're both free. It's fated, you see?"

A long time ago, before Meredith and long before Chase, Carter was married to Isabel, who was small and fair and thin and rich, truly beautiful and chronically unfaithful. In those days, Carter was a graduate student at the university, in business administration, which these days he teaches. They lived, back then, he and Isabel, in a fairly modest rented house out on Franklin Street, somewhat crowded with Isabel's valuable inherited antiques; the effect was grander than that of any other graduate students', or even young professors', homes. As Isabel was grander, more elegant than other wives, in her big hats and long skirts and very high heels, with her fancy hors d'oeuvres and her collection of forties big-band tapes, to which she loved to dance. After dinner, at parties at their house, as others cleared off the table, Isabel would turn up the music and lower the lights in the living room. "Come *on*," she would say. "Let's all *dance*."

Sometimes there were arguments later:

"I feel rather foolish saying this, but I don't exactly like the way you dance with Walter."

"Whatever do you mean? Walter's a marvelous dancer." But she laughed unpleasantly, her wide, thin, dark-red mouth showing small, perfect teeth; she knew exactly what he meant.

What do you do if your wife persists in dancing *like that* in your presence? And if she even tells you, on a Sunday, that she thinks she will drive to the beach with Sam, since you have so many papers to grade?

She promises they won't be late, and kisses Carter good-bye very tenderly. But they are late, very late. Lovely Isabel, who comes into the house by herself and is not only late but a little drunk, as Carter himself is by then, having had considerable bourbon for dinner, with some peanuts for nourishment.

Nothing that he learned at The Citadel had prepared Carter for any of this.

Standing in the doorway, Isabel thrusts her body into a dancer's pose, one thin hip pushed forward and her chin, too, stuck out—a sort of mime of defiance. She says, "Well, what can I say? I know I'm late, and we drank too much."

"Obviously."

"But so have you, from the look of things."

"I guess."

"Well, let's have another drink together. What the hell. We always have fun drinking, don't we, darling Carter?"

"I guess."

It was true. Often, drinking, they had hours of long, wonderful, excited conversations, impossible to recall the following day. As was the case this time, the night of Isabel's Sunday at the beach with Sam.

Drinking was what they did best together; making love was not. This was something they never discussed, although back then, in the early seventies, people did talk about it quite a lot, and many people seemed to do it all the time. But part of their problem, sexually, had to do with drink itself, not surprisingly. A few belts of bourbon or a couple of Sunday-lunch martinis made Isabel aggressively amorous, full of tricks and wiles and somewhat startling perverse persuasions. But Carter, although his mind was aroused and his imagination inflamed, often found himself incapacitated. Out of it, turned off. This did not always happen, but it happened far too often.

Sometimes, though, there were long, luxurious Sunday couplings, perhaps with some breakfast champagne or some dope; Isabel was extremely fond of an early-morning joint. Then it could be as great as any of Carter's boyhood imaginings of sex.

But much more often, as Isabel made all the passionate gestures in her considerable repertoire, Carter would have to murmur, "Sorry, dear," to her ear. Nuzzling, kissing her neck. "Sorry I'm such a poop."

And so it went the night she came home from Sam, from the beach. They had some drinks, and they talked. "Sam's actually kind of a jerk," said Isabel. "And you know, we didn't actually do anything. So let's go to bed. Come, kiss me and say I'm forgiven, show me I'm forgiven." But he couldn't show her, and at last it was she who had to forgive.

Another, somewhat lesser problem was that Isabel really did not like Chapel Hill. "It's awfully pretty," she admitted, "and we do get an occasional good concert, or even an art show, But, otherwise, what a terrifically overrated town! And the faculty wives, now really. I miss my friends."

Therefore Carter was pleased, he was very pleased, when Isabel began to speak with some warmth of this new friend, Meredith. "She's big and fat, in fact she's built like a cow, and she's very Southern, but she has a pretty voice and she works in the music department, she teaches there, and she seems to have a sense of humor. You won't mind if I ask her over?"

Meeting Meredith, and gradually spending some time with her, Carter at first thought she was a good scout, like someone's sister. Like many big women (Isabel's description had been unkind), she had a pleasant disposition and lovely skin. Nice long brown hair, and her eyes, if just too closely placed, were the clear, warm brown of Southern brooks. With Carter, her new friend's husband, she was flirty in a friendly, pleasant way—the way of Southern women, a way he was used to. She was like his mother's friends, and his cousins, and the nice girls from Ashley Hall whom he used to take to dances at The Citadel.

Meredith became the family friend. She was often invited to dinner parties, or sometimes just for supper by herself. She and Isabel always seemed to have a lot to talk about. Concerts in New York, composers and musicians, not to mention a lot of local gossip.

When they were alone, Carter gathered, they talked about Meredith's boyfriends, of which she seemed to have a large and steady supply. "She's this certain type of Southern belle," was Isabel's opinion. "Not threateningly attractive, but sexy and basically comfy. She makes men feel good, with those big adoring cow eyes."

Did Isabel confide in Meredith? Carter suspected that she did, and later he found out for certain from Meredith that she had. About her own affairs. Her boyfriends.

Although he had every reason to know that she was unhappy, Carter was devastated by Isabel's departure. Against all reason, miserably, he felt that his life was demolished. Irrationally, instead of remembering a bitter, complaining Isabel ("I can't stand this tacky town a minute longer") or an Isabel with whom things did not work out well in bed ("Well, Jesus Christ, is that what you learned at The Citadel?"), he recalled only her beauty. Her clothes, and her scents. Her long blond hair.

He was quite surprised, at first, when Meredith began to call a lot with messages of sympathy, when she seemed to take his side. "You poor guy, you certainly didn't deserve this," was one of the things she said at the time. Told that he was finding it hard to eat—"I don't know, everything I try tastes awful"—she began to arrive every day or so, at mealtimes, with delicately flavored chicken and oven-fresh Sally Lunn, tomatoes from her garden, and cookies, lots and lots of homemade cookies. Then she took to inviting him to her house for dinner—often.

As he left her house, at night, Carter would always kiss Meredith, in a friendly way, but somehow, imperceptibly, the kisses and their accompanying embraces became more prolonged. Also, Carter found that this good-night moment was something he looked forward to. Until the night when Meredith whispered to him, "You really don't have to go home, you know. You could stay with me." More kissing, and then, "Please stay. I want you, my darling Carter."

Sex with Meredith was sweet and pleasant and friendly, and if it lacked the wild rush that he had sometimes felt with Isabel, at least when he failed her she was nice about it. Sweet and comforting. Unlike angry Isabel.

. . .

They married as soon as his divorce was final, and together they bought the bargain house, on a hill outside town, and they set about remodeling: shingling, making a garden, making a kitchen and a bedroom with wonderful views. Carter, like everyone else in the high-flying eighties, had made some money on the market, and he put all this into the house. The house became very beautiful; they loved it, and in that house Carter and Meredith thrived. Or so he thought.

He thought so until the day she came to him in anguished tears and told him, "This terrible thing. I've fallen in love with Adam." Adam, a lean young musician, a cellist, who had been to the house for dinner a couple of times. Unprepossessing, Carter would have said.

Carter felt, at first, a virile rage. Bloodily murderous fantasies obsessed his waking hours; at night he could barely sleep. He was almost unrecognizable to himself, this furiously, righteously impassioned man. With Meredith he was icily, enragedly cold. And then, one day, Meredith came to him and with more tears she told him, "It's over, I'll never see him again. Or if I do we'll just be friends."

After that followed a brief and intense and, to Carter, slightly unreal period of, well, fucking: the fury with which they went at each other could not be called "making love." Meredith was the first to taper off; she responded less and less actively, although as always she was pleasant, nice. But Carter finally asked her what was wrong, and she admitted, through more tears, "It's Adam. I'm seeing him again. I mean, we're in love again."

This time, Carter reacted not with rage but with a sort of defeated grief. He felt terribly old and battered. *Cuckold.* The ugly, old-fashioned word resounded, echoing through his brain. He thought, I am the sort of man to whom women are unfaithful.

When he moved out, away from Meredith and into an apartment, and Chase Landau fell in love with him (quite rapidly, it seemed), Carter assumed that she must be crazy. It even seemed a little nuts for her to ask him for dinner soon after they met, introducing themselves in the elevator. Chase lived in his building, but her apartment, which contained her studio, was about twice the size of Carter's and much nicer, with balconies and views. "I liked your face," she later explained. "I always go for those narrow, cold, mean eyes." Laughing, making it a joke.

Chase was a tall, thin, red-haired woman, not Southern but from New York, and somewhat abrasive in manner. A painter of considerable talent and reputation (no wonder Meredith was impressed). Carter himself was impressed at finding inquiries from *Who's Who* lying around, especially because she never mentioned it. In his field, only the really major players made it.

Her paintings were huge, dark, and violent abstractions, incomprehensible. Discomforting. How could anyone buy these things and live with them? As they sat having drinks that first night, working at light conversation, Carter felt the paintings as enormous, hostile presences.

Chase was almost as tall as Carter, close to six feet, and thin, but heavy-breasted, which may have accounted for her bad posture; she tended to slouch, and later she admitted, "When I was very young I didn't like my body at all. So conspicuous." Carter liked her body, very much. Her eyes were intense and serious, always.

As they were finishing dinner she said to him, "Your shoulders are wonderful. I mean the angle of them. This," and she reached with strong hands to show him.

He found himself aroused by that touch, wanting to turn and grasp her. To kiss. But not doing so. Later on, he did kiss her good night, but very chastely.

Used to living with women, with Isabel and then with Meredith, Carter began to wonder what to do by himself at night. He had never been much of a reader, and most television bored him. In the small town that Chapel Hill still was in many ways, you would think (Carter thought) that people knowing of the separation would call and ask him over, but so far no one had. He wished he had more friends; he should have been warmer, kinder. Closer to people. He felt very old, and alone. (He wondered, *Are* my eyes mean? Am *I* mean?)

He called Chase and asked her out to dinner. "I know it's terribly short notice, but are you busy tonight?"

"No, in fact I'd love to go out tonight. I'm glad you called."

His heart leaped up at those mild words.

During that dinner, Chase talked quite a lot about the art world: her New York gallery, the one in L.A., the local art department. He listened, grateful for the entertainment she provided, but he really wasn't paying much attention. He was thinking of later on: would she, possibly, so soon—

She would not. At the door, she bid him a clear good night after a rather perfunctory social kiss. She thanked him for the dinner. She had talked too much, she feared; she tended to do that with new people, she told him, with a small, not quite apologetic, laugh.

From a friend in the law school, Carter got the name of a lawyer, a woman, with whom he spent an uncomfortable, discouraging, and expensive half hour. What it came to was that in order to recover his share in the house, Carter would have to force Meredith to sell it, unless she could buy him out. None of this was final, of course; it was just the lawyer's temporary take on things. Still, it was deeply depressing to Carter.

Coming home, in the downstairs lobby of his building he ran into Chase, who was carrying a sack of groceries, which of course he offered to take.

"Only if you'll come and have supper with me." She flashed him a challenging smile. "I must have been thinking of you. I know I bought too much."

That night it was he who talked a lot. She only interrupted from time to time with small but sharp-edged questions. "If you didn't want to go to The Citadel, why didn't you speak up?" And, "Do you think you trusted Meredith at first because she's not as good-looking as Isabel?" The sort of questions that he usually hated—that he hated from Dr. Chen—but not so with Chase; her dark, intelligent eyes were kind and alert. He almost forgot his wish to make love to her.

But then he remembered, and all that desire returned. He told her, "It's all I can do not to touch you. You're most terrifically attractive to me."

By way of answer, she smiled and leaned to meet him in a kiss. For a long time, then, like adolescents, they sat there kissing on her sofa, until she whispered, "Come on, let's go to bed. This is silly."

Carter had not expected their progress to be quite so rapid. He hardly knew her; did he really want this? But not long after that, they were indeed in bed, both naked. He caressed her soft, heavy breasts.

Pausing, sitting up to reach somewhere, Chase said, "You'll have to wear this. I'm sorry."

"Oh, Lord. I haven't done that since I was twenty. And look, I'm safe. I never played around."

"I know, but Meredith did. A lot."

"I don't think I can—"

"Here, I'll help you."

"Damn, I'm losing it; I knew I would."

Strictly speaking, technically, that night was not a great success. Still, literally they had gone to bed together, and Carter's feeling was that this was not a woman who fell into bed very easily (unlike—he had to think this—either Isabel or Meredith).

The next day he had another appointment with the lawyer, who had talked with Meredith's lawyer, who had said that things looked worse.

"I don't know why I'm so drawn to you," Chase told him, "but I really am." She laughed. "That's probably not a good sign. For you, I mean. The men I've really liked best were close to certifiable. But you're not crazy, are you?"

"Not so far as I know."

Chase did not seem crazy to him. She was hardworking, very intelligent. Her two sons, with whom she got along well, were off in school, and she was surrounded by warm and admiring friends; her phone rang all the time with invitations, friendly voices. But, as Carter put it to himself, she did sometimes seem a little much. A little more than he had bargained for. Or more than he was up to right now.

Their sexual life, despite her continued insistence on—hated phrase—"safe sex," was sometimes great, then not. Chase complained, though nicely, that out of bed he was not affectionate. "I could use more plain, unsexy touching," she said, and he tried to comply, though demonstrativeness was not at all in his nature.

Carter's broker called with bad news, quite a lot of bad news. Carter, like most people in the market, had taken a beating.

Even Chase would admit that her work habits were a little strange. She liked to get up late and spend a couple of hours drinking coffee, phoning, maybe writing a letter or two. She would then go into her studio (a room to which Carter was never admitted). At times she would emerge to eat a piece of fruit, heat some soup, or, less frequently, go out for a short walk along the graveled paths of old Chapel Hill. Back in her studio, immersed in her work, quite often she would forget about dinner until ten at night, or eleven; she did not forget dinner dates, but she sometimes phoned to break or postpone them.

Carter argued, "But if you started earlier in the morning you could finish—"

"I know. I know it's impractical, but it's the way I seem to have to work. I'm sorry. It's not something I can change."

Along with feeling some annoyance, Carter was moved and a little alarmed by her intensity, her high purpose.

Sometimes, in bed, Chase cried out quick, impassioned words of love to him—which Carter did not answer in kind, nor did he take what she said at those moments too seriously. In fact, as he was later forced to recognize, he gave rather little thought to Chase's deeper feelings. "You didn't want to deal with what I felt," she accused him, and he had to admit that that was entirely correct.

"Adam and I aren't getting along at all," said Meredith to Carter, over the phone. I don't know—he's a lot more neurotic than I thought he was."

"Oh, that's too bad," was Carter's response. Not saying, *Now* you find this out, after wrecking our marriage and costing God knows what in lawyers' bills.

"He's very dependent," Meredith said. "I don't really like that. I guess I was spoiled by you."

"I don't know why she's telling me this stuff," Carter said to Chase when she called; the old instinct of compulsive honesty had forced him to repeat the conversation with Meredith.

"I think she wants you back," Chase told him. "You wait and see."

"You think so? Really?"

"Jesus, Carter, you sound sort of pleased. If she did, would you even consider it?"

"Well, I don't know." As always, the literal truth; he did not know.

"God, Carter, she slept with everyone. Everyone in town knows that. Why do you think I insisted on safe sex?"

She was furiously excited, almost hysterical, Carter thought. She was out of control. A little frightening—but he only said, "Oh, come on, now."

"How tacky can you get!" Chase cried out, And then she said, "Look, don't call me, I'll call you, okay?" And hung up.

True to her word, she did call him—once, very late at night. "I've had some wine," she said. "I shouldn't be calling, I mean, otherwise I wouldn't. But I just wanted you to know a couple of things. One, I was really in love with you. God, if I needed further proof that I'm seriously deranged. I always fall in love with the most unavailable man anywhere around. Emotionally. Mean eyes, good shoulders. *Shit,* why did I call? Good night!" And she hung up, loud and clear. A ridiculous and quite unnecessary conversation, in Carter's view.

Now, in the afternoon sunshine, Carter looks about at all the roses and the scented white wisteria—at their lovely house and at unlovely, untrustworthy, but deeply familiar Meredith. He finds that, despite himself, he is thinking of Chase. Of her passion (those cries of love) and her scornful rage and of her final avowals (but she was drunk). Is it now too late? Suppose he went to her and said that he was through with Meredith, would she take him back? Would she ask him to come and live with her? (So far, she has never suggested such a thing.) Could they marry?

No is the answer that Carter gives to all these questions. No, Chase would probably not take him back, and no, there is no way he could afford to marry her. Even if he were sure that he wanted to. Chase is crazy—she must be crazy. Look at those paintings. There in the warm sunlight he suddenly shivers, as though haunted.

"Yes," he says to Meredith, although she hasn't spoken for a while. "Yes, okay. All right."

The Haunted Beach

The room, in this old, West Coast Mexican resort hotel, is unspeakably shabby—a window broken, the bedside table precariously leaning sideways—and not entirely clean. Led there by the aging, barefoot busboy, Penelope Jaspers, an art dealer, and Ben Bowman, a superior court judge, both from San Francisco, exchange a heavy look. In the bathroom, which is not quite as bad as she feared, Penelope, who had requested this particular room (she has been here before, though not for several years), tries a faucet: no water. And then back in the bedroom she finds no electricity. She can see from Ben's face, and his stance, that he is prepared to tough it out if she is, but Penelope has more at stake in this trip, for her a possibly dangerous return to old haunts (although she has changed a lot since then, she feels), and so she rather quickly decides that discomfort will be less than no help. She tells the busboy, Alfonso, who does not seem to remember her (or is he being tactful?), "Things don't seem to work in this room, Alfonso. Could we see another?"

Alfonso does not recognize Penelope; they look so much alike, these North American women. Pale and too thin, they dress either in pants or in immodest bathing costumes. This particular light-haired woman has a smile more pleasant than the rest, and her voice is soft—he thinks that he may have seen her before, although with a taller husband, who had no beard. North Americans quite frequently exchange their husbands and wives with each other, he has been told. Nevertheless, as pleasantly as he can, he tells the woman, whose Spanish is fairly good, for a gringa, that he will return to the desk for another key; he will show them another room.

Penelope and Ben smile at each other, quickly, tentatively, and she tells him, with a gesture, "This room, with the Farquhars in it, you can't imagine the difference. They always came for a month, you know, and put their things around." Not telling him, And Charles and I were in the room next door. Ben "knows" about Charles, a painter; knows that she came here with him often, and that she felt "terrible" when she and Charles broke up (terrible for a couple of years, in fact; but now she is really okay, she has told him that too). "The room even seemed bigger," she adds.

"Empty rooms look smaller." Ben is given to such stray bits of information.

"Lucky there's another room. We hope."

"Probably. This is off-season," he reminds her.

There is another room, seemingly at the top of the flight of steps they have just come down—and which now, following Alfonso and their luggage, they climb again, in the almost stifling, unaccustomed April sunshine, among the still bravely flowering bougainvillea vines.

Happily, the new room is extremely nice. A new structure has been built over the old, existing structures, over the tiers of rooms—over all of them, in fact, except the lower row, where the Farquhars, and next door Penelope and Charles, used to stay. This room is large and white, with an alcove for bathing, another space for reading, or lounging about, with two sofas and a table. A king-sized bed, and a broad porch out in front, with a table and chairs and hammocks—and a sweeping view of the bay, the brilliant sea and its enclosing hills of jungle trees. The sea and the view for which they have come, essentially, to this place.

And how fortunate, really, that they have this room instead of the old one that Penelope asked for, the Farquhars' room. How lucky that the lights didn't work, Penelope is thinking, and the water. If things had been just slightly better they would have stuck it out, and suffered. Ben wanting to please her, to be a good sport, and Penelope, for her pride, pretending that everything was fine. But this is perfect, she thinks. Here we are in San Bartolomeo, but not in the same room or near those rooms. It is simply a much better version of what I had before, she thinks. How fortunate, all around.

She asks Ben, "Do you want a swim?"

He smiles. "Well, why not?"

. . .

"I'm over him, really, finally, I think. If I just don't go back to Mexico I'll be all right, probably." Penelope said this to her closest friend from time to time, with decreasing frequency, in the years that succeeded her disastrous breakup with Charles, with whom she had lived for five or six years (depending on whether you counted the months of quarrelsome separations). She said it a couple of times after entering into a "relationship" with Ben, a more or less respectable, though bearded, judge. And then this spring, now about three years "after Charles," as Penelope still thinks of it, she finds herself on a trip with Ben, not only to Mexico but to San Bartolomeo itself, the beautiful scene of too much, the scene of too many scenes.

What happened was an airlines deal, promotional: Go anywhere in Mexico for $199. Penelope and Ben read this, and they both began to say, Why not? We need a vacation, swimming, warm weather. In San Francisco, a long mild dry winter had been succeeded by a cold wet dark spring. And then they began to eliminate places: well, obviously not Cancún, and Cozumel's so far away. Acapulco is horrible, and Vallarta's much too crowded. Until at last Penelope said, more or less to herself, Well, why not San Bartolomeo? It's so much in my mind, I have to go back there sometime, why not now? with Ben? with whom, on the whole, she got along rather well—though not lately; lately she had felt rough edges between them.

San Bartolomeo was where every January, for a week, she and Charles struck a truce, or nearly. No really bad fights. Where everything was beautiful: the flowers; the green, encroaching jungle; the white beach and the sea. And the Farquhars, an elderly, distinguished couple, he an astronomer, she an actress, both long retired, were in the cabin next door—unlikely but close, and valued, crucial friends for wild Charles and frightened Penelope. With Carlotta and Travis Farquhar, Charles tamed down, drank less, and shouted not at all; he was, in fact, his best, most imaginative, entertaining, generous, and sensitive self. And beautiful; Charles was always more handsome than anyone else around. Penelope, losing fear, was more friendly and talkative than usual (she felt this to be so, with the Farquhars).

For those weeks in San Bartolomeo there had been not only the balm of the Farquhars' company but also that of the place itself, its extreme tropical, flowery, seaside beauty. The long days of nothing to do but swim and walk and eat and take naps. And make love.

The Farquhars had died a couple of years ago—as a dedicated couple will, within weeks of each other. And why, Penelope wondered in the weeks succeeding confirmation of plans for their trip, hers and Ben's, why had she so specifically asked for the Farquhars' room? Did she imagine that she and Ben (they sometimes spoke of marriage) might become, eventually, such a couple? Or did she want to be right next to, but not inside, the room that she and Charles had shared so happily? (It *was* true, they had been almost always happy in San Bartolomeo.)

In any case, it does seem fortunate that they are to be in quite another room—although, on the way down to go swimming that first day, and every day after that, they walk right past that well-known row of rooms, the bottom row. Vines and bushes have been allowed to grow up almost to the porches, interfering, Penelope supposes, with the view from those rooms.

On the plane down from San Francisco, Penelope had chatted somewhat nervously to Ben, extolling the virtues and beauties of their destination—indeed, until he patted her arm and told her, "Pen, it's okay, I'm sure it will be all right."

One of the attractions described by Penelope was Rosa's restaurant, a beach shack, at the foot of the path up to their hotel. "Rosa is wonderful," Penelope told Ben. "Very small and dark, this burnished skin. And such a great cook, the best seafood. She's so energetic! With this slob of a husband who lolls around in very clean clothes that probably she ironed."

As they reach the foot of the path, that first day, there indeed is Rosa's: a concrete floor with a thatched lean-to roof, some tables and chairs. And, swinging out into the breeze, several rickety cages, each housing a drowsy, shabby-looking parrot.

And there is Rosa! recognizing Penelope. "Ah, amiga!" and rushing toward her, as Ben stands off at some distance, discreetly, on the sand.

They embrace, as Penelope thinks that she had not remembered Rosa as being so small. Rosa's head barely reaches Penelope's breast.

And then, still embracing Penelope, Rosa bursts into tears. "My husband!" she cries out. "Now dead two years!"

"Oh, how terrible. My husband died too," Penelope lies—a double lie; she and Charles never married, and he did not die but ran off to Turkey, finally, with a pretty boy. She does not understand this lie that she herself has told.

"Ah, amiga." Rosa presses her closer, and then lets go.

"My friend Ben," Penelope gestures vaguely in his direction, as Ben, who knows no Spanish (and thus did not hear Penelope's curious untruth), smiles.

"Ah, good," says Rosa, vaguely.

"We'll see you later; we'll come down for dinner," Penelope promises.

"Good."

But Penelope senses that Rosa has already lost interest in her. Rosa only wanted to say that her husband had died, wanted the drama of that moment. Her husband, the slob in his clean freshly ironed clothes, whom Rosa loved.

Having promised, though, they do go down that night to Rosa's for dinner, Penelope in her long white flowered dress, bought years ago, down here, in a funny store recommended by Carlotta Farquhar. "You look really pretty," Ben tells her as they settle into rickety chairs, next to the view of the night-black, half-moonlit sea.

Rosa's has all been repainted, a bright yellowish green, but still the room seems much darker than before. At one end, the kitchen end, a large TV set emits a murky light and a lot of noise—a Mexican talk show, dancers in frilly costumes, tambourines, guitars, Rosa and a group of assorted, T-shirted adolescents—her children, now five years older than when Penelope last saw them, all huddled, transfixed. Rosa, who used to be always rushing in and out of the kitchen.

The food is good, good fresh fish browned in garlic, but not as good as Penelope remembered it.

Ben asks, "Have you ever been to Hawaii?"

"No, why?" Not asking, Do you wish we were there instead? already?

"I just wondered. I used to go there a lot."

"You liked it?"

"Oh yes. With, uh, Betty."

Betty is Ben's former wife, who behaved very badly; she drank, had affairs, all that. Ben almost never speaks of her, conveniently for Penelope, who does not wish to speak of Charles. She asks him, "Do you think of going back there?"

He hesitates—what Penelope thinks of as a judicial pause. "No, I guess not," he tells her.

The group clustered at the TV set seems indescribably sad, to Penelope. She considers the life of Rosa, a life of such hard work, so many children, but successful, in a way: her own good restaurant, there on the beach. Very popular with tourists; or she once was. But now seemingly all is in ruins; nothing is getting through to her but absence and pain, mourning, and noisy TV talk shows. Rosa is so terribly reduced that possibly she has indeed shrunk in stature, Penelope believes. In no sense is she now the woman she once was. All over Mexico, Penelope imagines, there must be women like Rosa, defeated women, bowing to sadness. The emotions that she herself felt after Charles were sufficiently like this to make her now shudder, and some shame for Rosa, for herself, for all of them makes her wish that Ben had not met Rosa in this state.

Ben and Charles are so totally unlike, as men, that Penelope almost never consciously compares them. Ben is dark, quite presentable but not handsome. He is thrifty, extremely thrifty. Intelligent rather than brilliant, tending to be quiet, almost taciturn. Judicial. His most annoying expression, to Penelope, is, "Well, I'd have to see the evidence on that."

His love for Penelope, a love to which he admits, though reluctantly, seems out of character, odd. At times Penelope can hardly believe in its truth, but then Ben is an exceptionally truthful man. She senses that he would prefer a more conventional woman, perhaps another lawyer?—but in that case what was he doing with crazy Betty?

He must wonder, it occurs to Penelope, if she is in fact thinking of Charles, and if so what in particular she remembers.

Actually, what Penelope most remembered about San Bartolomeo, in those years of not going there, was the flowers—the spills and fountains of bougainvillea, the lush profusion of bloom, in every color: pink red purple yellow orange. And the bright red trumpet vines, and other nameless flowers, everywhere.

This year, however, she notices on their way to breakfast that everything looks drier; the vines are brittle, the palm fronds yellowing. There are some flowers still, some hard fuchsia bougainvillea, but far fewer.

Can there have been a drought in Mexico that she had not read about, along with all that country's other, increasing problems? Corruption and garbage, pollution, overpopulation, and disease. Extreme, unending poverty.

In the dining room things are more or less the same. A buffet table with lovely fresh fruit, and boxes of American cold cereal. An urn of awful coffee, not quite hot. Pretty young maids, who take orders for Mexican eggs, French toast, whatever. Penelope scours the room for some maid that she knew before, but finds none, not beautiful Aurelia, or small smart friendly Guadalupe.

The other guests, on the whole, are younger than the people who used to come here. Younger and less affluent looking. Many couples with small children. They are all probably taking advantage of the new cheap fares—as we are, Penelope thinks, at that moment badly missing the Farquhars, their elderly grace, their immaculate dignity. "You would have liked the Farquhars," she says to Ben—as she has several times before.

Down on the beach, the scene is much the same as always, couples or groups lounging in various states of undress around their palapas, with their bright new books or magazines, their transistors, bottles of beer, and suntan lotion. Too many people. Most of the palapas are taken; the only one available to Penelope is at the foot of the steps, near Rosa's.

"There's not a lot of surf," Ben comments as they settle into uncomfortable slatted chairs.

"Sometimes there is." Does he mean that he would rather be in Hawaii, where the surf is higher?

"Those boats look dangerous," he tells her.

Penelope has to agree. Back and forth, perilously close to the swimmers, small motorboats race by, some hauling along waterskiers, others attached to a person who is dangling from a parachute, up in the sky. The boats are driven by young boys, sixteen or seventeen, from the look of them, who often turn back to laugh with their admiring girlfriends, on the seats behind them. In fact Penelope has always been extremely afraid of these boats—though Charles reassured her that they would not hit anyone (laughing: "They never have, have you noticed?"). But this year there seem to be more of them, and they seem to come in much closer than before.

A young Mexican woman with a bunch of plastic bottles, strung together, comes up to their palapa and asks if they want to buy some sun-tan lotion.

No, thank you.

A very small girl with enormous eyes comes by selling Chiclets.

No, thanks.

"It's odd about vendors this year," Penelope tells Ben. "There used to be lots of them, and they had some good stuff. Carlotta got some incredible necklaces. There was one in particular, a tall pretty young woman in a white uniform, sort of like a nurse. She had a briefcase full of lovely silver things. Pretty opal rings; it's where I got mine." And she spreads her fingers, showing him, again, the two opal rings, one pink and one green, each with seeming depths of fire, each surrounded by a sort of silver filigree. "About ten bucks apiece," Penelope laughs. "Augustina, her name was. I wanted to get more rings on this trip, but I don't see her."

"Why more?"

"Oh, they don't last. They dull and come apart. But I suppose I don't really need them." Though thrifty, Ben no doubt disapproves of such cheap rings, or so Penelope imagines—the wives of successful lawyers, and certainly of judges, do not wear ten-dollar rings. And in a discouraged way Penelope wonders why they have come to Mexico together, she and Ben. Most recently in San Francisco they had not been getting on especially well; there was a string of minor arguments, the more annoying because of their utter triviality—where to eat, whom to see, what to do—arguments that had left them somewhat raw, on edge. It comes to Penelope that she must have expected some special Mexican balm; she must have thought that somehow Mexico would make every-thing come right, would impart its own magic. And she thinks, Alas, poor Mexico, you can hardly heal yourself, much less me.

"Well, how about a swim?" Ben stands up, so trim and neatly made, in his neat khaki trunks, that Penelope sighs and thinks, He's so nice, and generally good; do I only truly like madmen, like Charles? Even as she smiles and says, "Sure, let's go."

As always, the water is mysteriously warm and cool at once, both nurturing and refreshing—and green, glittering there for miles out into the sunlight. But perhaps not quite as clear as before? Penelope thinks that, but she is not entirely sure.

Despite a passing motorboat, this one lolling at low speed, its owner smiling an invitation, drumming up trade—Ben strikes out into deep water, swimming hard. For an instant Penelope thinks, Oh Lord, he'll be killed, that's what this ill-advised (probably) trip is all about. But then more sensibly she thinks, No, Ben will be okay. He is not slated to be run over by a Mexican motorboat (or is he?). She herself, more and more fearful as another boat zips by, this one trailing a large yellow inflated balloon, astride which six young women shriek and giggle— Penelope moves closer to a large, wave-jumping group of Americans for protection.

She persuades Ben to go back to Rosa's for lunch, but the day scene there is even more depressing than what goes on at night: the same blaring TV, same group clustered in front of it—in broad daylight, the sun streaming outside on the beach, the lovely sea not twenty yards away. Rosa hardly looks up as they come in. And the food is indifferent.

Walking up the path to their room, Penelope observes, again, the row of empty rooms. And she remembers an elderly couple, the Connors, friends of the Farquhars, who always took the room on this end, that nearest to the path, and sat there, calling out to their friends who passed. The lonely old Connors, now very likely dead. But how easy to imagine them sitting there still, he with his binoculars, she with her solitaire cards. And, in the room after next, Penelope and Charles, and in the next room the Farquhars. It seems impossible, quite out of the question, for all those people to have vanished. To have left no trace in this air.

Instead of saying any of that to Ben (of course she would not), Penelope says, "I do wonder how come Augustina's not around anymore. Her things were great, and she was so nice."

During their siesta Penelope has a most curious dream—in which she and Charles and Steven, Charles's beautiful boy, are all good friends, or perhaps she and Charles are the happy parents of Steven. The dream is vague, but there they are, the three of them—cornily enough, in a meadow of flowers. And, as Penelope awakes, the even cornier phrase, "Forgiveness flowers," appears somewhere at the edges of her mind.

Nevertheless, it seems a cheering, on the whole restorative dream, and she awakens refreshed, and cheered.

That night she and Ben walk into the town for dinner, a thing that she and Charles almost never did, and they find the town very much as it was: dingy, rutted, poorly lit streets leading toward the center, along which wary old men loiter, sometimes stopping to rest on the stoop of a darkened house, to smoke a cigarette, to stare at the night. Then stores, small and shabby at first, little groceries, ill-equipped drugstores, with timid souvenirs, faded postcards, cheap cosmetics. And then more light, larger and gaudier stores. More people. The same old mix of tourists, always instantly identifiable as non-Mexican. And Mexicans, mostly poor, some very poor, beggars, pitiful dark thin women, holding babies.

At their chosen, recommended restaurant, no table will be available for half an hour. And so Ben and Penelope go into the small, white, rather austere church that they have just passed.

A mass of some sort is going on; a white-robed priest is at the altar; everywhere there are white flowers. Penelope and Ben take back-row seats, and she watches as three little girls clamber all over their mother, who prays, paying them no heed. The girls and their mother wear churchgoing finery, black skirts and embroidered white shirts, and all the family's black hair is braided, beautifully. Whereas, the more Anglo-looking (less Indian) families in the church are dressed more or less as tourists are, in cotton skirts or pants, camp shirts, sandals.

Their dinner, in an attractive open court, is mildly pleasant. A subdued guitarist plays softly in one corner; there is a scent of flowers every-where.

"Do you really think we should marry?" Ben asks, at some point.

At which Penelope more or less bridles. "Well no, I'm not at all sure; did I say that I did—?"

He pauses, just slightly confused. "I didn't mean you had, but—well, I don't know."

She laughs, "You mean, not in Mexico."

He looks less nervous. "Oh, right." He laughs.

The next morning, very early, Ben says that he wants to swim. "Before those damn boats are around," he quite reasonably says. "You too?"

"I don't think so." What she wants is just to lie there for a while, savoring the Mexican dawn, just now visible between the drawn window draperies. "I'll come down in a little while."

"Leave the key in the blue sack, okay?"

Penelope lies there, deliciously, for ten or fifteen minutes. Ben will want to swim for close to an hour, she knows. She lies there, thinking of nothing—and then she puts on her bathing suit, a red bikini, puts the room key in the small blue airline bag, and starts down the path—down past the empty row of rooms where they all used to stay (it now seems very long ago), past Rosa's restaurant, and out onto the beach, where she leaves the bag with the key on a table beneath one of the palapas. And she steps out into the water, the marvel of cool, of freshness. She thinks she sees Ben's dark head, far out to sea, but what she sees could as easily be a buoy.

She swims for a while, fairly sure that dark head is indeed Ben's. She waves, and whoever it is waves back. Looking to shore, for the first time she notices a sign, TOURIST MARKET, and she wonders what that is. She heads back in, stands up, and starts walking out of the water, up onto the beach.

She is trying to remember which palapa table she put the bag on, and does not remember. She does not see the bright blue bag on any table.

And slowly it registers on Penelope's frightened consciousness that the bag is not there. Gone. No key to the room. At the same moment, the moment of realizing her loss, she sees an old man, a sort of beach bum, wrapped in something orange, rags, hobbling down the beach. And Penelope, wildly out of character, for her, now thinks, I have to run after him, I have to chase that old man, who must have my key. Whether I get it back or not, I have to run after him.

And she does. She starts off down the beach, running as best she can, but clumsily, in the deep dry sand.

She is unused to running, but the man ahead of her is very old. She is gaining on him when suddenly he veers off the beach, to the left, and into the Tourist Market. Where Penelope follows, not far behind.

Getting closer, she begins to shout, "Stop! Stop!"

The market is a row of booths, now mostly empty, so early in the morning, but here and there a solitary figure pauses, putting aside a broom or a dusting cloth, a crate—to observe this chase. Penelope imagines herself, as she must look: A tall blond skinny American woman in a red bikini, chasing after a poor old man, a derelict, hysterically shouting. Why should anyone help her?

But there, ahead of her, at the end of the row of rickety booths, to her surprise she sees the old man wheel and turn. He is standing there on one leg, a tattered old bird, maybe too tired to keep on running.

His dark, grizzled face is all twisted, one eye is gone, the skin closed over, and most of his teeth are gone. His mouth contorts, and the bright remaining black eye stares out at Penelope. A dying Aztec, she thinks. She thinks, *Mexico,* I should not have come back here.

Over one of the old man's shoulders a large old brown leather sack is slung, zippered up. In which there must be her blue bag. Her room key.

But what she (ridiculously) says is, "Did you happen to see my bag? on the table?"

"No—" His voice is tentative, querulous, but his eye is challenging, accusing, even. Perhaps it was not he who took her bag but someone else, earlier, while she was swimming.

Penelope finds no way to say, Open your sack up; let me see what you have inside. How could she?

She says again, "My blue bag, are you sure you didn't see it?"

"Yes." He turns from her.

Defeated, Penelope begins to walk back through the market booths, past a sort of workers' restaurant, just opening up, past more booths, with jewelry, scarves, leather—to the beach.

Where bearded Ben is getting out of the water. Shaking himself, like a dog.

He frowns a little at what Penelope tells him, but then he says, "Well, it's not too bad. We'll go up to the room, and you wait there while I go to the desk for another key. They should have given us two. As I said."

However, after the fifteen or twenty minutes that Penelope has been standing there in the hallway, outside their room, in the gathering heat of the day, Ben comes back to inform her that it is not so simple, after all. They don't *have* another key. Honestly, Mexico. Someone has gone to find the housekeeper. God knows how long that will take. It's Sunday, remember?

Since there is no existing key to their room—many keys have been lost, they are told, or simply not turned in—the only solution to a keyless room is for Penelope and Ben to move into another room. Which, once the housekeeper has been found (an hour or so) and their old room wrenched open, they finally do: with the help of several maids they repack and move all their clothes.

The new room is lower down, and smaller, with less of a view. Not as nice.

However, they are only here for two more days. Ben and Penelope, over their much-delayed breakfast, remind each other of this fact.

That old man with his rags, his toothless twisted mouth, and his one defiant eye is in Penelope's mind all that day, however. How angry he must have been, she thinks, if he opened the blue bag, expecting money, to find nothing but an old key.

And was it, after all, that old man who took the bag, or someone else, some other stroller on the beach who had vanished in another direction before Penelope got out of the water?

That night in the bar a young woman, another American whom they have seen around, with her fat young husband and two very fat small children, comes up to them to say, "Are you the guys who lost a blue flight bag, with your room key? My husband found it, in back of that Tourist Market, and he couldn't find anyone to claim it, so he turned it in at the restaurant there. Just go and tell them it's yours."

The next morning Penelope, dressed, sets out for the Tourist Market. She approaches it from a back road she knows that passes Rosa's and leads to the corner where she and the ragged old man confronted each other. Where now for a moment she pauses, imagining him, and she looks around, as though he might have come back and been lurking around. But of course he has not; there is only the road, and back of the road the yellowing jungle brush, in the beating Mexican sun. Penelope continues to the restaurant.

A pleasant-faced, plump young woman tells her, "Oh yes, your bag. Right here."

Penelope thanks her very much, gives her some pesos, and walks on with her bag, in which she can feel the room key, still there. And she thinks again of the old man, how angry he must have been to find only a key. Crazily, for a moment this seems to Penelope unfair; she even thinks of trying to find that old man, to give him some money— and she smiles to think of what Ben would make of that gesture, combining as it would two of her (to him) worst qualities: thriftlessness and "irrationality."

She continues through the booths, until she is stopped by a display of rings. She bends over, as always hoping for opals—and sees that there are several: opal rings of just the sort that she likes, the lovely stones with their fiery interiors.

A pretty Mexican woman in a yellow sweater, dark skirt, asks if she can help. These rings are about twenty-five dollars for two, but still so cheap! and so pretty. Penelope feels a great surge of happiness at having found them. The rings seem a good omen, somehow, though she is not sure of what: of this trip? that she was right, after all, to come back to Mexico, and to this particular place?

Negotiations with the young woman concluded, rings chosen and pesos paid, Penelope then asks her, on some whim, "Did you ever know a very nice woman who used to sell jewelry along the beach, named Augustina?"

"But I am Augustina!" *Yo soy Augustina.* The woman laughs, and the two of them embrace.

"Ah, amiga," says Augustina.

"I didn't recognize you; you always wore that white uniform," Penelope tells her. "I bought these rings from you!" and she shows Augustina her hand.

"Amiga, this time you come back very soon," Augustina says.

"Oh, I will. Very soon. Augustina, thank you." And with her rings, and the bag with its key, Penelope walks back to the hotel.

Their new room, she realizes as she goes out onto the balcony for a dry bathing suit, directly overlooks the old tier of rooms, where once she stayed with Charles, next door to the Farquhars.

On their last night in San Bartolomeo, Ben and Penelope have dinner in the hotel dining room, where, as always, the food is very bad—and the view magnificent; glittering black water, down through palm fronds. Stars, and a partial moon.

"Well, it's not the worst place I've ever been," is how Ben sums up their trip. Judiciously.

"It was really okay," Penelope tells her closest friend, a couple of days later, on the phone. "I'm glad we went. As a matter of fact, I hardly thought about Charles. He wasn't there." Then she laughs. "Actually I didn't think much about Ben either. I don't think he liked it very much there. But I thought a lot about Mexico." And then she adds, "But not thinking about Charles is the same as thinking about him all the time. If you see what I mean."

The friend does see.

"Anyway, the trip made me feel a lot better," Penelope continues. "About everything. More free." She adds, with a laugh, "I can't think why."

Great Sex

"And then of course there was, uh, great sex," says Sheila Williams, a young pediatrician, to her friend Alison Green. She is trying to explain the long presence in her life of a man who in many ways made her unhappy. Dick, a very smart, politically visible young lawyer, with whom she has just broken up. Dick is white, Sheila black. Small and neat and trim, from Roxbury, Massachusetts, Sheila is from a religious family, and tends to be somewhat prim; this conversation is unusual for her.

Alison is also young, although her long dark-blond hair, knotted up, is streaked with white. She edits a small art magazine, which does not take up a lot of her time. She is also an unmarried mother (Jennifer is four), which does take time. She has reacted to her friend's last remark, about great sex, in several ways: relief that Sheila is no longer seeing Dick, who sounds mean, and some surprise at the last phrase, "great sex"—that not being taken for granted by herself, or by anyone she knows. She further observes that "great sex" has become in some instances one word. "We had greatsex," some people say.

The two women are seated in a pretty, still-cheap French restaurant out on Geary Street, in San Francisco. Drinking white wine, as they wait for their dinner. They are long-term friends, with a shared Berkeley past, but busyness now prevents their seeing much of each other, and so their visits always have a catching-up quality; they discuss work, love affairs, Alison's daughter, and sometimes Sheila's two dogs—in a usually jumbled order; the categories overlap. Sheila, who is basically shy, reluctant as to personal revelation, has a lot to say about her work, which is at the San Francisco General Hospital and also involves the parents of her patients, most of whom are poor: black, Asian, or Hispanic. Some battered mothers. They do not ordinarily talk, Alison and Sheila, even generally about sex. It was unusual for Sheila to say what she had. But breaking up with Dick has made her more vulnerable, more open, perhaps.

Earlier they had been comparing their just-passed day; a bad one all around, they had agreed, bad for them both. Alison that morning had taken Jennifer to the airport, for a weekend in Santa Barbara with Alison's mother, the grandmother whom Jennifer adores. A friend of Alison's had been going there too and offered to escort Jennifer, who was thrilled at the whole prospect. But the planes were all delayed because of fog—planes to anywhere, Paris or Jakarta, Singapore or just Santa Barbara. Sheila had had terrible, terminal trouble with her car.

Nothing earthshaking for either of them, solvable problems, just annoying. Alison called and canceled her appointments, told her assistant to reschedule, and she finally put a very excited Jennifer on the plane. And Sheila called Triple-A for rescue, and in the meantime got a cab to her office.

But now, with the wine, Sheila's phrase about great sex begins to reverberate in Alison's brain. She has not been "seeing" anyone for at least a couple of years, and perhaps for that reason her mind returns to three instances of sex that was the greatest.

"Holy screwing," was how her first lover used to put it; he was a grad student at Berkeley, in mathematics; they smoked a great deal of pot together and made love effortlessly, wonderfully. Later, somehow, their connection fell apart, and he went East to a teaching job.

After that, graduated, Alison worked at part-time gallery jobs in San Francisco, and tried for journalism assignments. In that uncertain period of her life she fell in love with an older (twenty years older than she was) sculptor, semifamous, and with him too the sex was—great. An earthquake, with deeper aftershocks.

Out of bed they also got on well; much talk, many small jokes, and some glorious High Sierra hikes. They moved in together and planned to marry, "sometime, when we get around to it." But then he was killed, at the corner of Market and Franklin Streets, "senselessly," by a hit-and-run red-light runner, who was never caught but whom Alison, even now when she is "better," dreams of killing.

After that, for Alison there was hard work and some slow success— publication of articles in increasingly prestigious art magazines. And scattered, occasional love affairs. Sometimes great sex, sometimes not so great. And then, all inner wisdom notwithstanding, she fell in love with a man who was married—"happily," or at least comfortably enough, conveniently, so that he told her from the start that he could not, or would not, dislodge himself. Besides, there were three children. But with him, once more, there was holy, earthquake sex. She liked him very much, and he her. He worked in Washington, D.C., in an environmental agency, and often came to San Francisco—sometimes alone, sometimes not. Seeing each other was often difficult, but for a time they managed. Alison lived on Potrero Hill, conveniently near the freeway. And even an hour together was worth anything, they felt.

When Alison became pregnant, Jack was sympathetic: bad luck, he saw it as, and of course she would have an abortion. Of course he would pay, and he would do everything possible, supportively.

But Alison could not. She had had one abortion, the result of carelessness during a somewhat feckless affair. She had voted and marched for women's right to choice. But this time she could not, not possibly. Jack quite reasonably argued that he too should have a choice, since the baby was also his—and Alison saw that this was true. Still, she had to go ahead with this pregnancy. And she did, and lovely Jennifer was born; sometimes Alison even thought that she had somehow known that this baby would be *Jennifer,* so beautiful, so loved.

Sheila, her friend, just then starting in pediatrics, became their doctor.

Now Sheila, really out of character, is still talking about great sex. And Dick, the man she no longer sees, who was an ungiving, emotionally stunted person, as Sheila had always known. "Sometimes I thought he got some sort of charge out of having a black girlfriend," Sheila said. "A liberal credential. *So* correct. But there were other sides to him. Moments of kindness, generosity, and these flashes of amazing insight. Enough of all that to make me stick around. What I'm saying is, he's not all bad." Sheila laughs, but her dark-brown eyes are wide and serious.

"We're supposed to think that no one is, aren't we?" Alison laughs too.

The waiter brings their food; they seem to have ordered a lot.

Somewhat later Sheila more or less continues. "I think it's these moments of nice, of goodness, that all men have, or almost all, and that's what keeps us around. We all think that that's the real person. That what we're seeing is a window into who he really is." She adds, "I mean it's one of the things. With really battered women of course there's also fear, no self-esteem, and often no money."

"Oh, you're right," Alison tells her. She is struck by what sounds wise and accurate, although she herself has not experienced much meanness from men.

"Battered women," Sheila now says. "People think, or some people think, they hang around for sex, but it's not that, mostly. I was always hoping that Dick would turn into the person I sometimes saw."

Alison finds herself very moved by the fact of Sheila saying all this; it is so unlike her to talk of intimate matters in this way. She is in fact more moved by Sheila herself than by what Sheila is saying, although she sees its truth. But possibly, also, Sheila is theorizing in part as a way out of pain?

Sheila now asks Alison, "You've got plans for your childless weekend?"

"I've got to work," Alison grins. "Probably I should have planned more." And indeed she should have, she now thinks. She is unused to weekends without Jennifer; it is not as though she had longed for such unfettered time.

The somewhat antiquated or at least other-era impression made by this restaurant, with its worn white linen tablecloths, white ruffled curtains, and fake white daisies in the decorative fake-brick windows—all that is increased by the music, which is thirties and forties; at the moment Charles Trenet is singing, "Vous—qui passez sans me voir—"

The room at this hour, about eight, is filling up. Alison, absorbed in their conversation, and then her food, has not paid much attention to the other guests.

But she looks up just in time to see a new couple come in, a short plump woman in black, a tall thin man with familiar shoulders. They come in slowly, as though in a horror film. Alison's own oft-imagined worst dream: Jack and his wife. At the instant in which she recognizes him he turns and sees her, and starts toward their table. As his wife, long bright blond hair swinging, goes on to a table across the room.

Smiling widely, as Alison also is, he arrives. He bends toward her—

can he have meant to exchange a social kiss? Alison extends her hand, as she says, "How nice to see you. You remember Sheila?"

"Yes of course." He shakes hands with Sheila too, and says, "Nice place!"

They have been there together several times.

"Oh, very."

"Well, uh, everything okay?"

He must be asking, Is Jennifer okay? Alison nods, and then he is gone, and Alison feels the crocodile smile which has stretched her face recede.

She looks down at all the food on her plate, says, "I can't eat this," and she adds, "Oddly enough," with a very small laugh.

"Of course not." Understanding Sheila. "Take some deep breaths."

Alison does breathe deeply, managing too to glance across the room. At her. And she thinks, I'm prettier than she is. An out-of-character thought: Alison is not especially vain, nor for that matter is *pretty* the word for her, as she knows. She is often described as attractive, tall and thin, with an interesting, angular face. Good bones. But Jack's wife is too old for her very bright long blond hair, and too plump for her very short black dress.

Sheila, who has also managed a look, now whispers, "Could it be a wig?"

Alison laughs softly. "I suppose, but I doubt it." She adds, "Jesus, the end of a perfect day."

Four years ago—or five by now, it must be five—when Alison was pregnant, she and Jack quarreled a lot, and each said melodramatic, bad things to the other.

"You're ruining your life—"

"It's my life, you're completely insensitive—"

"You're crazy—hysterical—you have no sense—"

"I never want to see you again—just stay away—"

Since then, and since Jennifer's birth, there has been a polite, some-what stilted, occasional exchange of notes—Alison's sent to Jack's office, of course, as in fact her notes always were. For a while he sent money, checks that in her high pride Alison never cashed. Besides, by then she was doing pretty well on her own. The magazine, though tiny, paid her a good salary; its backer needed the tax loss. And she sold more and more articles.

Jack had never asked to visit, although she assumed that he still came to San Francisco from time to time.

Now Alison asks Sheila, "What shall we do with all this food? Would your dogs eat it?"

"No, the bones are too small. We'll have the waiter wrap it and we can leave it in a package for some homeless person."

That night Alison's sleep is broken, very troubled. She is plagued with dreams that vanish at the slightest touch of her conscious mind. She believes that Jack has been the focus of these dreams, but she is not entirely sure; nothing is clear. And when in her waking mind she thinks of him, his image is confused, as possibly it always was. There is the sensual memory of him, his weight, his bones crushing into hers, the hot smooth skin of his back, in her clutching hands. And then there is the loud-voiced angry Jack, who insists that she have an abortion. She finds, though, still another man, Jack the kind and super-intelligent good friend, with whom for hours she discussed almost everything in life—the environment; their childhoods; Bosnia, Zaire, and Haiti; Jack's relations with the Sierra Club and other local environmentalists; Alison's magazine; local painters. And sometimes, even, their own connection (both disliked the word *relationship*). They alternated between celebration (it was so good; they cared so much for each other) and sadness (it was necessarily limited; they could not, for instance, travel together, or, more to the point, live together).

Alison thinks too of what Sheila was saying, describing those windows of niceness that keep even battered women going (Did even O.J. have moments of niceness? she wonders). As she stuck around with a man who meant to and probably would stay married, for whatever responsible, guilty reasons of his own.

She wonders, What will I do when he calls tomorrow, as he most likely will? She thinks, At least Jennifer's out of town, I don't have to lie about that.

. . .

At breakfast, raw with sleeplessness, she decides to spend as much of the day as she can on a long city walk. When Jack calls, her answering machine will pick it up, and she can do as she likes. She does walk, in the bright cool windy day, fog lingering on all the horizons of the city. Perfect for walking. She hikes down to the Embarcadero, and along all that way to the Ferry Building, past the new incongruous row of palms, and the old decaying empty wharves.

When she gets home, having walked for a couple of hours, she finds no messages, not one on her machine. Digesting what feels like keen disappointment, not relief, she simply stands there in her kitchen for a moment, looking out to her view of the Bay Bridge, the bay, and Oakland hills. And the Embarcadero, where she just was.

The phone rings. She hesitates, answers on the third sound.

Jack. After a polite exchange of greetings, he says, "In a way I'm sorry about last night. I hope you weren't as shaken up as I was. But you know, I've wanted to see you. To be more in touch. And Jennifer—"

Some honest quality of pain in his voice is very moving to Alison; it was good of him to say that he was upset. She tells him, "I'm really sorry, Jennifer's down in Santa Barbara with my mother."

A long pause before he says, "Could I just see you for a little? I really want to."

She too pauses, and then says, "In an hour. I've just got back from a walk. I have to take a shower."

As he comes into her living room, and they shake hands—again, Alison observes what she had almost forgotten: that Jack is rather shy, and his glasses tend to slip down his longish nose. He is very tall, his posture bad, and he is still too thin.

He says, "You're really nice to let me—"

"Well, of course—"

"No, not of course—"

Both wearing their shy smiles, they sit down at opposite ends of her sofa (as they have before). Alison tells him, "Jennifer. I'm sorry she's not here; a friend was going to Santa Barbara for the weekend, Susan, I don't think you met her. And it seemed such a good chance for Jennifer, she likes Susan and she really loves her grandmother, and she thinks Santa Barbara is great, the beach and all—"

She is babbling to stave off the sudden and unaccountable tears that threaten her eyes, and her voice. Alison realizes this, but she is afraid to stop. She adds, "She's really nice—"

Looking at her with his slow shy smile, Jack says, "Of course she is."

"Well, tell me how your work's going! You're still happy in Washington, and mad at most of the Bureau?"

"Well, yes and no."

He talks for a while, and Alison does not hear a word he says, as she thinks, He's a very nice man; he really is. It wasn't "just sex," whatever that means. I think we can be friends, and he can come and see Jennifer sometimes. *Friends.* And I'm not going to cry, and we won't make love.

But Alison is wrong.

After she has made tea, Twinings English Breakfast, which they drink, and after a lot more civilized conversation, Jack gets up to go, and as, staring at her with his very dark, myopic, and beautiful hazel eyes, he starts to say good-bye, Alison distinctly hears the smallest catch in his voice, and she sees the effort at control that he makes.

Which is just enough, at last, to set off her tears—a minute before he truly meant to leave.

Jack puts his arms around her, intending comfort, friendliness, but it does not work out that way.

They begin to kiss, and minutes later they have moved to Alison's bedroom, where, on her bed, once more, they have great—the greatest sex.

Raccoons

Every evening, despairingly, Mary Alexander, a former actress, puts out tin bowls of food for Linda, her cat, who is lost: stolen, starving somewhere, locked in a strange garage—maybe dead. In any case, gone. And every morning, on the deck of her small house in Larkspur, California, Mary examines the bowls and sees that nothing is gone, and her heart seems to shrink within her, her blood to chill. Out there among all the pots of luxuriant roses, bright geraniums, and climbing, profusely flowering bougainvillea, Mary looks blindly at all that color, that bloom, and at her pretty house, in the rare fine August sunlight, and she mourns for Linda; she is inhabited, permeated with loss. She takes in the plates and washes them off; she makes and eats her own breakfast, and then goes out for a walk. She spends the day in an effort to pull herself together, as she looks and looks, and calls and calls for Linda. And then at night she puts out the food again, and she waits, and hopes. For lovely Linda, who is as beautiful and as shy as a little fox.

This is very neurotic, Mary lectures herself, rather in the voice of her very helpful former shrink, a gentle, kindly, and most courteous man from Louisiana, who spoke in those attractive accents, and whose sternest chiding was, "That's just plain neurotic." And he would smile, acknowledging that they both already knew she was neurotic; that very likely most people are, including himself.

For comfort, Mary sometimes thinks of a man she considers the least neurotic among her friends: Bill, a biologist. Internationally known, he goes to conferences all over; he does a lot of work in Africa on AIDS. Bill is absolutely devoted to Alison, his wife, herself a distinguished watercolorist. Bill is also intensely attached to Henry, their cat. Once, in fact (this is the memory from which Mary takes comfort), Henry was reported missing by their housesitter; Bill and Alison were on a rare vacation in Paris. Many transatlantic phone calls ensued; Bill was almost on the plane to come back from Paris, to walk every block of their San Francisco neighborhood—when, of course, Henry strolled into their house, insouciant and dirty. But Bill, this internationally famous scientist, had been poised to cut short a trip with his much-loved wife, to come home from Paris to look for Henry, his cat. All of which now makes Mary feel a little less crazy, less "neurotic," but no less sad.

Mary's own life, viewed by any friend or acquaintance, would be judged comparatively rich, and in many ways successful. Early days in New York included occasional Broadway parts, some off-Broadway, and mostly good reviews. Too little money, usually, and too many (but generally good) love affairs. Then the move to San Francisco, the Actors Workshop, and ACT, plus some TV ad work, boring but well paid. More love affairs, some of which became rewarding friendships. Even now, at what she herself considers an advanced age, there is a man with whom she sometimes sleeps (Mary much dislikes the phrase *to have sex,* but they do), a man of whom she is most extremely fond (which surely beats being in love, has been Mary's conclusion). They would see each other more, except that he has a very mean, vindictive lawyer wife; it is not all perfect, but then, what is? In any case, Mary's life does not fit the stereotype of the lonely old woman whose only companion is her cat.

Mary was never beautiful; as a very young woman she was too thin, almost gaunt, with a long thin nose, a wide and sensual mouth. But she was both intelligent and talented, capable of projecting passion, irony, and humor, qualities that she could be said to contain within herself. Her friends, including fellow actors, generally liked her, and several men loved her extremely.

Aging is easier, somewhat, for a not-beautiful actress, Mary has thought; critics are less apt to point out that you are not as young as formerly. But this must be true for all women, not only those in her own narcissistic profession? You do not suddenly observe that heads are not turning, if few or any ever did. These days Mary could have more TV ad work than she does, if she would accept more happy-grandmother shots. The problem is that her capacity for tolerating boredom has diminished, she finds. She can no longer endure certain endless hours before hot cameras—as she can no longer listen raptly at dull dinner parties. She cannot escape into steamy trash fiction as she once did, in dressing rooms, awaiting calls. (She has lately been rereading Colette, and has recently discovered Carl Hiassen, who makes her laugh aloud.) The move from San Francisco up to Larkspur constituted a sort of retirement; she lives mostly on residuals, a little stock. She believes that she lives fairly well, with Linda.

Still, certain things have happened, inevitably, to her face and body that she does not like, and cannot much change. Mostly she objects to dry skin, and increasing fatigue.

Mary has—or she used to have, with Linda—certain small rituals. Rituals of love and intimacy, you might say. One was that whenever Mary went upstairs, Linda would race ahead of her, and then stop and lie across a step, in Mary's way, so that Mary had to stop. And to pet Linda, to scratch her beautiful yellow stomach as Linda stretched along the step. They always did this, and now, as Mary walks up the stairs alone and unimpeded, she misses Linda as acutely as she has ever missed a lover, and she thinks, in somewhat the same way as she used to think, He's gone!

So that now she thinks, I must be truly mad. All this about a pretty little cat? I carry on as though it were a major love affair?

Linda now has been gone for five days, and nights. Mary continues her nightly routine of putting food out on the deck and bringing in the untouched dishes in the morning. Washing them out.

Getting through the days.

And then one night, as she lies upstairs in bed, alone, she hears from down on her deck the rattle of tin plates—her plates, with Linda's food. *Linda!* In an instant she grabs up a robe, shoves her feet into slippers; she runs downstairs and flicks off the burglar alarm. She rushes to the french doors that lead to the deck. Where she sees, to her horror, three raccoons. Two large, one smaller, all with their round black staring unfrightened eyes and their horrible bent clawed feet. At times Mary has argued that raccoons are cute, nice little visitors at picnics. But tonight she sees that they are hideous intruders, feral and dangerous, fearsome.

She is afraid that if she opens the door they will run in, searching for more food (they have eaten all of Linda's), and so she only bangs on the glass, afraid too that it will break, and she will be defenseless. But the raccoons, having eaten, now leave, loping, ungainly on their short legs and ugly feet, back across the deck.

Very slowly Mary goes upstairs, and gets back into bed.

Raccoons attack cats; they sometimes hurt or kill them. Everyone says that.

Mary gets up, and in her bathroom she takes a tranquilizer, then gets into bed again.

She lies there, coping as best she can with the probable fact of Linda's death (later she does not understand how she did this). Linda must be dead, killed by horrendously ugly, murderous raccoons; if not those, some others, equally hideous. Mary only hopes that it was quick, as one hopes for air-crash victims. Poor crazy fearful Linda could well have died of fright before she was hurt, Mary thinks.

She tries to sleep, and at last she does, and she wakes in the morning very calm, and much, much more sad.

And although she has more or less accepted the fact of Linda's death, she continues in a minor way to look for her, and she still puts out the food.

"What you need is another cat," the few friends in whom she has confided begin to say, and in theory Mary agrees; she does need another cat.

One day (it is now September, Linda gone for a week) the sun comes out earlier than usual, burning through fog and leaving only a few white mists that hang above the tall dark trees, above the town of Larkspur. Mount Tamalpais is sharp and clear, less distant, more inviting. And Mary's mail comes earlier than usual, just before lunch. In it there is a check that she has been owed and has needed for some time, from her agent in L.A. These are all good signs, she thinks; Mary has certain unvoiceable, eccentric superstitions. Perhaps this should be the day when she goes to the animal shelter and finds a new beautiful cat.

She cannot resist the further superstitious thought that *maybe* getting a new cat will bring Linda magically home to her, rather in the way that couples with a fertility problem at last adopt, and then become pregnant.

In the animal shelter, which is encouragingly clean, well kept up, and staffed by very nice and cheerful young women, Mary looks through the rows of cages, all containing cats with one or another sort of appeal, any one of whom she would no doubt in time learn to love. But no cat there is as beautiful as Linda is (or was); there is no one whom she instantly, totally loves. In the last cage, though (of course the last), there is a thin, lithe, graceful gray cat named Fiona—to Mary an appealing name; years ago she had a friend, an English actress, Fiona Shaw (just as she once had a friend named Linda, years back). A small typed notice states that Fiona has just been spayed; she is fine, but not quite ready for adoption—a few days more. Mary watches Fiona for a little while; she is an exceptionally pretty little cat, shy and graceful. (And if Linda *should* come back, they might get along?)

On the way home Mary sees some new neighbors, a nice young couple, both architects, who have heard and been kind and sympathetic over Linda.

"I saw this very pretty cat in the shelter," Mary tells them. "A small gray one. She's named Fiona."

Almost in unison they say, "But Linda might come—"

"No," Mary tells them, very firmly. "The raccoons got her. They must have."

At which the young man frowns. "I've seen a couple around. Mean-looking little bastards."

And the woman, "I think they're sweet. And I could have sworn I heard a cat outside last night."

"Well, you'll have to come for tea very soon and meet Fiona," Mary tells them.

Every return to her house, which now does not contain Linda, is sad for Mary, and as she walks in, the raccoons now return to her mind, unbidden; she sees them vividly again, their hideous claws and their small mean shining eyes. Firmly she forces herself instead to imagine pretty Fiona as she walks through her house to the deck, and down the steps to her garden.

Where she is just in time to see a flash of brown fur, a plumey tail—Linda!—who tears across the grass and into Mary's basement, which contains a clutter of broken, discarded furniture, empty boxes, old luggage. Where Linda instantly hides herself.

The basement entrance is wide, with no door; there is no way to block it off, to prevent a bolting Linda—except for Mary herself to stand across it, or to sit down, as she does, and to stretch her legs across the opening.

But was that really Linda, that flash of fur? Mary begins to doubt her own vision. Could it, God forbid, have been a raccoon?

Raccoons

In her softest, most caressing voice she calls to Linda; she calls and calls, a stream of loving syllables that Linda must know (if cats know anything) and always her name. "Linda, Linda-loo, lovely Linda—" On and on, with no answer.

She would like to go upstairs and phone the nice neighbors for help; she could block the escape route while they went in and banged around, but she does not dare leave. She would also like a glass of water. But she has to go on. "Linda, loopy Lou, Linda-pie—" On forever.

At last, after maybe ten minutes, there is a sort of rattling among the boxes; an old broken bamboo table moves, so that Mary sees a glimpse, a quick tiny glimpse, of what is surely Linda.

After another five minutes, probably, of calling, and of small but increasingly certain sighting, Linda emerges into a small cleared space, a safe twenty feet from where Mary sits. Linda emerges, she stares, and retreats.

She repeats all that several times, each time flicking her tail, back, forth.

And then she emerges into another, smaller space, about ten feet from Mary. Looking at Mary, she rolls over—the first sure friendly signal, or even acknowledgment that she has ever seen Mary before. She does this three or four times, each time somehow managing to roll though still poised for flight.

And so Mary does not reach out to grab her, restraining herself until she is absolutely sure of reaching and grasping Linda. Which at last she successfully does, with a firm, strong, loving, and furious grip.

"You rotten little slut, where in God's name have you been, you little bitch?" She whispers these harsh new words, rising and clutching Linda, who is struggling hysterically to get away—away from this sudden stranger who has seized her unawares.

But this time Mary wins. She carries fighting Linda out of the basement, up the stairs, and across the deck and into her house.

Dumping her onto the rug she asks, "Oh Linda, how come you're so *crazy*?" and, again, "Where on earth have you *been*?"

No answer.

And Linda, in character, runs off and hides. She does not even seem very hungry, nor does she have the look of a starving lost cat. She has obviously done well for herself, but Mary will never know where, or how.

Or *why.* Mary pours herself a glass of white wine and collapses on the old chintz sofa, thinking, God*damn* Linda, anyway.

How much, or what, do cats remember? Can anyone comprehend at all the memory of a cat? Over the next few days Mary wonders and ponders these questions, sometimes staring into the round yellow eyes of Linda as though there might be a clue. As though Linda knew.

She considers too the fact that both she and her friend Bill the biologist have chosen cats of their own gender for major loves. Could this mean that love of one's cat is really love of one's self? Was it she herself who she feared was lost and hungry, possibly dead?

At other times she simply holds her hands around that small warm vibrant body, the delicate strong rib cage and the drum-tight rounded belly, and she thinks, and she says aloud, "You're home, darling Linda. You came *home.*"

Mary has had the wit not to talk much to her friends about the loss of Linda, and so now she does not make much of her return. Only to her sometime lover, who is also in a way her closest friend, she confides, "I'm embarrassed, really, when I think how upset I was. And that night when I was sure the raccoons had got her, well—"

"Mary dear, you were great," he says. As he might have said, as people did say, of some performance of hers, which, come to think of it, in a public way it had been. No one really knew that for Mary the loss of Linda had been the end of the world, or nearly. None of her friends or her lover knew that she would have sacrificed any or all of them for her cat.

Or at least at moments she would have.

Soon after Linda's return there is a small dinner party for some visiting old friends from New York, and at which Mary very much enjoys the sort of theatre gossip that she is used to: "But Maria's always great. . . . I hear Edward's new play is even better. . . . Poor Colin is really sick. . . . No, Gilbert's still okay . . . they are not getting a divorce . . . the problem was that she loathed L.A. . . . I must say, you're looking wonderful. . . ." She comes home in a mood of slightly wistful but pleasant nostalgia. She goes upstairs and finds Linda, as usual, curled on the foot of her bed. She pats Linda, who looks up, blinks, purrs briefly, and goes back to sleep. Soon Mary too is sound asleep.

She wakes an hour or so later, and at first she thinks, I should never have had that last glass of wine, I didn't need it. I know I can't drink red. But then she hears a scratching, rustling sound on her deck, which may have been what woke her up.

She gets out of bed, slowly puts on slippers and robe, noting as she passes that Linda is not there. She goes downstairs, flicks on lights—and there on her deck, lined up, are four raccoons, one large, three smaller. They keep a certain distance, and perhaps for that reason are not quite as threatening as they were before. They look both formal and expectant; they could be either judges or penitents—impossible to tell. Or, they could be asking for Linda. Demanding Linda?

Mary turns off the lights and goes back upstairs, where she does not find Linda anywhere in her bedroom; she even looks under the bed. She spends an anxious half hour or so in this search for Linda, at this ungodly hour, at the same time telling herself that this is ridiculous. There is no way that Linda could have gotten out; all the doors are locked, her bedroom window is only opened a crack. She also thinks: I cannot go through this again, I really can't—as she calls out softly, "Linda, darling Linda, where are you?"

She at last finds Linda asleep on the studio couch in her study, a not unlikely place for her to be, though more usual in the daytime. As Mary approaches, Linda wakes and raises her head; she blinks and looks at Mary as though to say, This is the middle of the night; I was sleeping here quietly. What is your problem?

The next night, after feeding Linda, Mary is moved to put out a little food for raccoons, really for whatever creature wants it. She puts a little plate of dried kibble and one of water down in the garden, where she cannot hear if the plates are rattled.

And whether the impulse that moved her is one of simply nurturing or of a more complex propitiation, or some dark exorcism, Mary has no idea.

Old Love Affairs

Mildly upset by a phone call, Lucretia Baine, who is almost old but lively, comes back into her living room and stares for a moment into the large white driftwood-framed mirror there, as though to check that she is still herself. Reassured, she smiles briefly, but continues to look at the mirror. In the soft, kindly lamplight—this is an early evening, in October—she is beautiful, still, even to her own harshly critical (large, green) eyes. But she knows perfectly well how she looks in her cruelly accurate bathroom mirror, first thing in the morning. Now, though, she looks all right, just upset; on the other hand, she may look better than usual. A little more color?

The disturbing call did not involve bad news; it was simply that Lucretia momentarily confused two men: Simon, whom she is crazy about (hopelessly, irreversibly, it seems), with Burt, who in his way is crazy about her. He loves Lucretia permanently, he says. Burt called, and just for an instant she thought he was Simon. Although she would have thought that two men more unlike did not exist, including their voices: Burt's deep and friendly, Midwestern, and Simon's very New England, Cambridge, slightly raspy.

"Crazy about." Like many people, Lucretia tends to think in the argot of her youth, in her case the forties. However, in this instance, the instance of Simon, the phrase seems accurate. At her age, to harbor such feelings is crazy indeed, and so, for that matter, are Burt's feelings for her, at his advanced age. Lucretia sighs. If only Simon were gay and in love with Burt the circle would be perfect, Shakespearean, she thinks. She sighs again, at what seems the silliness of it all. Simon is not gay, and the two men have never met. And she only confused their voices because she was expecting a call from Simon, sort of.

She did not do anything so crude as calling Burt "Simon"; she was only a little cool at the onset of the conversation, cool with disappointment. But then poor Burt was probably used to cool, from her.

This living room of Lucretia's, though comfortable and exceptionally pretty, too often called "charming," in a sense resembles an archaeological dig; there are layers, and remains. Traces of former husbands, three of them, two divorced, one dead. Tokens and presents from former lovers, quite a few of those, and from good friends, even more. And clear signs of a long and steadfast career: Lucretia is a reporter, a dedicated newspaperwoman. She has always worked in that way. The driftwood mirror is, in fact, a present from her longtime editor, now an elderly gentleman, who is gay—a much-loved friend; Lucretia is less sure how she feels about the mirror.

Thus the room, which has never exactly been "decorated," is full of trophies, of carefully, tastefully selected objects, and of whimsically, impulsively bought *things*. A jumble of books and pictures, lots of framed photographs; anyone can see that Lucretia, young, was quite ravishing, and that most of the men she knew were tall and good-looking. Pots and vases of flowers stand about, more carefully arranged than they look to be: a great clump of growing gold chrysanthemums, smelling of earth, and of fall—and a slender silver vase of yellow roses, unscented but beautiful, chosen by Lucretia, for herself. She sometimes wonders how she could feel lonely in such a room, and, for that matter, in such a house, but sometimes she does.

Souvenirs, then, of love and friendship, but also of work. Lucretia has done a lot of travel writing for many years, as the assistant travel editor of her paper; shelves of travel books, as well as atlases and stacks of maps, attest to those years, along with one wall's collection of masks, from Mexico and from Haiti, from India and Africa and Egypt. For idle pleasure Lucretia sometimes picks up a map of Italy, say, and goes over it carefully, naming out favorite towns to herself: Orvieto, Todi, Arezzo, Fiesole, as another person might read a familiar novel, happy to recognize Barsetshire again.

She was working throughout all those marriages and love affairs, which no doubt kept her sane (she herself is sure of this), but these days her work creates certain problems in "relationships" when the men involved are retired, as Burt is—Burt especially, demanding, intrusive (more "in love"), does not like to hear about Lucretia's deadlines, her work obligations. He has often suggested that she retire. What he means is, marry him. But Lucretia plans to postpone retirement for as long as she can, and in the meantime to take whatever assignments the paper offers. She has gone back lately to doing more interviews than travel writing, although last December she wrote a long piece about Christmas in Venice, lights in the Piazza San Marco, processions of gondolas. Extremely handsome gondoliers.

Lucretia's first marriage took place when she was eighteen. There should be a law against marriages under thirty, she has sometimes thought, and said. Surely under twenty, and probably twenty-five. Jim, the young husband, was in law school; her second, Tommy, a reporter. Years later, speaking of marriage, she also said, "I married the first two times for sex. How dumb can you get?" Sometimes adding, "Tommy was dear, well, really they both were, Tommy and Jim. But Tommy drank so much, and besides, I really needed to get out of Boston."

She divorced poor, dear Tommy in Reno, and continued to San Francisco, where, with some money from a grandmother who providentially died around that time, she bought a small house in an alley on Telegraph Hill—with such a view! And she got a job on the *Examiner.*

There then followed for Lucretia many happy years. Telegraph Hill and, indeed, the whole city were seemingly full of the relatively young and unmarried. There was great cheap Italian food and wine in North Beach restaurants, and great cheap Chinese along Grant Avenue, Chinatown, with wonderful jazz at the Blackhawk, the Jazz Workshop. And good bars all over the place. Not to mention the prettily romantic city itself, a perfect backdrop. Lucretia had quite a few very pleasant but not serious love affairs; to herself, she thought, Well, good, I'm beginning to take sex not quite so seriously; it's just very good, very affectionate fun.

Sometimes, though, she was assailed by much darker thoughts, one of which persistently was: I'm really too old for all this silliness; my friends are doing serious things like bringing up children. (In those days thirty-five was viewed as too old for almost anything, including love affairs and certainly children.) Also, the fact was that she still did take sex seriously. Her affairs were never so casual as she tried to make herself believe; she sometimes suffered extreme pangs of missing whoever was just gone. Pangs of longing to hear from someone who did not phone. (In those days women were not supposed to telephone men.)

In those blacker moods Lucretia tended to forget her own considerable professional success. She was extremely good at her work; she had won citations and prizes, along with the occasional raise. And she liked it very much, especially the interviews, which she was more and more frequently assigned. She liked the work and mostly she liked her fellow reporters. But as she waited for her phone to ring, waited for *him* to call, she forgot all that.

Jason was first described by Lucretia to her friends as "this terribly nice man who lives next door." A tall, skinny young (her age) architect from Tennessee, Jason had a serious girlfriend, Sally, who was not around much. Jason and Lucretia went to movies at the Palace and to the New Pisa for long, half-drunken dinners together; when she broke up with whomever, Jason was always comforting. And she was nice to him, making homey meals and listening a lot when he broke up with Sally, although by then Lucretia was seeing someone else.

By the time they fell in love and decided to marry, Jason and Lucretia had been friends for several years. So sometimes she wondered, Why didn't I know all along how I felt about Jason? Why did we waste all that time?

In both earlier marriages, to Jim and then to Tommy, sex had been the greatest bond. Especially with Tommy, a true sexual explorer, an inspired and tender lover—when sober. But then, he was so often drunk. With Jason, after the early raptures of mutual discovery, when in effect they both said, "You've been here all along, and I didn't *know*?—after some months of that, the sexual energy between them seemed to taper off to a twice-a-week nice treat. Lucretia often felt that she was more enthusiastic than Jason was, that perhaps she was basically a sexier person, which she found a little embarrassing, although she still liked Jason better than anyone in the world. And for the three years of their marriage they were mostly happy, both busy with separate work, and enjoying vacation trips together.

Then, cruelly, Jason, who was still a relatively young man, was diagnosed with colon cancer. Invasive. Inoperable. But he took a long time dying, poor darling; near the end Lucretia moved him down to the living room, where he could see the friends he still wanted to see, and she could more easily bring him trays. He complained sometimes about sleeping down there alone, and so Lucretia would cuddle against him, there on the couch.

Unhappily, that is what she most clearly recalled of Jason, his dying. How pitifully thin he was, his eyes so huge and needful. His bony hands. She remembered less of his good jokes and general good sense. Their trips. Lovely Italian wine and, at times, good sex.

Mourning Jason, a truly loved and irreplaceable friend, Lucretia mourned, too, what she felt to be the end of love in her life. By that time she was in her early fifties; even to think of love affairs was ridiculous, despite what she read here and there. And so she did something very ridiculous, or worse: she fell violently in love with a man almost twenty years younger than she was, a beautiful Italian, Silvio. Not only twenty years younger but married, and a Catholic, of course.

Oddly enough, it was he who loved first. Or he who said it first, pressing her fingers as they held a wineglass, at lunch, in Fiesole. Looking up at him, she saw him laugh in a slightly embarrassed way as he said, "You mustn't laugh, although it is a little funny. But I find myself seriously in love with you."

She did not laugh, but she smiled as she said, "Oh Silvio, come on—" even as her heart began to race, her blood to surge forward.

She was aware that they looked a little alike, she and Silvio, a northern blond; some people must think them mother and son. Many people must think that.

Lucretia was staying at a small hotel on the Arno, not far from Harry's Bar; she had a penthouse room, with a lovely view of the river. From her balcony, in early evenings, she observed the long ovals formed by the bridges and their reflections in the water. She and Silvio had drinks there the first night he came to call, quite properly, to take her to Harry's for dinner. He was the friend of a friend; his wife and children were off at Viareggio. After they became lovers, they had drinks on that terrace every night.

"You have the most marvelous skin in the world," he told her. "Your back, and here. Like hot velvet." He laughed. "My poor English. I sound like the TV."

"Your English is fine."

"You are fine. However can I let you go?"

But he did. They let each other go at the end of Lucretia's two weeks: a week of exploratory friendship, another of perfect love. Or, vividly recalled by Lucretia in San Francisco, that is what it seemed, all perfect. Beautiful, sexy Silvio made love to her repeatedly, over and over, at night, and then again in the morning, before driving off to his own house across the river. Just love and sex; they never spoke of anything foolish and alien, like divorce. Only, once or twice Silvio asked her, "If I should come to San Francisco, you will remember?"

She laughed at him. "Always, my darling." She feared that that would indeed be true. And she thought, Suppose he calls when I'm really old, too old to see him again, although I still remember? (She forgot that at that time he, too, would be much older.)

In her pretty Telegraph Hill cottage, then, with the doleful sound of foghorns strained through her dreams, Lucretia often woke to a painful lack of Silvio, a missing of him that was especially sexual. And none of the obvious solutions to this crying need appealed to her at all. Only Silvio would do, and at times, at the worst and most painful predawn hours, she thought of flying back to Italy. To Florence, where she would say to Silvio what seemed at the moment to be true: I can't live without you.

Of course, she could and did live without him, and all the prescribed cures worked. She joined a health club and exercised fiercely; she walked whenever and for as long as she could. She intensified her efforts at work; she took on more assignments. And she thought, Well, that will have to be that. Enough of sex and love. I've surely had my share, and maybe more. Except that every now and then she would read some tantalizing, romantic account of a woman even older than she was falling in love, getting married. Or an article about the sexual needs and activities of the old, "Geriatric Sex." Lucretia's very blood would warm and flare, and she would think, Well, maybe. Even as a more sensible voice within would warn her, Oh, come *on*.

"He's not exactly your type, but he's nice," said a friend, by way of introducing Burt McElroy into her life. "He's dying to meet you."

"Good Lord, why?"

"Oh, don't be like that. You're sort of famous here, and he likes blonds. His wife was blond."

"Old blonds."

"His wife was older than you. They were married forever."

"I just don't feel like meeting anyone. I've given up all that stuff. Or maybe it's given me up."

"Well, just come for dinner. I won't lock you up in a closet together or anything." She added, "He was a trial lawyer. Now retired."

The lawyer, Burt McElroy, was a very large man, at least six three, and heavy. Thick white hair and small bright-blue eyes, a big white beard. Jolly, at first glance, but on second not jolly at all—in fact, somewhat severe. Censorious. And a little sad.

At dinner that first night, at the house of the friend, Burt talked considerably about his wife, and a music foundation that he was establishing in her honor; apparently she had been a noted cellist. As he spoke of this dead woman, this Laura, Burt often looked at Lucretia, and she understood that he was announcing his feelings: I will never be really untrue to Laura.

And so she laughed, and was flirtatious with him; she, in her way, was saying, "Look, don't worry, I'll never be serious about you either."

A few days later he called and asked her out to dinner. They went, and again he talked a lot about Laura and his children. At her door he said, "You know, you're really a knockout lady. As we said in my youth, 'I could really go for you.' "

"Oh, don't do that." She laughed up at him.

Later, thinking over the evening, Lucretia saw that she did not like him very much, despite his good qualities. He talked nonstop and rather self-importantly, a man accustomed to having the floor. To delivering opinions. And he did not listen well; in fact, he showed very little curiosity about her or anyone else. In short, he bored her; it was true, he was not her type at all. Except for being tall.

But she recognized, too, with some shame, a certain sexual pull in his direction. She looked forward to when he would kiss her. She put this down to sheer sexual starvation—it had been a long time since she had kissed anyone.

Their next dinner was less boring for Lucretia, because of the kissing that she now looked forward to. Just that, kissing, for the moment.

They went from a good-night kiss at the door to some very enthusiastic kissing on the sofa, and then, because such adolescent necking seemed ridiculous at their age, they went to bed.

Where, after several long, futile minutes of strenuous efforts on his part, and some effort on hers, Burt said, "I'm sorry. I had this prostate surgery, and I was afraid, but I had hoped—"

He was breathing hard, from exertion rather than from lust, Lucretia felt, as she thought, Poor guy, how embarrassing this must be. And depressing.

"Here," he said, "Let me—" He moved heavily, laboriously, down her body, positioning himself.

This is not something he usually does, Lucretia thought. Oral sex was not on the regular menu with Laura, the wife. Though, of course, Lucretia could have been wrong.

Feeling sorry for him, she pretended more pleasure than she actually felt; also, she wanted him to stop.

He moved up to lie beside her; he whispered into her ear, "It's wonderful to give you pleasure. You're wonderful."

Without spelling things out, without saying, "Look, I'm sorry, but I just don't like you very much. And sexually, I know it's not your fault and I'm sorry you have this problem, but it just doesn't work for me. I'm sorry I pretended," Lucretia hoped he would somehow understand. It did not occur to her until later that she could just have not seen him again, without apology.

Because he did not understand; he seemed now to want to see her all the time.

He took her to a banquet at which he was the guest of honor, long tables at the Fairmont Hotel, important political people. Men whose names, at least, she knew.

Lucretia, in her proper, "appropriate" black dress and her proper pearls, felt fraudulent; she wanted almost to announce: I'm not his lady friend, we are not, not, *not* getting married.

Burt's friends were roughly the same age as Lucretia was, like Burt himself, but they all seemed considerably older. She thought this could be delusional on her part, a delusion of youth, although she knew that she was generally a realist in that way. Vain, perhaps, she surely was that, caring too much about how she looked. But not kidding herself that she was a kid anymore.

She was not quite sure what this "older" quality consisted of; the best she could do was to describe it as a sort of settled heaviness, in both minds and bodies. They all looked pleasantly invulnerable, these people, Burt and his friends. No longer subject to much change. Or to passion. They did not much mind being overweight. Or that their expensive clothes were out of style.

Lucretia was not exactly smug about looking younger, and better; she knew it was largely accidental. She had been born pretty, and most of it had lasted. She ate almost what she wanted to, and nevertheless stayed fairly thin. She exercised, but not immoderately. She had not had anything "done" to herself in a surgical way, although she had thought about it.

"You're the sexiest woman I ever met. I'm crazy for you," Burt breathed into her ear.

"But—"

"Maybe a little cruise somewhere? Alaska, maybe, or Baja."

"Cruises—"

"Look, forget you're a travel writer. Just come along. Enjoy."

At the time of the cruise conversation (she had been on a number of cruises and very much disliked them all) Lucretia was much involved in writing a series of articles on shelters for battered women. She tried to tell Burt just how involved she was, how she cared about this particular piece.

Which did not go over well with Burt. "You should throw your weight around more," he told her. "Such as it is," and he laughed at his own mild joke. He often teased her about being what he called "under-weight." "You've been there long enough and won enough prizes," he scolded. "You should be calling the shots. Not taking these really tough assignments."

I'm trying my best to call the shots with you, she thought, but did not say. And I like writing this piece; I like these women.

It was Burt's mouth that gave his face its severity, she decided. A small mouth, set and firm, made smaller-seeming by the surrounding beard. Had someone long ago said that small mouths were a bad sign, that they meant an ungiving, stingy nature? Actually, Burt was somewhat stingy, she had come to see; "careful" would be the kinder word, but he was super-careful, hyperconcerned with prices, costs, and he was surprised and somewhat annoyed by her ignorance of these things.

"It's not that I don't care what things cost," she tried to explain. "It's just that I get confused. I'm not good with numbers."

She tried going to bed with him a few more times, deeply knowing this to be a mistake but saying to herself that this time it might work; she might feel the pleasure she pretended (and she knew her pretense to be a serious error, politically incorrect). But, because of what he referred to as his "problem," Lucretia found it hard to put him off entirely; she understood how much his pride was involved, and she was reluctant to hurt that pride, and his feelings.

When he said, as he sometimes gloomily did, that if they broke up she would be the last woman in his life, she also understood that this had less to do with the great love that he professed for her than with his secret, his "problem." Lucretia, the only person privy to that secret, had to be the last in line.

In the women's shelter Lucretia felt herself stretched between extreme emotions: between pity and fear, admiration, sometimes disgust. And occasionally sheer boredom: encouraged by her questions, some of these women would have talked for hours, not always coherently. But many of them were coherent, many interesting, some even funny. A marvelous elderly black woman—from Montana, of all places. A shriveled Mexican-Jewish woman from L.A., with raucous, horrifying tales of endless boyfriends.

Lucretia's story in four installments ran in the Sunday paper, and most of her friends called to say how good it was, congratulations. Edwin, the editor and her old friend (the donor of the white-framed mirror), was highly pleased. Lucretia noted with interest that Burt was among those who did not call.

But Simon did call. Simon Coyne, at that time a voice from her remote past, from Jim and Cambridge days, law school. Although Simon had not been in law school. Eccentrically, everyone felt at the time, he was getting his doctorate in philosophy. Lucretia had heard that he married a Boston girl, and that broke up, and he married someone else. He taught in several small schools around the South. She had not really heard of him for years now, although when he called she realized that he had remained a romantic image in her mind: so tall and fair, with his pipe and tweeds and slightly odd way of speech. He was from Toronto, originally, Lucretia remembered, but he seemed rather "English" than Canadian. More distant than Canadians generally were. More impeccably, remotely courteous.

He was teaching in Berkeley now, Simon said, and yes, he liked it very much. He had found a nice house up on Euclid. His cats liked it, too; he had three. No, he was not married, but two of his three sons were living close by, as it happened.

Why didn't you call me before? Lucretia wanted to ask him. And, When can we see each other? Are you busy tonight? But she managed simply to say, "I'd love to see you; could you come over for supper sometime soon?"

He was terribly busy, as he was sure that she was, too, and besides, he insisted on taking her out to dinner. He would call.

And then she didn't hear from him for a couple of weeks, during which she saw Burt more than she had meant to. She did manage at last to say, "Look, Burt, we can have dinner sometimes if you'd like to, but we can't, uh, go to bed."

His whole face tightened. "I can hardly blame you for that. With my problem."

"It's not that. Honestly." And honestly it was not, not his impotence but his whole severe, self-centered, somewhat hostile character. She would have liked to say, I just don't like you very much, but she said instead, "My heart just isn't in it. I'm sorry."

She should have been rewarded, Lucretia believed, by a phone call from Simon, asking her out to dinner at last. But she was not. Burt called several times, still wanting to see her, and each time the phone rang she imagined that it would be Simon, but it was not. After some time of this she thought, I am much too old to wait for phone calls. And so she called him.

As she had more or less known that he would be, Simon was gallantly contrite. He had meant to call her, he had looked forward to seeing her, but had been stuck with crazy busyness. Department politics, plus high-level university trouble.

She reassured him. Perfectly all right—she had been busy, too. She invited him to dinner.

Oh, no, he said, they must go out, and he named a place that he wanted to try. On the waterfront. Supposed to be excellent food, and also attractive. Hard to get reservations, but he would try, and call her back. They settled on a night. He did call back, to say that he could get a table only at seven, too early, but worth a try. He would pick her up at six-thirty; he would very much look forward to seeing her.

Like a nervous girl, Lucretia wondered what to wear. She was tempted to buy something new and wonderful, but she did not like the styles of that year. She settled on her best old black dress that everyone liked.

At about six her phone rang, and Lucretia's heart sank as she thought, It must be Burt, or worse, it's Simon, canceling.

It was Simon, not canceling but apologizing: A meeting was holding him up, could they possibly meet at the restaurant?

Driving down Broadway, through all the mess of lights and traffic, it occurred to Lucretia that she should have taken a cab; this way they would have to part publicly in some parking lot.

The restaurant was in an old wharf building, remodeled: low, dark ceilings, low lights, a long, rich bar and spectacular view of the bay and the Bay Bridge, Oakland. Black water and huge, dim, looming boats.

At first, coming in, Lucretia could not see Simon, but then she said his name, and she was directed: there, he could have been no one else— tall, lean, fair Simon, with his narrow face, long nose, sardonic mouth. He was standing, smiling, and then coming toward her, hands outstretched to her.

They both said, "Oh, I'm so glad—" and stopped, and laughed.

Their dinner was much in that key, enthusiastically friendly, with good laughs. And relatively impersonal. Simon gracefully deflected anything verging on the personal, did not discuss his two marriages. Instantly sensitive to his mood and needs (this was one of her major skills), Lucretia was amusing. She told funny stories about the paper, about people she had interviewed. And they exchanged travel notes; they both loved the South of France, the North of Italy, and they laughed at the unoriginality of their tastes.

Simon's hair, though still thick, was actually white, not blond, as

Lucretia had remembered. But, as she sat with him there, she was seeing not the elderly man whom another person might have described as distinguished but rather a young, blond, athletic Simon, with his fair hair and dark-brown eyes, his high, white intellectual brow, and his clever, sensual mouth. She was seeing and responding to a very young man, but also to an aging man, with white hair, whom she hardly knew. With whom she had an animated, no-depth conversation. But to whom she responded, deeply.

As she had imagined, and feared, they parted at her car, though, bending down to her, Simon asked anxiously, "Should I follow you home? See that you get there safely?"

"Oh no, I drive around all the time. I'll be fine."

A brush of mouths on cheeks. Good night.

Lucretia *knew* that she was much too old to wait for the phone to ring, and yet the next day, a Saturday, she found that that was what she was doing. Despite the fact that her answering machine was functioning, she kept herself within range of her telephone, postponing the small weekend tasks that would make enough noise to drown it out. Postponing neighborhood errands.

Until she thought, This is absolutely, utterly ridiculous, And she went out for an extended walk, doing errands, and even appreciating the beautiful day.

Coming home, though, and noting her machine's nonflashing light, no messages, she experienced a sinking of her spirits: he had not called.

This was crazy, she knew that; she thought, I cannot let myself do this. I will simply have to take charge. I'll call him. This is the nineties, no matter how old we are.

"Simon, it's Lucretia. I just wanted to thank you for dinner. It was really terrific. I had a marvelous time, so lovely to see you, really, I wondered, could you come here for dinner, do you think? Maybe next Friday? Well, actually Saturday's fine. Even better. Great! See you then."

Rack of lamb? Steak *au poivre*? Or were those too show-offy, obvious? Maybe just cracked crab and a salad? But that showed off nothing at all, no cooking. And then she thought, Dear God, it doesn't matter. I'll make something good. Whatever.

But she spent the next week in elaborate fantasies of the possible evening with Simon. In which, sometimes, they went from passionate kissing at the door directly to bed, where things went well.

So obsessed was she that she wondered, Have I fallen in love with Simon? At my age? Is that what this is all about?

She noted that in her dreams several other men appeared whom she had not thought of for years. She dreamed of Jim and of Tommy, of poor dead Jason, of beautiful Silvio. And of several others.

By the actual night on which the actual Simon came to her house for dinner, Lucretia was exhausted, emotionally, so drained that preparing the rack of lamb, God knows an easy dish, had taken great effort. Not to mention blow-drying her hair, brushing it.

It was partly from fatigue, then, that later, in her pretty living room, a familiar and perfect backdrop for love, Lucretia found herself regarding Simon with the most terrible sadness. She was not in love with Simon, she really was not—although he was perfectly nice and in his way quite handsome, still, and interesting. It was simply that he reminded her of love. Some hint of all the men she had ever loved was in his aura, like a scent. One sniff of it and she thought, Ah, love!

That knowledge, or insight, though sad, was relaxing to Lucretia, and she said, "I hope you won't mind if we eat unfashionably early? I'm sort of tired."

"Not at all. It's a terrible thing about age," he said, with his attractive, crooked smile. "I find that I'm tired a lot."

"Oh, I am, too!" and she flashed her answering bright smile, as she thought, Oh good, I won't have to pretend anymore. And I won't even think about falling in love.

But of course she did.

A Very Nice Dog

A few weeks ago, somewhat against my better judgment, I went to a Sunday-lunch party in Sausalito, at which I was deeply bored by the guest of honor, an actor whom I had not especially wanted to meet, and at which I ate very little lunch. But where I met a very nice black dog, an aging Lab, slightly grizzled around the jaw, with large, kind, gentle, and hopeful dark-brown eyes. There he was, lying out in the sun in a corner of my friend Patrick's deck, in the ravishingly beautiful and warm late-October sunlight.

Patrick and I are old, old friends; a very long time ago we were undergraduates together, in Charlottesville, and now we like to say (sometimes we like it) that we are aging together, transported out here to California. I live by myself in San Francisco, and Patrick lives with his friend Oliver in the dark-shingled old Sausalito house, with its newly added cantilevered deck, and its stunning view of the bay and boats, and Alcatraz and Belvedere.

Because of Oliver's allergies they have no pets, although before Oliver entered his life Patrick had Burmese cats, and sometimes a handsome poodle as well. I have three cats. This new dog was not Patrick's, then. "He lives across the street," Oliver explained, when I asked, surprised at finding a dog there. That day Oliver was serving, since Patrick had chosen to cook, and they both seemed a little harassed by this change of roles, Oliver being the better and more usual cook. They had little patience for pet conversations—at first.

Patrick is an architect, talented and energetic when he has a project going, depressed when he does not. Genuinely witty, often kind, and sometimes mean, he retains friendships with many old clients. And makes new ones: he had just done a house for this actor, Tom Something, in the Napa Valley. He truly loves his friends, all of them, although he is capable of some manipulation, a little mischief. On the lunch-party day he had clearly enjoyed my discomfort when he would not tell me who was stopping by to pick me up; since I don't drive, some friends and especially Patrick insist on arranging my transportation, when I would really rather do it myself; there are buses to Sausalito, and even a cab is not all that expensive.

At this point I must go back and introduce an element new to this story: a man whom for quite a while I had wanted to know. Just that: he looked interesting, and the little I knew of him was appealing. The appeal was not sexy; he looked to be at least ten years older than I am, and I am too old to be turned on by older men. We had met at some large gathering or other, some time ago, and now when our paths literally crossed on city walks—we both are walkers, we live in the same neighborhood—we would exchange a few words. But he gave an impression of chosen solitude, of great reserve. Justin Solomon, a small dark man with a shock of white hair, and a very slight limp, although he still walked even faster than I did, and I walk fast. He had been a civil rights lawyer, not flamboyant but quietly, wisely effective, and was rumored to give most of his money, earned and inherited from a family brokerage, to those causes. His wife of many years had recently died; she had been a distant friend-connection of Patrick's; thus Patrick knew Justin much better than I did. I thought Justin looked lonely, as well as wryly intelligent—and too thin.

It seems to me simpleminded to label all nurturing impulses "maternal," especially in this instance, but I do like to cook, and I would have liked to ask Mr. Solomon to dinner. However, I felt that I didn't know him well enough, and there is always the female dread (still!) of being misinterpreted, of being perceived as predatory, a sexual aggressor. Or just as lonely.

But since Patrick had this Justin Solomon connection, when he asked me for lunch and began to go on about drivers, I thought, and then said, "What about Justin Solomon?"

"Oh! Well! I hadn't exactly planned to invite dear Justin, it's not exactly his kind of party, but I'll think about it."

"You'll let me know?"

"Of course." He laughed. "Or I may leave it to be a surprise. I'll surprise you with a driver." He laughed again. "I'll send a stretch limo."

The neurotic truth is that I don't much like surprises. I like to know pretty clearly what's going to happen. A kind A.A. friend tells me that this comes from having had alcoholic parents, but I did not want to get into any of that with Patrick. Also, I really thought it likely that he would ask Justin, and had only wanted to tease me.

In the interval between that phone call and the Sunday of the lunch, I had many fantasy conversations with my new best friend, Justin Solomon, as we drove from my house, on Green Street, to Patrick's, in Sausalito. In the course of these talks just possibly he could point to some spot of hope in what I saw as the hopeless awfulness of most recent events, in Russia and Bosnia, in Africa. In Washington, and even L.A.

But as a terrible corrective to this intimate fantasy, I thought too about the stereotype that I feared, of the eager, elderly woman, and I cringed. There must be a lot of such ladies "after" Justin, I thought.

And so I was rather torn about the prospect of my drive to Sausalito, with whomever, and I gave it far too much thought.

What actually happened was that Patrick's friend Oliver picked me up; he had to get some special bread for the lunch at a delicatessen down on Chestnut Street, and so he combined the two errands, me and the special Italian bread.

I was deeply disappointed. I tried not to think about it, or to show it.

Which brings me back to the lunch, the boring too-young actor, Tom, and the nice dog over in the corner of the deck, near the still-flowering azalea.

"Venice is like, like really beautiful," said Tom, as I thought, It's not *like* beautiful, you silly jerk. It *is*.

Tom is very handsome, I guess, with a round blond unlined and (to me) entirely uninteresting, unsexy face, and a deep insistent voice. "Then we did a shoot in Dubrovnik," he said, intoning. "A tragic city—" (At least he did not say it was like a tragic city.)

Many years of practice have enabled me to smile at what I believe and hope are appropriate pauses, though with this Tom it hardly mattered, so concerned was he with his speech, so little aware of his victim-audience. Unless, as I have sometimes suspected of considerable bores, he was doing it on purpose; having sensed my perhaps unusual failure to respond to his charm, he set out to bore me to death.

The lunch was not very good, although Patrick's intentions were generous; gray, overdone slices of cold lamb, and underdone potato salad. Patrick, a somewhat competitive person, does not like to admit that Oliver is the better cook. (Earlier I had even wondered if some misplaced competitiveness with Justin for my friendship had made Patrick not invite Justin to this party.)

I looked over at the dog, who was looking wistfully in the direction of the party, the people, I thought. I also thought how polite of him not to come over and beg for food. And then, as though acknowledging my thought, he turned his head away, showing a profile that was both proud and noble.

"But hey! I really love those guys!" said Tom the actor. Serbs? Bosnians? Venetians? No matter, he was now talking to someone else, and I no longer had to pretend that I was listening.

Very carefully and (I hoped) unobtrusively, then, I packed all my lamb into my napkin, and as though heading into the house I got up and went over to the dog. I knelt beside him and began to feed him the nice cold meat, whose toughness he did not seem to mind. He took every piece very tidily from my hand, with no slobber or visible greed. He looked at me with his beautiful dark-brown-purple velvet eyes, and I felt that an important connection between us had been established.

After maybe five minutes I went back to my table, and the party continued much as before.

And later Oliver took me home at a reasonably early hour, although I could happily have left even earlier. I did not see the dog around as I left.

The next day I called Patrick to thank him for the lunch, and I also said, "What a nice dog that was; I really liked him."

And Patrick said, "Oh, that's Max. Poor baby, he is. Terribly nice, and his people have deserted him. Moved back into town, except on weekends."

"Couldn't you and Oliver adopt him?"

"Well, *I'd* love to. But you know, Oliver's allergies. And the poor dog's so lonesome, he howls all night."

That wrenched my heart; I truly could not bear it. Lonesome Max at night. And although I do have three cats, one of whom is skittish to a point of near psychosis, I was thinking that maybe I could take Max. Emma was already so crazy; she would just have to cope, as the rest of us do.

But at that moment a small and vivid memory filled my mind: on a recent walk in Cow Hollow, where Justin Solomon and I both live, I had come upon him on Jackson Street, near Alta Plaza park. In his old brown sweater and chinos, Justin did not look like a lawyer, even retired. Together for a few moments that day, we observed the frisking dogs whose recreational terrain that park is, and Justin sighed as he said, "I should get a dog. I'd really like one, but I don't seem to get around to it."

Excitedly I now told Patrick, "Listen! Justin Solomon wants a dog; he told me. You know him. Call him and tell him about Max. Max would be perfect for Justin, they're both so polite."

As I might have known he would, Patrick saw this as a less than wonderful idea. "In the first place," he told me, "the Fowlers probably have their own idea for Max. They may have left him there on purpose. To guard the house."

That seemed a reasonable point, although I argued, "But couldn't you call them? Say that Max is keeping you awake?"

That last was inspired; Patrick likes to complain. A legitimate gripe makes him very happy.

I was right. Patrick agreed to call the Fowlers.

"And if that doesn't work you could call the SPCA," I suggested.

But, hanging up, I felt a little glum as to the possible outcomes of my interference, although at that point I saw my motives as pure. Very likely nothing good would come of this, and I could have made things worse for Max if the SPCA got into it; they might haul him off to a shelter. I considered taking a cab to Sausalito, somehow finding Max and luring him into the car. Taking him home, and even sedating Emma.

Typically, Patrick did not call for several days, during which I had more bad, sad thoughts about lonely Max, howling in Sausalito.

And then Patrick called, and he asked me, "Are you sitting down? I have some really, truly great news."

Well, he did. He had called the Fowlers, and Mrs. Fowler, who turned out to be nice but a little silly, told Patrick that she was so sorry, she too was sad over Max. But they had to be in town most nights. If only they could find a nice home for Max, who was no longer young; he was six, she said. Patrick said he would try to help; he was sorry that his friend was so allergic. And then he actually called Justin Solomon and said that he had heard ("I didn't think you'd want me to say it was you") that Justin might want a dog. And ("this is the part you won't believe")

Justin just happened to have an errand in Marin County *that very day;* and Justin came over and met Max and *took him home.* "On approval, he said," said Patrick. "But I could tell that he was in love."

"Patrick, that's really the best story I ever heard." And it was, a totally satisfying story, marvelous: lonely nice Max in a good kind home, and lonely Justin with a very nice dog.

The only missing element for me, and I had to admit this to myself, was my own role. I actually would have liked it if Patrick had given me the proper credit, of course I would. Better to be thought a little indiscreet than to remain almost invisible, I thought.

In fantasy, then, I saw myself again running into Justin—and Max!—somewhere in the neighborhood. It was too much to expect that Max would remember me, despite all the lamb, but I would certainly know him, and his name. And in greeting Max I could explain to Justin how it all came about. Taking full credit.

But would that necessarily lead to our becoming friends? Might not Justin, a somewhat formal man, simply say, "How very kind of you to have thought of me." So that we would continue as before, acquaintances who rarely saw each other, and then only by chance.

What I probably needed, I thought a little sadly, was a dog of my own. A really nice dog, with beautiful eyes. Like Max. Even Emma would get used to him in time, probably. The one needing a dog is me.

More immediately, though, I could telephone Justin Solomon? Identifying myself, I could include knowing Patrick. I could tell him about the lunch, the lamb. Me and Max. "I'd really love to see him again," I could say. "Should we meet for a walk, or something?"

That seems the best plan, and that is what I will do tomorrow, if not sooner. And then, in the course of the walk, I'll invite him to dinner, and I'll cook something good, with bones—for Max.

The Visit

"She's just dying to see you, so excited, and you really can't refuse a ninety-two-year-old," said Miles Henry to his old friend Grace Lafferty, the famous actress, who was just passing through town, a very quick visit. Miles and Grace were getting on too, but they were nowhere near the awesome age of ninety-two, the age of Miss Louise Dabney, she who was so very anxious to see Grace, "if only for a minute, over tea."

"I really don't remember her awfully well," Grace told Miles. "She was very pretty? But all Mother's friends were pretty. Which made her look even worse. Miles, do we really have to come for tea?"

"You really do." He laughed, as she had laughed, but they both understood what was meant. She and the friend whom she had brought along—Jonathan Hedding, a lawyer, retired, very tall and a total enigma to everyone, so far—must come to tea. As payment, really, for how well Miles had managed their visit: no parties, no pictures or interviews. He had been wonderfully firm, and since he and Grace had been friends forever, if somewhat mysteriously, it was conceded that he had a right to take charge. No one in town would have thought of challenging Miles; for one thing, he was too elusive.

The town was a fairly small one, in the Georgia hill country, not far from Atlanta—and almost everyone there was somewhat excited, interested in this visit; those who were not were simply too young to know who Grace Lafferty was, although their parents had told them: the very famous Broadway actress, then movie star, then occasional TV parts. Grace, who had been born and raised in this town, had barely been back at all. Just briefly, twice, for the funerals of her parents, and one other time when a movie was opening in Atlanta. And now she was here for this very short visit. Nothing to do with publicity or promotions; according to Miles she just wanted to see it all again, and she had carefully picked this season, April, the first weeks of spring, as being the most beautiful that she remembered. Anywhere.

It was odd how she and Miles had stayed friends all these years. One rumor held that they had been lovers very long ago, in the time of Grace's turbulent girlhood, before she got so beautiful (dyed her hair blond) and famous. Miles had been studying architecture in Atlanta then, and certainly they had known each other, but the exact nature of their connection was a mystery, and Miles was far too old-time gentlemanly for anyone to ask. Any more than they would have asked about his two marriages, when he was living up North, and his daughter, whom he never seemed to see.

If Grace's later life from a distance had seemed blessed with fortune (although, four marriages, no children?), one had to admit that her early days were not; her parents, both of them, were difficult. Her father, a classic *beau* of his time, was handsome, and drank too much, and chased girls. Her mother, later also given to drink, was smart and snobbish (she was from South Carolina, and considered Georgia a considerable comedown). She tended to say exactly what she thought, and she wasn't one bit pretty. Neither one of them seemed like ordinary parents, a fact they made a point of—of being above and beyond most normal parental concerns, of not acting like "parents." "We appreciate Grace as a person, and not just because she's our daughter," Hortense, the mother, was fairly often heard to say, which may have accounted for the fact that Grace was a rather unchildlike child: precocious, impertinent, too smart for her own good. Rebellious, always. Unfairly, probably, no one cared a lot for poor wronged Hortense, and almost everyone liked handsome bad Buck Lafferty. Half the women in town had real big, serious crushes on him.

Certainly they made a striking threesome, tall Grace and those two tall men, during the short days of her visit, as they walked slowly, with a certain majesty, around the town, Grace's new friend, or whatever he was, Jonathan Hedding, the lawyer, was the tallest, with heavy, thick gray hair, worn a trifle long for these parts but still, enviably all his own. Miles and Grace were almost the exact same height, she in those heels she always wore, and in the new spring sunlight their hair seemed about the same color, his shining white, hers the palest blond. Grace wore the largest dark glasses that anyone had ever seen—in that way only did she look like a movie star; that and the hair, otherwise she was just tall and a little plump, and a good fifteen years older than she looked to be.

Several times in the course of that walking around Miles asked her, "But was there something particular you wanted to see? I could take you—"

"Oh no." Her throaty voice hesitated. "Oh no, I just wanted to see—everything. The way we're doing. And of course I wanted Jon to see it too."

Miles asked her, "How about the cemetery? These days I know more people there than I do downtown."

She laughed, but she told him, "Oh, great. Let's do go and see the cemetery."

Certainly Grace had been right about the season. The dogwood was just in bloom, white fountains spraying out against the darker evergreens, and fragrant white or lavender wisteria, across the roofs of porches, over garden trellises. Jonquils and narcissus, in their tidy plots, bricked off from the flowing lawns. As Grace several times remarked, the air simply smelled of April. There was nothing like it, anywhere.

"You should come back more often," Miles chided.

"I'm not sure I could stand it." She laughed, very lightly.

The cemetery was old, pre–Civil War; many of the stones were broken, worn, the inscriptions illegible. But there were new ones too, that both Grace and Miles recognized, and remarked upon.

"Look at those Sloanes, they were always the tackiest people. Oh, the Berryhills, they must have struck it rich. And the Calvins, discreet and tasteful as always. Lord, how could there be so many Strouds?"

It was Jonathan who finally said, "Now I see the point of cemeteries. Future entertainment."

They all laughed. It was perhaps the high point of their afternoon, the moment at which they all liked each other best.

And then Grace pointed ahead of them, and she said, "Well for God's sake, there they are. Why did I think I could miss them, totally?"

An imposing granite stone announced LAFFERTY, and underneath, in more discreet lettering, Hortense and Thomas. With dates.

Grace shuddered. "Well, they won't get me in there. Not with them. I'm going to be cremated and have the ashes scattered off Malibu. Or maybe in Central Park."

Five o'clock. Already they were a little late. It was time to go for tea, or rather to be there. Grace had taken even longer than usual with makeup, with general fussing, though Jonathan had reminded her, "At ninety-two she may not see too well, you know."

"Nevertheless." But she hadn't laughed.

Miles lived in a small house just across the street from Miss Dabney's much larger, grander house. It was thus that they knew each other. As Grace and Jonathan drove up he was out in front poking at leaves, but actually just waiting for them, as they all knew.

"I'm sorry—" Grace began.

"It's all right, but whyever are you so nerved up?"

"Oh, I don't know—"

Inside Miss Dabney's entrance hall, to which they had been admitted by a white-aproned, very small black woman, where they were told to wait, Jonathan tried to exchange a complicitous look with Grace: after all, she was with him. But she seemed abstracted, apart.

The parlor into which they were at last led by the same small silent maid was predictably crowded—with tiny tables and chairs, with silver frames and photographs, loveseats and glassed-in bookcases. And, in the center of it all, Miss Dabney herself, yellowed white hair swathed about her head like a bandage but held up stiff and high, as though the heavy pearl choker that she wore were a splint. Her eyes, shining out through folds of flesh, were tiny and black, and brilliant. She held out a gnarled, much-jeweled hand to Grace (was Grace supposed to kiss the rings? She did not). The two women touched fingers.

When Miss Dabney spoke her voice was amazingly clear, rather high, a little hoarse but distinct. "Grace Lafferty, you do look absolutely lovely," she said. "I'd know you anywhere; in a way you haven't changed a bit."

"Oh well, but you look—" Grace started to say.

"Now now. I'm much too old to be flattered. That's how come I don't have handsome men around me anymore." Her glance flicked out to take in Miles, and then Jonathan. "But of course no man was ever as handsome as your daddy."

"No, I guess—"

"Too bad your mother wasn't pretty too. I think it would have improved her character."

"Probably—"

Miss Dabney leaned forward. "You know, we've always been so proud of you in this town. Just as proud as proud."

The effect of this on Grace was instant; something within her settled down, some set of nerves, perhaps. She almost relaxed. Miles with relief observed this, and Jonathan too.

"Yes, indeed we have. For so many, many things," Miss Dabney continued.

A warm and pleasant small moment ensued, during which in an almost preening way Grace glanced at Jonathan—before Miss Dabney took it up again.

"But do you know what you did that made us the very proudest of all?" Quite apparently wanting no answer, had one been possible, she seemed to savor the expectation her non-question had aroused.

"It was many, many years ago, and your parents were giving a dinner party," she began—as Miles thought, Oh dear God, oh Jesus.

"And you were just this adorable little two- or three-year-old. And somehow you got out of your crib and you came downstairs, and you crawled right under the big white linen tablecloth, it must have seemed like a circus tent to you—and you bit your mother right there on the ankle. Good and hard! She jumped and cried out, and Buck lifted up the tablecloth and there you were. I don't remember quite how they punished you, but we all just laughed and laughed. Hortense was not the most popular lady in town, and I reckon one time or another we'd all had an urge to bite her. And you did it! We were all just so proud!"

"But—" Grace protests, or rather, she begins to protest. She seems then, though, to remember certain rules. One held that Southern ladies did not contradict other ladies, especially if the other one is very old. She also remembered a rule from her training as an actress: you do not exhibit uncontrolled emotion of your own.

Grace simply says, "It's funny, I don't remember that at all," and she smiles, beautifully.

Miles, though, who has known her for so very long, and who has always loved her, for the first time fully understands just what led her to become an actress, and also why she is so very good at what she does.

"Well of course you don't," Miss Dabney is saying. "You were much too young. But it's a wonder no one ever told you, considering how famous—how famous that story was."

Jonathan, who feels that Grace is really too old for him, but whose fame he has enjoyed, up to a point, now tells Miss Dabney, "It's a marvelous story. You really should write it, I think. Some magazine—"

Grace gives him the smallest but most decisive frown—as Miles, watching, thinks, Oh, good.

And Grace now says, abandoning all rules, "I guess up to now no one ever told me so as not to make me feel small and bad. I guess they knew I'd have to get very old and really mean before I'd think that was funny."

As Miles thinks, Ah, that's my girl!

The Last Lovely City

Old and famous, an acknowledged success both in this country and in his native Mexico, though now a sadhearted widower, Dr. Benito Zamora slowly and unskillfully navigates the high, sharp curves on the road to Stinson Beach, California—his destination. From time to time, barely moving his heavy, white-maned head, he glances at the unfamiliar young woman near him on the seat—the streaky-haired, underweight woman in a very short skirt and green sandals (her name is Carla) who has somewhat inexplicably invited him to come along to this party. What old hands, Benito thinks, of his own, on the wheel, an old beggar's hands. What can this girl want of me? he wonders. Some new heaviness around the doctor's neck and chin makes him look both strong and fierce, and his deep-set black eyes are powerful, still, and unrelenting in their judgmental gaze, beneath thick, uneven, white brows.

"We're almost there," he tells the girl, this Carla.

"I don't care; I love the drive," she says, and moves her head closer to the window, so her long hair fans out across her shoulders. "Do you go back to Mexico very often?" she turns now to ask him.

"Fairly. My very old mother still lives there. Near Oaxaca."

"Oh, I've been to Oaxaca. So beautiful." She beams. "The hotel—"

"My mother's not in the Presidente."

She grins, showing small, white, even teeth. "Well, you're right. I did stay there. But it is a very nice hotel."

"Very nice," he agrees, not looking at her.

His mother is not the doctor's only reason for going to Oaxaca. His interests are actually in almost adjacent Chiapas, where he oversees and has largely funded two large free clinics—hence his fame, and his nickname, Dr. Do-Good (to Benito, an epithet replete with irony, and one that he much dislikes).

They have now emerged from the dark, tall, covering woods, the groves of redwood, eucalyptus, occasional laurel, and they are circling down the western slope as the two-lane road forms wide arcs. Ahead of them is the sea, the white curve of beach, and strung-out Stinson, the strange, small coastal town of rich retirees; weekenders, also rich; and a core population of former hippies, now just plain poor, middle-aged people with too many children. In his palmier days, his early, successful years, Dr. Zamora often came to Stinson from San Francisco on Sundays for lunch parties, first as a semi-sought-after bachelor ("But would you want your daughter actually to marry . . . ?" Benito thought he felt this question), and later, less often, with his bride, the fairest of them all, his wife, his lovely blond. His white soul. Elizabeth.

After Elizabeth died, now some five months ago, in April, friends and colleagues were predictably kind—many invitations, too many solicitous phone calls. And then, just as predictably (he had seen this happen with relatives of patients), all the attention fell off, and he was often alone. And at a time impossible for trips to Mexico: rains made most of the roads in Chiapas impassable, and he feared that he was now too old for the summer heat. Besides, these days the clinics actually ran quite well without him; he imagined that all they really needed was the money that came regularly from his banks. (Had that always been the case? he wondered. Were all those trips to Chiapas unnecessary, ultimately self-serving?) And his mother, in her tiny stucco villa, near Oaxaca, hardly recognized her oldest living son.

Too much time alone, then, and although he had always known that would happen, was even in a sense prepared, the doctor is sometimes angry: Why must they leave him now, when he is so vulnerable? Is no one able to imagine the daily lack, the loss with which he lives?

And then this girl, this Carla, whom the doctor had met at a dinner a month or so before, called and asked him to the lunch, at Stinson Beach. "I hope you don't mind a sort of last-minute invitation," she said, "but I really loved our talk, and I wanted to see you again, and this seemed a good excuse." He gratefully accepted, although he remembered very little of her, really, except for her hair, which was very long and silky-looking, streaked all shades of brown, with yellow. He remembered her hair, and that she seemed nice, a little shy; she was quiet, and so he had talked too much. ("Not too unusual, my darling," Elizabeth might have said.) He thinks she said she worked for a newspaper; it now seems too late to ask. He believes she is intelligent, and serious. Curious about his clinics.

But in the short interval between her call and this drive a host of fantasies has crowded old Benito's imagination. She looked about thirty, this girl did, but these days most women look young; she could be forty-two. Still a long way from his own age, but such things did happen. One read of them.

Or was it possible that Carla meant to write about him for her paper? The doctor had refused most interviews for years; had refused until he noticed that no one had asked, not for years.

"What did you say the name of our hostess was?" he thinks to ask her as they round the last curve and approach the first buildings of the town.

"Posey Pendergast. You've never met her?"

"I don't think so, but the name—something goes off in my head."

"Everyone knows Posey; I really thought you would. She's quite marvelous."

"Quite marvelous" is a phrase that Benito (Elizabeth used to agree) finds cautionary; those marvelous people are almost as bad as "characters." All those groups he is sure not to like, how they do proliferate, thinks old Benito sourly, aware of the cruel absence of Elizabeth, with her light laugh, agreeing.

"I'm sure you'll know some of her friends," adds Carla.

Posey Pendergast is a skinny old wreck of a woman, in a tattered straw sun hat and a red, Persian-looking outfit. She breathes heavily. Emphysema and some problems with her heart, the doctor thinks, automatically noting the pink-white skin, faintly bluish mouth, and arthritic hands—hugely blue-veined, rings buried in finger flesh. "I've been hearing of you for years," she tells Benito in her raspy, classy voice. Is she English? No, more like Boston, or somewhere back there, the doctor decides. She goes on. "I can't believe we've never met. I'm *so* glad Carla brought you,"

"This is some house," he says solemnly (using what Elizabeth called his innocent-Indian pose, which is one of his tricks).

It is some house, and the doctor now remembers walking past it, with Elizabeth, marveling at its size and opulence. It was right out there on the beach, not farther along in Seadrift, with the other big, expensive houses, but out in public—a huge house built up on pilings, all enormous beams, and steel and glass, and diagonal boards.

"My son designed it for me," Posey Pendergast is saying. "Carla's friend," she adds, just as some remote flash is going off in the doctor's mind: he used to hear a lot about this Posey, he recalls, something odd and somewhat scandalous, but from whom? Not Elizabeth, he is sure of that, although she was fond of gossip and used to lament his refusal to talk about patients. Did he hear of Posey from some patient? Some old friend?

This large room facing the sea is now fairly full of people. Women in short, silk, flowered dresses or pastel pants, men in linen or cashmere coats. Rich old gringos is Benito's instant assessment. He notes what seems an unusual number of hearing aids.

He and Carla are introduced around by Posey, although Carla seems already to know a number of the guests. People extend their hands; they all say how nice it is to meet the doctor; several people say that they have heard so much about him. And then, from that roster of Anglo-Saxon names, all sounding somewhat alike, from those voices, nasal Eastern to neutral Californian, Benito hears a familiar sound: "Oh." (It is the drawn-out "Oh" that he recognizes.) "Oh, but I've known Dr. Zamora *very* well, for a *very* long time."

He is confronted by an immense (she must weigh two hundred pounds) short woman, with a huge puff of orange hair, green eyeshadow, and the pinkish spots that skin cancer leaves marking her pale, lined forehead. It is Dolores. Originally Dolores Gutierrez—then Osborne, then Graham, and then he lost track. But here she is before him, her doughy face tightened into a mask, behind which he can indistinctly see the beauty that she was.

"Benito Zamora. Benny Zamora. What an absolutely awful name, my darling. So *spic,*" said Dolores, almost fifty years ago.

"How about Dolores Gutierrez?"

"I can marry out of it, and I certainly plan to. Why else would I even think of Boy Osborne, or for that matter Whitney Satterfield? But you, you simply have to change *yours*. How about Benjamin Orland? That keeps some of the sound, you see? I really don't like names to begin with 'Z.' "

"This is an extremely ugly room," he told her.

She laughed. "I know, but poor dear Norman thinks it's the cat's pajamas, and it's costing him a fortune."

"When you laugh I feel ice on my back." He shivered.

"Pull the sheet up. There. My, you are a gorgeous young man. You really are. Too bad about your name. You don't look so terribly spic."

They were in the pink-and-gold suite of a lesser Nob Hill hotel, definitely not the Mark or the Fairmont, but still no doubt costing poor Norman a lot. Heavy, gold-threaded, rose-colored draperies, barely parted, yielded a narrow blue view of the San Francisco Bay, the Bay Bridge, a white slice of Oakland. The bedspread, a darker rose, also gold-threaded, lay in a heavy, crumpled mass on the floor. The sheets were pink, and the shallow buttocks of Dolores Gutierrez were ivory—cool and smooth. Her hair, even then, was false gold.

"You know what I'd really like you to do? Do you want to know?" Her voice was like scented oil, the young doctor thought, light and insidious and finally dirty, making stains.

"I do want to know," he told her.

"Well, this is really perverse. *Really*. It may be a little too much for you." She was suddenly almost breathless with wanting to tell him what she really wanted, what was so terrifically exciting.

"Tell me." His breath caught, too, although in a rational way he believed that they had surely done everything. He stroked her smooth, cool bottom.

"I want you to pay me," she said. "I know you don't have much money, so that will make it all the more exciting. I want you to pay me a lot. And I might give it back to you, but then again I might not."

After several minutes, during which he took back his hand, Benito told her, "I don't want to do that. I don't think it would be fun."

And now this new Dolores, whose laugh is deeper, tells him, "This is a classic situation, isn't it, my angel? Famous man runs into an old lady friend, who's run to fat?" She laughs, and, as before, Benito shivers. "But wherever did you meet my darling old Posey?"

"Just now, actually. I never saw her before."

"The love of my life," Dolores declaims, as the doctor reflects that this could well be true, for he has just remembered a few more lines from their past. "I really don't like men at all," Dolores confided back then. "I only need them, although I'm terrified of them. And now I've fallen in love with this beautiful girl, who is very rich, of course. Even thinner than I am. With the most delicious name. Posey Pendergast. You must meet her one day. She would like you, too."

Wishing no more of this, and wishing no more of Dolores, ever, Benito turns in search of Carla, who seems to have vanished or hidden herself in the crowd that now populates this oversized room, milling around the long bar table and spilling out onto the broad deck that faces the sea. As he catches sight of the deck, the doctor instinctively moves toward it, even as Dolores is saying, "You must come back and tell me how you made all that money, Dr. Do-Good."

"Excuse me," he mutters stiffly, making for the door. He is not at all graceful in the usual way of Latins; Elizabeth said that from time to time.

From the deck San Francisco is still invisible; it lurks there behind the great cliffs of land, across the surging, dark-streaked sea. The tall, pale city, lovely and unreal. Benito thinks of his amazement at that city, years back, when he roamed its streets as an almost indigent medical student—at Stanford, in those days a city medical school, at Clay and Webster Streets, in Pacific Heights. How lonely he used to feel as he walked across those hills and stared at massive apartment houses, at enormous family houses—how isolated and full of greed. He *wanted* the city, both to possess and to immerse himself in it. It is hardly surprising, he now thinks—with a small, wry, private smile—that he ended up in bed with Dolores Gutierrez, and that a few years later he found himself the owner of many sleazy blocks of hotels in the Tenderloin.

But that is not how he ended up, the doctor tells himself, in a fierce interior whisper. He ended up with Elizabeth, who was both beautiful and good, a serious woman, with whom he lived harmoniously, if sometimes sadly (they had no children, and Elizabeth was given to depression), near St. Francis Wood, in a house with a view of everything—the city and the sea, the Farallon Islands.

Nor is that life with Elizabeth how he ended up, actually. The actual is now, of course, and he has ended up alone. Childless and without Elizabeth.

The doctor takes deep breaths, inhaling the cool, fresh wind, and exhaling, he hopes and believes, the germs of self-pity that sometimes enter and threaten to invade his system. He looks back to the great Marin headlands, those steep, sweeping hills of green. Far out at sea he sees two small, hopeful white boats, sails bobbing against the dark horizon.

Looking back inside the house, he sees Carla in intimate-seeming conversation with withered old Posey. Fresh from the intimations of Dolores, he shudders: Posey must be even older than he is, and quite unwell. But before he has time for speculation along those lines, he is jolted by a face, suddenly glimpsed behind the glass doors: bright-eyed and buck-toothed, thinner and grayer but otherwise not much aged, in a starched white embroidered shirt (Why on earth? Does he want to look Mexican?), that lawyer, Herman Tolliver.

"Well, of course they should be condemned; half this town should be condemned, are you crazy?" Tolliver grinned sideways, hiding his teeth. "The point is, they're not going to be condemned. Somebody's going to make a bundle off them. And from where I'm sitting it looks like you could be the guy. Along with me." Another grin, which was then extinguished as Tolliver tended to the lighting of a new cigar.

In that long-ago time (about forty years back) the doctor had just opened his own office and begun his cardiology practice. And had just met a young woman, with straw-blond hair, clear, dark-blue eyes, and a sexy overbite—Carole Lombard with a Gene Tierney mouth. A young woman of class and style, none of which he could ever afford. Elizabeth Montague: her very name was defeating. Whoever would exchange Montague for Zamora?

None of which excused Benito's acquiescence in Tolliver's scheme. (Certain details as to the precise use of Tolliver's "hotels" Benito arranged not quite to know, but he had, of course, his suspicions.) It ended in making the doctor and his wife, Elizabeth Montague Zamora, very rich. And in funding the clinics for the indigent of Chiapas.

. . .

After that first encounter with Herman Tolliver, the doctor almost managed never to see him again. They talked on the phone, or, in the later days of success and busyness, through secretaries. Benito was aware of Tolliver, aware that they were both making a great deal of money, but otherwise he was fairly successful in dismissing the man from his mind.

One morning, not long before Elizabeth died, she looked up from the paper at breakfast (Benito only scanned the *New York Times,* did not read local news at all) and said, "Didn't you used to know this scandalous lawyer, this Tolliver?"

"We've met." But how did Elizabeth know that? Benito, shaken, wondered, and then remembered: some time back there had been phone calls, a secretary saying that Mr. Tolliver wanted to get in touch (fortunately, nothing urgent). Just enough to fix the name in Elizabeth's mind. "Is he scandalous?" Benito then asked his wife, very lightly.

"Well, some business with tax evasion. Goodness, do all lawyers do things like that these days?"

Aware of his own relief (he certainly did not want public scandals connected with Tolliver), Benito told her, "I very much doubt it, my darling."

And that was the end of that, it seemed.

Carla is now talking to both old Posey and Herman Tolliver, but the doctor can see from her posture that she doesn't really like Tolliver, does not really want to talk to him. She is barely giving him the time of day, holding her glass out in front of her like a shield, or a weapon. She keeps glancing about, not smiling, as Tolliver goes on talking.

Is she looking for him? the doctor wonders. Does she ask herself what has happened to old Benito? He smiles to himself at this notion—and then, almost at the same moment, is chilled with longing for Elizabeth.

A problem with death, the doctor has more than once thought, is its removal of all the merciful dross of memory: he no longer remembers any petty annoyances, ever, or even moments of boredom, irritation, or sad, faded acts of love. All that is erased, and he only recalls, with the most cruel, searing accuracy, the golden peaks of their time together.

Beautiful days, long nights of love. He sees Elizabeth at their dining table, on a rare warm summer night. Her shoulders bare and white; a thin gold necklace that he has brought her from Oaxaca shines in the candlelight; she is bending toward their guest, old Dr. McPherson, from med-school days. Benito sees, too, McPherson's wife, and other colleague guests with their wives—all attractive, pale, and well dressed. But none so attractive as his own wife, his pale Elizabeth.

"Oh, there you are," Carla says, coming up to him suddenly.

"You couldn't see me out here? I could see you quite clearly," he tells her, in his sober, mechanical voice.

"I was busy fending off that creep, Tolliver. Mr. Slime." She tosses her hair, now gleaming in the sunlight. "I can't imagine what Posey sees in him. Do you know him?"

"We've met," the doctor admits. "But how do you know him?"

"I'm a reporter, remember? I meet everyone."

"And Posey Pendergast? You know her because—"

But that question and its possible answer are interrupted, cut off by the enormous, puffing arrival of Dolores. "Oh, here's where you've got to," she tells Benito and Carla, as though she had not seen them from afar and headed directly to where they stand, leaning together against the balcony's railing. "Carla, I'm absolutely in love with your hair," says Dolores.

Carla giggles—out of character for her, the doctor thinks—and then, another surprise, she takes his arm for a moment and laughs as she asks him, "Why don't you ever say such flattering things to me?"

Is she flirting with him, seriously flirting? Well, she could be. Such things do happen, the doctor reminds himself. And she seems a very honest young woman, and kind. She could brighten my life, he thinks, and lighten my home, all those rooms with their splendid views that seem to have darkened.

"Don't you want some lunch?" she is asking. "Can I get you something?"

Before he can answer (and he had very much liked the idea of her bringing him food), Dolores, again interrupting, has stated, "He never eats. Can't you tell? Dr. Abstemious, I used to call him."

"Well, I'm really hungry, I'll see you two later." And with an uncertain smile (from shyness? annoyance? and if annoyance, at which of them?), Carla has left. She is pushing back into the room, through the crowds; she has vanished behind the glass.

Looking at Dolores then, the old doctor is seized with rage; he stares at that puffy, self-adoring face, those dark and infinitely self-pitying eyes. How he longs to push her against the railing, down into the sand! How he despises her!

"My darling, I believe you're really hungry after all," is what Dolores says, but she may have felt some of his anger, for she deftly steps sideways, on her high, thin, dangerous heels, just out of his reach.

"Not in the least," says Benito rigidly. "In fact, I think I'll go for a walk on the beach."

Down on the sand, though, as he walks along the dark, packed strip that is nearest to the sea, Benito's confusion increases. He feels the presence of those people in that rather vulgar, glassed-in house behind him—of Dolores Gutierrez and Herman Tolliver, and God knows who else, what other ghosts from his past whom he simply failed to see. As though they were giants, he feels their looming presences, and feels their connection to some past year or years of his own life. He no longer knows where he is. What place is this, what country? What rolling gray-green ocean does he walk beside? What year it this, and what is his own true age?

Clearly, some derangement has taken hold of him, or nearly, and Benito is forced to fight back with certain heavy and irrefutable facts: this is September, 1990, the last year of a decade, and the year in which Elizabeth died. He is in Stinson Beach, and if he continues walking far enough along the coast—he is heading south, toward the Golden Gate— he will be in sight of beautiful, mystical San Francisco, the city and the center of all his early dreams, the city where everything, finally, happened: Dolores Gutierrez and his medical degree; Herman Tolliver and those hotels. His (at last) successful medical practice. Elizabeth, and all that money, and his house with its fabulous views. His fame as Dr. Do-Good.

His whole San Francisco history seems to rise up then and to break his heart. The city itself is still pale and distant and invisible, and he stands absolutely still, a tall figure on the sand, next to an intricate, crumbling sand castle that some children have recently abandoned.

Hearing running feet behind him, at that moment the doctor turns in fright—expecting what? some dangerous stranger?—but it is Carla, out of breath, her hair streaming backward in the wind. His savior.

"Ah, you," he says to her. "You ran."

"And these are not the greatest running shoes." She laughs, pointing down to her sandals, now sand-streaked and damp.

"You came after me—"

She looks down, and away. "Well. It was partly an excuse to get out of there. It was getting a little claustrophobic, and almost everyone I talked to was hard-of-hearing."

"Oh, right."

"Well, shall we walk for a while?"

"*Yes.*"

Walking along with Carla, the doctor finds that those giants from his dark and tangled past have quite suddenly receded: Dolores and Tolliver have shrunk down to human size, the size of people accidentally encountered at a party. Such meetings can happen to anyone, easily, especially at a certain age.

Benito even finds that he can talk about them. "To tell you the truth"—an ominous beginning, he knows, but it is what he intends to do—"I did some business with Herman Tolliver a long time ago, maybe forty years. It came out very well, financially, but I'm still a little ashamed of it. It seems to me now that I was pretending to myself not to know certain things that I really did know."

"You mean about his hotels?"

"Well, yes. Hotels. But how do you—does everyone know all that?"

"I'm a reporter, remember? Investigative." She laughs, then sniffles a little in the hard, cold ocean wind. "He had an idea a few years back about running for supervisor, but I'm sure he was really thinking mayor, ultimately. But we dug up some stuff."

"Here, take my handkerchief—"

"Thanks. Anyway, he was persuaded to forget it. There were really ugly things about preteenage Asian girls. We made a bargain: the papers would print only the stuff about his 'tax problems' if he'd bow out." She sighs, a little ruefully. "I don't know. It might have been better to let him get into politics; he might have done less harm that way."

This walk, and the conversation, are serving both to calm and to excite the doctor. Simultaneously. Most peculiar. He feels a calm, and at the same time a strange, warm, quiet excitement. "How do you mean?" he asks Carla.

"Oh, he got in deeper and deeper. Getting richer and richer."

"I got richer and richer, too, back then. Sometimes I felt like I owned the whole goddam city." Benito is paying very little attention to what he is saying; it is now all he can do to prevent himself from speaking his heart, from saying, "When will you marry me? How soon can that be?"

"But that's great that you made so much money," Carla says. "That way you could start those clinics, and do so much good."

Barely listening, Benito murmurs, "I suppose . . ."

She could redecorate the house any way she would like to, he thinks. Throw things out, repaint, reupholster, hang mirrors. His imagination sees, all completed, a brilliant house, with Carla its brilliant, shining center.

"How did you happen to know Dolores?" Carla is asking.

By now they have reached the end of the beach: a high mass of rocks left there by mammoth storms the year before. Impassable. Beyond lies more beach, more cliffs, more headlands, all along the way to the sight of the distant city.

"Actually, Dolores was an old girlfriend, you might say." Since he cares so much for this girl, Benito will never lie to her, he thinks. "You might not believe this, but she was quite a beauty in her day."

"Oh, I believe you. She's still so vain. That hair."

Benito laughs, feeling pleased, and wondering, Can this adorable girl be, even slightly, jealous? "You're right there," he tells Carla. "Very vain, always was. Of course, she's a few years older than I am."

"I guess we have to turn around now," says Carla.

"And now Dolores tells me that she and Posey Pendergast were at one time, uh, lovers," Benito continues, in his honest mode.

"I guess they could have been," Carla muses. "On the other hand, it's my impression that Dolores lies a lot. And Posey I'm just not sure about. Nor any of that group, for that matter. Tolliver, all those people. It's worrying." She laughs. "I guess I sort of hoped you might know something about them. Sort of explain them to me."

Not having listened carefully to much of this, Benito rephrases the question he does not remember having begun to ask before, which Dolores interrupted: "How do you know Posey?" he asks Carla.

"It's mostly her son I know, Patrick. He's my fiancé, I guess you could say. We were planning to make it legal, and I guess we will. Any day now." And she goes on, "Actually, Patrick was supposed to come today, and then he couldn't, and then I thought—I thought of you."

The sun has sunk into the ocean, and Benito's heart has sunk with it, drowned. He shudders, despising himself. How could he possibly have imagined, how not have guessed?

"How nice," Benito remarks, without meaning, and then he babbles on, "You know, the whole city seems so corrupt these days. It's all real estate, and deals."

"Get real," she chides him, in her harsh young voice. "That's what it's like all over."

"Well, I'll be awfully glad to get back to Mexico. At least I more or less understand the corruption there."

"Are you going back for long?"

The wind is really cold now. Benito sniffs, wishing he had his hand-kerchief back, and unable to ask for it. "Oh, permanently," he tells Carla. "A permanent move. I want to be near my clinics. See how they're doing. Maybe help."

The doctor had no plan to say (much less to do) any of this before he spoke, but he knows that he is now committed to this action. This permanent move. He will buy a house in San Cristóbal de las Casas, and will bring his mother there, from Oaxaca, to live in that house for as long as she lasts. And he, for as long as he lasts, will work in his clinics, with his own poor.

"Well, that's great. Maybe we could work out a little interview before you go."

"Well, maybe."

"I wonder if we couldn't just bypass the party for now," says Carla. "I'm just not up to going in again, going through all that, with those people."

"Nor I," the doctor tells her. "Good idea."

"I'll call Posey as soon as we get back. Did she tell you the house was up for sale? She may have sold it today—all those people . . ."

Half hearing her, the doctor is wrestling with the idea of a return to the city, which is suddenly unaccountably terrible to him; he dreads the first pale, romantic view of it from the bridge, and then the drive across town to his empty house, after dropping Carla off on Telegraph Hill. His house with its night views of city hills and lights. But he braces himself with the thought that he won't be in San Francisco long this time. That as soon as he can arrange things he will be back in Chiapas, in Mexico. For the rest of his life.

And thus he manages to walk on, following Carla past the big, fancy house, for sale—and all those people, the house's rich and crazily corrupt population. He manages to walk across the sand toward his car, and the long, circuitous, and risky drive to the city.

The Islands

What does it mean to love an animal, a pet, in my case a cat, in the fierce, entire, and unambivalent way that some of us do? I really want to know this. Does the cat (did the cat) represent some person, a parent, or a child? some part of one's self? I don't think so—and none of the words or phrases that one uses for human connections sounds quite right: "crazy about," "really liked," "very fond of"—none of those describes how I felt and still feel about my cat. Many years ago, soon after we got the cat (her name was Pink), I went to Rome with my husband, Andrew, whom I really liked; I was crazy about Andrew, and very fond of him too. And I have a most vivid memory of lying awake in Rome, in the pretty bed in its deep alcove, in the nice small hotel near the Borghese Gardens—lying there, so fortunate to be in Rome, with Andrew, and missing Pink, a small striped cat with no tail—missing Pink unbearably. Even blaming Andrew for having brought me there, although he loved her too, almost as much as I did. And now Pink has died, and I cannot accept or believe in her death, any more than I could believe in Rome. (Andrew also died, three years ago, but this is not his story.)

A couple of days after Pink died (this has all been recent), I went to Hawaii with a new friend, Slater. It had not been planned that way; I had known for months that Pink was slowly failing (she was nineteen), but I did not expect her to die. She just suddenly did, and then I went off to "the islands," as my old friend Zoe Pinkerton used to call them, in her nasal, moneyed voice. I went to Hawaii as planned, which interfered with my proper mourning for Pink. I feel as though those islands interposed themselves between her death and me. When I needed to be alone, to absorb her death, I was over there with Slater.

. . .

Slater is a developer; malls and condominium complexes all over the world. Andrew would not have approved of Slater, and sometimes I don't think I do either. Slater is tall and lean, red-haired, a little younger than I am, and very attractive, I suppose, although on first meeting Slater I was not at all drawn to him (which I have come to think is one of the reasons he found me so attractive, calling me the next day, insisting on dinner that night; he was probably used to women who found him terrific, right off). But I thought Slater talked too much about money, or just talked too much, period.

Later on, when I began to like him a little better (I was flattered by all that attention, is the truth), I thought that Slater's very differences from Andrew should be a good sign. You're supposed to look for opposites, not reproductions, I read somewhere.

Andrew and I had acquired Pink from Zoe, a very rich alcoholic, at that time a new neighbor of ours in Berkeley. Having met Andrew down in his bookstore, she invited us to what turned out to be a very long Sunday-lunch party in her splendidly decked and viewed new Berkeley hills house. Getting to know some of the least offensive neighbors, is how she probably thought of it. Her style was harsh, abrasive; anything for a laugh was surely one of her mottoes, but she was pretty funny, fairly often. We saw her around when she first moved to Berkeley (from Ireland: a brief experiment that had not worked out too well). And then she met Andrew in his store, and found that we were neighbors, and she invited us to her party, and Andrew fell in love with a beautiful cat. "The most beautiful cat I ever saw," he told Zoe, and she was, soft and silver, with great blue eyes. The mother of Pink.

"Well, you're in luck," Zoe told us. "That's Molly Bloom, and she just had five kittens. They're all in a box downstairs, in my bedroom, and you get to choose any one you want. It's your door prize for being such a handsome couple."

Andrew went off to look at the kittens, and then came back up to me. "There's one that's really great," he said. "A tailless wonder. Must be part Manx."

As in several Berkeley hills houses, Zoe's great sprawl of a bedroom was downstairs, with its own narrow deck, its view of the bay and the bridge, and of San Francisco. The room was the most appalling mess I had ever seen. Clothes, papers, books, dirty glasses, spilled powder, more clothes dumped everywhere. I was surprised that my tidy, somewhat censorious husband even entered, and that he was able to find the big wicker basket (filled with what looked to be discarded silk underthings, presumably clean) in which five very tiny kittens mewed and tried to rise and stalk about on thin, uncertain legs.

The one that Andrew had picked was gray striped, a tabby, with a stub of a tail, very large eyes, and tall ears. I agreed that she was darling, how great it would be to have a cat again; our last cat, Lily, who was sweet and pretty but undistinguished, had died some years ago. And so Andrew and I went back upstairs and told Zoe, who was almost very drunk, that we wanted the one with no tail.

"Oh, Stubs," she rasped. "You don't have to take that one. What are you guys, some kind of Berkeley bleeding hearts? You can have a whole cat." And she laughed, delighted as always with her own wit.

No, we told her. We wanted that particular cat. We liked her best.

Aside from seeing the cats—our first sight of Pink!—the best part of Zoe's lunch was her daughter, Lucy, a shy, pretty, and very gentle young woman—as opposed to the other guests, a rowdy, oil-rich group, old friends of Zoe's from Texas.

"What a curious litter," I remarked to Andrew, walking home up Marin to our considerably smaller house. "All different. Five different patterns of cat."

"Five fathers." Andrew had read a book about this, I could tell. Andrew read everything. "It's called multiple insemination, and occurs fairly often in cats. It's theoretically possible in humans, but they haven't come across any instances." He laughed, really pleased with this lore.

"It's sure something to think about."

"Just don't."

Andrew. An extremely smart, passionate, selfish, and generous man, a medium-successful bookstore owner. A former academic: he left teaching in order to have more time to read, he said. Also (I thought) he much preferred being alone in his store to the company of students or, worse, of other professors—a loner, Andrew. Small and almost handsome, competitive, a gifted tennis player, mediocre pianist. Gray hair and gray-green eyes. As I have said, I was crazy about Andrew (usually). I found him funny and interestingly observant, sexy and smart. His death was more grievous to me than I can (or will) say.

"You guys don't have to take Stubs; you can have a whole cat all your own." Zoe Pinkerton on the phone, a few days later. Like many alcoholics, she tended to repeat herself, although in Zoe's case some vast Texas store of self-confidence may have fueled her repetitions.

And we in our turn repeated: we wanted the little one with no tail.

Zoe told us that she would bring "Stubs" over in a week or so; then the kittens would be old enough to leave Molly Bloom.

Andrew: "Molly Bloom indeed."

I: "No wonder she got multiply inseminated."

Andrew: "Exactly."

We both, though somewhat warily, liked Zoe. Or we were both somewhat charmed by her. For one thing, she made it clear that she thought we were great. For another, she was smart; she had read even more than Andrew had.

A very small woman, she walked with a swagger; her laugh was loud, and liberal. I sometimes felt that Pink was a little like Zoe—a tiny cat with a high, proud walk; a cat with a lot to say.

In a couple of weeks, then, Zoe called, and she came over with this tiny tailless kitten under her arm. A Saturday afternoon. Andrew was at home, puttering in the garden like the good Berkeley husband that he did not intend to be.

Zoe arrived in her purple suede pants and a vivid orange sweater (this picture is a little poignant; fairly soon after that the booze began to get the better of her legs, and she stopped taking walks at all). She held out a tiny kitten, all huge gray eyes and pointed ears. A kitten who took one look at us and began to purr; she purred for several days, it seemed, as she walked all over our house and made it her own. This is absolutely the best place I've ever been, she seemed to say, and you are the greatest people—you are my people.

From the beginning, then, our connection with Pink seemed like a privilege; automatically we accorded her rights that poor Lily would never have aspired to.

She decided to sleep with us. In the middle of the night there came a light soft plop on our bed, which was low and wide, and then a small sound, *mmrrr,* a little announcement of her presence. "Littlest announcer," said Andrew, and we called her that, among her other names. Neither of us ever mentioned locking her out.

Several times in the night she would leave us and then return, each time with the same small sound, the littlest announcement.

In those days, the early days of Pink, I was doing a lot of freelance editing for local small presses, which is to say that I spent many waking hours at my desk. Pink assessed my habits early on, and decided to make them her own; or perhaps she decided that she too was an editor. In any case she would come up to my lap, where she would sit, often looking up with something to say. She was in fact the only cat I have ever known with whom a sort of conversation was possible; we made sounds back and forth at each other, very politely, and though mine were mostly non-sense syllables, Pink seemed pleased.

Pink was her main name, about which Zoe Pinkerton was very happy. "Lordy, no one's ever named a cat for me before." But Andrew and I used many other names for her. I had an idea that Pink liked a new name occasionally; maybe we all would? In any case we called her a lot of other, mostly P-starting names: Peppercorn, Pipsy Doodler, Poipu Beach. This last was a favorite place of Zoe's, when she went out to "the islands." Pink seemed to like all those names; she regarded us both with her great gray eyes—especially me; she was always mostly my cat.

Worried about raccoons and Berkeley free-roaming dogs, we decided early on that Pink was to be a house cat, for good. She was not expendable. But Andrew and I liked to take weekend trips, and after she came to live with us we often took Pink along. She liked car travel right away; settled on the seat between us, she would join right in whenever we broke what had been a silence—not interrupting, just adding her own small voice, a sort of soft clear mew.

This must have been in the early seventies; we talked a lot about Nixon and Watergate. "Mew if you think he's guilty," Andrew would say to Pink, who always responded satisfactorily.

Sometimes, especially on summer trips, we would take Pink out for a semiwalk; our following Pink is what it usually amounted to, as she bounded into some meadow grass, with miniature leaps. Once, before I could stop her, she suddenly raced ahead—to a chipmunk. I was horrified. But then she raced back to me with the chipmunk in her mouth, and after a tiny shake she let him go, and the chipmunk ran off, unscathed. (Pink had what hunters call a soft mouth. Of course she did.)

We went to Rome and I missed her, very much; and we went off to the Piazza Argentina and gave a lot of lire to the very old woman there who was feeding all those mangy, half-blind cats. In honor of Pink.

I hope that I am not describing some idealized "perfect" adorable cat, because Pink was never that. She was entirely herself, sometimes cross and always independent. On the few occasions when I swatted her (very gently), she would hit me right back, a return swat on the hand—though always with sheathed claws.

I like to think that her long life with us, and then just with me, was a very happy one. Her version, though, would undoubtedly state that she was perfectly happy until Black and Brown moved in.

Another Berkeley lunch. A weekday, and all the women present work, and have very little time, and so this getting together seems a rare treat. Our hostess, a diminutive and brilliant art historian, announces that her cat, Parsley, is extremely pregnant. "Honestly, any minute," she laughs, and this is clearly true; the poor burdened cat, a brown Burmese, comes into the room, heavy and uncomfortable and restless. Searching.

A little later, in the midst of serving our many-salad lunch, the hostess says that the cat is actually having her kittens now, in the kitchen closet. We all troop out into the kitchen to watch.

The first tiny sac-enclosed kitten to barrel out is a black one, instantly vigorous, eager to stand up and get on with her life. Then three more come at intervals; it is harder to make out their colors.

"More multiple insemination," I told Andrew that night.

"It must be rife in Berkeley, like everyone says."

"It was fascinating, watching them being born."

"I guess, if you like obstetrics."

A month or so later the art historian friend called with a very sad story; she had just been diagnosed as being very clearly allergic to cats. "I thought I wasn't feeling too well, but I never thought it could be the cats. I know you already have that marvelous Pink, but do you think—until I find someone to take them? Just the two that are left?"

Surprisingly, Andrew, when consulted, said, "Well, why not? Be entertainment for old Pink; she must be getting pretty bored with just us."

We did not consult Pink, who hated those cats on sight. But Andrew was right away crazy about them, especially the black one (maybe he had wanted a cat of his own?). We called them, of course, Black and Brown. They were two Burmese females, or semi-Burmese, soon established in our house and seeming to believe that they lived there.

Black was (she is) the more interesting and aggressive of the two. And from the first she truly took to Pink, exhibiting the sort of clear affection that admits of no rebuff.

We had had Pink spayed as soon as she was old enough, after one quite miserable heat. And now Black and Brown seemed to come into heat consecutively, and to look to Pink for relief. She raged and scratched at them as they, alternatively, squirmed and rubbed toward her. Especially Brown, who gave all the signs of a major passion for Pink. Furious, Pink seemed to be saying, Even if I were the tomcat that you long for, I would never look at you.

Black and Brown were spayed, and relations among the cats settled down to a much less luridly sexual pattern. Black and Brown both liked Pink and wished to be close to her, which she would almost never permit. She refused to eat with them, haughtily waiting at mealtimes until they were through.

It is easy for me to imagine Black and Brown as people, as women. Black would be a sculptor, I think, very strong, moving freely and widely through the world. Unmarried, no children. Whereas Brown would be a very sweet and pretty, rather silly woman, adored by her husband and sons.

But I do not imagine Pink as a person at all. I only see her as herself. A cat.

Zoe was going to move to Hawaii, she suddenly said. "Somewhere on Kauai, natch, and probably Poipu, if those grubby developers have kept their hands off anything there." Her hatchet laugh. "But I like the idea of living on the islands, away from it all. And so does Gordon. You guys will have to come and visit us there. Bring Pink, but not those other two strays."

"Gordon" was a new beau, just turned up from somewhere in Zoe's complex Dallas childhood. With misgivings, but I think mostly goodwill, we went over to meet him, to hear about all these new plans.

Gordon was dark and pale and puffy, great black blotches under his narrow, dishonest eyes, a practiced laugh. Meeting him, I right off thought, They're not going to Hawaii; they're not going anywhere together.

Gordon did not drink at all that day, although I later heard that he was a famous drunk. But occasionally he chided Zoe, who as usual was belting down vodka on ice. "Now Baby," he kept saying. (Strident, striding Zoe—Baby?) "Let's go easy on the sauce. Remember what we promised?" (We?)

At which Zoe laughed long and loud, as though her drinking were a good joke that we all shared.

A week or so after that Zoe called and said she was just out of the hospital. "I'm not in the greatest shape in the world," she said—and after that there was no more mention of Gordon, nor of a move to Hawaii.

And not very long after that Zoe moved down to Santa Barbara. She had friends there, she said.

Pink by now was in some cat equivalent to middle age. Still quite small, still playful at times, she was almost always talkative. She disliked Black and Brown, but sometimes I would find her nestled against one of them, usually Black, in sleep. I had a clear sense that I was not supposed to know about this occasional rapport, or whatever. Pink still came up to my lap as I worked, and she slept on our bed at night, which we had always forbidden Black and Brown to do.

We bought a new, somewhat larger house, farther up in the hills. It had stairs, and the cats ran happily up and down, and they seemed to thrive, like elderly people who benefit from a new program of exercise.

. . .

Andrew got sick, a terrible swift-moving cancer that killed him within a year, and for a long time I did very little but grieve. I sometimes saw friends, and I tried to work. There was a lot to do about Andrew's bookstore, which I sold, but mostly I stayed at home with my cats, all of whom were now allowed to sleep with me on that suddenly too-wide bed.

Pink at that time chose to get under the covers with me. In a peremptory way she would tap at my cheek or my forehead, demanding to be taken in. This would happen several times in the course of the night, which was not a great help to my already fragile pattern of sleep, but it never occurred to me to deny her. And I was always too embarrassed to mention this to my doctor when I complained of lack of sleep.

And then after several years I met Slater, at a well-meaning friend's house. Although as I have said I did not much like him at first, I was struck by his nice dark-red hair, and by his extreme directness—Andrew had a tendency to be vague; it was sometimes hard to get at just what he meant. Not so with Slater, who was very clear—immediately clear about the fact that he liked me a lot, and wanted us to spend time together. And so we became somewhat involved, Slater and I, despite certain temperamental obstacles, including the fact that he does not much like cats.

And eventually we began to plan a trip to Hawaii, where Slater had business to see to.

Pink as an old cat slept more and more, and her high-assed strut showed sometimes a slight arthritic creak. Her voice got appreciably louder; no longer a littlest announcer, her statements were loud and clear (I have to admit, it was not the most attractive sound). It seems possible that she was getting a little deaf. When I took her to the vet, a sympathetic, tall, and handsome young Japanese woman, she always said, "She sure doesn't look her age—" at which both Pink and I preened.

The vet, Dr. Ino, greatly admired the stripes below Pink's neck, on her breast, which looked like intricate necklaces. I admired them too (and so had Andrew).

Needless to say, the cats were perfectly trained to the sandbox, and very dainty in their habits. But at a certain point I began to notice small accidents around the house, from time to time. Especially when I had been away for a day or two. It seemed a punishment, cat turds in some dark corner. But it was hard to fix responsibility, and I decided to blame all three—and to take various measures like the installation of an upstairs sandbox, which helped. I did think Pink was getting a little old for all those stairs.

Since she was an old cat I sometimes, though rarely, thought of the fact that Pink would die. Of course she would, eventually—although at times (bad times: the weeks and months around Andrew's illness and death) I melodramatically announced (more or less to myself) that Pink's death would be the one thing I could not bear. "Pink has promised to outlive me," I told several friends, and almost believed.

At times I even felt that we were the same person-cat, that we somehow inhabited each other. In a way I still do feel that—if I did not, her loss would be truly unbearable.

I worried about her when I went away on trips. I would always come home, come into my house, with some little apprehension that she might not be there. She was usually the last of the three cats to appear in the kitchen, where I stood confused among baggage, mail, and phone messages. I would greet Black and Brown, and then begin to call her— "Pink, Pink?"—until, very diffident and proud, she would stroll unhurriedly toward me, and I would sweep her up into my arms with foolish cries of relief, and of love. *Ah, my darling old Pink.*

As I have said, Slater did not particularly like cats; he had nothing against them, really, just a general indifference. He eventually developed a fondness for Brown, believing that she liked him too, but actually Brown is a whore among cats; she will purr and rub up against anyone who might feed her. Whereas Pink was always discriminating, in every way, and fussy. Slater complained that one of the cats deposited small turds on the bathmat in the room where he sometimes showered, and I am afraid that this was indeed old Pink, both angry and becoming incontinent.

One night at dinner at my house, when Slater and I, alone, were admiring my view of the bay and of romantic San Francisco, all those lights, we were also talking about our trip to Hawaii. Making plans. He had been there before and was enthusiastic.

Then the phone rang, and it was Lucy, daughter of Zoe, who told me that her mother had died the day before, in Santa Barbara. "Her doctor said it was amazing she'd lived so long. All those years of booze."

"I guess. But Lucy, it's so sad, I'm so sorry."

"I know." A pause. "I'd love to see you sometime. How's old Pink?"

"Oh, Pink's fine," I lied.

Coming back to the table, I explained as best I could about Zoe Pinkerton, how we got Pink. I played it all down, knowing his feelings about cats. But I thought he would like the multiple-insemination part, and he did—as had Andrew. (It is startling when two such dissimilar men, Andrew, the somewhat dreamy book person, and Slater, the practical man, get so turned on by the same dumb joke.)

"So strange that we're going to Poipu," I told Slater. "Zoe always talked about Poipu." As I said this I knew it was not the sort of coincidence that Slater would find remarkable.

"I'm afraid it's changed a lot," he said, quite missing the point. "The early developers have probably knocked hell out of it. The greedy competition."

So much for mysterious ways.

Two days before we were to go to Hawaii, in the morning Pink seemed disoriented, unsure when she was in her sandbox, her feeding place. Also, she clearly had some bad intestinal disorder. She was very sick, but still in a way it seemed cruel to take her to the vet, whom I somehow knew could do nothing for her. However, at last I saw no alternative.

She (Dr. Ino, the admirable vet) found a large hard mass in Pink's stomach, almost certainly cancer. Inoperable. "I just can't reverse what's wrong with her," the doctor told me, with great sadness. And succinctness: I saw what she meant. I was so terribly torn, though: Should I bring Pink home for a few more days—whatever was left to her—although she was so miserable, so embarrassed at her own condition?

I chose not to do that (although I still wonder, I still am torn). And I still cannot think of those last moments of Pink. Whose death I chose.

I wept on and off for a couple of days. I called some close friends who would have wanted to know about Pink, I thought; they were all most supportively kind (most of my best friends love cats).

And then it was time to leave for Hawaii.

Sometimes, during those days of packing and then flying to Hawaii, I thought it odd that Pink was not more constantly on my mind, even odd that I did not weep more than I did. Now, though, looking back on that trip and its various aftermaths, I see that in fact I was thinking about Pink all that time, that she was totally in charge, as she always had been.

We stayed in a pretty condominium complex, two-story white buildings with porches and decks, and everywhere sweeping green lawns, and flowers. A low wall of rocks, a small coarsely sanded beach, and the vast and billowing sea.

Ours was a second-floor unit, with a nice wide balcony for sunset drinks, or daytime sunning. And, looking down from that balcony one night, our first, I saw the people in the building next door, out on the grass beside what must have been their kitchen, *feeding their cats.* They must have brought along these cats, two supple gray Siamese, and were giving them their supper. I chose not to mention this to Slater, I thought I could imagine his reaction, but in the days after that, every time we walked past that building I slowed my pace and looked carefully for the cats, and a couple of times I saw them. Such pretty cats, and very friendly, for Siamese. Imagine: traveling to Hawaii with your cats— though I was not at all sure that I would have wanted Black and Brown along, nice as they are, and pretty.

Another cat event (there were four in all) came as we drove from Lihue back to Poipu, going very slowly over those very sedate tree- and flower-lined streets, with their decorous, spare houses. Suddenly I felt— we felt—a sort of thump, and Slater, looking startled, slowed down even further and looked back.

"Lord God, that was a cat," he said.

"A cat?"

"She ran right out into the car. And then ran back."

"Are you sure? She's all right?"

"Absolutely. Got a good scare though." Slater chuckled.

But you might have killed a cat, I did not say. And for a moment I wondered if he actually had, and lied, saying the cat was okay. However, Slater would never lie to spare my feelings, I am quite sure of that.

The third cat happening took place as we drove down a winding, very steep mountain road (we had been up to see the mammoth gorges cut into the island, near its western edge). On either side of the road was thick green jungle growth—and suddenly, there among the vines and shrubs, I saw a small yellow cat staring out, her eyes lowered. Frightened. Eyes begging.

Slater saw her too, and even he observed, "Good Lord, people dumping off animals to starve. It's awful."

"You're sure she doesn't live out there? a wilderness cat?"

"I don't think so." Honest Slater.

We did not talk then or later about going back to rescue that cat—not until the next day, when he asked me what I would like to do and I said, "I'd like to go back for that cat." He assumed I was joking, and I guess I mostly was. There were too many obvious reasons not to save that particular cat, including the difficulty of finding her again. But I remembered her face; I can see it still, that expression of much-resented dependence. It was a way even Pink looked, very occasionally.

Wherever we drove, through small neat impoverished "native" settlements (blocks of houses that Slater and his cohorts planned to buy, and demolish, to replace with fancy condos), with their lavish flowers all restrained into tiny beds, I kept looking at the yards, and under the houses. I wanted to see a cat, or some cats (I wanted to see Pink again). Realizing what I was doing, I continued to do it, to strain for the sight of a cat.

The fourth and final cat event took place as we walked home from dinner one night, in the flower-scented, corny-romantic Hawaiian darkness. To our left was the surging black sea and to our right large tamed white shrubbery, and a hotel swimming pool, glistening darkly under feeble yellow floodlights. And then quite suddenly, from nowhere, a small cat appeared in our path, shyly and uncertainly arching her back against a bush. A black cat with some yellow tortoise markings, a long thin curve of a tail.

"He looks just like your Pink, doesn't he?" Slater actually said this, and I suppose he believed it to be true.

"What—Pink? But her tail—Jesus, didn't you even see my cat?"

I'm afraid I went on in this vein, sporadically, for several days. But it did seem so incredible, not remembering Pink, my elegantly striped, my tailless wonder. (It is also true that I was purposefully using this lapse, as one will, in a poor connection.)

I dreaded going home with no Pink to call out to as I came in the door. And the actuality was nearly as bad as my imaginings of it: Black and Brown, lazy and affectionate, glad to see me. And no Pink, with her scolding *hauteur,* her long-delayed yielding to my blandishments.

I had no good pictures of Pink, and to explain this odd fact I have to admit that I am very bad about snapshots; I have never devised a really good way of storing and keeping them, and tend rather to enclose any interesting ones in letters to people who might like them, to whom they would have some meaning. And to shove the others into drawers, among old letters and other unclassifiable mementos.

I began then to scour my house for Pink pictures, looking everywhere. In an album (Andrew and I put together a couple of albums, early on) I found a great many pictures of Pink as a tiny, tall-eared, brand-new kitten, stalking across a padded window seat, hiding behind an oversized Boston fern—among all the other pictures from those days: Zoe Pinkerton, happy and smoking a long cigarette and almost drunk, wearing outrageous colors, on the deck of her house. And Andrew and I, young and very happy, silly, snapped by someone at a party. Andrew in his bookstore, horn-rimmed and quirky. Andrew uncharacteristically working in our garden. Andrew all over the place.

But no middle-year or recent pictures of Pink. I had in fact (I then remembered) sent the most recent shots of Pink to Zoe; it must have been just before she (Zoe) died, with a silly note about old survivors, something like that. It occurred to me to get in touch with Lucy, Zoe's daughter, to see if those pictures had turned up among Zoe's "effects," but knowing the chaos in which Zoe had always lived (and doubtless died) I decided that this would be tactless, unnecessary trouble. And I gave up looking for pictures.

Slater called yesterday to say that he is going back to Hawaii, a sudden trip. Business. I imagine that he is about to finish the ruination of all that was left of Zoe's islands. He certainly did not suggest that I come along, nor did he speak specifically of our getting together again, and I rather think that he, like me, has begun to wonder what we were doing together in the first place. It does seem to me that I was drawn to him for a very suspicious reason, his lack of resemblance to Andrew: Whyever should I seek out the opposite of a person I truly loved?

But I do look forward to some time alone now. I will think about Pink—I always feel her presence in my house, everywhere. Pink, stalking and severe, ears high. Pink, in my lap, raising her head with some small soft thing to say.

And maybe, since Black and Brown are getting fairly old now too, I will think about getting another new young cat. Maybe, with luck, a small gray partially Manx, with no tail at all, and beautiful necklaces.

The Drinking Club

Harsh, powerful sunlight strikes the far edge of the giant pink bed on which Karen Brownfield, a pianist, now lies alone, Karen, on a concert tour. It must be midmorning, or nearly. On the other hand, perhaps early afternoon? Karen seems to have removed her watch; no doubt she has thrown it somewhere, or maybe given it away to someone (she did that once in Paris; she clearly remembers the boy's fair pretty face), However, wherever she is now and whatever time it is, what day, she is not in Paris. Karen is sure of that much.

Would knowing any more, though, improve her head, which threatens to split open like a watermelon in the sun? If she knew where she was, for example, would she feel any better?

She does not really believe that any such knowledge would help her. If she rang room service, and they told her, This is the Palmer House, in Cincinnati (if there is a Palmer House in Cincinnati), why would that improve her day? She doesn't see it, although her husband, a psychiatrist, undoubtedly would. Julian, Karen's husband, is committed to what he calls emotional information.

If she phoned Julian could he possibly tell her what went on last night here in her room? Well, of course not.

If she had played a concert, though, she would remember; she always does. And so, did she cancel a concert? That seems likely; quite possibly she canceled at about this same time yesterday, perhaps from this room, this bedside pink princess telephone. Noon is Karen's usual canceling time, her cop-out hour.

Whatever it was she did last night, for which she must have canceled her concert, made the most incredible whirlwind mess of the room.

Karen closes her eyes against the sight of it: wadded-up clothes (hers), and sheets, so many sheets! all also wadded up. And knocked-over lamps, two of them on the floor. Full ashtrays. Karen doesn't smoke; they smell awful. Reeking glasses, partly filled with undrunk booze. Lord God, did she throw a party? *Who?*

What she can least well face, Karen has learned from other such mornings, is the sight of her own face. *I can't face my face,* she once thought, on some other occasion, and it almost made her laugh. She is surely not laughing now, though. She is seriously concerned with the logistics of getting in and out of the bathroom with no smallest glimpse of herself in any mirror. She knows that even if you wrap yourself in a sheet you are apt to see, but she manages not to.

Once back from the bathroom, where she found her watch (stopped), and where she was able to braid her hair without looking at it—she is good at this—Karen decides that what she really needs is something to drink. Then she can begin with the guilt over whatever went on last night. But first she will telephone Julian, in California.

If another person should enter that room, for instance the elderly black waiter delivering the wine that Karen is about to order (this hotel, which is famous, is in Atlanta), he would see, in addition to the mess, a woman whose face is the color of white linen. A crazy-looking woman, with the whitest face and the biggest eyes, dark lake-blue, and the longest, thickest rope of red hair that he has ever seen.

It is actually only about nine-thirty in Atlanta. Karen has slept less than she thinks she has. Thus in California it is about six-thirty.

It is early for a phone call, especially since Julian is not alone in his bed, their bed, his and Karen's. He is there with his lover, Lila Lewisohn, also a psychiatrist. ("Julian's *girl,*" would be Karen's phrase for what Lila is—*girl,* with ugly emphasis—if Karen actually knew what she now only strongly suspects.)

This is something that Julian and Lila have never done before, slept together at Julian's house. Usually there are children at home, as well as Karen, and until recently there was Lila's husband to whom she had to return, Garrett Lewisohn, a lawyer.

And tonight, after dinner in Sausalito, they had meant to go back to Lila's house, on the western, seaward slope of San Francisco. However, as they approached the Golden Gate, the yellow fog lights and heavy traffic, they learned from another motorist that there had been an accident on the bridge, and it would be closed for at least another half hour. Not long to wait; ordinarily they would have done just that: Lila and Julian are accustomed to postponements, to deferral of pleasure. Tonight, though, for whatever reasons, an unusual mood of urgency was upon them (the wine, and the fact that they hadn't been together for several weeks, Julian having been occupied with holding Karen together for her tour). In the restaurant their hands often met, eyes meeting too, laughing but complicitous, sexual.

And so, "I don't want to wait, do you?" Julian.

"No. But—"

Julian however had begun to turn the car about and to head too fast toward Mill Valley. Up the winding road to his very large, ultracontemporary house, all glass and steel, among giant redwoods, mammoth ferns.

Lila has been there before, of course. She and Julian, after all, are colleagues. And the two couples, Julian and Karen, Garrett and Lila, were for a time ostensibly friends.

As lovers, though, Lila and Julian have mostly gone to motels for love, always as far from the city as they have had time for: Half Moon Bay, Bodega Bay—they seem to seek the coast. More recently, since Garrett left (moving down to Atherton with his pregnant young girlfriend), they have enjoyed the privacy—the incredible luxury, it seems to them— of Lila's small but pleasant house.

Tonight, though, Julian's house. Or Karen's house. Her room. Her bed.

.   .   .

Just before the phone rings and long before any sunlight penetrates the morning fog that envelops Julian's house, naked Lila's very long brown legs are entangled in sheets, her upper body pressed to Julian's bare bony back. They breathe in unison, deeply.

(This is a scene that Karen has often imagined. Her most frequent and blackest fantasies are of Lila and Julian, in sexual poses. She has also thought of Julian with female patients; she has imagined him with some sad woman on the worn brown leather sofa in his office, humping away—although this seems much less likely than Julian with Lila.)

The phone bell. A soft, sudden, and terrible sound.

Both Julian and Lila, trained doctors, are instantly awake. And both, in the second before Julian answers it, think, Karen. Or maybe a patient; they both hope it will be a patient.

"This is Dr. Brownfield. Well Karen, of course I'm here, but my dear it is rather early. Six-thirty. Well, I know it's later where you are. Tuesday, you must be in Atlanta." He laughs, then coughs. "How is Atlanta? The concert? Well Karen, I'm really sorry. No I didn't—No I don't. Karen, I'm sorry. No I didn't. No of course I don't blame you. No one will—of course you can't play when you're sick. Yes it is unpredictable. No Karen, I am not mad at you. Yes, I do. No, I don't think I should come to Atlanta, even if I could. No. No. If you need a doctor—No Karen, I am not mad. Yes. Right. Good. Good for you. Goodbye. Love."

Hanging up, he leans back against the headboard and looks at Lila.

She sees that he is utterly, totally exhausted.

"Karen has a bad cold," says Julian. "She says."

"Oh." As though Karen could see her, Lila begins to pull sheets up around herself, covering bare breasts.

"She had to cancel the concert. Of course."

"By the way, what's your name?" Karen, in Atlanta, is speaking to the man who has brought her the wine, a man who is large and old and black, with big gnarled hands. The bottle that he has brought on a napkined silver tray is tall and green, cold, glistening rivulets running down its sides.

"Calvin Montgomery, ma'am."

"Oh Lord, please don't call me ma'am. My name is Karen, Mrs. Brownfield. But you have a beautiful name."

"Thank you, Mrs. Brown. Field."

Karen laughs. "And now if you could just open it. I'm a pianist, but I feel all thumbs today. Plus which I've got a cold." She laughs again.

As she watches him closely, eagerly, Calvin Montgomery with his big hands uncorks the wine in a single practiced gesture. "There you are. There's your cold cure."

They both laugh.

"Oh, Mr. Montgomery, thank *you*."

"Shall I make breakfast here?" Julian asks this of Lila. They are now sitting up in bed, both with sheets drawn up around them.

Looking at Julian, his thinning gray-brown hair, large sad and gray eyes, Lila thinks as she has before of the deep affinities binding them to each other. We could be brother and sister, she has sometimes thought. Blood ties.

"I don't think breakfast," she tells him. "I don't feet quite, you know, easy here." Knowing that he must feel the same about her being there. "I'd rather my house. If we have to eat breakfast."

"Well, something? Orange juice?" Julian has gotten up, is pulling on a robe. "You'll feel better after some juice," he reminds her.

Lila smiles, grateful. "Or I could just go home. But my car." Her car of course has been left in San Francisco, and suddenly this transportation problem seems both insuperable and highly symbolic. They are surely not supposed to sleep in this house.

Tendrils of fog reach around the smallest branches of Julian's huge redwoods, mysterious white feathers. And from somewhere comes the gentle, ambiguous sound of mourning doves, their softly descending notes.

I am simply not used to being here, Lila thinks, standing up and beginning to get into her clothes. I've never seen it before in the daytime, or almost day. All this fog. Julian is right, she thinks, I need some juice. Blood sugar.

· · ·

The wine makes Karen feel at the same time physically improved and considerably worse in her head. As shadows disperse and she begins to remember.

An interview. Yesterday about this time, or was it later? At lunch? Yes, lunch. In any case, she was being interviewed in a strange restaurant in the below-street-level part of this hotel. A more famous, possibly preferable restaurant is billed as "rooftop," to Karen a terrifying word. And so, this subterranean room, all stones and small calculated water-falls, and walls of sheet water, quite effective really but slightly scaring.

Her interviewer is a pale and puffy young man, with a small rosy mouth and blinking white-blue eyes. A Southern, very Southern voice.

At first he was hard to understand, but gradually, after the skirmishes of small talk, he began to come through. "Married to a psychiatrist," he was saying. "Must be extremely interesting. Though I don't suppose they talk a lot about their cases, not supposed to anyways. But don't you find it just the least little bit of what you might call a threat?"

"Oh, I do," Karen said. No one, certainly not the shrink that she herself once went to, though not for long, has ever quite asked this. And Karen realized that from the start she had felt something very sympathetic about this young man. Karen likes fat people; she finds them comforting. Julian is so extremely thin, all sharp bones and stretched dry skin.

"I don't need to tell you that the question is solely motivated by a personal curiosity," the young man assured her, blinking, signaling his commitment to truth. Hal, did he say his name was? Yes. Hal.

"I've just put in so much time with those fellows and lady shrinks too, that for the life of me I can't imagine a home life with any one of them," said Hal.

"Oh, you're absolutely right," Karen told him. And then she confided, "I think I'm coming down with a really bad cold. Can you hear it in my voice?"

"Oh, I sure can. Well, maybe this here ice tea was a mistake." At first this seemed an odd remark, and then not odd. Karen recognized a certain gleam in those pale eyes, along with a certain timid question in his voice.

"I'm sure you're right," she told him, laughing lightly and tossing her long braid back over her shoulder. "We need some stronger stuff.

What do folks around here mostly drink?" (Lord, where had she suddenly got that accent?)

"Bourbon, mostly. Although I've gone off that hard stuff myself." Righteous Hal. "But I can tell you, there's a certain very nice concoction—" He snapped his fingers for the waiter.

The concoction when it came was fairly sweet and very strong. Karen could tell it was strong. And watching Hal as he drank, his eager quick repeated sips, she thought, No wonder I like you.

They had a couple of concoctions, all the time talking in a very civilized way about Karen's professional history, Hal taking notes: Wellesley, Juilliard, the Paris Conservatory. Brahms, Chopin, Debussy.

And then, maybe on the third of those drinks, they returned to the question of shrinks. Living with them. Talking to them. The terror.

"Most probably in their spare time they ought to just only talk to each other," Hal said (fatally).

"Oh, you are so right," Karen told him. "My husband, Julian Brownfield, has this big friend, and when I say big I mean really, really big, you never in your life saw such a big tall woman. Name of Lila Lewisohn." And out it all poured, in that crazy new sweet Southern voice. All Karen's worst fears, her ugliest, most powerful fantasies.

"I can just see her big long legs in some great big old bed, some motel I guess, all wrapped around my skinny white old Julian."

Along with the new accent Karen seemed to have acquired a new persona, and one that she liked a lot. She liked being a silly, pretty, somewhat flirty, complaining little woman, talking to that nice big fat old boy. Telling him just about everything.

Her cold by then was making her sniffle and sneeze, and quite naturally Karen had a lot to say about her condition. "It's still just coming on strong. I can feel it all over me," she told Hal. "Although these concoctions of yours are really something else. But you know if you'll just excuse me I think I've got to call my agent. There's just no way I can play a concert tonight. As a matter of fact I think I'd better make the call from my room. Why don't you just come on up with me, give me some moral support? Lord God, will he be *mad*! I'm telling you, fit to kill."

So far Karen remembers it all, the whole conversation now plays as precisely as a tape, in her grimed, exhausted mind.

Now, continuing in her new Southern voice, she thinks, Julian wasn't very nice to me on the phone. He tells me he cares how I feel, but he doesn't, not really. All he really cares about is his patients, and that awful old Lila.

Julian and Lila have left Mill Valley, crossed the bridge, and reached San Francisco, Lila's house. But although alone in those familiar sur- roundings they are not quite restored to each other. For one thing there is almost no time. Both have morning patients; Julian must leave. And for another Karen is so present to them both, having just arisen from her bed, been awakened by her voice.

Lila has made coffee and heated two bagels. With this small nour- ishment they are perched at Lila's round kitchen table. It would be pleas- ant simply to enjoy the moment for what it is, but the fact of what they are, what they do, prevents an avoidance of the subject. Of Karen.

Julian. "Amazing, really amazing. I still feel a certain amount of guilt over not going to Atlanta."

Lila. "Julian the caretaker."

"I know; we seem to have struck a perfect balance, she and I."

"Right. Whereas Garrett and I were so unbalanced that he had to leave. Or one of us did and it turned out to be him." But they have already talked a great deal about Garrett—of course they have. They have even discussed at some length the possibility of their needing Gar- rett for some balance of their own: Since Julian is married to Karen, how will things work out in terms of Julian and Lila, now that Lila is unmar- ried? They talk a lot, they speculate.

Not so long ago, all four of those people sat at that same round kitchen table, Lila and Garrett playing host to Julian and Karen. All drinking champagne, good French stuff bought by Garrett. And they were eating something fancy that he had whipped up, crab and mush- rooms. After a concert of Karen's, in Berkeley.

Karen had played beautifully. Brahms, Mozart, Debussy. A silly Satie. A safe concert, as reviewers would hasten to point out (Karen was unpopular with local critics; her habit of cancellation did not win friends), but still, Karen's particular lyric flow was present. Playing, she sang. Wonderfully.

That night Lila, as she looked at Karen, the small exhausted woman hunched over the table, her fallen silk hair a mess, white hands gripping the stem of her glass (Karen tended to break glasses; she did so later, a good glass from Lila's mother; Garrett was angry)—watching Karen, then, it seemed astounding to Lila that she could have played at all.

Karen's beauty, too, was always astounding, even totally disheveled, entirely tired. That white, translucent skin, the very wide, dark-blue eyes, small nose, and long delicate mouth. The amazing long red silk hair.

Sometimes, envisioning Karen, Lila has thought, Well, no wonder. No wonder Julian wants her around just to look at, even if she is so often drunk, impossible. She is so beautiful, and impressively talented. He feels what I would feel, probably.

"I have this really wonderful group of friends at home," Karen now remembers telling Hal, once they were up in her room and she had made the phone call. "All people who like to drink, well, you know, too much. And who've tried the shrink route, A.A., Betty Ford, all that grim stuff. Well, we all got together and we formed this little club, we called it the Drinking Club. We meet every now and then and we really drink, I mean we just drink up a storm. But the rest of the time, stone-cold sober."

By the time she had finished all this about her club, both Karen and Hal were laughing so hard they were crying, she sitting up on her big pink bed and he in a chair near the window—a huge piece of floor-to-ceiling glass that seemed to slant into the room.

"Only trouble was," Karen continued, "we got to having our meetings all the *time.*"

"You know what?" Hal said, when either of them could speak. "You know what, I'm going to start me a branch of your club right here in Atlanta, and I'm going to start promoting the first meeting right here in this room, right *now.*"

And Hal picked up the bedside pink princess phone and began to tap out numbers, and to talk. In the mirror across the room Karen could see herself as he did so: a pretty little woman lying back on the bed, her loosened hair fanned out, prettily (the same bed which is now such a horrible mess).

Yesterday afternoon? Last night? As Hal talked and talked on the phone Karen lay back and laughed and laughed, his voice sounded so funny to her, just killing. And his fat was so nice, so reassuring.

After that her memory is vague, more spotty.

Other people came to her room. All men? Karen thinks so, but just as she thinks, All men, she remembers a woman. Was that a maid, with more drinks, bottles? Ice?

Drinking. Smoking. A lot of them smoked, a lot.

Then something about the air conditioner not working. Too hot.

People undressing?

But no sex. Nothing like that.

Or was there?

At that moment, two things happen to Karen simultaneously. Her memory closes down. Black. Blank. And her stomach lurches, then tightens like a fist.

In the bathroom nothing comes to her mouth but bile, thin and bitter, greenish. Her stomach contracts again, and again. More bitterness, more thin bile.

Very clearly then, to herself Karen says, This must never happen again. Not any of it. Not ever.

She begins to repeat, "I am an alcoholic. I am not in control of my life."

In San Francisco, in the heavy early-morning fog that will probably last all day, the trees around Lila's house drip moisture, water running down pine needles, slow drops from eucalyptus leaves. And from out in the bay comes the heavy, scraping sound of foghorns.

Lila has pulled a dark gray sweater over the silk shirt that she wore to dinner last night, with Julian, but even so she is cold as they stand there in her doorway, saying good-bye.

"Well, in any case, tonight, okay?" asks Julian. "We'll stay here? Do you want to make dinner, or should we go out, do you think? It might be better—"

This tentativeness of Julian's tells Lila that he is not at all sure what to do about Karen, who might telephone—anywhere.

Surprising herself—she, too, had assumed this night for them together—Lila hears her own voice saying, "Well, maybe not? I mean maybe not tonight at all?" She laughs to lighten the effect of what she has said: they have never before not seen each other when they could. "Let's talk on the phone instead." She laughs again.

"Well. Oh. Well, okay." Looking hard at Lila as he says those few words, Julian too seems to strive for lightness. But then he says, "Or I could make dinner at my house? We haven't done that for a while. I'll bring you home early, I promise."

Meaning that he can't quite let her go, not now? He needs some sort of help from Lila?

No time for talking about it, however, and so she temporizes. "Well, let me call you later, okay?"

They kiss, both with the thought that they will see each other that night after all. Probably.

Julian walks over to his car, and Lila goes back inside her house, where she will clean up their few dishes before heading over to her study, ready for the day's first patient.

Cleaning up her room, which seemed to Karen a first step, is not quite as terrible as she imagined it would be. To start with, there are not as many sheets lying around as she thought there were. She pulls the sheets and a couple of towels into a bundle that she then thrusts out into the hall—seeing no one in the corridor, luckily.

She empties the ashtrays into the toilet, along with the inches of booze in the several glasses. Flushes it all away. Gone. She considers washing the ashtrays and decides against it, imagining that wet-ash smell. She just stacks everything there in the bathroom and closes the door.

Well. Already a huge improvement.

She will call her agent and apologize; in fact she will call a lot of people, explaining, apologizing. But there is no way, not now, that she could go on to New York today, as she was meant to do.

She will call down for some food, a tray of tea and eggs, some yogurt, all healthy stuff. Maybe that nice black man will bring it up to her, the one who brought the wine. (Wine. She will never drink wine again, or anything else.) How surprised and pleased he will be to see how she has tidied up the room! And to see her looking so much better! How surprised everyone will be when they see her.

She very much hopes it will be the same waiter. She really liked him. If only she could remember his name.

Earthquake Damage

Stretching long legs to brace her boots against the bulkhead as the plane heads upward from Toronto into gray mid-October air, Lila Lewisohn, a very tall, exhausted psychiatrist—a week of meetings has almost done her in, she feels—takes note of the advantages of this seat: enough leg room, and somewhat out of the crush. Also, the seat next to hers is vacant. At least, she thinks, the trip will be comfortable; maybe I can sleep.

But a few minutes into the air the plane is gripped and shaken. Turbulence rattles everything, as passengers clutch their armrests, or neighboring human arms, if they are traveling with friends or lovers. Lila, for whom this is a rather isolated period, instead grips her own knees, and grits her teeth, and prays—to no one, or perhaps to a very odd bunch: to God, in whom she does not believe; to Freud, about whom she has serious doubts; to her old shrink, who is dead; to her mother, also dead, and whom she mostly did not like. And to her former (she supposes it is now former) lover, Julian Brownfield, also a shrink.

Lila and Julian, in training together in Boston, plunged more or less inadvertently from a collegial friendship into heady adulterous love— a love (and a friendship) that for many years worked, sustaining them both through problematic marriages. But in the five or six years since the dissolutions of those marriages a certain troubled imbalance has set in. Most recently, Julian has taken back his ex-wife, Karen, an alcoholic pianist who is not doing well with recovery and has just violently separated from another husband. *Sheltering* might be Julian's word for what he is doing for Karen—Lila would call it *harboring,* or worse: if Karen behaved well, she might stay on forever there with Julian,

Lila at least half believes. She has so far refused to see Julian, with Karen there.

In any case, Lila now prays to all those on her list, and especially to Julian, to whom she says, I'm just not up to all this; I'm really running on empty. *Please.*

Her meetings, held in the new Harbourfront section of Toronto, in an excellent hotel with lovely, wide lake views, were no more than routinely tiring, actually; Lila was forced to admit to herself that it was the theme of the conference that afflicted her with a variety of troubled feelings. It was a psychiatric conference on the contemporary state of being single, though of course certain newspaper articles vulgarized it into "A New Look at Singles," "Singles: Shrinks Say the New Minority." Whereas in fact the hours of papers and discussion had ranged about— had included the guilt that many people feel over their single state; social ostracism, subtle and overt; myths of singleness; the couple as conspiracy; plus practical problems, demographics, and perceived changes over the last several generations. And Lila found that she overreacted—she was reached, touched, shaken by much that was said. She had trouble sleeping, despite long lap swims in the hotel's glassed-in pool, with its views of Canadian skies across Lake Ontario.

Now, very tired, she braces herself against the turbulence, and against certain strong old demons in her mind. And then, as though one of those to whom she has prayed were indeed in charge, the turbulence ends. The huge plane zooms peacefully through a clear gray dusk. Westward, toward San Francisco. A direct flight.

Lila must have fallen asleep, for she is startled awake by the too loud voice of the pilot, over the intercom: "Sorry, folks. We've just had news of a very mild earthquake in the San Francisco area, very mild but a little damage to the airport, so we'll be heading back to Toronto."

An instant of silence is followed by loud groans from the rows and rows of seats behind Lila's bulkhead. Groans and exclamations: *Oh no, Jesus Christ, all we need, an earthquake.* Turning, she sees that a great many people are standing up, moving about, as if there were anything to do. One man, though—trench-coated, lean, dark blond, almost handsome—makes for the telephone up on the wall near Lila's seat. Seizing it, he begins to dial, and dial and dial. Lila gestures that he can sit down in the empty seat, and he does so, with a twisting grimace. Then, "Can't get through, *damn,*" he says. "My family's down on the Peninsula." He dials again, says, "Damn," again, then asks Lila, "Yours?"

"Oh. Uh, San Francisco."

"Well, San Francisco's better. Guy with a radio said the epicenter's in Hollister."

"I wonder about that 'mild.' " Lila leans toward him to whisper.

"No way it could be mild. They're not closing down the airport for any mild earthquake."

Which is pretty much what Lila had already thought.

"Well, I guess I better let someone else try to phone."

"There's one on the other side," Lila tells him, having noticed this symmetrical arrangement on entering the plane.

"Oh, well then." But after a few minutes, muttering, he gets up and goes back to his seat, as Lila realizes that she wishes he had stuck around—not that she was especially drawn to him; she simply wanted someone there.

People are by now crowding around the two phones, pressing into the passageway between the aisles. A man has managed to get through to his sister-in-law, in Sacramento, and soon everyone has his news: it is a major quake. Many dead. The bridge down.

At that last piece of news, about the bridge, Lila's tired heart is drenched with cold, as she thinks: Julian, Julian, who lives in Mill Valley and practices in San Francisco, could be on the bridge at any time. Especially now, just after five in San Francisco. Commuter time.

On the other hand, almost anyone *could* have been on the bridge, especially anyone who lives in Marin County. Fighting panic, Lila says this firmly to herself: anyone does not mean Julian, necessarily. A major disaster involving the bridge does not necessarily involve Julian Brownfield. Not necessarily. She is gripping her knees, as during the turbulence; with an effort she unclenches her fingers and clasps her hands together on her lap, too tightly.

"How about the game?" someone near her is saying.

"No stadium damage, I heard."

"Lucky it wasn't a little later. People leaving, going back to Oakland."

As, very slowly, these sentences penetrate Lila's miasma of anxiety, she understands: they are talking about the Bay Bridge. The Bay Bridge was damaged, not the Golden Gate. Traffic to the East Bay, not to Marin, Mill Valley.

What Lila feels then, along with extreme relief, is an increase of exhaustion; her nerves sag. And she has, too, the cold new thought that Julian, an unlikely fan, could well have gone to the game. (Taken Karen to the game?) Could have left early, and been overtaken by the earthquake, anywhere at all.

Rising from her seat, intending to walk about, she sees that everyone else is also trying to move. They all seem to protest the event, and their situations, with restless, random motion. Strangers confront and query each other along the packed aisles: Where're you from? Remember the quake last August? The one in '72? In '57? How long were you in Toronto? Like it there? But not enough to make you want to go back right away, right?

At last they begin the descent into Toronto, strapped in, looking down, and no one notices the turbulence that they pass through.

In Julian's house, high up on the wooded crest above Mill Valley, there is total chaos: in the front hall, two large suitcases lie open and overflowing—a crazy tangle of dresses and blouses, sweaters, silk nightgowns, pantyhose, and shoes thrown all over.

"Anyone coming in," Julian comments from a doorway, "anyone would think the earthquake, whereas actually—"

"Well, in a way it is the fucking earthquake," Karen unnecessarily tells him, in her furious, choppy way. "Closing the fucking airport."

"Whereas, really, we were lucky," Julian continues, more or less to himself. He is tall and too thin, gray-haired. His skin, too, now looks gray: three weeks of Karen have almost done him in, he thinks. In character, she has alternated her wish to leave with a passionate desire to stay with Julian—forever. Only a day ago she had decided firmly (it seemed) to leave. And now, on the verge of her departure, an earthquake. "The airport might open in a couple of hours," Julian tells Karen, and he is thinking of Lila, the exact hour of whose return he is uncertain about. Perhaps she is already here? "Or tomorrow," he says to Karen, hopefully.

"But how would we know, with the phone out?" Karen complains. "It might be a couple of weeks." She is visibly at the end of her rope, which is short at the best of times. "A couple of weeks with no lights or electricity!"

It is clear to Julian that whatever controls Karen has managed to place on herself for the course of her stay are now wavering, if not completely gone. She has not behaved badly; she has not, that is, got drunk. He himself, at this moment, acutely longs for a drink. An odd longing: Julian is generally abstemious, a tennis player, always in shape. And he wonders, is he catching Karen's own longing, her alcoholic impulse? Karen, opposing A.A. (she did not like it there), believes that alcoholics can cut down, citing herself as an example—every night she has one, and only one, vodka martini.

Karen is very beautiful, still. All that booze has in no way afflicted the fine white skin. Her face shows no tracks of pain, nor shadows. Her wide, dark-blue eyes are clear; looking into those eyes, one might imagine that her head resounds only with Mozart, or Brahms—and perhaps in a way it still does.

"Well, come on, Julian, let's find some candles. You know perfectly well that this is the cocktail hour," she says to her former husband, and she laughs.

Down on the ground in Toronto, disembarked, all the passengers from the flight to San Francisco are herded into a room where, they are assured, they will be given instructions. And in that large, bare room rumors quickly begin to circulate, as people gather and mutter questions to each other.

No one is sitting or standing alone, Lila notices, although surely there were other solitary travelers on that plane. And she finds that she, too, begins to attach herself to groups, one after another. Is she seeking information, or simple creature comfort, animal reassurance? She is not sure.

Three businessmen in overcoats, with lavish attaché cases, having spoken to the pilot, inform Lila that it may be several days before the San Francisco airport opens. And that the reason for not going on to L.A., or even to Reno or Salt Lake City, has to do with flight regulations—since theirs was a Canadian carrier, they had to return to Canada.

In an automatic way she looks across to the man in the trench coat, at the same time wondering why: Why has she more or less chosen him to lead her? She very much doubts that it is because he is almost handsome, and she hopes that it is not simply that he is a man. He looks decisive, she more or less concludes, and then is shaken by a powerful memory of Julian, who is neither handsome nor decisive, and whom she has loved for all those years.

The trench-coated man seems indeed to have a definite group of his own, of which he is in charge. Lila reads this from the posture of the four people whom she now approaches, leaving the didactic businessmen. But before Lila can ask anything, the loudspeaker comes on, and a voice says that they are all to be housed in the Toronto Hilton, which is very near, and that the airline will do everything possible to get them to their destination tomorrow. A van will pick them up downstairs to take them to the hotel. Names will be called, vouchers given.

Lila has barely joined her chosen group when she hears her name called; they must be doing it by rows, she decides. She is instructed to go through a hall and down some stairs, go outside, and meet the Hilton van there.

And after a couple of wrong turns Lila indeed finds herself outside in the semidark, next to a dimly lit, low-ceilinged traffic tunnel, where a van soon does arrive. But it is for the Ramada Inn, not the Hilton.

And that is the last vehicle of any nature to show up for the next ten or twelve minutes, during which time no people show up, either. No one.

Several taxis are parked some yards down from where Lila has been standing, pacing, in her boots, by her carry-on bag. Drivers are lounging on the seats inside. Should she take a cab to the Hilton? On the other hand, maybe by now everything has been changed, and no one is going to the Hilton after all.

It is very cold, standing there in the dark tunnel, and seemingly darker and dingier all the time. Across the black, wide car lanes are some glassed-in offices, closed and black, reflecting nothing. Behind Lila is the last room through which she came. It is still lit, and empty.

Something clearly is wrong; things cannot be going as planned. Or, she is in the wrong place. Then, dimly, at the end of the tunnel, she sees a van moving toward her. It will not be a Hilton van, she thinks, and she is right: HOLIDAY INN, its sign reads. It passes her slowly, an empty van, its driver barely looking out.

Earthquake Damage

Lila is later to think of this period of time as the worst of the earthquake for her—a time in which she feels most utterly alone, quite possibly abandoned. It is so bad that she has forgotten about the earthquake itself almost entirely; she is too immediately frightened and uncomfortable to think of distant disaster.

After perhaps another five minutes, during which everything gets worse—the cold and the darkness, Lila's anxiety and her growing hunger—she hears voices from the room behind her. Turning, she sees what she thinks of as her group: the trench-coated man and his charges, followed by the other passengers, all coming out to where Lila stands, shifting her feet in boots that no longer seem to fit.

As though they were old friends, Lila hurries toward him. "Where've you been? What happened?"

"Bureaucratic foul-up," he tells her. "Some stuff about whether or not the airline would spring for the hotel. Who cares? And some confusion about whose flights originated in Toronto." With a semismile he adds, "You were really lucky to get out first."

"Was I? I don't know."

"Anyway. Look, there's our van. Toronto Hilton."

In the candlelit kitchen of Julian's house, Julian and Karen are drinking vodka and orange juice, Karen's idea being that they have to use up the orange juice before it goes to waste in the powerless refrigerator. "Besides, the C makes it good for you." She laughs, and Julian hears a sad echo of her old flirtatiousness as she adds, "But why am I telling a doctor anything like that?"

He sighs. "Yes, I am a doctor."

This is not a room designed for such romantic illumination. The shadows on the giant steel refrigerator are severe, menacing, and the flickering candlelight on the black-tiled floor looks evil—they could be in jail. Julian feels nothing of the vodka, and Karen's face, across the round, white, high-gloss table, shows mostly fatigue. She looks vague, distracted.

In a sober, conversational voice she remarks, "Funny to think back to old times in this kitchen. With Lila and old Garrett." Garrett: Lila's former husband, a mean and somber lawyer.

"This kitchen?" asks Julian. "I don't remember . . ."

"Sure you do. We were all drinking champagne, and later I broke a glass."

"I think it's Lila's kitchen we were in." The whole scene has indeed come back to Julian, a flash, immobilized: the other kitchen, so unlike this one, all soft wood, some copper bowls, blue pillows on a bench. Prim, pale Garrett—and Lila, her gray hair bright, brushed upward. Lila laughing and talking, he (Julian) talking, each of them, as always, excited by the other's sheer proximity. "It was somebody's birthday," he tells Karen, knowing perfectly well that it was Lila's. "You had on a green dress."

"Well, you sure do have a great memory for details."

"I have to, it's my job." And you always broke glasses, he does not say.

"You mean, my green dress is what you might call a professional memory? Holy shit, Julian, holy shit, you're, you're . . ." She begins to cough, unable to tell Julian what he is. He gets up and moves to pat her back, but Karen gestures him away.

"Don't, I'm okay, don't hit me!" She laughs a little hysterically, as Julian, too late, realizes that she is getting drunk. Is drunk. "You know what the earthquake was like for me?" She is looking blearily across at him, tears pooled in those great, dark-blue eyes. "*Fun.* The most fun in the world. I loved it."

"Good, Karen, I'm glad." It no longer matters what he says, Julian knows, as long as it is fairly neutral. "I thought it was more like turbulence in an airplane," he mutters, more or less to himself.

At which Karen giggles. "I like turbulence," she tells him. "Remember? I think it's a kick." And then, quite suddenly, she bursts into tears. "Julian, I've never loved anyone but you," she sobs, reaching out to him. Blindly.

Descending from the van at the Toronto Hilton, Lila and her new friends see that the lobby inside is very crowded. Everyone is gathered around a single small television screen, and in a room beyond there is a coffee shop, apparently open. "Hundreds killed," the announcer is saying. "Devastation."

"The restaurant's out of food," someone says.

There is a line at the reception desk, but it seems to move quickly;

within minutes Lila is being assigned a room. "I wonder about phoning," she says to the man in the trench coat, Mark. They have all introduced themselves.

Lila's room, at the top of the Toronto Hilton, is actually a small suite, to which she pays no attention as she heads for the phone. Without considering consequences (Karen could easily answer), she dials the familiar Mill Valley number. Dialing directly, not bothering with credit cards or operators, she gets at first a busy signal and then an operator saying that she is sorry, all the circuits are busy. Lila dials again, gets more operators who are sorry, more busy signals. She goes into the bathroom to wash up, comes back and dials the number again, and again. She orders a sandwich from room service, and continues to try to phone.

A couple of hours later, in Mill Valley, Julian awakes with a sudden jolt: he is in his kitchen, still, and every brilliant light in the room is on, as is the television. Bottles and sticky glasses on the table. Gradually he remembers carrying Karen into the guest room. She is light enough in his arms, but a total dead weight; his back feels strained. And then he came back into this room. Surely not, he hopes, for another drink?

The TV screen shows a very large, white apartment building that has buckled and is rent with cracks and gaps. A background of black night sky, and a cordon of police. Cars, flashing lights. Dazed people standing around in clumps. Julian gets up to turn it off when, at that moment, the phone rings. In his confusion, he stumbles, just catches it on the third ring.

"Lila? My darling, my Lila, wherever . . . ? We're here, I mean I'm here, no damage, really. Well, I imagine I do sound odd, but no, of course I'm not drunk. Karen was just on the point of leaving—actually packed, then the damn thing hit. I guess she'll go tomorrow; by now I suppose I mean today. And you? You'll be back today! For sure?"

Smiling, still breathing hard with the effort of so much futile dialing before at last getting through, Lila offers a silent prayer to all those on her curious private list: she prays that she can fly out of Toronto tomorrow, or whatever day this now is—and that Karen can fly, finally, out of San Francisco.

She sleeps fitfully and wakes early, knowing that she is awake for good. She thinks of telephoning Julian again, but does not. She showers and dresses as hurriedly as possible, and goes down to the hotel lobby.

There people are sitting around, or milling about, aimlessly. The TV seems still to be showing the news from the night before; Lila glimpses the same bridge shots, fire shots, the broken apartment house. All around her in the lobby the faces are pale, clothes a little disheveled, as hers must be. From a small, plump woman who is sitting near the front desk she hears, "They say we're getting out today, but I don't believe it."

Lila, too, has trouble believing that they will escape. As she looks around at the tired clusters of people—no one, she observes again, is going it alone—she imagines that they will be there for months, that they are in fact refugees from some much larger disaster.

In the coffee shop, she finds Mark, and another man, and joins them. Mark got through to his wife, in Saratoga, who said that their chimney had fallen off, and that everything in the house that could break was broken. "But she's okay," says Mark, with a grin. "And the kids. You should have seen the waves in the swimming pool, she told me. You wouldn't believe it. Tidal."

From the lobby then, at first indistinctly, they hear an announcement: ". . . vans will begin to leave this hotel at nine-forty-five. Repeat: the San Francisco airport is clear."

Lila's seat on the morning plane is not nearly as good as the one the day before. Pushing her way down the aisle with her carry-on, she takes note of this fact, though today it seems extremely unimportant. And she does have a window seat.

Everyone on the plane is in a festive mood. People smile a lot, though many faces show considerable fatigue, the ravages of a long and anxious night. But an almost manic mood prevails: the airport is clear, we're going home, the city has more or less survived. To all of which Lila adds to herself, and Karen is going back East, probably.

Everyone is seated, buckled in. The pilot's voice is telling the flight attendants to prepare for departure. The engines start their roar; they roar and roar. And nothing happens.

This goes on for some time—ten minutes, fifteen—until the engines are turned off, and they are simply sitting there on the runway, in the

October Canadian sunlight. But the atmosphere on the plane is less impatient than might be imagined; it is felt that at least they are on their way. There may even be a certain (unacknowledged, unconscious) relief at the delay: San Francisco and whatever lies ahead do not have to be faced quite so soon.

The pilot announces a small mechanical glitch, which will be taken care of right away. And, perhaps twenty minutes later, the engines start again. And they are off, almost: the plane starts down the runway, gathering speed, and then, quite suddenly, it slows, and stops.

Jesus Christ. Now really. What now? We'll never. What in hell is going on? These sentiments echo around the cabin, where patience has worn audibly thin, until, apparently starting at the front row, where a smiling stewardess is standing, the rumor spreads: a dog has somehow got loose on the field; it will be a minute more. They have already been cleared for takeoff.

And then, with a motion that seems to be decisive, the plane moves forward, again. Glancing from her window, quite suddenly Lila sees—indeed!—a dog, running in the opposite direction, running back to Toronto. A large, lean, yellowish dog, whose gallop is purposeful, determined. He will get back to his place, but in the meantime he enjoys the run, the freedom of the forbidden field. His long nose swings up and down, his tail streams backward, a pennant, as Lila—watching from her window, headed at last back to San Francisco (probably)—begins in a quiet, controlled, and private way to laugh. "It was just so funny," she will say to Julian, later. "The final thing, that dog. And he looked so proud! As though instead of getting in our way he had come to our rescue."

A NOTE ON THE TYPE

The text of this book was set in Simoncini Garamond, a modern version by Francesco Simoncini of the type attributed to the famous Parisian type cutter Claude Garamond (c. 1480–1561). Garamond was a pupil of Geoffroy Tory and is believed to have based his letters on the Venetian models, although he introduced a number of important differences, and it is to him we owe the letter that we know as old style. He gave to his letters a certain elegance and a feeling of movement that won for their creator an immediate reputation and the patronage of Francis I of France.

Composed by Stratford Publishing Services
Brattleboro, Vermont

Printed and bound by Berryville Graphics
Berryville, Virginia

Designed by Dorothy S. Baker